THE
threadbare
HEART

**Center Point
Large Print**

Also by Jennie Nash
and available from Center Point Large Print:

The Last Beach Bungalow
The Only True Genius in the Family

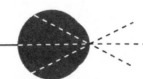

**This Large Print Book carries the
Seal of Approval of N.A.V.H.**

THE
threadbare
HEART

JENNIE NASH

CENTER POINT PUBLISHING
THORNDIKE, MAINE

The text of this Large Print edition is unabridged.
In other aspects, this book may vary
from the original edition.
Printed in the United States of America
on permanent paper.
Set in 16-point Times New Roman type.

ISBN: 978-1-60285-774-2

Library of Congress Cataloging-in-Publication Data

Nash, Jennie, 1964–
   The threadbare heart / Jennie Nash.
      p. cm.
   ISBN 978-1-60285-774-2 (library binding : alk. paper)
   1. Disaster victims—Fiction. 2. Loss (Psychology)—Fiction. 3. Psychological fiction.
   4. Large type books. I. Title.
PS3614.A73T47 2010b
813'.6—dc22
                                          2010000547

For my sweet sister Laura

Acknowledgments

Thanks to Jackie for her enduring support, her clarity of thought, and for sharing her passion for fabric; to Faye, of course, for everything; to the whole team at Berkley for doing what you do so well; to Kitty Felde, whose stories about sewing were so inspiring, and who helped me design Lily's dress; to my dad for that key week in Colorado, and to Bonnie Inouye, weaver, whose looms got me into this story; to Jane Broket, Jennifer Balis, and Elaine Murakami for talking about their fabric collecting habits; to Chuck Marso at F&S Fabric in Los Angeles for helping me pick real fabric for my fictional dress; to Stacy Lantagne, for insight into Red Sox Nation; to Lynn Solaro for walking and talking about these characters as if they were real; to Annie Webster, ceramic teacher at Chadwick School, for helping me get the clay right, and to Shelley Frost for showing me how it's done. (The pots with arms and legs that I describe were designed by Erica Reiss in her senior year at Chadwick School; I saw them at a school art show in 2008, and couldn't get them out of my head.) Thanks to all the members of the Wellesley College Club of Houston's BookClub (Georgina Armstrong, Jesse Berger, Anna Grassini, Suzanne Jester, Jackie Kacen, Lydia Luz, Maneesha Patil, Rebecca

Saltzer, Martita Schmuck, Sandy Simmoms) who read and critiqued an early draft of this story, and helped me get it right. Thanks to Laura for helping me with the timeline, the details of academia, the record of the Harvard baseball team and a hundred other facts; to Carlyn and Emily for helping me with the beginning and for challenging me to write a character with two sons; to my mom and Doug for being willing to let me take their story and run; to Hannah for insisting that the dog had to live; and finally, to Rob, for teaching me so much about love.

THE
threadbare
HEART

·1·

Lily

LOVE was the one thing Lily always thought she did better than her mother. She believed that she knew exactly what love took, what it cost, and what it meant, and she thought of her long marriage to Tom as proof of it. But in the short period of time between Christmas and the start of fire season, everything she understood about love unraveled, the way jeans do at the hem, the way tweed does so that it reveals the intricate relationship of the warp and the weft, and she realized how very little she knew about the way love worked. People naturally assumed, after everything that happened, that it was a bitter revelation, but they were wrong.

"Would you do it all again, knowing what you know now?" her mother, Eleanor, asked. Eleanor was, at that moment, seventy-five years old, about to be married again herself, and hoping that this time she might get it right.

"In a heartbeat," Lily said—not only because she believed it, but because she knew it was what her mother needed to hear.

IT had started, simply enough, in December of 2007 in a bookstore in Burlington, Vermont. She and Tom still had a few weeks of classes left to teach before the end of the semester—he in biology, she in math—and they had come into town to meet some old friends for dinner. Church Street was at its most charming—lights in the trees, snow dusted on the ground, the shops warm and welcoming. Even though they were wearing gloves, they held hands as they walked home.

"I didn't get you a Christmas gift," Tom said. "Again."

Lily smiled. After twenty-six years of marriage, what was there to get each other? She had recently brought home Tom's favorite cinnamon bread from the bakery because she knew how much he liked to toast it for breakfast, and he had replaced the broken birdfeeder that hung from the big elm tree outside the kitchen window because he knew how much it delighted Lily when the jays came, and the woodpeckers, and the cardinals. These small gestures gave them as much surprise and indulgence as they needed. "Then we're even," she said.

"And we'll have less to haul out to California."

"I don't have anything yet to give to Brooke," Lily said. "It's as if I never had a two-year-old. I can't remember what two-year-olds like."

"Cardboard boxes," Tom said. "Don't you remember the way Luke used to pile all his pillows in boxes, and sleep in there? And how Ryan made that castle in the basement?"

She laughed. "I'd forgotten that."

"We could get her a book," Tom said. They were coming up on the Burlington Bookshop. There were pine boughs encircling the window and the sound of jingle bells as someone came out the door.

"A book would be good," Lily said. She stopped in front of the shop, Tom held the door for her, and they went in. They each meandered through the tables and the stacks, drawn in by titles and covers as if by a magnetic field. Lily got pulled toward a table where the cookbooks were displayed. She loved the idea of cooking—and the fact that there could be an entire cookbook featuring nothing but tacos or mushrooms or cup-cakes—but she wasn't much of a cook herself. She made soups and stews, salads and sand-wiches. When the boys were home, she would roast a chicken with herbs from Tom's garden, but she didn't need a recipe for that. She wan-dered over to a section of art books, and picked up one on master quilters. She sat in a chair, and lost herself in the photos of intricately made quilts that looked like pointillist paintings, and abstract murals, and in the words of the artists who spoke about layering fabric and layering time.

The owner of the shop came quietly up to her. "Can I bring you a cup of hot chocolate?" he asked.

Lily looked up, surprised to find herself in a bookstore and not in an art gallery.

"It's Lake Champlain," the man said, referring to the brand of artisanal chocolate. "Aztec spice."

"Sure," Lily said. "Thank you. That would be nice."

But chocolate was, in fact, a dangerous thing. She had been struck with debilitating headaches when she got pregnant with Ryan, at age twenty-six, and they had never gone away. Over the years, in an effort at self-preservation, she had figured out exactly what triggered them: the glare of lights from oncoming traffic, chocolate, strawberries, bananas, aspartame, sleeplessness, and red wine. She learned the combinations that would cause the most damage, the inherent risks of every offending food or situation, and then she set out systematically to avoid them. She politely declined strawberry daiquiris and walnut brownies, late-night parties and late-start movies, night driving, and Diet Coke. Far from feeling deprived, she felt that she had become master of her migraines, and she had a strange affection for the strict logic of it, and the power she wielded.

That night, however, she'd already had two glasses of sauvignon blanc at dinner. She felt happy—so much a part of the holiday, and the warmth of the store, and the charm of the town where she and Tom had lived for so long—that she couldn't imagine anything going wrong. She couldn't imagine a headache. What harm could a bit of chocolate do? She accepted the mug gratefully, and took a sip.

A few minutes later, Tom caught sight of Lily across the store—his wife, curled up in a soft chair like a child, a book in her lap, her brow knit together in concentration—and he was overcome with a rush of love. He had picked out some books for their granddaughter, and he approached Lily to show her his discoveries. When he got up closer, he smelled the chocolate and the hot spice of the drink Lily held in her hand. He bent down next to her chair.

"What are you doing?" he whispered—his voice a quiet demand.

"Reading about quilts," she said, turning the book so that he could see what she was seeing. "Look at these colors."

"But you're drinking hot chocolate." He knew what would happen if Lily got a migraine: she would turn inward toward the pain, hold her head in her hands, lie down in the dark, and hope that if she lay perfectly still, she could keep the pain at bay. An hour later, or three, or maybe in the middle of the night, she would be crouched on the bathroom floor, crying out in pain, begging for mercy, begging for him to help. And he would help, because that's what Tom did. He would hold her. He would get her ice. He would remind her to breathe.

"I'll be okay," she said.

"You don't know that, Lily."

"Tom," she whispered. "Please. I'll be okay."

"I think you're making a mistake."

"Then I'll deal with the consequences."

"No," he said, standing up and speaking too loud now for a bookstore. "I'll deal with the consequences. *I* will. Your headache will be *my* problem."

She stared up at him. He had never spoken to her like this before. "Can we talk about this later?" she whispered. "Outside?"

"I'm not going to stand here and watch you drink that," he said.

She clenched her teeth and took a deep breath through her nose. It smelled of dark chocolate and chili, but in that breath she also sensed vulnerability—her body's vulnerability in its fifty-first year, and the vulnerability that came from loving another human being. She was bound to Tom, beholden to him, and there were good things that came from that, and compromises, too. She wordlessly set the hot chocolate down on the table.

"I found something for Brooke," Tom said. "A collection of Richard Scarry books. Isn't that perfect?"

"Well," Lily said, "it was perfect for the boys, but for a girl? I don't know." She remembered how Ryan and Luke would pore over the pages of their Richard Scarry books, naming each truck and airplane, each job undertaken by one of the enterprising townsfolk, but she wasn't sure whether the books would have the same appeal to a little girl. Ryan and Olivia had moved to California when Brooke was just three months old. Lily had missed Brooke's first steps, her first teeth, her first words, and because she had missed those milestones, she wanted to give a gift that Brooke would adore.

"Everyone loves Mr. Fixit and Sergeant Murphy," Tom said.

It was true; they did. But the whole thing made her suddenly tired—the whole business of being a wife, a grandmother, a daughter about to go home for the holidays. She wanted to get out of the shop and go home. "Okay," she said. "Fine." She figured that she would have enough time to sew something for Brooke, maybe a little flannel blanket for her bear. She'd pieced together a quilt when Brooke was born—nine log cabin blocks in a riot of colors and patterns sewn in a square. Perhaps she would make a dress or a pillow from some of the floral prints she had in her stash.

"You're right," she said. "Let's get the Richard Scarry books. And I'm going to get this quilt book. It can be my Christmas present."

He smiled. "I'm going to get this gardening book," he said. "It can be mine."

● ● ●

WHEN they were back out in the cold, Tom began to talk about the book he had just purchased. It was a treatise on the importance of preserving heirloom seeds. The author was arguing for the beauty and integrity of food grown without intervention. Lily listened, and agreed that it was a timely and necessary argument, but she was waiting for a pause in the story, a chance to make a different point. When Tom seemed finished talking, she said, "What did you mean when you said, *Your headache will be my problem*?"

"Just what it sounds like," Tom said. "You can be cavalier about chocolate or wine or whatever, but I'm the one who has to deal with it."

"I'm the one who'll have the headache."

Tom shifted his feet on the snowy ground. He looked off into the dark night. "You think it's been easy for me all these years?" he asked. "To stand by watching?"

"Well, no," she said. "Of course not." None of it was easy—watching someone have doubt or have the flu, watching them lose their nerve or lose their parents. Even just watching Tom's hair turn gray, or watching his skin become more susceptible to the cold, dry air, or watching his knee become stiffer by degrees. It was all hard. All of it.

"You think I *enjoy* hearing you beg for the pain to stop, hearing you moan about wanting to die?" Tom said.

She stopped. She could see her breath forming in the cold air in front of her face. She had had only a few migraines a year these past several years. She had begun to think, in fact, that maybe she was becoming immune to headaches, that maybe this was something that got better as she got older. She had begun to think that she could risk a mug of hot chocolate. Tom's display of doubt rubbed up against her hard-won hope and caught her off guard. "I didn't know how much it was bothering you," she said.

Tom laughed—a kind of snort that meant, *How on earth could you* not *know?*

"I don't get this sudden concern, Tom," she said. "Is something wrong?"

He shrugged. They were older now. Their boys were grown and gone now. Things that used to flit past Tom like clouds or birds bothered him now. Things he used to handle without much thought now seemed insurmountable. Lily's headaches were something he had handled for years without complaint. But the last few times, they had grabbed hold of him in a way that frightened him. He had imagined Lily spiraling farther down into pain than she had ever gone before, spiraling so far away that she was out of reach. It made him think about her dying and his being alone. That wasn't something he felt like he could endure.

"It's nothing," he said. "I'm sorry I said anything. Let's get out of the cold."

• • •

BUT Lily knew that it wasn't nothing. She had lived with Tom for a long time. As they moved through December, through their classes and departmental parties, through final exams and holiday cheer, she had a feeling of unease. She thought, for a while, that it was the fact that they were going through their first holiday season with no children in the house. Things were so quiet, and so strange without the boys, and she noticed that Tom was taking extra long treks in the snow by himself, and coming back to the house pensive instead of exhilarated. Perhaps he missed the kids more than she knew. Later, she thought that the unease was due to the fact that when she and Tom came back from vacation neither of them would be teaching a full course load. She had won a grant to update her textbook and he had been tapped to help the university write a plan for transitioning to an integrated science curriculum. Maybe they were both just feeling a little untethered.

When she looked back at it all, however, and tried to figure out when everything began to unravel, she would go back to that moment in the bookstore when her sense of contentedness was so quickly replaced by a feeling of unease. One minute she was sipping hot chocolate like any holiday reveler, reading about fabric and design, knowing that her husband was happily wandering the bookstore aisles, and the next moment, she felt the full weight of the ordinary dangers of the world—chocolate, a holiday in her mother's house, marriage itself.

·2·

Tom

THEY all gathered at Eleanor's house in Santa Barbara for the holidays. It was a three-story red-tiled town house with five bedrooms, a dining room that looked out at the mountains, and a living room that looked past the landmark court-house down to the sea. Luke, Lily and Tom's younger boy, lived only a half hour away from Eleanor now; Ryan, Olivia, and Brooke were two hours to the north in San Luis Obispo; and there was nothing Eleanor liked better than organizing meals and outings, especially during the holidays. Each day, she had a full lineup of events, from a trip to the zoo, to wine tasting in Santa Ynez Valley, to a seating at Seagrass, the new seafood restaurant that had opened around the corner. Eleanor had a seven-foot noble fir erected in her living room, and another one on the rooftop deck, both of which she had hired a florist to decorate. Under the tree in the living room was a pile of gifts, all expertly wrapped by the department stores where they had been purchased. There could never be enough revelry for Eleanor, or enough people in the house, or enough gifts. She adored a party.

Four days before Christmas, after Brooke had

been put to bed, Eleanor announced that she was thinking of ordering a girl-sized dress to match the one on the doll she had already purchased for Brooke's gift. The doll came with storybooks, satin slippers, and a wardrobe that included a plaid pinafore, white nightgown, and red velvet party dress. Her eyes and hair were the same color as Brooke's—green eyes, curly dark hair. "The girl-sized party dress is darling," Eleanor said, "and there's still time to have it FedExed if I call right away. What do you think?"

Ryan, who was twenty-five years old and didn't know enough about his daughter and dresses to comment, turned toward his wife for help.

Olivia smiled. "You were so generous to get the doll," she said. "Please don't feel that you need to do anything more."

All Lily and Tom had for Brooke were the Richard Scarry books—and Lily felt suddenly that this wasn't enough. She hadn't sewn anything, hadn't picked out anything memorable, anything girlish and sweet. The fact that her mother had hit upon such a fantastic gift—a beautiful doll, with a matching girl-sized dress—made jealousy rise in Lily like a fever. Eleanor had always had such an easy way with people, such a natural way of charming them. She always knew just what to bring to a party, what to wear, what to say, and Lily, more often than not, would spend the entire time just wishing she could go home. "I could make a red velvet dress," she blurted out.

"You sew?" Olivia asked.

Lily smiled wryly, and nodded. How odd that there was someone in her life who didn't know that she sewed. "I sewed all my own clothes in high school and college," she said. "I used to love it. It was the perfect hobby for a mathematical mind—all those angles and shapes."

"The point of this dress," Eleanor said, "is that it's exactly the same as the doll's."

"I'd actually like to do it, Mom," Lily said with a casualness she did not feel. "I can go to Beverly Fabrics tomorrow morning."

Eleanor sipped her wine. "We were invited to the Hailwoods' for brunch tomorrow morning," she said, and turned toward Tom to explain that the Hailwoods lived on an avocado ranch in the foothills, with a sweeping view of the Channel Islands. "And besides," she added, "I don't own a sewing machine. I never have."

"You own a factory full of high-speed looms in Italy, but you don't own a sewing machine?" Luke asked. The boys loved to poke fun at their grandmother. She looked like a woman whose silver hair was never out of place, but Ryan and Luke knew better. Eleanor would fly across the country to take them to a baseball game, swim in frigid water on a dare, and beat the pants off any of them in a hand of bridge.

"I run a multinational company," Eleanor said with a theatrical flourish. "I don't do manual labor." Ryan laughed at Eleanor's perfect description of herself, and Luke said, "Touché."

"I can buy a sewing machine," Lily said. "I've been thinking about getting one of the programmable ones they use now for quilting."

Tom glanced up, curious at what his wife was saying—she wanted a new sewing machine? Something besides her grandmother's clunky cast-iron Singer that swung up from a wooden cabinet? Lily was devoted to that machine, and always said that adding bells and whistles to a sewing machine didn't equal progress.

Lily caught Tom's eye and silently implored him to be quiet while she made her argument. "I can just ship it home when I'm done with the dress," she said.

Tom got the hint and said nothing.

Olivia said, "That sounds wonderful."

Eleanor stood up, waved her hand dismissively through the air, and said, "Fine. Whatever you like. I'm going to bed."

BY the time Tom had finished breakfast the next morning, Lily was dressed and ready to head to the fabric store.

"You don't mind if I go to the brunch, do you?" Tom asked. "I'd like to see that avocado ranch."

"No," Lily said. "You should definitely go."

"You sure you don't want to join us? You could buy your fabric this afternoon."

She shook her head. "I want to get started on the dress while Brooke is out of the house."

Tom had grown up walking in the green woods of New England, and he and Lily had raised their boys there among the evergreens and the birch. The silver sage colors and Mediterranean climate of Lily's hometown had at first seemed alien to him, but over the years, over many visits, he had come to find their spare beauty captivating.

As they drove to the Hailwoods', Tom drank in the scenery. Behind them was the whole glittering ocean. In front of them were sandstone peaks, chaparral-choked canyons, and stands of towering eucalyptus trees. The road wound gently upward toward a neat grid of avocado trees, which spread over the hills in stately procession, their leaves flat and shiny, their fruit black and gnarled.

At the party, kids ran around eating fistfuls of tortilla chips. Adults gathered around the bartender, drinking margaritas made with fresh limes, even though it wasn't yet noon, and even though back in Vermont a lime would cost at least a dollar. Ryan and Luke slipped into the crowd, and discussed how Marian Jones's drug scandal would impact track sponsorships. Olivia followed Brooke around like a shepherd, making sure she didn't fall off the deck, keeping her fingers out of the salsa bowls, which sat on low tables, as tempting as candy. Eleanor introduced Tom to their hosts, Gail and Ted Hailwood, and Tom immediately started asking questions about the trees.

"The ranch is twenty-seven acres," Ted said. "Three hundred mature trees. We're contract growers, so all our fruit goes straight to the Calavo warehouse down in Carpinteria."

"Has your yield been impacted by the diminishing bee population?" Tom asked.

"Everything impacts the yield," Ted said, "the bees, the drought, and now you have to think about the market demand for organic on top of it."

"You're running conventional, then?"

"For now," Ted said. "Times are changing, though, they're definitely changing. But you should taste these beauties." He stepped over to a table nearby, and Tom followed. A woman in an apron was scooping the green flesh of an avocado from the black skin, mixing in minced garlic and onion, and mashing it in a stone bowl to make guacamole.

Tom took a chip; his forehead was creased in thought. "You harvest in winter?" he asked.

"Harvest year-round," Ted said. "There's a variety called Fuerte. It's got a thicker skin that can withstand just about any frost. We've got half Fuerte, half Haas."

Tom's eyes opened wide. "I'd like to see the difference between the trees, if you don't mind."

They slipped off the deck and into the orchard, and by the time Tom emerged, he was thinking about mashed avocados and running a small ranch in a place where fog was the worst weather you would ever expect and no one cared a whit about an integrated science curriculum or the role that freshman biology played in weeding out students who couldn't handle the premed curriculum.

WHEN they got back to Eleanor's house, Lily had hidden away her purchases and her project. She asked everyone how the party had been. Tom smiled. "Ted Hailwood gave me a tour of the property," he said. "There's a variety of avocado that thrives in the winter, and they've got those trees planted on the southern sector to take advantage of the winter light. The roots actually like to be dry, which is why the hillside location is ideal. It was fascinating."

Eleanor put down her purse and, with the air of someone telling a secret she knew wasn't hers to tell, said, "The ranch is for sale. Ted told us on our way out. They're moving to a retirement community as soon as they can find a buyer."

For a heartbeat, no one said anything. Tom and Lily both turned to look at Eleanor—Tom shocked that Ted's offhand parting comment had registered with Eleanor, and Lily shocked at what she felt certain her mother was gearing up to say. And then Eleanor looked at Lily and said it: "Maybe you and Tom should snatch it up."

"Snatch it up?" Lily said. To Eleanor, a cross-country move, a new occupation, a radical change in lifestyle, required as much thought as buying a new lipstick, but to Lily it was as if her mother had proposed a trip to the moon.

Ryan, who had grown up working in his dad's summer garden, picking tomatoes and stringing peas, said, "You'd be the perfect gentleman farmer, Dad, with your straw hat and your tools, tramping through the trees."

"Yeah," Luke added, "and it would give you an excuse to buy as many trowels as you'd ever want."

Tom laughed. "I do like trowels," he said, "and tramping through trees. Maybe someday I'll get my hands in the dirt of an orchard of my own."

Lily gaped at her husband. He taught biology, and grew tomatoes and peas and sunflowers in the backyard. She couldn't recall a single time he had talked about farming. He wanted to travel when they retired. And walk in the woods. And he often mentioned getting involved with the board at Burlington's Intervale Community Farms so that he could help raise funds for their school garden programs—but wanting an *actual* farm? Wanting a new occupation? This was completely new. She spoke to him quietly, as if no one else were in the room. "Tom?" she said. "You want to be a farmer?"

Tom shrugged and looked at his wife with such affection and longing that Eleanor and Olivia and the boys all looked away; the moment seemed too intimate to watch. "It was a spectacularly beautiful spot," he said. "I could just picture us there—walking through the trees in the morning, taking stock of the birds and the bees, the sun and the rain."

"Wow," Lily said breathlessly, as if the air had suddenly been sucked from the room and she was struggling to get enough. "I had no idea that's something you wanted."

Tom got up and went over to Lily and took her head in his hands and kissed her. "I'm a man of many surprises," he said, and Ryan and Luke both burst out laughing, because their dad was so clearly not.

"Well, listen, Tom," Eleanor said. "If you're serious about wanting to buy that farm, I'll help foot the bill. I don't need to die with all my money in the bank."

"You can give it to me," Luke said, and they all laughed again, because Luke had just graduated from college, and five months ago had moved from Vermont to take a job at Bertasi Linen, his grandmother's textile company. He was still in shock about how taxes eviscerated his paycheck, about how hard it was to pay the rent on his tiny apartment. Everyone laughed, that is, except Lily.

"What are you all *talking* about?" she asked. She and Tom owned their house in Burlington outright. They were each five years away from earning their full pensions at the University of Vermont. They were not planning a move, and certainly not a move back to the hometown she had once left for good. Just because Tom had been inspired by an avocado farm didn't mean they were going to buy it.

"I'm talking about investing in real estate," Eleanor said.

"That's obvious," Lily said, "but are you *serious*? Did you happen to forget that your moving from place to place on a whim was one of the central realities of my childhood? Tom and I have worked hard to build our life in Burlington, and it's a good life and a stable life and we're not just going to up and move because you can write a check."

"Having the money to do the things you want isn't a crime, Lily."

Lily turned, fuming, and then spun back toward her mother, but Tom spoke before Lily could open her mouth. "Stop," he said, raising his hand like a traffic cop. "Both of you. Please. I was just musing about a beautiful spot on the map."

AT the end of the day, when they were alone in the guest room on the third floor, Lily turned to

Tom. "Thank you for calling my mom off this morning," she said.

"You take her too seriously," Tom said. "She doesn't mean any harm."

Lily laughed. "I think my mother would like nothing better than to cause a little harm. She causes harm for sport. I hope Luke knows what he got himself into, signing on to work for her."

"It's a good opportunity for him," Tom said, "and I wouldn't worry about Luke. He can hold his own."

She sat down on the bed. "I miss him," she said. "I didn't realize how lucky we were to have him so close to home for college."

"Yes you did," Tom said, smiling. "You talked about it every time he brought friends home for dinner. You talked about it every time he brought you a duffel bag full of laundry."

"I guess," she said. "It just went so fast. And now here he is—my baby, out in the world." She slipped off her shoes, and thought again about the conversation from the morning. "Tom?" she asked. "You *were* a little serious about that avocado farm, weren't you?"

He shrugged, shy like a little boy who had been caught red-handed. "You should have seen those trees," he said, "that view."

•3•

Ryan

RYAN and Olivia were encamped in the guest room on the first floor. They had a portable crib for Brooke set up against the wall. By the time Ryan had finished playing cards with his grandmother that night, Olivia and Brooke were fast asleep. He brushed his teeth, pulled off his clothes, and slipped into bed beside his wife.

Being with his parents was more difficult than he had anticipated. They were a constant reminder to him about what a poor job he was doing as a husband and father. His parents just seemed to get it right; they always had. When he was a teenager and other kids' parents argued about money, went on separate vacations, and took other lovers, his parents seemed to be as devoted to each other as they always had been. No matter what was happening, they were good to each other—kind and caring. They respected each other. And they had plenty of affection left over for him and his brother. Ryan had lately been thinking that maybe he just wasn't cut out for marriage.

Some days he came home from running a late workout at the pool and Olivia and Brooke would be giggling and playing some private game, and he would just stare, wondering who the little girl in pink was and what she was doing there in his house. Other days, when he hugged his wife and cupped her breasts in his hands, she recoiled the way she had sometimes done when she was still breast-feeding Brooke. Some nights when he came home late, Olivia didn't even look up from the book she was reading. He often wondered if she even *liked* him anymore.

He squeezed his eyes shut, and then opened them and turned to look at Olivia. She was so sound asleep that she was hardly moving. Her breathing was deep and even. He fit his hand over her hip bone and lay against her and listened to her sleep. He tried to imagine what it would be like if she was just suddenly gone, and his throat constricted and he pressed harder against her because he wasn't sure he could bear it. She was his wife, the mother of his child. He slid his hand over her pelvis to the soft hair between her legs, and he entwined his fingers there and felt her breath move in and out of her body. She shifted, and he felt her body press against his hand—a small show of desire. He groaned, and pressed against her and moved his fingers farther down. Now she moaned, and shifted her weight so that she could receive his hand. Then she woke up. She lifted her head. She pulled up her knees. "What are you doing?" she said—groggy, confused, displeased.

"Making love to my sexy wife," Ryan said.

Olivia pulled herself up on the pillows, pulled up the sheet to cover herself. "Brooke's right there," she said—and it was true: Brooke was asleep in a portable crib against the far wall.

"She's asleep," Ryan said.

"She could wake up any second."

"We have sheets," he said. "Blankets." He reached his hand to her hip again, an invitation.

"I can't," she said, turning away from him. "I'm sorry."

He flung the covers off. "I'm tired of all your excuses, Olivia."

"Shhh," she said. "You'll wake her."

"I'm tired of that, too—turning our lives upside down for a two-year-old."

"That's what parents do," Olivia said. "That's the job definition."

"I'm pretty sure the job definition involves having sex more than once in a blue moon. You used to like it, you know. You used to want it."

"Ryan," she said. "There'll be time for that later. She's so little."

"I think it's bullshit," he said, and stood up. "I know plenty of guys whose wives still put out after they have a baby."

"Put out?" she scoffed. "Are you kidding me? You dare to talk to me like that? I'm the mother of your child."

"I'm just calling a spade a spade."

"Fine. Then if you want it so badly, go out and get it somewhere else, Ryan. Go out and find some sweet thing who'll *put out* for you."

He stood up, picked up his pillow. "I've come that close," he said, holding his thumb and forefinger a quarter inch apart. "That close."

The air in the room got thin then, as if they were in a plane that had suddenly lost pressure. She had to concentrate on breathing. "Don't bother holding back on my account," she finally said. "Brooke and I will be just fine without you."

"Is that what you want?"

"Apparently it's what *you* want."

"I didn't do it yet, Olivia. I just said I had come close."

"Congratulations," she said. "Your mom and dad would be so proud."

Just then, Brooke lifted her head, and then she lifted herself up and stood at the side of the crib. Olivia flung back the covers on her side of the bed, scooped Brooke up in her arms, and kissed her hot and sweaty cheeks.

"I'm going to sleep on the couch," Ryan said, and walked out the door.

·4·

Lily

ON the day she picked out the velvet for Brooke's dress, Lily walked up and down the aisles of the fabric store in a state of rapture. Surrounded by meaty wools, diaphanous silks, and row after row of vibrant cotton prints made her pulse quicken, and her mind spin. *I could make a quilt,* she thought, *I could make a coat, I could make a dress, a tablecloth, pillows.* She had once heard an interviewer ask Willie Nelson where he got his ideas for songs, and Nelson had said, "The air is full of tunes; I just reach up and pick one." Lily felt that same sense of possibility here in the store. All she had to do was choose the yardage, and the project would suggest itself. She had stopped sewing regularly when the boys were small, when the demands of teaching and raising children had overwhelmed her. She stopped buying fabric, too, convincing herself that she had enough for a lifetime, that the basement could hold nothing more. Standing in the store, on a mission to buy red velvet, she realized that she was wrong; she could never have enough fabric.

She reluctantly left behind the riotous cotton prints from Anna Maria Horner's latest collection, the block print silk from Japan, and the improbably thin merino wool from Milan, and bought three yards of ruby red velvet and three yards of muslin. She picked out an electronic Singer sewing machine that seemed more akin to a rocket ship than it did to her grandmother's cast-iron workhorse, and grabbed an eight-inch zipper, a pair of Gingher scissors, a box of pins, a spool of thread, and a package of needles.

"No pattern?" the saleswoman asked.

Lily smiled. *You sew? No pattern?* She used to sit in her grandmother's sewing room rearranging the wooden spools of threads as if they were soldiers, and listening to the sounds of the sewing machine as if it were a choir, singing them off to battle. She loved everything about Hattie's room—the color, the sound, the smell, the feel of the fabric, and the way that her grandmother could unfold a bolt of muslin, make a few cuts, and suddenly have the pattern for a princess's dress, a witch's cape, or a thick red wool peacoat that would keep her warm all winter. When she was eight, her grandmother taught her this magic trick. She guided Lily to cut a pattern from newspaper, to hold it up to her waist, to leave an allowance for the seam. "It's all a matter of getting the vision right," Hattie said. Lily pinned her pattern to a piece of red-checked cotton with long, thick straight pins. Hattie showed her how to use pinking shears to cut out the shapes, and then how to thread the sewing machine—over, under, around, and through. When Lily began to sew, her whole body became involved as she pressed the pedal to make the machine hum and leaned forward to guide the fabric underneath the needle: her hands, her feet, her arms, and her mind were all working together to make something that she could use that very night. That was what she loved most about sewing—the wholeness of it.

In high school, during the summers when her mother traveled the world to visit mills and factories and to secure the business of new hotels, Lily traveled to Boston to stay with her grandmother, and to sew. At the end of each summer, Eleanor would have a whole new wardrobe, custom-made by tailors in London and Milan, and Lily would have a whole new wardrobe made by hand on her grandmother's black Singer sewing machine. Each year, she tackled more and more complicated designs—from simple dresses and A-line skirts to lined jackets and collared shirts. The year she turned sixteen, Lily made a knockoff of a Pucci dress, a miniskirt, and a caftan, whose neckline she embellished with beads. Hattie, appalled at the loose designs, suggested that Lily learn how to make a formal, fitted dress suitable for a dance.

"I don't go to dances, Grandma," she said.

"They don't dance in California?"

Lily thought about the funky dances everyone was doing now—the Twist, the Boogaloo. "They dance," Lily said, "but not the way you're thinking. And I don't go to the dances anyway."

"Why on earth not?"

She shrugged, thinking of the loud music, the frantic couplings, the hemlines that were up and then down, the whole hazy frenzy of it all. It reminded her so much of her mother. "I guess I'm too shy," she said.

"A pretty dress will fix that," Hattie said. She got up, opened a cedar chest under the window, spent several minutes moving cloth around, and finally took out a parcel of brown butcher paper. There was lace inside. It was silvery white, with wide, open flowers, whose petals formed the scalloped edges of the cloth. Around the flowers, delicate ribbons curved and spun like tiny shimmering roads, and in the center of each flower was a burst of seed pearls.

Lily reached out to feel the embroidered petals, and trace the ribbon with her fingers, "What is it?"

"Hand-embroidered, hand-beaded French lace. My father brought it back for my mother when he was in the war, but she didn't live to see it."

"It's gorgeous."

"I was going to make a dress," Hattie said, "to wear to a dance, but after Mother died, things started going badly with my father's business and then there were no more dances."

"Why didn't you make something else?" Lily asked.

Hattie shrugged. "When Grandpa asked me to marry him, I designed five different wedding dresses, and dozens of veils, but I could never bear to cut the lace. I ended up using machine-made lace from Stein's. I almost used this to make a gown for a charity ball during the years when Grandpa and I went to those sorts of things, but you can see that I never did."

"So you just kept it?"

"I liked imagining the possibilities more than I would have liked making it into any single thing. Maybe you'll be braver than me." She held the lace out toward Lily.

"Oh no," Lily said, backing away as if the fabric had sharp edges. "No way; I'm not touching that fabric."

"It would be lovely over a petal pink shift. That's how the flapper dresses were made—lace over silk."

"I can't," Lily said, thinking how preposterous pink silk and hand-embroidered lace would be at a time when girls were wearing go-go boots, cutoff jeans, and wooden beads. Still, she let her grandmother take her down to a fabric store in Lynn, not far from the original family mill. They selected five yards of a soft pink satin, and three yards of tulle, and Lily made a party dress that looked like something from the fifties, like some kind of costume. She tried hard to sew her seams as straight as her grandmother's, to press her darts as sharply, to finish her hems as neatly. She did not use a pattern and she did not use the lace.

She never wore the dress.

When Hattie died in the spring of Lily's junior year in college, Lily went and sat on her floor and carefully went through the fabric in the cedar chest. Eleanor didn't want any of it; she called it dusty, old, useless junk. There was a length of beautiful black cashmere. A yard of rich Harris tweed. At the bottom of the chest, still wrapped in butcher paper, was the lace. Lily stuffed a suitcase full of fabric and wrestled the sewing machine into the trunk of a borrowed car.

She had her grandmother's blood in her veins and her grandmother's fabric in her stash; she did not need a pattern to sew her own granddaughter a Christmas dress. She turned to the fabric saleswoman in Santa Barbara. "No thanks," she said. "I don't need a pattern."

WHILE the rest of her family went to the party at the Hailwoods' ranch, she learned how her new sewing machine worked, and sketched out patterns on the newspaper. In the afternoon, while her mother, Olivia, and Brooke went to the zoo and the boys went sea kayaking, she measured and cut, basted and stitched. On Christmas Eve, she stayed up by herself to hem the velvet dress.

The fabric was soft and substantial. It was a deep crimson red, the kind of color that had once been reserved for nobility. Brooke would feel like a princess when she put it on, and Lily felt a secret thrill that the gift she made with her hands would equal the gift her mother had bought with her money. When she was done with the dress, she wrapped it up and put it under the tree. She poured out the milk Brooke had set out, and ate the sprinkled sugar cookies they'd brought home from the bakery, and hoped that having sugar so late at night wouldn't keep her up or give her a migraine.

IN the morning, Eleanor and Ryan got up at dawn to go down to the beach for their annual Polar Bear swim. They were back sipping coffee by the time the rest of the family was awakened by Brooke's cries of glee.

"Santa came," Brooke called. "Santa came!"

They made their way downstairs, and even though no one but Eleanor knew that Ryan had slept on the couch, Lily noticed that while Olivia crouched down with Brooke to examine the cookie crumbs and the empty glass of milk, Ryan sat on the couch, his hair still wet, looking as if he'd rather be anywhere else. It was a split-second observation of a tiny moment of discord, but it lodged in Lily's brain, and would stay wedged there, like a thorn.

Brooke turned her attention to the gifts under the tree, to the big red box wrapped in a white satin bow. She ripped the paper off the doll. Her mouth formed a perfect "O" when she held the beautiful doll in her hands.

"It's from Nana," Olivia said, and Brooke threw herself at her great-grandmother, squeezing the doll between them. Lily stared at her mother's sun-spotted hand stroking her grandchild's gleaming hair, and felt a wave of jealousy. Brooke returned to opening her other gifts, including the red velvet dress, but as soon as everything was opened, she retreated to a corner of the living room, where she laid out the doll's clothes and shoes and storybooks, and fell into a world of her own making. The red velvet dress, *The Busy Town of Richard Scarry*, and the other toys and gifts were left untouched.

"Brooke," Olivia said, "your grandma Lily made this beautiful dress so you could match your doll. Why don't you try it on?"

Brooke ignored her mother. She was talking softly to the doll, stroking its hair.

"Brooke," Olivia said sharply, but still the girl did not turn around.

Olivia stood up and walked over to her daughter. She crouched down.

"I'd like to help you try on Grandma Lily's dress."

Brooke shook her head. "No," she said.

Olivia took the doll, set it up high on a book-shelf, and Brooke began to scream. She flung herself on the ground, wailing.

Ryan brought his hands to his face as if he could block out the scene, and Olivia simply picked up Brooke and marched downstairs to the room where they were staying.

Lily quickly got up and went to the kitchen to make pancakes.

Tom followed her. "The dress is pretty, sweetheart," he said. "You did a nice job."

Lily waved her hand, dismissing his comment. "It was silly of me to make it," she said. "A two-year-old doesn't care about clothes."

"Don't be so hard on yourself. A few years from now she'll be able to appreciate your skill."

Lily raised herself up on her toes and kissed him on the cheek.

"That's nice of you to say," she said, but she still felt the sting of the rejection, and the shame of how she had been so jealous of her own mother.

Tom reached down and wrapped his arms around her. Just then, Ryan walked in.

"Whoa, sorry to interrupt," Ryan said, skidding to a halt as he rounded the corner. Lily and Tom smiled at their son.

"I just wanted to make sure you were okay, Mom, about the dress and everything."

"Don't worry about me, Ryan. You just take care of your sweet family."

He shrugged, and a shadow crossed his face. "I'm trying," he said.

Lily got out the flour and the eggs, the butter and the syrup. Tom pulled bacon from the refrigerator.

"You and Dad have set the bar pretty high for family happiness," Ryan said.

"The secret to a good marriage," Tom said, "is breakfast."

Lily and Ryan both raised their eyebrows in question.

"It's the small things," Tom said. "The daily things that make life a little easier because you're sharing it."

"Is that from *Old Tom's Almanac?*" Ryan teased.

Lily laughed.

"Very good," Tom said, and laughed, too. "*Old Tom's Almanac.*"

THAT night, Tom got into bed, took off the round glasses that made him look like a caricature of a professor, and did not pick up the book he had been reading on the horrors of modern food production. He just lay there, staring at the ceiling. Lily washed her face and brushed her teeth as if it were any other day, but her mind was spinning. She slipped in beside Tom and then turned out the light.

She thought about her headaches, her mother,

her son, the avocado farm, the red velvet dress. She thought about how infrequently she and Tom made love anymore, and how, when they did, it was like a chore—grade the papers, attend the meeting, stroke the thigh, kiss the lips. After a while, she spoke into the darkness. "Are you happy?"

"It was great to be with all the kids," he said. "I get such a kick out of seeing Ryan with Olivia and Brooke, and Luke with a job now. God, it seems like just yesterday when they were making snow forts in the front yard."

Lily smiled wryly in the dark. "I meant on a more cosmic scale."

"Oh," he said. "Am I happy? I don't know. I keep thinking about a short story I once read about Gregor Mendel."

"The Andrea Barrett story? The one about how Mendel was duped."

He turned to face her, thrilled that she knew what he was talking about. It was proof of how connected they were, how interdependent they were. Who else would know all his obscure references? Who else would agree when he lamented the changing face of biology? "Exactly," he said. "There was some very good science in that story. But it also depicted a very old man, a man who had lost his mind. People kept having to convince him of who he was, and what he had contributed to the world. Sometimes I feel like that man."

"You haven't lost your mind, Tom," she said, and reached out and stroked his hair, which was still quite thick. "Far from it."

"I know that," he said, "but sometimes I can't remember what the point of it all is."

"You've educated generations of students. You've been a pillar of our community. You're a wonderful father and husband. Grandfather, too. And you grow the best tomatoes in the state of Vermont. That's point enough, I would think."

He leaned over and kissed her. "Thank you," he said, and then, "Good night."

She lay there in the dark while Tom slept.

Is something wrong? she had asked that night in front of the bookshop.

You want to be a farmer? she had asked yesterday.

And just now, *Are you happy?*

The truth was that Lily wasn't sure of so many of the things she had once been sure of. She had always thought that the longer you were married, the closer you would get to the other person—that the gap between you would close over time. But it didn't. There was, even now, a part of Tom she could never reach. She accepted that, but at the same time, she wanted to make sure that the gap didn't widen. Even though it had been her mother's idea, even though it was such a radical departure from the road map they had made for their lives, she found herself playing with the idea of buying the avocado ranch the way a child works a loose tooth. She would present the ranch to Tom as if it were a gift tied up with a bow. She would make an impassioned speech about following one's heart. And while Tom tramped through the trees in the California sunshine, she would sit by the window and sort through her fabric and imagine the possibilities, and at night, they would talk about the things they were making, the problems they were solving, and how lucky they were to still be together after so many years.

·5·

Eleanor

AFTER everyone in her family had come and gone for the holidays, Eleanor felt bereft. The problem with being the life of the party, she thought, is that every time the party comes to an end, you die a small death. On December 28, she sat in her empty kitchen, looking at the Tupperware containers filled with leftover chili and slices of roast beef, and at the Christmas tree, whose needles were now yellow and dry, and she realized that what she had to look forward to in the New Year, for the most part, were other deaths and dissolutions.

The death part was a given. She was nearly seventy-five years old, and everyone around her was dying. They moved with increasing frequency out of their houses into assisted living facilities, or they moved in and out of the hospital, until one day, there was a phone call, or an e-mail, or a short paragraph on the obituary page of the newspaper, and they were gone. It was starting to really get to her. This year, she expected to have to say good-bye to two more people from the group of six who she always thought would live forever. There was her old college roommate, Gracie, whose cancer had migrated to her brain and taken up permanent residence there. And there was Judy Vreeland, who kept falling and breaking bones, and each time it took her longer and longer to recover. These were the people who most remembered the noise and the pop and the chaos of the prime of her life, and over the years, Eleanor had always joked that when they were gone, she might as well go, too. Now that it was actually here, however, she didn't feel sorry for herself so much as she felt angry at all of them for leaving.

She had counted on her friends far more than she had counted on her husbands or her family— counted on them to understand her, to entertain her, to always be there for her—and for years and years, it had been a smart choice. Her husbands were all gone, her daughter had taken off to live a quiet, academic life in the northern woods, but her friends remained. With one phone call, she could have a place to go for the holidays, get counsel on a business matter, find a companion to travel to the ends of the earth, or just enlist someone who would stay up late to play a hand of bridge. Eleanor thought that friendship was the most enduring relationship of all, until the calls started coming in—cancer, stroke, heart attack— and she began to see that she would be left alone in the end anyway, cursed by long-lasting genes and short-lived marriages.

The dissolution part of her premonition for the

New Year was just a suspicion—something she could smell in the air like the sea. She had lived a long time, and it was her experience that marriage didn't last. She married Billy Edwards because he had gone to Harvard and because his future looked bright, and although they had a child and gave dinner parties and traveled to the Cape in the summer, she never really loved him, not the way Judy loved Gordon, not the way she imagined love to be. When he fell to the floor of the airport in Buenos Aires, dead of a heart attack at the age of thirty-five, it was a liberation. Her relationship with her second husband, Elliot Taft, had been based wholly on desire, and before long, their marriage burned itself out. There was another husband after that, an art dealer who considered Eleanor a beautiful investment, and she used him to increase the reach of her business the same way he used her. After just four years into their marriage, the art dealer had doubled his list of exclusive contracts and Eleanor was selling high-thread-count sheets and towels to hotels on five continents, instead of just two. They agreed to divorce when there was no advantage left for either of them.

It was one thing for Eleanor to have handled marriage so recklessly, but now she smelled trouble with her grandson, Ryan, and she didn't like it. She didn't want to leave a legacy of botched love. Lily had proved capable, somehow, of a good, long marriage—a relationship that Eleanor both envied and cherished. Envied because she'd never had it herself, and cherished because her daughter's success at marriage vindicated Eleanor's many failures. But now she could see Ryan standing apart from his wife and his daughter, as though he lived in the same territory but not the same tribe. He had married too young, and for the wrong reason. It wasn't going to last. And she felt a desperation about it that surprised her.

ON Christmas morning Eleanor and Ryan got up in the dark, at dawn, and drove down to Miramar Beach for the annual Polar Bear swim. Eleanor had been a record-holding backstroker in college, and still swam three mornings a week with a Masters Group. Ryan had been an age group sprinter in Vermont, and when he was in high school, there was some talk of his being able to make an Olympic qualifying time. He never did and never succeeded to recover, completely, from the disappointment. He was now the assistant swim coach at Cal Poly, where he put young athletes through their paces and recalled, daily, what it was like to be that strong, and that free. Swimming was a language grandmother and grandson both understood—the way the body slipped through the water, the way the sensory assault of the world stopped when you were underwater—and there was no reason for them to speak as they drove.

When they got to the beach, they walked out on the sand and joined the other early-morning risers, who slapped shoulders and called out, "Merry Christmas," in voices too loud for morning. The sky was clear and cool, and out in the channel, perched in front of the islands, the oil rigs looked like giant, brooding black birds. When the swimmers ran into the waves, the cold of the water was a shock. People whooped and hollered as they made their way out to the buoy, around it, and back to the beach. Eleanor was the oldest female swimmer who'd come out that day. The skin on the undersides of her arms sagged and her legs were crisscrossed with purple veins, but she was trim, and her lungs were strong, and she didn't mind the cold. She was, still, the kind of woman that men called a good sport, the kind of woman that men adored because she was both small and beautiful, and game for a good time. She swam just behind Ryan, making her way through the choppy sea, thinking how good it was to move her arms and her legs, to take air into her lungs, to swim in the same water as the dolphins.

On the way back in, they waited at the break line for a good wave to ride, and chose to kick out on the same smooth-breaking swell. They let the water carry them along, feeling the pull on their feet, the froth in their face. Ryan stood up quickly when he got to shallow water, and was right beside Eleanor to give her a hand and help her get her legs underneath her. Bob Shafer, who came in on the wave behind them, said, "Good idea to bring your grandson again." Bob lived on a yacht in the harbor, and swam every morning in the sea. Sometimes, when Eleanor needed an escort to a party, Bob would put on his tuxedo and accompany her. Every so often, he invited Eleanor to come back with him to his boat, but she would toss her thick silver hair, flash her blue eyes, and say, "Oh, Bob, you don't really mean that," even though she knew he did.

John O'Hara, who swam three mornings a week at the club with Eleanor, was already standing on the beach. He looked at Ryan and said, "Chip off the old block, is he?"

"God, I hope not," Eleanor said, and they all laughed, because everyone knew how many times she had been married, and how many hearts she had broken in between.

But later, in the car, Ryan said, "Turns out I *am* a chip off the old block, Nana."

"How so?" Eleanor asked. She had come upon Ryan sleeping on the couch only a few hours before, with nothing more than a pillow. She knew exactly what that meant.

"Things aren't going so well with me and Olivia," he said.

"You have a toddler," Eleanor said. "Sleep deprivation magnifies every chink in the armor. You have to just wait it out."

Ryan kept his hands on the wheel of his grandmother's white Lexus, and looked straight ahead at the road. "There are more than chinks," he said.

"What's wrong?" Eleanor asked.

"I don't know," Ryan said. "It's hard to say." And then after a while, he said, "There are other women."

"Other women?" Eleanor repeated, and felt the dread she had been fearing settle on her shoulders.

"Just friends I see sometimes after work."

"Failing to keep your pants on is what got you into this situation," Eleanor said. "Don't make the same mistake twice. You have no idea what it costs to walk away."

"You're talking about money?" Ryan asked. "We don't have any money so that's not really an issue."

"Money?" she repeated. "Dear God, no, I'm not talking about money." She was talking about the shock of being old and alone, the slow dawning of understanding about the ways in which your actions and decisions reverberate through your family. "Money comes and money goes," she said.

She turned and looked out the window. She was talking about seeing the repercussions of your actions played out in the next generation, and the next. She hadn't paid much attention to Lily, and maybe Lily had paid too *much* attention to Ryan and Luke. Everyone expected a mother to be perfect, to give the child exactly what that child needed, and no mother could ever live up to it. Then the children grow up and go out and try to make up for what was missing—by living a carefully structured life the way Lily had done, free of risk, free of fun. Or by giving up on having as good a marriage as your parents when you were only twenty-five, the way Ryan was doing now.

Ryan snorted. "That's what Mom always said you believed about men."

Eleanor laughed bitterly. "I'm sure it looked that way to her, but I . . ."

"Nana," Ryan said, "you've said it a hundred times—*love is just an illusion, you can't count on love.*"

THAT phrase rang in Eleanor's head throughout the holidays. *You can't count on love.* She wondered if it was really true, and tried to think through all the couples she knew who had proven her wrong. She came up with just two. Her old friends Judy and Gordon. And Tom and Lily, her only child. But then, on the day before Christmas when the family came back from a party at the Hailwoods', there was the tense exchange about an avocado ranch, and Eleanor began to wonder even about them.

• • •

AFTER everyone went home, Eleanor called Gracie in New York. "What will we resolve this year?" she asked.

"I'm going to resolve not to die," Gracie said. "It works, since I never was very good at keeping my resolutions."

Eleanor was tempted to say, "You're not going to die, Gracie," just as she had said in college, "You're not going to fail." But it was too late for all that now. Gracie was dying, and they both knew it. "Just be sure you make it till Opening Day," Eleanor said.

"As long as you can wheel me to a skybox, honey, I'm going to Opening Day," Gracie said.

They had been making a party of the Red Sox Opening Day since the spring of 1952. That was eight months after they arrived at Wellesley College, with their wool kilts, their cardigan sets, their pearl necklaces. Gracie knew a baseball player from her hometown who was starting that fall at Harvard, and on the weekend of the Harvard-Yale football game, he brought two friends with him—a shortstop and a first baseman—so that Eleanor, Judy, and Gracie could each have a date. The six of them piled into a two-tone four-door Studebaker Commander with flasks of hot buttered rum, and drove out from Wellesley to the game. The couples were paired off by height, because that seemed the easiest thing to do, and because Eleanor took an instant liking to Billy Edwards, the shortest of the three boys. He was strong and athletic and wore his blue blazer and penny loafers as if they were his birthright.

"Do you know much about football?" Billy asked.

"Not a thing," Eleanor said coyly, "except that the men look ridiculous in those helmets. I far prefer baseball."

The boys hooted and whistled. "Do you now?" Gordon Vreeland asked. He was driving, and spoke without taking his eyes from the road.

"That's my girl," Billy said to the other boys— already claiming Eleanor, already staking his turf.

"Her daddy owns one of the big mills in Lynn and he has box seats at Fenway," Gracie blurted out, and the boys cheered again. The war was over, and life was good for all of them.

"And she swims, too," Judy said, just so she would have something to add to the conversation. "She swims fast! Isn't that right, Eleanor?" Gracie and Eleanor had been paired as roommates, and Judy lived down the hall from them, with a girl whose glasses were thick as Coke bottles and who preferred to spend her evenings in the library.

"But she doesn't know a thing about football," Gordon said to Billy. "She said so herself. So that means you've got some coaching to do today, sport."

The boys took the girls to three other football games that fall, and to a winter dance at Winthrop House, and when baseball season started in the spring, they invited them to their first game against Dartmouth—a game they lost quite badly, as they would so many games that season and the next. In exchange for all their kindnesses, Eleanor invited all six of the group to watch Ted Williams in the Red Sox Opening Day game, and they sat behind home plate on the first base foul line and ate hot dogs and felt like royalty. When Williams was called up to the Korean War a few weeks later, they were shocked and sobered, and their sense of having experienced something special was solidified.

"We should make this a tradition," Gracie said during the seventh inning stretch. "We should come back every year to Opening Day at Fenway, no matter where we are in our lives."

"It's a deal," Billy said, grabbing Eleanor's hand and squeezing.

Eleanor married Billy in June of the year they graduated. Judy married Gordon later that summer, but Gracie would choose a Yale man over Bucky Harrington. Still, they kept their promise as often as they could, returning to Fenway, as jobs, children, wars, and the vagaries of life allowed. Other friends from college joined them, now and again, and sometimes friends they made at work, or in their communities. Eleanor was accustomed to eating at fine restaurants all over the world, but there was little she liked better than a hot dog and a cold beer at Fenway Park.

NOW, some sixty years later, Gracie asked her old friend, "Are you resolving anything this year?"

"I'm swearing off men," Eleanor said.

Gracie laughed, and it sounded as though it made every bone in her body hurt. "That's a new one."

"I'm serious," Eleanor said. "It used to be fun; now it's just pathetic. Now they just want someone to keep them company or to nurse them in their old age."

"I'm not seeing you in that role," Gracie said.

"No," Eleanor agreed. "And I think I'm going to resolve to invest in a new family venture."

"So you're too old for men, but not too old for business?"

"I didn't say I was too old for men," Eleanor said. "I said they were too old for me. And family businesses have paid off quite handsomely for me, in case that's slipped your mind." She had helped run her father's textile company after Billy died, and took it over completely after her second husband died, too. In four years, she turned a regional operation into a multinational one.

"It hasn't slipped my mind," Gracie said, "believe you me. So what's the business this time? Anything to do with baseball? Fine art? Four-hundred-thread-count sheets?"

"No," she said. It was about making sure that Lily and Tom had reason to thank her, to include her, to be near her. It was about making sure that she would have someone in her life after her last best friend was dead and gone. "Avocados."

·6·

Lily

BACK in Burlington, it was cold and wet. There was no ice on Lake Champlain, but each night, the tree branches would become encased with ice and they would creak and moan under the added weight. The students weren't due back until January fourteenth and it was unnaturally quiet on campus. Lily walked through the cold to her office. She flicked on the lights and turned up the heat.

Marilyn, one of her colleagues, poked her head inside the door. "Hey," she said. "Welcome back to winter. How was Santa Barbara?" Lily considered telling Marilyn about Tom and the avocado ranch and what happened with Brooke and the red velvet dress—but she decided against it. Maybe Marilyn used to be the kind of friend she would confide in, but she wasn't anymore. No one was. All the friends Lily had when the boys were young—other mothers who went to swim meets and Little League games and who baked birthday cakes and nursed kids with the chicken pox—had drifted out of her life as her boys had grown up and moved away. Sometimes she would run into one of the women in the grocery store, and they would ask each other about their children and share the headlines of their lives, but then they had nothing left to say to each other, and they would smile and say good-bye. She often went on walks with Marilyn, and in the winter sometimes swam laps with a woman who worked in admissions, but they never really talked about anything more than the weather, the goings-on in the department, the new crop of freshman.

"Good," Lily said. "Fine. And did you survive the twins?"

"One of them bit me," she said, and held out her hand for proof.

Lily laughed, relieved that there were other people besides herself who didn't automatically get along with their grandchildren, who weren't automatically adored.

"And Jerry and I decided to separate," Marilyn said, but her voice was no longer light.

"Separate?" Lily said, more loudly perhaps than she needed to, because she was surprised to hear this sudden pronouncement. Hadn't she just seen Jerry holding a coat for Marilyn as they left a party a week before Christmas? Hadn't Marilyn just bought Jerry a new set of cross-country skis? "I didn't know you were having trouble."

Marilyn shrugged. "It's my own damn fault," she said matter-of-factly. "We got tangled up with another couple, and Jerry would rather be with her than with me."

"Oh," Lily said. Her mind raced for the next appropriate thing to say. Didn't Marilyn *mind* that everyone would know this private business about her life? Wasn't she the least bit *embarrassed* by what she was saying? "Are you . . ." Lily asked. "I mean, are you and this other man . . ."

"God, no," Marilyn said. "The whole thing was just a diversion for me, something I agreed to in order to keep Jerry happy. I had no idea it would end like this."

Lily just stared at her, stumped now.

"I was an idiot," Marilyn said. "I should have just done whatever the hell I wanted to please myself. The result would have been the same anyway."

Lily nodded. "I'm sorry," she said. She felt like she had so many times in her childhood—naïve, clueless, embarrassed at how much she hadn't seen or even guessed. Just a few weeks after Lily's father died, she had walked in on her mother, naked in bed with another man. Lily was ten years old—which was old enough to have some understanding of what she was seeing, but too young to fully comprehend. "This is Elliot Taft," her mother had said. "Elliot, this is my daughter, Lily," as if it were the most normal introduction in the world. Two years later, when her mother told her that Elliot was going back to Houston and they would be staying in Santa Barbara, Lily was stunned again. She hadn't seen it coming. She had grown to like Elliot Taft. He helped her with her homework, kept her mother somewhat grounded. She thought she might never understand the world of adults—a belief she felt again now that she was decidedly a part of it.

Marilyn shrugged again. "Life goes on," she said. "You starting work on that textbook website yet?"

"Today's the day," Lily said, relieved to be moving on to another topic. "What about you? What brings you into the office during winter break?"

"I'm on the search committee for a new assistant professor," Marilyn said. "We've got candidates coming in from Florida and Texas for the start of classes and I'm trying to make sure all the logistics are set."

"It's supposed to snow," Lily said.

"Well," Marilyn said, "it's not like we're pretending to be a tropical island."

Marilyn left, and again Lily's office was quiet. She turned her mind to *Discoveries in Geometry*. She needed to hire a web designer because her publisher wanted everything to be interactive, but she kept circling back to what Marilyn had said: *I should have just done whatever the hell I wanted to please myself.* That could have been Lily's mother talking. And it was, Lily thought with a certain amount of smugness, precisely the thing

Lily had resolved not to do in her marriage, and precisely why she was still married to this day.

AT noon, she gave up searching for a web guru who understood geometry and went home for lunch. She ate a turkey sandwich while reading about a quilt artist who worked exclusively with vintage fabrics, and when she was done, she went down into the basement. She had piles of fabric sealed in Rubbermaid boxes, impervious to mice and moths and sunlight. She had collected fabric everywhere her mother dragged her, and when she traveled by herself. One bin contained nothing but tablecloths—pristine white damask, hand-embroidered linen, woven cloth from India, and the brightly colored cotton cloth she and Tom had bought in Lyon. It was threadbare at the edges now, and at the creases, consigned to the Rubbermaid containers in the basement after a long life of service. She took it out, unfurled it like a flag. They had purchased it when they were in their midtwenties, in the days before they decided to marry. Tom had finished his graduate studies, and gone to Ethiopia with the Peace Corps to teach beekeeping. Lily had stayed on at the University of Denver, where she had done her graduate work, and was now teaching and working with an older mathematician on the text-book project she would ultimately inherit. She met Tom in Paris and they took the train to Lyon.

In the previous six months, they had written each other letters every week, talking about their work. They were worlds apart, and they had each begun to forget the spark of connection they had felt when they met in the mountains of Colorado the previous summer. Tom would write about pollen counts in African tribal hives and she would write about the difficulties of using English to describe math and they would each read the other's letters and think, *He is so far away; she is so far away.* In Lyon, however, they wandered through the street markets, took long walks along the river, and remembered how easy it was to be together, how easy it was to talk about everything, from what kind of cheese to buy for lunch to the probability of whether or not there was a God to what would become of their friends who had gone to work on Wall Street. They began to talk about looking for jobs at the same university, starting a family. One day, in a stall on a shady street, they saw a tablecloth printed in a bright cacophony of red and cream paisley swirls. Lily stopped to look, and Tom stood beside her, trying to see what she was seeing.

"It's printed cotton," Lily explained, "similar to the kind of cloth Matisse draped on the table of his still lifes. He was a huge collector of textiles. He painted them again and again, and called them his 'noble rags.'"

"Let's buy it," Tom said.

She laughed. "You want to buy a tablecloth?" she asked. They were young, just starting out in the world. They didn't have a house, a table, a set of silverware.

"First the tablecloth, then the table, then the house," Tom said, "and then a garden, of course."

While the woman at the stall rang up their purchase, she chatted with Lily about Bohain-en-Vermandois, the town where Matisse was born, several hundred miles to the north. "An ugly, industrial town," the woman said, "but they say that the river used to shimmer with a rainbow of impossible colors from all the dyes from the weavers' shops. Can you imagine it? A bright magenta river?"

Lily and Tom always repeated that part of the story, when they told it, time after time—*Can you imagine it? A bright magenta river?* Their friends would comment on the tablecloth, and Lily and Tom would talk about finding it in Lyon, which was really a story about how they found each other, how they committed to each other, and how they shared a love that sustained them.

SHE closed up her tubs, brought the tablecloth up from the basement, got out her ironing board, and set it up in the kitchen. She used to bring out the Lyon tablecloth for special occasions—birthdays and when they got their tenure appointments and promotions. The boys always liked it, and the stories that would follow about Tom and the bees and Lily trekking to France.

When Tom walked in, he said, "Hey, I haven't seen that in a while."

"It's been in the basement," she said, "but it's funny because I can't remember putting it down there."

"I find things down in the basement that I haven't seen in twenty years," Tom said.

Lily laughed. "That could come in handy if you ever wanted to find a *National Geographic* from the bicentennial."

"I remember that issue, actually," he said.

"Tom! I was kidding!"

"No, I do. There was an article by Isaac Asimov about life on a space colony fifty years in the future. It was fantastic, and people actually believed that's what the future would bring. I remember that there were these illustrations accompanying that article, and there was this girl in a minidress on a moving staircase. She kind of looked like you."

"You remember that?"

"Sure," Tom said.

Lily began to press the iron to the old tablecloth. "You're amazing," she said, "and a little frightening."

Tom got out a plate, made himself a sandwich, sat down at the table. "What were you doing down in the basement anyway?" he asked. "Have you been here all morning?"

"No," she said, "I went to the office to try to start my research for the website."

"I take it that didn't go well."

Lily set the iron down. "Nothing's changed in geometry," she said, "but I still have to find a way to modernize it. As if Euclid alone isn't enough."

"What would happen if you told them you weren't going to do it?"

"My book would become even more obsolete. I'd have to teach from a book written by someone who drank the 'make math whiz-bang' Kool-Aid."

Tom got up from the table. "You and I," he said, "are old school. We are definitely old school."

"Oh," she said, "speaking of that. Marilyn Mason came by my office this morning. Did you know she and Jerry are separating?"

"No," he said, "I hadn't heard that."

She decided not to tell him the rest of the story just now, and he didn't ask. She was still thinking about what Marilyn had said: *I should have just done whatever the hell I wanted to please myself.*

LILY did not go to the office the next day. She went instead to visit Elizabeth Stewart, her neighbor down the street. Elizabeth was a potter, a tea drinker, a dog lover, a mother, a widow, a third-generation New Englander. Although they mostly only waved at each other as they passed on the street, or knocked on each other's door when there was an emergency with the electricity or a deer trapped by a fence at the end of the street, Lily considered Elizabeth to be one of the only people with whom she could still have a meaningful conversation. Elizabeth was practical, grounded, kind.

"You're just in time," Elizabeth said when she let Lily in. "I'm glazing today. You can keep me company."

The older woman led Lily through her house to the studio out back. On the workbench, there were fifteen pots made out of a gritty clay the color of wet sand. Some were small creamers and pitchers, others traditional urn-shaped vessels. Each pot looked like a little pear-shaped human, with either legs and feet, or arms and hands. Some of the smaller bowls stood upon little feet, or sat upon outstretched legs. One pitcher had two arms that wrapped around itself in a hug; the elbows were the handles. The bowls and vases looked like they might come to life at any moment and walk away, or start clapping. Lily laughed.

"Strange, aren't they?" Elizabeth asked.

"Strangely wonderful," Lily said.

"A gallery over on Church Street asked me to do a series for them, and this is what came to me.

I love the color of the clay, so I'm giving them a clear glaze."

"They're really great," Lily said. She perched on a stool near the window, and got right to the reason she had come. "I'm supposed to be working on a website for my textbook today, but you can see that I'm not doing that."

"Creativity is not a linear process," Elizabeth said. "Maybe you're solving a problem you're not even aware you're solving."

Lily shrugged. "It's not that," she said, not bothering to explain how little creativity had to do with a digitized version of a geometry textbook. "There's an avocado ranch for sale in Santa Barbara."

Elizabeth was stirring a barrel of glaze on the floor with a wooden stick. She lifted her face and raised her eyebrows. "Don't go," Elizabeth said.

Lily laughed at her neighbor's directness. "Why not?"

"New Englanders don't do well out there. I can't tell you the number of people I know who moved to California, and came back within a year. They keep waiting for the fall, and it never comes."

"Luke's there now. And Ryan. They love it."

"Luke is twenty-two years old, Lily. Ryan has a young family. They're in a different phase of life."

"Tom asked me the other day what would

happen if I gave up my textbook project, and I keep thinking about it. About what I would do instead."

"You'd farm avocados?"

Lily shook her head. "No, that's Tom's thing," she said. "I would sew. And I might make an art quilt. God knows I have enough fabric."

"You don't have to move to Santa Barbara to make a quilt."

"I was also thinking about getting a dog," Lily said, although the idea had just occurred to her. When their last shepherd died during Luke's junior year of college, they didn't get a new dog, the way they had done so many times before. By mutual, silent consent she and Tom decided to be without a pet, now that they were so decidedly without kids in the house. It was easy enough to make the decision; they simply didn't visit any kennels where they would be swayed by the big brown eyes of a pup; they didn't respond to any DOGS FOR SALE signs that would lead them to a sweet, loving dog in need of a home; and they didn't go out of their way to notice dogs with dis-tinguished dispositions around town who might have sisters or puppies. When Ryan or Luke came to visit, the boys would comment on how silent and still the house was, and they would ask about a dog, and Tom would mumble something about being too busy and Lily would change the subject because she didn't want to look too closely at what it all meant—a life with no kids, no dogs, a life that would grow increasingly quiet. A dog, all of a sudden, seemed emblematic of what they had lost, and what they might gain.

"And there are no dogs in Vermont?" Elizabeth asked.

"I know it sounds crazy," Lily said, "but I think everything would come together on the avocado farm." Having said it out loud, now, it suddenly didn't seem so crazy at all.

THE wind was howling as she walked home from Elizabeth's house. She remembered how cold she had been when they first moved to Vermont. They were living in a third-floor apartment of an old house on Brattle Street, and the cold came through the windows as if it, too, were paying rent. She was cold at night, cold in the morning. She was happy the winter she was pregnant with Ryan, because she felt better insulated, and after Luke was born, they left the apartment with the thin windows and moved to a small, well-built house. The cold, however, was always a threat, and being well organized was Lily's best defense. She had a basket for hats, gloves, and scarves just inside the door. She always had chili or stew in the refrigerator for a fast, warm dinner. In just a few winters, she became as resilient as a native New Englander. Her home was worlds away from mild and easy California, and she liked it like that; each passing season proved to her how far she had come from her mother's world—a place where fabric was just a means to an end and marriage was something that didn't last.

IN the middle of night, the wind blew hard off the lake. There was a thundering crash in the backyard, which sounded like an explosion and shook the house like an earthquake. "What was that?" Lily gasped. Tom leapt out of bed and they raced down from the bedroom to see what had happened. They turned on the outdoor lights, peered out the window, and lurched back. The big elm tree had fallen, crashing through the branches of two other trees, crushing the fence around Tom's garden, and coming to rest just feet from the kitchen door. The leaves knocked against the windows, whipped by the wind, scratching and scrabbling as if they were alive.

They stood at the window for a moment, transfixed by how close they had come to a disaster. Had the wind been blowing at a slightly different tack, the tree would have fallen on them where they slept. "Jesus," Tom said.

They went to the closet to get boots and coats, and Tom fished a flashlight from the drawer in the kitchen. They walked out the front door, leaned into the wind, and made their way around to the back. The wind was bitter and cold, and the rain drove down into their faces. They surveyed the damage, and determined there was nothing they could do until morning.

They got back in bed, but they did not sleep. They sat up and talked about who they could call to come with a chainsaw in the morning, and who could haul away the debris. They talked about what would have happened if the tree had fallen through the kitchen, and what would have happened if it had fallen on the roof over their bedroom. They talked about other times they had narrowly escaped tragedy—the time the ice cracked when they were skating on the lake, the time Ryan's car skidded out on black ice the night of his junior prom, the time they were supposed to be on the Metrolink train that ended up in a twisted mass of steel.

"I guess we're just lucky," Lily said.

Tom nodded and wrapped her tightly in his arms, and they fell into a fitful sleep.

THE next day, while chainsaws buzzed in the backyard, Lily slipped away, picked up the phone, and called her mother. She took a deep breath while she waited for the call to go through. When Eleanor answered, Lily said hello and told her about the tree, and then she said, "Were you serious about buying that avocado ranch?" She spoke quickly, before there was time to change her mind.

"Funny you should ask," Eleanor said. "I spoke

to Ted Hailwood at the Farmer's Market the other day."

"About the avocado ranch?" Lily asked, as if there might be something else in question.

"Well, no one was interested in a lemon ranch that I knew of," Eleanor said.

"Oh my God," Lily said, and she flopped down on the couch. She couldn't believe her mother's presumptuousness, her mother's ability to trump her every move, her mother's knack for having an answer to everything. "You're going to *buy* it, aren't you? I should've known you would do this. I should've known."

"It's a good investment," Eleanor said. "And I was inspired. That's a combination that can't be beat."

"And you think Tom and I will just say, *'Great! Let's pack up and move to Santa Barbara?'* like it's nothing?" Even saying the words out loud made Lily's throat go dry; suddenly the thing she had been dreaming about was a real possibility, and she was going to have to face it.

"I think it's a good bet. Otherwise I wouldn't have made an offer."

Lily shook her head. "Before I picked up this phone," she said, "buying that ranch was just a vague idea. I mean, I've thought about it," she said, refusing to betray that she had, in fact, been turning it over and over in her mind. "But it's not like it's something I'm convinced I want to do."

"That's poppycock," Eleanor said.

Lily laughed. "Poppycock, Mom? No one says *poppycock* anymore."

"I do," Eleanor said, "and it *is* poppycock. You know why you called. You know what you want."

"Well, maybe I've thought about the ranch," Lily said, "but most people don't act on whims like that. There have been a thousand times when I've dreamed of something, or wanted something, and didn't do anything about it. I remember falling in love with this bolt of merino wool in Como. It was the most exquisite fabric, printed in an exaggerated paisley pattern. I can still picture the exact colors—browns and golds and a beautiful rust. Every cell in my body screamed out for me to buy that fabric, but we had spent all our money just getting there. I couldn't have it. But I had the experience of seeing it, and of wanting it, and in some ways they amount to the same thing."

"When you get to be my age," Eleanor said, "there's no time for regret like that. There's only time for action."

"I'm not your age."

"No, but you can learn something from your own mother, can't you? Tom loves that ranch. You didn't see his face when he was out there that day, but my guess is that you wouldn't have to see his face to know what he's thinking."

"What's that supposed to mean?"

79

"That you know what makes your husband happy."

"Why would you say that?"

"Because it's true," Eleanor said.

"Wait, Mom," Lily said, suddenly wondering if her mother was sick, if she was going to die. "Why are you doing this?" Lily had been trying for years to talk seriously about what steps they would take when Eleanor could no longer live by herself. Eleanor would mention friends who had brought in caregivers when they could no longer drive, and people she knew who had sold everything and moved into beautiful apartments that came with twenty-four-hour nursing care, but she would never talk about her own plans or her own wishes. "I'm healthy as an ox," she insisted whenever Lily brought it up, "so why waste time thinking about it?" *Because,* Lily thought, *I don't like surprises. I can't stand uncertainty.*

"Everyone I know is dying," Eleanor said, "all my old friends. Mostly, I just go to funerals these days. I need a better reason to throw a party."

Lily laughed. "You're crazy, Mom."

"So I've heard."

"Fine," she said. "Fine. I'll talk to Tom."

·7·

Ryan

RYAN stayed late at the pool to meet with the team trainer and a sophomore butterflyer whose shoulders were giving him problems. He had helped recruit the swimmer from Texas, and suspected he was making up his ailment because he didn't like the weight training the coaching staff had added onto the workouts. Going into the last phase of the season, the kid was swimming fast and complaining hard. The head coach was not pleased. The trainer worked with the kid's shoulder and cleared him to keep training. When the meeting was over, Ryan lingered in his office. He read the headlines on ESPN. Cleaned out his personal e-mail. He knew that once he got home, there would be no time for any of that— no time to rest, to breathe, to recharge for the next day.

When he got back to the apartment, Brooke was dressed in pink footie pajamas. She was sitting on the floor with her new doll. When she heard him, she dropped the doll, ran to him, and threw her arms around his legs. "Daddy!" she yelled.

Ryan eyed Olivia. She was sitting on the couch paging through *Newsweek* magazine, and she barely looked his way.

"Your dinner's on the table," she said. "You probably want to heat it up."

Ryan stepped over the doll, gave Olivia a kiss. He could feel the anger coming off her in waves.

"Sorry I didn't call to say I would be late," he said.

She shrugged.

"Remember that kid Tad I was telling you about? He claimed he had sore shoulders again. I had to talk with the trainer."

Brooke had padded off to her room and come back with *Harold and the Purple Crayon*, which she held up toward Ryan. "Read to me," she said.

He was starving. The last thing he'd eaten was a handful of almonds around three o'clock. It was eight o'clock now. "After I eat the dinner Mommy made," he said.

Brooke turned on her heel and faced Olivia. "Read to me," she said.

Olivia glared at Ryan. She stood up. She slapped the magazine on the coffee table. "Come on, pumpkin," she said, scooped up Brooke, and walked out of the room.

She had said only three words—*Come on, pumpkin*—but they contained a whole argument. Ryan could hear the whole thing as if it had been spoken word for word: *I've been with her all day, entertaining her all day, and I let her stay up past her bedtime so that she could at least* see *you today, and the least you could do is take ten minutes to read her a bedtime story.*

He closed his eyes. He wondered how anyone survived having a toddler. He wondered what his life would be like, now, if Olivia had never come to him, trembling, and whispered, "I'm pregnant." He couldn't believe that he was twenty-five years old, and responsible for not only himself, but two other people besides. He thought about how his own father had read him endless books when he was a boy—Richard Scarry and Robert McCloskey and then Twain, Kipling, London. How had Tom had such energy at the end of the day? How had he had the time? He heard Olivia's soft voice falling into the rhythm of the story, and he wanted to go to his wife and child, he wanted to cross the divide that separated him from them, but he was hungry, he was tired, and he felt as though he wouldn't be entirely welcome.

He cracked open a beer, and then heated up the bowl of pasta left for him, and sat alone at the table. There was a pile of mail there—a bill from the water company, a reminder that he needed to get his teeth cleaned. In the pile was a letter from his grandmother. Ryan recognized her cream-colored Crane stationery and knew how heavy it would be when he picked it up, and how the texture of her address, embossed on the back of the envelope, would feel against his fingers. Eleanor was always sending him clippings about swimmers who had performed amazing feats, or about trips she thought he should consider taking, or about an interesting wine she had tried on a trip to Seville or the Seychelles. Sometimes she just wrote little notes of encouragement—quotes from John Wooden, or from Coco Chanel. They always made him smile.

He opened the envelope and pulled out the card.

Dear Ryan,

I would like to give you and Olivia a gift for the New Year. It's a little late, I realize, but sometimes it takes me a while to hit on the right thing. I would like to buy you the services of a chef. I will leave it to you to select one that is appropriate, as I know that Olivia is very careful about what she eats. A check is enclosed.

Love,
Nana

Olivia came out of Brooke's room while he was still eating. He got up, went in to kiss Brooke good night, and then came back to his place at the table.

"So she saw you for, what? Three minutes today?"

"I said I was sorry," Ryan said.

"And you're leaving for a meet on Thursday, right? For three days."

"Yes," he said, and because he knew he was in trouble, he added, "Will you be okay?"

"It's actually easier when you're gone," Olivia said, and he felt as though a knife had been slipped in under his ribs, but he also recognized the truth in what she was saying. It was easier for him when he was gone, too. It was easier not to come home. Last week, he had actually stopped at a bar on the way home. There was a Patriots' game on, and he stopped in for one quick beer, but he found that the room was full of guys his age who hadn't yet married and women who didn't yet have pink children at home, and he stayed for a few hours, enjoying the relief, awash in the guilt.

"You're saying you'd rather I didn't come home?" he asked.

"No, I'm just stating a fact. It's easier when you're gone. Then we're not expecting you, we're not waiting up for you. I don't make a real dinner."

"Speaking of that," he said, and held out the card to her.

She read it without smiling. "So she's going to bail you out?"

"Bail me out?" Ryan asked. "She's trying to do something nice for us, Olivia. What the hell's wrong with that?"

"Sure, it's nice, but it lets you off the hook, doesn't it? You don't have to worry about coming home, you don't have to choke down the dinner I made with a screaming kid on my hip."

"Olivia," he said, "you're a great cook. This isn't a statement about your cooking."

"No, but I'm supposed to interview chefs? After I spend four hours transcribing tapes, take Brooke to the pediatrician, do the laundry, pick up all the toys in the house, and find a plumber?"

"You think I'm doing nothing all day?"

"I don't know what you do all day."

"You know what?" Ryan said as he went to the refrigerator for another beer. "I don't get you. You wanted a baby, you wanted to stay home with her," he said. "We're bending over backwards so you can do that. And here my grandmother has offered us this gift and you're pissy about it? What's the matter with you?"

"I didn't think I'd be a single mom," she said.

"A single mom doesn't have someone going out every day earning a living for her," he said.

"You think that's all I want from you? Money?"

"Seems pretty spot on to me."

She started to cry then, and went into the bedroom and shut the door.

Ryan had another beer, and turned on ESPN. He

figured he wasn't welcome in bed with his wife, so he stayed on the couch, under a thin blanket, and in the morning, he took a shower and left for work without waking her up to say good-bye.

·8·

Eleanor

THE second week of January, the carcass of a blue whale washed ashore on Miramar Beach. Eleanor heard the news at swim practice at the Harbor Pool, and when Bob Shafer said he was going to drive down to the beach after their workout to see it, Eleanor went along.

She felt that the death of the whale was somehow personal. She first moved to Santa Barbara in 1966 when Union Oil began erecting the oil platforms in the channel. Her new husband, Elliot Taft, was in charge of communications for the company, and they wanted him on hand during the development phase. He sent out press releases about the technological advances being put to use and spoke to reporters about the numbers of barrels of oil being pumped every day. In 1969, there was a massive oil spill. There was a buildup of pressure on a Union Oil platform, and a rupture on the ocean floor. For eleven days, thick crude oil bubbled to the surface, creating an eight-hundred-mile slick, and a death trap for marine animals. The community rallied together to try to save the thousands of shore birds, whose feathers were matted with crude oil, who floundered in the black waves and on the contaminated beaches. College students, businessmen, hippies, society women, and surfers flocked to the beaches to lift the helpless birds into their cars and drive them to emergency treatment centers. The rest of the country watched, transfixed by the sight of the thick oil lapping on the beach and the army of people who refused to stand by and let the birds die.

Elliot was in charge of the heated public relations effort. He was part of the team that held press conferences and tried to minimize the damage being done by such a photogenic disaster. While Elliot was holed up in conference rooms and television studios, Eleanor and Lily, who was thirteen years old, went down to the beach to watch the rescue effort. Lily cried at the sight of seals and shorebirds covered in oil. She begged to join the swarm of people trying to help. Eleanor said no, but they kept returning to the beach to stand and stare—and finally, four days later, Eleanor relented; she put on a pair of blue jeans and a clean white pair of Tretorn tennis shoes, and took Lily down to Miramar Beach. They spent the afternoon lifting oil-covered seagulls and cormorants into the company car so that they could take them to the zoo for rescue. Eleanor and Lily were a very attractive pair—a petite girl with a thick black ponytail and tear-stained cheeks, and her slim, animated mother with a chic bob—and their picture was snapped by the *Santa*

Barbara News-Press. It went out on the national wires—an emblem of the emblematic disaster—and Elliot was fired by the end of the week. When he packed to leave town, Eleanor refused to go with him.

"How can you just walk away from this disaster?" she asked.

"I was fired," he said. "I have no business here."

"I want to stay," she said.

"If you stay, our marriage is over," Elliot said.

Eleanor shrugged. Her marriage was already over. Elliot had divorced his first wife in order to marry Eleanor, but he had never actually given her up. All the upheavals happening in the world—the marches and the protests, the movements and the demand for equality—proved to Eleanor that she didn't need a husband, particularly not one like Elliot Taft. She owned a majority stake in Bertasi Linen. She still had money from Billy's life insurance policy. "Then so be it," she said.

THREE weeks later, before any papers had been filed or any actions taken, Elliot dropped dead of a heart attack in the driveway of his first wife's house. Eleanor flew back to Houston, baked the rum cake her mother always made when someone died, served it to well-wishers, and pretended that she was bereft. She wasn't, but neither was she completely relieved. Behind her back, Eleanor's friends chattered on about the bizarre circumstances of her husbands' deaths—two husbands, two bad hearts? Was there something more to it than mere coincidence? Secretly she wondered the same thing. Perhaps she wasn't meant to be loved.

ELEANOR sold the Houston house, and purchased a modern home in Santa Barbara—all white stucco and windows. She announced to the board of Bertasi Linen that she would be taking control of the business, moved the headquarters to State Street, and began a mission to woo more clients all over the world. She traveled everywhere, with samples of sheets tucked into her suitcase, and charmed hoteliers wherever she went. A year later, on the anniversary of the oil spill and on a day that would later come to be known as the first Earth Day, Eleanor took Lily on a whale watching boat in the Santa Barbara Channel. They cruised out to Santa Rosa Island, and on the way back, when they were in the middle of the shipping lane, a mother humpback whale and her calf approached the boat. The captain announced that he had to cut the engine because the whales had ventured so close. The boat floated free in the sea and the two whales came up to the boat, dove under, circled back, and then repeated their circuit again and again. For half an hour, the mother and baby swirled around them, and all the passengers on the boat scrambled to the railing to get a better view.

"Come on, Lily," Eleanor said, grabbing her daughter by the hand.

Lily refused to leave her seat. "I'm going to throw up," she said.

Eleanor led her to the small bathroom, and then dashed to the rail so she could see the whales. She felt the spray from the whale's blowholes, counted the barnacles on their rubbery skin, looked the mother directly in the eye when it poked its head out of the water. She was dazzled by their size and their grace and their presence in the ocean. For years, she and Lily would argue about the trip—with Lily saying how Eleanor had dragged her to a new city, away from her friends and her school, and dragged her away from a chance at having a normal family after her own dad had dropped dead; and then abandoned her in the middle of the ocean during her time of need. Eleanor would say how she had left her for only a moment, and that the experience of seeing the whales had been so precious to her that she would do the same thing again.

She was telling the truth: she would do the same thing again. But that didn't mean that she was proud of her behavior. She found being a mother agonizingly difficult. Other women seemed content to dote on their children, to spend hours in the kitchen making noodle casseroles and sewing pinafores and witch costumes. Eleanor couldn't sit still long enough for any of that. She could take Lily to the boulevards of Paris and to the small mill towns in Italy, and she could take her to museums and shops and parties—anything as long as she was moving—but sitting alone in a room, where the air stayed still and the hours ticked slowly by, made her feel trapped, and being trapped was something she couldn't bear.

She felt safest at work. She felt relieved when Lily went back East to college, and when she married Tom. She felt absolved, somehow, of responsibility for any life but her own.

THE road out to Miramar Beach was jammed. Eleanor and her swimming friends had to park nearly a quarter mile to the south. They could see the whale before they could smell it—a creature so big, it defied comprehension. It lay heavily in the sand. A group of people stood by its side, talking and gesturing to a woman who sat atop its back. This woman, who seemed to be the scientist in charge, was clad in a white tank top and yellow rubber overalls. It was a warm day, and her skin glistened with sweat. From time to time, she bent over and seemed to be whispering to the whale, as if she was coaxing it, and Eleanor had the sense that the whale might lift its head, turn over, and slip back into the sea.

She stopped on the road above the beach, and held her breath, and when she finally inhaled again, the smell hit her—salt and sand and the sweet, gut-twisting odor of decay. She looked out at the vast blue ocean and tried to imagine other whales out there, swimming and mourning. She scanned the crowd, who were dressed in bikinis and cover-ups, board shorts and flip-flops. Despite the fact that they were dressed for a day at the beach, she felt their collective grief and awe. No one was rushing toward the whale, hoping to touch the barnacles on its snout or look into its antediluvian eyes. No one was standing at the yellow tape, peppering the scientists with questions. Even the young children, who clung to their parents' hands or stood solemnly by their sides, had an aura of reverence about them.

Eleanor couldn't help it; she began to cry. Tears poured from her eyes, and she stood there silently thinking about her friends Gracie and Judy, and how death would be coming for them one day soon, too.

Bob, her friend from swimming, came up to her, and put his arm across her shoulders. "It's a hell of a thing," he said.

She reached up and squeezed his hand, and nodded.

"Would you like to go for lunch at the Nugget? Nothing like a great burger to soothe the soul."

"No, thank you, Bob," she said. "I need to be getting to the office."

"You ever going to stop working so hard?" Bob said.

"Why should I?" she said. "I love my business, and I have good people. Even my grandson works for me now, did you know?"

"You're something else, Eleanor," Bob said, and he shook his head and walked away.

THE next day after breakfast, Eleanor headed down the hill to the beach. This time she had to park even farther away. They were performing the autopsy of the whale right on the beach, as if the sand were a stage and the cars on the highway an audience. There were more people inside the yellow caution tape, and several trucks parked on the sand. There were bystanders near the rocks, people lining the road, and a slow stream of cars making their way along the highway, where the shimmer of heat rose in distorted waves. The scientists were stripping the skin on the whale's flank, revealing a wall of pure white blubber. Blood pooled in the sand. She guessed that they were looking for bruises and contusions, and that they would soon learn what the whale had eaten, how old it was, where it had traveled, and how, exactly, it had died. She felt a wave of affection for these men and women, and deep grief for the whale.

ON the way home, Eleanor stopped off at Vons to get the ingredients to make rum cake. It was the perfect cake to set out for guests, to take to a church reception hall, to leave off on a porch, but Eleanor wasn't going to do any of those things this time. After years and years of eating it and baking it, the cake defined comfort for Eleanor and she just wanted to smell it baking. It was an old-fashioned yellow cake, made from a boxed mix, baked in a Bundt pan, and soaked in butter, pecans, and Mount Gay Barbados Rum, which she had first tasted on the actual island of Barbados. She didn't cook much anymore. She never had, really. So she had to buy a bottle of vegetable oil, a bag of nuts, and a dozen eggs. She felt as though she were preparing for a siege.

While she was standing at the checkout line, she heard someone call her name. She turned around to see Gail and Ted Hailwood.

"I was going to call you tomorrow," Ted said as he fell into line behind her. "I've got another offer on the ranch. A movie producer. Seems pretty eager. You still want to move forward with the deal?"

WHILE the cake was in the oven, Eleanor called Lily back in Vermont. This was something Eleanor almost never did—called just to say hello. She usually called if there was a decision to make, some legal matter, a discussion about plane flights. Lily was immediately on guard.

"Do you remember the whale watching trip we went on when you were thirteen?" she asked.

"Every minute of it," Lily said.

"A blue whale died in the channel yesterday. It washed up on a beach. I went down there to see it, and it got me thinking."

"About throwing up?"

"Lily, don't start . . ." Eleanor said.

Lily could hear the wounded tone in her mother's voice—a kind of neediness that was new, and that worried her. "Sorry," she said. "What did it get you thinking about?"

"It got me thinking about all the contrivances of being human," Eleanor said, because it was the closest she could come to saying what she was feeling about death and longing, and wanting her family nearby. "Whales don't worry about real estate and they don't plan funerals and they don't sit up at night fretting about the price of cotton. They just swim, you know? They just swim and then they die. I was envious."

Lily didn't know what to make of this phone call. It was so unlike her mother. It felt like some kind of confession, but Lily wasn't sure of what. "The whales are probably envious of you, too, Mom," she said, but then she replayed the conversation in her head and stuck on one of the

97

phrases her mother had used: *worry about real estate.*

"Is something happening with the ranch, Mom? Because I haven't found the right time to bring it up with Tom. Things have been a little crazy here. They canceled Tom's only class this semester due to low enrollment and gave him more responsibility on the curriculum integration committee instead."

"I saw Ted Hailwood yesterday," Eleanor said. "He has another offer on the ranch. He needs an answer."

ON the third day after the whale's death, Eleanor read in the morning paper that the scientists had concluded that the whale had been struck by a ship. Its bones had been crushed, its body bruised. It had probably been dragged for some time through the channel. The experts decided that the best course of action was to bury the carcass of the whale right on the beach, where bacteria and natural forces would break it down over time. Eleanor felt a sense of outrage as she imagined the whale, the biggest creature in the ocean, overcome by a thing that was a hundred times bigger, a thing that would only rust and never die. She thought about calling Gracie to tell her that the largest creature on earth was suffering from broken bones, too, but she decided against it. She decided to go back to the beach again instead.

98

When she pulled up alongside the rocks on the road, she saw a gangly bulldozer bent over a massive hole at the surf line. It reached out its long neck, grabbed a mouthful of sand, and spit it out into the hole. The carcass of the whale was no longer visible, although you could still sense its shape under the sand. Eleanor parked and got out and sat down on the rocks to watch the end of the hot day and the end of the drama. She sat there until the last rays of sunlight had disappeared, and when she stood to go, she paused to let her knees adjust, and then drove silently home.

SHE cut a slice of rum cake and called Gracie, even though it was late in New York. The home nurse answered, and it took some time for Gracie to come to the phone.

"I was just thinking about you," Eleanor said.

"Is this a deathwatch?" Gracie asked. "You're calling to see if I'm still here?"

"I'm calling to make plans for Opening Day," Eleanor said. "Did you hear where the game is going to be played?"

"Detroit?"

"Japan!"

"What in hell are they thinking?"

"Something about being ambassadors for the sport and letting Matsuzaka and Okajima play in their home country. It's looking like we'll be having the first ever Opening Day *breakfast*."

"You're talking about flying to Japan?" Gracie asked, and Eleanor could hear the resignation in her voice; Gracie could make the trip from New York to Boston, even if it killed her, but a trip to Japan was out of the question.

"I'm talking about having breakfast in Boston and watching the game. A six a.m. start, they say."

"Good lord."

"So do you think pancakes or hot dogs?"

"Hot dogs," Gracie said. "It has to be hot dogs. By the way, how's the new business venture going? The avocados."

"Slipping away," Eleanor said. "Due to inaction by certain parties."

"Ah. So you have no control over the family?"

Eleanor laughed bitterly. "No," she said. "I don't."

·9·

Lily

AFTER dinner, Lily asked Tom if he wanted to go for a walk in the snow. They put on their boots and their coats and gloves and walked out into the dark, cold night. They walked, as if by agreement, to the center of the central green. The wrought iron lamps along the pathways glowed in the cold air, and yellow light shone from isolated windows in the stately old buildings that lined the square. Someone had built a snow sculpture, with turrets and tunnels. Tom began to explore it, walking around to see where the entrances and the exits were. Lily just stood at the place where the paths crossed the green, and closed her eyes and felt the cold creep into her fingers and her toes.

She watched Tom poking around the snow tunnels. She loved him. She loved his constancy, his loyalty. She loved his green eyes, his methodical brain.

"Tom?" she called.

He came around a snowbank, and stood beside her, his breath visible in the air.

"Were you serious about wanting to own that avocado ranch in Santa Barbara?"

He laughed, and she could see his teeth—the

gold crown on the back molar. "Is this a hypothetical question?"

"No, actually," she said. "It's not. My mother made an offer on it."

He shoved his hands deeper in his pockets, kicked his boot into the snow. "She did what?"

"She ran into Ted Hailwood, though I'm not entirely sure that it wasn't by design. She made an offer."

"Sounds like your mom."

"I know," she said, "but it also sounded tempting. To be near the boys again. To forget about curriculum integration and interactive textbooks and just . . . walk away and start something new. I was thinking it could be good for us."

"You're serious?"

"I was thinking about maybe getting a dog," she said, and hoped that the comment conveyed everything she felt about their marriage and their home and who they had become.

"A dog?" he said, peering at her. "Why a dog?"

"I miss the noise of a family," she said, "the energy. I miss the way we were with each other when we had all that. I guess I thought that the ranch and the dog would bring some of that back."

"If you want a dog, we could get a dog," he said.

"Tom, come on. That's not what I meant. What

I want is something completely new, something that we can do together."

"It was a beautiful ranch," he said.

"So you'll think about it?"

He shrugged. "I will."

WHEN they got back to their house, Tom ripped off his jacket, and his sweater, and scratched at his forearms, which had bloomed with a scaly eczema as the temperature plummeted. Sometimes Lily would wake up at night because there was a movement, and a sound, and it would be Tom, sound asleep, scratching.

He asked Lily if she would like tea.

"Tea would be nice," she said.

He got the new teapot and filled it with water. While it was heating, he got out two of the stoneware mugs they had bought from a potter in Maine—two left out of a dozen—and unwrapped two tea bags. She didn't really know what was in Tom's heart. She knew that he liked chamomile tea with honey and oatmeal cookies with walnuts, and that he loved the first day of classes, when the students came in, so eager and young. She knew that skin rashes plagued him and that he got blisters in the summer when he gardened and that he pressed flowers and leaves between the pages of books and put them in envelopes and sent them to his granddaughter. But she knew, too, that even after twenty-six years of marriage, one person couldn't really know another.

Tom set the mugs on the table, then looked up at his wife. "You would really take your mother's money?"

"After an entire lifetime of turning it down?" Lily asked. "Of letting her stew in it and telling her I didn't need it, and didn't want it? I'm thinking I would."

"Why now?"

"Because I care more about making sure we're okay than I do about the power she might have over me."

"You would really just—go? It's so not like you."

"I know," she said. "But I think it could be good for us—for you and me."

Tom took her in his arms and pulled her into his warmth. "We're okay," he said.

"I know," she said, "but okay is never what I was after."

THE next day, she came home for dinner and found Tom sitting in the living room reading a book on tree grafting. Another on organic composting lay nearby, and she saw that he had printed out articles on the nutritional makeup of the avocado and the origin of guacamole.

He looked up. "Okay was never what I was after either," he said.

One call later, it was a done deal.

• • •

THEY listed their house with a woman who lived around the corner and told their department heads that they were resigning their duties. Tom's only class had already been canceled, so covering for him was a matter of finding someone else to head the curriculum integration committee—a physicist or a chemist. Lily had no classes that semester, and had the distinct feeling that the math department was secretly happy they were getting rid of a senior professor, whose salary was so costly. When Lily told her textbook editor that she was ceasing work on the interactive project, there was a flurry of phone calls to try to talk her out of it, but she was resolute. She just kept saying, "No," until there were no more questions, and no more calls.

Lily began to sort through their belongings. She started making piles in the basement—things to throw away, things to give away, and things to take with them. She kept calling Olivia out in San Luis Obispo.

"I found a ski jacket Ryan used to wear," she would say. "Can you use it for Brooke?" "I found a trophy Ryan won in college; do you have room for it?" "There's no reason to send out a sled, is there?"

Olivia could hear the excitement in her mother-in-law's voice, and she tried to stay upbeat as she said, "No, thank you," "I'll ask Ryan," and "I don't think so."

Tom was more difficult. He wanted to keep everything—towering stacks of *National Geographics*, a trekking pole that no longer had a mate, and all his gardening tools, whether their handles were splintered, their tines were rusted, or their blades as dull as a piece of wood.

"It doesn't hurt anything to throw the stuff in the moving van," Tom said.

Lily disagreed. "Yes it does," she said. "We'll just have to sort it all out when we get to Santa Barbara. And besides, it's good to cast off old junk."

"To make room for new junk?"

She pointed to a floor mat that had mildewed during the last big storm. She'd washed it, bleached it, but the dark splotches remained. "You'd rather hold on to things like that?"

He shrugged. She had a point. "Okay," he said. "But this doesn't give you free rein to get rid of everything you always wanted me to get rid of. No secretly giving away my *National Geographics*."

She smiled. "As long as I get to take all my fabric."

THE second week in March, their colleagues threw Tom and Lily a party, and didn't bother to conceal their jealousy at their spontaneous departure.

"A gentleman farmer, eh?" Pat Cordoba said as he slapped Tom on the back.

"So you'll really have a view of the ocean?" Janet Barnes asked three separate times.

Marilyn came up to Lily, lowered her voice, and said, "What are you going to do, now that you've let the textbook go?"

"You make it sound like a crime, Marilyn."

"Not at all," Marilyn said. "I envy you. But I know you; you're not going to sit on your hands while Tom picks avocados."

She shrugged. "I've been thinking about making a quilt," she said.

"A quilt? I envy you," she said again, and Lily knew that her friend was not just talking about a creative undertaking. Lily and Tom were setting off on an adventure together. They had made a new plan together. They were, still, together.

"Take care of yourself, Marilyn," Lily said. "Don't let the faculty right out of grad school get you down."

Marilyn laughed, took Lily's hands in her own, and kissed her friend good-bye.

ONCE the house was completely empty, they walked through the rooms one last time, saying farewell to the views they had looked at for so many years, and following the paths their boys had followed as they learned how to walk, and standing on the raw dirt patch where the roots of the big elm tree had once grown.

Out of habit, Tom noticed all the things that

needed repairing—the water stain on the down-stairs bathroom ceiling, the faded paint in the family room, the light in the basement that flick-ered when you turned it on. Lily looked one last time at the view from the living room window and at the backyard where Ryan had broken both his arms when he leapt off the swing from the top of its arc, where Luke had tried to plant dinosaurs, and where Tom had grown his peas and tomatoes.

"This was a good house," Lily said.

"Very good indeed," Tom agreed.

THEY spent their last few nights at the Sheraton, with a room that had a view of the lake. They had thrown out truckloads of things they no longer needed, given away bags of clothes. The furniture they were keeping—their dining table and chairs, the brass bed, the entry table with its inlaid wood edging, Hattie's old Singer sewing machine—was on a truck to California, along with seven-teen plastic tubs of Lily's fabric and twenty-three boxes of books. Lily had the unsettling feeling that something was going to go wrong with the truck carrying all their possessions. She kept imagining that it wouldn't make it, somehow, to California, and that without all the furniture and fabric she had spent her whole life collecting and caring for, without her steadfast coats and shoes, without her well-aged sheets and wool blankets, she would feel adrift. She tucked a few things into her suitcase that she couldn't bear to lose—a tin sugar scoop Luke made in shop class, the small stone Ryan had presented to her after he and Tom and Luke finished their mountain climbing challenge, the Matisse tablecloth, and her grandmother's six yards of hand-embroidered French lace.

Before they went to sleep, Lily went over to where Tom was sitting in a green leather wing-back chair, reading the town newspaper that had been neatly folded on the coffee table. She took the newspaper from his hands and laid it back down on the table. She sat on his lap, and leaned in to kiss him. He kissed her back more deeply. He lifted her up, and laid her down on the bed. He lifted her nightgown over her head, and she raised her hands to allow it. He ran his hands over her small breasts and her narrow hips, kissed her collarbone, then removed his own clothes and lay on top of her.

"You excited?" she said.

"About this," he said, "or about the move?"

"Both," she said.

He kissed her again, on the ears, the nose. "Yes," he said.

·10·

Eleanor

JUDY Vreeland died the first week of March. Gracie called to tell Eleanor the news, and to report that the funeral would be on Saturday and that Gordon was expecting them both. Within a few hours, Eleanor had a plane ticket, a room reserved at the Pierre, and her suitcase opened on her bed.

Eleanor was an expert at funerals. She had buried both her parents, all three of her husbands, a younger sister, and friends from every phase of her life. She knew that the worst possible thing a guest could do was to show up in a somber black outfit, sip chardonnay, and say in a whispered voice how sorry they were for the person's loss. For the funeral of Judy Vreeland, Eleanor packed a claret-colored, formfitting knit dress, patent leather slingbacks, and a pair of chandelier diamond earrings. She sat in St. Thomas Church on Fifth Avenue and listened to the soaring hymns and the raspy readings of Corinthians 12 and to the old relatives cough and wheeze, and then afterward, she went straight to the bar at the Pierre and ordered a scotch. She delivered it to Gordon discreetly while he stood in a receiving line listening to a blue-haired lady wax on about losing her husband in the war. Gordon winked, mouthed *thank you*, and then Eleanor went to find Bucky Harrington and Gracie Dooley to talk about the Red Sox's abysmal performance in the play-offs.

Gracie found her first. "You owe me five bucks," she said.

"Whatever for?"

"On the day Gordon married Judy in 1956, you bet me that it wouldn't last."

Eleanor took a sip of scotch. "Why on earth did you take such a sucker bet?"

Gracie shrugged. "I always like a long shot."

"And why would you still remember it fifty-two years later?"

"I never forget a bet," Gracie said.

Eleanor opened her beaded evening bag and pulled out a five-dollar bill. "Well, you certainly earned it," she said, handing over the cash. "Gordon never so much as looked at another woman in all these years."

"Poor thing," Gracie said. "He looks horrible. He looks downright bereft."

"I guess that's the price you pay for love," Eleanor said, and Gracie looked at her and shook her head and laughed.

Bucky Harrington walked up then, and kissed each woman on the cheek. "Evening, ladies," he said. "How nice of you to come to mourn the Red Sox." Bucky had been the pitcher for the Harvard baseball team, a member of the original Great Date, and he was now a congressman from Massachusetts.

"We're in Yankee territory," Gracie said.

"Ah, but the failures of the Sox are so colossal they cannot be contained," Bucky said.

"Quite true," Eleanor said, "quite true. Were you at Game 7 last year?"

"I'm at every game," Bucky said. "It's part of my job description. Mingle with the constituents, you know."

"I should run for Congress," Eleanor said. "It's the cushiest job in America."

"No one in Congress is as beautiful as you, my dear. You'd be out of your league. And the pay cut would kill you."

Eleanor laughed. "You flatter me, Bucky," she said. "Which is why I adore you."

THE after-memorial party went on into the night. There were crab cakes, buttermilk rolls, and chocolate cake, and toasts and speeches by the family. Everyone talked about how sweet Judy had been, how loyal, how generous. Eleanor sat listening and thought that Judy probably deserved such praise. Judy was the perfect housewife, a Betty Crocker mom. She organized bridge games, ran the charity ball at the hospital, deferred to her husband when asked her opinion on everything from finance to what color to paint the walls.

Judy had been all the things girls in their generation were raised to be, all the things Eleanor could never bear. When the crowd thinned, Eleanor got up from the table where her old friends still sat.

"Brunch at eight a.m. tomorrow," Gracie said. "And then the Cézanne show at the Met."

"I'm looking forward to it," Eleanor said, and went to find Gordon.

HE was standing near the bar, trapped by a plump woman in a pantsuit. He was much taller than she was—he was taller than most everyone—and he had to stoop and turn slightly to hear her with his good ear. His shirt was clean and crisp and his wingtips were polished enough to pass inspection, but his eyes were sad and drawn, and the skin of his face seemed as if it had been drained of color. He looked like a general who had carefully dressed to sign the treaty of his own defeat. He pulled himself away from the woman by saying, "Excuse me, Gwen," and stepping toward Eleanor.

He held out his big hands, palms up, and she placed her small hands in his. He pulled her toward him, and when they embraced, she could smell Ivory soap and starch, and she had the thought that Gordon smelled like a whole era— that his scent defined the whole generation of people who had gone to college before anyone had even dreamed of the sixties and who were growing old in the age of YouTube.

"Thank you for the scotch," he said, "and for coming all this way. It means the world to me."

She pulled back and looked up at him. "It was a lovely service," she said, "and believe me, I've been to a lot of funerals, so I would know."

Gordon laughed, a tired laugh that belied his exhaustion. "I guess you would," he said. He fidgeted with the change in his pockets, and with his keys. "I dread it being over, actually."

"Today?" she asked.

He nodded, and swallowed, and tried to hold back the tears.

"You don't have to be brave," Eleanor said.

He looked away. "I've had to be brave all my life."

"And you've been good at it, Gordon. But you're almost seveny-five years old. Your wife just died. You can stop."

He laughed. "You make it sound so easy."

"It can be," she said. "When everyone goes home, we'll go on a walk. We'll walk down to the Oak Room and have a drink. And we'll see if they can conjure up a rum cake. It works wonders."

"That would be nice," he said.

She smiled. She remembered seeing Gordon for the first time standing under the porte cochere at Tower Hall in the fall of 1951. He was the tallest of the group of boys, with arms that looked like crooked wings, and a shy smile. Her eyes passed over him that day and settled on Billy, a boy who had grown more quickly into his skin and whose feet seemed like less of a liability. She considered herself fully mature at age eighteen and wasn't interested in a boy like Gordon who was a work-in-progress. But now such distinctions were irrelevant. Gordon was one of the last of her oldest best friends.

At eleven o'clock, they stepped out of the Pierre and headed south down Fifth Avenue. They hadn't gone half a block when Gordon stopped, and gasped. He buried his face in his hands, and slumped against the limestone wall. "How will I live without her?" he sobbed.

Eleanor didn't answer the question. She was a good nine inches shorter than Gordon, even in her heels. She stepped toward him, and embraced him, and then she pressed her hand on his back to guide him back to the Pierre, where she asked the doorman to hail them a cab.

They sat on either side of the backseat as the cab slipped through the streets of Manhattan. Gordon looked out the window on his side, and Eleanor looked straight ahead at the stoplights and the buildings and the people. When they got to Seventy-third Street, the driver opened the door for Eleanor, and Gordon fished in his pocket for a tip while the doorman waited without a trace of curiosity on his face.

"Evening, sir," he said. "Evening, ma'am."

"Evening, Marvin," Gordon said.

"Everything okay, Mr. Vreeland? With the evening and all?"

Gordon turned to the man who had served him and his wife steadfastly for the past seven years. He reached out and put his hand on the doorman's shoulder, and his face screwed up in pain.

"It was a fine funeral," Eleanor said. "Judy would have approved."

When they got to his apartment, Gordon opened the door and went to the couch and folded himself forward, his elbows resting on his knees, and his head resting in his hands.

"Do you still keep the liquor in the dining room?" Eleanor asked crisply, as if she were about to dress a wound—an actual tear in the flesh, an insistent flow of blood.

He nodded.

Eleanor clipped across the walnut floors in her heels. She had been in this apartment ten years ago for Gordon's retirement party and not much had changed. The dining room chairs had been refinished in a bold blue-green brocade and the walls were painted a deep navy blue. There was a new photographic portrait of the entire Vreeland family on the wall over the fireplace. Every member of the family, from the smallest baby to Gordon himself, was dressed in khakis and a plain black shirt. They were a handsome group—

predominantly blond and tall with straight noses, strong chins, and good teeth.

Eleanor brought back a silver tray that held a crystal decanter of scotch and two highball glasses. "Did you eat anything at the Pierre?" she asked.

Gordon waved his hand through the air as if eating were a trifle he couldn't be bothered with.

"I'll call the doorman," she said.

"I'm fine," he said.

"Pizza? Steak? Soup? What sounds good?"

"Soup," he said. "Coconut lime soup."

"Thai?"

"Thai Palace. Marvin will know what I mean."

While Eleanor called for food, Gordon took his keys and his phone out of his pocket and set them on the table, loosened his tie and unbuttoned the top button of his shirt, and slipped his feet out of his shoes. When he sat back, his phone rang. He watched it ring three, four, five times, then reached to pick it up.

"Hello?" he said. "Yes, of course. No, I'm fine. Okay. Right. Thank you. I have another call, Joel. I'll call you later."

He paused, then launched into a similar conversation: "Hello? Fine. Yes, thank you. Okay."

He set the phone back down on the table, then shoved it across the glass as if it were a hockey puck.

"People are so nice," he said, as if it were a condemnation.

Eleanor picked up Gordon's phone and turned it off, and then she fished in her beaded evening bag for her phone and turned it off and set it beside his.

"People don't like death," she said. "It makes them uncomfortable."

"Why do you think that is?" Gordon asked.

"Lack of imagination, I suppose," she said. "They can't see what will come next."

A short while later their food arrived. They sat on the couch and drank their scotch and sipped their soup, and talked about Judy and their children and the grandchildren, and how one had autism and one was born with a missing toe, and they talked about the Red Sox and the Yankees, and about the exhibit of Edward Weston photos that had been at the Getty in Los Angeles, and how the price of real estate in Santa Barbara was relatively affordable again. Eleanor got up to make coffee sometime after midnight, but when she came back out to the living room, Gordon was asleep on the couch. She found the linen closet, got a blanket, and laid it over him. She got another blanket and curled up in a nearby wing chair, where she could watch the lights of the city twinkle, and where the light from the reading lamp wouldn't fall on her friend. There were newspapers in a basket by the coffee table, with crosswords that were not yet done. She sat there keeping watch, trying to crack a code that had something to do with college sports teams.

When the sun began to rise, Eleanor got up, splashed water on her face, and went downstairs to ask the doorman where to buy bagels. It had rained during the night and the streets were damp. The air was full of the smell of just-wet cement, freshly liberated dust, and damp garbage. There were people out walking their dogs, and people jogging with gloves on their hands, hats on their heads, and iPods in their ears. There was nowhere better in the world to be on the day after a funeral, Eleanor thought, than New York City. Life was relentless here, on full display. Someone may have died, but someone else would be up at the crack of dawn boiling dough to make the perfect crust on a bagel. She said good morning to the businessman who held the door open for her, and stepped into the light and the heat of the bagel store. Its windows were steamed, and there were four people standing in line at the counter, and two others reading the paper at small tables. She bought a dozen bagels that were still warm from the oven, a tub of cream cheese, lox, and two tall coffees.

The doorman at Gordon's building held the door for her, pressed the elevator button for her, and bade her to send his condolences to Mr. Vreeland. Gordon, however, was still asleep on the couch. He looked so still and seemed so silent that Eleanor got down close to him to make sure that he was still breathing. She could see the flattened tops of his teeth, the gold fillings in his molars, the white hairs in his nose, the places where his skin seemed translucent. She didn't miss living with a man. She didn't miss having a man come home on Friday night to say that they would be having eight people for brunch the next morning. She didn't miss having to talk to the dull wives of men her husband found interesting. She liked spending long hours in her own company, having the entire crossword puzzle to herself, being able to invite whomever she wanted to a party.

She put the food on the coffee table, and felt suddenly very tired. She sat back in the wing chair, pulled the blanket over herself, closed her eyes, and fell asleep.

WHEN she awoke, it was after noon and she was starving. Gordon had showered, eaten a bagel, folded the blanket, and was sitting on the couch with the unfinished crossword puzzle.

She sat up abruptly. "I must have fallen asleep."

"Three hours that I know of," he said, and lowered the paper.

"Three hours! What time is it?"

"Twelve thirty."

"Oh no!" she said, and stood up. "Did Gracie

call? I was supposed to meet her for brunch."

Gordon smiled and shrugged. "You turned off the phones, remember?"

"My glory!" she said, and reached to flip her phone on.

Gordon reached forward, clutched her wrist, and said, "Don't."

"Don't?"

"Please. It's been so peaceful."

She sat back. "Okay," she said cautiously. "So you must have slept, too?"

"I did. I think that's the longest I've slept in six months. I'd forgotten how good it feels."

Eleanor nodded toward the crossword puzzle folded on the table in front of him. "Did you figure out the one about North Carolina? Peter Collins is diabolical."

Gordon put on his glasses, picked up the paper, scanned the crossword, and read aloud: " 'Jacket material for a mixed-up North Carolina athlete.' Well," he said, "North Carolina are the Tar Heels. Letterman jackets are made of leather. You can get 'leather' out of 'Tar Heel.' "

She reached for the paper to verify his entry on 38-Across. "Impressive," she said.

"I spent an hour on it. I kept wanting to shout out to Judy for help, but then I'd look up and I'd see you sleeping there and I'd remember that she was dead. She's died a hundred deaths this morning."

"That doesn't sound very peaceful."

"It was," he said, and looked straight into her eyes. "Thanks to your being here."

Eleanor felt the heat of his gaze, and she blushed. She raised a hand to her cheek as if she could feel the heat there. Gordon reached out and took her hand and pulled it toward him and pressed his lips to the back of her hand. Her skin was dry and speckled with age spots, and his lips were thin and dry, too, but his lips lingered on her skin and he stared into her eyes, and she recognized that look of longing and desperation and thought, *Oh no.*

·11·

Lily

WHEN Tom and Lily got to Santa Barbara, they slept in Eleanor's guest room and borrowed her sedan until Tom's truck and the Subaru arrived from Vermont. They drove over to their new house, and stood on the deck in the sunshine, looking down at the avocado trees and at the ocean far below, and walking through the empty rooms, thinking of where their furniture would fit and how their lives would be in those rooms. Later that afternoon, Lily offered to drop Tom off at the warehouse while she went out to buy a doormat, a dish drainer, a garbage can, a broom. It was a gorgeous drive along East Valley Road, with its towering eucalyptus trees, fruit trees, and horse ranches, and then they popped out onto the freeway that ran along a cliff above the ocean. The water sparkled in the afternoon sunlight, and across the channel were the islands—Santa Cruz and Santa Rosa.

"Calavo is like a co-op," Tom had explained. "We agree to sell our fruit to them and they sort it and weigh it and ship it out to retailers. We split the profit, which rises and falls, of course, with demand. Our first harvest should be in about a month."

"That sounds great," Lily said, although she wasn't really paying attention. Her head was full of thoughts about the new house, the drive, the view.

"The Hailwoods didn't try to maximize yield. Nadine says she thinks I should be able to double it, no problem, and that's even taking into account a switch to organic, which will cause a drop in yield as a matter of course."

"Nadine?" Lily asked.

"Our Calavo rep. The one I've been talking to on the phone. She seems like a really nice gal."

Lily knew, before she even stepped into the warehouse, what Nadine would look like. Perhaps not the details, but the type. And she was exactly right. Nadine was about twenty-four years old. Her long red hair was pulled back into a ponytail, her plaid flannel shirt flapped open over a braless blue tank top, her colorless Birkenstocks were caked with mud. She had probably been an environmental studies major, the kind who would hang around Tom's office, soaking up his knowledge, hoping to win his favor.

"How nice to finally meet you!" Nadine sang out when Tom introduced himself.

"Tom's been talking about how much you're helping him learn the ropes," Lily said.

Nadine beamed. "You'll love the community of avocado growers. We're a tight group. We all really look out for each other."

Lily looked across the warehouse, to the industrial scales, the crates of fruit, the skip loaders. This was a temple, and these were the tools of worship. She understood that. She had been in such places many times before, but they were warehouses where fabric was milled and loomed, or living rooms where quilts were being stitched, and where the language spoken had to do with color and pattern, thread and weave. That was a world she knew and loved. She thought back to the summer when she met Tom, in a tiny town called Gothic, on the western slope of the Rockies. He was interning at the Rocky Mountain Biological Labs, and she was taking a break from her graduate studies in Denver to meet a famous weaver who she thought might have something important to teach her about fabric and geometry. Her name was Jenny Wood, and she wove intricate silk twill in the cramped second story of an unassuming wooden shed. Three large looms were positioned in that space, and when Lily saw them crammed together, with spools of yarn set on shelves up under the eaves, she thought of a ship built in a bottle.

"How did you get your looms up here?" Lily asked, thinking of the dirt road, the narrow staircase.

"We built them in this room. My husband, Jacques, and I."

"He's a weaver, too?"

"No, no," Jenny said, "a biologist. He runs the labs in the summer. That's why we come."

Jacques came home that afternoon with one of his graduate students—Tom, a tall, serious young man with a beard and a sunburned face. The moment Tom stepped in the door of the ramshackle house, Lily could feel the high mountain air change, and she wanted to laugh at how improbable it was that in this unassuming cabin in the woods, there were both sophisticated looms and the possibility of love. She smiled at Tom as if she had a secret, and he shook her hand and peered at her. "Do I know you?" he asked.

"I don't think so," she said.

"From Columbia?"

"No," she said, and shook her head. "I went to school in Boston."

"You seem very familiar," he said.

She smiled again. "I know what you mean."

They picked lettuce and tomatoes from the sloping garden out the back door, and while Lily washed the lettuce, and dried it and tore it, Tom stood next to her in the tiny, narrow kitchen, slicing the tomatoes with the precision of a surgeon, and sprinkling coarse pepper and rock salt on them as if he were performing some kind of ancient ritual. She wanted to stop and gape at the dirt under his fingernails, at his elegant hands. She wanted to sit and simply watch. She had traveled all over the world with her mother, visiting beautiful hotel properties and soaring cathedrals, but she felt that evening as if she had traveled to the ends of the earth—to another place and time—and she felt, at long last, at home.

They talked about vegetables and garden pests, about research funding and the job market for mathematicians. They argued about *Star Wars*, and what was going to happen to the relationship between Luke and Leia in the sequel. They stood around Jenny's looms, and watched her demonstrate how archeologists could prove from the pattern in the weft that as far back as the Neolithic era, women worked together to weave cloth. They sat in chairs on the dirt in the front of the house and watched the last licks of daylight fade out from the sky and the mountains cloak themselves in dark, brooding shadows.

Tom paid Lily no special attention. He was, after all, a somewhat shy young man at dinner with his boss. A little after ten, Tom stood and said that he had to go back to his bunk to get some sleep. Lily stood, too, worried sick that she would never see him again. "I suppose I should be going, too," she said. Her mind was racing to come up with something to say, some reason for them to have to meet again.

They said their thank-yous and good-byes to Jenny and Jacques, and walked down the dirt path to the dirt road where Lily's car was parked. While she dug her key out of her bag, Tom looked at his mud-caked shoes. "If, uh, you're free tomorrow afternoon," he said, "there is a little waterfall about three miles from the research center. I've been following the blooming patterns of the columbines up there."

She had to try hard not to throw her arms around him. "I'd like that," she said. "Very much."

He turned and walked off into the night, and she drove in the other direction through the aspen groves and back to the main town of Crested Butte, singing "Rocky Mountain High" at the top of her lungs.

THAT first week in Santa Barbara reminded Lily of those five days in Gothic. They each had only a suitcase full of clothes, and the few possessions that they had decided to carry with them on the plane. They knew virtually no one in town, had nowhere they had to be. On Monday, they went up to the new house and walked through the orchard and picked a crate full of avocados. On Tuesday morning, when it was still dark, they got up and walked the six blocks from Eleanor's town house to the Farmer's Market.

"Why are you going so early?" Eleanor asked.

"That's when the farmers arrive," Tom said, "and the chefs. That's when the real action takes place."

"How does he know that?" Eleanor asked.

Lily shrugged. "That's just Tom."

They picked out yellow heirloom tomatoes with veins of green, tomatillos with paper skin, bulbs of garlic that smelled like heaven, sweet Maui onions, lemons, limes, cilantro, and five kinds of hot peppers. They watched one chef move through the market at the speed of light, buying bushels of vegetables with the flick of his fingers, and another who moved slowly, touching, smelling, tasting everything before she laid down her cash.

Back in Eleanor's kitchen, Lily made coffee while Tom set out his recipes on the marble countertops.

"Avocados," he pronounced, "have been prized for centuries for their high fat and protein content."

Lily minced garlic, grated lemon zest, and listened to Tom go on.

"When the Spaniards came and conquered the Aztecs, they believed guacamole to be an aphrodisiac."

"Those Spaniards were evil, but clever," Eleanor said.

Tom sent Lily out to buy organic, full-fat sour cream, fresh tortilla chips, and a six-pack of Tecate. At lunchtime, he had six different types of guacamole arranged on the countertops, and rating cards for each one. How was the texture, the taste, the balance of flavors, the heat? They ate and debated, and could not agree—but later, when it mattered, they would remember exactly the mix of lemon and spice in the particular mix that Tom most adored.

·12·

Eleanor

WHEN the moving truck arrived, Eleanor came to stand in silent witness with Lily and Tom as the men moved the furniture and the boxes from the truck into the house. The movers were experts; they lifted and turned furniture through doorways and hallways as if they had navigated those exact corners a hundred times.

"Where do you want these?" one of the men asked, hefting a Rubbermaid tub in the air.

Lily glanced at Tom. They had decided to turn the big room off the kitchen into a study, but it was the place where Lily planned to sew as well. She would set up a machine in there, and an ironing board. She would put cork board on one wall so that she could pin up swatches, move around pattern and color. She would be able to work while looking out across the avocado trees, and the ocean, and she would know that Tom was out there, examining bugs, measuring water levels, talking to the trees. She wanted her fabric nearby. It made her feel safe, protected, settled. It made her feel a sense of possibility. "Is the garage okay?" she asked Tom. Her containers would take up so much room that they wouldn't be able to park a car inside; they wouldn't be able to install a workbench.

"Fine," he said, smiling, "but only because I've got the shed."

The men began to parade by with the tubs. "Is *all* of this fabric?" Eleanor asked.

"It's like you and shoes," Lily said.

"You can wear shoes," Eleanor said. "Fabric just sits there collecting dust."

"That's what the tubs are for."

"What's *in* them?"

Lily pictured her green-blue tub, her orange tub, her fuchsia tub, each with gorgeous printed cottons in complementary shades. There were tubs with nothing but black-and-white geometric prints, tubs filled with wool from the Scottish highlands that was so dense it would resist water in a driving rain. There were tweeds and gauzy chiffons, dots and stripes and solids. "Just fabric," she said.

"It's just like my mother," Eleanor said. "I never understood it."

Lily looked at her mother—at the lines that fanned out from her eyes, at her earlobes weighed down by silver earrings, and her sun-spotted skin. "It's because you never learned to sew," she said, and then lowered her voice and added, "which I always thought was strange."

"My father owned a mill," Eleanor said. "He wanted so badly to make it in the world, and he understood how much depended on appearances. My mother never did. She insisted on sewing her own clothes. She'd go to Boston's fanciest parties in a homemade gown. Other wives wore the latest outfits from Filene's or Bonwit Teller, but she insisted on homemade. She never understood how society judged her for it, and how it embarrassed my dad."

"And you?" Lily asked. "It embarrassed you?"

"Of course it did," Eleanor said.

They stood there, watching the parade of tubs go by as if it were a river and they were watching from the bank. Tom walked in with a floor lamp. He plugged it in, then unplugged it, moved it across the room, and plugged it in again.

After a while, Lily said, "I was proud of the clothes Grandma made me."

"That was obvious," Eleanor said.

"I carried her lace on the plane with me," Lily said, "because it's one thing I couldn't bear to lose."

"A piece of old lace?"

"It's not just lace," Lily said. "It's our family history. Does that mean nothing to you?"

Eleanor shook her head. "No," she said. "It doesn't. It's only proof of how stubborn my mother was."

"Stubborn? I think it's sentimental. A man brings this piece of fabric home from the war for his wife, who dies before she ever sees it, and his daughter can never bear to make anything from it because it is so precious to her. She can't even bear to make her own wedding dress. I love that story."

"Being sentimental," Eleanor said, "doesn't get you anything in this world."

"Maybe the point isn't to get something, Mom. It's just to *feel* something. To hold that lace in your hands and feel something."

Eleanor had been excited that Lily and Tom were moving to town. But standing there watching those tubs go by, she wondered if her excitement had been misplaced. What, besides blood, bound them together? Lily was not a woman Eleanor would choose as a friend. She was her daughter, but they were nothing alike. Eleanor would never hold on to a piece of fabric for fifty years just because of the story it carried in its threads. She would never have stayed married to someone as long as Lily had stayed married to Tom. Being that sentimental, after all, left you wide open for all kinds of hurt. "Feeling," Eleanor said, "is overrated."

Lily burst out laughing. "You're impossible, Mom."

ON their second Saturday, Eleanor hosted a welcome party. She invited people to Tom and Lily's back deck for cocktails and grilled scallops, stuffed mushroom caps, and endive with herbed cream cheese. Eleanor's employees were there, and her friends from the museum, and her friends from the pool, and Lily and Tom's new neighbor, Mary Hazelton, who lived in the house down the hill. Two women whom Lily had known in high school came, and after reminiscing about the time one of them wrote a paper on the history of the ukulele and about how good the peanut butter cookies in the cafeteria had been, they invited her to play bunco with them on the first Tuesday of the month. The Hailwoods stopped by, and raised a toast and said how glad they were that Lily and Tom had come. Nadine arrived with two men from the warehouse. Her hair was washed, her jeans clean, a bra still not visible under her beaded tunic.

Lily smiled and shook Nadine's hand and offered her wine.

"Just water," Nadine said sweetly. "Thanks." Lily wondered briefly why Nadine didn't drink wine. Was she a recovering alcoholic? Or did it give her migraines, the way it did Lily? Before she could start a conversation, another woman rushed up to her and said, "Lily? I'm Shilpa. I'm Eleanor's yoga instructor at the club, and I've found the perfect dog for you."

Lily watched Nadine make her way toward Tom, who was leaning against the railing and looking out over the sweep of water.

"It's an Australian shepherd," Shilpa said, "about ten years old. From a family who will be moving to Brussels next week. This dog will love it up here on the hill."

Lily smiled. "We've never had an Australian shepherd," she said. "Ours were always German."

"This is a special dog," Shilpa said. "She has one milky blue eye and one brown. A spirit dog. A protector."

Lily continued to watch Tom talking to Nadine. "A protector?" she asked. "That sounds good."

·13·

Lily

BUNCO turned out to be a simple game of probability, and the point of the evening seemed to be to complain about men. One woman's husband had recently walked out on her because he had fallen in love with her sister. Another woman had just hired a detective because she suspected her husband was carrying on with someone at work. And then there was the endless parade of powerful men in politics who had fallen for their interns, their secretaries, a call girl, another man's wife. "Men are all a bunch of assholes," someone said, and Lily was jolted from her complacence.

She set down her wine. She looked at the woman who had just made the proclamation. "Not all," she said.

The room went quiet. Everyone looked at her and waited for an explanation. Were men in Vermont different from men in California?

"It's just that I know a lot of good men," she said. "Men who would never cheat on their wives."

"Just give 'em time," someone said. There was laughter, and more wine was poured, and Lily's defense was soon forgotten.

But her old friends from high school had gotten to her. Over the next few weeks, she couldn't help but notice how eager Tom was to ask Nadine for help, how eager she was to give it. One night, Tom and Lily were slated to have dinner with Eleanor, and Tom stayed late at the warehouse to help Nadine with some formulas for compost. He called Lily at the house. "Go on without me," Tom said. "I'll come by later."

Lily drove down the hill to her mother's house, and sat nervously while Eleanor prepared gazpacho and chilled shrimp salad she had picked up from the gourmet deli. She felt as if she were on trial, sitting there without Tom.

"Where's Tom?" Eleanor asked.

"At the warehouse," Lily said, "with some of the other growers. He can't get enough of it. He loves it so much." She had told her tale, and her mother had believed it, but Lily could barely touch her food. She hadn't known Tom was tired of her headaches. She hadn't known that Tom wanted to be a farmer. Maybe she didn't know a whole lot else about Tom as well.

TEN days after their arrival, they met Shilpa on a Wednesday evening at the animal shelter in Goleta—Tom and Lily, and Eleanor, who had never owned a dog, but still considered herself an expert in identifying good disposition. The shelter was a small bungalow, with a maze of dog runs out the back, and the moment they stepped outside, the dogs started to howl.

"She's waiting for you," Shilpa said of the Australian shepherd. "I told her you were coming. Her name is Luna."

Tom looked at Lily and she smiled, because she knew that Tom didn't believe that dogs could understand human speech, although he believed they could understand something else about humans—their moods, their desires, their souls. Eleanor saw the look pass between Tom and Lily and felt a flash of envy at that kind of wordless communication, that depth of understanding between two people. She'd never had it. She wondered what it was like.

Luna was large, with three colors of fur spreading out across her head and chest. She had brown speckles on a white muzzle, and just as Shilpa had described, one milky blue-white eye, and one brown one. She came right up to them when they opened the door, and licked Tom's hand, and nuzzled Shilpa's leg, and circled Lily and Eleanor with her tail wagging.

"The family says she's high-spirited. She chases blackbirds. She apparently likes Popsicles."

Tom knelt down to look more closely in the dog's mismatched eyes, and to look at her teeth and her paws. "She's beautiful," he declared.

"I told you that she's ten years old," Shilpa said,

"didn't I? Her life expectancy is about four more years."

Lily nodded. "That's okay," she said, "because we're old, too."

Eleanor coughed in an exaggerated way, as if to say, *If you're old, then what am I?*

"You could count your age in dog years, Eleanor," Tom said, "and no one would be the wiser."

They all laughed, and walked back to the front office to complete some paperwork, and to pick up Luna's dog dish and leash. There was a man behind the counter, who hadn't been there before. He looked up. "Lily Peters," he said, and grinned. "I'd recognize that smile anywhere. What the hell are you doing here?"

It was Jack Taylor. She hadn't seen him in thirty-four years but she would have recognized him anywhere, too. He was fit and tan. His blond hair had gone gray and was cropped close to his head. He squinted out from blue eyes that had spent a lifetime looking into the sun. In high school, Jack used to skip classes when the winter swells were breaking at Miramar Beach, and Lily, who went to class even when she was sick, would note his absence as if part of her own body were missing. She rarely spoke to him, would have sworn that he hadn't known who she was—the small, pale girl who was devoted to math and never went to dances.

"Oh," Lily said, feeling nervous again. Her heart was beating hard in her chest. "We just moved back, actually. My husband, Tom, and I." Lily glanced at Tom, who was holding the dog on a tight leash. "This is Jack," she said. "Jack Taylor. We went to high school together."

"She used to beat the crap out of me in math," Jack said.

"She tends to do that," Tom said, smiling.

"And this is my mom," Lily added, waving her arm toward Eleanor.

"What a pleasure," Eleanor said, holding out her hand as if Jack might kiss it. He leaned over the counter, took her hand, and pumped it.

Lily remembered exactly the feeling of walking into calculus and looking forward to seeing Jack. He used to sit slumped in his desk chair, his long hair flopping, but whenever Dr. B called on him, Jack had the answer. He couldn't be tripped up. Lily used to love the power play between teacher and student, and would secretly cheer for Jack. It was far more interesting to listen to the two of them wrestle with math than it was for Lily to give Dr. B exactly what he was looking for, and to receive his empty praise. "Did you go into math?" Lily asked. "After high school? I always thought you might."

Jack laughed. "I went into surfing," he said.

"Did you?" Lily said. She wasn't sure whether or not he was kidding.

Shilpa chimed in to explain. "Jack's head of the sports ambassador program for Patagonia," she explained. "He travels all over the world for them."

"Shilpa," Jack teased, trying to call her off, "what's the harm in these people thinking I'm just a surf bum?"

Shilpa lowered her voice and, in a theatrical whisper, said, "He's actually a VP. He has an office at the headquarters in Ventura. And he volunteers with stray dogs every other Sunday. He's no maverick."

"I *surf* the big water at Maverick, baby," Jack said with a sly grin. He turned his gaze on Lily, and she felt his eyes boring straight into her, and her cheeks grow hot. "And you?" he asked. "What brings you back to paradise?"

"Avocados," she said. "We bought an avocado ranch up near Sheffield Drive."

"You're a rancher, then?"

"Tom taught biology at the University of Vermont for twenty years," she said. "This is a second career."

Jack nodded. "Nice," he said, and stood up and came around to rub the dog behind her ears. "And now you're taking home this great shepherd. She's a beauty."

"She really is," Tom said.

Lily felt suddenly embarrassed, with Jack standing so close to her on one side, and Tom so close to her on the other. She could lean one way and brush the skin of her husband's arm, and that was accepted, allowed, and she would feel nothing but the familiarity of his touch. She could lean the other way the same number of inches, and brush the skin of this former golden boy, and that was illicit, forbidden, and she would feel . . . what? She didn't know. She had never dared such a thing. She was appalled that the question had even entered her head—and sickened by what the bunco ladies would say about it—and couldn't wait to get out of that dog shelter and away from Jack.

"See you at the beach," Jack said, and Lily knew that he must say the phrase to everyone he met, that it was as benign as saying, *Have a nice day, we should have lunch,* but she found herself thinking about Tom meeting Nadine for lunch, and Tom working late with Nadine at the warehouse. She found herself thinking about Jack.

Before they even made it to the car, Eleanor spoke up. "I don't remember that boy from high school. I think I would have remembered such an attractive boy."

Lily opened the back of the car for Luna; she scratched the dog's ears. She remembered how every time she used to mention anything having to do with a boy—that she was studying with one, working on a science project with one, going with a group of them to get root beer floats at A&W—Eleanor would question her about whether the boy was handsome, available, interested. It got to the point where Lily stopped mentioning boys at all, and then Eleanor grilled her about *that*. "He wasn't my friend," she finally said, in response to the comment about Jack. "He was just a boy from math class."

TOM spent the afternoon in the orchard with Luna, while Lily went to the pet store to buy some chew toys and dog food. She looked for Jack at the end of each aisle, behind each cash register. She was disappointed and relieved when she didn't see him. When she got home, she wandered through the trees calling out to Tom. She finally found him at the compost pile behind the shed. He was turning the pile with a pitchfork, and sweat poured from his brow. The dog was chasing birds that neither Tom nor Lily could see.

"She's crazy," Tom said, nodding at the dog with a smile.

She was so crazy, in fact, that after the sun went down, she raced around the house like a puppy. Lily gave her the chew toy, which helped for a little while, but the dog was wound up as tight as a top. Tom took her out for a walk, which seemed to calm her a little, but by the time they got back, he was exhausted.

"Go to sleep," Lily said. "I'll stay up with her."

Lily sat with her laptop on the living room

couch, and Luna sat at her feet, alternately putting her chin on Lily's knee, and leaping up to
bark at the moon as it rose in the sky. It was a
full moon, big and bright, and Lily didn't mind
having to stay up. She scrolled through websites
of art quilters, finding one whose designs of
aspen trees looked like a photograph, and another
whose abstract patterns reminded her of Escher.

The dog was so transfixed by the moon out the
window that, by midnight, Lily understood
exactly why she was named the way she was.
Soon after, Lily dragged the dog bed she had
just bought into the bedroom, where Tom was
asleep. Luna followed, but she refused to go
near the dog bed. Lily closed the shades so that
there was no sign of the moon, and no light
whatsoever. The dog finally leapt onto the bed,
settled on Tom's feet, and went to sleep.

LILY dreamed of Jack. She dreamed that she had
gone down to the beach to help save the birds
who had been covered with oil, and that Jack had
been there, too, out on his surfboard, immune
somehow from the black goo that lapped at the
shore. In 1969, in actual fact, the birds made Lily
nervous, and the oil stank, and she thought her
mother was only doing it to make a point. In her
dream, however, she was the hero. She was
saving the birds. And Jack, who appeared the
same way he looked in 1969—young and tan, his

145

long blond hair flopping over his face—walked up the beach to Lily, took her in his arms, kissed her without saying a word, and then he peeled her clothes off, and he gently laid her on the sand, and it was a tropical island then, and there was no oil, and they were alone, and she gave herself up to him.

When she woke, she rolled toward Tom with guilt and desire. She fitted her body into the curve of his spine, and kissed him where her face pressed into his shoulder blades. She reached her hand around Tom's body and placed her palm over his heart. He rolled over, pressing his chest against hers, his belly against her belly, his thighs against her thighs. They had been married for so long that there was no mystery in the way they touched. It was as if they had agreed to play a symphony, and she knew her part, and he knew his, and they both knew how things would sound when played together, but they played, still, for the pleasure of knowing.

But at a certain point, that morning, in the middle of a certain movement, Lily stopped playing the part she normally played. No longer the eager wife, the grateful wife, the bored wife, the playful wife, the conciliatory wife, the merely willing wife, she wasn't a wife at all. She was an earnest girl on her way to study math, and the man in bed with her was a boy named Jack who planned to study the waves, and it was Jack who was kissing her and stroking her, and it was Jack who made her hips insist on more, and Jack who made her cry out.

"Wow," Tom said. "Retirement suits you well, Mrs. Gilbert."

She laughed nervously, but inside her head, things were popping—bubbles of guilt, little pockets of shame.

·14·

Olivia

AS soon as Brooke learned that her grandparents had a dog, she wanted to visit them. She loved dogs. She chased small white dogs in the park, laughed at the long, lean ones on the street, tried to offer the big, mean ones a Cheerio. Ryan was gone every weekend scouting at high school swim championships up and down the state, and so Olivia thought a trip to Santa Barbara to see the new dog was a good idea. It would, at least, be a diversion; instead of asking endless questions about where her daddy was and when he was coming home, Brooke was asking endless questions about the dog and where it was going to sleep and who was going to feed it.

They began to pack twenty-four hours in advance of their trip—Olivia so that she didn't forget some crucial piece of toddler gear, and Brooke so that she didn't forget her bear, her blanket, the Cheerios she intended to give to the dog.

"You can't feed the dog the food that you eat," Olivia said.

"Why?"

"It will make her sick."

"Why?"

"Because dogs like dog food, not people food."

"I want dog food."

"No, silly," Olivia said. "You eat people food."

"Why?"

"Because you're a person."

"Anna cooks it."

"Well, yes," Olivia said, realizing that, in addition to stopping the mail and the newspaper, she had to call to cancel meals for Thursday and Friday. "Anna cooks our dinner sometimes when we're here, but she won't be cooking our food at Grandma's house. Maybe Grandpa Tom will make you some guacamole."

" 'Molee!" Brooke sang out.

ON the night before they left, Ryan called from Mission Bay. He and Olivia hadn't spoken in two days.

"Hey," he said. "It's me. Is Brooke still up?"

"No," Olivia said.

"How are you guys doing?"

"Fine."

"Up to anything fun?"

"We're going down to see your mom and dad," Olivia said, as if she were a reporter reciting the news, "and to meet the new dog."

"Oh," Ryan said. "Okay. I wanted to stop off and see them on my way down here, but I didn't have time. How long will you be there?"

"I don't know," she said.

"If you're mad at me, Olivia," Ryan finally said, "why don't you just say it."

"I've said it."

"You're mad that I have a full-time job, is that right? That's the complaint? That I'm not home for dinner every night?"

"This isn't what I wanted," Olivia said.

"Believe me, it's not what I wanted either," Ryan said. "I'm out here busting my butt and nothing seems to make you happy. A bigger pay-check, being able to stay home, food from my grandmother . . . none of it makes you happy?"

She paused for a moment to let the thoughts in her head come together, but they were like high, thin clouds, dispersed by the wind. She couldn't pull them into shape. "I don't know," she said, and pressed her lips together and squeezed her eyes shut and wondered if she would ever feel like herself again.

SHE had planned the drive so that Brooke would sleep, but Brooke didn't sleep. She wanted to listen to *Baby Beluga* over and over again, she wanted to know what the big truck next to them was carrying and where it was going, she wanted to know when they were going to go past the cows. Olivia drove, and answered, and drove, and answered, and when she drove up the narrow road that led to Tom and Lily's house on the hill, and saw the avocado trees spread out before her in neat, shimmering lines, she felt a sense of deliverance; someone would be here to help her.

The dog came bolting up to the car, barking, and Brooke started to chant, "Luna, Luna, Luna."

Tom came around the side of the house, waving and carrying a rake. He grabbed Luna's collar and pulled her back from the car. Olivia got out, kissed her father-in-law on the cheek, opened the back door, unlocked Brooke from her car seat, and hoisted the child on her hip. Brooke leaned over precipitously to try to pet the dog, so Olivia set her down and said, "Let Luna come to you, sweetie."

Luna stepped up to Brooke and sniffed her and circled her, and wagged her tail, and Brooke laughed, and Olivia never took her eyes off Luna's speckled snout or her mismatched eyes, alert to any sign that the dog would lunge, bite, attack. Olivia quickly realized that there would be no deliverance—not here, not anywhere, at least not until Brooke was five, or ten, or sixteen, or twenty-one.

Lily came out and threw her arms around Olivia and lifted Brooke into the air, where it seemed she didn't want to be. Lily set her down. While Brooke and the dog continued to circle each other and sniff each other out, and Tom and Olivia monitored them, Lily took the duffel bags from the car, and carried them into the guest room, which had new Bertasi sheets on the bed, a new bedspread, a big, red stuffed chair from the house in Vermont, and wildflowers in a vase beneath the window.

Olivia came in, hauling the port-a-crib. "This is a beautiful room," she said. "You've done such a nice job with it."

"It doesn't feel real," Lily said. "That this is our house, that's our dog, and you can just drive down to see us." She smiled. "I love it."

"It's wonderful to have you so close," Olivia said, "and the dog is obviously a big hit. Brooke would give anything for a dog."

"You're not a dog lover?"

"Oh I am," Olivia said. "We had Saint Bernards growing up. Five of them, over about ten years. It's just that . . ." She stopped, and turned toward the window so that Lily couldn't see her face, which had cracked open. She busied herself with unzipping the portable crib, composed herself, then stood up and faced her mother-in-law with tears in her eyes. "It's just that I can't handle a dog," she said. "I can barely handle Brooke."

Lily stepped up to Olivia and embraced her. The two women were nearly the same height and build, and Olivia fit in Lily's arms as if she were her own child. Olivia stepped back and sobbed. "It's just so hard," she said. "I'm so tired. And Ryan, you know, he's gone a lot. For his job. And when he's home, we're mad at each other all the time."

"Remember how after you gave birth to Brooke, you were shocked that no one had warned you how much it would hurt?"

Olivia nodded.

"It's the same deal with a toddler. There must be something in our brains that doesn't hear the stories other women tell, because everyone warns you how tired you're going to be. Everyone talks about how hard it is to keep your marriage whole. But every new mother is shocked. It will get better. I promise."

They heard Brooke begin to wail, and the sound got closer, and then Tom was there with Brooke in his arms and Luna at his heels. "Luna licked her face," Tom said.

Brooke reached out her arms for her mother, and Olivia took the girl, and felt her body shaking and heaving. "Shhhh," she said, "you'll be fine," and then to Tom and Lily said, "She skipped her nap. She was so excited to see you. I'll just lie down with her until she goes to sleep."

Tom and Lily left the room, and Olivia lay down with her overwrought child on the crisp new sheets, and fell asleep before Brooke did.

·15·

Eleanor

BUCKY Harrington hosted the Red Sox Opening Day party at his house on Charles River Square in April. Everyone arrived when it was still dark and the temperature hovered at 33 degrees. The caterer they used had hot coffee and strudel at the ready, and soon the voice of Jerry Remy warmed everyone up.

"Sounds like summer," Gordon said, and everyone smiled and nodded.

They watched as Dice-K took several pitches to warm up his arm, and as Manny tied the game with a big double in the sixth inning. They grumbled when Keith Foulke stepped onto the mound for Oakland, since he had been a Red Sox not so many years before. In the eighth inning, Jacoby Ellsbury went up for a catch, making a huge leap into the wall and coming down with the ball. The crowd in Bucky Harrington's living room went crazy.

Throughout the game, other parties and other baseball games were relived. Eleanor could no longer remember the name of a certain friend's child or the title of a book she read or which street she needed to turn on to get to a favorite restaurant, but she remembered events from college and her young life in Boston with crystal clarity. It was as if she were retaining only the memories that really mattered.

Gracie used a walker because she couldn't risk a fall. She sat in a big wing chair behind the couch, and never touched the strudel or the fruit salad or the hot dog that was presented to her. Eleanor wasn't sure Gracie was even following the game. During a commercial break, Eleanor pulled up a folding chair next to her old room-mate. "We've never had an Opening Day quite like this one, have we?" she said.

Gracie turned and looked at Eleanor. "No, ma'am," she said.

"You're not eating your hot dog."

"I'm dying," Gracie said.

"I know that," Eleanor said, "but that's no reason to ignore a hot dog."

"I think it will be soon," Gracie said.

"Poppycock."

Gracie reached out her hand and took Eleanor's in hers. Gracie's skin was paper thin, and her hand shook. "I'm trying to say good-bye," she said.

Eleanor shook her head. She felt frantic. "I'll come to New York," she said. "I'll sit by your side."

"No," Gracie said, "I couldn't stand that. It will be easier this way."

Eleanor leaned over and put her arms around her friend. She could feel the thinness of her frame, the laboring of her breath. "Damn you, Gracie," she said.

"Next year at Fenway, have a hot dog for me, will you?"

"Until they cart me away," Eleanor said, and she pulled back and squeezed her friend's hand softly, being careful not to crush her bones.

The game came back on, and Eleanor couldn't watch as Papelbon attempted to close it out. She went to the kitchen for a Bloody Mary she didn't want, stepped outside to the small patio out back. She took a gulp of air and closed her eyes to keep in the hot tears. Suddenly, she felt a hand on her shoulder. It was Gordon.

"She's in terrible pain," he said.

"I know," Eleanor said, and wiped the tears that had run down her cheek. "Are you doing okay today? Judy would have loved this crazy breakfast, although she wouldn't have let on. She would have pretended to be offended."

Gordon shrugged. "I hardly sleep anymore," he said, "which is just as well. I hate waking up and having to realize, again, that she's gone."

"It was always something of a blessing to me," Eleanor said, "to realize I was finally rid of my husbands."

Gordon laughed. "You weren't easy to be married to," he said.

She smiled. "I always said love never lasts."

"You still playing the field out there in Santa

Barbara?" Gordon asked, and Eleanor had the distinct sense that he was nervous. He shifted his weight from foot to foot, and swirled his Bloody Mary around his glass.

"Good God, no," Eleanor said.

Gordon cleared his throat. He looked at his shoes. "Eleanor," he said. "Before Judy died, she told me I should remarry."

"That's just like Judy," Eleanor said. "Always thinking of everyone else first. You have any prospects? A distinguished navy man like you would be quite a draw, I would think. That, and the apartment on Seventy-third Street."

Gordon looked up. "She told me I should marry you," he said.

Eleanor was holding her drink in her right hand in a crystal highball. She dropped it on the patio and it smashed and sprayed tomato juice on her black patent flats and on Gordon's khaki pants. People came to the door to see what had happened, and to see if everyone was all right, and then the caterers came with sponges, and a maid came with a mop. They eventually all went back inside, and by that point the game was over, and the after-game interviews were going on, and people were talking about going back to their hotels for naps, or going over to the museum of art to see the Winslow Homer exhibit or going over to the Harvard baseball field to see what might be going on.

"Will you join me for lunch?" Gordon asked Eleanor.

"I'm sorry," Eleanor said, "I'm going with Gracie and her nurse to the train station."

"I'll have them hold us a table at the M Bar," he said. "They do a great poached lobster."

She closed her eyes. What could Judy possibly have meant by doing this? "Fine," she said.

SHE and Gracie sat on the benches at South Station and watched the people coming and going.

"The world has gotten faster," Gracie said.

Eleanor smiled. "I think we've just gotten slower."

"Look at everyone," Gracie said, "headphones and cell phones. It's ridiculous. They never get a moment's peace."

"It's fantastic," Eleanor argued. "I have a new BlackBerry. It has its own little global positioning system. Tells me exactly where I am in any city in the world." She fished the gadget out of her bag, and held it out on her palm.

Gracie scowled. "What on earth are you doing with a thing like that?"

"Luke gave it to me for Christmas. Look," she said, pressing the screen. "Look, here are pictures of Brooke, and of the house on the avocado ranch. I can even play hearts."

"Against a computer?"

"Try it," Eleanor said, holding out her phone.

Gracie waved her hand dismissively. "I'd rather just watch the passersby."

Eleanor turned off her phone and slipped it back into her bag. "Gordon says that Judy told him to marry me," she said.

Gracie chuckled.

"Why would she do such a thing?"

"Oh come on," Gracie said. "She probably just wanted to know he'd still be loved."

"Loved? You can't suddenly decide to love someone because someone else said you should."

"Why is that any worse a reason than any other?"

"Since when are you so philosophical?" Eleanor asked, and immediately wished she hadn't.

In the light of the station, Gracie's skin looked translucent. Eleanor thought she might be able to trace one of her friend's veins from her hand, up her arm, and straight into her heart. "I'm dying," Gracie said. "It tends to make you wax on about things."

"And what do you know about love anyway?"

"I know I never had it," Gracie said. "Nothing like Gordon and Judy. I was too damn stubborn. Just like you."

Eleanor looked at the board announcing the train arrivals and departures. The train Gracie would be taking back to New York was only seven minutes away. "What am I going to do?" Eleanor asked.

Gracie looked at her. "Say yes," she said.

"I've known him practically my whole life as Judy's husband. And I've botched every relationship I had. What good would it do him? And what good would it do me?"

"You might surprise yourself," Gracie said.

Her nurse stood, and said it was time to make their way to the tracks. Eleanor stood and helped Gracie to her feet. They walked slowly through the terminal, toward the archway leading to the train, and then down onto the platform. They felt the warm wind of the train as it pulled into the station, and Eleanor thought of the moment she first laid eyes on her friend. She was eighteen years old. Her mother had driven her out to Wellesley, and carried her suitcases to Room 28 in Tower Court. When they stepped into the small room with the sloped roof, there was a blond-haired girl sitting on a chair, her suitcases on the floor in the middle of the room. She was wearing a plaid skirt, a blouse with a Peter Pan collar, a navy blue sweater. She leapt up. "I've been waiting for you," she said. "I'm Gracie Dooley from Charleston, South Carolina. We're going to be great friends!"

"Good-bye, Gracie," Eleanor now said.

"Good-bye, Eleanor."

160

Eleanor stood on the platform while everyone settled onto the train, and she watched Gracie sit by the window in a first-class seat. She waved while the train pulled out of the station, and then she walked slowly out to the street and called a cab to take her to the Mandarin.

GORDON stood when she walked in. He pulled out the wicker chair for Eleanor, and called the waiter over to order her a drink. "Black coffee, please," she said. "It's only twelve thirty and I'm exhausted."

"Opening Day will do that to you," the waiter said, and Gordon laughed and raised his glass.

They talked about the game and about their friends who had been at the party and about the city of Boston and how good it was to be there. Eleanor told Gordon about the whale that had died on the beach in Santa Barbara, and how it reminded her so much of the oil spill of 1969, and how she couldn't stop thinking about it—oil-covered birds, and the great hulking carcass of the whale. She chatted like a nervous schoolgirl through soup and sandwiches, until finally, when the waiter brought coffee for the second time, Gordon circled around to the reason for their being there together.

"Judy made lists for each of us on a yellow legal pad," Gordon said. "There were lists of things she wanted each of the children to have, and lists of things she wanted them to remember—*stand up straight, look people in the eye when you speak to them.* That was for the grandkids."

Eleanor nodded.

"My pages were letters about various things," Gordon said. He reached into his pocket, took out his wallet, and unfolded a piece of yellow lined paper. "She gave me this one last."

Dearest Gordon,

I can't bear to think of you being alone. You have been such a good husband, and your talent should not go to waste just because I'm leaving this earth. You should marry again. Soon. And you should marry Eleanor Peters. Good friendship is a fine foundation for good love, I think. You won't have to defend your obsession with the Red Sox to her, and you won't have to explain why you sometimes break into songs by Gilbert & Sullivan, and the kids won't have to take time to get to know her since they've known her all their lives. I suppose that she will try to say no; I don't think she feels that she has been very good at love. But love, as you surely know after so many good years together, is a choice. There is no reason why Eleanor can't choose it, and

I hope you can get her to see this. It would give me great peace to know that you are not alone.

Forever,
Judy

After he finished reading the words, he handed the piece of paper across the small table to Eleanor. She read Judy's familiar left-leaning scribble, noting how erratic her lines were, how lightly the pen had moved across the page. She folded it and handed it back. "It's a lovely letter, and you know how I treasure our friendship, and how I treasured Judy's, but you can't expect me to just say yes, Gordon. You can't."

"I know that," Gordon said, "but I wanted to show you the letter, and to tell you that I think she was a genius."

"No woman has ever been more adored by a man," Eleanor said.

"I mean that I think she's right."

"About which part?"

"That love is a choice."

"Even if I agreed to marry you, Gordon, which I'm not agreeing to do, falling in *love* with you is a whole other matter. People don't just decide to fall in love, and then that's that. I mean, we're talking about love, Gordon! People search for love their entire lives and never find it."

"I don't think it's that hard," he said, "and I don't think Judy thought so either."

"Not that hard?"

"We made a decision every day that it was going to work."

"You were extraordinary. You must know that. You were gifted, blessed."

"It's true," Gordon said, "but it could be true for you and me, too."

She shook her head. "All my husbands either dropped dead or walked out on me," Eleanor said, "or both. And I was happy every time they left. There was always someone else I found more attractive, more interesting."

"You liked the hunt."

"I suppose I did."

"But you said you weren't playing the field in Santa Barbara. There are no other men in the wings, are there?"

"I swore off men," Eleanor said. "It was my New Year's resolution."

"I see," Gordon said, and he put the yellow piece of paper away, but Eleanor had the distinct feeling that the conversation was far from over.

ELEANOR took a nap that afternoon and then met the others for a walk around Harvard Square and hamburgers at Charlie's Kitchen. Gordon kept his distance the rest of the day, giving no indication of the conversation they had had at lunch. They shared a cab back to the hotel, and when they got into the elevator, Gordon said, "What floor, Eleanor?"

"Twenty-two," she said.

They rode in silence to her floor, and he held the door while she stepped into the vestibule, and he stepped out behind her, and walked by her side to her room.

"You're like a puppy," she said when they got to her door.

He shrugged. "I've come to loathe the night," he said. "I can't sleep, and when I do, I have nightmares. Are you good for one more drink?"

"Come in, come in," she said, relenting, and she led him to the sitting area by the window.

She sat down on the bed and took off her shoes while he called room service to order something from the bar. She was so tired, she didn't care about propriety. They talked for a while about dinner, and the view, and when the drinks came, Gordon went to the door to pay the bellman. When he turned around, Eleanor was resting on the pillows, asleep.

He debated leaving. It was a tricky question because Eleanor was a tricky woman. She was the most spontaneous woman he knew, on the one hand—a lover of parties, of travel, of early morning swims in the ocean and of love affairs that did not take into consideration the rules of the world. She was, on the other hand, someone who stood by ceremony—who believed that men should open doors for women, pay for dinner, and mix a strong martini, and that women should know how to wear pearls and set a proper table. She might think nothing of his sitting up all night in her room, or she might take great offense. She had recently sat up all night in his living room, so he was inclined to think she wouldn't mind his returning the favor. Besides, he felt desperate. When Judy gave him the note on the yellow legal pad, he immediately understood her impulse. He would have wanted to do the same for her. A good, long marriage made you believe in love. It made you depend on it. It made you crave it. Judy's directive to him had brought them both a measure of peace in her last days, and had brought him a sense of hope in the days that followed her death. If Eleanor refused him, however, he felt certain he would be completely lost.

He pulled the comforter across the bed and laid it over Eleanor. He turned off the main light in the room, and turned on the reading lamp by the window. Then he sat down, picked up the newspaper, and began the long wait for morning.

·16·

Lily

ON the morning of that same day, Tom got up at 6 a.m., made a cup of coffee, and immediately went out to be with the trees. There was a shed at the bottom of the hill—a small house, really—filled with wooden crates and picking poles and racks and clippers. He went through trying to understand the purpose of each of the tools, and he studied the irrigation system, and the compost pile behind the shed. At lunch, he came in and gave reports to Lily.

"There's a raccoon family that lives under the shed," he said. "The trees on the downhill side of the slope have more fruit. There's some kind of beetle in the bark on some trees by the eastern fence line."

At four o'clock, he called Lily to say that he was going to work through dinner at the warehouse with Nadine.

"You've been spending a lot of time there," Lily ventured. There had been early-morning trips to the warehouse, lunch at the warehouse, meetings at the warehouse. And except for when she had instigated it, there had been very little sex in their new bed. When they moved into their first apartment in Vermont, they had made love in every room, on every surface, and they had laughed, and gone out into the world each day filled with each other, and smug about their love. Now, it was as if they were brother and sister.

"Nadine's putting together a presentation on the benefits of organic composting," Tom said, "and I'm just helping her out."

Lily couldn't help it. She pictured Tom slowly stripping the flannel shirt off braless Nadine. It was a hot day and her skin would be sweaty, and his skin would be sweaty, but they wouldn't care because their desire for each other would be so great.

"We'll probably order something in," Tom said, "so you should go ahead and eat without me."

"Okay," Lily said, but what she was thinking was, *Of course.* What she was thinking was, *Love is just an illusion.* What she was thinking was, *I am such a fool.*

SHE put Luna into the back seat of the Subaru and headed down the hill. She would never have admitted that she was going to the beach to look for Jack, but that was exactly what she was doing. She wanted to know what it was like to act on a whim. She went to Eucalyptus Lane, parked the car, and walked down the shady street to Miramar Beach. Cement steps with a rusted railing led down from the end of the lane to the sand. She held Luna on a tight leash and made her way down. When they hit the sand, Luna went wild. She pulled on her leash, leaping at the seagulls who darted on the ground and flew through the air. She lunged toward a little terrier, whose fur was wet and matted.

"Whoa, girl," Lily said. She scanned the crowd. There were families with umbrellas and coolers, who looked like they'd been camped out all day, and couples lying bronze and sleek side by side in the late sun. In the water, there were toddlers running in the froth, kids with boogie boards, body surfers. A few surfers bobbed in the waves farther to the south. She turned in that direction and walked just beneath the houses that lined the sand. *It's a beautiful afternoon,* she told herself. *I'm just taking my dog for a walk.* When she got closer to the surfers, she slowed down, and scanned the people sitting on their boards, bobbing in the waves. Luna yelped, struggling to move toward a pile of seaweed abuzz with flies. She reached down to pet Luna on the head, and when she stood up again, she heard someone behind her calling, "Lily!"

She turned. It was Jack. She had come to find him, but she hadn't expected him to actually appear. She was startled and embarrassed. She thought about pretending not to hear him, or turning and running back to the car, but Jack was jogging toward her, waving. "Hey," he said when he caught up to her, "I recognized the dog." He leaned down and took Luna's nose in his hand. "How you doing, girl?" he asked, and then he let Luna lick his salty skin.

Lily felt her heart leap. She felt an electric jolt, and it was so strong that she was certain Jack felt it, too. How could he not?

Lily swallowed. "She's crazy," she said, "barks all the time. But we've already fallen in love with her."

"Excellent," Jack said. "I can't own a dog because I'm gone so much, but dogs are so much easier to be around than people, don't you think?"

"They can be," Lily said.

He looked her full in the face, and she thought she wouldn't be able to stand the intensity of his gaze. "You look exactly the same as you did in high school," he said. "Your smile, it's exactly the same. The years have been good to you."

She looked at the sand, at Luna's paws. "Thank you," she said very quietly.

"I always liked you," he said. "You were so serious, so dead set on going out into the world. Did you find whatever it was you were looking for?"

Lily swallowed. It felt like an incredibly intimate question from a man who was essentially a stranger. But she had come here for this. She had come to the beach for exactly this. "I'm not sure," she said.

He put a hand on her arm, and his skin felt hot

and charged—the way it had in her dream. She didn't flinch or pull away. She noticed how Jack's arms were so much thicker than Tom's, how they were darker, stronger, more firmly set in their sockets. She was lost for a moment, in the fact of Jack's hand on her skin, and then he stepped back.

"Our offices are in Ventura," he said. "Come by and see me sometime."

She swallowed. Her throat was dry. "I will," she said in a quavering voice, and then she turned on her heel and walked quickly back to the car.

SHE burst into her kitchen, opened a bottle of the zinfandel left over from her mother's welcome party, poured herself a glass, downed it, and stood at the counter waiting for the moment when she would begin to feel weak, when her heart would begin to pound and her head would begin to throb. Red wine did that to her. She was counting on it.

IT was ten thirty when Tom got home that night, and still hot. The moon was high in the sky, and the stars were coming out strong. Luna was wound up again, and the moment Tom walked into the house, Luna came bounding up to him, circling him and yelping.

"Hey, Luna," he said, squatting to nuzzle her nose. "How's my girl?"

Luna trotted toward the back deck, and when Tom saw a light on outside, he followed. Lily was sitting on a chaise longue, part of a teak set they had purchased from the Hailwoods, with apricot-colored pillows.

"What are you drinking?" Tom asked, thinking he might join her. When she didn't answer right away, he picked up the bottle. "Red wine?" he said, as alarmed as if she had been drinking arsenic. "Why are you drinking red wine?"

"I guess I just felt like flirting with danger."

"I think that's a decision you're going to regret," Tom said.

She turned to look at him and, with great tenderness, said, "You know that, don't you?"

Tom picked up a wedge of cheese. "Know what?" he asked.

"How I can't drink red wine. Exactly how sick I get. I mean, you know that very specific thing about me."

"It's not a big mystery, Lily."

"Oh, but it is," she said, and gulped more wine. "It is. I mean I could tell someone that red wine makes me sick, but they wouldn't have any idea what that meant. You know all about how ice helps, and when it's time to go to the emergency room. You know all that."

"Why don't you just go to bed, Lily," he said. He didn't know if she would get a headache or not, but either way, he loved his wife. He was the kind of man who faced whatever came to him, who handled things, who got things done.

"I'm not tired," she said. "I'm the opposite of tired."

"Well, I'm exhausted," he said. "I'm going to go to bed."

"For the first time tonight?" she asked.

"Now you've completely lost me," he said.

She sat forward in her chair and spoke quietly. "Have I?" she asked. "Lost you, Tom? Do we not love each other anymore? Did we make this whole move for nothing?"

"Lily," he said, and his voice was gentle and pleading. He wanted her to stop babbling, to go to sleep, to try to cheat the headache she had invited into the hot night.

"Well, it's true," she said. "It's like we're roommates. I mean, we moved across the country together. We picked up and moved, and you hardly want to touch me anymore, and you spend all your time with Nadine and maybe we don't really love each other, or not enough anyway. Maybe we never did. Maybe it was all just convenience."

Tom lowered himself into the chair next to Lily, and Luna came and put her nose on his knee. "Roommates?" he ventured. "I never had a roommate who acted the way you did the other night."

She felt the blood rush to her creeks, and

173

awkwardly waved her arm across the night. "Usually when I touch you now, it's like you're not there. I thought this move was going to help us, but now I'm thinking I was wrong." Silence settled over the back deck and the stars seemed to crackle in the hot sky. "I've been wondering if you've been sleeping with someone else," she said.

"What are you talking about?"

"Nadine," she said. "I'm talking about braless Nadine."

Tom got up from the chair so abruptly that it had the effect of a punch to Luna's nose. The dog reeled back and howled. "Are you kidding me?" Tom asked.

"About which part? Her being braless?"

"No," Tom said, "about what just came out of your mouth."

"I wasn't kidding," Lily said. "We walked away from our house, our jobs, our whole life because I thought somehow this move might be good for us, but all it did was free you up to hang out with braless Nadine."

"That's not fair," Tom said, "and you know it."

Lily threw back some more wine. "I don't know what I know anymore," she said. "Especially about you."

"Come on, Luna," Tom said. "We're going for a walk."

Tom and Luna walked out the front door, and

into the parched hills. There was a trail that went up the bone-dry creek bed and cut off onto the shoulder above the house. It was speckled with the shadow of oak trees swaying in the wind and alive with the sounds of summer—frogs thirsty for water, crickets wondering about the heat. Unaware of anything but the night, Luna put her nose into the unseasonably hot wind, and followed Tom up the trail.

Lily sat for a moment on the back deck, stunned at what she had done and what she had said, and stunned that Tom had actually walked out. She missed Luna's presence by her side, and felt an irrational sense of gratitude that Luna would not be able to tell Tom the secret of what Lily had done on the beach—why she had gone, who had appeared, what she had felt. She got up and made her way to the front door.

"Luna?" she called. "Luna?" She listened to the air moving through the brush, and to the crickets.

"Tom?" she called. "Tom?"

When there was no answer, she went back to the bedroom, got into bed, and waited for the headache to come find her.

·17·

Tom

TOM had friends who had taken lovers, who had swapped wives, who had taken advantage of the proximity professors have to young, eager girls, but Tom had never been interested in making a mess of things for a few small, extramarital pleasures. He didn't think it was worth it. He wanted what he had now: a comfortable, familiar marriage; an earthbound challenge that stimulated a dormant part of his brain; and a driveway that did not need to be shoveled. He realized that he had no idea anymore what Lily wanted. She had wanted to move. She had pushed for it. Why was she so suddenly unhinged?

When Tom got back to the house, he went immediately to the deck to see if Lily was still there, and if she was okay. He picked up the bottle of zinfandel, which still had a glass left in it, then set it down, and walked toward the bedroom. Lily was curled into a ball under the covers, her arms tucked under her body like fine-boned wings. She was a small woman who looked even smaller when she was asleep. The accusation she had made seemed to be hovering around her, like a tangible thing, thick and black. He stood over the bed for a while, watching, as Lily slept and Luna curled up on the carpet by the door. He was so sweaty and hot, he couldn't imagine climbing into bed. He walked out back to the deck, lay down on a lounge, finished off the wine, and after studying the stars, closed his eyes and fell asleep.

AT two o'clock in the morning, Tom swam up out of a deep sleep, awakened by the barking of a dog. He sat up slowly, confused. He couldn't remember why he was alone and outside, wearing jeans and a T-shirt. He didn't understand whose dog was barking, and why. He opened his eyes and saw Luna standing there giving short, sharp bursts of warning. In seconds, Tom was on his feet. "What is it?" he asked the dog, and began to walk through the dark house. He could hear things—groaning, something loud like thunder, and he had the thought that it could be raining —and still Luna kept barking and barking.

He found Lily crouched in front of the toilet, vomiting and sobbing and gasping for air.

"It will be okay," he said to her, and then to Luna, "It will be okay." They had been here a hundred times before, and they knew how it went: Lily would stay in the bathroom, sobbing and vomiting and pleading for the pain to stop, and when the pain ebbed, she would say she was sorry for drinking the wine, and then the cycle would start all over again, perhaps with a new twist this time: she would say she was sorry for what she had said, and Tom would say not to worry about it, and they would go back to the way they were—bound together, connected by the way they felt pain and the way they gave pleasure and by the fact that they had chosen to love each other for so long.

The dog was standing in the doorway, barking even more urgently, inching backward into the bedroom. She bolted out to the living room, and circled back. She did this two times before Tom realized that Luna was trying to tell him something more. He followed her back through the dark rooms, and now he could hear it even more clearly—a kind of insistent hum, and then he could smell it: something burning, something on fire. Tom left Lily retching in the bathroom and walked to the windows by the front door. Luna padded after him, still barking madly. He opened the door, and smelled the smoke—which smelled sweet and benign, like a campfire. It was, after all, fragrant stuff burning in the hills: sage, manzanita, eucalyptus. He stepped outside, and walked a few steps out into the driveway to see what he could see. The wind was still blowing hot down the canyon, and there was that sound of something buzzing in the air. He thought about helicopters, a swarm of bees. When he got up onto the road, he saw his neighbor, Mary Hazelton, an older woman who lived alone in a house that looked as if it belonged in 1974. She had been at Eleanor's cocktail party a few weeks before. She stood about two hundred feet below him, in the dark, but he knew her by her white hair, and her proclivity for cardigans. Luna raced down to Mary to greet her, and then raced back to Tom, her ears pricked up, her tail alert.

"Can you see anything?" Mary shouted in his direction.

"No," he shouted back. The sky to the southeast was shifting with patterns of light and dark, which could have been fog, or clouds, or smoke. "Maybe something going on across the creek?"

"I expect we better get out," she said. "With this wind, anything could happen."

"Wouldn't the fire department tell us if we had to leave?" he asked. He imagined a bullhorn, a truck driving urgently up and down the road. He had grown up in New York City, where subways failed and buildings burned and sometimes the snow fell in enormous dirty drifts. Once, because of a fire in the incinerator, they had to evacuate the building where his family lived on East Eighty-sixth Street, but they were out of town and missed the drama.

Mary had lived in the Santa Barbara foothills for most of her life. She had friends who had lost houses in the Sycamore Canyon Fire and Painted Cave. "I wouldn't count on it," Mary said. "I'll call nine-one-one, then I'm packing up."

Her use of the word *packing* made him think of suitcases, neatly folded shirts. When he and Lily had packed up the Burlington house, Lily had carefully weighed each item—*Do we still need it? Do we still want it?* She was glad to get rid of the boys' old ski helmets, old oilcloth jackets, the pasta maker they never used, the textbooks they held on to in case they needed them someday. Tom hadn't been so discriminating. He nodded as Mary turned back to her house. "Wait!" he yelled into the wind. "How long do you think we've got?"

She tipped her nose in the air just like Luna. "I'd say twenty minutes."

He ran back down the driveway and through the front door, with Luna on his heels. He ran back into the study, pulled open a drawer, and started flinging files on the floor—taxes, insurance, and bank accounts—then he left it all and ran into the bathroom, where Lily was crouched in a ball, her forehead pressed against the floor.

"Get up," he commanded. "Get up."

She raised her head and looked at him through small reptilian eyes. He reached out and grabbed her elbow and pulled her up, and she collapsed back to the floor. "Please don't," she said weakly, waving him away.

"Get up, Lily," he said. "There's a fire. We have to leave."

She stood up, then bent over the toilet and heaved.

Tom left her. He ran to the laundry room, grabbed a white laundry basket, and went back to the study to load in the files. He threw in a baseball that was sitting in a stand on his desk—he'd caught it at a Yankee game on his twelfth birthday—and a framed card that Ryan and Luke had made for him one Father's Day when being a father was something he *did* rather than something he was. He carried the basket out to his new truck, hoisted it in the bed, and ran back to the bathroom. Lily had gotten up, pulled on a pair of sweatpants and a T-shirt, slipped on her old sheepskin slippers, and was sitting on the edge of the bed, holding on to the mattress as if she were at sea.

"Come on," he said. He lifted her, propped her up. She moaned while she shuffled along: "It hurts so much, it hurts so much." When they got outside, the hot wind and the smell of smoke hit Lily full in the face, and she put her hand over her eyes to try to shut out the assault on her senses. She groaned. She stepped to the Ford and held on to the edge of the truck bed, and then her stomach seized again.

Tom pointed at Luna. "Stay," he said. "Stay with Lily."

Luna sat on the driveway at the door of the truck, whining as if she, too, were in pain.

Tom flew back into the house, to the bedroom to grab his wallet and car keys, and then pulled down a duffel bag from the top of the closet and bolted for the study. He shoved in the mortgage papers, their passports, and their laptops, and then he started pulling out Lily's bins of fabric. He riffled through them until he found the Matisse tablecloth and cardboard tube Lily had carried by hand from Burlington, and he shoved these in, too. He hoisted the duffel on his shoulder and walked as fast as he could out to the truck, ignoring the sweat that poured from his face and soaked his clothes, and the fear that pumped through his veins.

Lily was sitting in the front seat, feverish and reeling from the pain, and Luna was sitting on the ground beside her door, exactly where she had been told to stay. Tom dumped his load in the back, pressed the car keys into Lily's hand, said, "Don't move," to Lily and Luna both, then turned and ran back into the house through the front door. He thought he would get some books, the photo of the boys that hung in the front hallway, but when he got inside, there was smoke swirling in the air, and he coughed, and he changed his mind about trying to salvage anything else. He headed out the side door to get the hose to water down the roof, but when he rounded the corner, a hot ember the size of a baseball pelted his leg. He stumbled back from a wall of flame. The fire hissed and crackled and seemed to suck the hot night toward it like a black hole. He stood there, unable to move, and thought, *So this is how it will end,* but then he heard Luna barking in the driveway, and a siren wailing, and he turned and ran back around the side of the house to see Lily standing in the driveway yelling, "Tom! Tom!" Luna bolted through the front door, where he had disappeared just moments before.

"Start the truck!" Tom yelled to Lily, and then he took off after the dog.

Luna followed the path Tom had taken through the house. She skidded straight through the living room, out the side door, and directly into the fire.

Tom stopped again in the doorway.

"Luna!" he called, but the fire roared so loudly in his ears that he couldn't hear his own voice. He turned to go back the way he had come, but all he could see was smoke and all he could take into his lungs was smoke. He got onto his hands and knees and crawled across the hardwood floor of the living room toward the front door. He knocked the edge of the glass coffee table with his head, and realized he had gone the wrong way. He gulped the thick air. He coughed, and gasped, coughed and gasped, and then everything went black.

·18·

Ryan

WHEN he got the call at 5 a.m., Ryan was eating a bowl of cereal in the dark kitchen of his cold apartment. He had on his swimsuit, sweatpants, a fleece top—a uniform that felt like a second skin after twelve years of competitive swimming. On the mornings he swam with the masters' team, he came back to the apartment for a second breakfast with Olivia and Brooke, and then drove back to the pool to run the morning workouts for his college team.

"Hello?" he said. He was expecting a swimmer to be calling to say that she was sick, or that his car wouldn't start.

"He's still at the house," his mother said—her voice rushed, panicked, raspy. "It was engulfed in flames, Ryan. Totally engulfed."

His mind was still foggy with sleep. "Mom," he asked, "what's going on?"

"A fire," she said, and then she coughed, and sobbed, and whatever she said next was incomprehensible.

He stood up. He could hear voices in the background. "Where are you?" he asked.

"Emergency room," she said. "Daddy went back in the house; it was totally engulfed."

"Okay," he said. "Okay."

She moved away from the phone, and he could hear her retching.

"Mom," he shouted. "Mom."

She came back on the line, and moaned.

"Have you called Nana?"

"She's gone," Lily said, and Ryan felt a wave of panic move through his body, the hot flush of knowledge that no one else was in charge.

"What about Luke?" Ryan asked, but he couldn't hear what she was saying. "I'll be there in two hours," he said. "Hold tight, okay? Hold tight."

HE threw some shirts in a daypack, then went to wake Olivia.

"Stop it," she mumbled when he put his hand on her freckled shoulder. Brooke was up in the middle of the night every night now with nightmares—about alligators, sharks, a giant gorilla—and Olivia was living in a state of total sleep deprivation. He no longer touched her for anything less than an emergency.

"Wake up," he said, shaking her again.

She pulled a pillow over her head.

"Olivia, wake up," Ryan demanded. "Something's happened to my mom and dad."

She recognized the sound of terror. It was a sound that reverberated in her own head now, all day long, and all night long. Was Brooke eating enough, was Brooke sleeping enough, would Brooke fall into the pool, was the baby-sitter trustworthy? People always said that staying at home with a toddler was the hardest job in the world, but what they never said was what averting disaster all day long did to your soul—how it lost some of its protective coating, and became raw, exposed. She sat bolt upright. "What's wrong?" she asked, swinging her legs over the side of the bed, ready to solve the problem.

"It's my mom," Ryan said, and Olivia stopped midstride; she hated to be so callous, but she had to conserve her energy. This wasn't her problem to solve.

"There was a fire," Ryan said. "I have to go."

"Right now?" Olivia asked.

"My dad might not have gotten out."

"Oh my God," she said, and stepped toward him and threw her arms around him. She was wearing a thin nightgown, with spaghetti straps. He could feel her breasts and her soft tummy pressed against his body. She felt warm and she felt as if she weren't his anymore. It wasn't that long ago when the slightest touch from Olivia sent him into a frenzy. They couldn't kiss without ripping each other's clothes off. They couldn't sleep through a whole night without climbing on top of each other. Now he held his wife in his arms with a kind of caution.

"You'll be okay?" he asked. He wasn't sure what Olivia and Brooke did every day. There were groups of moms they met with, and some kind of class they went to that had something to do with music. Olivia bought organic fruit and vegetables at the local market, and cubed and steamed them for Brooke. When Brooke was asleep, or watching something on TV, Olivia transcribed notes for a medical office. He figured they would be fine without him. He wondered if he would even be missed.

She nodded. "We'll be fine."

"I'll call you when I get there," he said.

WHEN he got on the road, he felt a cold sense of dread. He dialed his parents' new phone number—a phone at a house where he had never lived—but there was no answer. He knew his parents had an answering machine. It had his father's voice on it: *We're not here right now, but leave us a message and we'll be sure to get back to you soon.*

"Fuck," Ryan said.

He plugged in his iPod and listened to Sting. He was used to seeing his mother distraught. When he was younger, she used to get migraines all the time—three, sometimes four times a month. She would cry out in pain, vomit. He couldn't stand the smell, or the fact of his mother being ill, and he would go in his room and put his music on. Luke took after their dad. He would wade right into the storm with a bucket and an ice pack.

While Sting's mournful voice filled his head, Ryan tried to imagine his dad caught in a fire. His mind wouldn't let it happen. His dad was quiet, reserved, a guy who planned everything out in advance, considered everything that could go wrong, and focused on whatever problems arose until they were solved. Ryan remembered a time when he had accidentally cast a fish hook through Luke's thumb. They were in the middle of a remote lake in the White Mountains in the heat of summer. While Luke howled, and Ryan sat there pale and stricken, his dad calmly assessed the wound, opened his tackle box, got out a pair of needle-nose pliers, broke off the barb, and slipped it out the way it had gone in.

Olivia won't come, he thought. *If something's happened to my dad, she won't come to Santa Barbara.* And he realized that his marriage, which was so new, was never going to last as long as his parents' had. As he drove over the pass into Santa Barbara, he saw the smoke that blanketed the hills like a shroud and he stared out at the mocking blue sky, the sunshine, the sparkling sea. When he got down onto the freeway, he could see actual flames on the hills—angry lines of them, marching along the hill—and he could see people driving in both directions, their cars hastily piled with whatever belongings they had grabbed before they fled.

WHEN he got to the hospital, Ryan bolted inside and demanded to see his mother. A receptionist directed him upstairs; a nurse walked him down a hallway. He found her lying in a hospital bed. Her eyes were closed, and her face, usually so pretty and composed, looked as if was bruised. Her dark gray hair, which usually swung around her ears and her chin, was matted against her head. There was an IV stuck in her arm, and a bag of clear fluids on a post near her head. Luke was sitting on a chair beside the bed, slumped forward, the whole weight of his head in his hands.

Luke looked up. "He's dead," he said quietly. "The doctor just told us. The firemen got him out but there was nothing they could do."

·19·

Eleanor

WHEN Eleanor woke up at daybreak the way she always did, she was startled to find that she was still fully clothed, and that Gordon Vreeland was asleep in the chair by the window. She was irritated that he had stayed. He was mooning after her the way all the rest of them were, and in one of her oldest and dearest friends, it was pathetic. She got off the bed, showered, and changed into a pair of slacks and a sweater. These things took her longer than they used to, because her bad knees made it hard to bend down in the morning. Getting her shoes off the floor required her to sit first, and if she dropped the soap in the shower, she would be in real trouble. She had a flight to catch at eleven o'clock, and she refused to eat breakfast at the airport. She would have a proper breakfast downstairs before catching a cab. When she was packed and ready to leave, she placed a hand on Gordon's shoulder and shook him awake.

"Get up, Gordon," she said.

"What?" he said. And then, "Oh, right, good morning, Eleanor."

"Why are you here?" she asked, her hand on her hip.

He sat up. "I was watching you sleep," he said,

as if it were the most normal thing in the world. "I must have fallen asleep. I'm sorry."

"I'm going down for breakfast," she said, and she began to collect her keys, her purse, her suitcase.

Gordon stood up and asked if he could use her bathroom. He washed his face, and smoothed down his thin gray hair, which stuck straight up from his head like a little boy's. He followed Eleanor to the elevator.

"Look," she said while they stood there waiting in the hallway, "I'm sorry I can't accept your offer."

"Does that mean I can't have breakfast with you?"

"Of course you can have breakfast with me," she said, "for crying out loud."

After they had ordered, she pulled out her phone and switched it on. Sometimes the airlines called with flight information, and she quickly scanned her messages. There were fifteen messages from yesterday alone. She wrinkled her forehead and studied them—and then she panicked. Both her grandsons had called, and they usually only did that on her birthday. She listened to just two frantic messages from Ryan—*Where are you? Answer your goddamn phone!*—before she excused herself from the table, stepped out of the restaurant into a vestibule in the lobby, and dialed Ryan.

"What's going on?" she demanded.

Ryan's voice was void of any emotion. He sounded flat, hollow. "There's been an accident," he said. "A fire."

"What?" Eleanor whispered.

"There was a wildfire in the hills."

"Are they okay? Lily and Tom?"

"They knocked her out. She was hysterical."

"Are you *there*, Ryan? In Santa Barbara?"

"We've been trying to reach you for hours, Nana. We didn't know where you were."

Eleanor began to walk back to the table in the restaurant, still talking on the phone. It was a habit she loathed when she saw other people doing it—carrying on conversations in public. "It was a wildfire?" she asked.

"The house is gone," Ryan said. "She doesn't know yet."

"Dear God," Eleanor said.

Gordon was standing, leaving money on the table, wheeling Eleanor's suitcase.

"And Dad . . ." Ryan said.

Eleanor had heard enough bad news in her life to know what was coming. Something in Ryan's tone, in the way he said that one word—*Dad*—said everything.

"Dad didn't make it out," Ryan said.

She felt something snap inside—some thread, some stitch that held her heart in place. She stopped in the middle of the restaurant, where the other diners were now staring at her, aware that something dramatic was happening while they ate their waffles and bacon. "Are you saying Tom's dead?"

"Yes," Ryan said.

"I have a flight in two hours," she said. "I'm on my way."

Gordon pressed his hand on her back and guided her into the lobby. He took her room key and dropped it at the front desk, then led her out the front door into the busy morning air. She was shaking. Her teeth were chattering, and her heart was pounding. She gulped in a drink of air, and when she let it out, it came out as a shuttering sob. Gordon put his arm around her and asked for a cab. When the cab pulled up, he got in next to her in the backseat and said to the driver, "Logan Airport, please."

They were in the tunnel before she spoke.

"There was a fire," she said, "in the hills. Lily's husband was killed."

Gordon pressed his lips together, and looked out the window of the cab at the tiled walls of the tunnel, and the dim light. Sometimes hours would go by when he forgot that Judy had died, or forgot to remember that she was dead, but mostly, he was reminded of it time and time again, and the pain never diminished. It was the same hurt, time after time. He had begun to recognize it, to see it coming, to brace for it. But sometimes—like now—the pain crashed over him unexpectedly, and he felt as if he were drowning. He drew in a large breath and let out the air in a kind of sputtering gasp.

Eleanor had been trying to be matter-of-fact. She thought that if she could just get to the airport and get on the plane and get to Santa Barbara, it would somehow be okay. But when she heard Gordon sigh, she could not hold it together anymore. Tears spilled from her eyes, and she reached out and squeezed his hand in solidarity, and in thanks.

Once they got to the airport, Gordon used his phone to find news about the fire. It was only 80 percent contained. Eighty-three structures had burned. There was a shelter set up at the high school, and the insurance companies had already rolled in mobile units to help people process their claims. He fed her this information in small bits as they stood in line, and she only nodded in response. She had lived in Santa Barbara through several fires. She knew how it went: the hot winds whipped down the canyons at sundown, the eucalyptus trees burst into flame, the fire raced along the ridges like a voracious beast and the only thing you could do if you were in the way was to run. She'd known people who escaped from their homes with nothing but the clothes on their backs. She'd known others whose house was left standing while every structure around it was burned to the ground. The power of the fires was so awesome that the entire population of the town entered into a kind of reverent hush. Smoke filled the sky, ash filled the air, and people sat in front of their televisions transfixed by the images of flame and the specter of burned houses. They listened as their fellow citizens talked about their great good luck at being alive, and proclaimed their resolve to continue to live in the fragrant hillside chaparral, despite the fact that fire might come again.

When Eleanor had a boarding pass in hand, she made her way to the security line. Gordon followed her as far as he could, but then there was a uniformed security guard asking to see ID and boarding passes, and he was unable to continue.

"Will you call me when you arrive?" he asked.

She nodded dismissively, and turned to go, but then she stepped out of the stream of people, and turned back to face him. "Tom and Lily were like you and Judy," she said. "They were one of those couples that made you believe in marriage. It used to drive me crazy that she had exactly the thing I had never been able to get. I had husbands die and husbands disappoint, and I took lover after lover trying to fill the void, and she just sort of fell into this beautiful, lasting relationship like it was nothing. I know I shouldn't have thought this about my own child, but I didn't think it was fair." A rim of red rose up around her eyes as if someone had drawn it in, and her nostrils flared. She gulped at the air, once, as if she was going to dive underwater and needed her breath.

"You'd better go," he said. He put his hand on her back, and gave her a small push toward the gate.

She turned into the sea of people surging toward the security check, slipped off her shoes, and was gone.

SHE normally loved to ride on planes. She loved the hum of the engines and the clouds out the window and the way the entire country seemed within grasp when you were thirty thousand feet above it. But the trip to Santa Barbara that day was torture. She had one flight from Boston to Denver, and another from Denver to Santa Barbara. She felt faint on the first leg of the trip, and nauseous. The flight attendant brought her a 7Up, and some crackers and a warm towel.

She knew what it was like to have a husband suddenly die. She had been with Billy when his heart stopped. They were on their way home from Buenos Aires, where he had been playing an exhibition baseball game. They were at the airport, walking along, and then suddenly he was no longer next to her. He was slumped on the floor at her feet, and she knew before anyone could tell her that he was dead. She was secretly relieved. Once he made the major leagues, his love of baseball eclipsed his love of anything else. Eleanor didn't know yet how easy it was for a woman to walk out on a marriage, and sudden death was an elegant solution to her dilemma.

Elliot Taft must have sensed her glee. A Harvard classmate of Billy's, who did not have the good fortune to be on the Great Date, came calling within weeks of the funeral, and said he had been trying to keep his hands off her ever since they had met. He was married, with three children, and Eleanor took him as a lover. One day that fall, Lily came home early from school and found them naked in bed. Eleanor could see confusion and betrayal flash across her daughter's face, and so she told Elliot that he had to marry her, or leave her. By that point, Elliot couldn't give her up. He left his wife and children, got Union Oil to transfer him to a new city, and started a new life with Eleanor and Lily. But Elliot Taft wanted it all—his first wife, his new wife, and any other woman that struck his fancy. When he died after the oil spill debacle, Eleanor thought that he got exactly what he deserved.

Her third husband, Jacques, walked into her office one day and said he wanted a divorce. He had been a stately, polished man, an architect, an art collector, and he had picked Eleanor much the same way he would have picked a painting—for the way it would look in his home, for the prestige, for the investment. Many of his friends and colleagues were architects and designers, and through them, she was able to broaden the reach of Bertasi Linen all over the world. "That sounds reasonable," she said, and she called a lawyer, and he was gone within a matter of weeks.

As her plane touched down in Denver, Eleanor kept trying to imagine what it would be like to lose a husband with whom you were actually in love.

IN Denver, she watched the planes taking off and landing as she waited for her flight, and she kept imagining them falling out of the sky, and people raining down. She checked her phone, and saw that Gordon had called three times, but she did not call him back. She called Luke, and Ryan, and heard that they were waiting to see the body, and deciding what to do with it.

The trip to Santa Barbara took forever. She felt as though the canyons below her and the clouds above continued to go by as if on a conveyor belt, as if the landscape was moving in a circle, and they were just standing still in the sky. She didn't know what she would do to help Lily through this, but she would come up with something. Despite all the ways they had let each other down over the years, and the distance between them, and the fact that it was, in so many ways, her fault that Tom had been in the path of the fire, Eleanor would come up with something.

·20·

Olivia

OLIVIA'S nerves were frayed. That was the word she kept saying to herself, and the picture she kept imagining—the end of a rope, frayed, its individual threads exposed. A strange array of thoughts flitted across her mind like static on a TV screen—*we need to call a plumber about the drain in the bathtub, maybe Franny can watch Brooke on Wednesday, if Ryan's dad is hurt what will happen to Ryan's mom?* She couldn't remember the last time she'd slept through the night. Every night, as she brushed Brooke's teeth, changed her diaper, changed her into pajamas, read her *Harold and the Purple Crayon* again and again and again, she thought, *Maybe tonight.* But every night, Brooke awoke because her diaper was wet, or she'd had a bad dream, or she was thirsty, and Olivia would get up and stumble through the dark house to do whatever had to be done, and she would lie in bed and, instead of going to sleep, would wait for the next assault.

Things were easier with Ryan gone. She didn't have to wash her hair, didn't have to come up with something to say when he asked how her day had been, didn't have to feel guilty when she got in bed and he reached out for her and she rolled away and said, "No." She could concentrate, simply, on getting through the day. All morning, Brooke had been asking where Ryan was, and all morning, Olivia had been lying to her.

"Where's Daddy?" Brooke asked.

"He had to go away for a little while," Olivia said.

"Where?" Brooke asked again.

"He went to see Grandma and Grandpa."

"Why?"

Olivia panicked. Why? What could she possibly say that a two-year-old would understand? "Because they needed his help," she said.

"Why?"

"Because Grandpa Tom isn't feeling well."

"He's sick?"

"Yes," Olivia said. "He's sick."

She put Brooke down for her morning nap and backed out of the room so as not to disturb her. She sat down at the computer to search for plumbers. When the phone rang, she jumped. "Hello?" she said softly.

"It's me," Ryan said, and she could tell from his voice—gravelly, hollow—that something was very wrong. The thought she had just had—that things were easier without Ryan—was swept away, and she felt a wave of concern and affection for him.

"What's wrong?" she said. "What's happened?"

"It's my dad," Ryan said. "He's dead."

She sucked in air and instantly felt the burn of tears in her eyes. "Oh my God, Ryan," she said. "Oh my God."

He hadn't cried until then, but the sound of Olivia's voice made him remember that he had his own family now. He was a father. And he needed to be there for his child the way his dad had been there for him. "There was a fire," he said through his tears. "In the hills. I guess he went back for something. He was trying to get something out."

"He was trapped?" Olivia whispered.

"The firemen said it was the smoke," Ryan said. "It was the smoke that killed him."

She had seen pictures of California wildfires. From her home in Boston, they had seemed like exotic, far-off catastrophes. But here was something very specific—smoke, probably black, probably toxic, smoke that could kill. Ryan was sobbing, and Olivia realized that she had never heard him cry. She closed her eyes. "Oh Ryan," she said. "How's your mom?"

"Fucked up," he said, "totally fucked up." And then, "Olivia? Will you and Brooke come down?"

Her eyes welled up with tears again at the way he asked—as if she might not say yes. "Of course," she said, "of course we'll come down." She looked around the apartment at the diaper bag spilled on the floor, the food left out on the counter, the laundry that still needed folding. She imagined just picking up Brooke and walking out the door. "Should we come right now?"

"Tomorrow might be better," Ryan said. "We're meeting with the coroner. We have to get Mom into Nana's house. You should fly, don't you think?"

"That'll be expensive."

"It'd be stupid to have two cars here. Just fly. And can you bring me another pair of jeans?"

She got up, got a piece of paper, started a list. "Anything else?"

"My razor, I guess. Deodorant."

She nodded. She remembered when she and Ryan first started spending nights together. The presence of a razor in her bathroom was momentous. The presence of deodorant meant everything. She remembered wanting the tokens of Ryan's life to be a part of her life, too—to belong in her bathroom, to mingle with her lavender lotion and her peppermint soap.

"What's my mom going to do?" Ryan asked. He spoke so softly now that she could barely make out the words.

"Your mom will come through," Olivia said. "She's a strong woman. Did the house burn down?"

"Burned to the ground. A fireman told me. A guy in a yellow rubber jumpsuit just like you see on TV. I kept wanting to say, 'Are you for real?' "

Ryan laughed then, a sick, hollow sound. "I kept wanting to say, 'Dude, it's not Halloween.'"

She laughed along with him, just to make him feel better.

"Kiss Brooke for me," Ryan said.

"I will."

"Tell her I love her."

"I will."

"And you, too," he said. "I love you so much."

She licked the tears that ran down her face and they tasted salty. She hated to admit it in light of everything that happened, but they tasted good. "I love you, too," she said.

·21·

Lily

LILY and the boys slumped down the hall and into the white room where Tom's body lay under a sheet. Gritting his teeth, Ryan stepped forward to lift the edge of the sheet. Luke put an arm around his mother's shoulders and ushered her forward. He was glad to have something to do with his hands.

Tom's skin was smudged with ash, covered in soot. He smelled of smoke. Lily's first thought was that Tom would sit up and shake off what was ailing him and go back to being Tom. She counted her own breath—in, out; in, out; in, out; in, out—and when he didn't breathe during that whole time, she thought, *Okay. They're right. He's dead.* She lifted his hand and held it, and with her other hand, brushed her fingers lightly on Tom's cheek. "He's so cold," she said, and squeezed her eyes shut because she could hear him in her head saying, *I don't think I would miss the cold.*

"You know what I keep thinking about?" Luke asked. He was tall like his father, not as beefy as his brother. "How much he loved his stupid garden, all those goddamn peas and kale."

"I keep thinking about how much he loved

Mount Mansfield," Ryan said. When Ryan was in high school, Tom set out to climb every peak in the state of Vermont over four thousand feet. Luke accompanied him on almost every climb, but because of his swimming, Ryan was rarely free to go. In August, when the swim team took its only break, he joined his dad and his brother on the last big climb. *We saved the best for last,* his dad declared, and when they got to the top of Mount Mansfield, he grew very quiet as he looked out over the scoured valleys and the green-padded hills. After a while, he said, *"When I die, cremate me and throw my ashes from this peak."*

"He's *dead*," Lily said, and neither of the boys said, *"Smart, Mom,"* or *"Good observation, Mom,"* the way they might have under other circumstances. They just stood there over the body, feeling small and fragile, as if they, too, could at any moment simply stop walking and talking and breathing.

Ryan cleared his throat. "I'll take his ashes to the top of Mount Mansfield," he said. "I can do it before the snow falls, unless you want to come with me, Luke. We could do it next summer."

Luke nodded. Surely his grandmother would give him enough time off to help scatter his father's ashes. "Maybe we could take some of the ashes over to Apple Tree Point, too. To that cove he loved. Mom could come with us, and Olivia and Brooke."

Lily rested Tom's hand back next to his body, and stepped away from the table. Tom's family had a plot at Mount Auburn Cemetery in Boston—a neatly manicured row of granite tombstones shaded by elm trees and hydrangeas in the lush green park where proper New England families buried their dead. The Gilberts had a relative who had been an astronomer and a telescope maker. His was the first grave in the family plot at Mount Auburn—*Charles Gilbert, 1755–1838, Patriot, Scholar, Scientist*. But Tom didn't like Mount Auburn Cemetery. He didn't like the dates carved in granite, the gargoyles on the mausoleums, the way the gardeners so carefully manicured the ancient, haunted leaves. "Just cremate me," he always used to say after a visit to Mount Auburn. "Scatter my ashes in the garden where they'll do some good, or on a mountain where they'll blend into the scenery."

Lily had always intended to do as he wished. She and Tom had thought their deaths through with as much attention to detail as they lived their lives. They had generous life insurance policies, an airtight will that would preserve the family money in a trust, durable powers of attorney so that each of them could pull the plug on the other should they end up in a vegetative state. When the boys were young, they had long, somber conversations about the importance of staying the course if tragedy were to strike. If one of them were to slip on the ice and hit their head, run off the road and hit a tree, receive a sudden diagnosis of pancreatic cancer and be gone in a month, the surviving spouse would stay in the house, stay in Burlington, keep everything as stable as possible. Death itself might be unknowable, but Lily Gilbert thought she knew just what to do if Tom—who never got sick, who never complained, who never seemed as if he were even susceptible to death—were to be the first to die: she would simply follow the plan they had made as if it were a road map. Now here she was, alone, somewhere far off the map. *Damn him,* she thought.

She looked at Tom's blackened body and it seemed to her as though it was already on its way to ash; it didn't have that much further to go. "No," she said, and both boys looked up as if someone else had walked into the room and spoken that word. "We're not going to cremate his body. I'm going to bury him at Mount Auburn."

Ryan felt as if his whole body were a high-tension wire. It seemed to vibrate, to sizzle. "You can't do that, Mom," he said sharply.

She stared at her son as if he were underwater and the sound he'd made had been too distorted to hear. He'd been a quiet teenager, the kind of boy who slipped out of bed on dark winter mornings to get himself to swim practice, who holed up in his bedroom listening to music for hours on end, but when he decided he had something to say, he said it with force and conviction, and he found that he often got his way. He was never the loudest member of the team, or the one who stood out in a crowd, but he was always elected captain. He had a sureness about him that drew people in. Now that he was in his twenties, that sureness had hardened into something sharp-edged that Lily found suddenly ugly.

"You can't do it," Ryan repeated. "Because it's not what he wanted."

"It's what *I* want," she said.

Ryan turned away from his father's body to the white wall of the hospital, and then he turned back to his mother. "But it's not what he asked us to do."

Lily looked again at Tom's body—cold, inert, lifeless. "He's not here anymore," Lily said.

"Which is why we have to honor his wishes."

Lily shook her head. "No we don't," she said. She looked into her son's eyes—hazel, flecked with gold, totally different from his dad's solid green eyes. "We couldn't save him from the first fire," she said. "But we can save him from this one."

Luke looked again at his dad's body. Tom's hair was matted with ash. His fingernails had half-moons of black under the rim. "She's right, Ryan," Luke said quietly.

Ryan looked up, shocked that his younger brother had spoken, shocked to see that Luke was a man, too, grown-up and opinionated. They were so old, so suddenly.

"Dad would never break someone's trust," Ryan said, "and I don't see how we can break his now."

Lily jerked her head up. Why had Ryan chosen those words—*Dad would never break someone's trust*? Had he emphasized the word *Dad*? *Dad* would never break someone's trust—but *Mom* was another story? Mom would go to meet another man, fantasize about another man, imagine leaving a perfectly good marriage to a perfectly good man just because *good* somehow didn't seem like it was good enough anymore?

"Let it go," Luke said.

"I can't have any more fire," Lily said.

Ryan pressed his teeth together again. He thought of Olivia and of Brooke, and of everything slipping through his fingers like water. "Fine," he said, and turned away from his dad's lifeless body, and his mom's battered face.

SHE made arrangements for Tom's body to be embalmed and shipped back to Boston, where they would have a small family ceremony to put him in the ground. She liked the idea of him resting under all that snow, in a place that would be green and leafy all spring. She thought of all the things that burn—books, photographs, rugs, furniture, walls, flesh and bone. It gave her some measure of comfort to think that nothing could burn the piece of granite that would bear Tom's name.

"What about a funeral out here, Mom," Luke asked, "or a memorial service of some kind?"

Lily imagined sitting in a borrowed dress in a borrowed church, and then she thought of guacamole. All spring, Tom had thrown himself into the study of avocados—their history, their uses. *"The preferred way of eating avocados has always been to mash them up. The Aztecs called this mix ahuaca-mull."* Lily would look up from her computer, or from the soup she was stirring on the stove, and say, "Really? I had no idea." When their knives and cutting boards and mixing bowls came off the moving truck in Santa Barbara—safely arrived, after all—Tom began to cook. He had never shown any interest in cooking before, but suddenly, he was bringing back exotic peppers from the Farmer's Market and slow roasting them over an open flame, mincing garlic and cilantro, and buying specially curved knives with which to deseed heirloom tomatoes. He set down bowls of guacamole in front of anyone who walked into the house, pushing baskets of chips across the table, cracking open cold beers. It was a strange invitation from a man who wore wool socks with his sandals.

Within the first week, Tom developed a favorite recipe. It was the one that elicited the most praise, for its chunky texture and its lively taste. Even Eleanor, who usually preferred more refined fare, said that it tasted like summer.

"What's in it, Tom?" Eleanor asked.

"Ah," he said, pleased to have piqued her interest. "A man who shares his secret guacamole recipe is a man who is a fool."

Now he was dead, and Lily imagined re-creating his guacamole. It would taste like summer, and they would all stand around and remember how much Tom wanted to become a gentleman farmer, and how he had gotten his wish, however briefly. "I think we should just have a small gathering for now," she said.

WHEN they left the hospital in the late afternoon, the sky was orange and opaque. The fire was still burning in the hills and smoldering in the canyons. Hundreds of families had fled, and were huddled on friends' couches watching the news, crouched in front of other people's computers scrolling through lists of burned properties, camped out in the Red Cross shelter at the high school giving thanks for dinner and a blanket. Lily and the boys got in Luke's truck in solemn silence. It was Lily, sitting in the front passenger seat, who spoke first.

"What happened to Dad's truck? Someone

drove me down the hill in it, but then an ambulance came because I couldn't stop vomiting."

"It's parked up on Sheffield Drive behind the police line," Ryan said. A fireman had come up to him in the hospital to tell him about the truck and to tell him about the house. *It's gone,* the man had said. *We couldn't save any of it.*

Lily nodded, and then after a moment, she said, "The house is gone, isn't it?"

Ryan cleared his throat. "Yeah," he said. "That's what they told me."

"All of it?" She knew that sometimes it was only a wall that burned, or a room.

"It sounds like it," he said.

Lily laughed, a short, sharp burst of sound. "I'm homeless," she said. "I'm a homeless widow."

"Nana's on her way," Ryan said, because it was, at least, an answer to the question of where they would sleep. "She said to go to her house."

Images flashed into Lily's mind—the socks in her sock drawer, the washing machine and dryer that had just been delivered, the stack of books in the study. Was all of it really gone? And if so, where did it go to? She looked out the window of the truck at the greasy sky, and at the ash that gathered on the windshield like snow. Was that the remains of her teapot, her kitchen table, the blown-glass ornaments she brought back from Venice? "I don't have a toothbrush," she said.

Luke turned on the ignition. "Grandma probably has one," he said.

"I don't have underwear."

"Then I'll go to Target," Luke said. "I'll get you whatever you need."

WHEN they got to her mother's house, Lily went straight to her mother's office. It was on the first floor, just beyond the entryway, with a window that looked out onto a patio with bougainvillea-covered walls. There was a drawer with pens and paperclips and stamps and tape and scissors, and a wooden tray for correspondence. She took a piece of blank paper out of the printer, wrote "Bedroom" at the top, and started to make a list:

Cherry spindle bed
Organic cotton flannel blanket
Susan Sargent Blue Birds duvet cover and
  pillow
L.L.Bean cotton flannel sheets, blue
L.L.Bean cotton flannel sheets, green
Bertasi Linen cotton sheets, navy blue piping
Bertasi Linen cotton sheets, white
Alarm clock
Flashlight
Art Quilts of Lancaster County
A Quilter's Guide to Pattern Design
Organic Farming
The Journal of American Agriculture

Gold-framed mirror
Painting of winter birch trees
Photo of Luke and Ryan
Photo of Ryan, Olivia, and Brooke
Grandma Hattie's pearls
Grandma Hattie's garnet ring
Cashmere gloves
Black leather gloves
Tom's loose coins
Tom's Patriots' hat
Tom's collection of fountain pens—Pelikan Steno (Xmas 1973), Waterman Phileas (20th anniversary), Parker Sonnet (Xmas 1985), the obsidian Montblanc, the silver Cross

She filled up one page, then got out another, and wrote the things she had shipped from Santa Barbara to Burlington and back again:

The new Singer
Gingher scissors—old, new
Box of pins
Ruby red thread

"What are you doing?" Ryan asked.

"I don't want to forget anything," Lily said. It suddenly seemed important that she remember every single thing that she and Tom had purchased, and packed, and moved out to California.

If she could name all of those items—the furniture, the clothes, the books, the cups, the toiletries—then perhaps she could know exactly what it was that she and Tom had, all those years together, and what it all meant. She would never have said it out loud, or even admitted it to herself, but she had the tiniest hope that if she could name every single one of the things that brought life to their home, they would somehow add up to Tom himself.

Ryan held open a laptop. "I found the house on a list of lost properties," he said solemnly. "It's on the city's website."

She peered at the screen. There was a list of street numbers. She didn't know whom most of the houses belonged to. She had only briefly met a few of the neighbors, shaken their hands, and said hello at her mother's welcome party.

"There's also a map of the burn area on the *Independent* website," Ryan said, "and I've got Google Earth up so you can compare the two; you can see how the fire came right down the canyon."

They looked at the maps and pointed at the streets and zoomed in on the photograph of the house, which was taken six months ago, when Ted Hailwood was still worrying about bees, and Lily and Tom were finishing up their fall semester classes. "You can see the furniture on the back deck," Lily said, "and the shed at the bottom of the hill. Can you print that out, Ryan?"

"Sure," he said.

Lily turned back to her list. She and Tom had negotiated to buy that patio furniture, because the Hailwoods couldn't take it to the assisted living community where they were moving, and it was beautiful furniture, in fine shape. She wrote "Back Deck," and then added:

Teak table
4 teak chairs
4 teak longues
Carnival striped patio umbrella
Terra-cotta pots
Hummingbird feeder
Wind chime
Sisal doormat

The boys stepped into their grandmother's kitchen to find something to eat. There was hardly anything in the refrigerator—eggs, butter, a chunk of cheese.

"Let's just order pizza," Luke said.

Ryan nodded. He was worried about Olivia and Brooke coming down from San Luis Obispo—he had an irrational fear that their plane would crash—and he was worried about his mother. Her eyes had looked hollow and haunted, and her obsession with writing everything down that she had lost in the house had a creepiness to it that frightened him. He had never actually believed it would come to this—his dad dead? His mother crazy with grief? "Do you think Mom will eat?" he asked.

Luke took a deep breath and let the air out in a loud rush. "Probably not."

"I don't know what the fuck she's doing making all these lists," Ryan said. "It's not like it's going to bring him back."

Luke didn't respond. He was worried about something else. "I don't understand why she got out and he didn't," he said. "It doesn't make any sense. I can't figure it out."

"They were loading things into the truck, right?" Ryan asked.

Luke nodded.

"So he must have gone back for something. Made one last trip."

"Went back for what, though? I mean, what would be that important? His Bean boots? His maps? His pens? He wouldn't be that dumb. Don't you remember how many times he made us come down from a hill because there was lightning, or stop skiing because the visibility was bad?"

"I always thought he was so anal," Ryan said, and his voice broke. "I always used to wish that he would just cut loose and ski after midnight, or stand on a mountaintop in a thunderstorm."

Luke reached out and put his arm around his older brother's shoulders. "Maybe he did," Luke said. "Maybe that's what buying the avocado ranch was for him."

Ryan dropped his head in his hands and wept.

·22·

Luke

THE next day, Luke was desperate for something to do—anything that would make his head stop spinning, anything that would help him to breathe. He drove to Target and headed for the toothbrush aisle. He grabbed the first toothbrush that caught his eye—purple, shimmery, with words on the packaging that claimed the bristles would be soft and long-lasting. He selected a tube of the same toothpaste he used, which was the same toothpaste he had used throughout his childhood in Vermont. As he stood there, toothbrush and toothpaste in hand, he remembered the way his dad would stand at the sink brushing his teeth and shaving his face as if precision and control, even in this small daily endeavor, were of the utmost importance. It used to fascinate Luke—that every morning of his life, his dad got up and did exactly the same thing in exactly the same way, whether there was a blizzard outside, or blazing sun, whether he would be going fishing or going to teach a class called Cooperation and Conflict in the Biological Sciences. Once, Luke swiped his brother's swimming stopwatch to time his dad's morning routine. He found that over five days, the routine never varied more than twenty seconds from the norm. When Luke himself learned to shave, he tried to adopt the same precision. He believed it was one of the things that made you a man.

Next, Luke made his way to the area where women's underthings were displayed. He stood on the tile at the edge of the carpet and tried not to think about what he was doing. It was just a chore, an errand, something he had to do. He also tried not to think of Franny Jones and her petal pink underwear and the petal pink bra in tenth grade, and how he had learned to unhook it without even looking. He plunged ahead, trying not to catch the eye of any of the other shoppers. He found a display of Jockey underwear—three pairs wrapped in plastic, one white, one beige, one black. He shuffled through until he found a small. He knew his mother would be a small. He took two packages.

On his way to the cash register, he walked by a display of jeans and sweatshirts at the edge of the women's clothing department. He stopped, and grabbed a pair of Levi's and a plain blue hoodie sweatshirt, then went to pay for his purchases.

The woman in front of him had her cart piled high with toilet paper and paper towels. Underneath the paper goods was a layer of cleaning supplies—dishwasher soap and soap for the laundry, toilet bowl cleaner, and Clorox—and also bottles of shampoo and conditioner. The last item she put on the black conveyer belt was a single can of shaving cream. It was red-and-white-striped Barbasol: the exact kind of shaving cream his dad used. He would shake the can exactly five times, cup his hand, deliver a ball the size, color, and shape of a Ping-Pong ball, set down the can, rub the tips of his fingers together exactly five times, apply the cream to his face, and then, starting on the left side, near the ear, would start his first stroke down.

Luke closed his eyes. He felt them burn. He stood like that—eyes closed, eyes burning—until the cashier asked if she could help him, and then he opened his eyes, brushed away the tears, and set down the toothbrush, toothpaste, clothing, and underwear he had selected for his mother, the homeless widow.

The cashier was a young woman with a name tag that read DARLENE. Luke braced himself for her to look at him with contempt or pity, or for her to ask, "Are you okay?" but she simply scanned and bagged his items, punched the keys on the cash register, made change from the hundred he handed over, and turned to her next customer.

"Thank you very much," Luke said, and hoped she understood how much he meant it.

·23·

Eleanor

ELEANOR'S plane touched down at the Santa Barbara airport a few minutes after ten. Ryan was there to meet her. He was sitting at an outside bench drinking Heineken and watching the strange glow of the lights in the smoky sky. When he saw his grandmother step onto the tarmac, he stood up. He was almost two feet taller than she was.

"Hey, Nana," he said, leaning down to embrace her. His eyes were red, his face heavy. "How was your flight?"

"Longest trip of my life," she said.

He nodded.

"And you?" she asked. "Are you okay?"

He shrugged. "It's hard to believe any of it is real." He took her suitcase and wheeled it along, and led her out to the car.

Eleanor wanted to say, *"Believe it, child,"* because she had lived long enough to know that everything can change in an instant, that people are always dying when you least expect it. "I know," she said, "I know."

RYAN put the suitcase in the trunk of the car, and held the door for his grandmother. When he got into the driver's seat, she looked over at him. "He was doing exactly what he wanted," she said. "At least there's that."

"I know," Ryan said. "That's what Mom keeps saying."

A feeling of guilt flashed across Eleanor's consciousness like a meteor. *It was my fault,* she thought. *It was my fault that they were living in the foothills of Santa Barbara in the sixth year of a drought, on a piece of property that was primed to burn. Were it not for me, they would be back in Vermont, awaiting the spring.* She felt her stomach clench, and grew slightly faint.

"She's doing okay, then?" Eleanor asked.

"She's pretty messed up," Ryan said. "She's just sitting there, making lists."

ELEANOR dropped her purse by the front door and headed directly to the third-floor guest room, where she found Lily with a notepad perched on her knees.

"Oh, my sweet girl," Eleanor said, sweeping into the room. She threw her arms around Lily's neck, and kissed her on the cheek, and clutched her hand as if she would never let go.

"He's dead," Lily said, and even though her body did not move, her face screwed up, and tears spilled from her eyes. "And it's all because of me."

"No, no," Eleanor said, but she didn't say,

You're wrong, it was all because of me. "No, Lily. It was an accident, an act of nature."

Lily shook her head. "I had a migraine," she said. "I couldn't even see straight."

"A headache doesn't cause a wildfire," Eleanor said.

"I can't live without him," Lily said, looking straight into her mother's eyes in order to make her point as clear as possible. "I can't."

"You can and you will," Eleanor said. "I will see to it." But even as she spoke the words, she knew that there were limits to what one person could do for another. She knew that there was always a space you couldn't cross—a great divide. She had never bridged it with any of her husbands or lovers. She had never bridged it with Lily. She had come the closest with Gracie, who was dying alone in her beautiful apartment in New York City. But she was Lily's mother and she would do whatever it took to help her daughter recover from this blow.

"Have you eaten?" Eleanor asked.

Lily shook her head once.

"What about some Thai soup?" Eleanor said, recalling how that had worked with Gordon on the night of Judy's funeral. "Coconut lime soup?"

"I'd throw it up," Lily said.

"Toast?"

"No."

Eleanor felt panic rise in her like a fever. She

224

wasn't good at doing nothing. "What are you writing?" she asked, nodding at the notepad, and thinking about the piece of yellow legal paper that Gordon had shown her just twenty-four hours before.

Lily tipped the pad so that her mother could see it. At the top of the page was the word "Kitchen." Underneath it was a list:

Walnut cookie jar
2 ceramic mugs from Maine
12 Blueberry Hill dinner plates
10 Blueberry Hill salad plates
9 Blueberry Hill bowls
Cast-iron skillet
Green-handled ice cream scoop
New dish drainer
New garbage can

"I have nothing left," Lily said. "Nothing."

Eleanor nodded, and brushed Lily's dark hair behind her ears. "You have us," she said, and even as she said it, she felt another jolt of guilt. She had wanted this: to have her family near, to have a role to play. She had asked for it. She had orchestrated it. This tragedy was, in many ways, completely her fault.

ELEANOR got up early the next morning and went to her office on the first floor. There were dozens of phone messages on Lily's cell phone—friends and neighbors and relatives calling from all over the country to see if the fires had affected her, to see if she was okay; and people from town—old friends from high school, people from the avocado warehouse. On Eleanor's home phone, there were dozens more. The last one had been from Gordon.

"Please call," he said. "I'm worried sick about you."

She answered all the other calls first. She had learned a thing or two about sudden and public tragedy, and so she knew just what to do: she told everyone about her son-in-law's death, that Lily's house had burned to the ground, and that in lieu of flowers they should send money to the Santa Barbara Fire Department.

Ryan was up early, too. He sat in the office where his grandmother worked the phones—first her home phone, then Lily's cell phone—and looked up information on how to file insurance claims on a house that no longer stood. In between calls, he looked up at his grandmother. "Nana," he said. "What the hell's wrong with flowers?"

Eleanor spoke in the voice of a master passing on a deep secret. She said simply, "They die."

When every call had been made, Eleanor finally called Gordon.

"I miss you," he said.

Eleanor wondered if Gordon had eaten anything besides bagels since she left. She wondered if he had sent his clothes to the cleaners. He was a lonely old man, used to having people around to look after him, cook for him, give a sense of purpose to his days. He no longer worked, was no longer married, no longer mattered in his children's lives. "No, you don't," Eleanor said. "You miss Judy."

"I miss her desperately," he said. "I do. But I also think she was right. What's the point of being alone, when we could be together? You're out there dealing with this terrible thing all alone. It doesn't have to be that way."

"Don't worry about me," she said. "I'm good at dealing with tragedy."

"I'd like to come see you," he said.

Her daughter was locked in the guest room. Her grandson was brooding in her office. There was going to be a memorial party in five days, and she needed to get the gardener to come out and prune the rosebushes on the patio and take the dead leaves off the palm trees. "I don't think that's a good idea," she said, and hung up.

After the phone call, Ryan spoke again. "My dad loved flowers," he said. "He grew these huge sunflowers and he'd cut off the heads and leave them out on the deck for the chipmunks. He planted tulips every year along the stone wall at the edge of the property, even though the deer were the only ones who really got to see them."

Eleanor looked at her grandson. She'd visited Lily's home in Vermont every couple of years for Thanksgiving, and occasionally in July when the garden was in full flower. She often gave Tom things related to the garden for gifts—gardening books that had been written about in the *Times*, a beautiful trowel from Smith & Hawken.

"That's right," she said. "I'd forgotten that."

ELEANOR left the house and went to Vons. She got a cart, and flew through the store, selecting butter, sugar, a box of yellow cake mix, and a bottle of Mount Gay Rum. When she got back to the house and started mixing the ingredients in a bowl, Luke came and stared. "You bake?" he asked.

"Usually only when people die."

Lily came downstairs when the cake was almost done.

"This is for Tom?" she asked. "The cake is for Tom?" Eleanor could see a thousand emotions flicker across Lily's face, and she wasn't sure whether Lily was going to wail or scream or laugh or burst out in an angry tirade.

Eleanor nodded.

Lily didn't speak. She walked directly over to her mother, and collapsed into Eleanor's body like a flower falling off its stem.

Eleanor was not used to her daughter's body in

her arms. She was not used to the weight, to the smell, to the look of her graying hair, to the feeling of her shoulders shaking. She put her arms around Lily, first one, then the other, as if she were trying to feel her way.

·24·

Lily

THE jeans and sweatshirt reminded Lily of ones she'd had in college. There was something comforting about getting up every day and putting on the most basic, generic clothes. Her mother kept offering to go to Saks or Nordstrom to buy her a nice pair of pants or a skirt, but having her mother pick out clothes for her brought back too many memories of being a child in her mother's house, and so Lily just kept wearing the clothes Luke had bought, and she kept saying, "Please don't."

Lily slept on and off during the day, and at night, she sat up cataloging. Once, when she heard sirens, she went to the front door, and then settled again on the couch, across from where Luke had fallen asleep. Around 4 a.m., she stopped writing down things she remembered from her house on the hill and began to write out guacamole recipes. Some had three roasted peppers, and others had four. Some used lemon and some used lime. Tom had begun experimenting the moment they got to town, using ingredients from the Farmer's Market, and pushing the guacamole on everyone he met. At dinner, he would recite the recipes to Lily, and she realized now that she hadn't really been listening. She remembered the peppers—Anaheim, Pasillo, Serrano—but she couldn't remember whether Tom had paired the mild chiles with lemon, or the hot ones with lime.

"The avocado is considered the most highly nutritionally evolved of all food plants," Tom once told her. *"With the biochemical profile of a nut rather than a fruit, the average avocado provides enough protein to replace the meat or cheese in a light meal."* He had started a journal that he wrote in every night—notes about the trees and the weather, the soil and the fertilizer. It was a black Moleskine notebook with blank pages, and he poured his thoughts into it like a modern-day Ben Franklin writing the almanac. *Old Tom's Almanac.* She turned back to her list and wrote at the bottom of one column:

Tom's Moleskine farm journal

SHE awoke at 8 a.m to the smell of frying eggs and immediately felt nauseous. She imagined throwing up—just sitting there and throwing up, the way second graders sometimes do at their desks, when they are totally overcome by sudden sickness. She remembered the red wine she'd drunk on the back deck, and how Luna sat with her under the hot sky, and she remembered the cold tile on the bathroom floor when Tom came in to say that there was a fire and they had to leave.

Underneath all her thoughts, like an infection that won't back down, were thoughts of Jack. She had gone to look for Jack. She had sought him out. And her skin had buzzed under his touch. She drank the wine because of Jack. Maybe Tom had died because of Jack. And the truly insidious part of the thought was that she wasn't sure she regretted it. Maybe there was some divine plan at work. Maybe the move to Santa Barbara wasn't supposed to buoy up their marriage. Maybe the move was meant to end it. Maybe the move was meant to deliver her into the arms of someone new. Maybe she had been given an excuse to behave the way her mom always did—tossing out one person for another, acting on what felt good in the moment.

She was horrified at her own thoughts. She threw off the covers, took a freezing cold shower as punishment, and then charged down the stairs to the kitchen.

"I want to go see the house," she said. She needed pain to yank her back to a proper place of mourning. She needed to see where the house had been, where Tom had died.

Her whole family turned to look at her. Ryan put down a cup of orange juice, Luke swallowed a bite of pancake, Eleanor turned off the stove.

Luke cleared his throat. "I can take you up there in my truck," he said.

"Nana and I can follow in her car," Ryan said,

"and one of us can drive Dad's truck back."

Lily had forgotten about Tom's truck and the ride down the hill, and the transfer to an ambulance. Her head had been exploding. The firemen had left the truck at the side of the road when the ambulance met them. At the time she had thought, *When Tom comes down, he'll see it and he'll bring the truck down to the hospital. He'll bring Luna.*

Eleanor looked at Lily's slippered feet. "You'll need shoes," she said. Lily nodded, because this time her mother was right.

WHEN they got to Nordstrom's shoe department, Lily went straight toward the clogs. They were heavy, practical. They would last fifteen years. She asked the sales clerk if she could to try on a black pair, size 6 1/2, and when the salesman brought them out, she was pleased at how compact they seemed. She slipped them on and walked a few steps around on the carpet. She listened to the discussions the other shoppers were having with each other—*that was a steal, they're so cute, you look amazing in them.* Living with Tom had permanently cured her of shopping for pleasure. He was a true New Englander, the kind of man who valued owning the same pair of Bean boots for thirty years, and who thought nothing of depending on a twenty-year-old hat. Tom could patch an oiled canvas jacket, caulk an old wooden boat, rewire a washing machine that got stuck on the rinse cycle. Lily fell into his thrifty ways. She would spend money on a beautiful wool coat, but with the intention of owning it for fifty years. She would buy a length of fabric to make a skirt in a timeless cut, knowing that it would look good for decades.

"What about these?" Eleanor said. She approached Lily carrying a copper-colored sandal similar to the ones she had on her feet, and a black patent leather ballet flat.

"I'm getting the clogs."

"You can get more than one pair of shoes, Lily."

"I don't need more than one pair of shoes."

"For goodness' sake, you lost everything. Buy a few pairs of shoes!"

"I don't need them," she said.

Eleanor handed the strappy sandal and the pretty flat to the saleslady, dramatically rolled her eyes, and said to everyone and to no one in particular, "How on earth did I end up with a daughter who doesn't love shoes?"

THEY drove in silence toward the police line on East Valley Road, and when they got there, a policeman leaned into view and asked them for ID.

She handed him her driver's license, and while he checked it against the list on his clipboard, she remembered Tom carrying boxes, thumping them in the bed of the truck. She remembered him yelling at her to get in the truck, and ordering Luna to stay by her side. When the policeman came back, he said, "Officer Tippet will accompany you to your property."

Luke noted how the man said *property*, not *house*. "We also have a truck," Luke said, "a white Ford, parked on Sheffied Drive."

The policeman looked at another page on his clipboard, then stepped away and spoke into his walkie-talkie. There was crackling, a conversation. The policeman confirmed that the escort would take them to the truck as well.

Luke followed the black-and-white police car for a mile through an unscathed grove of trees, and Ryan drove his grandmother's Lexus behind them. They could smell the scorched ground, and they could feel the looming blackness, even though they couldn't see it. It was an aching emptiness, a void, a place where there had recently been something and now there was nothing. Lily remembered taking the boys to see the Grand Canyon when they were in middle school. They drove out to the South Rim very early one morning, scattering elk in the darkness. Tom kept saying, "Can you feel it coming?" and the boys, wild with excitement despite the hour, kept saying, "What? What?" But they knew; you could feel it—something big out there. A big space. And then there it was—the canyon, the ground falling away, the eons of time exposed before them, the void.

This was exactly like that.

THEY came first to the pickup truck. It had been pulled onto the dirt at the side of the road, by a row of scraggly orange trees at the edge of someone's property. It was wrapped with yellow caution tape and there was a sticker slapped onto the windshield warning people that this was police property. Officer Tippet parked his cruiser, got out, snipped the tape. Lily climbed out of Luke's truck and walked to the back of Tom's Ford. She stood at the tailgate and peered into the back. "This is what he saved," she said in a small voice. "This is what he chose to save."

There was a laundry basket filled with paper and a duffel bag, all of it smelling of smoke and covered in fine white ash. She spotted the Matisse tablecloth and the cardboard tube that contained her grandmother's lace, and she closed her eyes. She saw again the wall of fire coming around the side of the house, saw Tom disappear into the smoke and the flames. She turned away from the truck and sank to the ground, squatting like a child, her face in her hands. *He saved all this for me,* she thought. *He saved all this for me.*

LUKE walked over, pulled down the tailgate, pulled his mother to her feet, and guided her to sit down. He sat next to her, weeping, too, his arms tightly around her shoulders. Ryan, watching his brother, suddenly thought what a good father Luke would make. Luke would be just like their own dad—calm, kind, connected. Perhaps Ryan didn't have what it took. Perhaps he hadn't paid close enough attention to how it was done when his dad was still alive to show him how. He put both hands on the side of the truck, as if he might push it away, and closed his eyes.

Eleanor walked toward them all and began to gather up the caution tape, because she knew someone was eventually going to have to drive this truck somewhere when all the crying stopped. Later she and Lily would argue about it—how Eleanor was always fixing things, always doing things, how she couldn't stop and just *feel*, how crazy she was, how cold, and how it had always been that way.

·25·

Lily

THEY left the truck on the side of the road, got back in the cars, and drove up into the hills. They waited in silence for the scorched earth to present itself, and then suddenly it was before them—bald and blackened hills, half-burned trees, the gutted-out houses of people who just days before had been making toast in those houses, folding laundry, writing bills, arguing about dinner, touching each other with hands that weren't entirely honest. "Oh my God," Lily said. Cement foundations marked out their phantom rooms, and chimneys stood as tall as giants in a black Lilliputian land. Everything was absolutely gray and absolutely still.

Luke drove slowly up the road thinking that this was the way the moon must look, that this was the way a landscape looked when it had been bombed off the face of the planet. He took a turn to the left, then a fork to the right, and Mary Hazelton's house stood before them, miraculously whole and untouched. Across the street, Tom's avocado orchard, with its neat rows of bright shiny green trees, continued to do its work of turning sun-shine into chlorophyll, and chlorophyll into green-fleshed fruit.

Lily couldn't help thinking that everyone had gotten it wrong: her house did not burn, her husband did not die. She would round the corner, and Tom would be there with Luna on the front step, talking about bark beetles or the latest news on global warming. She would run up to him and throw her arms around his neck and say that she was sorry for what she had said and what she had done and what she had thought, and he would say, "It's okay." They would go on comfortably ignoring each other and counting on each other, drawing on the investment of love they had made as if it were a bank account.

On the other hand, she kept imagining the lot where their house had been, wiped clean as if by a giant's hand. She pictured it smoothed over. She remembered seeing footage once of a house that had been lifted off its foundation by a tornado, exactly like Dorothy's had been. This one, however, had been a real house, a little two-bedroom cottage built on the banks of the Missouri River. The owner stood on the threshold, talking to the TV cameraman, saying, "As God is my witness, we went to bed in this house a full half mile away and woke up right here where y'all are standing." Maybe her house had been lifted away like that, by the fire.

She held her breath. Luke drove on, and when they rounded the final bend, she exhaled.

It was all true.

She sat holding one hand over her mouth and nose, because ash was still falling from the sky like snow, and she didn't want to breathe in burned pieces of people's homes, of pine trees that had lived a hundred years, of someone's flesh and bone. Her eyes stung, her nostrils flared. There was the place where Tom had died, there was where she had sat in the truck waiting for him to come out of the house, there was where the fireman who saved her had stood as he pushed her out of the driver's seat. She sat next to Luke, saying nothing, until Ryan came and opened her door, and the smell of smoke and ash and charcoal, which had been strong enough inside the car, exploded with full force upon them.

Lily stepped out of the car. She waited a moment, expecting Luna to come bounding out of the flattened house, barking her greeting, but there was no sound besides the soft rustling of the wind in the avocado trees, which stood there, green and mocking. The policemen had cautioned them against doing anything more than taking a brief look at the property. There were live embers, open gas lines, toxic smoke. In a few days they could come back to sift through the ash to see if anything could be salvaged. For now, they just stood in the driveway, staring at the wreckage, trying to comprehend everything that had been lost.

After a while, when the silence and the stench

became too much to bear, Eleanor said, "Why don't we go now?"

Ryan was quick to agree. "You can drop me off at Dad's truck," he said. "I'll drive it down to Nana's."

Lily shook her head. "I want to stay," she said.

Ryan and Luke glanced at their grandmother, because someone had to dissuade Lily, and they figured it would be Eleanor.

Eleanor coughed. "Sweetheart," she said, "I don't think that's a good idea. The policemen said—"

Lily cut her off. "I know what they said. I'm not going to do anything stupid. I just want to pick some avocados so they'll be ripe for the party."

Luke was the first to speak. "Maybe we should wait, Mom," he said.

"For what?"

"For everything to cool down." They could hear hissing and popping where things still simmered. There was a palpable sense of instability. But there was also the knowledge that Tom had died in a spot just a few feet in front of them, and that knowledge bore down on them in a physical way. It seemed like it might be difficult to stand there very much longer and not get crushed.

"I'll just be a few minutes," Lily said.

Luke coughed—his lungs protesting the gritty air. "I'll stay with you," he said.

Ryan, relieved to be released from the strange

scene, said quickly, "Nana can take me down to get the truck."

Luke stepped up to his mother and took hold of her hand. "Come on," he said, and led her toward the trees.

·26·

Luke

THEY walked around the smoldering remains of the house to the orchard. The first two rows of trees were charred and stripped of leaves. The damaged trees stood out like skeletons against the rest of the orchard, which was still green and vibrant, dusted with ash.

"You want to pick the ones with the blackest skin," Lily said as she walked down a row of trees. "They should fall right off in your hands."

Luke squinted up. "Is there something we can put them in? A bag or something?"

"There are crates in the shed," she said. "If the shed is still there."

They walked to the bottom of the hill, and the shed stood before them, unscathed. For a moment, Lily thought that Tom would step out from behind the shed and say something about raccoons or beetles or red-tailed hawks. She stood there, waiting, and then Luke rolled back the big barn door and stepped inside. He grabbed a crate, and one of the long poles with a picking basket on the end. "You want one?" he asked.

Lily nodded.

They went back into the trees, and set the crate on the ashy ground. The air was acrid, and they coughed as they worked. They reached into the trees and pulled down avocados, one by one. When their crate was full, they took it to the shed and used the hose—neatly coiled against the outside wall—to rinse the ash off the fruit. Luke carried the crate up the hill and put it in the back of his truck.

Lily stayed by herself at the shed and touched everything that was still there—the hose that Tom had coiled, the old rake that Tom had brought from Vermont, the ball of twine that Tom had barely begun to use. She thought of things she had lost over the years—glasses, keys, a white enamel casserole pan, a scratchy green wool shawl given to her by a friend in college whom she never really liked. She was forever losing pens, which was her argument against owning anything other than a simple Bic ballpoint, but Tom always said that if you invested in fine writing instruments, you wouldn't lose them. Their mere expense would keep them safe.

But she had lost expensive things, too. She once lost one of a pair of black pearl earrings her mother had lent her to wear to dinner in Milan. One minute, they were adorning her ears, the next, the left one was gone. The waiters searched the floor under the table while Eleanor grew more and more dismayed, but nothing was ever found. Eleanor forgave her, but Lily never forgave herself.

"They're just *things*," people always said, to soothe the dismay of loss. "You can replace things."

That was true about a Bic pen. But why, then, did she remember that casserole pan, with its chips on the handle? Why did she remember that shawl—its exact color of pea soup green, its bulky knit-purl pattern, the loamy way that it smelled when it was wet? Could the loss of an object give it meaning?

"Ready to go?" Luke asked.

Lily jumped. She placed her hand over her heart, which was beating wildly. "You scared me," she said.

He put his arm around her, and she noted how he had the same build as Tom, the same long arms, the same smell. "Sorry," he said.

They walked back up past the charred remains of her home—the washer and dryer warped and twisted, the kitchen reduced to nothing. It was as if someone had come and carried away the refrigerator, the sink, the bay window, the cabinets, the pots and pans and plates they had so carefully covered in bubble wrap so that they wouldn't be damaged on their cross-country trip.

"Remember when Oreo ran away that one Christmas?"

Luke nodded. "That was the worst," he said. "How Ryan made up those flyers and walked around on Christmas Day posting them every-where."

"But it worked."

"Yeah," Luke said.

Lily stopped right in front of Luke's truck—right in the spot where Tom had told Luna to stay, and where she had stood and yelled at Tom not to go back into the house. "I think Luna must have died," she said. "They never found her body, but she ran straight into the fire. The flames were huge on that side of the house." She pointed to her left. "She was probably incinerated."

"Why would she have run into the fire?" Luke asked.

"Because Tom went in. She was going after Tom."

"Maybe she got out. Maybe someone found her."

Lily shook her head.

"There must be people who rescue animals after a fire, some kind of shelter. I'll find out. I'll go look."

BACK at his grandmother's house, Luke searched for information on animal rescue. It only took him two phone calls to learn that there was a central holding area for animals rescued from the fire.

"Luna had tags, didn't she?" he asked his mom.

"Yes," Lily said, "and mismatched eyes. You can't miss the eyes."

He grabbed a cold piece of pizza, got back in the truck, and drove out to Goleta. He walked through the pens and the dog runs for forty-five minutes looking for an Australian shepherd with one blue eye and one brown, but there was no such dog to be found.

WHEN Luke reported that he hadn't seen Luna, Lily thanked him for trying, and she had to stop herself from thinking, *I have to remember to tell Tom how Luke took on the search for the dog, how hard he tried, how good he was.* She had to stop herself from thinking, *I have to remember to talk to Tom about Ryan and how worried I am about him.* Instead, she got out her list and added a page:

Luna
Dog bowl
Dog mat
Dog brush
Dog bed
Gnawed rope toy
Leash

·27·

Ryan

RYAN sat on the same airport bench where he had greeted his grandmother, and waited for Olivia and Brooke to arrive. He drank Heineken in the warm night air and thought of his wife and child hurtling through the sky. He thought of a girl he used to know who set a school record in the 500 Free, and how she had died on the plane that hit the Pentagon. She had gone back to school late that year, because on the day she was originally planning to fly, she'd had an acute attack of appendicitis.

When the little plane touched down, Ryan stood up. Brooke had called Tom Pop-Pop. Olivia said it was because making the *Grr* sound at the beginning of the word *Grandpa* was something that didn't develop in children until later. Olivia had read this in a book. Everything Olivia knew about being a parent she'd read in a book. She didn't have much of a relationship with her own mother, and so she set out to learn it all herself. Ryan loved Brooke. He liked the way she smelled and the way she climbed onto his lap and curled into a ball when she was tired. But he wasn't a student like his brother, Luke. He wasn't a scholar like his dad. He didn't want to have to work so hard to understand why Brooke called his dad Pop-Pop.

He saw Olivia at the top of the stairs that descended from the plane. She had Brooke's pink backpack slung over one shoulder, and her enormous canvas bag in the crook of her arm. She held Brooke on her hip, and held the railing of the stairs as she descended. Ryan felt as if he might jump out of his skin as he waited for them to make their painstaking descent down the stairs, and walk across the tarmac.

When they stepped through the gateway, he swept Olivia and Brooke into his arms, and there was a subtle transferring of weight so that he held Brooke now and he breathed in the scent of her soft hair.

"How was the flight?" he asked.

"Good," Olivia said. "Brooke had a snack and we read some stories."

"We read *Olivia*," Brooke said, and Ryan knew she was referring to the book about a pig who thought she was a diva, "the *other* Olivia."

This was something Brooke always said when she spoke about this particular book—the *other* Olivia—and so Ryan laughed, and Olivia laughed, and Brooke beamed.

THEY collected all the luggage, and strapped the car seat into the back of Nana's car, and then Brooke said she wanted juice.

"You can have juice when we get to Nana's," Ryan said.

"But you promised," Brooke said, and Ryan could hear her voice escalating in tone and intensity, and he felt the muscles in his neck tighten.

"I did," Olivia said to Ryan, and then to Brooke, "I promised you could have the juice when we got to Nana's."

"I want my juice," she said, and her voice now began to waver. She was on the verge of throwing a fit. "You promised!"

"I did," Olivia repeated, and then she turned to Ryan and said, "I promised."

Ryan turned to look out the driver's side window as Olivia unsnapped her seat belt, got out of the car, went around to the back, and unloaded all the suitcases he had just loaded in. She dug around until she found the juice, and then she unwrapped the straw, thrust it through the hole, and handed the box to Brooke.

Olivia got back into her seat, Ryan started the car, and before they even got out of the parking lot, the juice was gone.

"I want more," Brooke said.

Olivia turned backward to face Brooke. "I'd like it if you said, *Please. Please may I have more juice.*"

"Please may I have more juice," Brooke said, and Ryan thought he might scream. The feeling of happiness and connectedness he had felt when

Brooke had talked about the pig book was gone, replaced by the familiar dread of his child's demands, his wife's endless calm, and his own place outside of their circle.

LATER, when Brooke was telling her uncle Luke about her airplane trip, and Ryan and Olivia were taking the luggage in from the garage, Ryan lowered his voice and said, "My mom's been obsessed with making these lists. She's pretty messed up."

"What kind of lists?" Olivia asked.

"Stuff that was in the house."

"She has to do that for insurance, right?"

"Yeah, but these lists have everything on them. You know that drawer everyone has with scissors and rubber bands and the twisty things from plastic bags? She has a list for that drawer. And a list of all the cleaning stuff. The toilet cleaning brush and the Clorox."

"I'd do the same thing," Olivia said.

"You would?"

She nodded. "Write it all down so that your memory doesn't surprise you later, so that the story is all right there."

Ryan rolled his shoulders backward and then rotated his left ear toward his left shoulder to try to stretch out his neck. "I think she's crazy," he said, and then he added, "I don't know how much patience she's going to have for Brooke."

251

"She's not crazy," Olivia said. "I totally get it. I'd do the same thing. And I bet she'll be fine with Brooke."

"I'm just saying you might want to wait until morning before Brooke goes in there."

Fifteen minutes later, Brooke started asking when she was going to see her Nana and Pop-Pop, and Olivia launched into a careful explanation of how Pop-Pop had died and that's why they had come on the trip, and how Nana was sad and didn't want to see them right now. She had said the same words, or words like them, a dozen times since they started out on their trip.

Brooke went to her lime green duffel bag and pulled out Bear, the stuffed teddy bear she slept with every night. "I want to show Nana Bear."

"Nana's sleeping," Olivia explained. "She's just down the hallway in her own bedroom, asleep, and we should go to sleep, too. You can show her Bear in the morning."

"I want to show her Bear now."

"Sweetie . . ." Olivia said, but before she could continue, Ryan said, "Oh for God's sake."

"What?" Olivia snapped.

"The answer is *no*," Ryan said. "Just tell her no. She can't do it."

"Ryan, she doesn't understand what's going on. You can't just tell her *no*. You have to explain . . ."

"You can just tell her no. My mom has refused everything that's been offered to her for the past two days—tea, soup, toast, back rubs, sleeping pills. If Brooke goes in there—"

"Can I finish my sentence?" Olivia demanded.

"If you'll let me finish mine."

While her parents stood locked in battle, Brooke turned and bolted out the door. She ran down the hallway, glancing in each door, and when she got to a door that was closed, she opened it and ran in. The shades were drawn, the room was dark. It smelled of fire, and of sweat, and of despair. Lily sat on the bed, propped up by two thick pillows. The white down comforter was drawn up to her chin. To Brooke, her grandmother looked similar to her bear. Her hair was dirty and limp. The light in her eyes was dim and flat. Her limbs looked as if they were incapable of holding her up. She had been intending to introduce Bear to Nana—to say, "This is Bear." But Brooke had a child's instinctive understanding of pain. She stopped at the side of the bed and wordlessly handed Bear over.

Lily smiled. She reached out and accepted Bear with one hand, and with the other, she reached out and gently stroked her granddaughter's silken hair.

"Thank you," she said.

·28·

Lily

LILY got up in the middle of the night, left the teddy bear, and went down to her mother's garage, where the things Tom had saved from the fire were sitting on the cold cement floor. The boys had immediately gone through the documents to locate the insurance papers they needed to file claims, and they had begun to sort through the rest of what was there. It was all covered in a white ash, which looked benign, but left a greasy residue whenever it was touched. Next to the duffel bag and the laundry basket were a pile of microfiber rags and a bottle of Simple Green, which they had been using to try to clean things off.

She turned on the light and saw that one of the boys had tried to clean the cardboard tube that held Hattie's lace. It was no longer dusted with ash, but there were dark, greasy streaks down its sides. She snapped off the plastic end of the tube and peered at the lace. It was still neatly wound inside archival tissue, totally undisturbed. The cardboard tube had done its job—as cocoon, as armor, as shield. She felt a wave of gratitude for the simple tube, and for her grandmother's impulse to preserve the piece of cloth, and for how well her husband had known her and loved her. As the fire bore down and the danger closed in, he had thought to save the one object that meant the most to her—that defined her. It was a piece of possibility. She closed the tube back up and set it down again on the garage floor.

Next, she found the Matisse tablecloth and took it inside. It hadn't fared as well. It was covered with ash, it smelled of smoke. She carried it through the dark house to the laundry room. She carefully set it in the washing machine, turned the dial to "cold" and to "soak," measured out a capful of Ivory, and pushed the start button.

While the washer started its work, she grabbed her purse, snuck out of the house into the still-dark morning, and went to the Farmer's Market.

SHE hadn't been paying attention to Tom's guacamole obsession. She had minced garlic when he asked her to, chopped onions, held a Pasillo chile over an open flame to char it, but she hadn't read his recipes, didn't know the alchemy that went into his successes. She was determined, however, to re-create the guacamole he had thought was best. She remembered that it had been chunky and smoky, with a kick of lime and a wave of heat that followed the first cool taste.

She bought limes first, then onions, garlic, and three kinds of chiles. She walked by three tables piled with red cherry tomatoes and thick beefsteak tomatoes until she got to a stand offering a wide variety of shapes and colors. The banner on the awning read TUTTI FRUITI FARMS: HEIRLOOM TOMATOES. She stopped to taste the samples the farmers had set out on a folding table. There were a dozen glass bowls of sliced tomatoes, with toothpicks for sampling. She speared a small green tomato, a piece of thick yellow striped tomato, and one that was pear-shaped and golden yellow. The one she liked best was a small round red one labeled JAPANESE. It popped in her mouth—a burst of sweet, vibrant flavor. She bought three pounds, and felt a thrill when the farmer beamed at her and said, "These are very good in guacamole."

THE only person awake back at her mother's house was Eleanor. She was sitting at the table reading the newspaper. "You missed Ryan," she said. "He went out for a swim. I figured you were on a walk."

"To the Farmer's Market," Lily said, and held up her bags. "I'm making Tom's guacamole."

"He had one that tasted just like summer," Eleanor said. "But a little smoky? With a roasted pepper?"

"And lime."

"Can I help wash things, or chop?"

Lily nodded. She knew her mother didn't have the patience to cook. She took Eleanor's offer for what it was—a gesture of solidarity. "Maybe you can start by squeezing the limes and chopping the garlic," she said. "I've got a tablecloth in the washing machine I need to rinse."

"I did that," Eleanor said, and instead of being worried that her mother had done it wrong, or that she had done it at all, Lily just nodded, and thanked her.

They chopped and sliced and mixed things in different combinations, trying to match what was in front of them to what they remembered Tom had made. They argued about the amount of lime, the degree of charring necessary for the pepper. By the time Olivia and Brooke and Luke came out to the kitchen, there were six large bowls of guacamole. The smell of garlic filled the air, and the tang of roasted pepper.

" 'Molee!" Brooke squealed.

"Huevos rancheros?" Luke asked.

"How long have you two been *up*?" Olivia demanded.

"Too long," Lily said, "but I think we got it."

"Got what?" Luke said.

"Daddy's favorite guacamole."

The mood in the room suddenly shifted. Tom's spirit had been alive in the chopping and the mixing, but now that they were done, it was clear that it would take more than a recipe to bring Tom back. Lily washed her hands, and announced that she was going back to bed.

"What about your tablecloth?" Eleanor asked.

"I'll get it," Lily said.

She walked slowly to the laundry room, got out the clean, damp tablecloth, and took it to the guest room upstairs. She spread it out on the bed to dry, and then climbed underneath the sheets and cried herself to sleep.

·29·

Nadine

NADINE was bereft. She hadn't known Tom for very long, and she hadn't known him very well, but she felt his death keenly. She circled around Tom's ranch for days before she got the courage to drive up the hill, and turn into the driveway. She wanted to see if the trees were still standing. She sat in her truck, tears rolling down her cheeks, and scanned the blackened scene. There was Tom's stone fireplace, still ready to warm the night, and the foundation of the house still sturdy and whole. Beyond where the house had been was a row of burned trees, looking naked and gnarled, and beyond them, the untouched orchard. After a few moments, Nadine became aware of a high-pitched yelping. She got out of her truck and tried to piece together what it was. A baby crying? A woman yelling? A siren coming up the street again to fend off another fire? Yes, she decided, it was an inconsolable baby suffering from colic, caught in a rhythmic wail, but then she remembered that there were no babies in this neighborhood; there were no people; there were no houses.

A moment later, Luna appeared from the thick light like an apparition. Thin, her fur matted and soiled, she seemed to float out of the trees as if she, too, were made of smoke. "Luna?" Nadine asked, and blinked. She stepped forward and held out her hand. "Luna," she said softly. The dog raised her head, stepped slowly toward Nadine, and changed her howl to something that sounded more like weeping.

Eleanor's defenses were so strong that when Nadine called in the afternoon about the dog, she almost didn't get through. "It's *Nadine*," she finally said. "Nadine from the Calavo warehouse. We met at the cocktail party."

"I know who you are," Eleanor said.

"Then may I please speak to Lily?"

"She's indisposed at the moment," Eleanor said. Lily had barely gotten out of bed for the last forty-eight hours. She hadn't showered, had only eaten a piece of toast, a scrambled egg. Whenever anyone asked her if she wanted some soup, or to go on a walk, or to watch TV, she just shook her head no, and continued to stare out the window at the charred hills.

"I have Luna," Nadine said.

It took Eleanor a moment to process what she was hearing. "Dead or alive?" she finally asked.

"Alive," Nadine said. "But barely."

Eleanor felt a jolt of joy—a sudden belief that redemption was at hand. Dogs were better suited for grief than people were. They didn't try to talk to make things better. They didn't ask how things were going or if they could help. Luna could give Lily what Eleanor never could.

She took the phone up to the third floor, tapped on Lily's door, and stepped in without waiting to be invited.

Eleanor held the phone out toward her daughter.

"No," Lily mouthed, and shook her head. She didn't want to speak to anyone. She didn't want to hear them say they were sorry, didn't want to hear them wonder what they could do to help.

"It's Nadine," Eleanor said, "from Calavo. She has some good news."

Lily sat up. She took the phone. "Yes?"

"Luna came home," Nadine said.

When Lily didn't respond, Nadine offered more: "I went up to check on the trees, and she was there."

"She's dead," Lily said.

Nadine reached down and stroked Luna's back. Her fur was singed and matted and she was covered with burrs. "She's sleeping right here on my kitchen floor."

Lily sat up higher on her pillows and looked wildly around the room. She hadn't slept more than a few hours in a single stretch since the fire. She felt like everything was folding over on itself—time and reality and even the organs inside her body, which gurgled and churned in protest of food she wasn't eating. Several nights, in the middle of the night, she could have sworn she heard Tom calling to her. She strained her ears, got out of bed, opened the windows, walked down the stairs, only to be reminded by the emptiness and the darkness that Tom had died, and Luna had died, and their house and everything in it had burned to the ground.

She had the odd sense that Nadine had conjured Luna up like a witch doctor, or a shaman. She believed it was Nadine's doing somehow that the dog was alive. And she remembered how Tom had been with Nadine on the night of the fire—how Tom's staying at the warehouse had been the reason Lily had gone down to the beach in the first place. It was Nadine that had justified Jack in her mind. Nadine and the whole crashing reality of how you can never know what your husband is doing or thinking. You can never be sure that love is real. You can live with someone for almost thirty years and love them and be loyal to them and feel loved in return, but you will never know how they truly feel about you, how much space they leave open in their heart for other people, other things.

"It can't be her," Lily said.

Eleanor was still standing by the bed, waiting to spring into action—to go get the dog, to bathe the dog.

"It can't be her," Lily repeated.

Eleanor walked over to the bed, took the phone from Lily's hand, and spoke to Nadine. "This is

Eleanor," she said, "Lily's mother. I'd like to come see the dog."

Eleanor rummaged in a drawer for a piece of paper and a pen, but while she was writing down Nadine's address, Lily spoke up.

"It can't be her," she said.

"Just a moment," Eleanor said to Nadine, and she looked over at Lily and saw that there were tears streaming down her face, falling from the edge of her face to her collarbone.

"Eleanor?" Nadine was calling. Her voice was coming through the receiver of the phone. "Eleanor?"

"I'm sorry," Eleanor said to Nadine. "We're going to have to call you back." She hung up.

"Tom ran back after her," Lily said. "She ran through the front door, and he ran in after her. She can't be alive."

"Dogs have a sense for danger," Eleanor said. "She may have escaped. She may have tried to help Tom escape."

Lily could picture Jack leaning down to scratch Luna behind her ear. She could hear him saying, *I'd recognize that smile anywhere; See you at the beach; Come by and see me sometime.* She could see herself smiling back, and going to the beach, where she knew she would find him.

"I don't want to see her," Lily whispered.

Eleanor sat on the edge of the bed, and reached

out to smooth Lily's hair behind her ears. Lily turned her face from her mother's touch.

"It would remind me too much of him," she said, and although Eleanor did not know it, the *him* she was talking about wasn't just Tom—it was also Jack.

·30·

Lily

AFTER the phone call about the dog, Lily got out of bed, eased her wedding ring off her finger, and set it on the bathroom counter. She usually never removed it, and the skin underneath was pink, and dented to fit the shape of the platinum and gold band. The ring featured a two-and-a-half-carat diamond, a miner's cut that had originally been set in a man's platinum dinner ring. "A hideous old ring," Eleanor always said. It had been in her father's family for generations. When Billy Edwards proposed to Eleanor, he did everything the proper way. He asked her parents for permission, and when they gave it, they gave him the dinner ring to do with as he wished. Billy removed the diamond from its ornate embrace and had a spectacular ring designed—a band of diamonds, a swirl of platinum and gold that held the diamond aloft. He had the jeweler remake it three times before he deemed it acceptable for his young bride. Eleanor always said that she liked the ring better than the man; she continued to wear it on her right hand through her second marriage. She wore it until Lily brought Tom home. At dinner that night, Eleanor slid the ring off her delicate finger, and handed it to her daughter.

"What is this?" Lily asked.

"Following a hunch," Eleanor said, "that you're going to be needing that ring soon."

"Mom!" Lily cried. She loved the ring; it was the one thing of her mother's that she wished was hers, but she was mortified that Eleanor was behaving this way in front of her boyfriend. She tried to hand the ring back.

"Okay, then," Eleanor said. She took the ring from Lily's hand. "Have it your way." She slid it into Tom's palm. "That is my gift to you," she said, "should you decide to marry my daughter. Should you decide otherwise, I expect you'll return it. And if your marriage doesn't last, I'd like it back, as well."

LILY and Tom argued ceaselessly about the ring. Lily felt guilty about accepting it, and she felt strange about slipping something on her finger that her mother had worn for so long. She also worried that the ring would be bad luck to her marriage, since her mother's marriages had all ended so badly. But Tom was planning on their marriage lasting forever, and thought the ring was beautiful on her hand. "Besides," he said, "I like the idea of a family stone. It gives it a certain meaning, a certain weight that we couldn't get just walking into a jewelry store."

"The weight," Lily said, "comes from the fact that it's two and a half carats."

"What if there was some way of putting our own stamp on it? Making it a talisman of lasting love."

She burst out laughing at his corny statement. "A talisman of lasting love? You've got to be kidding me."

But he wasn't. Tom took the ring to a jeweler to be engraved. When he got it back, he marched her outside, got down on his knees, and said, "Say I do."

"About what exactly?"

"About marrying me."

"I do," she said. "Of course I do."

He handed her the ring and a flashlight so that she could see how he had changed the family heirloom.

Lily took the ring, took the flashlight, and read the immortal words that Yoda had uttered to Luke during his Jedi training:

Do or do not—there is no try.

She threw back her head and laughed. "Okay," she said. "You win." She helped him up out of the snow and he slipped the ring on her finger. She hadn't taken it off—until now.

AFTER she slipped off the ring, she called her friend Elizabeth back in Vermont. She had been thinking about fire—about what burns and what

267

explodes, and what melts and what survives. It seemed important for her to know more concretely about the reality of fire's impact on rock and metal, wood and skin, on paper and leather, fabric and hair, on pots and pans and refrigerators.

"How hot does your kiln burn?" she asked.

"Three thousand degrees," Elizabeth said.

"Is that as hot as a wildfire, or hotter?"

"About the same."

"So if I put in a fountain pen, what would happen?"

"If there was air caught inside, it might explode. Otherwise, it would turn to ash."

"What about a leather shoe?"

"There would be nothing left."

"A fork?"

"Nothing left."

"But it makes the clay stronger, that kind of heat?"

"Yes. The molecules realign themselves into stronger chains."

"And besides clay, what doesn't burn? What can't burn?"

"Diamonds," Elizabeth said.

What Lily loved was that Elizabeth never asked why Lily was asking. She never said, *I'm worried about you.* She never indicated that she had any concern at all for her friend's sanity. A few hours later, Elizabeth called back to say that there was an artist in Mission Canyon—a friend of a friend—who was willing to let Lily come work in her studio a few mornings a week, if she was interested. Her name was Shelley, and she was waiting for her.

WHEN Lily got to Shelley's studio, she felt transparent, as if Shelley knew that she had come to play with fire, as if she knew what was in her pocket.

"What type of work are you interested in doing?" Shelley asked.

Lily looked at the bowls and cups and vases on the studio shelves. She thought about how her boys used to play with fire when they were young. On the Fourth of July they'd light red rocket firecrackers and she would watch them from a safe distance back and think, *Boys.* When Luke was in eleventh grade chemistry, he developed a fascination for hydrogen and helium and dry ice and baking soda, and was constantly making small explosions in the garage. That was before fire became something that toyed with them instead of the other way around.

"I don't know," she said. "I didn't really think about that. I just thought it would be a good thing for me to do."

"To work with clay?" Shelley asked.

Lily nodded. She felt like an idiot.

But then Shelley said, "It can be very healing."

They took a chunk of fast-drying clay and set it on the worktable. It was red and cold and smelled of dampness and something organic.

"What about a house?" Shelley asked. "We can make a house from a block of clay."

Lily shook her head. Her house had been obliterated. She wasn't interested in resurrection.

"An angel?" Shelley asked. "You can shape one from a simple cone."

"I don't believe in angels," Lily said. She didn't believe that Tom was floating around somewhere, looking over her. He was in a box that would be buried under the ground at Mount Auburn Cemetery, marked by a piece of granite that would never burn.

They were silent for a while. Lily watched her hands working the clay, and she felt the warmth of the clay as it took heat from her fingers.

"What about a little round bowl?" Lily asked. "With a lid."

Shelley nodded. "A very sensual shape," she said, "very organic. Perfect."

They rolled the clay into a ball, and then pinched and pulled it, being careful to avoid stretching it too thin so that it wouldn't collapse. Lily felt the way the clay moved and turned as she pressed and kneaded, and it felt good in her hands. She liked how it yielded, how it took the shape she gave it. Shelley showed her how to cut a lid to match the opening of the bowl, which was like cutting dough for cookies. When she was done, Lily had something that looked like a lumpy teacup.

"I'd like to put something inside," she said, and pulled her ring out of her pocket.

Shelley stared at the diamond ring. She didn't have to ask if it was real. She could tell by the way Lily held it, and by the way the light hit it, and by the energy that seemed to come off it. Elizabeth had told her that the woman who was coming to her studio had lost her husband in the fire, and her house, too, so she had expected strong emotion, but she hadn't expected this—a sacrifice, a cremation.

"It will burn to ash," she said.

"I know."

"Not the diamond, of course, but the ring. The band."

"I know."

"You're sure you want to do it?"

"I am," Lily said.

Lily dropped the ring onto the wet clay. Neither woman said anything while they washed their hands and cleaned up the worktable, but when Lily was ready to go, Shelley stopped her. "The bowl will take a few days to dry," she said, "and I will put it into the first bisque firing. Then you can come back to glaze it."

Lily nodded. "Would you do it?" she said. "Put a clear glaze on it?"

"Sure," Shelley said, and then: "You're sure about the ring?"

"Yes," Lily said. "Very sure."

·31·

Lily

AN hour before the guests were set to arrive at the house, Luke was sitting with Brooke looking at pictures of his father that friends from Vermont had e-mailed when they learned that all of Tom and Lily's photos had burned. There was Tom at the tops of mountains, in the garden, in the snow, in the classroom, with Lily, with the boys, with their dogs. Luke had printed out some of the photos and arranged them on a poster board, the way he had done for projects when he was a boy. Lily thought that Luke had chosen the photos well; you could look at the board and see the things that had made up Tom's life, the things he had loved.

In the kitchen, Olivia chopped onions and garlic for the guacamole, carefully following the instructions Lily had left for her—mince the garlic very finely; strain the lime juice; leave the pits of the avocados in the guacamole to keep it from turning brown. Whenever Lily walked by, Olivia offered her a taste, but Lily just kept saying, "I'm sure it's fine."

Around dusk, flowers were delivered to Eleanor's door. There were forty large white rosebuds packed into a square of glass like perfect sugary confections. Eleanor set them on the marble counter not far from where Lily was mincing cilantro, and although Lily had paid little attention to the cards and bouquets that had been arriving all week, she looked up from the cutting board at the spectacular roses and instantly thought: Jack. *Jack has sent me these flowers because he loves me, he can't live without me, and I will no longer have to bear this grief alone.*

She reached for the card, which was tied on a white silk ribbon, and tried to pretend that her heart wasn't beating wildly.

With sympathy, Gordon Vreeland

Lily held the card out to her mother. Her hand, which was wet and stuck with small bits of herbs, was shaking. "It's for you," she said.

Eleanor took in everything—her daughter's crestfallen face and the vast amount of air between them—and quickly glanced at the card. "No," she said gently, "they're for you, Lily."

"His wife died, what?" Lily asked. "Two weeks ago? Three?"

"Lily," Eleanor said.

"No," Lily said. "I just want to know what the rules are, you know? Because it used to be that you had to wait three or four months after your spouse died before choosing a new one. That was considered a polite period of mourning when Dad died, wasn't it, Mom? So now it's just a week or so, which I guess means I should keep my eyes open today when everyone comes to help me get over the fact that my husband just died trying to save our fucking dog, because Prince Charming might walk through the door and sweep me away. And oh," she went on, "you always said you wanted the wedding ring back when my marriage was over. Perhaps you're wanting it now for yourself? For marriage number four?"

Eleanor said nothing. She just stood there, mouth agape.

"I burned it," Lily said. "It's gone. Ashes to ashes and dust to dust."

A wave of incredulity swept across Eleanor's eyes. She had never had a marriage like Lily's marriage to Tom. She didn't know what that kind of love and that kind of loyalty felt like. But that didn't make her worthy of such derision. That didn't make her unable to provide her child comfort during a tragedy. "Don't you dare speak to me that way," she hissed.

"Why?" Lily asked. "Because it's too close to the truth? Because you're hoping to snatch Gordon Vreeland up?"

"No," Eleanor said. "Because I may not have been as lucky in love as you were, and I may not have been the mother you hoped for, but I was never cruel."

Eleanor swiped the florist's white card off the counter, turned, and left the room so fast she seemed to disappear into thin air.

•32•

Eleanor

ELEANOR climbed the stairs to her rooftop deck. In one direction, you could see out across the red tile roofs of Santa Barbara to the courthouse bell tower—a tiled square tower modeled after the Alhambra in Spain. Beyond the courthouse was the harbor, with its curl of seawall and its sea of masts. To the west were the mountains, charred now, but Eleanor knew that fire was what renewed the chaparral. Even now, under the scarred earth, seeds were shaken loose from their hard casings and roots were primed to grow in the spring. People would rebuild their houses and their lives, and the hills would grow green again. One thing you figured out when you'd lived as long as she had was that it always happened that way.

She stepped out into the shadowy night, sat in one of the wrought iron chairs, and called Gordon in New York.

"Well, you put me in a fine pickle," Eleanor said.

"The flowers?" he asked.

"Lily thinks I've gone and plucked a widower straight from his wife's funeral. She thinks this is what I've done all my life, you see, so it fits into her vision of me."

"She thinks you've chased widowers?"

"She thinks I've been opportunistic when it came to men. It's because all the men I married were rich, and because many of the other ones I became involved with were married."

"So she's right, then," Gordon said.

Eleanor sighed. "But look what it's gotten me. I get to sit here in my old age and remember all the adventures, all the good times. I chose my path, every step of the way. It's not her right to judge it after the fact."

"Eleanor," he said. "She's just had something yanked away that you've disregarded your whole life."

"You're on her side?"

"Well, no," he said. "But I understand what she's feeling."

"You think I've disregarded love? I've loved, Gordon. I've loved extremely well. And it's presumptuous for you to assume that you know anything about it. In fact, I'm offended."

"I know I'm going out on a limb," he said. "I do. And I'm sorry if I've offended you. But time is running out for both of us."

"I can't replace Judy," Eleanor said.

"But have you ever let anyone love you, Eleanor?" Gordon said softly. "Do you know what I'm offering? Do you know what it feels like to be cherished?"

She thought, strangely, of Gracie, and the

friendship they had shared for sixty-four years. Gracie had cherished her, and she had cherished Gracie. But it was easier with friends than it was with lovers. There was a natural distance that never had to be bridged—and Eleanor needed that distance, because without it, she was afraid she would lose herself. "I don't think I'm going to answer that question," she said.

"But will you at least think about it? Can you promise me that?"

"I will," she said, and then there was just silence between them. They might have hung up; it was a natural break in the conversation, but neither was ready to end it. Gordon spoke into the silence.

"I sent the flowers because I just wanted to send my sympathies," Gordon said. "It's how I was raised."

"I know," she said. "As was I."

"I miss you," Gordon said.

She stared out across the darkened city. She had come to Santa Barbara during her second marriage, when Lily was still young, and it had felt like home from the start. She loved the feel of the air and the smell of the sea and the way everyone in town, whether they were locals or visitors, seemed acutely aware that they were in on something good.

"Are you still there?" Gordon asked.

"I am."

"I haven't been able to sleep since you left. I haven't been able to complete a crossword puzzle."

"You miss Judy," she said.

"I miss you, too," he said. "May I come visit?"

"It would be too awkward, Gordon, to have you here courting me when you know I don't really want to be courted. This is Lily's home now, too," she said. "And it would just be awkward all around. I'm sorry."

·33·

Olivia

OLIVIA dressed Brooke in a navy blue dress for the memorial party, and patent leather Mary Janes. She braided her hair, and made sure Brooke washed her face. For her own part, Olivia just threw on the same black wrap dress she'd worn for every party, funeral, or function she'd been invited to since giving birth. No one at this party would know the difference, except for Ryan. A number of Tom and Lily's close friends and colleagues were flying in from Vermont, and there was an aunt and uncle from New York, and some cousins from the Midwest. Most of the people coming today seemed to be friends of Eleanor's who had known Lily as a child. Olivia couldn't help wondering how many more people would have come if the party had been held in Burlington. Tom could never go out in that town without running into people whom he was teaching, or had taught, or had worked with, or hiked with. The house was filled with letters from them, and cards, and flowers.

"Is there going to be a party in Burlington, too?" she asked Luke. He was the safest person to talk to, the only one who didn't seem brittle.

"I have no idea," Luke said. "I guess if Mom wants one."

"Will she stay here, do you think?"

"I wouldn't, if I were her."

"You'd go back?"

"I'd go somewhere, that's for damn sure."

BROOKE followed her great-grandmother around the party, to the delight of everyone gathered, but when anyone spoke to Brooke, she would say, "Pop-Pop died," and they would all grow silent, for fear of saying the wrong thing.

At one point, Brooke broke away from Eleanor to come up to the island where the guacamole was set out. " 'Moleee," she said.

"You want to try Pop-Pop's guacamole?" Lily asked.

Brooke held her hands up in answer, and Lily took a chip and scooped up a bit of the gua-camole. "It's hot," Lily said. "Hot, hot, hot."

Brooke took the chip and bit it, and her brow wrinkled as she tried to reconcile the cool dip with her grandmother's warning about it being hot. Then the taste hit her tongue, and she began to hop up and down. "Hot," she said. "Hot, hot, hot!" And then she looked back up at Lily and said, "More 'moleee!"

Lily laughed, the first time all week, the only time that night, and handed her another chip.

• • •

RYAN drank margaritas all night and talked to anyone who would listen about camping in the Vermont woods with his dad. He told one of Tom's New York cousins about the things his dad had saved from the fire—the jumble of paper and the old baseball and the duffel bag stuffed with fabric.

"That's a hell of a thing," the man said. "Having a few minutes to choose what to save from a whole house full of memories."

Ryan shrugged. "I'd just get my car keys and walk," he said.

Olivia was standing nearby, rocking Brooke back and forth on her hip. The child was on her way to sleep, her thumb in her mouth, her eyes closed. Olivia turned to face her husband.

"You'd walk away from Brooke's room?"

Ryan shrugged. "You can always get another crib."

"What about Bear or her blanket?"

"It's all replaceable."

The cousin caught the eye of another guest and moved toward the bar, leaving Ryan and Olivia alone.

"Us, too?" she said softly.

Ryan swigged the end of his margarita and didn't answer, which was answer enough for Olivia. *I came out here because Lily lost her husband,* she thought, *but I think I may have lost mine, too.*

· · ·

AFTER the enchilada dinner Eleanor had brought in to go with the guacamole, she stood up and thanked everyone for coming, and for the donations they had made in Tom's name. She told the story about Tom and the engagement ring, and about the look on his face the day he first saw the avocado farm. Ryan was afraid he might cry, and so he held Brooke on his hip like a shield, and spoke quickly about how he hoped he could be as good a father as his father had been. Luke surprised everyone by reading a prepared speech that wove together remembrances of Tom in the garden, in the woods, and in the classroom. It ended with a vow that Luke was going to learn how to grow something, in his dad's honor, even if it was just a houseplant—a line that made everyone laugh.

Lily did not speak. She couldn't speak. She sat on the couch in between her sons, wearing the teal dress her mother had purchased, smiling at her friends and family, and holding back her tears the way she might hold off a headache in the middle of teaching a class. She kept thinking about getting up and pouring herself a glass of red wine, and cutting herself a slice of the chocolate torte her mother had ordered from the bakery, because physical pain seemed to her the most appropriate thing to feel right then, but she held off doing that, too.

At the end of the night, after Brooke had gone to bed, Olivia sat with Lily on a couch by the window, alone.

"You okay?" Olivia asked.

"I used to love to go to parties with Tom," she said, "because he would remember everything that I forgot. I would just have to turn to him and ask, and he would whisper the name of a neighbor, or where someone's child ended up moving, or how I knew the woman in green. It's like half my memory is gone."

Olivia nodded. She thought she understood.

"But the worst part," Lily said, "is that, with the house gone and everything in it, there's no proof that I lived my life."

"You don't need proof," Olivia said.

"Maybe you do," Lily said. "Maybe that's why we all rush around collecting things and cramming our house full of things. So that we'll have proof."

"Did anyone ever tell you that you think too much?"

Lily looked up at her son's wife and nodded. "Tom," she said. "He used to say that to me all the time."

Olivia pressed her lips together and looked at the ground. "I'm sorry," she said.

"It's okay," Lily said. "I miss him. It's unspeakable what happened to him, and my own part in it is unforgivable." She stopped, and breathed in and breathed out. "But I'm not sure our marriage was okay," she said quietly. "I'm just not sure."

"What do you mean?" Olivia asked quietly.

Lily shrugged. "Sometimes I think the only reason we stayed together was because we were afraid of coming apart."

"There could be worse reasons."

"But it didn't feel like what I imagined a long marriage to be—rich and vibrant and passionate. It just felt . . . familiar."

"But that sounds lovely, actually. I would like that—a marriage that felt familiar. Mine feels like it still needs to be broken in. Or maybe like it's the wrong fit altogether."

Lily looked up, surprised. So it was true. Her son and his wife were having trouble.

"Sorry," Olivia said quickly. "I shouldn't have said that to you. We'll be fine. We're just going through a rough patch because of the baby. We'll be fine."

"I guess you can't ever really know if you're going to be fine or not," Lily said.

They could hear Luke and Ryan downstairs watching a ball game. There were occasional shouts at the television, waves of cheers.

"What did you mean when you said that your part was unforgivable?" Olivia asked. "Weren't you sick when the fire broke out?"

Lily had told no one what had really happened that night. She said she'd had a migraine. She said she'd never smelled the fire, never heard it, never sensed it, never would have gotten out if Tom hadn't come for her. Everyone knew the things that Tom had taken out of the house—they were stacked in the garage downstairs, dusted with ash and with tragedy. Everyone knew that Tom went back in for the dog. But the fact that the last time Lily had slept with Tom, she had imagined another man in his place? The fact that Lily had gone to the beach to see that man in the flesh? The awful things she had accused Tom of doing before she saw him disappear into the hills, the dog trotting by his side? No one knew.

"It's just unforgivable," she said, "that after all this time, I can't control my migraines." She knew Olivia would buy her lie, and she was right.

"Don't be so hard on yourself," Olivia said, and Lily just pressed her lips together and nodded.

·34·

Lily

THE next afternoon, Lily told her family that she was going out, and then she walked out to the curb and got in the truck. Before she could close the door, Olivia appeared with Brooke. They had been walking around the block because Brooke had been crying, and Olivia thought a little fresh air might help calm her down.

"Hey," Olivia said. "Where are you off to?"

"To do some errands," Lily said, but the way she said it, it sounded more like a question than a statement.

Olivia cocked her head. "Did you tell the boys?"

"I told them," Lily said, "and my mother. Living here is like being back in high school, only worse. Everyone watching my every move, everyone gauging every word that comes out of my mouth."

"We're all so worried about you," Olivia said.

"Worried about what?" Lily said. "That I'm not sleeping? That I'm not eating? That grief might make me insane?"

Olivia shifted Brooke from one hip to the other. The girl had her head on her mother's shoulder, her thumb in her mouth, and a glassy look in her eyes. "Well, yes," Olivia said.

"So what if I am?" Lily said. "Please tell the rest of them when you go back inside. Tell them to stop watching me so closely. I can't stand it."

"We love you very much," Olivia said.

Lily shrugged, and her eyes filled with tears. "It doesn't help," she said.

SHE drove to the Patagonia world headquarters, which was housed in a series of old industrial buildings a half mile from the beach in Ventura, California. There was a meatpacking building and an old railroad station with brick walls and high, open-beamed ceilings. Patagonia had transformed the warehouses into a hip, eco-friendly campus. All the buildings were painted a bright saffron yellow and acted like a beacon to adventurers, rock climbers, river runners, and surfers who believe that a jacket can last a lifetime and that a clothing company can save the world.

Lily parked her truck in front of the main building and walked up the wide front steps. There was a large mural of a rock climber clinging to a granite wall. The climber looked like a spider, like a monkey, like a creature born to move through the world vertically. Lily stepped through the glass doors and up to the receptionist, who was young and fit and wholesome, which was a prerequisite for employment.

"I'm here to see Jack Taylor," she said.

"Is he expecting you?"

Lily thought about answering, *Yes, he is; he ran up to me on Miramar Beach.* Instead, she said, "No."

The receptionist pressed some buttons, listened at her phone, hung up. "He's not at his desk," she said. "May I take a message?"

"No," Lily said, trying not to look disappointed. "Thanks anyway." She turned and walked back by the spider woman, and toward her car. She had just put her hand on the door when Jack called her name. He was standing on the steps of the building she had just left, shielding his eyes from the sun.

"Hey," she said, and moved back around the car. "I thought I'd stop in and say hello. I should have called . . ."

"No," Jack said. "It's great. Come in."

She followed him past the wholesome receptionist and down the hall, which was lined with more posters of more people doing amazing things in amazing locations—flying through the air in a kayak over a waterfall, trekking across a glacial ridge. He stepped into his office, offered her a seat on a couch, and took a chair across from her.

"I was thinking about you during the fires," Jack said. "You said you lived in that area. Everything okay back at the farm?"

"Our house burned to the ground," Lily said. It was a phrase she had heard before, but she'd never known exactly what it meant—that every part of a house could burn and everything in it, and that there could be nothing left except the ground on which it was built. She didn't know that when a house burned to the ground, the people who lived there would be forever going to get a certain mug from a certain cupboard, or a certain shirt from a certain drawer, or a certain spool of thread from a certain plastic fisherman's case in a closet where a sewing machine had been kept, and that they would forever be faced with the fact that there was no certainty. She had the urge to add, *But I have lists of everything; I'm making lists.* Because the lists were the only things that were keeping her from flying apart. Her one link to sanity was remembering what was in each room, and where it had sat in relation to other things, and that those things had made up her life.

"Oh my God," Jack said, and leaned back in his chair. "I'm sorry."

Lily took a deep breath. "My husband was killed," Lily said, and looked at the yellow stitching on her Levi's. Her legs were shaking, up and down, up and down.

"Jesus, Lily," Jack said, and stood up and closed the door. Lily could feel her face screw up and she could feel the heat building behind her ears, and then she started to cry. Jack came and kneeled beside her, and when she didn't stop crying, he put his thick arm around her shoulders in an awkward gesture of comfort. He didn't really know Lily. She didn't really know him. But that was why she had come. Jack was someone with whom she shared a blank history. He was a player on the stage of her life, but besides that one strange interlude on the beach, neither of them had spoken any lines or played any scenes. Jack could be whoever she wanted him to be, and what she wanted was to believe that he would rescue her from her doubt and her confusion, from her guilt and her grief.

When he said, "I'm so sorry," she nodded her thanks.

"That doesn't help much, does it?" he asked. "People being sorry?"

"No, it does," she said, looking up. "Of course it does."

"Is there anything I can do, to, you know, help you get back on your feet? Hey, what about some clothes and jackets and things? We've got a whole warehouse."

"It's okay," she said. After all, she had her sweatshirt, her jeans, her clogs.

She wasn't sure what to do next. She thought, suddenly, that she should stand up and tell Jack that it had been a mistake to come, that it had been a terrible mistake, and that she needed to pretend like it had never happened. Then she thought she might confess—explain how she had gone home right after seeing him on the beach, and opened the bottle of wine, and said unforgivable things, and that the reason Tom was dead was because of that. Finally, she circled back to the reason that she was sitting there in Jack's office in the first place: he could love her. She could leap from one love to another as easily as if love were stones on a path. She could make it through the same way her mother always had.

She looked up. "Are you free for dinner?" she asked. "I don't think I've eaten anything in three days."

Jack stood up, leaned back against his desk, crossed his arms. He didn't understand marriage. He had been married briefly once, and thought it was a ridiculous charade. But he understood something about desire. "There's a great burger place down the way," he said. "Burgers and beer."

She nodded, and swallowed. "That sounds good," she said.

WHILE they ate, they talked about people they knew in high school and about the successes and disappointments of their own lives. Jack told how he had started out as a surfer sponsored by Patagonia, moved up to sales rep, did a stint in marketing, and was now in charge of managing the relationships the sportswear giant had with top athletes. Lily explained about teaching, and the textbook she had abandoned, and the decision she and Tom had made to buy the avocado farm. Jack was wide-shouldered, tan, tattooed, his body buffed by wind and water, and she was petite, gray-haired, and as reserved as if she had been born and bred in New England. No one would have imagined they were a couple, and yet as they sat together, they felt the spark of connection. It was the same spark Lily had felt when Jack spoke to her at the dog shelter, and when he had stood near her at the beach—a tugging, a buzzing. She felt nervous and excited and somewhat sickened by it. She remembered making love to Tom and thinking about Jack, and she tried to remember the last time Tom's touch had felt so electric.

They had another beer after dinner, and sat out in the warm night. They were careful not to talk about fire or about sex or about how Lily was living, again, at her mother's house, just as if she were in high school again. Jack paid the bill and said, "My house is just a few blocks that way. We can walk."

Lily nodded, and then she walked with him. She did not touch him as they walked, but she did not change her mind either. She knew exactly what she was doing.

JACK lived in a little bungalow just off Main Street. It had a screen door that banged and surfboards in the garage. His walls were covered in photographs of oceans. There were so many

292

colors of blue and white, and so many kinds of sand, and waves that curled and rose and crashed and sparkled. Lily stood in the center of the room and stared and was about to ask questions the way an academic would—*What are the locations of the photographs? What kind of camera did you use?*—and then Jack was behind her, and his arms were around her waist, and she felt him press against her back. She took a quick breath in, surprised by his touch, and the strength of his arms, and how he wasn't Tom, but she was still Lily.

He pressed his palm flat against her belly, his fingers reaching under the waistband of her jeans, and she did not move, she did not lift her hands or move her arms. She just stood, and let him hold her and stroke her, because that was why she had come. He turned her around so that she was facing him, and leaned down and kissed her on the mouth, and now she pressed back with her lips and her tongue. He slipped his hand under her shirt and around to the small of her back, and she felt him hard against her belly.

"I know how to make you feel alive," he boasted, and he kissed her neck, and her collarbone.

Her whole body was buzzing, from the beer and from the sense of abandon—such an alien, dangerous thing. His touch felt electric, and all she could think of was his fingers and where they were moving, and she wanted to dive into that feeling, to feel only that. She reached down and unbuckled his belt, and unbuttoned his jeans, and he groaned and she thought, *Good.*

He took her into the bedroom, which was surprisingly neat. The bed was neatly made with a chocolate brown cotton comforter, and there were matching pillowcases, and one large photo of a wave on the wall. He lifted off her hoodie sweatshirt, helped her step out of her clogs, slid her Levi's down to her ankles. He flung back the covers on the bed, and she sat on the edge of the sheets. He was still wearing an old plaid pair of boxer shorts, and he kneeled on the carpet and began to suck on her toes, very slowly. She wanted to scream, *No, no, no,* because her brain was about to explode with desire and with fear, and she wanted it to end quickly. She didn't want to *enjoy* it.

Jack's tongue was hot, and his patience was firm. He took each toe one at a time into his mouth, and rolled it around, and licked it. He kissed all the way up one of Lily's legs, over her hip, to her breast, and then he kissed her mouth and moved back down the other side of her body. "Who knew that the smartest girl in the class of 1974 had curves like this?" he said. What he was doing was a kind of performance; she sensed this. She understood that her role was to just lie there and appreciate it. It was different from what she had in mind, but she gave in to it. It was such a relief for something other than her brain to be throbbing.

He climbed on top of her, and rolled his hips, and slid inside, and then he slid out and she groaned—it was a kind of agony—and he kept up the kissing and the licking, moving closer and closer to the center, to the point between her legs where everything converged.

He climbed on top of her again, and rolled his hips again, and thrust inside her, once, twice, three times. This was more what she had hoped for—the urgency and the heat, the pleasure that was so close to pain, and when he pulled out again, she missed it, and she said, "Do that again," in a voice that was a command.

He did, and she cried out, and he cried out, and then her gasps turned into actual sobs, and she was lying under a man she didn't really know, weeping for her husband.

·35·

Eleanor

WHEN Lily got back, she half expected Olivia to be waiting up for her, but it was Eleanor who was sitting at the dining room table, the *New York Times* crossword puzzle in front of her, and a pen, and a dictionary.

Lily walked through the darkness and stood in front of her mother. When she was a teenager, she would do the same thing, but back then, she had nothing to hide. She was the kind of girl who would stay out all night at parties, drinking nothing. The kind of girl who would go on a date with a boy and just talk. Sometimes Lily thought that her mother was disappointed by her strait-laced ways. Sometimes she thought her mother was waiting up for her with the hope that Lily might actually come home tipsy, with smeared lipstick, a shirt buttoned the wrong way.

"What are you doing?" Lily asked. The light coming in from the night was hazy, gauzy, from all the smoke still in the air.

"You weren't running errands, were you?" Eleanor asked.

Lily raised her hand in the air as if to say, *So what?* and let it fall against her thigh with a slap. "No," she finally said.

Eleanor knew how comforting desire could be, how easy it was to go to it, and to give in to it. She knew how easy it was to get what you wanted when all you wanted was to be held, for a time. She guessed where Lily had gone, and she felt a shock of recognition now that she knew she was right. This daughter, who was so different from her, who had gone through the world on such a different path, had the same impulse in grief that she herself had once had—to reach out to someone else, to find instant comfort wherever you could find it. In the end, maybe they weren't so different after all. "You went to see that boy Jack," she said.

"Jesus, Mom," Lily said. "He's more than fifty years old. He's not a boy."

"Am I right?"

"Right? Right? Of course you're right. And you love that, don't you?"

"Lily . . ."

"You probably actually *love* that Tom died, too, because didn't you tell me it wouldn't last? That he couldn't give me everything I wanted? Well, you're right about all that, too. It's all over. And I have nothing."

Eleanor stood up in the eerie glow. "What I was going to say was that I understand this thing with Jack. I was going to tell you that it's okay. You take comfort where you can find it."

Lily held her breath. The words her mother was

saying were so perfect, so exactly right, but she couldn't accept them. It was too much for her mother to be so right. "By the way," she said, "I'm going to fix up the shed and move back up there." Her voice was crisp and matter-of-fact. "I'm going to put a refrigerator and a stove in the front room, and a bed in the back."

Eleanor took a step forward. She wanted to wrap her arms around Lily's shoulders, to stroke her cheek. "You don't have to do that," she said. "You're welcome to stay here as long as you'd like." She swallowed and looked at the ground. "I like having you here," she said quietly.

"I know," Lily said. "I just think it would be best for us both."

SHE dreamed of fire, of flame, of smoke, of heat. She dreamed of angels—cartoon angels with cartoon wings—who lift people gently from the earth and fly them through the sky like Peter Pan and Wendy, over a glittering lighted earth. She was sometimes in the audience watching with amazement, and she was at other times in the wings of the stage watching with worry to see if the wires might break. In both instances, the angels smiled down at her, but the people they carried just flew; they never looked back.

In the morning, she got out the yellow legal pad. On a fresh piece of paper, at the top in the center, she wrote one word:

Tom

A few days later, Shelley called to say that Lily's bowl had been fired. Lily drove to the studio to pick it up. Shelley had set it on the worktable with the lid on top. It was just as misshapen as when Lily had made it, but there was a sense of permanence about it now, as if nothing could change it. She lifted the little lid, and inside was a ring of ash, and a two-and-a-half-carat diamond.

·36·

Eleanor

AFTER everyone had gone home again and Eleanor and Lily were left by themselves, Gordon called to say that he was in Santa Barbara. He had booked a room at the Biltmore Hotel, and wondered if Eleanor was free for dinner.

Eleanor said, "No, I most certainly am not," and Lily looked up in alarm.

"What was that about?" Lily said.

GORDON called the next day, and again asked if Eleanor was free for dinner.

"Gordon," Eleanor said. "You must stop this."

"Just let me come for a drink," he said. "One drink."

She relented. At six o'clock, he arrived in a crisp Thomas Pink shirt and a pair of khakis with a perfect crease. He leaned down and kissed his old friend on the cheek when she opened the door, and then he stood up and said, "Your place looks good, as always."

"Thank you," she said, and invited him inside.

Lily came downstairs to say hello. Gordon took both of Lily's hands in his own, looked her straight in the eye, and said, "I recently lost my wife of fifty-five years. I know that nothing I can say will make you feel any better, but I did want to say that I'm sorry for your loss."

Lily felt her throat constrict, and her eyes burn. She wanted to fall into Gordon's arms and be comforted, like a child. She pressed her lips together and nodded. "Thank you," she said quietly, and then, in order to change the subject, in order to pay her mother back for all the manipulative things she'd done in her life, in order to throw a rope to this kind, gray-haired man, she said, "So you two are going to dinner?"

"No," Eleanor said. "Gordon just stopped by for a drink."

"I have a reservation at the Wine Cask," Gordon said to Lily, "and no company. Would you care to join me?"

Lily had no interest in eating, and no interest in being out in public, where people might ask how she was doing, or if she was having a nice day, or whether or not her husband would be joining them. But she felt more comfort in the presence of Gordon Vreeland than she had felt in the past ten days. She said yes.

"Fine," Eleanor said. "That's just fine." But she felt jealousy rise up in her like a wave.

·37·

Lily

THEY ordered the halibut and an expensive bottle of pinot grigio. They talked about Lily's father, and Gordon told stories of the things Billy did in college—how he got an A on a history test he didn't study for, how he once hit three home runs in a row in practice. They talked about Opening Day parties at Fenway Park, and how Lily had never cared much for baseball. Then they talked about death—how final it was, how surprising, how silent.

"Do you think it's better to lose someone slowly, the way you lost Judy, or to lose someone quickly, the way we lost my dad?" Lily asked.

"Slowly," Gordon said. "Not being able to say good-bye is agonizing."

Lily nodded. "It's not only that," she said. "It's that everything's unresolved. I'm not even sure that Tom and I were doing okay."

Gordon set down his fork. "Your mother said you had a very good marriage."

"How would she know?" Lily asked, and Gordon laughed gently.

"Good point," he said. "Your mother was so different from other girls her age. She had this restlessness, this mischievousness. I actually told your father after that first night to watch himself with her. I told him she was dangerous. Billy didn't care, though. He liked that about her."

"Do you think she loved him?"

"Your mother? Love your father?" He took a sip of wine. "Wild horses couldn't keep the two of them apart. Do you know that he climbed out the second-story window of Winthrop House to go see her? Broke about five house rules."

"You're talking about lust, though, not love."

"She wanted him," Gordon said, "as if he were a prize. And he wanted her for the same reason. They were well suited to each other."

"But it wasn't love. It was something else."

"Who can say what love looks like from the outside?" he said. "I think love is only recognizable when you're in it."

The waiter came and took their orders for coffee, and when he had left, Gordon said, "Lily. I want you to know that your mother is not chasing after me. I'm chasing after her."

"It's a familiar scenario, either way," Lily said. "Someone dies, and my mother suddenly has a new man. I thought it would stop when she hit seventy. I thought it would be over."

"You've got it all wrong, sweetheart," Gordon said. "And I'll tell you why. Do you know what Judy said to me before she died?" he asked.

Lily shook her head.

"She told me I should marry your mom."

Lily looked up. "Why?"

"She thought it would make us happy."

"Would it?"

Gordon shrugged. "I'm an old man," he said, "and I'm not good for much anymore. But I am good at love. I've known your mother for almost fifty years. I've always adored her. It would be a small leap for me to love her. And yes. I think it would make us happy."

Lily thought of Jack, and how she had imagined the same thing—that she could trade one love for another, make a quick swap, stop her grief before it gained steam. She thought of the wedding ring her father had made for her mother, and how Eleanor had worn it for so long, and how Lily had worn it for even longer. She should have given it back to her mother. She should have saved it for someone else. It was a talisman of lasting love and she had willfully destroyed it. "I'll talk to her," Lily said.

"You think that will help?"

Lily smiled. "Probably not."

"Neither do I," Gordon said. "But go ahead. Try. I'm going home on Wednesday."

AFTER dinner, she did not go back to her mother's house. She drove out to Ventura, to the beach cottage with the screen door that banged. It was nine thirty. The lights were blazing in the living room and the bedroom. She rang the bell,

304

stepped back, and waited. She was cold suddenly and wished she had brought a sweater.

Jack opened the door. "I wondered when you would come back," he said.

"You didn't wonder *if* I'd come back?"

He shrugged. "It was pretty hot sex, Lily. Not many people will stay away from that. Are you coming in, or what?"

It was much rougher this time, much faster. He pulled off her clothes and pressed her against the wall, and she felt her skin pull where it was dry and where he thrust against her. When it was over, he asked if she wanted to stay and have a drink.

She shook her head, put on her clothes, and slunk back into the night.

·38·

Lily

THE news the next morning was filled with reports of an unseasonable cold snap. Citrus farmers were worried about their crops. "My trees can withstand a little frost," one orange farmer said, "but two nights, or more, and the damage will be deep." Lily got up from the breakfast table, agitated and upset. She didn't know a thing about avocado farming, or if the trees were in the same danger, and the only person she thought might know was Nadine.

She called the Calavo warehouse, but Nadine was not in.

"I'm going up to the house," she said, unable to call the charred remains of her home what it was.

"What are you going to do?" Eleanor asked.

"I'm not sure."

"Do you know anything about avocado trees?"

"No," Lily said, "but I'm going to find someone who does. Those trees are all I have left."

WHEN Lily pulled into the driveway, there was an unfamiliar truck already there. It was white, clean, with four doors and big tires. On the back were two bumper stickers: one that said LOCAVORE and one that featured the Sierra

Club's iconic sugar pine tree. Lily walked quickly through the rows of trees, peering along them, unsure of what she would find. She felt nervous—as if the person who had arrived before her was an intruder intent on doing her harm.

She walked toward the shed at the base of the orchard, and as she drew closer, she heard footsteps, the crack of someone dropping a wooden crate on the bare cement floor. She stepped into the doorway.

Nadine was at the far end of the shed next to a stack of wooden crates. A picking stick was propped up on the workbench at her side. Her hair was pulled back in a ponytail, and her flannel shirt—red plaid, with tiny black stripes—hung like a flag from her body. She wore Birkenstocks that were flattened and dusty, and she wore, as usual, no bra. Her breasts hung inside her white tank top like ripe fruit. Lily's gaze darted to them, and then came to rest on Nadine's face. "What are you doing?" she asked.

"The fruit will all die," she said. "I'm harvesting it."

Lily peered through the dusty air. She could see dust mites dancing in the shafts of light that came through the old window, and thought about batting them out of the way.

Nadine stepped toward her. "Lily," she said, "I'm sorry about Tom. I'm sorry about your loss."

Lily closed her eyes. Despite the lists she had

made on the yellow lined paper, she was tempted to say, *I didn't lose anything.* Losing implied some kind of game, like hockey, baseball, crazy eights—or some kind of carelessness, like keys left in a lock, glasses left behind on a desk. She felt, in that moment, the full flowering of guilt. She felt, suddenly, that she had killed Tom. She had betrayed him, and then she had killed him— by her negligence, her selfishness, her indulgence. She opened her eyes.

"Were you sleeping with him?" she asked. She said it gently, the way you might ask someone if they had recently been ill.

Nadine looked directly back into Lily's eyes. "No," she said. "We were working on a presentation together. He was a smart man, Lily, a good man. He wouldn't have done that to you."

Lily picked up an avocado from the full crate on the workbench, and cupped it in her hand. It was rough and heavy. She let its weight pull her hand down to her side. "But did you want to sleep with him?" she asked.

"Lily . . ." Nadine said.

"It's important that I know the truth," she said.

Nadine shifted her weight from one leg to the other. "Okay," she said. "No. I wasn't attracted to him in that way."

Lily nodded. She set her avocado on the workbench, and it rolled toward the back and stopped against the Peg-Board. A crow called outside the

308

shed, and both women glanced toward the door, as if the bird might be right there, speaking directly to them. When Nadine looked back, there were tears on Lily's face.

"The last time I had sex with Tom," Lily said, "I imagined another man in his place."

She said these words, and then she stood there in the dust and the dim light, letting the tears stream down her cheeks. "I can't seem to forgive myself for that. I can't stop wishing I could have the chance to apologize for that."

Nadine stepped toward Lily and gathered the other woman up in her arms. Lily leaned into her—her free-hanging breasts, her free-hanging plaid shirt, her beaten-down shoes that held her so solidly on the ground—and sobbed.

THE next thing she knew, Luna was there. The dog bounded through the trees, barking, and Lily just stood and watched her approach through the dappled light. Luna circled her, yelping and jumping on her legs, and Lily felt unsteady.

"Stop," she said sharply.

Luna hesitated for a moment, then barreled into Lily, jumped on her, and knocked her down onto the loamy ground. Luna yelped and licked her hands and her face and her neck, and Lily put her hands over her face, and tried to turn away.

"No," she said, "Luna, no!"

The dog sat down a foot from where Lily lay, and waited, panting and whining.

Lily sat up and brushed the dead leaves from her sleeves, and looked into Luna's face, and her mismatched, knowing eyes. Maybe Luna had been with Tom when he died. Maybe she stayed by his side until she knew the firemen had come to pull his body out, and then bolted through the flames to save herself. Lily put her arms around her dog, buried her face in her fur, and smelled the smoke of the fire and the bitterness of her despair.

Nadine turned and walked back into the trees and left them alone.

·39·

Eleanor

GORDON knocked on her door just after noon on Tuesday.

"Gracie died," he said.

Eleanor backed across her foyer, sat on the kilim bench, and rested her head against the wall.

Gordon closed the door, and came and sat next to her. Neither of them said anything for a long time. They just sat, remembering their friend, and their lives, and all the people they knew who had lived and died.

After a while, Eleanor stood up. "I have to go to the store," she said, "to get the ingredients to make a cake."

"A cake?"

"It's what I do when people die. Make rum cake."

"Can I drive you?"

She closed her eyes. She already had the cake mix, the rum. All she needed were a few more eggs. "Okay," she said.

WHEN they came back to the house, Lily was sitting at the dining room table. She was staring at a vase the size of a large pear, and at her feet was a box, a pile of packing bubbles, and a torn pile of brown paper wrapping. She looked at Eleanor. "It's from my friend Elizabeth," she said. "My old neighbor."

Eleanor stepped closer, and saw that the handles of the little vase were arms. It appeared that the vessel was hugging itself.

"She's a potter," Lily said. "Do you know what that means?"

Eleanor shook her head.

"It means that she knows something about fire."

Eleanor put her shopping bag on the floor, and sat in a chair opposite Lily. Gordon stayed where he was, a short distance apart, as if he knew he didn't belong at the table.

"Listen to what she says," Lily said. She reached into the pot and pulled out a slip of paper like a fortune from a cookie.

"Fire destroys, but it also galvanizes. Tom may be gone, but the love he had for you is fused to you like a glaze."

Eleanor held out her hand, and Lily placed the slip of paper in it. Eleanor read it, laid the paper down, then reached for the vase and turned it so that she could see its perfect symmetry, its human curves. "It's lovely," she said.

Lily nodded. "I love the word *galvanized*. The word *fused*. I love the way this vase has been burned, but it still feels like it's been loved."

Eleanor nodded.

"I'm choosing to believe it," Lily said.

"What?"

"That the love Tom and I had for each other is fused to me like a glaze."

THAT evening, the three of them gathered in the kitchen. Eleanor had the rum out on the counter, and Gordon asked where the glasses were kept so that he could make them drinks.

"This rum is for making cake," Eleanor said, "not drinking. I've got vodka, gin, and scotch and enough wine for a party, if you'd like."

"But this is good rum," Gordon said. "A little soda, a twist of lime. It could be a new tradition to drink rum while you make rum cake."

"I saw limes on the neighbors' tree," Lily said.

"Aha! A bit of pirating will make this cocktail perfect. Did you know that the British Navy considered rum to be so critical that they gave every sailor a half-pint-a-day ration?"

"And the Americans handed out Hershey bars . . ." Eleanor said.

"We had our fair share of rum," Gordon said. "Don't you worry."

They drank their rum while they beat the cake batter forty-two times by hand. "It has to be forty-two," Eleanor explained. "I don't know why, but that's what my mother always told me."

"She said the same thing about lemon meringue

pie," Lily said, "and she made the most amazing lemon meringue pie."

"I'm not a big fan of lemon meringue," Gordon said. "Judy's specialty was a coconut cream. It was divine."

"All I know how to bake is rum cake from Duncan Hines Yellow Cake Mix," Eleanor said. "When I die, you'll know just what to do."

Lily raised her glass. "And I'll drink the rum like the British sailors do and toast a thanks to Gordon."

"I'll be dead, too, no doubt."

"Nonsense," Eleanor said. "You're going to live to a hundred."

Gordon smiled. "Could be. We'll have to see."

"Gracie always wanted to live that long. She used to always talk about how we would drink a bottle of champagne even if we had to sneak it into the hospital." Eleanor sipped her rum, looked straight at Gordon. "Damn her," she said.

The smell of the cake permeated the kitchen now—sweet and powerful—and Lily remembered how she had smelled that on the day after Tom had died, and how she had thought, *That can't be for Tom,* as if it had all been a mistake. "I never imagined Tom would die first," she said to no one in particular. "I never imagined it. Not once."

Gordon stood up and made his way around to the bar stool where Lily sat, and he set his glass down and took her in his arms without saying a word. Eleanor followed him, and came up to her daughter, and leaned over and gently kissed her forehead. Lily took hold of her mother's hand—small and frail, with loose, wrinkled skin—and squeezed it in thanks.

When the cake was done, they put slices on Eleanor's Limoges plates, which she said Gracie helped her pick out at Filene's in Boston when they were just twenty-one years old. They sat out on the balcony, where the air still smelled like fire, and ate their cake and drank more rum until they could no longer keep their eyes open.

GORDON slept that night on Eleanor's couch. When she came downstairs in the morning, she said, "People will talk about us, Gordon."

He laughed. "What people? We're practically the only ones left."

"Is that why you won't leave me alone?"

"It's not a bad reason," he said.

She walked up to him and reached up on her toes and kissed him on the cheek. "You're very sweet, Gordon. I adore you. We will always be great friends."

"But you're not going to marry me, are you?"

"I'm sorry," she said.

"You're kicking me off your couch, then?"

"I am."

"Good," he said. "It's uncomfortable as hell."

·40·

Gordon

HE was nearly seventy-five years old, but Gordon had never been rejected by a girl. He had been an awkward, unformed boy when he arrived at Harvard in the fall of 1951, a kid who understood that the long arms and legs that helped him on the baseball field were a liability everywhere else. He stayed away from dances, from drive-ins, from any event where the boys were required to be smooth. When Judy Wyeth wiggled in next to him in the front seat of the Studebaker that day in front of Tower Court, he felt the curve of her hip, smelled the sweetness of her hair, saw the kindness in her eyes, and within moments decided that he wanted her the way he had wanted nothing else in his life. He wanted to hold her, to lie down next to her, to take her in his arms and never let her go. At nights, in his ivy-covered dorm, he would lie awake and dream of having a job, a house, and Judy as his wife.

He asked Judy to marry him on Tupelo Point. It was on a leafy rise on the path that circled Wellesley's Lake Waban. His knees knocked, his voice shook, and he felt certain that the birds in the trees were there just to mock his intention with their "caw, caw." But Judy threw her arms around him, and she cried, "Oh yes." It was then that he made a vow to himself: he would be a good husband. He would adore Judy until the day he died. He was twenty years old, and he never imagined that she would die first. He never let himself imagine it, until she became so ill that he couldn't ignore it.

And now, Eleanor Peters had kicked him off her couch and told him to go home. He felt crushed, deflated, embarrassed that he had come all that way and failed. It seemed as if the wind had been knocked out of him. As he packed his suitcase to go back to New York, his mind cascaded back through the years, remembering friends whose hearts had been broken. There was a fellow sailor in the navy whose sweetheart had let him go in a letter that arrived on his birthday, who talked of flinging himself overboard. There was a trumpet player at Harvard who sat out in the quad playing Taps when he found out that his girl had betrayed him. Gordon even remembered a boy in the sixth grade clutching a homemade valentine, a look of absolute shock on his face because the girl had shaken her head and said no, she wouldn't accept it. He couldn't remember the boys' names, but he remembered the looks on their faces. Only now did he know what it felt like in the gut.

He wished he could go back to all those moments and provide better comfort to his friends. He didn't know how physical a feeling it was, how strongly it registered in his stomach and his legs and the intricate space behind his eyes. He went to the hotel bar and ordered a drink, and when he told the bartender that he was in town for a girl but that the trip hadn't gone well, the bartender gave him a second on the house. Gordon smiled wryly, understanding, at long last, what a perfect temporary antidote scotch and a sympathetic stranger could be. He was seventy-four years old and still learning about love and life. He was seventy-four years old and alone for the first time.

He was going to fly home the following day, and he knew that when he got there, the doorman would ask if he'd had a nice trip. There was nothing else he could do other than nod, and lie, and say, "Yes, indeed."

·41·

Ryan

BEER was no longer enough to numb Ryan's pain. He poured himself a shot of tequila as soon as he walked in the door every night, and had another before he went to bed. He didn't try to hide it, and always offered Olivia a shot, too, and that way he nearly convinced himself that he didn't have a problem—not with the drinking anyway.

It was harder to pretend with his marriage. On the night of his father's memorial party, Ryan did not sleep in the downstairs bedroom where Olivia and Brooke were sleeping. He slept on the couch in Nana's TV room. He just stayed there after watching the Dodgers' game with Luke, as if he had passed out from exhaustion, as if he didn't even have the wherewithal to get up and brush his teeth. The truth was that he knew he wasn't welcome in bed with his wife after what he had said, and he wasn't sure he wanted to be there anyway.

"Marriage is fucked up," he said to Luke, during a lull in the eighth inning, "It's so damn hard to get it right, and when you get it right like Mom and Dad, all you get is heartbreak because someone's always going to die first."

"Mom seems pretty tweaked."

"See?" Ryan said. "It's fucked up."

"But Olivia is great," Luke said. "You and Olivia are great."

"Wrong," Ryan said.

"Wrong? What do you mean, wrong? She's sweet and pretty, and she's great with Brooke."

"She won't let me touch her."

"No shit?" Luke laughed. "And here I thought that was the best part of being married."

"Maybe it is for someone who knows what they're doing, but that's not me, bro. I don't have whatever it is that Dad had."

Luke shook his head. "I can't believe he's gone."

"I know," Ryan said. "It's fucked up."

HIS grandmother called one night after they returned to San Luis Obispo. She was calling, she said, to check up on them.

"We're great, Nana," Ryan said. "Things are great."

"Don't lie to me, Ryan Gilbert," she said.

"What?" he asked.

"I called to ask how you're doing. I'm quite serious about the question."

Ryan sighed. Olivia was reading to Brooke in the bedroom in the back of the house, but he wanted to make sure they didn't overhear him. He stepped out onto the front porch. "I'm sleeping on the couch. I'm eating food you're paying someone else to cook. My daughter won't let me near her. She constantly says, 'Mommy do it, Mommy do it.' And Olivia is happy to oblige because it makes her feel superior."

"It's that bad?" Eleanor said.

"It's that bad."

"I'll pay for counseling," Eleanor said, "if you think it would help."

"You and your money," Ryan said.

"Well?"

"The truth is," Ryan said, "I won't go. I don't want to sit there and have someone ask me about my family because then I'll have to tell them what a great dad I had and how he was such a great husband, and how he just died in a wild-fire and there's just no way in hell I'm ever going to live up to him."

"You don't have to live up to anyone, Ryan. You should know that. But walking away from a marriage . . ."

"I know," he said. "I know. I have no idea what it will cost."

WHEN he got off the phone, the house was silent. He walked down the hallway, pushed open the bedroom door, and saw that both Olivia and Brooke had fallen asleep in the rocking chair. He stood and watched them from the doorway, wondering if he should turn out the light, wake them up, walk away. After a while, he stepped toward them. He reached down and lifted Brooke out of Olivia's arms. Brooke's skin was sweaty. Her soft hair was matted to her forehead. She smelled like soap. He closed his eyes and held her to his shoulder, and just stood there, holding her, until his arms grew numb, and then he gently laid her on the bed, and kissed her and said good night. He felt like a thief who had stolen something precious.

He walked out of the room, turned off the light, and headed for the couch.

•42•

Lily

AFTER the avocados were safe from the frost, Lily went back to Beverly Fabrics. She wandered through the aisles, stopping at bolts of fabric that caught her eye, considering the possibilities. There were burnout velvets, Italian wools so fine they felt like silk, silk in a cacophony of color, weight, and texture. Every bolt offered something new to Lily's imagination—a coat, a skirt, a dress—and every possibility reminded her of a piece of fabric she had lost in the fire. There was so much fabric and so many things she had never made! She thought that she could list them all on her yellow pad of paper—Hattie's gray tweed that had not become a jacket, the sage green flea market silk that had not become a skirt, the white dotted Swiss that she had bought in Boston when she thought she might have a little girl. She had one Rubbermaid tub that was stuffed with swatches of printed cotton in different shades of blue. There were stripes, dots, florals, swirls, and geometric prints, and taken all together, they had looked like the sea. Lily had always thought that she would make a beautiful quilt with all that blue. She would design the horizon, the sky and the water, and somehow, it would cease to look like bits of cotton stitched together, and would look, instead, exactly the way the beach did on a clear summer day.

"I should have done it," she said, and she realized too late that she had spoken out loud.

"May I help you?" a saleswoman asked. She wore jeans and a chambray blouse, and her hair was cropped straight across as if she'd cut it herself. Pinned on her shirt was a name tag that said JANET.

"I'm looking for some silk," Lily said, which she knew was the equivalent of walking into a bookstore and saying, *I'd like a story,* but it was all she could manage to say.

Janet looked at Lily kindly. "Ah," she said. "Are you making something for a special occasion?"

"I think so," Lily said.

"Well, let's see," said Janet. "We have some beautiful new dupioni silk, and I think the blue is particularly pretty."

Lily touched the slags in the silk, felt the stiffness of the fabric. "I'm thinking of something that drapes," she said.

"Did you see the Japanese chiffons up front? They're very popular."

"I did," Lily said, "but I don't think I want a pattern."

Through this back-and-forth, Lily figured out what she was looking for. She ended up in front of the wall with the solid-colored silks. She scanned them, and pointed to a bolt above her head—a dark silver gray double-sided satin. Janet brought a step stool, pulled down the bolt, laid it across a cutting table. The fabric shimmered like an iridescent sea creature. Lily reached out to touch it—it was slippery, thick—and the light bounced off it as if it were alive. It looked like mercury, set free. She held it across her body and it moved and flowed over her breasts and over her belly like something magic.

"It looks wonderful with your hair and your coloring," Janet said. Lily couldn't see herself, but she could picture it—the silver gray fabric playing off the gray of her hair, playing off the blue of her eyes.

"This is it," Lily said. "I'd like four yards."

She bought the same sewing machine she had bought just five months before, and needles, thread, scissors, pins. She bought muslin and button forms. She realized, as she made her purchase, that she was amassing things—things that would need to be stored somewhere, things that would be there when she wanted to use them rather than phantom objects that were burned, gone. She realized, too, that these new items would not be shared with Tom. They would be, simply, hers. Everything she bought from here on out would be like that. As Janet rang each item up and put them all in a bag, Lily stood at the counter and tried, unsuccessfully, not to cry.

• • •

WHEN she got back to her mother's house, she went to the garage and got the cardboard tube of fabric that Tom had saved from the fire. She spread the pewter silk over the back of the couch, spread the lace out over it, then spread the muslin on the dining room table. She closed her eyes and pictured the dress her grandmother would have made to wear to a dance. She pictured a shift made of silk, an overlay of lace, a dress that would skim over her body like water.

Eleanor came down from her bedroom several hours later, when the muslin dress lay stitched together on the back of a chair and Lily was draping the iridescent silk across her body. Eleanor stopped, startled at the presence of so fine a fabric in the hands of her jeans- and grief-clad daughter. "What are you making?" she asked.

"A dress," Lily said.

Eleanor had never understood the appeal of sewing or felt the impulse to create. It seemed like so much frustration, so much effort, and no matter how good the seamstress was, the result always had the air of homemade about it. She remembered her mother going out with her father to Red Sox games and to the Head of the Charles wearing handmade dresses and suits, and she remembered wishing that her mother would go down to the shops on Newbury Street and buy dresses like the other wives. Her father was a prominent businessman in town, a man who had made it, and his wife still made her own clothes. But at least Lily wanted something new, something pretty. At least she was thinking about how she looked. "Good," Eleanor said, nodding with approval. "That's very good."

THE next morning, there were two muslin pieces—a shift and a piece that would overlay it—and Lily pieced together the silk. In the afternoon, she finished the seams, hemmed, and ironed. The following day, she laid the lace out on the table. She walked around it, considering the scalloped edges, the pearls, and considering all the things that this piece of fabric had never become. Hattie had never danced in it. She hadn't gotten married in it, hadn't dressed her child in it. The life of the lace had been one of longing, of waiting, of stories not told—an experience just the opposite of hers. Life was a risk. Love was a risk. And she saw now, very clearly, that it was one well worth taking. She lifted her scissors and cut right through the lace. Pearls fell to the floor like hail, and Eleanor looked up from where she was sitting and reading, and said, "Sounds like rain."

"It's Hattie's lace," Lily said.

Eleanor got off the couch, came over to the table. "So it is," she said, and then after a moment, she said, "It looks good."

"You can't ever write off a piece of fabric," Lily said, "or the possibility of love."

"What's that supposed to mean?"

"That Gordon loves you. He wants to marry you. I think you should say yes."

Eleanor stood at the table, silently, thinking that Lily sounded like Gracie, and then missing Gracie, and missing Judy and feeling, suddenly, very old.

"Do you have any idea what it feels like to be loved the way he loves you?" Lily asked.

Eleanor walked to the windows that looked out at the blackened hills, where the fire had swept down, and where, even now, the seeds in the soil would be preparing to sprout. She thought about the kind of love that doesn't end, that doesn't bend, that is just there, solid as an oak tree. She had never wanted it before now. She had thought that it would cost her something she couldn't afford to lose—her sense of self, maybe, her pride. Whatever it was, it seemed so silly now that she had lived so long and never allowed love in. It seemed so pointless. It seemed so sad. "No," she said quietly. "The truth is that I don't have any idea."

"I do," Lily said. "Because that's the way Tom loved me. It wasn't flashy, or loud, but it was constant. It was relentless. Nothing was going to get in its way. And I lived with that love for our entire marriage. I came to count on it. To take it for granted actually. But now that it's gone, I know exactly what I had, and I can tell you this, Mom: it feels very nice."

Tears were streaming down Lily's face, but she stayed where she was seated, behind the sewing machine. Eleanor walked back toward her and then Lily stood up and held the dress out in front of her. "It's for you," she said, "from me, and from Hattie, to wear when you say *I do*."

"You think I should say yes, then? Say yes to Gordon?"

Lily nodded. "I do."

WHEN the dress was pressed and hanging on the back of the door, and when the sewing machine was snapped into its case and the pins all stuck back in the pincushion, Lily drove out to see Luna, whom Nadine was taking care of until the shed was ready for her to move into. She took the dog on a walk along the dirt roads in the hills behind the Calavo warehouse, and sat with her awhile under the shade of one of the avocado trees near where her car was parked. Luna barked at the birds, leapt at the leaves on the ground, full of life. Lily might have been tempted to say that the dog had no clue that Tom was dead—the man who had agreed to take her home, who thought she would be a good partner for tramping through the trees, who went back into a fiery house because he wanted to save her. But there was something in the way Luna behaved around her that convinced her otherwise. Luna seemed to be watching her, and watching the world around her, alert for signs of trouble, ready to head them off. This dog, she thought, whom Tom had touched and loved, was never going to leave her side.

"You're a good dog, Luna," Lily said, looking into Luna's mismatched eyes. "I'm glad you came back."

·43·

Eleanor

AFTER Lily went to see Luna, Eleanor sat on the kilim bench just inside her front door and cried.

She used to always say that love was an illusion. Love always dissolved in the face of everyday pressures, in the face of time. You couldn't pin it down, couldn't hold on to it, couldn't count on it. Something so ephemeral, she used to say, was not a good investment. But she had never been loved the way Lily had been loved by Tom. She had no idea what it felt like to give your heart over so completely that even death couldn't steal it away.

After a while, she got up, and called Gordon. It was evening in New York, and he was getting ready for bed.

"Who is this?" he demanded.

"It's Eleanor," she said. "Calling from California."

"Something's wrong?" Gordon asked. In his experience, tragedy was the only reason people phoned in the middle of the night.

"No," she said. "I've just been thinking about Judy."

Gordon cleared his throat. So it was tragedy, after all. A reminder of his loss. A moment in the middle of the night when he had to realize, once again, that she was gone and he was alone. He waited.

"Judy and I took a class together our first semester of college. Beginning French. She insisted that we speak nothing but French to each other when we were in the dorm. She said it would be the best way to learn the language. I thought it was just another one of Judy's crazy ideas and laughed at her and told her she was being silly. So she sat in her room every night and spoke to herself. Had conversations with herself. We all laughed even louder at her while we played bridge and smoked our cigarettes. Well, you know it turned out. Judy spoke French like a native, and I always sounded like a schoolgirl. Still do, in fact."

He was more awake now. "Eleanor," he said. "It's the middle of the night."

"My point is that I've been thinking about how often Judy was right."

He sat up straighter in bed. He thought he understood now what was happening. "She was indeed," he said.

"About love, too, Gordon. I think Judy was right about love, too. So I'd like to marry you," she said. "I'd like to accept your kind offer. I don't know how we will work it out with my house and Lily and the boys all here in California, and your apartment and all your children there in

New York, but I don't see any reason why we should be alone, Gordon, when we can be together. What I'm saying is, I'm choosing love, just like Judy said I should. I'm choosing you—that is, if your offer is still good."

He smiled. "Will I have to sleep on your couch?"

"Of course not," she said. "I am taking you to be my husband, not my houseboy."

"Good," he said, "because my back ached for days after that night."

HE met her at the airport when she arrived two days later. He stood in the baggage claim area at LaGuardia, his arms filled with white roses. When she came down the escalator, he bent down on one knee, and everyone around him stared at the white-haired man with the white roses who appeared to be proposing marriage, but he couldn't balance there, and then he had trouble getting up, and Eleanor had to help him. He stood up finally, and presented her with the bouquet, and the people who had been watching—who had flown in with her from Los Angeles, or flown all the way from Kyoto—broke into applause. He took her in his arms, and just stood there, holding her and thinking of the ways in which she felt different from Judy, and thinking of the ways in which she felt exactly the same.

·44·

Lily

ELEANOR and Gordon planned an early June wedding at the church by the sea.

A few days before the event, Eleanor stopped Lily in the kitchen before she went up to bed. "You'll need a dress for the ceremony," she said.

"I guess you're right," Lily said.

"And you'll need shoes."

"That's true."

"Come on," Eleanor said. "We're going shopping."

"But not to Nordstrom."

"They have the best dresses in town and the best shoes."

"I want something old."

"You mean something used?"

"Exactly. Something with history. Something with a story."

"God help me," Eleanor said.

They walked to a consignment store tucked into one of the downtown paseos. There were beautiful shoes in the window, and jeweled purses, and a display of couture dresses.

"Can I help you?" the woman asked. "Are you looking for something special?"

"Yes," Lily said. "Something for an afternoon wedding."

The shopkeeper led them to a rack of dresses and began to suggest things—chiffon and silk. Eleanor noted with pleasure the quality of the designers and the range of styles. She and the shopkeeper got into a discussion about how well Chanel holds its value, and Lily slipped off to another rack, and ran her hands along the fabric, feeling her way through the clothes. When her fingers landed on something particularly rich, she stopped. It was a pair of light wool cream-colored palazzo pants. She held them to her waist, and then turned to look for a top. She zeroed in on a crisp, short-sleeved cappuccino wraparound silk blouse. She slipped into the dressing room, tried the outfit on, and walked out, barefoot, into the shop, where her mother and the shopkeeper were still talking. They stopped their conversation and stared.

"Oh," the shopkeeper said.

Eleanor nodded, and bit her lip to keep from crying. "You look beautiful," she said.

A few hours before the ceremony, Gordon was nervously pacing the parking lot outside the chapel.

"How are you doing?" Lily asked.

He darted his eyes at her. "This is a big day," he said.

"It's a very big day," she said, but then she remembered why they were there—because his wife had died, and wanted him to keep loving. "You must be thinking about Judy," she said. She knew it was so, because she couldn't get Tom out of her mind. She kept thinking she would see him, getting out of a car, walking around the corner of the church, walking down the sidewalk, but time after time, Tom wasn't there.

Gordon stopped pacing. "I can't get her out of my mind," he said.

"She can be part of this day," Lily said. And she smiled and added, "Her love can be fused to you like a glaze."

"Like a glaze?"

"That's a line from a potter friend of mine," she said, "who sculpts things out of earth and fire."

"That's good," Gordon said, and his wild eyes calmed down in their sockets, and he stopped moving. "That's very good."

THE gray lace dress appeared to be a part of Eleanor—not so much something she had put on as something she had become. The silk flowed across her small body, and the lace floated over it like flowers scattered on a shimmering lake. Her white hair picked up the silver threads in the fabric and threw off an energetic light. She wore pumps with a strap that buttoned over her feet, and a soft plum lipstick, and everyone said she looked stunning.

Luke was there with a new girlfriend, and Ryan and Olivia, who sat together in willful misery, wondering about dissolution, reconciliation, the myriad paths that lay before them. Lily had made Brooke a blue satin dress with a white bow, and Brooke twirled around like a princess until Lily took her hand and helped her to stand still and watch what was happening before them.

"Nana's pretty," Brooke whispered.

"All brides are pretty," Lily said, and she felt her eyes fill with tears, and her throat constrict as she remembered Tom and the day in Lyon when she promised to love him until death do them part. She had had no idea, then, that she would love him so well, that she would lose him so hard. She'd had no idea that love was so much stronger than death.

"Then how come you're crying?" Brooke asked.

Lily wanted to say that it was because it was such a rare thing to love and be loved, and such a joyful thing, and such a fragile thing, and she wanted to say that she had never thought she would see her mother stand up to receive love like this, and to give it, and that she was grateful to be alive to witness it. She wanted to say how much she had loved Tom, and how much she missed him, and how she woke up every day thinking he would be there beside her again, but there were no words for that kind of longing. "Because," she said simply, "I'm happy for her."

THEY had dinner at the Biltmore, where they could hear the waves of the ocean crashing onto the sand. On the way home, Lily said she would see everyone back at her mom's, and left by herself. Instead of driving north, toward Eleanor's town house, she drove south, to Jack's.

"Ah," he said when he opened the door, "the grieving widow back for more?"

"No," she said, "actually, no. This was all a mistake, Jack. I used you, and I just wanted to come by to tell you that I'm sorry."

"Come on in," he said. "Use me all you want. You look fantastic."

"No," she said, staying where she was on the front steps. "I can't anymore."

He stepped through his door and put one hand around the back of her neck, and another on the curve of her bottom. He pulled her roughly toward him and kissed her, hard, on the mouth. She tasted beer and desire, and pulled away, but he did not let go.

"You know you liked it," he said.

She nodded. "I did like it," she said. "It's true. But it's not going to make me feel better about what I lost. My grief deserves more respect than I've been giving it. If we lived in another time and place, I guess I'd be wearing black so everyone would know."

Jack let his hands fall to his sides. "That's the girl I remember from high school," he said. "The good girl. The rule follower."

She smiled a mirthless smile. "I'm afraid so," she said, and turned and walked away.

·45·

Lily

AT the end of June, Lily moved into the shed on the burned-out lot. There was nothing to throw out this time, nothing to assess. All her possessions could fit into four cardboard boxes. Eleanor brought home a set of eight-hundred-thread-count white sheets for the new bed, and Luke insisted on going to Target and buying towels for the little bathroom. "I'm all over Target now," he said. "I've got that place wired."

Gordon put the boxes in the back of Luke's truck, and they all drove together up the hill. The closer they got to the lot, the quieter they got, until they weren't speaking at all. When Luke pulled into the driveway, Eleanor turned around to look at Lily in the backseat. "Are you sure about this?" she asked. "Gordon and I are happy to have you stay with us for as long as you'd like."

Lily nodded, and gasped for air, because she was crying so hard and it was hard to breathe. "Tom and I moved to this piece of land because we wanted to be together. We didn't want to get complacent about our love or our lives. We didn't want to take any of it for granted." She gulped more air. "I still feel all that here. I feel him."

"He would be glad that you're going to keep the ranch, Mom," Luke said.

"I don't know how I'll do managing the trees and all, but I'm going to try. And I want to be with Luna," Lily said. "I know it sounds strange, but I feel safe with her."

"It doesn't sound strange," Eleanor said. "It doesn't sound strange at all." She remembered when Lily and Tom first moved to Burlington, to a terrible little apartment with windows that barely kept out the cold. She kept wanting to give them money for a better house, better furniture, better window coverings, and they kept refusing. Eleanor was certain their marriage would crumble under the strain of those conditions, but it never did. She had been so wrong about them.

They all got out of the truck and carried the boxes past the burned-out house, down through the dappled shade of the avocado trees, and into the shed. There was a small box on the doorstep, wrapped in the comics from the newspaper and tied with twine. The card was from Nadine, and it said simply, *Welcome home.* Lily tore off the paper to reveal a pair of goatskin leather gardening gloves, women's size small.

Lily stepped into the shed, set the gloves on the workbench, and then placed her lumpy little ceramic bowl beside it. She dug into one of the boxes and got out a new stainless steel dog bowl,

341

a red webbed leash, and a rubber bone, and set them on the floor.

"That's it," she said to her mother and her younger son. "That's everything."

THE next morning, Nadine arrived at eight o'clock, and from the shed, Lily could hear her truck stop, her door slam, and then Luna yelping. The noise grew closer and closer until the dog was at her door. Luna threw her body at Lily, her paws clawing her legs, her tongue wagging. Lily sat down on the floor and wrestled with Luna, and rubbed her belly and her ears, and Luna lapped at her face.

"This is one crazy dog," Lily said when Nadine appeared. She was carrying a chain saw in one hand, and a length of rope in the other.

"You're telling *me*?" Nadine asked. Luna lunged from one woman to the other and back again. "I'm just glad she's your problem now."

"Thanks for taking such good care of her," Lily said.

Nadine shrugged. "My pleasure."

"What's the saw for?" Lily asked.

"To remove the damaged branches from those trees," Nadine said. "We'll have to paint them with a calcium-lime mix to prevent bugs and decay."

Lily nodded. "Let me get my gloves," she said.

The three of them walked through the shade of

the trees toward the part of the orchard that had burned.

"Tom was planning on going organic," Nadine said, "but I don't know if you want to make the switch right away. It will take a few months to complete the transition, and we'll lose some yield along the way."

"I want to make the switch," Lily said.

Nadine stopped and set down her saw. "He would have been a very good farmer," she said.

Lily's eyes teared up. She was so tired of being surprised, time and again, that Tom was really gone. Sometimes she was mad at him, and other times she just desperately missed him, and she wanted to yell at him, and to take him in her arms, and to tell him she was sorry, and to ask him to forgive her. Her relationship to Tom was still so complex, and yet he was no longer here for all the ordinary things—the chores and the meals, the discussions about what was going on that day. That was the part she missed the most.

She turned toward Nadine. "He was a very good husband," she said.

READERS GUIDE

DISCUSSION QUESTIONS
PLUS
TWO BEHIND-THE-SCENES MOMENTS
FROM THE AUTHOR

1. *The Threadbare Heart* explores the intersection of marriage and love, and the same question seems to lurk in each of the character's minds: What makes marriage work? Which character has the answer you most agree with?

2. Throughout *The Threadbare Heart*, Lily and Tom alternate between cherishing their knowledge of each other and wondering if they are capable of knowing each other at all. What does it mean to truly know someone?

3. Eleanor and Lily both see the avocado farm as the answer to their familial problems, but for different reasons. Eleanor has money to burn and wants her loved ones near, whereas Lily sees the opportunity as a fresh start that could reinvigorate her marriage. Are their expectations met?

4. Lily is emotionally attached to the fabric she has collected throughout her life. She observes that Eleanor never holds on to things—or

people—because holding on leaves a person vulnerable to pain. Lily says that for Eleanor "fabric is just a means to an end." What does she mean?

5. Were you surprised at Gordon's feelings for Eleanor? Why or why not?

6. Lily's friend Marilyn and her mother seem to share the belief that you should put yourself first in marriage and in life. Lily feels differently; she credits her willingness to compromise as one of the keys to her long marriage. Whose beliefs serve them better?

7. The theme of love in marriage is at the core of *The Threadbare Heart*. According to Eleanor, love is an illusion and you're better off keeping it at a safe distance. On the opposite end of the spectrum is Gordon, who believes that love is a choice. Where does Lily fall on the spectrum? What effect does losing Tom have on her perception of love?

8. Ryan constantly compares his marriage with Olivia to that of his parents, and constantly comes up short. Can Ryan and Olivia's marriage be saved? Where do you think they might be five years from now?

9. At one point Eleanor refers to her first hus-

band's sudden death as an "elegant solution" to the dilemma of her unhappy marriage. Is her brutal honesty refreshing, cold, or somewhere in between?

10. Do you agree with Lily's decision to send Tom's remains back to Vermont to be buried in a cemetery instead of cremated?

11. Discuss the physical relationship between Jack and Lily. What do you think of Jack? Is he an opportunist taking advantage of a vulnerable person, or is there legitimacy to this informal sort of therapy known as sexual healing?

12. Why do you think Lily decides to incinerate her wedding ring? How is the process therapeutic for her?

13. Grandma Hattie's lace becomes a significant metaphor for untapped potential. As Lily puts it, "The life of the lace had been one of longing, of waiting, of stories not told." How do you think Lily would describe the story she ultimately tells with the lace?

BEHIND-THE-SCENES MOMENT #1
THE GREAT DATE

This story was inspired, in part, by a real-life romance. My parents met on a blind date on their first weekend of college in 1956—and just like the characters in this story, they drove off in an old Studebaker, the girls sitting on the boys' laps. My mom had just started at Wellesley College and my dad at Harvard. There were four other couples on that same date, and two of the couples were married right after their college graduations—including my mom and dad. That was June 1960. Although my parents are both great individuals, they didn't have a great marriage— or at least not a long-lasting one. They were divorced when I was thirteen years old.

One of the other men on the original date was my dad's roommate, Doug. He married a lovely woman named Lesley and stayed happily married to her for thirty-eight years until her death from lung cancer. Six years ago, in 2003—which was forty-seven years after the weekend they met— Doug and my mother were married at a church by the sea in Santa Barbara. They make a wonderful couple, and I'm very happy that Doug is now part of our family.

BEHIND-THE-SCENES MOMENT #2
SANTA BARBARA'S WILDFIRE SEASON

I grew up in Santa Barbara, and have carried an image of the terrible beauty of wildfires in my head my whole life. I vividly remember standing outside our house in the dark, looking at the angry flames, the burning hills, the billowing smoke, and I remember hearing the adults talk about plans for escape, and plans for what to save. No one talked about moving away from the tinder-dry hills; it was considered well worth the risk to live in that beautiful red-roofed town.

When I was in the middle of writing this book, and after I had written the fire scenes, Santa Barbara was struck by two devastating wildfires. I live two hours to the south of the city, so I watched on TV, filled with the special horror of knowing that the devastation I made up on the page was actually happening to real people in real time. There was something very strange about that reality—as if my writing—my act of imagination—had somehow contributed to the fact of the fire in the real world. It's hard to explain what I mean, but it was a disturbing few days, where I questioned whether or not I should keep the fire in my book. I could choose whether or not my house stood or my character lived, whereas there were hundreds of people who could not.

And then my mother called to tell me that she had half an hour to evacuate from her home in Santa Barbara, and that she was packing her car and would be at my house by dinner. Suddenly, the lists I had made up of things my character remembered from her destroyed home were instructive. "Don't just take what you need," I told my mom. "Take some things you want, too." Along with clothes and some paperwork, she took the seal coat she's had since she was eighteen years old.

Her house was fine, in the end—at least this time. And I was left with the awesome knowledge of exactly how life mirrors story, and story informs life.

Center Point Publishing

600 Brooks Road ● PO Box 1
Thorndike ME 04986-0001 USA

(207) 568-3717

US & Canada:
1 800 929-9108
www.centerpointlargeprint.com

STUDIES IN HISTORY, ECONOMICS AND
PUBLIC LAW

Edited by the
FACULTY OF POLITICAL SCIENCE
OF COLUMBIA UNIVERSITY

———

NUMBER 416

*AMERICAN OPINION OF ROMAN CATHOLICISM
IN THE EIGHTEENTH CENTURY*

BY

SISTER MARY AUGUSTINA (RAY), B. V. M.

AMERICAN OPINION
OF ROMAN CATHOLICISM IN THE
EIGHTEENTH CENTURY

SISTER MARY AUGUSTINA (RAY), B.V.M.

OCTAGON BOOKS

A DIVISION OF FARRAR, STRAUS AND GIROUX

New York   1974

Copyright 1936 by Columbia University Press

Reprinted 1974
by special arrangement with Columbia University Press

OCTAGON BOOKS
A DIVISION OF FARRAR, STRAUS & GIROUX, INC.
19 Union Square West
New York, N. Y. 10003

140661

Library of Congress Cataloging in Publication Data

Ray, Mary Augustina, Sister, 1880-
 American opinion of Roman Catholicism in the eighteenth century.

 Reprint of the ed. published by Columbia University Press, New
York, which was issued as no. 416 of Studies in history, economics, and public law.

 Bibliography: p.
 1. Religious liberty—United States. 2. Catholics in the United
States. 3. United States—History—Colonial period, ca. 1600-
1775. 4. Public opinion—United States. 5. Religious tolerance.
6. Prejudices and antipathies. I. Title. II. Series: Columbia
studies in the social sciences, no. 416.

BX1406.R35   1974   301.15'43'28273   74-5254
ISBN 0-374-96723-7

Manufactured by Braun-Brumfield, Inc.
Ann Arbor, Michigan

Printed in the United States of America

FOREWORD

THAT most Americans of our colonial era, who were religious at all, were definitely—not to say aggressively—Protestant is well known. What is not so generally realized is the extent and intensity of anti-Catholic feeling. This state of mind, originating in old-world controversies, came across the sea with the seventeenth-century pioneers, was reinforced by subsequent immigrant groups, as well as by the international rivalries of the eighteenth century, and still later found expression in several state constitutions of the early republic. The writer of the following monograph has given us for the first time a comprehensive, thoroughly documented, and accurate account of this phase of early American history. The study is not of course concerned with the merits or demerits of particular religious systems—the truth or falsity of the ideas expressed by their respective advocates. Prejudices and justified opinions are equally facts with which the historian has to reckon.

The ecclesiastical *imprimatur* prefixed to this monograph is required by the rules of the society of which the writer is a member. It was secured after the manuscript had been recommended by members of the Faculty of Political Science in Columbia University as a work of sound historical scholarship, worthy of inclusion in the series of which it forms a part.

EVARTS B. GREENE.

5

PREFACE

DURING the last quarter of the eighteenth century, the period of the making of our first state constitutions, religious liberty was an ideal which only a small minority of our legislators were willing to make a reality for all. The goal had been set, however, and the next fifty years saw the gradual removal of most legal discriminations. Unfortunately their disappearance from the statute books did not produce a corresponding change in the mental attitude of the American public, as periodic waves of religious bigotry have testified. Something further was needed to eradicate hereditary or acquired antipathies, on the one hand, and to create or strengthen the cordial relationships of the various religious denominations, on the other.

To this end the efforts both of individuals and of organized groups have been directed; with what success it is difficult to say. Positive achievement in such an undertaking is not easy to measure. Whatever the accomplishment, much remains to be done. Better understanding should make for more kindly feeling, for to know all is to forgive all. Towards this better understanding it is hoped that this study will make some slight contribution, since it has assayed not only a survey of early American opinion of Roman Catholicism, but also an investigation of its origins. Given such opinions with such derivations, the wonder is not that Roman Catholics have been the subject of religious discriminations, but that these have been removed as quickly and as completely as they have.

7

It is a pleasure to acknowledge the unfailing courtesy and helpfulness of various library staffs throughout the country. To the librarians of the Newberry Library, Chicago, of the manuscripts division of the New York Public Library, and of the various divisions of the Library of Congress, I am especially indebted. The courtesy of Mr. Walter Briggs of the Widener Library, Harvard University, placed at my disposal manuscript copies of the Dudleian Lectures. The kindness of Dr. Earl G. Swem made available the second volume of his Virginia *Historical Index* while it was still in manuscript. To Professor J. A. Krout of Columbia University and to Reverend J. McCormick, S.J., of Loyola University, Chicago, I owe special thanks for their careful reading of the manuscript and for helpful criticisms. My greatest debt is to Professor Evarts B. Greene at whose suggestion this study was begun. To his scholarly guidance and kindly encouragement it owes much.

S. M. A.

Mundelein College, Chicago.

TABLE OF CONTENTS

CHAPTER I

The English Historical Tradition to 1688

The mother country of the United States was England in the first half of the seventeenth century, or, at most, England before the Revolution of 1688. From the English spoken in the days of the Stuart kings came our primitive speech, and the opinions, prejudices and modes of thinking of the English of that day lay at the bottom of what intellectual life there was in the colonies.—Edward Eggleston, *Transit of Civilization from England to America in the Seventeenth Century* (New York, 1901), pp. 1-2.

If the passage quoted above be true of the intellectual life of our Revolutionary forefathers—and there are few who will not grant it—much more is it true of their religious preconceptions. In a very special manner does it apply to the colonial and Revolutionary attitude towards the Church of Rome and her followers. One needs to read neither long nor widely in the early history of our country to realize that one of the strongest of these characteristic " prejudices " was a deeply instilled hatred of " Popery " and of everything which that term connoted.

Religious persecution did not of course begin with the Protestant Revolt. The history of Christianity—to go back no further—furnishes too many instances of a misguided zeal which would force its beliefs upon others, presumably less enlightened, in order to secure their salvation. Nor did the controversial methods, which were so popular in the sixteenth century and later, owe their origin to that period of religious turmoil. As early as the fourteenth century Wycliffe and his followers had set the fashion for coarse invective against the Papacy.[1] This is not to hail him as the " Father of the Reformation," nor to establish a direct tradition between his followers and those of Luther. The latter, like the former, were the children of their own age. Polemics in those days were intolerant, abusive, and concentrated not so much upon the elucidation of truth as on proving one's enemy in the wrong. With individual exceptions, no single sect or nation was free from these undesirable traits; to say that they were characteristic of the Protestant reformers is but to class them with their own generation. To make good their claim to have restored Christianity to its primitive simplicity, they undertook to prove that the Church from which they had seceded was false, and not only false, but the embodiment of all evil, the source of all corruption.

Begun by Luther and Calvin on the continent, the " No-Popery campaign " was taken up in England by Barnes [2] and Bale [3] who were quick to see the advantage, for purposes of

---

[1] John Wycliffe, *Select English Works*, Thomas Arnold, ed. (3 vols., Oxford, 1869-71). See index under papal bulls, celibacy, indulgences, infallibility, monks, papacy, pope, sacraments, tithes, Urban VI. Mark Tierney, *Dodd's Church History of England from the Commencement of the Sixteenth Century to the Revolution in 1688. With Notes, Additions, and a Continuation* (5 vols., London, 1839). (Cited hereafter as Dodd-Tierney), vol. i, pp. 147-49, n. *Cf.* T. C. Hall, *The Religious Background of American Culture* (Boston, 1930), pp. 23, 32.

[2] Robert Barnes, "The Works of Doctour Barnes" in *The Whole Works of W. Tyndall, John Frith and Doct. Barnes*... (London, 1572), pp. 177-376 and *passim*. *Cf.* Robert Barnes and John Bale, *Scriptores duo Anglici, Coaetanei ac Conterranei, de Vitis Pontificum Romanorum*... Lugduni Batavorum (1615). (Copy in Union Theological Seminary, New York), *passim*.

[3] John Bale, *The Apology of John Bale agaynst a ranke Papyst, aunsering both hym and hys doctours, that neyther their vowes nor yet their priesthode are of the Gospell, but of antichrist* (Anno D. 1550), *passim. Pageant of Popes* (London, 1574), *passim. Select Works*... containing the Examination of Lord Cobham, William Thorpe, and Ann Askewe, and the Image of Both Churches*, Parker Soc. (Cambridge, 1894). See " Image ", pp. 249-640.

popular appeal, of the historical over the theological argument. In their avowed purpose of exposing the iniquities of " Popish tyranny ", special prominence was given to those authors who shared their anti-Papal complex. Their highest meed of praise was bestowed upon those writers whose indictment of the Church seemed most convincing and comprehensive. It remained for their more popular contemporaries, Foxe [4] and Knox,[5] to complete this campaign of education in hatred and to instil their religious prejudices into the minds and hearts of thousands whom their less widely read rivals failed to reach. Such were the beginnings in England of that " poisoning of the wells of thought ", of that coloring and distorting of a " great national literature ", which became for non-Catholic English writers a " controlling tradition." [6] It is the purpose of this chapter to indicate some of the salient features of this tradition and the processes by which it was built up.

If the average Englishman of the sixteenth or seventeenth century were asked to sum up the policy of the Catholic Church on educational or intellectual matters in general, he had at his fingers' tips a formula, clear, terse, and, to his mind, comprehensive: " Ignorance is the mother of devotion." By that he meant that Rome deliberately kept her children in the grossest ignorance that she might the more easily exact from them a blind adherence to her teachings. Superstition, he would tell you, took the place of an enlightened piety which it was one of the glories of the Reformation to have stimulated. In proportion as the masses were both ignorant and superstitious were they the more effective instruments in the hands of their unscrupulous guides.

---

[4] John Foxe, *Acts and Monuments* (8 vols., London, 1843-49), *passim.*

[5] John Knox, *The Historie of the Reformation of the Church in Scotland* (London, 1644), *passim.*

[6] Michael Williams, *Shadow of the Pope* (New York, 1932), pp. 20-22. *Cf.* Herbert Thurston, S.J., *No-Popery* (London, 1930), chs. i, xiv.

In the realm of morals, perhaps the adjectives " unmoral "
or " non-moral " would best describe the Protestant Englishman's notion of a religion whose tenets tended to deaden in
its votaries all sense of right and wrong. For not only
were the grossest vices practiced with impunity; the Church's
traffic in dispensations and indulgences offered positive encouragement to a vicious life. This corruption pervaded all
classes, but was especially rife among those who made profession of a blameless life; that is, among the clergy and
the religious orders. So numerous were their opportunities
for spreading vice under the cloak of religion, that their
presence in a community might be likened to a hidden cancer
secretly spreading its virus through the entire social organism.
Against the ancient Church as a religious system the reformers preferred many charges. Of these the following
pages will furnish numerous examples. After several generations of controversy, exigencies of time and space demanded briefer treatment than was the custom in the early
years of the revolt, so the indictment came to be summed up
in two words: tyranny and idolatry.[7] In virtue of her claim
to infallibility and by means of manifold and minute pre-
scriptions, the Church of Rome so " forced the consciences
of men " as to destroy completely the liberty of the children
of God. Under her tutelage theirs was the servile homage
of a slave rather than the filial devotion of a child. As to
the spiritual food which this despot gave her children, it was
the grossest idolatry. Whatever portion of the truth " delivered to the saints " had been hers in the primitive ages of

---

[7] For an example of one of the earlier Elizabethan indictments of the
Church see Bishop Jewel's *Challenge*, drawn up under twenty-seven
heads, the last of which is " ignorance is the mother or the cause of true
devotion." *Documentary Annals of the Reformed Church of England;
being a Collection of Injunctions, Declarations, Orders, Articles of
Inquiry, etc., from the Year 1716; with notes historical and explanatory*
by Edward Cardwell (2 vols., Oxford, 1844), vol. i, p. 287 et seq.

Christianity, Rome had so perverted the teaching of Christ,
so encumbered it with doctrinal and ritualistic observances
of her own invention, that she had become the very antithesis of what she claimed to be—Antichrist.   Nor was this
term as applied by the reformers to Roman Catholicism a
mere figure of speech.   Quite literally the Church had become in their opinion unchristian, so that they habitually
classed her with pagans, Mohammedans, Turks.   Theirs was
the lesser sin, indeed, since to them, presumably, had never
been vouchsafed that revelation of the truth which Rome
had bartered for a mess of pottage.   She was the " Beast ",
the " Scarlet Woman " of the Apocalypse, who, usurping the
throne of the Almighty, had demanded for herself the homage due to Him alone.

To this conception of Roman Catholicism as an intellectual, moral and religious system, must be added another
feature without which much of the fear which she inspired,
much of the hatred with which she was regarded would be
unintelligible.   Rome wielded temporal as well as spiritual
power.   In domestic as well as in international politics she
was a force to be reckoned with.   For centuries she had
been the arbiter of Christendom, had made and unmade
kings.   The friend of absolutism in temporal no less than
in spiritual affairs, she was nevertheless the foe of any government which she could not control for her own ends.   If
kings were not amenable to her suggestions, it were no great
task to persuade their subjects that *vox populi* was *vox Dei*.
And did not Rome absolve subjects from their allegiance?
Did she not teach that faith need not be kept with heretics?
Worse still, were not the Jesuits justifying tyrannicide, and
teaching that the end justifies the means?

In an age when the establishment of state churches was
one of the many manifestations of the strong current of
nationalism in European politics, when with few exceptions

it was conceded by Catholic and Protestant alike that religious dissent was a standing menace to national unity, the international interests of the Papacy, a bond of union in a united Christendom, were naturally regarded with distrust by Protestant England. The superior allegiance which Catholics presumably owed the Pope even in civil affairs, their enthusiasm for his far-reaching schemes, religious or secular, were looked upon as dangerous diversions of an interest which might otherwise have been utilized to swell the tide of national consciousness. The Papal alliance with her traditional enemies, France and Spain, tended but to strengthen England's suspicions. Too often were these fears confirmed; when they were not, popular imagination, ever ready to transfer to a nation or a religion the real or imaginary qualities of a hero or villain, supplied the deficit. At the close of the seventeenth century hero and villain had become stereotyped: the hero, " Protestantism and English liberties," was embodied in the person of Elizabeth; the villain, " Popery and Slavery," was typified not by a single individual but by three, with the central figure holding the place of honor—Guy Fawkes, the Pope, the Devil.

In the production of this composite picture the clergy and the official pronouncements of the Reformed Church of England played no inconsiderable part. A good beginning was made in the short reign of Edward VI. The *Book of Common Prayer* had this petition in the Litany: " From the enormities of the Bishop of Rome, Good Lord, deliver us." [8] From time to time directions or " Injunctions " were issued to the clergy, who among other things were admonished to observe the statutes for abolishing the " pretended and usurped power " of the Bishop of Rome. Four times a year

---

[8] E. Cardwell, *Doc. Annals*, vol. i, p. 211. *Cf. Dodd-Tierney*, vol. ii, pp. 31-33; H. N. Birt, *The Elizabethan Religious Settlement* (London, 1907), p. 27. The petition was omitted in the Elizabethan revision.

they were to preach against the same bishop as well as on the " idolatry " inherent in the use of candles, images, and the like.[9] Under Elizabeth these exhortations became monthly, while in 1604 the " Constitutions and Canons Ecclesiastical " decreed that they should form part of the regular Sunday service.[10] To supply the lack of trained preachers as well as to form a " pattern and a boundary, as it were, for preaching ministers," [11] a collection of sermons or " Homilies " was prepared. Compiled partly in the reign of Edward and partly in that of Elizabeth, they received the sanction of both sovereigns. Later when the Forty-two Articles were superseded by the Thirty-nine, article thirty-five of the latter code honored the " Homilies " with a special recommendation.[12] These sermons ran the entire gamut of the Reformation charges against the Papacy— civil, political, religious. He would be dull indeed who, having listened to them over a period of years and having no other influence to counteract their teaching, would fail to be convinced that Roman Catholicism was a deadly menace to the individual, to the state, and to the world at large.[13]

It is to be noted that one of the reasons for the composition of the " Homilies " and for the insistence on their being read without " enlargement or comment," [14] was to prevent the more intemperate preachers from " exasperating the op-

[9] E. Cardwell, *Doc. Annals*, vol. i, pp. 4, 211.

[10] E. Cardwell, *Synodalia. A collection of articles of religion, canons, and proceedings of Convocations in Canterbury* (2 vols., Oxford, 1842), vol. i, pp. 273, 275.

[11] E. Cardwell, *Doc. Annals*, vol. ii, p. 20. *Cf.* vol. i, pp. 202, 205, 251, 306.

[12] *Ibid.*, vol. i, pp. 4, 49, 211; *Dodd-Tierney*, vol. ii, pp. 38-39.

[13] *Certaine Homilies appointed to be Read in the Churches*, G. E. Corrie, ed. (London, 1850), pp. 113, 168-272, 551, 584, 589.

[14] E. Cardwell, *Synodalia*, vol. i, pp. 273, 275.

posite party." [15]   Elizabeth herself, at least in the early years of her reign, and the more moderate reformers, wished to conciliate the Catholics rather than drive them to retaliation. So the "Homilies", extreme as they are from a Catholic viewpoint, represent a *via media,* if not a closer approach to conciliation.[16]

If the unlicensed [17] clergy were obliged to adhere to the text of the "Homilies", the licensed preachers, provided they kept within the bounds of orthodoxy, were apparently unfettered.   Called forth not infrequently by some event of local importance, such as the opening of Parliament, a public fast or thanksgiving, or as a contribution to the well-nigh perennial controversies of the age, these occasional discourses reveal none of that hesitancy which presumably restrained the writers of the "Homilies."   High Churchman or Low Churchman, the speaker too often availed himself of the opportunity to invite invidious comparisons with the ancient Church.

Typical of the extreme High Church position is that of Archbishop Laud.   His effort to invest the church services with beauty and dignity called forth many attacks from the Low Church party, as well as from Non-conformists.   For one of these, *News from Ipswich,* the author, William Prynne, had been cited before the Star Chamber.   After the

---

[15] *Dodd-Tierney,* vol. ii, pp. 38-39.

[16] *Ibid.*

[17] Owing to the dearth of licensed preachers it was often necessary to utilize the services of laymen or of unlicensed clergymen.   There was danger that the zeal of the latter might exceed the bounds of prudence and that their lack of learning might result in an unorthodox (from the Reformation viewpoint) exposition of the new religion.   These unlicensed preachers were therefore instructed to adhere strictly to the Book of Homilies and to read without comment the Homily designated for the day.   See the Injunctions of Edward VI (1547) and of Elizabeth (1559) in *Dodd-Tierney,* vol. ii, pp. xxxix, xlv, cclv-cclvi, cclxxi.

trial, Laud took occasion to deliver a speech in defense of his measures. He indignantly denied the existence of plots to overthrow the " Orthodox Religion established in England. . . . As if the externall decent worship of God could not be upheld in this Kingdome, without the bringing in of Popery." [18]   With equal fervor he answered the charges of double dealing preferred against the clergy. They are not " so base," he exclaimed, " as to live Prelates in the Church of England, & Labour to bring in the Superstitions of the Church of Rome." [19]   The last " innovation " of which the *News from Ipswich* complained was the omission of the prayer for the navy. Since there was at the time no enemy on the sea, the archbishop explained, he saw no objection to the omission; unless, he added, those who make it intend to bring in " the whore of Babylon." [20]

Representative of the Latitudinarians, but of a generation later than Laud, was Archbishop Tillotson, whose charity towards the dissenters did not however extend to Catholics. A dissenter before he became an Anglican, his early affiliation doubtless accounts for his sympathy for the former and his antipathy to Rome. A note in an unknown hand on the flyleaf of one of his sermons [21] describes him as " distinguished for his opposition to popery both in preaching and from the press." His sermons leave no doubt as to the

[18] William Laud, *A Speech Delivered in the Starre-Chamber, on Wednesday, the xivth of June, 1637* (London, 1637), p. 11. *Cf.* W. H. Hutton, *The English Church from the Accession of Charles I to the Death of Anne, 1625-1714* (London, 1903), pp. 67-69.

[19] Laud, *op. cit.*, p. 13.

[20] *Ibid.*, p. 40. *Cf. A. Relation of the Conference betweene William Laud, . . . And Mr. Fisher the Jesuite, by the Command of King James of ever Blessed Memorie* (London, 1639). Henry Sacheverell, *Perils of False Brethren, both in Church and State* (London, 1709).

[21] John Tillotson, *A Sermon Preached at Lincolns-Inn-Chapel, On the 31st of January, 1688* (London, 1689). Copy in Library of Congress (L. C.).

truth of the characterization. The very titles often reveal their viewpoint. *A Seasonable New-years Gift against Popery* [22] has for its thesis that to the essentials of Christianity one may make such additions as may endanger one's salvation. Of this the Church of Rome is the outstanding example. To the fundamental doctrines of Christianity she has added infallibility, purgatory, Transubstantiation, deposition of a heretic king and absolution of his subjects from their allegiance, and so on. In another discourse he speaks of " the restless and black Designs of that sure and inveterate Enemy of ours, the Church of Rome." It was through her " unwearied Malice and Arts " that the " seeds of Dissention were scattered early among us." Had it not been for the " Popish alliances " of the Stuarts this foe would in all probability have been exterminated.[23]

To these illustrations of the attitude of Anglican churchmen towards Roman Catholicism might be added many others which undoubtedly would have weight as cumulative evidence but which would add little that is new. A catalogue of discourses published by Anglicans and Non-conformists during the short reign of James II lists 228 titles for the former. Even a cursory reading of titles and authors is sufficient to convince one that the views expressed by Laud and Tillotson are not isolated instances of anti-Catholic bias but representative rather of the Anglican clergy as a whole.[24]

[22] John Tillotson, *A Seasonable New-Years Gift against Popery. A Sermon preached at Whitehall before King Charles the Second* (London, n. d.).

[23] Tillotson, *Sermon Preached at Lincolns-Inn-Chapel.* Cf. *Works* (10 vols., London, 1820), vol. ii, pp. 223-29, 245-47, 266-67, 279.

[24] Edward Gee, *A Catalogue of All the Discourses published against Popery, During the Reign of James II by the Members of the Church of England, and by the Non-conformists* (London, 1689).

If Roman Catholicism was a thorn in the side of the Established Church it was not the only source of irritation. There was Non-conformity in all its varying aspects. As the Puritans emerged from the dissident ranks of the Anglicans, as they in turn ramified into Presbyterians, Independents, Separatists, Baptists, Quakers and other shades of dissent, the Establishment found itself confronted with a multiplicity of sects whose very existence challenged its privileged position. Out of the numerous and well-nigh endless controversies which arose from the conflict of opinion thus engendered, there emerged what was perhaps the only common ground between Conformity on the one hand and the various aspects of Non-conformity on the other—their hatred, deep and abiding, of Catholicism. If Puritan taunted Anglican for retaining in his services the "rags of Popery," if he characterized the English *Prayer Book* as an "unperfect book, culled and picked out of the popish dunghill, the Portuise and mass-book," [25] the Churchman retorted that "running into conventicles" and thereby "worshipping God according to an imagination of their own erecting," was idolatry and therefore "Popery." [26]   Nor did he fail to point out the "Popery" inherent in the Nonconformist's objection to the doctrine of passive obedience and non-resistance.[27]   The controversial literature of the period is full of contemptuous, not to say scurrilous, references to all that Catholics hold sacred.   In an age when polemics were anything but urbane, Quaker [28] and Anabap-

---

[25] W. H. Frere, *A History of the English Church in the Reigns of Elizabeth and James I, 1558-1625* (London, 1904), p. 179, *cf.* pp. 196, 203.

[26] A. A. Seaton, *The Theory of Toleration under the Later Stuarts* (Cambridge University Press, 1911), pp. 192-93.

[27] *Ibid.*, pp. 126-27.

[28] George Fox, *The Arraignment of Popery* (1669), pp. 23, 81, 84, 96, *et seq.* Cf. Robert Barclay, *Anarchy of the Ranters, and other Libertines; the Hierarchy of the Romanists and other Pretended Churches,*

tist,[29] no less than Churchman [30] and Presbyterian,[31] contributed to the building up of that tradition which identified the Papacy with " that highest distinction in the Puritan vocabulary "—Antichrist.[32]

But the religious conditions of the age were not the only factors which contributed to the evolution of that tradition. Politics, domestic and foreign, played an important part. If today men do not hesitate to utilize religious passion for political ends, they did so all the more readily in an age when national security was thought to be bound up with religious unity.[33] Catholics were already suspect because of their spiritual allegiance to the Pope. The line between ecclesiastical and political loyalty was by no means clearly drawn. The ambiguity of the oaths of supremacy and of allegiance worried not a few, Protestants as well as Catholics; their lack of clarity offered to others the opportunity

equally refused and refuted (London, 1733), sec. 8. William Penn, "A Seasonable Caveat against Popery," in *A Collection of the Works of William Penn. In Two Volumes. To Which is Prefixed A Journal of His Life. With many Original Letters and Papers Not Before Published* (2 vols., London, 1726), vol. i, pp. 467-85.

29 Benjamin Harris, ed., *Protestant (Domestick) Intelligence, or News both from City and Country. Published to prevent false reports* (London, 1679-80), *passim. Cf. Protestant Tutor* (London, 1679), *passim.* A. A. Seaton, *op. cit.*, pp. 98-104.

30 *Supra*, pp. 18-20. See also sermons of Bishop Burnet and Archbishop Tenison.

31 Richard Baxter, *Jesuit Juggling. Forty Popish Frauds Detected and Disclosed* (First American edition with an Introductory Address, New York, 1835), *passim.* (The viewpoint of the Introduction is substantially that of Baxter.) *Cf.* F. J. Powicke, *Life of Richard Baxter, 1615-1691* (London, 1924), pp. 195, 258, 259. M. Sylvester, *Reliquiae Baxterianiae* . . . (London, 1696), bk. i, pp. 112, 118; bk. ii, p. 373; bk. iii, pp. 181, 183.

32 W. H. Frere, *op. cit.*, p. 311; W. H. Frere and C. E. Douglas, eds., *Puritan Manifestoes* (London, 1907). (Church Historical Society, vol. lxxxii), *passim.*

33 A. A. Seaton, *Theory of Toleration*, pp. 30-35.

of attesting their whole-hearted loyalty to their sovereign. Catholics there were without number who were willing to die for Elizabeth, but who could not in conscience acknowledge her as head of the Church. To these it became increasingly evident, that, given the legal toleration for which they repeatedly petitioned, they might be loyal English subjects as well as faithful children of the Church.[34] To the mass of English Protestants, on the contrary, it was just as evident that every Catholic, in proportion to his fidelity to his religion, was a real or a potential traitor.[35] This conviction, strengthened by the papal bull of excommunication against Elizabeth and the freeing of her Catholic subjects from their allegiance,[36] received fresh confirmation from a series of events, domestic and international, the interaction of which did incalculable harm to the Catholic cause. The plots, real and fictitious, centering around Mary Stuart, the Northern Rising, the advent of the Jesuits and the seminary priests, the assassination of the Prince of Orange, the massacre of St. Bartholomew, the Spanish Armada—these by no means exhaust the catalogue of such occurrences in the long reign of Elizabeth. They may serve to indicate, however, the type of event which, fathered or fostered by individuals, groups or nations, but never by the whole body or even by a majority of English Catholics, was nevertheless attributed to the

---

[34] J. H. Pollen, "English Post-Reformation Oaths," *Catholic Encyclopedia*, vol. xi, pp. 177-180. "Politics of English Catholics in the Reign of Elizabeth," pt. vi, "After the Armada," *The Month* (Aug., 1902), vol. c, p. 176 *et seq.* *Cf.* Dodd-Tierney, vol. ii, p. 130; vol. iv, pp. 66-83. W. H. Frere, *Eng. Church*, pp. 330, 336, 338, 345, 373. P. Guilday, *English Catholic Refugees on the Continent, 1558-1795* (New York, 1914), pp. 242, 243, 248, 250.

[35] W. H. Frere, *op. cit.*, pp. 93-94. *Cf.* W. K. Jordan, *Development of Religious Toleration in England...to the Death of Elizabeth* (Harvard Univ. Press, 1932), pp. 119-26, 163-211.

[36] *Supra*, note 34.

entire group and was cited as an example of the practical effects of Catholic teaching.[37]

Upon the penal laws they acted at once as cause and effect. Every domestic intrigue, every political crisis on the continent, was the signal for fresh reprisals which in turn drove their victims to desperation. Oppressor and oppressed were slow to learn the lesson of the futility of force. The English government saw in the Gunpowder Plot [38] not the effects of its own harsh system nor the last desperate gamble of a group of fanatics, but fresh evidence that in the extermination of the Catholics lay the safety of the realm. During the interregnum Puritan logic reached the same grim conclusion save that it would purge the country of " prelacy " as well as of " Popery."

At the Restoration there was a change of actors but not of methods. Catholic hopes ran high. Charles had promised the Pope and the Catholic powers of Europe that he would do his utmost to have the penal laws repealed. Attempts to fulfill that promise proved that he had reckoned without his host. Declarations of Indulgence, even though

[37] For the activities of English Catholics during the reign of Elizabeth, see the series of articles by Rev. J. H. Pollen, S.J., " The Foreign Politics of English Catholics during the Reign of Elizabeth," *The Month*, vols. xcix, c (Jan.-Aug., 1902). Also, " Religious Persecution under Elizabeth," *The Month*, vol. civ (July-Dec., 1904), pp. 501-517. " Religious Terrorism under Elizabeth," *The Month*, vol. cv (1905), pp. 270-287. *Cf.* R. B. Merriman, " Some Notes on the Treatment of English Catholics in the Reign of Elizabeth," *American Historical Review*, vol. xiii (April, 1908), pp. 480-500. W. H. Frere, *Eng. Church*, pp. 3-4, 52, 74-96, 80-94, 134, 143, 176, 206-21. H. N. Birt, *Elizabethan Religious Settlement*, p. 473 *et seq.* H. Thurston, *No-Popery*, pp. 191-210. J. W. Thompson, *The Religious Wars of France* (Chicago, 1909), pp. 422-453. P. Guilday, *Eng. Cath. Refugees, passim.*

[38] W. H. Frere, *Eng. Church*, pp. 324-340. Dodd-Tierney, vol. iv, pp. 35-65. J. Lingard, *History of England*, rev. ed. edited by Hilaire Belloc (11 vols., New York, 1912). Cited hereafter as Lingard-Belloc, vol. vii, pp. 38-85.

they included all sects, were interpreted as intended primarily to relieve the " Romanists." The demand for their withdrawal was followed by new statutes which bore heavily upon dissenters as well as Catholics. When in 1672 Charles again attempted to suspend the penal laws, this time in virtue of his " supreme power in affairs ecclesiastical," Parliament, keenly alive to the monarch's leanings to French absolutism, pointed out the connection between " Popery, France and arbitrary power." The slogan was to grow in popularity and effectiveness for generations to come. The frenzy evoked by the Titus Oates plot did not die out until 1681, when Charles, defeated in every effort to relieve religious oppression, declared that he " dare not " save its last victim, Archbishop Plunket of Ireland. That year parliament met at Oxford. The London members as they marched from town wore on their hats streamers bearing the words, " No Popery, No Slavery." So strong was the anti-Catholic animus at the end of the reign that it was evident that a Catholic sovereign would have to walk warily if he wished to avoid disaster.[39]

Unfortunately James II pursued an opposite course. In doing so he acted contrary to the advice of influential Catholics at home and abroad. Even the reigning pontiff, Innocent XI, advised caution, lest a too precipitate policy should revive the fears of the Protestants. The results of his

[39] G. N. Clark, *Later Stuarts, 1660-1717* (Oxford, 1934), pp. 18-19, 21-22, 56, 72-77, 86-110. G. M. Trevelyan, *England under the Stuarts, 1603-1717* (London, 1925), pp. 428-434. Lingard-Belloc, vols. ix, x, ch. i. L. von Ranke, *History of England especially in the Seventeenth Century* (Eng. trans., 6 vols., 1875), vol. iii, pp. 496-497, 518. W. H. Hutton, *The English Church from the Accession of Charles I to the Death of Queen Anne, 1625-1714* (London, 1903), pp. 184-196, 202-208. F. J. Powicke, *Life of Rev. Richard Baxter*, pp. 195, 258-59, gives the attitude of the leader of the Presbyterian party. J. Pollock, *The Popish Plot* (London, 1903). *Cf.* J. G. Gerard, "History 'ex Hypothesi' and the Popish Plot," *The Month* (July, 1903), vol. c, pp. 2-22.

undoubtedly sincere, but, under the circumstances, rash course of action, are too well known to require more than the briefest mention here.   Almost from the King's accession, Protestants viewed with growing alarm his efforts to introduce complete religious toleration, his admission of Catholics to high office, civil and military, their entrance into Oxford and Cambridge, the opening of Catholic educational institutions, and above all the imprisonment of the seven recalcitrant bishops on their refusal to promulgate the King's last Declaration of Indulgence, 1688.   The climax came with the birth of an heir who undoubtedly would be reared a Catholic.[40]

The foreign policy of the later Stuarts tended in no way to weaken religious prejudice or to gratify national pride. That French subsidies enabled both monarchs to act independently of Parliament was known by some, guessed by others.   In the secret articles of the Treaty of Dover (June, 1670), Charles had agreed to make public profession of his conversion to Rome, at such time and under such circumstances, as he should deem expedient.   Should this avowal cause disturbances in England, Charles was to receive, if necessary, subsidies and troops from Louis XIV.[41]   When

[40] Henry Foley, S.J., *Records of the English Province of the Society of Jesus* (6 vols., London, 1875-80. Later edition, 7 vols., London, 1882), vol. v, p. 157.   Lord Acton, *Lectures on Modern History* (London, 1906), pp. 219-232.   Michael Ott, "Innocent XI," *Catholic Encyclopedia*, vol. viii, pp. 21-22.   H. Belloc, *James the Second* (New York, 1928), pp. 175-226.   G. M. Trevelyan, *England under the Stuarts*, pp. 428-439. L. Ranke, *Eng. in Seventeenth Century*, vol. iv, pp. 215-372.   W. H. Hutton, *Eng. Church*, pp. 217-233.

[41] The text of the Secret Treaty is given in Lingard's *England* (Edinburgh, 1902), vol. ix, Note B, pp. 503-510.   Article 2, reads in part:

2. Le seigneur roy de la Grande-Bretagne estant convaincu de la vérité de la religion catholique, et résolu d'en faire sa déclaration, et de se réconcilier avec l'eglise Romaine aussy tost que le bien des affaires de son royaume luy pourra permettre . . . néantmoins comme il se trouve quelques fois des esprits brouillons et inquiets qui s'efforcent de troubler la tranquillité publique . . . sa majesté de la Grande-Bretagne . . . seroit d'estre

these secret articles became public the combination of
" Popery, France and arbitrary government " took on a new
significance. Even before the revocation of the Edict of
Nantes, the Protestant courts of Europe were protesting
against French persecution of the Huguenots. The emigrants who reached England had a harrowing, if one-sided,
tale to tell. Elsewhere in Europe, notably in Savoy and in
Hungary, Protestants were being oppressed. In the Palatinate the new elector was reinstating the Catholic Church.[42]
That politics rather than zeal for religion dictated much of
this policy, that the Holy See repeatedly protested against
this harrying of the Protestants, that the coolness of Innocent
XI towards James II was not lessened by the latter's approval
of the arbitrary methods of Louis XIV [43]—all this was either
forgotten or ignored by the molders of public opinion in
England, and by that small but influential group whose interests were so well served by the Revolution of 1688.
English statesmen needed no Daniel to interpret the hand-
writing on the wall. To them it was evident that the days
of British liberty, of Protestantism, were numbered; in their
wake would come inevitably " Popery and slavery."

assuré en cas de besoin de l'assistance de sa majesté trèschrestienne,
laquelle ... a promis et promet de donner pour cet effet au dit seigneur
roy de la Grande-Bretagne la somme de deux millions de livres tournoises
... et en outre ledit seigneur roy trèschrestien s'oblige d'assister de troupes
sa majesté de la Grande-Bretagne, jusq'au nombre de six mille hommes de
pied s'il est besoin ...

[42] G. N. Clark, *Later Stuarts*, p. 124. Lingard-Belloc, vol. x, p. 319
et seq. W. H. Lecky, *History of England in the Eighteenth Century*
(8 vols., New York, 1891), vol. i, pp. 20-25, notes 1 and 2. L. Ranke,
Eng. in Seventeenth Century, vol. iv, pp. 371-384. A. F. Pollard, *Factors
in Modern History* (London, 1926), pp. 204-5. Charles Gérin, " Le
Pape Innocent XI et la Révocation de l'Edict de Nantes," *Revue des
Quéstions Historiques,* vol. xxiv (1878). Lord Acton, *op. cit.,* pp. 219-232.

[43] As to papal knowledge of the preliminaries of the Revolution of
1688 see C. Gérin, " Le Pape Innocent XI et la révolution anglaise de
1688," *Rev. des Qués. Hist.,* vol. xx (1876). *Cf.* Lingard-Belloc, vol. x,
p. 320, n.

The average Englishman of the age of the Stuarts as of today was not interested in fine theological distinctions. Nor did he know much if anything of the interaction of religion and politics, whether national or international. He was ready to take his opinions second hand, without, of course, suspecting that he was doing so. Like the " man in the street " today, he was willing to believe without questioning almost any story, however far-fetched, suggestive of corruption in high places. It was the successful appeal to this trait in human nature that was largely responsible for the development of the Protestant tradition of the Pope as the " Man of Sin." The main outlines of the pattern once determined, the details could be filled in or modified as occasion required. Half truths, statements twisted out of their context, historical legends with or without a basis of fact, individuals of sufficient notoriety to serve as symbols, local events such as the burning of London—from such materials would the details be fashioned to make the picture intelligible and attractive to the common man.

Into the dissemination and perpetuation of the tradition many factors entered. The parts played by the Established Church and the Non-conformist groups, by the government, by national and international politics have been sketched briefly. To these might be added various other agencies the discussion of which would however take us too far afield. Happily we have two documents—*Domestick Intelligence* and *The Protestant Tutor*—which throw considerable light upon late seventeenth-century methods of propaganda. They furnish us with a concrete picture of what the lower middle-class Englishman of the period thought of the Church of Rome and of what he wished his children to think of her. In other words, it is the historical tradition which was current in the century of the great Puritan migrations.

Benjamin Harris, editor or compiler of the two documents
in question, was himself a member of one of the most radical
of the dissenting sects, the Anabaptists. Some allowance,
therefore, must be made for exaggerations characteristic of
the individual as of the sect. Taking the documents by and
large, however, there are few passages that could not be
matched by Puritan and Quaker tracts, or by the supposedly
more conservative productions of a Laud, a Tillotson, or a
Burnet. They are moreover of special significance for this
study, for their editor later emigrated to New England where
for some time his Boston book-shop served as a center for
his propaganda.[44]

Anabaptist by religious persuasion, author, publisher and
bookseller by vocation, Benjamin Harris attracted attention during the first six years of his career by the publication
of many attacks upon Quakers and Catholics. In 1679 he
joined Titus Oates in the exposition of the so-called Popish
Plot.[45] On July seventh of the same year he published the
first number of *Domestick Intelligence, Or News both from
City and Country,* to which title he added as a *raison d'être,
Published to prevent false reports.* The paper ran under
that title until January thirteenth, 1680, when the fifty-sixth
number appeared as *Protestant (Domestick) Intelligence, Or
News both from City and Country.* The change of title is
significant, for it was in a country still trembling with the
terrors of plots and counterplots that Harris carried on his
propaganda. The issues of the paper, though numbered
consecutively from one to one hundred fourteen, did not
appear regularly, the checkered events of the editor's career
being no doubt responsible for the irregularity. The longest interruption, from April sixteenth to December twenty-
eighth, 1680, was due to the arrest, trial and conviction of

[44] *Cf. infra,* pp. 33, n. 53; 118, n. 8; 170-71, 173.
[45] J. G. Muddiman, *The King's Journalist* (London, 1923), p. 214.

Harris for having published Blount's seditious pamphlet, *An Appeal from the Country to the City.*[46] Once in prison, Harris resumed his editorial duties.

In keeping with the change of title was the increased emphasis which Harris placed on "revelations" of the Popish Plot. Constituting by far the greater portion of the news, these "revelations" were supplemented by a great variety of anti-Catholic propaganda. There were clerical scandals for those who were so minded. Accounts of French tyranny[47] and of persecution of Protestants[48] on the continent were intended to intensify national and religious rancor. Politics and religion were skillfully combined in the publication of writs of election with exhortations to return the same Protestant members because of their skill in detecting "popish plots." Petitions to exclude the Duke of York from the throne, details of the arrest and conviction of shopkeepers for selling "popish primers" and other "Romish trash" and "trumphery", celebrations of November fifth— nothing was too trivial or too important to furnish grist for the anti-Popery mill of Benjamin Harris. His advertisements alone merit careful study.[49] They illustrate well the persistency with which he kept the Roman menace before the minds of his readers. Books, pamphlets, plays, pageants, playing cards, games, catechisms, primers—all are made to serve his purpose. To one of these advertisements we shall now direct our attention.

---

[46] *Miscellaneous Works of Charles Blount, Esq.* (London, 1695), "An Appeal from the Country to the City," pp. 2-3. *Cf.* J. Lingard, *History of England* (10 vols., Edinburgh, 1902), vol. ix, p. 454.

[47] *Protestant (Domestick) Intelligence, Or News both from City and Country. Published to prevent false reports.* Photostat pub. by Mass. Hist. Soc. (Boston, 1918). See nos. 8, 9, 10, 14, 16, 26, 30, 31, 43, 95, 113.

[48] *Ibid.*, nos. 27, 29, 30, 94, 95.

[49] *Ibid.*, nos. 27, 29, 30, 94, 95.

There is lately published by Benjamin Harris, a Book Intitled, *The Protestant Tutor.* Instructing Children to Spell and Read English, and Grounding them in the True Protestant Religion, and Discovering the Errors and Deceits of the Papists. . . .[50]

The rest of the advertisement is practically a table of contents. It is at once typical of the compiler's appeal to anti-Catholic prejudice and a tribute to his shrewd business sense. The English book-market was probably well stocked with primers, but Harris saw in the excitement over the Titus Oates plot an opportunity of selling a new work of the kind, which, while embodying a few educational features, would at the same time be " an unfailing encouragement to persecute Roman Catholics." [51]   The popularity of the book is attested by its various editions.

The title page gives the keynote of the tract—for such it is—and establishes the proper mental attitude. If the childish student, still struggling with the alphabet, be unable to read, the framework of illustrations will not fail to convey the desired impression. Two of these, companion pictures of the lower margin, are labeled respectively " Cruelty " and " Popery." In the former Catholics are industriously stirring up the fires which are consuming their Protestant brethren; in the latter, the monstrance is borne aloft in a procession of the Blessed Sacrament. The inference is plain; the religion which fosters such superstitious practices sanctions the persecution of those outside its fold.

With this orientation the child proceeds to the first lesson, " An Account of the Burning of the Pope at Temple Bar,

[50] *Ibid.,* no. 68.

[51] J. G. Muddiman, *King's Journalist,* p. 246 says that the *Tutor* filled a long felt want, " for there was no spelling book for children in existence," and that it ran through many editions. But see W. C. Ford, " The New England Primer " in *Bibliographical Essays: A Tribute to Wilberforce Eames* (Harvard Univ. Press, 1924), pp. 61-65.

Nov. 17, 1679." The date in question was the anniversary of the accession of Queen Elizabeth, a day celebrated in England with great pomp and pageantry. The account given in the *Tutor* is practically a reprint of that reported in *Domestick Intelligence* (November 18, 1679, No. 39), the day following the celebration. In 1679 the Popish Plot was the medium through which all public occurrences were viewed by Englishmen. What more natural, therefore, than to combine the celebration with a demonstration of the terrible plot? Besides interesting the populace, it would serve as an object lesson of what might be expected under a Catholic regime. The description of the pageant omits no detail of the fiendish design of the Papacy to subvert the civil and religious liberties of England and of all Europe. There were in the procession six Jesuits with " bloody consecrated daggers ", a priest who " gave pardons away very plentifully to all who would murder Protestants, and proclaiming it meritorious." Bringing up the rear was the Pope behind whom

stood the Devil, His Hollinesses Privy Counsellor, frequently Caressing, Huggling and Whispering him all the way, and often-times instructing him aloud to destroy His Majesty, to contrive a pretended Presbyterian Plot, and to fire the City again, to which purpose he held an Infernal sword in his hand. . . .

Arrived at Temple Bar the procession halted near the statue of Queen Elizabeth. Near by was a great bonfire into which the Pope was " decently tumbled." Throughout London could be heard

universal Acclamations, Long Live King Charles, and let Popery perish, and Papists with their Plots and Counter-Plots be forever confounded as they have hitherto been. To which every honest English Man will readily say, Amen.

Thus by a skillful combination of religious and patriotic elements the *Protestant Tutor* sketched for its young readers the traditional picture of Rome and her methods which for generations the mere mention of her name conjured up before the Protestant Briton. In another section of the primer ten additional pages are devoted to the details of the plot which is represented as the " Unanimous undertaking of the whole Romish Church." [52]

In the same vivid fashion the sufferings of the Marian martyrs are treated. Here, too, are the verses attributed to John Rogers and later incorporated into the *New England Primer*. There follow the story of the Armada, the Gunpowder Plot, the Rebellion in Ireland (1641), the Massacre of St. Bartholomew, the burning of London, 1666. This orgy of killing is relieved by a lesson from Holy Scripture, a syllabary and a " Catechism against Popery." [53]   The last question and answer of the catechism reads:

43. Q. May we joyn with Rome?

A. No. Rev. 18, 4, 5. I heard a Voice from Heaven, saying, Come out of her my People, that ye be not partakers of her Sins, and that ye receive not of her Plagues. For

[52] Pp. 83-93.

[53] This portion of the primer was reprinted in Boston in 1685 under the title of " The Protestant Tutor." It was printed by Samuel Green to be sold by John Griffith of Boston (1685). In 1686 Harris himself, obliged to flee from persecution in England, opened a book shop in Boston where he incorporated some features of the *Tutor* in his edition of the *New England Primer*. Although surrounded by seven other bookshops, Harris' "coffee-house", frequented by such local celebrities as the Mathers, not only held its own but became a center for the exchange of literary and political views. *Cf.* John Dunton, " Letters from New England " in *Publications of the Prince Society* (Boston, 1867), p. 143 *et seq. Life and Errors of John Dunton* (2 vols., London, 1818), vol. i, p. 217. W. C. Ford, note to photostat copy of *Domestick Intelligence,* Mass. Hist. Soc. (Boston, 1918). Frank Monaghan, " Benjamin Harris " in D. A. B., vol. viii, pp. 303-305.

her sins have reached unto Heaven, and God hath remembered her iniquities.

In the preface of the primer Harris acknowledges his indebtedness to Foxe. A further compliment to his master is " A Compendium of the Book of Martyrs in Verse." Foxe's influence is apparent all through the *Tutor*, but nowhere is it more evident than in the final series of horrors entitled, " A Short Account of the Variety of Popish Tortures Practised upon Protestants, with brief remarks of the Wicked Lives of several Popes of Rome." There is the same inaccuracy, the same exaggeration, the same one-sided presentation of events which won for the famous martyrologist's work the title of the Golden Legend.[54]

Small wonder that with such tutoring English emigrants should have brought with them to the New World the conviction that the Pope was indeed Antichrist; that his followers, cleric or lay, were the source of corruption to the godly, of treason to the state; that, finally, the preservation

[54] Convocation ordered this book to be placed with the Bible in all of the cathedral churches, and although Parliament failed to confirm the order, it was so generally complied with that even the parish churches had their copies chained to the desk like the Bible. In England the book went through edition after edition. Emigrant families brought it with them to America, where colonial booksellers included it in their regular stock. Sidney Lee says of it: " More than any other influence it fanned the flame of that fierce hatred of Spain and the Inquisition which was the master passion of the reign. Nor was its influence transient. For generations the popular conception of popery has been derived from its melancholy and bitter pages." *Ency. Brit.* (1904 ed.). See also Lee's article in *Dictionary of National Biography*. *Cf.* John Gerard, *John Foxe and his " Book of Martyrs,"* Catholic Truth Society (London). John G. Nichols, ed., *Narratives of the Days of the Reformation*, Camden Soc. Pub. (London, 1859), Pref. xxii *et seq.* H. Thurston, *No-Popery*, p. 257 *et seq.* The London ed. of *Acts and Monuments* (8 vols., London, 1843-49), ed. by Rev. G. Townsend, contains a life and vindication of the martyrologist. *Life of Foxe*, vol. i, pp. 1-161; answers to objections, vol. i, pp. 161-236.

of personal liberty as well as of the free institutions which are its guardians demanded that the adherents of the Church of Rome be excluded from the body politic. Nor is it surprising that with such convictions, the forebears of the Revolutionary generation should deem it their sacred duty to imbue their children's children with a deadly hatred of the old faith. Only thus, they reasoned, could they preserve intact the faith " delivered to the saints."

CHAPTER II

THE ENGLISH HISTORICAL TRADITION AFTER 1688

ENGLAND'S Catholic monarch was in exile. The kingdom was in a dilemma. The king *de facto,* champion of " the Protestant religion and the liberties of England," was a Dutch Calvinist who had repeatedly declared himself in favor of a " general toleration "—a toleration not so general, however, as to include Roman Catholics. Still more limited was the toleration envisaged by the peers who had extended the invitation to William. Since both Anglican and dissenter had sponsored the Revolution, and since the prince, a non-Anglican, was to rule not by divine hereditary right but by parliamentary title, obviously some concession would have to be made to Non-conformity. This was to be done, not by the removal of the disabilities which had so effectively curbed the social and political ambitions of the sectaries, but by the imposition of carefully defined conditions, the fulfillment of which, while granting certain exemptions, would in no wise endanger the " rule of the ascendency." These conditions, simple enough for those who could fulfill them, were embodied in the Toleration Act. Briefly, all non-conforming believers in the Trinity who took certain oaths, whose teachers subscribed to certain portions of the Thirty-nine Articles, and whose places of worship were registered with the bishops, were freed from all restrictions in their public worship. The Toleration Act did not repeal the penal laws; it granted merely certain exemptions on specified conditions.[1]

[1] Owen Ruffhead, *Statutes at Large from Magna Carta to the Twentieth Year of George III* (14 vols., London, 1763-1780. Index to tenth year of George III, London, 1772. All references are to this edition

To Catholics it brought no relief whatever; rather did it stigmatize them as a group who could not accept the revolution without renouncing their faith. The oath of allegiance, a simple attestation of loyalty, offered no difficulties. Appended to it was a second oath which denied the Papal power of excommunication and the civil or ecclesiastical authority of the Papacy within the realm, and a third, the Caroline declaration against Transubstantiation.[2] These no Catholic could take. The last two oaths were exacted of the sovereign by the Bill of Rights, which in another clause excluded from the throne Catholics or those marrying Catholics.[3]

It was not long before it was realized that further legislation would be needed to provide for the succession. In 1694 Mary had died without heirs. Even if William married again, there was little likelihood of his having issue. Moreover, the death on July 30, 1700, of the little Duke of Gloucester, son of Princess Anne, who was next in succession, made legal provision a necessity if the Catholic Stuarts were to be excluded. Parliament, therefore, in response to an invitation from William, passed the Act of Settlement or the Act for the Further Limitation of the Crown. It deliberately set aside the claims of the Catholic branch of the Stuarts and vested the crown in the Princess Sophia, electress of Hanover, the nearest Protestant successor of James I, and her heirs, "being Protestants." It was further provided that after the deaths of William and Anne, the

unless otherwise indicated. Cited as "Ruffhead"), vol. iii, p. 424 *et seq.*, 1 William and Mary, st. i, ch. 18. *Cf.* 10 Anne, ch. ii, s. 7, etc.

2 Ruffhead, vol. iii, p. 417 *et seq.*, 1 W. and M., st. i, ch. 8. W. S. Lilly and J. P. Wallis, *Manual of Laws Especially Affecting Roman Catholics* (London, 1893), p. 21.

3Ruffhead, vol. iii, p. 440 *et seq.*, 1 W. and M., Sess. 2, ch. 2. *Cf.* William Blackstone, *Commentaries on the Laws of England* (10th ed., 4 vols., London, 1787), vol. i, pp. 267-68.

ruler of England should thenceforth belong to the Anglican communion.[4]

If in previous reigns Stuart activities in Scotland, Ireland and France had complicated the position of English Catholics, Jacobite plots, actual or feigned, rendered it still more difficult after the Revolution. James II died in 1701. Immediately Louis XIV proclaimed his son James III of England. Parliament's answer was the passage of a Bill of Attainder [5] against the " Popish Pretender ", and the imposition of an oath of abjuration.[6] This oath was so worded that it could not be taken by those who believed in the hereditary title of the Pretender, even though they were quite willing to acknowledge the *de facto* government. England's alarm at the success of Louis on the continent and the anger of her merchants because of French discrimination against English manufactured goods, had already disposed the nation to war. But the proclamation of Louis in favor of James III added fuel to the flame, giving the contest the character of a dynastic and religious war. On January 10, 1701, Sir Edward Seymour moved in the House of Commons that the King be petitioned to have inserted in the several treaties of the Grand Alliance a clause to the effect

That no Peace be made with France, until his Majesty, and the Nation, have Reparation for the great Indignity offered by the French King, in owning and declaring the pretended Prince of Wales, King of England, Scotland, and Ireland.

Though William died before final action was taken, the signatories of the Alliance ratified the " Seymour Clause " early

---

[4] Ruffhead, vol. iv, p. 61, 12 and 13 William III, ch. 2.

[5] Ruffhead, vol. iv, p. 81 *et seq.*, 13 Wm. III, ch. 3. W. Cobbett, *Parliamentary History of England from 1066 to 1803*, continued from 1803 as *Parliamentary Debates*, vol. v, 1688-1702 (London, 1809), pp. 1331-1335; vol. vi, p. 94.

[6] Ruffhead, vol. iv, p. 83, 13 Wm. III, ch. 6.

in Anne's reign.[7] The religious implications of the war were heightened by the presence in England of over eight thousand Protestant refugees from war-ridden Europe who revived memories of Huguenot persecutions.[8] Papal subsidies for the restoration of the Pretender would not soften British bitterness towards Rome.[9]

Yet with the exception of such periods of national excitement there was relatively little active persecution during the reign of Anne. As in previous and in succeeding reigns, Catholics were double-taxed [10] and were rigorously excluded from office; [11] but Catholic noblemen were allowed to have chaplains, and priests in the discharge of their ministry [12] might come and go without molestation. And although Catholics were forbidden to carry arms [13] or to own a horse

[7] *Journals of the House of Commons ... From November the 8th, 1547 ... [to August the 14th, 1885].* [London] 1803-[85]. (140 vols. in 142. 7 vols. of index), vol. xiii, pp. 665, 855. The Latin and French texts of the "Seymour Clause" are printed in Onno Klopp, *Der Fall des Hauses Stuart und die Succession des Hauses Hanover in Gross-Britannien und Ireland* ... (14 vols. in 7, Wien, 1875-88), vol. ix, pp. 500-501.

[8] I. S. Leadam, *History of England, 1702-1763* (New York, 1909), pp. 141-42.

[9] G. M. Trevelyan, *England under Queen Anne* (3 vols., New York, 1930-34), vol. ii, p. 337. Leadam, *op. cit.*, pp. 239, 240, 264. Robert Chambers, *Domestic Annals of Scotland* (2 vols., Edinburgh, 1859), vol. i, p. 102; vol. ii, p. 55.

[10] Ruffhead, 1 Anne, st. 2, ch. 23, vol. iv, p. 130. *Cf.* 9 Geo. I, ch. 18, vol. v, p. 450; 9 Geo. I, ch. 24, vol. v, p. 465 (Scotland); 1 Geo. II, ch. 17, vol. v, p. 282 (ed. by John Raithby, London, 1811); 11-12 Wm. III, ch. 12, vol. iv, p. 13; 1 Geo. III, ch. 2, st. 56, vol. viii, p. 526.

[11] Ruffhead, 3 Jas. I, ch. 4, vol. iii, p. 38 *et seq.*; 3 Jas. I, ch. 5, vol. iii, p. 46; 3 Jas. I, ch. 6, vol. iii, p. 79; 25 Chas. II, ch. 2, vol. iii, p. 377; 30 Chas. II, st. 2, vol. iii, p. 395; 1 W. and M., Sess. 1, ch. 8, vol. iii, p. 417; 7 and 8, Wm. III, ch. 27, vol. iii, p. 617.

[12] Trevelyan, *op. cit.*, vol. i, p. 57. *Cf.* Charles Butler, *Historical Memoirs of English, Irish and Scottish Catholics* (4 vols., 3rd ed., London, 1822), vol. iii, pp. 139-40.

[13] 1 W. and M., ch. 15. *Cf.* Lilly-Wallis, *Manual of Laws,* pp. 29-30. T. C. Anstey, *Guide to Laws ... Affecting Roman Catholics* (London, 1842), pp. 50-51.

worth more than five pounds,[14] in practice they rode whatever
mounts they had and went about armed. There was a
renewal of persecution at the Jacobite uprisings of 1715 [15]
and 1745, followed by periods of comparative quiet.[16] Agitation for the repeal of penal legislation began in the reign
of George III.

In Scotland, as in England, devotion to the Stuart cause
brought disaster. Like their co-religionists to the south,
Catholics had been harassed by a series of penal enactments
the enforcement of which deprived them ultimately of every
vestige of civil and religious liberty.[17] Scotland did not have
as many martyrs as England, but the persecution fell heavier
on the rank and file of the faithful, since to the rancor engendered by religious differences there was added the hostil-

---

[14] 6 Anne, ch. 67, ss. 6, 9; 1 W. and M., ch. 15, s. 7.

[15] *Cf.* 1 Geo. I, st. 2 ch. 55, vol. v, p. 93; 3 Geo. I, ch. 18, vol. v, p. 164.

[16] Leadam, *Hist. Eng.*, pp. 239-266, 391 *et seq.* Lingard-Belloc, vol. xi,
p. 118 *et seq.*, 198 *et seq.* Lecky, *Eng.*, vol. i, pp. 143, 228, 294-99. *Cf.*
W. J. Amherst, *History of Catholic Emancipation* (2 vols., London,
1886), vol. i, pp. 23-24. J. O. Payne, *Records of the English Catholics
of 1715* (London, 1889), preface and *passim*. *Catholic Record Society
Publications* (34 vols., London, 1904-34), vol. vii (1909). R. Challoner,
Memoirs of Missionary Priests (London, 1844).

[17] Henry Home, Lord Kames, *Statute Law of Scotland, Abridged, with
Historical Notes* (2nd ed., Edinburgh, 1769), pp. 237-242, conveniently
brings together all the Scottish penal laws against Catholics from 1581
(xxiii Eliz.) to 1771 (x Geo. III). A reprint of this abstract may be
found in *Scots Magazine* (Edinburgh, Oct., 1773), vol. xl, pp. 513-517.
Cf. A. Bellesheim, *Geschichte der Katholischen Kirche in Schottland von
der Einführung des Christenthums bis auf die Gegenwart* (2 vols., Mainz,
1883), in vol. ii, pp. 378-380. *A Short View of the Statutes at Present
in Force in Scotland against Popery* (Edinburgh, 1778). For the operation of the penal laws in Scotland, see Robt. Chambers, *Domestic Annals
of Scotland*, vol. i, pp. 23, 73, 172-73, 219, 224, 315, 336-37, 352-53, 359,
402-04, 415-17, 421-22, 429, 465-66, 504, 514; vol. ii, pp. 20-28, 36-41, 57-60,
72, 145, 211, 283-84, 335-38, 499. Wm. Forbes-Leith, S.J., *Narratives of
Scottish Catholics under Mary Stuart and James VI* (London, 1889),
Part ii, *passim*. *Memoirs of Scottish Catholics during the XVIIth and
XVIIIth Centuries* (2 vols., New York, 1909), vol. ii, 139 *et seq.* C.

ity of clan for clan. Entire settlements were often evicted or destroyed. As a result, Protestantism took such root in Scotland that it has been described as " perhaps more vividly Protestant than any state in Europe." [18] The Lowlands were more thoroughly Protestantized than the Highlands. In both sections, however, there was a considerable number of Catholics, many of whom had been given important offices by James II. That these should fall from favor after the " rewards of power " had passed to " the ascendancy " in 1689, was to be expected. Perhaps it was to be expected also that their loyalty to the Stuarts and to the Church would not go unpunished. Their records show how dearly they suffered for their double treason—for so it was construed. One Highland clan, the Macdonalds of Glencoe, were all but exterminated.[19] As in England, the Jacobite efforts of 1715 and 1745 were the signals for renewed persecution.[20] When later the Catholic Emancipation movement began in England, riots in Edinburgh and Glasgow attested the strength of the prejudices which would have to be combated in the north.

The Revolution in Ireland has a history all its own. There the Catholic question was complicated by a racial antagonism rendered still more acute by a policy which has been vividly if not elegantly described as " land-grabbing." The greed which dictated this systematic confiscation, galling enough under any circumstances, was further motivated by the determination to degrade its victims. It has been pointed out by Lecky and by other historians after him, that this spoliation of a conquered majority by a victorious minority

---

Butler, *Hist. Mem.*, vol. iv, pp. 77-83. H. J. Somers, *Life and Times of Hon. and Rt. Rev. Alexander Macdonell* (Washington, 1931), p. 2.

[18] Lingard-Belloc, vol. xi, p. 24.

[19] Somers, *Life of Alex. Macdonell*, pp. 4-8. C. Butler, *Hist. Memoirs*, vol. iv, pp. 85-89. Trevelyan, *Eng. under Q. Anne*, vol. ii, pp. 208, 218. Lingard-Belloc, vol. xi, pp. 31-32.

[20] C. Butler, *op. cit.*, vol. iv, pp. 90-103. Lecky, *Eng.*, vol. iii, p. 552.

which supplemented its legalized theft by a code "deliberately intended to demoralize and degrade," constituted the distinguishing feature of the Irish penal legislation.[21] As regards the mere letter of the law, its severity could, unfortunately, be matched and even surpassed by the penal statutes of other countries; the unique distinction of the Irish code was the reduction of three-fourths of the population to a condition of abject servitude. The worst features of this system of oppression were enacted in the eighteenth century,[22] when the Catholics of England and Scotland, though still subject to fines, confiscations and civil disabilities, were, nevertheless, enjoying periods of comparative tranquillity.

It would be a mistake to think of the ferocious policy pursued in Ireland during the eighteenth century as a system sprung full-grown from the brains of the faction in control of affairs after the Treaty of Limerick. Rather was it the culmination of some two hundred years of misgovernment, signalized on the one hand by the Rebellion of 1641,[23] and on the other by the retaliation of the Cromwellian forces at Drogheda and Wexford. Cromwell's own account [24] is an unimpeachable witness of the religious fanaticism of the conquerors as well as of the unlikelihood of any hope of quarter for the conquered. As the event proved, *Vae Victis*

---

[21] *Statutes at Large, passed in the Parliaments held in Ireland from 1310 to 1798* (18 vols., Dublin, 1799). A digest of the penal statutes may be found in the Index, part viii, under "Papists." W. H. Lecky, *History of Ireland in the Eighteenth Century* (5 vols., New York, 1893), vol. i, pp. 36-168; *Eng.*, vol. i (1878), p. 256 *et seq.*

[22] Lecky, *Ireland*, vol. i, pp. 141-42. *Cf. supra*, p. 29, note 16.

[23] For causes of this rebellion see Lecky, *op. cit.*, vol. i, pp. 41-42, 79-100. Clark, *op. cit.*, p. 282. Ranke, *Eng. in Seventeenth Century*, vol. ii, pp. 283-89. Lingard-Belloc, vol. vii, p. 503 *et seq.* H. Hallam, *Constitutional History of England* (3 vols., London, 1877), vol. iii, pp. 361-64, 372n.

[24] Quoted in part by Lecky, *op. cit.*, vol. i, p. 102. *Cf. ibid.*, vol. i, pp. 36-39 for other instances of anti-Catholic animus.

might well have been inscribed on the Puritan banners.[25] With the Restoration there came such serious economic discrimination [26] as to cause considerable emigration—largely Protestant, but including some Catholics—to America. But so lax, comparatively speaking, was the enforcement of the penal laws, that when after the defeat of James II at the Boyne, the terms of the Treaty of Limerick were arranged, Catholics looked to the time of Charles II as the period of their greatest freedom since the Reformation. Their demand for the restoration of the privileges of this reign was granted. From those who elected to remain in Ireland, a simple oath of allegiance only was required. Catholics were confirmed in such estates as they possessed under Charles II.[27]

On the Sunday after the Treaty of Limerick was signed, the bishop of Meath, Anthony Dopping, preached in Christ Church Cathedral, Dublin. Touching on the civil articles of the treaty, he declared that since the Irish were themselves faithless, there was no obligation to keep faith with them.[28] How far his declaration voiced the sentiments of his colleagues or of his audience, does not appear. The fact remains, however, that without the shadow of an excuse the treaty was broken and there was inaugurated in Ireland a new era of persecution, the most merciless and the most degrading in its history. Although William III expressed his displeasure by the removal of Bishop Dopping,[29] and although he disclaimed all sympathy with the new penal code, he seems to have made no serious effort to prevent either its enactment or its enforcement. With him Parliament must

[25] Lingard-Belloc, vol. viii, p. 360 *et seq.*, 395-96. Lecky, *Ireland*, vol. i, pp. 103-106. Hallam, *op. cit.*, vol. iii (1877), p. 375.

[26] Clark, *op. cit.*, pp. 286-88. Lecky, *Ireland*, vol. i, p. 171 *et seq.*

[27] Lingard-Belloc, vol. xi, pp. 22-23. Lecky, *Ireland*, vol. i, p. 136. Clark, *op. cit.*, 297. Hallam, *op. cit.*, vol. iii (1877), p. 380.

[28] Clark, *op. cit.*, p. 298.

[29] *Ibid.*

share the odium of the persecution, for the Irish legislature
which passed the laws was subordinate to the English government, and the latter could prevent the passage of any bill
of which it disapproved.[30]

Lecky calls attention to the absolute loyalty of the Irish
during the Jacobite uprisings of 1715 and 1745, so that there
was not even a sham plot to urge in excuse.   The Irish were
leaderless and utterly without redress before the law.   Both
the lord chancellor and the chief justice had declared from
the bench " that the law does not suppose any such person
to exist as a Roman Catholic." [31]   The same historian, having analyzed the code in all its far-reaching consequences,
quotes with approval Burke's conclusion that

. . . all the penal laws of that unparallelled code of repression
were manifestly the efforts of national hatred and scorn towards
a conquered people whom the victors delighted to trample upon
and were not at all afraid to provoke. They were not the
effects of their fears but of their security.[32]

In the North of Ireland, especially in Ulster, the social
cleavage referred to by Burke was deeper perhaps than in
other parts of the island.   Here the English policy of dispossessing the native population by the naturally aggressive
Scottish Presbyterians had been attended by circumstances
which kept the racial and religious animosities of both conqueror and conquered almost always at white heat.   Each
succeeding generation added to its unhappy inheritance its
own contribution, so that the passage of years, instead of
softening, rather intensified the rancors of the past.   When
the Scotch-Irish—to use a much controverted term—became

[30] Lecky, *Ireland*, vol. i, pp. 142-145. *Cf.* Hallam, *op. cit.*, vol. iii
(1877), pp. 382-83.

[31] Lecky, *Ireland*, vol. i, p. 146.

[32] Lecky, *Eng.*, vol. i, p. 283. *Cf.* Hallam, *op. cit.*, vol. iii (1877),
p. 383 *et seq.* T. A. Hughes, *History of the Society of Jesus in North
America* (5 vols., New York, 1907-17), pp. 59-62.

in their turn the object of religious persecution and economic discrimination, and emigrated to America, they carried in their hearts two deadly hatreds, " Popery and Prelacy." [33] Here their scattered settlements along the frontier from New York to Georgia brought them again in contact with Catholic powers, France and Spain. Here, too, the difficulties of their pioneer environment, aggravated by the Indian problem, while giving full scope to their militant propensities, tended likewise to keep alive old-world memories which had best been forgotten.[34]

It is evident, then, that the Catholics of the British Isles derived no immediate benefit from the Revolution Settlement. Nevertheless, the Toleration Act was a step, and a very decided one, towards the desired goal of religious liberty. The civil disabilities of dissenters were not removed; the state still maintained its responsibility for religious error, persistency in which ought not to go unpunished; it recognized, however, that certain types of Non-conformity were not necessarily inconsistent with loyalty.[35] Roman Catholics, Unitarians, Jews, persons of no religious faith were still without the pale; membership in these groups still connoted disaffection, and in the case of the first, potential if not actual treason.

[33] Lecky, *Ireland*, vol. i, pp. 1-240, 422-438.

[34] William Willis, " Scotch-Irish Immigration to Maine and a Summary History of Presbyterianism," Maine Hist. Soc. *Coll.*, vol. vi (1859), pp. 1-37. W. H. Foote, *Sketches of North Carolina* (New York, 1846), pp. 111-113. *Records of the Presbyterian Church in the United States of America* (Phila., 1841), Introd. J. E. Vose, " Centennial Address, 1874," in W. R. Cochrane, *History of the Town of Antrim* (Manchester, N. H., 1880), pp. 121-130. Both the address and the history of which it forms a part furnish evidence of the vitality of old-world bigotry. C. A. Briggs, *American Presbyterianism* (New York, 1885).

[35] A. A. Seaton, *Theory of Toleration*, pp. 232-236. H. Harrington, " Catholic Emancipation in England," *Thought*, vol. iv (Dec., 1929), pp. 480-499.

With the ebb and flow of the tide of religious persecution, whether of Anglican against dissenter, of Independent against Churchman, or of both against the " Papist ", the cause of toleration was slowly, if at times obscurely, making headway. After the Restoration it was constantly in the air. Stuart policies alone would have kept the subject before the public, especially in its politico-religious aspect. Other considerations entered into the debate—economic, social, intellectual, moral.[36] From whatever angle the question was discussed, the Catholic problem was always present. Declarations of indulgence, as we have seen, were interpreted as subterfuges to restore " Popery." Most dissenters would have none of them if the " idolatrous Papists " were to be included. With some exceptions, Whig and Tory, divided on so many issues, were united on the undesirability of granting toleration to the Catholics. Extremists among the Whigs went so far as to point out that Catholics since the Reformation had tried to ruin the Establishment by advocating toleration, and " had made the dissenters their instrument for above six-score years." [37] Again, they argued, Non-conformists both preached and practiced resistance. What was that but the worst form of " Popery ", namely, " Jesuitry "? [38] On the other hand, there was John Corbet, Presbyterian rector of Bramshot, in Hampshire, pleading for an accommodation so that, united with the " Establishment ", they might offer an effective bulwark against the Catholics and the sectaries, both of whom he would exclude from toleration.[39]

---

[36] F. Pollock, *Essays in Jurisprudence and Ethics* (London, 1882), pp. 144-175.

[37] G. M. Trevelyan, *Eng. under Stuarts*, p. 377. Clark, *Later Stuarts*, pp. 97, 119. Seaton, *Theory of Toleration*, pp. 181, 271, 278, 321.

[38] J. N. Figgis, *Divine Right of Kings* (Cambridge, 1924), pp. 180-186.

[39] Seaton, *op. cit.*, p. 95; *cf. ibid.*, pp. 134, 138.

Within the State Church itself High and Low Churchmen were at loggerheads over the matter. Dr. Sacheverell, in a sermon which brought him much unenviable notoriety, attacked the Toleration Act and upbraided the Latitudinarians who, under the pretense of excluding " Popery ", were the more surely bringing it in. " The Papists," he contended, " wish to justle the Church out of her Establishment, by Hoisting their Toleration in its Place." Moreover, they demanded the repeal of the penal laws, " the only Security the Church has to depend upon." [40] Thus, on whatever grounds the question was debated, the Catholic plight was clear. Those who opposed toleration did so on the plea that it savored too much of Rome; those who favored it, would exclude Catholics.[41] The few exceptions would grant them only a limited toleration.[42]

While the battle for religious liberty was being waged in the study, in the market place, in the pulpit, at the court, John Locke was quietly systematizing the various theories in his first *Letter on Toleration*. It was published in Holland the same spring in which the Toleration Act was signed. In the autumn the English version was before the public. Though the *Letter* contained little that was new, Locke's grasp of principles, his ability to synthesize, to set forth his findings in a clear, orderly fashion, above all his discussion of the various aspects of the problem from an apparently non-partisan point of view, won for him at once a hearing which continued to grow through the remainder of the seventeenth and eighteenth centuries. Crossing the Atlantic, his theories became the inspiration of the political philosophy of the American Revolution.

[40] Henry Sacheverell, *The Perils of False Brethren*, p. 8. *Cf.* W. H. Hutton, *Eng. Church*, pp. 260-62.

[41] Seaton, *op. cit.*, pp. 62, 77, 95, 132, 134, 137, 149. Hallam, *Const. Hist.*, vol. iii (1877), pp. 167-68n.

[42] Seaton, *op. cit.*, pp. 97, 195.

The subject of Locke's inquiry was whether and to what extent the state is justified in suppressing religious opinions. His answer: purely speculative opinions and divine worship have an absolute right to universal toleration; practical opinions or principles have the same inalienable right in so far as they do not disturb the state, or cause greater inconvenience than advantage. It follows therefore that certain groups should be excluded from toleration: (1) Those whose opinions are destructive of human society; atheists, therefore, and those Roman Catholics, perhaps, who are not temporal subjects of the Pope, but whose divided allegiance might weaken their loyalty to their own country. (2) Those whose beliefs interfere with the civil rights of others; e. g., that faith need not be kept with heretics, that excommunicated princes forfeit their crowns, that dominion is founded in grace. (3) Those who, not believing in toleration, will not grant it to others; who may even seize the government for their own ends. Catholics do not tolerate the religious opinions of others; *ergo*. (4) Those whose tenets are incompatible with civil allegiance; that is, those who transfer their services to other princes, as the Pope. (5) Those who do not believe in the being of God; therefore atheists, who cannot be bound by the oaths that keep human society together. Locke nowhere specifically mentions Roman Catholics. To do so would be no more necessary in seventeenth- and eighteenth-century England than to explain who was meant by the " foreign prince and potentate " of the Test Oath.[43]

If the groups enumerated above should not be tolerated by the state, it followed that the state had a right to suppress

<hr>

[43] John Locke, *Letters Concerning Toleration* (London, 1765), pp. 58-59. *Cf.* Lecky, *Eng.*, vol. v (1879), p. 169. Seaton, *op. cit.*, pp. 236-72. Blackstone, *Commentaries*, vol. iv (1787), pp. 52, 55 *et seq.* H. F. Bourne, *Life of John Locke* (2 vols., New York, 1876), vol. ii, pp. 34-41, 180-187. T. A. Hughes, *Jesuits in North America*, text ii, p. 126n.

them. The state justified its suppression, not on religious, but on political or politico-social grounds; that is, because the presence of these groups in the body politic was inimical to the welfare of the state or of the Establishment. This was the official British theory of persecution. From Elizabeth's time until Catholic Emancipation in the nineteenth century, the government always disclaimed persecution for religion's sake. Just as today the governments of Mexico, Germany and Russia reply to protests against religious persecution that the culprits are being punished only for the violation of the law, so in England the technical charge was always treason. And the British public were no more deceived than are the peoples of the world today. Edmund Campion, whose loyalty was unquestioned, faced the issue squarely when he said, substantially, just before his execution, " If you esteem my religion treason, then I am guilty of treason." [44]

There were those among the British clergy and laity who sincerely believed in persecution for religion's sake. The belief that obstinacy in religious error should be punished, that when it was a question of securing a heretic's salvation the use of torture might somehow or other convince him of the error of his ways and lead him by a real conversion to embrace the truth, was common enough in the sixteenth century and later. It was on religious grounds that the Puritans justified their persistent harassing of the " Papists." From Elizabethan times they had always been the bitterest persecutors of the Catholics.[45] In time men began

---

[44] William, Cardinal Allen, *A Briefe Historie of Twelve Reverend Priests Father Edmund Campion and His Companions* . . . ed. by Rev. J. H. Pollen, S.J. (London and St. Louis, n. d.), pp. 2-3. *Cf.* W. H. Frere, *Eng. Church*, pp. 220-221. Hallam, *Const. Hist.* (New York, 1930), vol. i, p. 157, and note; 140.

[45] L. Pastor, *History of the Popes* (London, 1924), vol. xiv, p. 363; vol. xix, p. 470. P. Guilday, *Eng. Cath. Refugees*, p. 134. Seaton,

to think differently, and as we have seen above, ideas of toleration slowly gained ground. Throughout the entire penal period, however, the British government never took cognizance of religious persecution as such. Whether the violated law concerned the oath of allegiance, or a private opinion such as belief in Transubstantiation, or the replenishing of the royal treasury by the confiscation of "Papist" lands—danger to the things of Caesar was the all-sufficient justification.[46] Archbishop Laud, in a speech already referred to, protested against the confusion likely to arise from calling " Popery " rebellion. For, said he,

. . . if you make their Religion to be Rebellion, then you make their Religion and Rebellion to be all one. And that is against the ground both of State and of the Law. For when divers Romish priests and Jesuits have deservedly suffered death for Treason, is it not the constant and just profession of the State, that they never put any man to death for Religion, but for Rebellion and Treason onely? [47]

Later the Archbishop called attention to the statement of King James I in his " Premonition to all Christian Monarchies,"

I do constantly maintaine that no Papist either in my time or in the time of the late Queen ever dyed for his conscience.[48]

---

op. cit., pp. 9-13. Lord Acton, *History of Freedom* (London, 1904), " Protestant Theory of Persecution," pp. 165, 168-70. Hallam, *op. cit.*, vol. i (1930), p. 135. George Chalmers, *Revolt of the American Colonies* (2 vols., Boston, 1845), vol. i, p. 62.

[46] T. C. Anstey, *Guide to Laws . . . Affecting Roman Catholics*, pp. 30-33.

[47] William Laud, *Speech Delivered in the Starre-Chamber*, p. 37.

[48] *Ibid.*, p. 38. Cf. G. Burnet, *The Royal Martyr Lamented, in a Sermon preached at the Savoy, on King Charles the Martyr's Day, 1674-5* (London, 1710), pp. 14-15. Burnet quotes Charles I to the effect that neither his father nor Elizabeth ever put people to death for religion.

Upon the theory, then, of guarding for Caesar the things of Caesar, the British government built its harsh penal code. And having completed the structure, it was loath to tear it down. Men might debate theories of toleration as they would; England would have none of them save in so far as political expediency suggested their adoption. By the middle of the eighteenth century, other forces were at work—liberalism, rationalism, deism. Politics was becoming secularized. Those in power had ceased to be interested in the truth or falsity of doctrines like the Trinity or Transubstantiation. Nevertheless the laws which discriminated against Unitarians and the " Declaration against Transubstantiation " remained on the statute books. Some of the penal laws were allowed to lapse, others were only occasionally enforced. The system was retained, not so much as a working ideal, although it was by no means a dead letter, but as a reserve force which might be resorted to if the state were in danger.

As early as 1719 the first Catholic committee was formed to discuss with the government the removal of disabilities. Nothing came of it, however, for Jacobitism was not yet a dead issue. Even after it had ceased to be dangerous, recusancy fines were collected and confiscations were not unknown. The motive was political rather than religious. Should Jacobitism ever threaten the Protestant succession, its success would depend largely upon Papal subsidies and the contributions of Catholics. The continued impoverishment of the latter was one of the surest means of thwarting any such movement. So it was that the work of the first Catholic committee came to naught; the first English relief act was not passed until 1778.[49]

[49] H. Harrington, *Thought*, vol. iv (Dec., 1929), pp. 480-499. *Cf.* P. Hughes, *The Catholic Question, 1688-1829* (London, 1929), pp. 148-150.

14066

English and Scottish reaction to this first measure of alleviation shows clearly how far behind the liberalizing tendencies of the period were the masses of each nation. Moving southward from Glasgow and Edinburgh, pillaging and burning as they went, the violence of the " No-Popery " mobs increased as they approached London. Uniting there with the lowest elements of society they staged that series of anti-Catholic demonstrations known as the Gordon Riots. The terrors of those days became a tradition in Catholic annals. If the agitation for Catholic Emancipation thereafter proceeded slowly and haltingly, if Catholics at times seemed over-cautious, the memories of that nightmare of fanaticism offer at least a partial explanation. So evident was the desire of the rabble to destroy " Popery ", root and branch, that the liberals, Protestant or Catholic, could not ignore it with impunity.[50]

Meanwhile, how did the average Catholic of the British Isles live? Reference has been made to the relatively light enforcement of the penal laws—in England but not in Ireland—during the eighteenth century. The word " relatively " is important. Priests were no longer put to death for exercising their priestly functions, nor were they tortured on the rack nor subjected to other barbarous forms of punishment. They were, however, liable to fines and imprisonment. Until 1778 [51] informers who secured the conviction of a priest could claim a reward of a hundred pounds. They plied a lucrative trade, forcing the clergy to live like fugitives. Bishop Bonaventure Giffard who worked in the London district after 1702 was obliged to move continually

[50] J. Paul de Castro, *The Gordon Riots* (London, 1926), *passim*. Based on contemporary sources.

[51] P. Hughes, *op. cit.*, pp. 148, 150. D. Gwynn, *Struggle for Catholic Emancipation, 1750-1829* (New York, 1928), pp. 36-37. W. J. Amherst, *History of Catholic Emancipation*, vol. i, pp. 76-90, 107.

from place to place in order to avoid informers.[52]   On three several occasions he was arrested and thrown into prison. In 1767 in England a priest was condemned to imprisonment for life, and actually served for four years merely for performing his priestly functions.[53]   October 18, 1770, Father Watkinson of Middleton received the following notice:

. . . whereas you have taken upon you the office and functions of a Popish Priest as I am credibly informed, Therefore do I hereby give you notice that unless you do immediately Quit this Country you will be prosecuted as the law directs.[54]

It is apparent, then, that the law was not a dead letter. The machinery for persecution was on the statute books and might be put in operation at any moment.   Much depended upon the local justices of the peace.   Not all followed the example of Chief Justice Mansfield, who did everything in his power to prevent the persecution of English Catholics. Recusancy fines were collected in Yorkshire as late as 1782. There two poor laborers and their wives were fined a shilling each for non-attendance at Anglican services.   Since they were unable to pay the fine, the constable took some of their furniture in distraint and sold it at auction.   The bill presented to each family was five shillings—two for the fine, two for the constable's services, and one shilling for the warrant![55]

[52] B. Ward, *Dawn of the Catholic Revival in England, 1781-1803* (2 vols., New York, 1909), vol. i, pp. xxiv-xxv.   *Cf.* H. J. Somers, *Life of Alex. Macdonell*, pp. 7-8.

[53] Amherst, *op. cit.*, vol. i, p. 85.   William Hunt, *History of England, 1760-1801* (New York, 1905), p. 205.   *Cf. Catholic Record Society Publications*, vol. xiv (1914), p. 313 *et seq.*   R. Challoner, *Memoirs of Missionary Priests*, p. i.

[54] *Cath. Record Soc.*, vol. iv (1907), p. 271.   *Cf. ibid.*, vol. xxxii (1932), p. 254 *et seq.*, for Archbishop Blackburn's Visitation Returns.

[55] B. Ward, *op. cit.*, vol. i, p. 2 *et seq.*   *Cf.* P. Hughes, *op. cit.*, pp. 122-141.

This is admittedly an exceptional incident, but it illustrates how insecure were the lives of Catholics, especially the poor.   As the idea of toleration gained ground, as the discrepancy between its theory and practice diminished, the enforcement of recusancy laws grew more and more lax. But even after the Relief Act of 1778 [56] Catholics were still a proscribed people.   In 1788 their committee drew up a memorial which they presented to Pitt.   The list of disabilities therein mentioned, the memorialists state, does not include those laws which had been inoperative for some time. The grievances of which they complain, therefore, are presumably those which harassed their daily lives.   Briefly, they were as follows:

Catholics were prohibited under the most severe penalties from performing any act of religion according to their own form of worship.   Their priests might not exercise the functions of their office.   They might not have schools of their own nor were they permitted to educate their children abroad.   No Catholic could enter the army or navy.   They were excluded from the professions of law and medicine. Unlike other English free-holders, they might not vote at county elections, a disability which deprived them of representation in Parliament.   In the ownership of their property they were hampered by burdensome and expensive formalities in enrolling their deeds, the methods of which not infrequently entailed the exposure of secret family transactions.   They were excluded from all civil offices of honor and trust, membership in the House of Commons included. Catholic peers were deprived of their hereditary seats in the House of Lords.[57]   In other words, in the practice of their

[56] For the limitations of this act, see Anstey, *Laws . . . Affecting Roman Cath.*, pp. 1, 8, 9, 54, 61.   P. Hughes, *op. cit.*, pp. 148-150.

[57] C. Butler, *Hist. Mem.*, vol. iv, p. 7.   (It was Butler who presented the petition.)   B. Ward, *op. cit.*, vol. ii, pp. 266-68.   Appendix C.

religion, in the education of their children, in the social, civil
and political life of the community, in everything, that is,
which normally conduces to a useful, happy existence, the
Catholics of England were an outlawed race. In Ireland,
as we have seen, their condition was much worse.

Unless expressly extended by statute or by royal authority, the penal laws of England did not apply to her American
plantations. English common law, in so far as it was suitable or convenient to their new situation, followed the emigrants to their trans-Atlantic home; laws of a temporary or
territorial character, called forth by special circumstances of
time and place, had no force without the realm. The
English statutes which made Roman Catholicism an illegal
religion and its practice a crime were of this latter class;
hence they were not applicable to the colonies. In various
ways the crown might extend their force, however, or they
might be incorporated into colonial law by the local legislature. Only under such circumstances did the disqualifications which they imposed apply to the Catholic emigrant
or his descendants.[58]

Neither the home authorities nor the adventurers to the
new world were likely to overlook these necessary formalities. If, generally speaking, the " legal and administrative

---

[58] George Chalmers, *Opinions of Eminent Lawyers on Various Points of
Jurisprudence* ... (2 vols., London, 1814), vol. i, pp. 220, 295; vol. ii, pp.
31, 202. Anstey, *op. cit.*, pp. 167-184. J. Story, *Commentaries on the Conflict of Laws, Foreign and Domestic* (Boston, 1834), p. 97. Blackstone,
Commentaries, vol. i, p. 93 *et seq.* These pages may be found conveniently
summarized in *Ecclesiastical Records of the State of New York*, ed. by
H. Hastings (Albany, 1901), vol. ii, pp. 1080-82. C. J. Tarring, *Chapters
on the Law Relating to the Colonies* (London, 1893), pp. 4-11. W. Kilty,
*A Report of all such English Statutes as existed at the time of the first
emigration of the people of Maryland* (Annapolis, 1811), p. vi. St. George
L'. Sioussat, " The English Statutes in Maryland," *Johns Hopkins University Studies in Historical and Political Science*, ser. xxi, nos. 11-12
(Nov.-Dec., 1903), pp. 465-568.

traditions " of England [59] were easily and naturally transplanted, though not without modifications, her religious prejudices were transplanted with even greater facility but with less modification. Colonial charters, instructions to governors, test oaths, partisan legislation, popular uprisings—all testify that, as regards the Church of Rome, colonial " law, public policy, and popular sentiment " were but a reflex of those of the mother country. Occasionally colonial policy lagged behind that of England; at times it out-heroded Herod. There were few of the British penal laws that could not be paralleled by similar enactments of the mainland or island plantations. [60]

As in the home land, the Catholic clergy were singled out for special legislation. Massachusetts, New York, and Virginia enacted laws—almost verbally identical—proscribing priests. Adopted in 1647 and reenacted in 1700, the Massachusetts law decreed banishment for any priest or Jesuit found within the jurisdiction of the colony after a specified date; a second offense was punishable by death. The penalty for harboring a priest was two hundred pounds, one half to go to the informer. [61] The death penalty was never

[59] H. L. Osgood, *The American Colonies in the Seventeenth Century* (3 vols., New York, 1904-07), vol. iii, p. 14.

[60] For penal legislation of the island plantations, see N. Trott, *Laws of the British Plantations in America, Relating to the Church and the Clergy, Religion and Learning* (London, 1725), pp. 364-65, 388-90, 398-403. *Cf.* T. A. Hughes, *Jesuits in N. A.*, text ii, pp. 193-205, 575.

[61] *Acts and Resolves, Public and Private, of the Province of Massachusetts Bay* (21 vols., Boston, 1869-1922), vol. i, pp. 423-24. *Laws and Liberties of Massachusetts* (Boston, 1648). Reprint for H. E. Huntington Library (Cambridge, 1929), p. 26. *Cf.* N. Trott, *op. cit.*, pp. 335-36; 27 Eliz., ch. ii, 3 Jas. I, ch. 4, s. 3. For the Virginia law, see W. W. Hening, *Statutes at Large* (13 vols., Richmond, 1809-25), vol. i, pp. 268-69. For New York, *Acts of Assembly passed in the Province of New York, 1691-1725* (Bradford ed., 1726), pp. 42-44. *Cf. Colonial Laws of New York, from the Year 1664 to the Revolution* (Albany, 1894), vol. i, pp. 426-430. U. S. Cath. Hist. Soc., New York, *Records and Studies*, vol. ii, pp. 112-115. Trott, *op. cit.*, pp. 277-79.

inflicted, but clerical visitors on diplomatic missions were careful to avoid antagonizing the authorities by unduly prolonging their visit.[62]   New York in 1741 hanged an Anglican minister who was suspected of being a Catholic priest.[63]   The Jesuits who ministered to the Catholics of Virginia considered the mission to be one of great physical danger.[64]   In none of the British plantations could Mass be celebrated publicly save in tolerant Pennsylvania.   Even in Maryland Catholic services had to be conducted privately.[65]

The Catholic laity were subject to legislation as drastic as that of England.   Throughout British America they were disfranchised and excluded from offices of trust and honor.[66]   In Virginia, " Popish recusant convicts, negroes, mulatto and Indian servants, not being Christians," were incapable of being witnesses in any case whatsoever.[67]

[62] W. A. Leahy, *History of the Archdiocese of Boston* (Boston, 1899), pp. 12-22.

[63] Daniel Horsmanden, *The New York Negro Conspiracy, or a History of the Negro Plot, with the Journal of the Proceedings against the Conspirators at New York in the Years 1741-42* (New York, 1810).

[64] J. G. Shea, *History of the Catholic Church in the United States* (4 vols., 1886-1892), vol. ii, p. 87.

[65] Maryland Archives, W. H. Browne, ed. (Baltimore, 1883), vol. xxv, p. 341, vol. xxvi, pp. 591-92, 597-98, 630-31, 147-48. M. I. J. Griffin, " William Penn, the Friend of Catholics," Amer. Cath. H. S., *Records,* vol. i, pp. 71-85. J. L. J. Kirlin, *Catholicity in Philadelphia* (Philadelphia, 1909), p. 58. *Compleat Collection of the Laws of Maryland...* (Annapolis, 1727), p. 50 *et seq.* W. Kilty, *Laws of Maryland* (2 vols., Annapolis, 1779), acts for 1704, 1706, 1707.

[66] A. E. McKinley, *The Suffrage Franchise in the Thirteen English Colonies in America* (Philadelphia, 1905), *passim. Cf.* C. F. Bishop, *Elections in the American Colonies* (New York, 1893), p. 56 *et seq. Cf.* 3 Jas. I, ch. 5, ss. 8, 9; 25 Chas. II, ch. 2; 30 Chas. II, st. 2, ch. 1; 1 W. and M., sess. 1, chs. 1, 8; sess. 2, ch. 2, s. 3; 13 Wm. III, ch. 6, s. 10; 1 Geo. I, st. 2, ch. 13, ss. 16, 17; 10 Geo. IV, ch. 7, ss. 4, 5, 19.

[67] W. W. Hening, *Statutes at Large*, vol. iii, p. 298; vol. v, p. 480; vol. vi, p. 339.

Catholics were not allowed to be guardians or administrators.[68]   Excluded from the militia, they were forbidden to bear arms, but were double taxed in default of the service they would have rendered willingly.[69]   The social ostracism which motivated much of the penal legislation in England and Ireland was evident in the Virginia statute which forbade Catholics to own a horse worth more than five pounds.[70]

Maryland had the largest body of Catholics, who constituted approximately one twelfth of the population about the mid-eighteenth century.[71]   There the wealth and influence of many prominent families made it difficult to exclude them from the social and political life of the community. After the Revolution of 1688 an effort was made to enforce the worst features of the British penal code.[72]   So drastic was the legislation that much of it was disallowed by the King.[73]

[68] *Ibid.*, vol. iv, p. 285; vol. v, p. 449. *Journal House of Burgesses,* Feb. 22, 1727, pp. 24-25; June 25, 1730, p. 88. *Cf.* 3 Jas. I, ch. 5, ss. 22, 24; 12 Chas. II, ch. 24, s. 8. See *Tyler's Quarterly Magazine,* vol. iv (1923), p. 158 *et seq.*; *Virginia Calendar of State Papers,* vol. i, p. 31; L. M. Friedman, "Parental Right to Control the Religious Education of a Child," *Harvard Law Review,* vol. xxix (March, 1916), pp. 485-500; *Colonial Records of North Carolina, 1662-1790,* ed. by W. L. Saunders and others (26 vols. with 4 vols. of index), vol. xxiii, pp. 319, 416, 577.

[69] Hening, *op. cit.,* vol. vii, pp. 35-39. *Cf.* 15 Chas. II, ch. 9; 1 W. and M., ch. 15, s. 8; ch. 26, s. 7; 1 W. and M., sess. 2, ch. 1; 2 W. and M., chs. 2, 10; *Md. Arch.,* vol. vi, pp. 240, 297, 353, 419, 429, 496; vol. xxviii, pp. 314-315, 340.

[70] *Supra,* note 69.

[71] L. C., Mss. Div., Gr. Brit., *Archives of the Roman Catholic Diocese of Westminster,* vol. xli, no. 207. *Cf. Public Record Office, Col. Off.,* 318, vol. ii, pt. 1, p. 20, for "Comparative View of Different Religious Persuasions"; *Md. Arch.,* vol. vi, p. 497.

[72] *Compleat Collection of the Laws of Maryland,* ch. 59, acts of 1704. W. Kilty, *Report of English Statutes,* pp. 182 *et seq.* M. J. Riordan, *Cathedral Records* (Baltimore, 1906), pp. 6-12.

[73] W. T. Russell, *Maryland, Land of Sanctuary* (Baltimore, 1907), p. 370.

Queen Anne in 1704 suspended certain acts aimed at the complete suppression of Catholic worship and insisted on the passage of an act allowing priests to exercise their functions in private.[74] To prevent Irish Catholic immigration, Irish servants were taxed twenty shillings per poll. Later this fine was doubled.[75] Invading the privacy of the home, the laws prescribed that the children of mixed marriages should be reared Protestants. In case of the death of the non-Catholic parent, the children were to be removed from the guardianship of the survivor.[76] Besides making it illegal to employ Catholic teachers, the law imposed a fine of one hundred pounds for sending children to Catholic colleges abroad.[77] This by no means completes the tale of anti-Catholic legislation in Maryland, as even a cursory inspection of the laws will show. Although there were periods of relatively light enforcement, there were times also when the code, harsh as it was, fell short of the actual oppression to which Catholics were subjected.[78] Little wonder that the

[74] *Compleat Coll.* (1727), p. 50. *Cf.* T. A. Hughes, *Jesuits in N. A.*, text ii, p. 444, note 23; W. Kilty, *Laws of Md.*, 1704, 1706, 1707, 1708, 1715.

[75] *Compleat Coll.* (1727), pp. 157-58, 191-92.

[76] *Ibid.* (1727), p. 145. F. L. Hawks, *Contributions to the Ecclesiastical History of the United States of America* (2 vols., New York, 1836-39), vol. ii, pp. 125-27. *Md. Arch.*, vol. ii, p. 317. *Cf.* 11 and 12 W. and M., ch. 4, s. 7.

[77] *Compleat Coll.* (1727), p. 201. *Cf.* 27 Eliz. ch. 2, s. 6; 1 Jas. I, ch. 4, ss. 6, 7; 11 and 12 W. and M., ch. 4, s. 6. Anstey, *Laws . . . Affecting Roman Cath.*, pp. 36-59.

[78] John Sanderson, *Biography of the Signers of the Declaration of Independence* (9 vols., Philadelphia, 1827), vol. vii, p. 240. Latrobe, the author of this sketch, is said to have submitted it to Charles Carroll for his approval. *Md. Arch.*, vol. ix, pp. 315, 316, 322-23. *Maryland Gazette,* Nov. 28, 1754; Oct. 2, 1755. *American Historical Review*, vol. xxvii (Oct., 1921), p. 70. "Extracts from the Diary of Daniel Fisher, 1755," *Pennsylvania Magazine of History and Biography*, vol. xvii (1893), p. 274. *Cf. infra*, pp. 232-234.

Carrolls and other prominent families thought seriously of migrating to the Louisiana territory.[79]

In British America, as in the mother country, the severe or lax enforcement of the penal code was influenced largely by domestic and foreign politics. New-world politicians could wave the red flag of " No-Popery " with as much gusto as European statesmen. In New York the " Glorious Revolution " had little glamor for the Catholics who were the victims of Leisler's partisan activities.[80] The colonies had their own harvest of " Popish plots ", the seeds of which had been sown across the Atlantic.[81] Long after the excitement of the Coode-Waugh " conspiracies " had subsided in Virginia and Maryland, the " Papists " were under suspicion of being in sympathy with the Pretender.[82] Royal governors throughout the colonies were directed to enforce the test oaths the more effectively to exclude Catholics from the

[79] *Carroll Papers*, Md. H. S., boxes 1731-1760; 1760-1763. " Letters from Charles Carroll of Carrollton to his father," June 22, 1759; April 10, Sept. 16, 1760; Jan. 1, Feb. 13, July 20, Oct. 13, 1761. For revival of the penal laws, see letter of Charles Carroll of Doughoregan Manor to his son in K. C. Rowland, *Life and Correspondence of Charles Carroll of Carrollton* (2 vols., New York, 1898), vol. i, pp. 42-43.

[80] *Documents relating to the Colonial History of New York* (15 vols., Albany, 1853-87), vol. iii, pp. 583, 577, 599, 608, 665, 685, 882. *Cf.* J. H. Kennedy, *Thomas Dongan, Governor of New York, 1682-1688* (Washington, 1930), pp. 105-109; T. P. Phelan, *Thomas Dongan, Colonial Governor of New York* (New York, 1933), pp. 123-24.

[81] *Md. Arch.*, vol. viii, pp. 72, 77, 78, 79, 81, 83-84, 86, 94, 114, 117, 153. New Jersey Historical Society, *Proceedings*, n. s., vol. xvi (1931), pp. 257, 399 *et seq.* *Virginia Magazine*, vol. xx (1912), pp. 4, 11. *Virginia Historical Register*, vol. v (1852), pp. 142-43. American Cath. H. S. *Records*, vol. x (1899), pp. 208-228. S. H. Cobb, *Rise of Religious Liberty in America* (New York, 1902), p. 184.

[82] Hawks, *Eccles. Hist.*, vol. ii, pp. 53-58, 113-115. *Md. Arch.*, vol. viii, pref. v-vi; *cf. ibid.*, 115, 116, 124; vol. xxv, pp. 335. W. H. Browne, *Maryland: the History of a Palatinate* (Boston, 1884), pp. 133, 199. *Va. Mag., loc. cit. Va. Hist. Reg., loc. cit.*

civil and political life of the community.[83] Even in Pennsylvania the pressure of the home government secured the
passage of colonial legislation which had this much desired
effect.[84]

To these parallels between the anti-Catholic enactments
of Great Britain and those of her colonies, many others
might be added. Those already cited, however, sufficiently
establish the community of origin and purpose of the two
codes. In its legal aspect the English historical tradition,
the development of which has been traced in these two chapters, was transplanted intact to the new world. For a hundred and fifty years it continued to exercise an important
if not a controlling influence in the social and political life
of British America. Preserved in that portion of the
people's literature which has been characterized as " the
broadest, most authoritative expression " [85] of its national
life, it is an unimpeachable witness of the social, political
and intellectual degradation inflicted upon the Roman Catholic. When the Revolution with its levelling tendencies
brought in its wake the gift of religious liberty, the prejudices enshrined in the provincial penal codes had become a
heritage with which its possessors were slow to part. Indeed, so loath were they to do so, that vestiges of them were
retained in some of the state constitutions. Even yet, New

---

[83] *Public Record Office, Colonial Office,* Great Britain, Transcripts,
series 5, vols. 196-204. L. C.

[84] W. T. Root, *The Relations of Pennsylvania with the British Government, 1696-1765* (New York, 1912), p. 224, *et seq. Cf.* C. Stillé, "Religious
Tests in Provincial Pennsylvania," *Pa. Mag. Hist. and Biog.,* vol. ix
(1885), p. 382 *et seq.* Trott, *Laws of Brit. Plant.,* pp. 227-39.
L. Schrott, *German Catholic Immigrants in the Colonies* (New York,
1903), p. 19 *et seq.*

[85] H. Hitchcock, *American State Constitutions* (New York, 1887),
p. 9. *Cf.* H. Bronson, " Early Government in Connecticut," New Haven
H. S. *Papers,* vol. iii, pp. 293-403, 323.

Hampshire's Bill of Rights retains the word " Protestant." [86]
But there were factors other than legal which contributed to
the preservation of the European tradition.   To these we
now turn our attention.

[86] *Constitution of The State of New Hampshire, established October
31, 1783 . . . as subsequently amended and in force January 1, 1935* (Pub.
by the Dept. of State, Concord, N. H.), pp. 7-8.

CHAPTER III

The Tradition and the Colonial Clergy

One has only to read the list of patentees appended to the Virginia charters [1] or to dip into the promotion literature [2] put out by the Virginia Company to realize how lively was the interest of the Anglican clergy, individually and officially, in this first permanent British plantation. Nor was their interest confined to those colonies in which the Church of England was officially established; their proselytizing efforts in other plantations were more than once made a matter of reproach by the non-Anglican clergy, and the red man wherever found was always regarded as a legitimate object of their zeal. To further their missionary activities in the new world, there was chartered in 1701 a society whose instructions, journals and correspondence form our chief source of information for the work of the Anglican clergy in colonial America. This organization, the Society for Propagating

---

[1] The charters may be found in Samuel Lucas, *Charters of the Old English Colonies in America* (London, 1850), pp. 2, 18, 20. Also in W. W. Hening, *Statutes at Large*, vol. i, pp. 58, 97, 105.

[2] A list of the tracts sponsored by the company in 1609-10 may be found in *Abstract of the Proceedings of the Virginia Company of London, 1619-1624*, ed. by C. Robinson and R. A. Brock (2 vols., Richmond, 1888-89), vol. i, p. xv. Among them are two sermons, one of which was delivered before Lord Delaware on the eve of his departure for Virginia, the other before the members of the London Company. The titles of the sermons are: "Virginia," by William Symonds (London, 1609); "A Newyeeres Gift to Virginea," by W. Crashaw (London, 1610). Brown in his *Genesis of the United States* (2 vols., New York, 1891), pp. 282, 366 *et seq.*, analyzes the sermons and gives some excerpts, which, however, are wholly inadequate to give a correct idea of the animus of the two preachers against the Church of Rome.

the Gospel in Foreign Parts (S. P. G.), was an offshoot of
the Society for the Promotion of Christian Knowledge (S.
P. C. K.),[3] the scope of whose activities was, theoretically
at least, world wide.   By limiting the territory of the S. P.
G. to the British plantations in America, the new corporation, it was hoped, would better carry out the work of the
Society in the colonies.[4]

The specific reasons for the incorporation of the S. P. G.
as set forth in its charter, are: (1) The lack of sufficient
means to support a minister in many of the colonies, and the
consequent deprivation of the sacraments and other ministrations of religion.   (2) The encouragement given " Divers
Romish Priests and Jesuits . . . to pervert and draw Our
said Loving Subjects to Popish Superstitions and Idolatry." [5]
David Humphreys, general secretary of the Society, in his
account of the association, refers to the second of these
reasons as the chief cause of its organization.[6]   To offset
the efforts of Roman Catholic missionaries, the S. P. G.

---

[3] For an account of the S. P. C. K. and its interest in Catholic missionary activities, see W. O. B. Allen and Edmund McClure, *Two Hundred
Years: the History of the Society for the Promotion of Christian Knowledge, 1698-1898* (London, 1898), p. 41.   See the minutes of the meetings
for a record of the zeal with which certain members pursued " Popish
recusant convicts."

[4] The S. P. C. K. continued its work in England and later extended its
activities to India and other remote parts.   See *A General Account of the
Society for the Promotion of Christian Knowledge* (London, 1816), p. 4.

[5] David Humphreys, *An Historical Account of the Incorporated Society
for the Propagation of the Gospel in Foreign Parts, Containing their
Foundation, Proceedings, and the Success of their Missionaries in the
British Colonies, to the Year 1728* (London, 1730), p. xv et seq.   W. S.
Perry, *History of the American Episcopal Church, 1587-1883* (2 vols.,
Boston, 1885), vol. i, pp. 196-205.   Ernest Hawkins, *Historical Notices
of the Missions of the Church of England in the North American
Colonies, previous to the Independence of the United States: Chiefly
from the Ms. Documents of the S. P. G.* (London, 1845), Appendix A.

[6] Humphreys, *op. cit.,* p. 4.   *Cf.* Hawkins, *op. cit.,* app. A.

was to send Anglican ministers to the American plantations, to pay their salaries, and to furnish them with literature for their own needs and for their parishioners and neophytes.

The Society took great pains to keep in touch with its members in the new world. Besides the annual report which each clergyman was obliged to send to the general secretary, they were encouraged to write to their superiors when anything of interest or of consequence had happened. These letters and reports were discussed at the annual meeting of the Society. Often they were made the basis of instructions which were sent to the missionaries. To the latter, also, were sent abstracts of the proceedings of the Society as well as copies of the annual sermon usually delivered by one of the bishops or the archbishop of Canterbury. This sermon was one of the most important features of the yearly program. It was intended to keep before the members, whether present or absent, the ideals of the association, and to renew their enthusiasm for the prosecution of its designs. The major portion of this correspondence is now available in the hundred and fifty odd volumes of British Transcripts in the Library of Congress. A discussion of it with some excerpts will make clear the official attitude of the Church of England and of its individual members toward the Church of Rome.

The annual sermons extend over a period of eighty-three years, from 1702 to 1785, at which later date the Society announced that it would no longer be responsible for the salaries of Anglican ministers in the United States. Many of these discourses are not concerned with the Roman Catholic Church or her activities, or, at most, make only passing reference to them. Brief as the allusion may be, however, it is almost invariably hostile. An analysis of the other sermons reveals a certain similarity of viewpoint which affords a basis for grouping. The largest number, by far, decry the " popery and idolatry " of Rome, and deplore the zeal of her missionaries. This note is struck at the first annual meeting, when the speaker, referring to the lack of funds, expresses the hope that

the *Charity* of our *People* will now help to supply the defect, and take away this *reproach* from our Church and Nation, and that it shall never more be said that they of the Church of Rome are more zealous to promote Superstition and Idolatry in the world, than we are to promote the *true, uncorrupted* Religion of Jesus Christ.[7]

That was in 1702. In 1779 the bishop of St. David's was still bewailing the harm done the natives by

papal infallibility and supremacy, the idolatrous worship of the mass, the grant of indulgences to sin, and many gaudy accommodations of Christian worship to profane heathen ritual.[8]

A second group was concerned with the relation of the Church to the government. In 1777, British opposition to the repeal of the penal laws was reflected in the annual sermon by the archbishop of York, who admitted the severity of the statutes, but justified them, with Locke, on political grounds.[9] At the door of the Church, also, were laid the " cruelties of the Spaniards," as well as the " intrigues " of the Jesuits.[10] Bishop Moss gravely appended as a footnote to his sermon of 1772 the century-old charge that the French

----

[7] Richard Willis, *Sermon preached before the S. P. G. At Their First Yearly Meeting, Feb. 20, 1701* (London, 1702), p. 22. The Newberry Library, Chicago, has a complete set of these sermons, with abstracts of the proceedings of the annual meetings. For similar references, see sermons for 1705, 1706, 1708, 1709, 1712, 1716, 1720, 1721, 1730, 1733, 1748, 1757, 1762, 1767, 1779.

[8] James [Yorke], bishop of St. David's, *Sermon, Feb. 19, 1779* (London, 1779).

[9] William [Markham], bishop of York, *Sermon, . . . Feb. 12, 1777* (London, 1777), p. xviii.

[10] *Sermons*, 1706, 1711, 1730.

missionaries taught the Indians that the English crucified our Saviour, and that the books used by the Protestant ministers were written by the devil.[11]

In the discussions at the annual meetings of the S. P. G. of the issues involved in the French and Indian wars, the speakers were at pains to emphasize the connection between Protestantism and allegiance to the crown.   Should the colonists become Roman Catholics, there would be no reasonable hope of retaining their friendship.   Therefore the Society should take special care to foster a spirit of union with the plantations.[12]   Here we have a frank recognition of the service expected from a patriotic missionary in upholding the Hanoverian succession.   In the new world as in the old, difference of religious belief, it was thought, would weaken the bonds of political union.   The Society would fail in its duty were it to neglect any means calculated to strengthen the ties between colony and colony, between ruler and subject.   This is the burden of the instructions sent out by the S. P. G. in 1756 to its members in America.

In the first place, the clergy are exhorted to take every occasion to impress upon their people the blessings of a government under a Protestant prince, and the advantages they enjoy in the free exercise of their religion.   Secondly, they are urged to " promote Brotherly Love and Christian Charity," not only among the " Protestant Inhabitants " of the colony or district of which they have charge, but also between " the different Provinces," and this " not merely as a general Duty of fellow Christians," but especially to prevent their falling a prey to the " implacable Ambition " of France, who is seeking " the compleat Ruin, of all the British Settlements, invading their property, and destroying their Commerce."

[11] Charles Moss, bishop of St. David's, *Sermon . . . Feb. 21, 1772* (London, 1772), p. 25, f. n.

[12] Frederick Cornwallis, bishop of Lichfield and Coventry, *Sermon . . . Feb. 20, 1756* (London, 1756), p. 55. *Cf. Sermons* for 1759, 1762, 1764.

Under the third and fourth points, the missionaries are urged to impress their people with the necessity of self-sacrifice and of making cheerfully the requisite contributions. Sixthly, " That you carefully guard your Flock against all the seducing Wiles of Popish Emissarys, Priests and Jesuites. . . ." Finally there is emphasized the need of prayer for protection against the enemies of " our commercial free & Protestant colonies . . . Resolved . . . that 750 copies of these Instructions be printed & sent to the venerable Missionaries in America." [13]

The evidence furnished by these instructions; namely, that the British government consciously planned to use the S. P. G. missionaries for political as well as for religious ends, needs to be emphasized for two reasons. First, because it shows the other side of a picture which British colonial writers for the most part—and others after them—have treated either as non-existent, or if they have recognized it at all, have called by another name. Spain, France and Holland, as well as England, recognized the value of the missionary in developing a spirit of loyalty among their subjects; all of them, moreover, regarded it as a legitimate policy, " patriotic " if applied to their own nationals, " perfidious " if applied to an enemy. Of this inconsistency we have already seen more than one instance; the succeeding pages will furnish many others. Secondly, the instructions outline a political philosophy which was adopted, not only by Anglicans, but by other Protestant groups—a philosophy which was modified at the approach of the Revolution, and later incorporated with further modification, but with its basic principles still intact, into American life and letters. It forms the political creed of thousands of Americans today. In the mid-eighteenth century, this philosophy might have been formulated thus:

[13] *S. P. G. Journals,* vol. xiii (1755-57), pt. 2, p. 133 *et seq.* L. C. Mss. Div.

Protestantism, the Hanoverian succession, free institutions, individual initiative, *versus* Catholicism, France (Jacobitism), arbitrary government, slavery.[14] For France might bé substituted, as occasion required, Spain or any other " priest-ridden " country. It was all one to the liberty-loving Protestant.

Turning now to the reports which the S. P. G. missionaries were directed to send annually to the general secretary of the Society, we note that among other items of information, these accounts were supposed to include data on the number of Catholics in the parish, the number of converts from Catholicism, if any, a report of Catholic activities, and the like. The number and extent of such references vary with the location of the parish and with the date. Where Catholics were few in number, poor and obscure in station, as in New England, New York, the Carolinas, or Georgia, one reads year after year in the *Notitia Parochialis* the laconic " No Papists ", or, to quote a South Carolina report, " Happily free from papists." [15] This is occasionally varied by a note like the following from Boston:

Papists we have, Foreigners and Inhabitants, in no small number, I guess; but they very much conceal themselves from our notice.[16]

---

[14] A. Baldwin, *The New England Clergy and the American Revolution* (Durham, 1928), pp. 82 *et seq.*, 112, 119, note 43. J. T. Adams, *Revolutionary New England, 1691-1776* (Boston, 1923), pp. 8, 96, 288.

[15] On number of Catholics in the various Anglican parishes, see: S. P. G. *Journals*, vol. xv, pt. I, p. 25; vol. xvii, pt. 3, p. 359; vol. xix, pt. 2, p. 249; vol. xx, pt. 2, p. 87; vol. xxiv, pt. i, p. 72. S. P. G. *Transcripts*, series B, vol. iv, pt. 1, p. 127; vol. v, no. 186; vol. vi (Sussex, Del., Sept. 1, 1722) ; vol. xxiv, pt. 1, no. 78. Fulham Palace Mss. S. C. no. 186. *Cf. Col. Rec., Pa.*, vol. vii, pp. 447, 448. Pa. *Arch.*, vol. iii, pp. 144-45. Henry Watts, " Goshenhoppen: An early Jesuit foundation in Philadelphia," U. S. Cath. H. S., *Records and Studies*, vol. xxi (1932), pp. 138-169.

[16] Rev. Dr. Cutler to sec., S. P. G., Boston, July 6, 1739 in W. S. Perry, *Historical Collections Relating to the American Colonial Church*

Anglican clergymen whose ministrations took them to the New England frontier would come into contact with the Catholic Indians and the French Jesuits. While witnessing to the fidelity of the neophytes to their spiritual guides, the reports repeat the old charges against the latter, such as their instilling a hatred of the English, fomenting rebellion, and teaching them anti-Christian principles.[17]

It is in the reports and letters from Pennsylvania and Maryland that we find frequent reference to Catholics and their activities. The practical toleration of Pennsylvania had enabled the Jesuits to build between 1732 and 1763 six churches or chapels, two in Philadelphia, and one each in Conewego, Goshenhoppen, Lancaster, and Reading.[18] These activities would not pass unnoticed. In 1742, Rev. R. Backhouse, writing from Chester, Pennsylvania, to the secretary of the S. P. G., remarks that of late the " popish priests appear pretty numerous," and that in Lancaster a " Mass House " is being erected.[19] Three years later, Rev. Robert Jenny, writing from Philadelphia, says that the city is " very much infested with popery & sysmatical divisions." He calls attention to the " noble stand " which the New York authorities have taken, so that there is " not the least face of popery " in that colony.[20] Again from Lancaster in 1748 comes the complaint that " the country is so much over-run with Jesuitism, Moravians and New Lights, which get ground

(5 vols.), vol. iii, p. 329. For similar references, see pp. 349, 363, 366, 370, 396, 418, 421, 427, 433, 439, 441, 445.

[17] See report of Rev. Mr. Beach, 1749, in C. F. Pascoe, *Two Hundred Years of the S. P. G.*... (London, 1901), vol. i, p. 54; also letter from the same to S. P. G. in abstract of *Proc.*, 1762; *ibid.*, 1767, for report of Rev. Mr. Bailey; W. S. Perry, *op. cit.*, vol. iii, p. 365, Rev. Stephen Roe to sec. S. P. G., Boston, Aug. 28, 1742.

[18] Henry Watts, *loc. cit.*

[19] Perry, *op. cit.*, vol. ii, p. 232.

[20] *Ibid.*, vol. ii, pp. 236-37. For New York's horror at Philadelphia's toleration, see J. L. J. Kirlin, *Catholicity in Philadelphia*, pp. 24-25.

very much." [21] The " popish seminary " at Bohemia Manor
was too near the Pennsylvania boundary to escape comment.
It was a center of missionary activity from which the Jesuits
ministered to the Catholics scattered through Pennsylvania,
Delaware and New York. Apoquiniminck, Pennsylvania,
was one of the places they visited at intervals. The establishment there, about 1760, of an Anglican mission supported
by the S. P. G. put a " check " to these visits and elicited a
prayer of thanksgiving from the chaplain who rejoiced that
" His Majesty's Subjects are not seduced to the Popish Religion." [22] Itinerant missionaries would have a better opportunity than resident chaplains to gage the " great & daily
growth of popery." One of these, Rev. Mr. Craig, attributes the increase to the " unlimited toleration " which
it enjoys in the Quaker colony. [23]

The reports of the Maryland clergy complain of the gains
made by the Catholics. Writes one,

We have Popish Priests daily flocking in amongst us, and the
whole province smells of Popish superstition, & I wish these
Caterpillars were destroyed; they poison apace our young Plants
that are growing up . . . [24]

A few months later he voices an economic grievance against
the " Papists " who are petitioning the assembly to exempt
negro women from taxation. This, he says, " will reduce
the salary of the clergy." Socially, too, Catholics are undesirable, for " they are intolerably ignorant, even beyond
description." [25]

[21] Perry, *op. cit.*, vol. ii, p. 253.

[22] *Ibid.*, vol. ii, pp. 311-16; 468-69. S. P. G. *Journals*, 1773-76, vol. xx,
pt. 6, p. 410.

[23] S. P. G. *Journals*, vol. xiii, pt. 4, p. 285.

[24] Perry, *op. cit.*, vol. iv, pp. 233-34, 241-42, 251-52; letters of Rev.
Giles Rainsford, Apr. 10, Aug. 16, 1724; July 22, 1725.

[25] *Ibid.* For other reports of the same tenor, see vol. iv, pp. 86-126,
234-38, 317-18.

Of more significance, perhaps, than the criticisms of individual missionaries, whose opinions are likely to be colored by the personal equation,[26] is the attitude of the Maryland ministry taken as a whole. In 1753 two general meetings of the Maryland clergy were held at Annapolis. At the August meeting the Catholic question occupied an important place in the discussions. No action was taken, however, beyond expressing in their felicitations to the newly inaugurated Governor Sharpe the hope that he would have the glory of rooting out " that worst & most unnatural of Mischiefs, Popery, and those greatest Enemies to the Xtian Religion & to all Virtues, the Jesuits. . . ." [27] The question of addressing the proprietary on the " dangerous Encroachments of Popery, and its growth in this Province," was postponed to the October session.

At the second meeting the basis of the discussion was a paper which had been submitted at the August session by Rev. James McGill of Queen Caroline's Parish, Anne Arundel County. The paper contained seventeen queries relating to " Popery & Jacobitism ", queries which the writer meant to be accepted as facts. A motion to submit the paper to the Committee of Grievances was objected to on the ground that it was unwise to assert as facts what might be only rumors. The speaker [28] advised caution. " Popery," he argued,

was undoubtedly exceedingly dangerous in a double Respect, as it must naturally wage continual War with our excellent Constitution both in Church and State. . . . That as a religion it was absolutely incompatible with ours where it had the upper

26 Rev. Mr. Rainsford, referred to above, was evidently accustomed to dispute frequently with the Jesuits. His letter to the bishop of London, July 22, 1725, is one long complaint against the Jesuits and their arts.

27 *Calvert Papers*, vol. xxx, 1753, no. 509, p. 9, Md. H. S.

28 Rev. Thomas Bacon, rector of St. Peter's Church, Talbot Co., Md.

hand, and cou'd not be satisfied with less than an Extirpation
of Protestancy: and as a political Institution it could never
obtain an Establishment in the British Dominions without introducing an Arbitrary Power inconsistent with the civil Rights
and Liberties of the People, & removing the present Royal
Family (our best Barrier under God, against all these Evils)
from the Throne of England.

Here is the Whig political theory functioning as a practical
philosophy in Maryland three years before it was incorporated in the instructions mentioned above.[29]   Thus the soil
was well prepared for it.   Although the speaker conceded
the truth of all this, he again advised caution.   Inquiries
should be made as to the kind of danger likely to arise from
the presence of "Popery."   If of a civil nature, the state
would take care of it; if religious, arising from the learning,
skill in argument, or the sanctity of the priests, the Anglican
clergy could oppose similar remedies.   The result of the debate was that the motion to present Mr. McGill's paper to
the Committee of Grievances was thrown out.   The recording secretary (identical with the speaker mentioned above)
continues:

We then went on examining into such Facts as our Brethren
cou'd avouch, or adduce good evidence for.

Of the seven charges agreed upon, the report disposes of
three only.   To the first, that Catholic schoolmasters were
teaching Protestants as well as Catholics, it was answered
that a Catholic schoolmaster named Garroty had been employed in Dorchester County because the people could pro-
cure no other.   The second, that Catholics were trying to
influence Protestants to send their children to St. Omers,
was disproved.   The third, that Catholic priests were offici-

[29] *Supra*, pp. 67-69.

ating publicly at Port Tobacco, was found to have been at the request of a criminal about to be executed.

The minutes of this October meeting of the parochial clergy at Annapolis cover fourteen folio pages.[30]　No secretary was formally chosen for this session, so the report is unsigned.　The secretary of the August meeting was Rev. Thomas Bacon, rector of St. Peter's Church, Talbot County, and the compiler of Maryland's laws.　It is more than likely that he acted as secretary of the October meeting also.　A man of varied talents and broad sympathies, popular and influential, he represented the best traditions of the Anglican clergy in the South.　He was much interested in popular education and in the welfare of the negro.　Of his edition of the *Laws of Maryland,* Wroth says, " in many respects it formed the most elaborate and laborious piece of editorial work until that time undertaken in America." [31] Amid this gathering of his fellow clergymen he stands apart. His seems to have been the one dissenting voice.　It was he who urged caution, suggested investigation, and wished to include only such charges as were proved.　Even when the assembly voted nine to one in favor of the addresses on " Popery " to be sent to the governor and the Committee of Grievances, he tried to gain time, he says, by quibbling over formalities (p. 55).　He must have been gratified to learn that the report was lost in the Lower House.　Some important considerations emerge from these minutes:

The two meetings probably included the most influential members of the Anglican clergy in Maryland.　An overwhelming majority of them were persuaded that the Roman Catholics, lay and cleric, were a real danger to the province.

---

[30] *Calvert Papers,* vol. xxi, no. 510, Md. H. S.

[31] L. C. Wroth, *History of Printing in Colonial Maryland, 1686-1776* (Baltimore, 1922), p. 95 *et seq. Cf.* H. E. Starr in D. A. B., vol. i, p. 484.

So sure were they that they were quite ready to listen to popular accusations against Catholics and to invoke the execution of the penal laws against them. It is worthy of note, too, that the only liberal member of the assembly was convinced like his brethren that Roman Catholicism was a menace to both church and state. He agreed with them, also, that adequate measures should be taken to lessen or to counteract its evil influence. He differed with his colleagues in first of all demanding proof, and secondly, in restricting the clergy to spiritual weapons. It is not the right of the state to enforce the penal laws that he questions, but rather the expediency of such a course.

One other phase of the Society's activities remains to be considered—its distribution of books and pamphlets. Such was the emphasis placed by the S. P. C. K. upon the distribution of suitable literature, that it has been characterized, not too accurately, perhaps, as " primarily a book and tract society." [32] Certainly Dr. Bray, its founder, was a firm believer in the efficacy of the printed word, and one of the chief works of the Society was the founding and maintaining of parochial and catechetical libraries in England, and the distribution of books generally. In the colonies the need of libraries was even greater than in the old country; so it is not surprising that with his appointment as commissary of the Church of England in the British Plantations, Dr. Bray should make them one of his chief concerns. During his lifetime some thirty-four thousand books and pamphlets were sent by the S. P. G. to the colonies.[33] The titles were

[32] J. E. Jacobs, *History of the Evangelical Lutheran Churches in the United States* (5th ed., New York, 1907), p. 147. For the activities of the Society to counteract by the distribution of literature "the practices of the Priests to pervert his Majesty's subjects to Popery," see minutes of the meetings in Allen, *op. cit.*, p. 40 *et seq.*

[33] B. C. Steiner, " Rev. Thomas Bray and His American Libraries," *Amer. Hist. Rev.*, vol. ii (1896-97), pp. 59-75. John F. Hurst, *Parochial*

carefully chosen, and classified into two general groups, those intended for the clergy, and those suitable for the laity. Among the latter there was a special class devoted to the exposition of the errors and absurdities of " Popery." Well aware that among the laity, at least, the historical argument was much more effective than theological and philosophical distinctions, there were included among the tracts such titles as Bennett's *Epitome* of the *Discourses against Popery, Accounts of the Cruelties done to Protestants on board the French Galleys, with an Exhortation to Perseverance, The Jesuites Morals by Dr. Tonge* (1679), *Popery and Tyranny: Or the Present State of France, Popish Cruelty Displayed: being a full and true Account of the Bloody and Hellish Massacre in Ireland.*[34]

These and other books of the same class would devote little or no space to the exposition of dogma; rather would they specialize in lurid accounts of excruciating tortures inflicted upon Protestants by Catholics. It is this type of tract that was ordered by Rev. Henry Addison, in a letter dated to Potomack River, October 30, 1760:

. . . There being a pretty many of the Church of Rome in my Parish, I should be glad to have some of the most approved Tracts upon Popery, & such as are written to the level of the meanest capacities:—particularly some historical accounts of their cruelties towards Protestants in England & Ireland . . . [35]

Libraries in the Colonial Period (New York, 1890). Reprint of paper read before the American Society of Church History, New York, Dec. 30-31, 1889, p. 50. F. K. Brown, *The Annapolitan Library of St. John's College* (privately printed). W. W. Kemp, *The Support of Schools in Colonial New York by the Society for the Propagation of the Gospel in Foreign Parts*, Contrib. to Educ., Teachers' College, Columbia University, no. 56 (New York, 1913), p. 11.

[34] *Cf. infra*, p. 178.

[35] S. P. G., Md., 1693-1784. See also ser. B, vol. v, no. 227, for a request for books for Irish, French, and German Protestants who had

Books of the expository type were also in demand, as is evident from the proceedings of the society for 1742. Among the titles ordered for distribution were " 500 copies of the third edition of *A Protestant Catechism, showing the principal Errors of the Church of Rome* from the Incorporated Society for Promoting English Working-Schools in Ireland." [36] Many of these tracts went through numerous editions in Europe and in America. Little wonder that Catholics should be both feared and hated when generations of their non-Catholic countrymen were reared on such a mental diet.

Although Methodism finally severed its connection with the Church of England, John Wesley's early missionary efforts in the new world were under the auspices of the S. P. G. It was Wesley who induced George Whitefield to undertake the missionary activities which identified him with the " Great Awakening." Wesley's interest in the colonies continued after his return to England; like Whitefield, though not with his phenomenal success, many another missionary caught from Wesley a spark of his own zeal for the spiritual well-being of the British plantations. As one of the most successful preachers of the Anglican communion and as one of the founders of a movement which ultimately developed into an independent church, his opinion of Roman Catholicism is worth considering.[37]

A study of Wesley's sermons, journals, letters and hymns reveals for the most part the traditional viewpoint of Protestant England. The Church of Rome, as it existed in his day, was not founded by Christ. Her doctrines and prac-

immigrated to South Carolina. The letter is from Rev. Charles Martyn, Charles Town, Feb. 20, 1764. *Cf.* also no. 121, letter of thanks from Rev. Daniel Earle, dated March 26, 1770.

[36] S. P. G. *Abstracts of Proceedings*, 1742, p. 41.

[37] L. A. Weigle, *American Idealism* (vol. x, *Pageant of America*), New Haven, 1928, pp. 111, 147-49.

tices were "unscriptural and novel corruptions." The effects of her teachings he sums up in a pamphlet entitled *Popery Calmly Considered.* He finds that these teachings tend to destroy (1) the love of God; (2) the love of our neighbor; (3) justice; (4) mercy (here he cites Philip II of Spain, Bloody Mary, the Inquisition); (5) truth (faith need not be kept with heretics, " officious lies, that is, lies told in order to do good, are not only innocent, but meritorious "). Absolution tends to encourage crime, as do also plenary indulgences. "This single doctrine of papal indulgences strikes at the root of all religion."[38]

To counteract these undesirable negative effects there is no positive compensation. The Catholic Irish—a typical Catholic people, to Wesley's mind—know little more of religion " than the Hottentots."

They know the names of God, and Christ, and the Virgin Mary. They know a little of St. Patrick, the Pope, and the Priest; how to tell their beads, to say *Ave Maria* and *Pater Noster*; to do what penance they are bid, to hear mass, and pay so much for the pardon of their sins. But as to the nature of religion, the life of God in the soul, they know no more (I will not say, than the Priest, but) than the beasts of the field.[39]

Like all deeply religious natures, Wesley had his moments of self-annihilation before God. In these periods of abasement the lowest depths to which he can descend is to call himself a child of Rome. In the second stanza of Hymn I he cries out:

> O how shall I presume
> Jesus, to call on thee,

[38] *Works of the Rev. John Wesley, A.M. . . . With a life of the author by the Rev. John Beecham, D.D.* (11th ed., 14 vols., London, 1856), vol. x, pp. 135-152.

[39] *Ibid.*, vol. ix, p. 213.

> Sunk in the lowest dregs of Rome,
> The worst idolatry.[40]

John Wesley disclaimed all sympathy with the scurrilous attacks [41] in the name of religion so common in his day. Neither would he persecute Catholics for the mere practice of their religion. England, however, should be warned of the political dangers inherent in this *imperium in imperio*. " No government not Roman Catholic ought to tolerate men of the Roman Catholic persuasion," he wrote in a letter to the *Public Advertiser* in 1780, because the Pope and even a priest can pardon perjury and treason like any other sin; therefore, no government can be certain that a Catholic will keep his oath of allegiance. Furthermore, the Catholic teaching that faith need not be kept with heretics encourages every Catholic to violate such an oath.[42] The date of this public letter, it will be noted, was that of the Gordon riots, which Wesley was accused of inciting. In fact Wesley and his followers, up to the date of Catholic Emancipation in 1829, bitterly opposed the relaxation of the penal laws.[43]

[40] *Ibid.*, vol. xi, pp. 183-87.

> *Cf.* Hymn II, stanza 3 : Let the blind sons of Rome bow down
> To images of wood and stone...
>
> Hymn III, stanza 12: A murderer convict, I come
> My vileness to bewail;
> By nature born a son of Rome,
> A child of wrath and hell. *Cf.* stanza 13.
>
> Hymn III, stanza 18: Heathen, and Jews, and Turks, may I
> And heretics embrace;
> Nor e'en to Rome the love deny
> I owe to all the race.

[41] *The Journals of the Rev. John Wesley, A.M.* . . . (Standard ed., New York, 1909-1916, 8 vols.), vol. ii, pp. 262-64.

[42] John Wesley, *Works*, vol. x, pp. 153-55, 157-166, 167-68. *Journals*, vol. vi, pp. 267, 301, 302.

[43] W. H. Lecky, *England*, vol. ii, pp. 580-82, 641-42, 633, 698; vol. ii, p. 553 *et seq.* J. H. Overton and F. Relton, *The English Church from the*

Thinking what he did of the religious and political influence of the Church of Rome, it seems like the irony of fate that Wesley should have been accused of being a " Papist." Yet more than once had he to defend himself from that charge, both in England and America. In Georgia a group of prominent citizens formulated an indictment against him in a pamphlet entitled, *A True and Historical Narrative of the Colony of Georgia.* The reasons assigned for suspecting Wesley of being a Roman Catholic throw as much light upon the state of public opinion in Georgia as upon Wesley's transgressions. They were enumerated under four heads, the last of which reads:

As there is always a strict connection between Popery and Slavery, so the design of all this fine scheme seemed, to the most judicious, to be calculated to depress and debase the minds of the people, to break any spirit of liberty, and humble them by fastings, penance, drinking of water, and a thorough subjection to the spiritual jurisdiction, which, he asserted, was to be established in his person; and, when this should be accomplished, the minds of the people would be equally prepared for the receiving of civil or ecclesiastical tyranny.

All the jesuitical arts were used to bring the well-concerted schemes to perfection; families were divided in parties; spies were engaged in many houses, and servants of others bribed and decoyed to let him into all the secrets of the families they belong to; nay, those who had given themselves up to his spiritual guidance (more especially women) were obliged to discover to him their most secret actions, nay even their thoughts, and the subjects of their dreams.[44]

Accession of George I to the End of the Eighteenth Century, 1714-1800 (London, 1906), p. 216. See *Historical Magazine*, vol. x (1866), p. 363 *et seq.*, for letters from Wesley to James Rivington, denying all guilt in the matter. The editor calls attention to an item in the Methodist account books in New York, March 1, 1781: " Paid Mr. Rivington for advertising Mr. Wesley's letter, etc., 12 pounds, 16s."

[44] John Wesley, *Journals*, vol. viii, pp. 304-07. Also in Force's *Tracts*, vol. i, no. 4, pp. 30-31. For Wesley's reply to a similar charge made in

George Whitefield's influence in the religious movement known as the "Great Awakening" is attested both by the number of his devoted followers and by the many enemies he made. His evangelizing tours extended from New England to Georgia. Everywhere he talked to large audiences; everywhere he made numerous proselytes. Strongly Calvinistic in his theology, sympathetic with the German pietists by whom he was to some extent influenced, and fraternizing on occasion with Baptist, Quaker or Moravian, Whitefield, on the other hand, met with not a little opposition from the regularly established clergy, who viewed what they considered his innovations with anything but a friendly eye.[45] His ultimate designs and his methods were alike impugned. "I am fully persuaded," wrote Commissary Cummings to the secretary of the S. P. G., "he designs to set up for the head of a sect, and doubt not but that he is supported under hand by deists and Jesuits or both." [46]

Like many of his clerical brethren, Mr. Whitefield often made politics the handmaid of religious propaganda, and *vice versa*. At the time of the Louisbourg expedition, 1745, his ardor won for him an urgent invitation to accompany the troops as chaplain. Ten years later, at the outbreak of the French and Indian War, Mr. Whitefield was again in America. Bradford's *Pennsylvania Journal* for December 25, 1754, carries this item:

The Rev. Mr. Whitefield, having preached every day since his arrival from New York, set out for Georgia on Tuesday last. In his preaching he frequently enlarged on the danger to which

Bristol, England, see *Journals*, vol. ii, pp. 262-64, 342; vol. iii, pp. 46, 100, 122; vol. iv, pp. 14-15. *Cf.* Umphrey Lee, *Historical Backgrounds of Early Methodist Enthusiasm* (New York, 1931), pp. 129-31.

[45] C. H. Maxson, *The Great Awakening in the Middle Colonies* (Chicago, 1920), pp. 44-53.

[46] W. S. Perry, *A History of the American Episcopal Church, 1587-1883*, vol. i, pp. 238-39. Letter dated Aug. 29, 1740.

we are likely to be exposed and showed the horrible Principles & Practices of our Popish Enemies in strong and lively Colours.[47]

Here is a sample of the " strong and lively Colours " in which Mr. Whitefield could paint the threatened evil. After the failure of the Jacobite rebellion in 1745, the churches of America, like those of England, held services of thanksgiving for the timely discovery of the plot, " first hatched in hell, and afterwards nursed in Rome." [48]   On August 24, 1746, Mr. Whitefield preached in Philadelphia a sermon on " Britain's Duty."   Among the mercies for which Britain should be grateful, the preacher included deliverance from the rule of the Pretender, which inevitably would mean loss of English liberty and vassalage to Rome.[49]   But far worse than temporal evils were the " spiritual mischiefs " which " would soon have overflown the Church " to the injury of immortal souls.

. . . How soon would whole swarms of monks, dominicans and friars, like so many locusts, have overspread and plagued the nation; with what winged speed would foreign titular bishops have posted over, in order to take possession of their respective sees?   How quickly would our universities have been filled with youths who have been sent abroad by their popish parents, in order to drink in all the superstitions of the church of Rome? [50]

The passage continues, exclamation following exclamation, until all possible evils are cataloged.

[47] Quoted in J. W. Wallace, *An Old Philadelphian, Colonel William Bradford, The Patriot Printer of 1776* (Philadelphia, 1884), p. 473.

[48] George Whitefield, *Works* (8 vols., London, 1771), vol. v, p. 82.

[49] Whitefield, *op. cit.*, vol. v, p. 82.

[50] *Ibid.*, vol. v, p. 84. *Cf. Boston Gazette*, Monday, Feb. 8, 1768, for the effect of a similar sermon in London. J. L. J. Kirlin, *op. cit.*, p. 58. For further evidence, see *Works*, vol. iii, pp. 71, 73, 77 *et seq.*; vol. iv, p. 172 *et seq.*, 265 *et seq.*

It is clear, then, from this brief survey of Anglican opinion in colonial America, that the English historical tradition transplanted in 1607 was preserved intact for at least one hundred and fifty years. Whatever the medium of its expression, whether it be instructions from the S. P. G. or its annual sermons on the one hand, or on the other the yearly reports, the private correspondence of some obscure missionary, or the discussions of a more distinguished group such as the meeting held in Maryland, its substantial conformity to Reformation opinion is unmistakable. The one derives directly from the other. The Methodists, too, both before and after their separation from the Church of England, preserved that portion of their spiritual heritage, and in their turn transmitted it to others. Indeed George Whitefield's evangelical methods and Calvinistic sympathies would tend to increase the bitterness of his attack.

It has been pointed out in a previous chapter that in sixteenth- and seventeenth-century England the Puritans were by far the most caustic critics of the Church of Rome. Their spiritual descendants in the new world might claim the same distinction. The two most important English-speaking groups were the Congregationalists and the Presbyterians. Although at one time differing radically on the question of church polity, both groups accepted as a basis of doctrinal belief the *Westminster Confession of Faith* together with the Assembly's *Larger and Shorter Catechisms.*[51] With the adoption of the Savoy Declaration by the Massachusetts Synod at Boston in 1680 and by the Connecticut clergy at Saybrook in 1708, differences of opinion in matters

---

[51] W. Walker, *Creeds and Platforms of Congregationalism* (New York, 1893), pp. 340-408. W. B. Sprague, *Annals of the American Pulpit* (8 vols., New York, 1857-1885), vol. i, p. xvi *et seq.* Joseph Tracy, *The Great Awakening* (Boston, 1842), p. 19, f. n.

of church discipline were so minimized that the adherents of both denominations chose to ignore them.[52]

The Elizabethan revision of the *Prayer Book* and the " Articles of Religion " had satisfied neither the non-conservative element nor the radical group which was rapidly becoming the Puritan faction.[53] The dissatisfaction of the latter party found expression in the *Westminster Confession of Faith,* first drawn up by the Westminster Assembly and ratified by Parliament in 1648. It condemned in no uncertain terms various points of Catholic teaching and practice, among which may be mentioned the so-called worship of images, the veneration of the saints, the taking of religious vows, the supremacy of the Pope—" that Antichrist, that man of sin and son of perdition,"—the sacrificial character of the Mass, communion under one kind, prayer for the dead, and Transubstantiation.[54] Ten years after the ratification of this platform by Parliament, the Congregationalists, or Independents as they were then called, wishing to have a confession of their own, called a meeting at Savoy Palace in London and drew up the Savoy Declaration. The original work of this synod was in the thirty sections of church polity appended to the confession. Yet it did not long maintain its coveted position of preeminence. At the Restoration, the Savoy Declaration was largely superseded in England by the Westminster Confession. In Massachusetts and Connecticut, however, it was the Savoy Declaration

[52] W. Walker, *op. cit.,* pp. 340-408. Sprague, *op. cit.,* vol. i, p. xvi *et seq.* W. D. Woods, *John Witherspoon* (New York, 1905), pp. 144-45.

[53] Dodd-Tierney, vol. ii, pp. 31-33, 43, 132-34; app., nos. 38, 39, 40. H. M. Birt, *Eliz. Relig. Settlement,* p. 27. E. Cardwell, *History of the Conferences and Other Proceedings connected with the Revision of the Book of Common Prayer; from the Year 1558 to the Year 1690* (Oxford, 1849). W. H. Frere, *Eng. Church,* pp. 148-170.

[54] P. Schaff, *Creeds of Christendom* (3 vols., New York, 1877), vol. iii, pp. 598-673.

which prevailed and which, according to the historian of Congregationalism, Williston Walker, long continued to be a recognized standard for Congregational Churches of America. With a few "immaterial modifications" the Declaration was adopted by a Massachusetts Synod at Boston in 1680, and under the name of the Saybrook Platform or Confession by Connecticut in 1708. Established by law in the latter colony, it continued in force there until 1784.[55]

The official pronouncements of the orthodox Congregational churches, then, had naught but anathemas for Rome and her teachings. The question now presents itself as to how far this official attitude was shared by individual clergymen. It has been asserted by Sprague that as early as the close of the seventeenth century a so-called liberal party tending to Arminianism could be detected; that by the middle of the following century, after the "Great Awakening", liberalism had made such headway that the Congregational clergy could be divided into two parties, the Calvinists and the Arminians. These statements have been questioned,

[55] *Public Records of the Colony of Connecticut, 1636-1776,* J. H. Trumbull and C. J. Hoadley, comp. (15 vols., Hartford, 1850-1890), vol. vi, pp. 51, 97, 423. *Statute Laws of Connecticut* (Hartford, 1808), vol. i, p. 575. Walker, *Creeds and Platforms,* pp. 161-63, 340-408; *History of the Congregational Churches in the United States* (6th ed., New York, 1907), pp. 207-09. Sprague, *Annals,* vol. i, p. xvi *et seq.* The Savoy Declaration derives from the Confession of 1596 issued by the Separatists from Amsterdam. The exiles prefer a long list of charges against the Anglican Church, which they accuse of enforcing "the burdens and intollerable yoke of their popish canons & decrees." These thirty-eight "antichristian ecclesiastical offices" disposed of, the *Apologia,* for such it is, denounces the clergy of the Church of England, who having formerly opposed the Roman hierarchy, "have now so redely submytted themselves to the Beast, and are not only content to receive his mark, but in the most hostile maner oppose and set themselves against us..." For a proper understanding of the Separatist attitude towards the Roman Catholic and Anglican Churches the entire document should be read. (See Walker, *op. cit.,* pp. 161-63, 340-408. Compared with it the Saybrook Platform is "sweetness and light."

apparently on sufficient evidence by a later writer [56] who
contends that the truth or falsity of the accusation is a matter
of " close definition." Of more importance to this study is
the implication that Arminianism, in the opinion of its critics,
tended to prepare the way for " Popery." [57]   Reliance for
salvation upon good works rather than upon the merits of
Christ alone, subservience to the priesthood, the corruption
of the ministry through the exercise of excessive power, and
its final degeneracy into an anti-Christian caste — such
were the dangers, all savoring of " Popery ", which, according to the orthodox, would result from the preaching of
Arminianism.

As a matter of fact there seems to have been little or
no ground for such fears.   On the contrary, an examination
of the writings of three outstanding liberals reveals anything
but a sympathetic attitude towards the Church of Rome.
Rev. Charles Chauncy considered her a " foul and contaminated channel " through which was transmitted the idea
of an uninterrupted Episcopal succession.[58]

Rev. Samuel Cooper, D.D., noted divine and patriot,
in his *Sermon on the Reduction of Quebec, October 16,
1759,* denounced the French, in the approved pulpit fashion
of the day, as " inflamed with Romish bigotry." [59]   His
Dudleian Lecture of 1773 on the Pope, " the Man of Sin ",
was among the bitterest attacks in that series of lectures, one

[56] F. A. Christie, " Beginnings of Arminianism in New England,"
American Society of Church History, *Papers,* ser. 2, vol. iii, pp. 153-172.
Cf. Sprague, *Annals,* vol. i, p. xvii *et seq.*

[57] Joseph Tracy, *op. cit.,* pp. 8-9.

[58] Charles Chauncy, D.D., *A Letter to a Friend ... An Answer to the
Bishop of Landoff's sermon before the Society for the Propagation of
the Gospel, London, Feb. 20, 1767* (Boston, 1767; reprinted London,
1768).   Supplement.

[59] Samuel Cooper, *Sermon on the Reduction of Quebec, Preached Oct.
16, 1759* (Boston, n. d.), p. 53.

of the avowed purposes of which was to prove that " Popery is in the true and proper sense anti-Christian." Although he himself considered this sermon one of the " most indifferent " of his efforts, the popularity of the theme and the reputation of the writer caused a second edition to be called for in 1774.[60]

Rev. Jonathan Mayhew, whose liberalism went beyond Arminianism into Arianism, and whose defense of civil and religious freedom earned for him an international reputation, excluded the Church of Rome from the liberty he claimed for himself and others. He urged the conversion of the Indians, not only to rescue them from the darkness of paganism, but to keep them from falling a prey to the " Romish missionaries " who would make them " twofold more the child of sin." [61] His *Discourse Concerning Unlimited Submission and Non-Resistance* attacked the Anglican and Roman Churches alike, but with this difference; the latter was the guiltier of the two, since as the " mother of harlots ", she was the source of all of the iniquity of the former.[62] An eloquent opponent of the Stamp Act, Dr.

[60] Dr. Cooper's hatred of Rome did not blind him later to the advantages of the French alliance. He received a pension from the French king to foster friendly relations between the two countries. So well did he succeed that his Puritan congregation even prayed for his Christian Majesty! This change of front was not lost upon his Congregational compatriots. Ezra Stiles wrote in his diary:

> In Brattle St. we seldom meet
> With silver tongued Sam,
> Who smoothly glides between both sides,
> And so escapes a jam.

Diary, vol. i, Nov. 30, 1774. L. C., Mss. Div., Force Trans.

[61] Jonathan Mayhew, *A sermon preached in the audience of his excellency William Shirley, esq....* (May 29, 1754), pp. 31-32.

[62] Jonathan Mayhew, *A Discourse Concerning Unlimited Submission and Non-Resistance to the Higher Powers: With some Reflections on the Resistance made to King Charles I, and on the Anniversary of his Death: In which the Mysterious Doctrine of that Prince's Saintship and*

Mayhew celebrated its repeal with a thanksgiving sermon entitled *The Snare Broken*. British tyranny, if unchallenged and unchecked, he argued, not only would destroy the colonies and the mother country, but would involve in its fall all freedom and even Protestantism itself.

> . . . If Britain . . . should, in destroying her colonies, destroy herself, . . . what would become of the few states which are now free? What, of the Protestant religion? The former might, not improbably, fall before the Grand Monarch, on this side of the Alps; the latter, before the successor of the apostle Judas, and Grand Vicar of Satan, beyond them . . . [63]

The Dudleian Lectures, sponsored by Harvard and treated in connection with that institution,[64] afford a fairly complete analysis of what the Congregational clergy thought of Roman Catholicism and its danger to both church and state. The roll call of the preachers includes the most distinguished members of the " standing order." To these might be added many names more or less prominent in New England annals: Amos Adams of Roxbury,[65] the Mathers,[66] Jeremy

Martyrdom is Unriddled, Jan. 30, 1749-50 (Boston, 1750), p. 48 *et seq.* For the effect of this and other sermons of Dr. Mayhew, see Charles G. Washburn, " Jasper Mauduit, Agent in London for the Province of the Massachusetts Bay, 1762-1765," in Massachusetts Hist. Soc. *Collections,* vol. xxiii (1918), p. 74.

[63] Jonathan Mayhew, *The snare broken: a thanksgiving discourse, preached at the desire of the West Church in Boston, N. E., Friday, May 23, 1766. Occasioned by the repeal of the Stamp-Act* (2nd ed., Boston, 1766), p. 30.

[64] *Cf.* Sprague, *Annals,* vol. viii, pp. 26-29. See also *infra,* p. 126 *et seq.*

[65] Amos Adams, *Religious Liberty an Invaluable Blessing: Illustrated in Two discourses Preached at Roxbury, Dec. 3, 1767* (Boston, 1768). *Concise Historical View of the Perils, Hardships, Difficulties and Discouragements which have attended the planting and Progressive Improvement of New England* (Boston, 1769). Two sermons preached at Roxbury on the occasion of a general fast, April, 1769. For Tyler's estimate

Belknap, the historian,[67] Ezra Stiles,[68] Timothy Dwight,[69] and Samuel Langdon,[70] to mention but a few.

Scattered throughout the British colonies from Maine and New Hampshire in the north to the backwoods of the Carolinas and Georgia in the south, the Presbyterians represented various emigrations both in point of time and of nationality. But whether of English, Irish or Scottish origin, whether of the seventeenth or eighteenth century, each group brought with it, as a precious inheritance to be guarded as their lives, the religious traditions of the parent presbytery.[71]   Their

of Adam's work, see M. C. Tyler, *Literary History of the Revolution, 1673-1783* (2 vols., New York, 1897), vol. ii, p. 385.

[66] Cotton Mather, *Magnalia Christi Americana* (Hartford, 1820), vol. i, pp. 65, 75, 162, 454, 195, 229; vol. ii, p. 433, and *passim. Diary*, ed. by P. L. Ford. Mass. H. S. *Coll.*, 7 ser., vols. vii, viii (1911-1912); vol. i, pp. 149, 572, 594-95; vol. ii, pp. 207, 441-42, 445-46. Samuel Mather, Letter to Samuel Adams, Jan. 27, 1777, in *Samuel Adams Papers*, Bancroft Transcripts, N. Y. P. L., vol. v. *Cf.* his *Apology for the Churches of New England*, app., p. 149.

[67] Jeremy Belknap, "Correspondence between Jeremy Belknap and Ebenezar Hazard," Mass. H. S. *Coll.*, 5 ser., vol. iii, pp. 240-41. *Belknap Papers*, Mass. H. S. *Coll.*, 6 ser., vol. iv, p. 253 *et seq. History of New Hampshire*, ed. by John Farmer (3 vols., Dover, 1831), vol. i, chs. 10, 12, 14, 22, *passim*.

[68] Ezra Stiles, *Literary Diary*, ed. by F. B. Dexter (3 vols., New York, 1901), vol. i, pp. 455, 585-87.

[69] Timothy Dwight, *Travels*, vol. i, pref., p. xvi, p. 295, f. n.; vol. iii, p. 162. *Cf. Sermon preached at Northampton, on the twenty-eighth of November, 1781* (Hartford, 1781).

[70] Samuel Langdon, *Observations on the Revelation of Jesus Christ to St. John* (Worcester, 1791). F. B. Sanborn, *President Langdon: a Biographical Tribute* (Boston, 1904). Reprinted from Mass. H. S. *Proceedings*, 2 ser., vol. xvii (1904), pp. 192-232.

[71] For the British, see the declaration of the London Provincial Assembly, 1654, *The Divine Right of the Gospel Ministry* (London, 1654), vol. ii, p. 83. Cited in C. A. Briggs, *American Presbyterianism*, pp. 2-3. For the Irish, see P. Schaff, *Creeds*, vol. iii, pp. 526-544. W. H. Foote, *Sketches of North Carolina*, pp. 109-110. For the Scottish, see P. Schaff, *op. cit.*, vol. iii, pp. 437-485.

fidelity to these traditions may be gathered from the minutes
of the various synods held in America for the last two hundred years.   The synods of Philadelphia, 1729, 1735, 1758,
1788,[72] as well as the general assembly of the Presbyterian
Church in 1805 [73] and subsequent assemblies, all agreed to
accept the *Westminster Confession of Faith,* the Assembly's
Larger and Shorter Catechisms.   Individual churches asking
for membership in a synod were required to subscribe to the
same documents.   Nor was this adherence a mere formality,
as may be seen from the action taken upon a report that the
synods of New York and Philadelphia had discarded the
Larger Catechism and " with difficulty " had retained the
Shorter.   Investigation having proved the falsity of the
report, it was decided to punish the authors of the libel.[74]
Adherence to the spirit of the Westminster Confession and to
its Catechisms would alone make hostility to the Church of
Rome a living conviction in the Presbyterian ministry.
There were other documents, however, relating chiefly to
church polity which, with certain modifications irrelevant to
this study, were adopted by the various synods referred to
above.   One of these documents, the Second Scottish Confession of Faith (1580), is so permeated with hatred of the

---

[72] *Records of the Presbyterian Church in the United States of America*
(Philadelphia, 1841), pp. 94-95, 116, 155, 232, 238, 242, 244, 284, 286,
546-47.

[73] *The Constitution of the Presbyterian Church in the United States
of America, Containing, the Confession of Faith, the Catechisms, and the
Directories for the Worship of God: together with the Plan of Government and Discipline, as amended and ratified by the General Assembly
at their sessions in May, 1805* (Philadelphia, 1815).   Cf. *A Directory
for Church Government* (London, 1644), in Briggs, *op. cit.,* app., pp.
i. xxvii, xxxi.

[74] Foote, *op. cit.,* pp. 469-470. Cf. Briggs, *Amer. Presby.,* p. 328, app.,
xxvii. *Records, supra,* note 72. Maxson, *Great Awakening,* pp. 69-79.
Charles Hodge, *Constitutional History of the Presbyterian Church in
the United States of America, 1705-1788* (Philadelphia, 1851), pp. 145-163.

Papacy that it would be hard to find its equal in that respect. On that score, indeed, the first Scottish Confession (1560), would seem to have left nothing to be desired.[75] But the troubled reign of Mary Stuart (1561-1572), her efforts to relax the penal laws, and the premature uprisings in her favor, so fired the zeal of the Kirk for the advancement of the " trew Religioun" that the Second Confession or National Covenant was issued. It was subscribed by the king, the council, the court, by all ranks of society in 1580-81, and again in 1590 and 1683.[76] In America, too, it was adopted by various synods as late as 1821.[77] A few sentences from this document will illustrate its spirit better than any discussion. The signatories, having postulated the truth of their particular confession, continue :

And theirfoir we abhorre and detest all contrare Religion and Doctrine; but chiefly all kynde of Papistrie in generall and particular headis, even as they ar now damned and confuted by the word of God and Kirk of *Scotland*. But in special, we detest and refuse the usurped authorite of that *Romane* Antichrist upon the scriptures of God, upon the Kirk, the civill Magistrate, and consciences of men . . . His fyve bastard sacraments . . . His blasphemous opinion of transubstantiation, or reall presence of Christis body in the elements . . . His devilish messe . . . His blasphemous priesthood . . . His erroneous and bloody Decreets made at Trente . . . [78]

This was the spiritual background, so far as the Church of Rome is concerned, of those waves of Irish immigrants

---

[75] P. Schaff, *Creeds*, vol. iii, p. 437 *et seq.*

[76] *Ibid.*, vol. iii, p. 480.

[77] *Supra*, p. 90, note 73.

[78] P. Schaff, *Creeds*, vol. iii, pp. 480-85. *Cf.* Robert Chambers, *Domestic Annals of Scotland from the Reformation to the Revolution*, vol. ii, pp. 105, 116, 120, 123. John England, *Works* (7 vols., Messmer ed., Cleveland, 1908), vol. ii, pp. 368, 407, 423, 430 *et seq.*

who came from Ulster in the seventeenth and eighteenth centuries. Woven into it as the warp with the woof were the bitter recollections of the Ulster rebellion of 1641. The first presbytery in Ireland was organized, according to Foote, by the Presbyterian chaplains attached to the Scottish army which crushed the rebellion in the spring of 1642. " From this period," he continues,

the complete organization of the Presbyterian Church in Ireland takes its date . . . and the government and discipline then adopted continue in all essential points unaltered, and all are to be found in the Presbyterian Church in the United States, to which they have descended as from parent to child.[79]

The " father of Presbyterianism "[80] in America, Rev. Francis Makemie, was ordained by the Presbytery of Laggan in Ireland, not far from the scene of the final struggle between James II and William of Orange.[81] It is not surprising, therefore, that he " loathed popery with all his soul." In that respect, as well as in the zeal with which he made the Presbyterian cause his own, his mantle seems to have descended upon Samuel Davies. A native of America, Davies' education at Faggs Manor under the tutelage of Samuel Blair would be sufficient guarantee of the purity of his Calvinism. Equally evident was its militant quality. The growth of Presbyterianism in Virginia and the foundation of the presbytery of Hanover in 1755 were due largely to his efforts. His tour of the British Isles to collect funds for the struggling College of New Jersey was but another

---

[79] Foote, *Sketches of N. C.*, pp. 111-113. Charles Hodge, *Constitutional History*, pp. 214, 215, 414.

[80] Sprague, *Annals*, vol. iii, p. 4. *Ecclesiastical Records of the State of New York*, vol. ii, pp. 877-79.

[81] L. P. Bowen, *The Days of Makemie; or, the Vine Planted, 1680-1708* (Philadelphia, 1885), p. 169.

aspect of his zeal in the same cause. As president of the college, the "headquarters" of Presbyterianism,[82] he was able to exert an influence in intellectual circles far beyond the sphere of his former labors.[83] But it is as a preacher that he is best remembered. At his death in 1761 he had achieved the reputation of being " the greatest pulpit orator of his generation. For fifty years after his death," continues his biographer, " his sermons were more widely read than those of any of his contemporaries." [84]

A " New Light " Presbyterian, Davies made use of all the oratorical devices and emotional appeals characteristic of revivalist preaching. As recruiting agencies, at a time when the pulpit was recognized as a legitimate instrument of the state, his sermons were so successful that more volunteers offered than could be enrolled in a given regiment. In these appeals Davies restates, fervently, cogently, the Whig political philosophy with its glorification of the Protestant succession and liberty, and with its insistence upon the obligation to preserve those blessings, if need be, by the shedding of one's blood. *The Good Soldier,* preached to a company of Virginia volunteers at the beginning of the French and Indian War is typical. You are engaged, he cries,

. . . To protect your brethren from the most bloody Barbarities —to defend the Territories of the Best of Kings against the Oppression and Tyranny of arbitrary Power, to secure the inestimable Blessings of Liberty, *British Liberty,* from the Chains

---

[82] Wm. Willis, *Scotch-Irish Immigration,* pp. 29, 35. W. Gewher, " Rise of Popular Churches in Virginia," *South Atlantic Quarterly,* vol. xxvii (1928), pp. 175-192. *Cf. William and Mary Quarterly,* vol. vi (1897-98), pp. 186-87; vol. vii (1898-99), p. 1.

[83] For an account of Davies' administration, see *Memorial Book of the Sesquicentennial Celebration . . . of Princeton University* (Princeton, 1898), pp. 367-79.

[84] J. E. Pomfret, in *D. A. B.,* vol. v, pp. 102-03. Sprague, *Annals,* vol. iii, p. 140. C. H. Maxson, *Great Awakening,* p. 29.

of *French* Slavery—to preserve that for which you have toiled and sweat, from falling a Prey to greedy Vultures—to guard your Religion, the pure *Religion* of *Jesus,* streaming uncorrupted from the Sacred Fountain of Scriptures: . . . to guard so dear, so precious a Religion, against Ignorance, Superstition, Idolatry, Tyranny over Conscience, Massacre, Fire, Sword, and all the Mischiefs beyond Expression, with which Popery is Pregnant . . . [85]

In another recruiting sermon, *The Curse of Cowardice,* preached to the militia of Hanover County, Virginia, this same sort of propaganda runs through four pages of the printed discourse.[86]   To his rhetorical question, " Can Protestant Christians expect Quarter from Heathen Savages and French Papists? " he answered, " Sure in such an Alliance, the Powers of Hell make a third Party."   This passage is followed by a melodramatic appeal to come to the rescue of friends and relations.   When the sermon was over and the company over-subscribed, the men followed Davies to the tavern, where he again preached to them until he was exhausted.[87]

[85] Samuel Davies, *The Good Soldier. Extracted from a Sermon preached to a Company of Volunteers, Raised in Virginia, August 17, 1755* (London, 1756).

[86] Samuel Davies, *The Curse of Cowardice. A Sermon preached to the Militia of Hanover County in Virginia, at A General Muster, May 8, 1758, With a View to raise a Company for Captain Meredith* (London, 1758), pp. 9-12, 19 *et seq.*

[87] *Memoir of Rev. Samuel Davies, formerly President of the College of New Jersey* (Boston, 1832). *Cf.* Alice Baldwin, *New England Clergy and the American Revolution,* pp. 87-88, f. n. 17. For other sermons of Davies, see *Virginia's Danger and Remedy. Two Discourses. Occasioned by The severe Drought in sundry Parts of the Country; and the Defeat of General Braddock* (Williamsburg, 1756). *Religion and Patriotism; the Constituents of a Good Soldier. A Sermon Preached to Captain Overton's Independent Company of Volunteers, raised in Hanover County, Virginia, August 17, 1755* (Philadelphia, 1756). A complete list of Davies' writings, largely sermons and addresses, is given in John

The sermons of Davies are by no means unique in Presbyterian annals. The passages quoted might be duplicated in the writings of Rev. Aaron Burr,[88] one of Davies' predecessors at Princeton; Rev. Samuel Finley,[89] his immediate successor; of the Tennents [90] who were such important influences in the political, educational and religious circles of the mid-eighteenth century, and of scores of lesser lights. In their printed form these tracts, dedicated to important personages in Europe or America, often with forewords by other celebrities, were widely advertised in the colonial press, and sometimes printed simultaneously in London and the colonies.[91] Their influence was incalculable, especially in the middle and southern colonies, although it was by no means confined to these sections.

McLean, *History of the College of New Jersey* (2 vols., Philadelphia, 1877).

[88] Aaron Burr, "A Discourse, delivered at Newark," January 1, 1755. Synopsis given in *New York Mercury*, March 3, 1755. *Sermon preached before the Synod of New York, at Newark, Sept. 30, 1756* (New York, 1756).

[89] Samuel Finley, *The Curse of Meroz; or, The Danger of Neutrality in the Cause of God, and our Country. A Sermon Preached the 2nd of October, 1757* (Philadelphia, 1757). Preface by Gilbert Tennent.

[90] Gilbert Tennent, *Sermons on Important Subjects; Adapted to the Perilous State of the British Nation, lately preached in Philadelphia* (Philadelphia, 1758), pp. 51, 418. *The Blessedness of Peace-Makers represented; and the Danger of Persecution considered; in Two Sermons on Matt. v: 9* (Philadelphia, 1765). *The Happiness of Rewarding the Enemies of our Religion and Liberty, represented in a Sermon Preached in Philadelphia, Feb. 17, 1756, to Captain Vanderspiegel's Independent Company of Volunteers, at the Request of their Officers* (Philadelphia, 1756).

[91] When the patriot army reached Philadelphia in June, 1778, after the evacuation of the British, their need of cartridge paper was supplied from the garret of an old printing office. "Among the mass was more than a cart body load of *Sermons* on *Defensive War*, preached by a famous *Gilbert Tennent*, during the old British and French War, to rouse the colonists to indispensable exertions." Alexander Garden, *Anecdotes of the American Revolution* (Brooklyn, 1865), vol. ii, p. 318.

To the north it was much the same. In Maine and New Hampshire, where the Presbyterian element was largely of Scotch-Irish extraction, antipathy to Rome was kept alive from generation to generation by the same partisan methods which cherished the recollection of the sufferings endured in an Ulster massacre but conveniently forgot the reprisals of a Drogheda. Or if the latter were recalled, it was only to commemorate the victory of the elect over the children of Baal. Nineteenth-century local histories of Maine and New Hampshire and centennial commemorations of towns and churches were still largely concerned with biased accounts of old-world happenings. Not infrequently the authors were Presbyterian clergymen, descendants of the early settlers. As one reads the concentrated hatred with which these narratives are too often disfigured, even in the mid- and late nineteenth century, one can only guess what must have been its strength in the seventeenth and eighteenth centuries.[92]

The Huguenots in British America adhered to the " Confession of Faith Held and Professed by the Reformed Churches of France, received and enacted by their First National Synod, celebrated in the City of Paris, and the year

---

[92] To cite but a few, see "Centennial Address of the Honorable Jeremiah Smith, delivered at the celebration of the Second Century from the time Exeter was settled by John Wheelright and others, July 4, 1838," in New Hamp. Hist. Soc. *Colls.* (Concord, 1924), vol. vi, pp. 167-204. Gordon Woodbury, "The Scotch-Irish and the Irish Presbyterian Settlers in New Hampshire," in New Hamp. Hist. Soc. *Proc.* (5 vols., Concord, 1874-1917), vol. iv, pp. 143 *et seq.* Rev. E. L. Parker, *History of Londonderry, N. H., with a memoir of the author* (Boston, 1851), pp. 28, 32, 34, 55, 68. Bedford, *History of Bedford, 1737-1900* (Concord, N. H., 1903), p. 263. Isaac O. Barnes, *An Address delivered at Bedford, New Hampshire, on the One Hundredth Anniversary of the Incorporation of the Town, May 19, 1850* (Boston, 1850). L. A. Morrison, *History of Windham* (Boston, 1883), pp. 553-54, 558. Scotch-Irish Society of America, *Proceedings of the Scotch-Irish Congress at Columbia, Tenn.* (Cincinnati, 1889). *Cf. supra*, pp. 44-45, n. 34.

of our Lord, 1559." [93] Article XXIV of that platform denies belief in purgatory and in the efficacy of the intercession of the saints, branding these doctrines as deceits of Satan. Vows, pilgrimages, auricular confession, indulgences, are censured as coming from " the same shop." Article XXVII condemns meetings of Catholics:

Because the pure word of God is banished out of them, and for that in them the sacraments are corrupted, counterfeited, falsified or utterly abolished, and for that among them, all kinds of superstitions and idolatries are in full vogue. All who join in such ceremonies are " cut off from the body of Christ Jesus."

Canon XV, chapter XIV of the " Discipline of the Reformed Churches of France, 1559," cautions parents to exercise care in the education of their children:

. . . And therefore, such as send them to school to be taught by priests, monks, Jesuits and nuns, they shall be prosecuted with all Church censures.[94]

The antipathies engendered by adherence to these documents were not the only heritage which the French Protestants brought with them from beyond the seas. There were, as in the case of the Scotch-Irish, the Palatines, the Salzburgers, unhappy memories of religious wars which time and distance had divested of all political significance, but which had become for the descendants of the first emigrants cherished traditions calculated to strengthen and perpetuate inherited aversions. Witness the petition of the " minister, elders and deacons of the French Protestant Church in New York," March 7, 1763. Canada, it will be recalled, with its population overwhelmingly Catholic, had but recently been

[93] Text in W. H. Foote, *The Huguenots* (Richmond, 1870), pp. 605-623. *Cf.* P. Schaff, *Creeds,* vol. iii, pp. 356-382.

[94] W. H. Foote, *op. cit.,* pp. 624-26.

ceded to England. The petitioners, having expressed their satisfaction at the success of British arms, proceed to enumerate the reasons for granting a confirmation of their lands.

And as the French Protestants in general may boast of the most inviolable Fidelity to all those indulgent States & Powers who protected them from the merciless Rage of their Popish Persecutors. . . . They flatter themselves that a French protestant Church in this City may invite Forriegners of their Perswasion to come over and settle here increase the number of useful Inhabitants & be a Means to reclaim the Kings Popish Subjects in Canada who will visit these Parts from the Errors, Idolatry & Superstition of the Church of Rome & thus facilitate their hearty submission to the British government.[95]

They ask, therefore, a royal charter to confirm their previous land grants.

The papers and proceedings of the Huguenot Society of America furnish ample evidence that the sentiments of the French Protestant clergy, as expressed in the petition quoted above, were shared by the Huguenot ministers throughout the land. All through the eighteenth, nineteenth and until well into the twentieth century, important anniversaries, such as the massacre of St. Bartholomew or the revocation of the Edict of Nantes, were made the occasion of reviving the religious hatreds so characteristic of the sixteenth and seventeenth centuries.[96] In other words, in their attitude toward the Church of Rome, the Huguenot clergy of America were at one with the other Calvinistic groups.

[95] *Doc. Hist. N. Y.*, vol. iii, p. 489 *et seq.*

[96] Huguenot Society of America, *Proceedings* (New York, 1883-1906). *Tercentenary Celebration of the Promulgation of the Edict of Nantes, April 13, 1598* (New York, 1900). *Cf.* Eliza Fludd, *Biographical Sketches of the Huguenot, Solomon Legaré, and of his family* (Charleston, 1886), pp. 38-39. Rev. George Foot, *Address embracing the Early History of Delaware* (Phila., 1842. Reprint, Wilmington, Del., 1898), p. 17 *et seq.*

In the Baptist communion there is no authority which can impose upon all its followers a definite creed. Their confessions, therefore, are statements of what a given Baptist group believed at a given time, rather than a creed to which all Baptists, as a condition of membership, are obliged to subscribe for all time.[97] The absence of a central authority does not, however, prevent voluntary adoption of certain articles of belief, or their acceptance by other groups. One of the earliest of these was drawn up by the Regular or Calvinistic Baptists in London in 1643, was confirmed in 1688 and 1689, and adopted by the Philadelphia Association of Baptists in 1724, and again in 1742. It "became the most important and influential of all the Baptist Confessions."[98] It is a slight modification of the Westminster Confession of 1647 and of the Savoy Declaration of 1658.[99] Consistent with the creeds from which it derives is this sentence from the appendix to the Baptist Confession:

If the ten commandments exhibited in the popish Idolatrous service book had been received as the entire law of God . . . the second Commandment forbidding Idolatry had been entirely lost.[100]

This point of view, transplanted and translated into action, appears in the address of a group of Maryland Baptists to the governor and the court in 1742:

[97] W. J. McGlothlin, *Baptist Confessions of Faith*, Phila., c. d. 1911), p. xi.

[98] *Baptist Confession of Faith. First put forth in 1643; afterwards enlarged, corrected and published by an assembly of delegates (from the churches in Great Britain) met in London, July 3, 1689; adopted by the association at Philadelphia, Sept. 22, 1742; and now received by the churches of the same denomination in most of the American colonies. To which is added, A treatise of discipline* (Philadelphia, 1765). *Cf.* McGlothlin, *op. cit.*, p. 218. J. England, *Works*, vol. ii, p. 439 *et seq.*

[99] For the text of the Confession, see Schaff, *Creeds*, vol. iii, pp. 738-41. McGlothlin, *op. cit.*, p. 220.

[100] McGlothlin, *op. cit.*, p. 288.

We do also bind ourselves hereby to defend and live up to the protestant religion, and abhore and oppose the whore of Rome, pope, and popery, with all her anti-christian ways.[101]

Passing from group pronouncements to individual opinion, and from the South to New England, we have the recorded opinions of two outstanding Baptists, Roger Williams and Isaac Backus. Although Williams' connection with the Baptists was brief, he is generally conceded to have been the founder of the Baptist Church in America. His religious beliefs, like his political philosophy, defy rigid classification, as does the man himself. An extremist both in thought and action, he has been characterized by John Quincy Adams as "a combined conscientious and contentious spirit." [102] Although an ardent advocate of religious liberty, he frequently denounced beliefs other than his own, and while he would make no laws against the Quakers, they experienced the virulence of both his tongue and his pen.[103]

Roman Catholics fared no better. As a young man still in the thirties, he disdained not to champion his favorite cause—complete separation of church and state—by an appeal to the anti-Catholic prejudices of Puritan Salem. So effective was his harangue that Endicott immediately cut the cross out the king's colors as a " superstitious thing and a relique of antichrist." [104] Such utterances are always open

---

[101] D. Benedict, *A General History of the Baptist Denomination in the United States of America* (2 vols., Boston, 1813), vol. ii, p. 13. *Cf.* England, *Works*, vol. ii, p. 439 *et seq.*

[102] J. Q. Adams, "Address delivered before Mass. H. S., May 29, 1843," in *Memoir of the Life of John Quincy Adams*, by Josiah Quincy (Boston, 1858), p. 394.

[103] Roger Williams, *George Fox Digg'd out of His Burrows*, ed. by Rev. J. L. Diman, Narragansett Club Pub., 1st ser., vol. v (1875).

[104] John Winthrop, *Journal, 1630-1649*, ed. by J. K. Hosmer (2 vols., New York, 1908), vol. i, pp. 137, 147, 149-50, 174n. *Cf.* Cotton Mather, *Magnalia Christi Americana*, vol. ii, p. 433.

to suspicion, however, because of their popular appeal. They may or may not represent the private convictions of the speaker. But an examination of Roger Williams' correspondence proves conclusively that even after the lapse of half a century his conception of the " Romish wolf " gorging herself with " huge bowls of the blood of the saints " remained unchanged.[105] So scurrilous are some of the references in his private papers, as well as those intended for public consumption, that they have been not inaptly designated by one writer as " slime." [106] His attacks on other religious sects were never complete without some reference, real or fancied, to the " popish leviathan." Still, notwithstanding his private beliefs, notwithstanding his public invective, he professed himself willing to grant to Roman Catholics the same liberty in religious matters that he claimed for himself and his followers. He even went a step farther, and publicly demanded that privilege for them in a letter addressed to the representatives of religious persecution in the old world and the new.[107] It is true that Roger Williams'

[105] J. R. Bartlett, ed., *Letters of Roger Williams, 1632-1682* (Providence, 1874), pp. 306-311. Also in "The Winthrop Papers," 3 Mass. H. S. *Coll.*, vol. x, pp. 26-29, 37-42. *Cf.* 1 Mass. H. S. *Coll.*, vol. i (1792), pp. 275-283; vol. iii, pp. 313-316; 2 ser., vol. viii, pp. 196-198.

[106] Roger Williams, *The Bloody Tenent of Persecution, for cause of Conscience, discussed in a Conference between Truth and Peace. Who in All Tender Affection, present to the High Court of Parliament (as the Result of their Discourse) these (amongst other Passages) of highest consideration. Printed in the Year 1644*, Nar. Club Pub., 1 ser., vol. iii (1867), pp. 51, 100, 274, 376. *George Fox Digg'd out*, pp. 235, 262-64, 433-501. *Letters of Roger Williams*, pp. 307-311. J. Moss Ives, "Roger Williams, Apostle of Religious Bigotry," *Thought*, vol. vi (Dec., 1931), pp. 478-492. *Cf.* Stuart D. Goulding, "Honest Roger Williams," *Commonweal*, vol. xix (Jan. 19, 1934), pp. 317-319. *Cf. ibid.*, vol. xxiii (March 13, 1936), pp. 540-42.

[107] Roger Williams, *Bloody Tenent*, pp. 107, 142, 171, 181. The edition published by the Hansard Knollys Society, London, 1848, includes Cotton's letter. *Cf.* S. D. Goulding, *loc. cit.*

promises were never put to the test, but there is no reason to think that he would have treated Catholics less liberally than Quakers.

A century after Williams, another Baptist was pleading for religious liberty. The history of that struggle belongs to a later chapter. Here it is important to note merely the substantial agreement between Williams' opinion of the old faith and that of the eighteenth-century Baptist leader, Isaac Backus. Preaching in 1754 on the necessity of an internal call to preach the gospel, he warned his hearers of the danger of being content with an external call only. Such a procedure would savor of " popery ", for " the very Body of Antichrist consists in setting Man up in Christ's Place." [108] Like Williams, too, Backus retained in old age the convictions of his young manhood. In 1791 he once more admonished his listeners to avoid formalism lest in neglecting the " personal possession of faith in Christ " they follow Rome. " She is the *mother of harlots,* and all churches who go after any *lovers* but Christ, for a temporal living, are guilty of playing the harlot." [109]

Readers of *George Fox Digg'd out of His Burrows* are under no illusions as to what Roger Williams thought of the founder of the religious society called Friends. Yet George Fox's *Arraignment of Popery* [110] or William Penn's *Seasonable Caveat against Popery* [111] might well have been written by Roger Williams, or for that matter, by a score of other

[108] Isaac Backus, *The Nature and Necessity of an Internal Call to Preach the Gospel* (Boston, 1754), pp. 28, 74.

[109] Isaac Backus, *The Infinite Importance of the Obedience of Faith, and of a Separation from the World* (Boston, 1791), pp. 16, 26, 27.

[110] *The Arraignment of Popery ... By G. F. and E. H. Printed in the Year 1669.* See especially pp. 23, 81, 84, 96 *et seq.*

[111] William Penn, "A Seasonable Caveat against Popery. Or A Pamphlet, Entituled, An Explanation of the Roman Catholick Belief, Briefly Examined." In *Works of William Penn*, vol. i, pp. 467-485.

religious controversialists, so well did they conform to the accepted pattern of such writings. And just as Roger Williams' public utterances anent the Church of Rome were confirmed by his private correspondence, so those of George Fox and William Penn are substantiated by the *Journal*[112] of the one and letters of the other.[113] The views of these two outstanding Friends might in turn be paralleled by those of other prominent Quakers—a Howgill,[114] a Coale,[115] a Claridge,[116] or a Barclay.[117] *The Catechism and Confession of Faith* of the writer last mentioned, a popular text among the Friends in colonial and Revolutionary days, continued to

---

[112] George Fox, *Journal*, edited from Mss. by Norman Penny (2 vols., Cambridge Univ. Press, 1911), vol. i, pp. 21, 174, 323-26, 329-33; vol. ii, pp. 10, 51, 94-95, 104, 129-32, 138-47, 156-59, 272. Cf. *Gospel-Truth Demonstrated, in a Collection of Doctrinal Books, Given forth by that Faithful Minister of Jesus Christ, George Fox: Containing Principles, Essential to Christianity and Salvation, held amongst the People called Quakers* (London, 1706), pp. 201-04, 227-42, 994-98, 1086-89.

[113] William Penn, *Works*, vol. i, pp. 126-29.

[114] James Backhouse, *Memoirs of Francis Howgill, with extracts from his writings* (York, 1828), pp. 145, 146, 163-66.

[115] Josiah Coale, *The Books and Divers Epistles of the Faithful Servant of the Lord, Josiah Coale: Collected and Published, as it was desired by him the Day of his departure out of this Life* (1671). Cf. " The Whore Unvailed, Or the Mystery of the Deceit of the Church of Rome Revealed."

[116] Richard Claridge, *Life and Posthumous Works . . . Collected by Joseph Besse* (London, 1726), pp. 226-54, 491 *et seq.*, 550 *et seq.*

[117] Robert Barclay, *Anarchy of the Ranters, and other Libertines; the Hierarchy of the Romanists, and other Pretended Churches, equally refused and refuted, in a two-fold Apology for the Church and People of God, called in derision, Quakers* (London, 1733; also Wilmington, 1783, and other editions), sec. 8. There are some suggestive titles in Joseph Smith, *A Descriptive Catalogue of Friends' Books or works written by Members of the Society of Friends, commonly called Quakers, from their first rise to the present time, interspersed with critical remarks and occasional biographical notices* (2 vols., London, 1867), and *Bibliotheca Anti-Quakeriana; or, a catalogue of books adverse to the Society of Friends* (London, 1873).

be used until the close of the nineteenth century.   The Philadelphia edition for 1773 [118] contains also " The Ancient
Testimony of the People Called Quakers, reviv'd by the
Order and Approbation of the Yearly Meeting, held for the
Province of Pennsylvania and New Jersey, 1722." This
document reasserts the primitive belief of the society in the
doctrine of the inner light as a guide to conscience, their
rejection of original sin, of the sacraments, of a regularly ordained ministry, and their partial rejection of the
doctrines of the Trinity and the Atonement.   This was more
than enough to put them at variance with most of the divisions of Protestant Christianity.   Catholics being anti-
Christian, were beyond the pale, since they were the cause
of all the corruptions of the Protestant sects.   The yearly
meetings, besides reasserting their adherence to the " Ancient
Testimony ", renewed their acceptance of those principles as
set forth in Barclay's *Apology* and in the conclusions embodied in the *Book of Discipline*.[119]   Two brief quotations
from the last two titles will serve to indicate how closely the
Friends of Revolutionary America adhered to the society's
primitive view of Roman Catholicism.   The London, 1733,
edition of Barclay's *Anarchy of the Ranters,* or the *Apology,*
as it is briefly called, devotes Section viii to showing

How this Government altogether differeth from the Oppressing
and Persecuting Principality of the Church of Rome, and other
anti-Christian Assemblies.[120]

[118] Robert Barclay, *A Catechism and Confession of Faith* (Philadelphia, 1773). See the " Short Expostulation," p. 134.

[119] *The Book of Discipline, agreed on by the Yearly Meeting of Friends
for New England; containing extracts of minutes, conclusions and ad-
vices of that meeting and of the Yearly-Meetings of London, Pennsylvania and New Jersey, and New York; from their first Institution*
(Providence, 1785).

[120] Barclay, *Apology,* sec. 8.

The Book of Discipline adopted by the yearly meeting of New England in 1785 justifies among other practices the Quaker adoption of numerals to designate the days of the week and the month. After giving the " heathenish " origin of these names, the *Book* continues:

In the ages of Popish superstition, not only the use of such heathenish names and customs was indulged, but also other unfound and unscriptural practices in religion were invented and introduced.[121]

This was done by heathen priests, converts, whose interest it was to perpetuate these ceremonies.

From this corrupt source sprang the Popish sacrifice of the mass, the celebration of which, at particular times, and on particular occasions, gave rise to the vulgar names of Michaelmas, Martinmas, Christmas, and the like.[122]

The Friends, then, were at one with the other Protestant denominations in their opinion of Roman Catholic faith and practice. But there the parallel seems to end. Unsparing in his denunciation of a system which he deemed tyrannical, immoral, unchristian, William Penn nevertheless drew the distinction between the institution and its members. If with the one he would make no compromise, to the other he would accord the full measure of religious liberty which he demanded for himself. And notwithstanding the operation of the test laws, against which the Quakers made no protests save in so far as they affected themselves,[123] in no province

---

[121] *The Book of Discipline*, pp. 28-29.

[122] *Ibid.*

[123] This passivity of the Quakers in regard to the penal legislation of Pennsylvania was in direct contradiction to both the theory and practice of William Penn. For not only had he endeavored to obtain the repeal of the penal laws in England; when the opportunity offered, he repeatedly embodied his theories of religious liberty in the charters and laws of his

of British America did Roman Catholics have the freedom
in religious matters which they enjoyed in the Quaker colony.   Zealous Protestants in neighboring settlements might
protest,[124] the home government might express its displeasure
or renew its instructions for the enforcement of the penal
laws, the reputation of the colony might suffer, as in fact
it did, yet the " scandal of the Mass " was allowed to continue.   When in 1734 objection was made to the public celebration of Mass in St. Joseph's Church, Willing's Alley, the
Catholic appeal to the Charter of Privileges was sustained.[125]
In 1757 Father Harding repaired and enlarged St.
Joseph's.[126]   In 1763 a second Roman Catholic church, St.
Mary's, was erected in the City of Brotherly Love.[127]   The

colony. Yet such was the pressure of the home government that Penn
was forced to witness these liberal provisions give way to enactments
which reflected the intolerance of the authorities in England. The
Toleration Act, intended as a measure of relief to English dissenters,
was passed largely through his efforts. From 1705 to 1776 it was made
a test for all offices of trust and honor in the Quaker colony. *Charters
of the Province of Pensilvania and City of Philadelphia* (Phila., 1742).
*A Collection of all the Laws of the Province of Pennsylvania: Now in
Force* ... (Phila., 1742), pp. 310, 312, 403. Isaac Sharpless, *A Quaker
Experiment in Government* . . . *1682-1783* (Phila., 1902), vol. i, p. 123
et seq. W. R. Shepherd, *History of the Proprietary Government in Pennsylvania* (Col. Univ. Studies in History, Economics and Public Law, vi,
New York, 1896), pp. 351-387. Charles Stillé, "Religious Tests in
Provincial Pennsylvania," *Pa. Mag. Hist. Biog.*, vol. ix (1885), p. 382
et seq.

[124] The S. P. G. ministers were not at all in sympathy with the practical toleration of the Quakers. See letter of Rev. Colin Campbell to
secretary of S. P. G., Burlington, Nov. 2, 1742, in G. M. Hill, *History
of the Church in Burlington, N. J.* (Trenton, 1876), pp. 258-59.

[125] *Colonial Records of Pennsylvania*, vol. iii, pp. 545, 563. *Cf.* T. F.
Gordon, *History of Pennsylvania* . . . *to 1776* (Philadelphia, 1829),
pp. 570-71.

[126] J. L. J. Kirlin, *Catholicity in Philadelphia*, p. 84.

[127] P. S. P. Connor, "Early Registers of the Catholic Church in
Pennsylvania," American Cath. H. S. *Records* (referred to hereafter
as A. C. H. S. *Records*), vol. ii (1886-88), pp. 22-28.

TRADITION AND THE COLONIAL CLERGY   107

feeling of immunity from persecution is clearly evidenced in the address of the Roman Catholics to the lieutenant-governor, John Penn, upon his arrival in the province the same year. In what other province could Jesuits have ventured to sign the address in " Behalf of the Catholics "? To the Protestant governor of what other province could the Catholics as a body offer their " cooperation " in almost the same breath as that in which they begged his protection and a continuance of toleration? [128] That their confidence was justified is evident from a petition of the Roman Catholics of Northampton County who in 1767 asked for a license to solicit funds for the erection of a church.[129] The petition was, moreover, recommended by the justice of the peace.

Of the non-English sects on the eve of the Revolution, the Lutherans were the most numerous. Associated with them more or less closely, but decidedly Calvinistic in theology, were the German Reformed and the Dutch Reformed Churches. As the spiritual descendants of the leaders of the Protestant Revolution, as participants or victims of that series of politico-religious wars which devastated central Europe for so many decades, the Lutheran groups in America found themselves in complete accord with the anti-Catholic sentiment of these movements. To read the histories of their various settlements from Waldoborough in Maine to that of the Salzburgers in Georgia is to be convinced of how faithfully they preserved the traditions which had their inception in the Lutheran revolt.[130]

[128] *Newport Mercury* (Dec. 19, 1763), no. 276.

[129] *Pa. Arch.*, vol. iv, p. 279. *Cf.* J. G. Shea, *Hist. Cath. Church in U. S.*, vol. i, pp. 400-401.

[130] E. L. Hazelius, *History of the American Lutheran Church ... 1685-1843* (Zanesville, 1846), *passim.* E. J. Wolf, *Lutherans in America* (New York, 1890). W. D. Brown, *History of the Reformed Church in America* (New York, 1928), ch. 3 especially.

With the exception of the Augsburg Confession, the purpose of which was to emphasize the resemblances rather than the differences between the creeds of Luther and of Rome, the Lutheran confessions are permeated with anti-Catholic bias couched in the violent language characteristic of the monk of Wittenberg. The Augsburg Confession itself, for all its conciliatory diction, states clearly in part two its opposition to certain fundamental doctrines of the Church of Rome.[131] But it is to the Smalcald Articles and their Appendix that one must turn for the full flower of Lutheran hatred of that Church. By 1537 the breach between Luther and the Papacy seemed permanent; no longer was there need for the former to mask his true sentiments toward the latter. At the request of Frederick of Saxony, who deemed the language of the Augsburg Confession too temperate, Luther drew up the Smalcald Articles as a more complete expression of his doctrine. The Articles were approved by the Protestant princes in February 1537.[132]

As regards the Church of Rome and her teachings, let the document speak for itself. Article II . . . " of the Mass ", reads in part,

That the Mass in the Papacy must be the greatest and most horrible abomination . . . and above all other popish idolatries it is the chief and most specious. . . . Beyond all things this dragon's tail (I mean the Mass) has produced manifold abominations and idolatries.[133]

In Part II, Article IV, the Papacy is characterized thus,

131 P. Schaff, *Creeds*, vol. iii, p. 20 *et seq.*

132 H. E. Jacobs, ed., *The Book of Concord; or the Symbolical Books of the Evangelical Lutheran Church* ... (2 vols., Phila., 1882-83), vol. ii, pp. 41-45). *Lutheran Cyclopedia*, ed. by H. E. Jacobs and J. A. W. Haas (New York, 1899), pp. 427-28.

133 H. E. Jacobs, *Book of Concord*, vol. i, pp. 312-314.

For to lie and kill, to destroy body and soul eternally, is a prerogative of Papal government.[134]

This Article is amplified in the Appendix of the Smalcald Articles where all Christians are warned against the " godless doctrine, blasphemies and unjust cruelties of the Pope." The errors of " Popery " are denounced as the " doctrines of demons and of Antichrist." [135]   The Formula of Concord, the " amplest and most explicit " of the Lutheran confessions, though somewhat more temperate in expression, adopts substantially the point of view of the Smalcald Articles.[136]   In fact, all of the Lutheran confessions identify the Pope with Antichrist.[137]   In 1580 these documents, with the *Larger* and *Smaller Catechisms* of Luther, and the *Creeds* (Apostolic, Nicean, Athanasian) were incorporated into the *Book of Concord, or Symbolical Books of the Evangelical Lutheran Church.*[138]

Such was the European background of American Lutheanism.   During the seventeenth and until the closing decades of the eighteenth century, when the inroads of atheism, deism and rationalism fostered a reaction against all creeds and confessions, the various Lutheran immigrations adhered closely to the standards of the mother churches.   Governor Printz of the Lutheran colony at New Sweden on the Delaware was instructed to see

[134] *Ibid.*, vol. i, p. 320. For the Lutheran doctrine on monastic vows, see *ibid.*, p. 335; on human tradition, " the Pope's bundle of impostures," p. 336.

[135] *Ibid.*, vol. i, p. 346.

[136] P. Schaff, *Creeds*, vol. iii, p. 93 *et seq.* H. E. Jacobs, *Book of Concord*, vol. i, p. 667; ii, 51-63.

[137] *Lutheran Cyclopedia*, p. 16. G. E. Hageman, *Sketches of the History of the Church* (St. Louis, n. d.), pp. 243-44, 253.

[138] H. E. Jacobs, *Book of Concord*, vol. ii gives a history of the compilation and of the various symbolical books of which it is composed. It also affords evidence of the fidelity with which the spirit of the Lutheran confessions has been preserved.

that divine service be zealously performed according to the Unaltered Augsburg Confession, the Council of Upsäla, and the Ceremonies of the Swedish Church.[139]

The Swedish Church at the Council of Upsäla had adopted the " entire so-called Book of Concord." [140]

The Dutch pastors of the Lutheran congregations along the Hudson were directed to teach and preach " according to our Symbolical Books." The various churches under their care drew up constitutions which unequivocally acknowledged these standards of faith. Prospective preachers were required to sign a pledge that they would teach nothing contrary to the confessions of Lutheranism.[141]

The German Lutheran immigration, larger by far than that of the Dutch or Swedish, was distinguished for the confessional character of its churches. One of the earliest records is that of the Old Hill Church at Lebanon, Lancaster County, Pennsylvania. There the Lutheran and Reformed congregations, joint owners of the church, drew up a constitution called the " Rules of 1744." These included adherence to the Augsburg Confession and to the Symbolical Books.[142] Four years later, 1748, through the efforts of Henry Melchior Muhlenberg and his collaborators, the first Lutheran synod in this country was called under the title of " The Evangelical Lutheran Ministerium of Pennsylvania and adjacent States." The constitution drawn up by this synod required the subscription of every minister to " the Word of God and our Symbolical Books." Departures from

[139] John Nicum, " The Confessional History of the Evangelical Lutheran Church in the United States," *Papers of the Amer. Soc. of Church History* (New York, 1892), vol. iv, pp. 93-109, p. 97.

[140] *Ibid.*

[141] *Ibid.*, pp. 97-99. *Doc. Hist. N. Y.*, vol. iii, p. 590.

[142] Henry U. Heilman, *The Old Hill Church and a Court Trial* (Lebanon County Historical Society, vol. ix, no. 4).

these standards were punishable. Candidates for the ministry were to be examined for their knowledge of and their fidelity to these norms of faith and practice.[143] The synodical constitution of 1748 was duplicated by Lutheran congregations. The example of the Church at Lebanon was followed by that of St. Michael's, Philadelphia,[144] and other congregations throughout Pennsylvania. In Georgia the German Salzburgers kept alive Lutheran confessional traditions in the South.[145]

A canvass of the opinions of the minor religious groups, such as the Mennonites and the Moravians, warrants no change in the main outlines of the composite picture drawn by the sects already discussed in this chapter. Stemming from a common European source, the Protestant Revolt, the main outlines of the caricature, for such it was, would be much the same. Details might differ; nevertheless the monster called " Popery " was always recognizable. Emigration to British America would do little to soften its repulsive features; on the contrary, they would tend to become stereotyped in an atmosphere hostile to everything Catholic. Like the more numerous religious groups, these minor sects were to find hatred of Rome at times the only bond of union between them and their more influential brethren.[146] At times, too, it would prove a source of discord,

---

[143] W. Sprague, *Annals*, vol. ix, pp. v-viii. Hazelius, *op. cit.*, pp. 66-68. J. Nicum, " Confessional History," pp. 100-101.

[144] J. Nicum, " Confessional History," pp. 100-101.

[145] *Ibid.*

[146] Crèvecoeur, author of *Letters from an American Farmer*, more than once refers to the practical toleration of sect for sect, and to the growing indifference to religion of the second and third generations of immigrants. It does not appear, however, that this toleration was extended to Catholics generally. J. Hector St. John de Crèvecoeur, *Letters from an American Farmer*. Reprinted from the Original Edition. With a Prefatory note by W. P. Trent. And an Introduction by Ludwig

an excuse for persecution, for Mennonite and Moravian as well as Methodist and Episcopalian had more than once to endure the supreme insult—to be suspected or accused of being " Papists." [147]

This discussion of the attitude of the Protestant clergy towards Roman Catholicism may now be summarized briefly. And first of all there is to be noted the remarkable unanimity in their opinion of Roman Catholic doctrine and practice. Differ as they might and did on almost every other point, the various sects were sure to agree in their hatred of Rome. That hatred was no mere academic difference of opinion, but a very vital thing, kept alive by the methods of the early reformers whose child it was. There was the same theological appeal to the intellect, the historical appeal to the emotions; both were skillfully combined in the pulpit or on the printed page. In practice there was almost, but not quite the same unanimity. In theory every sect except the Baptists and the Quakers followed Locke in believing Catholics dan-

Lewisohn (New York, 1904), pp. 62-66. St. John de Crèvecoeur, *Sketches of Eighteenth Century America. More " Letters from an American Farmer"* (New Haven, 1925), pp. 63-66.

[147] The Mennonites in the articles of association drawn up for their settlement at Horekill in what is now Delaware County, Pa., would exclude among others, " all intractible people such as those in communion with the Roman See; Usurious Jews; English stiff-necked Quakers, Puritans, fool-hardy believers in the Millenium; and obstinate pretenders to revelation." George Smith, *History of Delaware County, Pa.* (Phila., 1862), p. 82. *Cf.* C. H. Smith, *The Mennonite Immigration to Pennsylvania in the Eighteenth Century* (Morristown, Pa., 1929), pp. 29-54, 308, 310 *et seq.*

The Moravian Indian mission near Sharon, Connecticut, was broken up by the government of New York in 1745, on the plea that the missionaries were " Jesuits and Papists, and emissaries of the pope and the French King." An act was passed requiring the Moravians to take the usual oaths, to have their places of worship certified, and to secure a license to preach to the Indian. *Doc. Hist. N. Y.*, vol. iii, p. 1023 (p. 603 in quarto ed.). *Cf. History of the Town of Litchfield, Litchfield County, Connecticut* (Phila., 1881), p. 569.

gerous to the civil government. The civil authorities were, therefore, justified in excluding them from every post of trust and honor. Strange to say, these two groups which alone pleaded for the inclusion of the Catholic in the same religious freedom which they demanded for themselves, also denied him political equality in the two provinces in which they exercised political control. In Rhode Island and Pennsylvania as in all the other British colonies, Catholics were disfranchised and ineligible for any office of trust and honor. Among individual clergymen who in other matters did not always see eye to eye with the official pronouncements of their church authorities, there was practically no difference of opinion as regards Catholics and the Church of Rome.[118] Considering the influence of the clergy in colonial and revolutionary America, considering, too, the importance of their sermons and other published writings in the history of the times, and their dominant position in the educational world, the conviction forces itself upon one that the almost universal execration in which the Catholic Church and her adherents were held in the period under discussion was due in no small measure to the fostering care of the Protestant clergy.[149]

[148] Ezra Stiles in the North and Jonathan Boucher in the South would seem to have been interesting exceptions. The former records in his *Diary* (vol. i, pp. 5, 7) two apparently enjoyable conversations with a "romish priest"; the latter on the eve of the Revolution made an impassioned plea that the Roman Catholics of Maryland be treated with toleration (*cf. infra*, p. 315). Sympathy with or for the individual Catholic did not however extend to the Church of Rome.

[149] *Cf.* P. Guilday, *Life and Times of John England* (2 vols., New York, 1927), vol. ii, p. 420.

CHAPTER IV

The Tradition in Colonial Education

However much the Reformation churches differed from
Rome on questions of doctrine and discipline, they agreed
with her in assigning to religion an all-important place in
the education of youth. Without a thorough knowledge of
the fundamental truths of religion, without that training in
the practice of virtue which such instruction presupposed,
the Christian ideal of love of God and one's neighbor, far
from becoming a reality, would remain but a beautiful
dream. The Protestant Revolt, with its heartsearchings on
either side, tended, for a time at least, to strengthen the
emphasis on the religious content of the curriculum. Flight
from religious persecution in the old world, although by no
means the only motive actuating the various emigrations,
would further deepen the conviction that the precious boon
of religious liberty must be guarded at all costs. "Liberty
of conscience," it is true, was a much abused phrase, since
to most of the sectaries it meant freedom for themselves
and persecution for others. But the very narrowness of
this conception, resting as it did upon the assumption that
they alone possessed the truth, made it all the more incum-
bent on the early settlers to transmit that truth unadulterated
to future generations. To this end education, formal and
informal, would be one of the most effective means. At
the foot of the educational ladder would be the elementary
school offering instruction in reading, writing and "cipher-
ing." This would be the minimum required of the members of a church which accepted the Bible as the sole rule
of faith and conduct. For subscription to the Westminster

Confession imposed upon parents and guardians the obligation of teaching their charges to read the Scriptures.[1] At the other end of the ladder would be the college or university with its chair or school of divinity. Thus an enlightened laity would cooperate with a learned ministry in the twofold task of excluding " the errors and superstitions of the Church of Rome," and of rearing in the wilderness a spiritual edifice which would embody Reformation ideals.

The so-called " public " school of the colonial and Revolutionary periods differed in many respects from the nonsectarian institution of today. It was essentially a church or a parochial school. Formal instruction in religion might, as in the case of the Boston schools, be relegated to the Saturday catechism classes; but the opening and closing of the daily program with prayer, the daily reading of the Scriptures, the appointment of teachers by the selectmen, usually with the approval of the ministers, supervision by selectmen and clergy—all this tended to the creation of a religious atmosphere which is entirely foreign to the public schools as we know them. In many of the smaller towns throughout New England—Rhode Island always excepted—where the town and the parish were often coterminous, the Congregational clergy exercised a controlling influence. Frequently the minister combined in himself the offices of teacher, administrator and supervisor. Where the Anglican church prevailed, teachers were licensed at various periods by the archbishop of Canterbury, the bishop of London, or the royal governor. In New York and Virginia teachers paid by the provincial government were to be examined by the ministers. This examination was intended, among other

[1] *Westminster Confession of Faith*, chs. vi-ix. P. Schaff, *Creeds*, vol. iii, p. 599. *Cf.* Burton Confrey, *Secularism in American Education* (Washington, 1931), pp. 3-14. S. E. Morison, *The Founding of Harvard College* (Cambridge, 1935), p. 150.

things, to insure the orthodoxy of the teacher.[2]   Possible heterodoxy was further guarded against by legislation which provided for religious tests for teachers and other educational officers.   The prospective teacher must give evidence of adherence to the Westminster Confession, the Thirty-nine Articles, the Doctrine, Discipline and Worship of the Synod of Dort, or the tenets of Quakerism.   To all of these creeds the Church of Rome was anathema.[3]

Orthodoxy in the personnel of the school was good, but not sufficient.   The texts, too, must be religious in character.   This, indeed, they were.   Hornbooks, primers, readers, spellers and even arithmetics, were made the vehicles of religious truths in general and of denominational instruction in particular.[4]   There were catechisms and primers without number.[5]   The use of many of them was limited

[2] S. W. Brown, *The Secularization of American Education* (New York, 1912), p. 5.   Confrey, *op. cit., passim.*   E. W. Clews, *Educational Legislation and Administration of Colonial Governments* (Columbia University Contributions to Philosophy, Psychology and Education, vi, nos. 1-4, New York, 1899), pp. 66, 69, 74, 79, 169, 223, 300, 314, 335, 352, 414, 416, 448, 461, 466, 480, 485-86.   M. W. Jernegan, *Laboring and Dependent Classes in Colonial America, 1607-1783* (Chicago, 1931), pp. 112-115.   N. Trott, *Laws of Brit. Plant.*, pp. 64, 198-203, 293, 318-19.   R. F. Seybolt, *Public Schools of Colonial Boston, 1635-1775* (Cambridge, 1935), pp. 28-29, 30, 58, 59, 67, 76.   S. Bell, *The Church, the State, and Education in Virginia* (Philadelphia, 1930), pp. 123-126.

[3] *Cf.* ch. III.

[4] G. F. Littlefield, *Early Schools and School-Books in New England* (Boston, 1904), pp. 69-73.   A. J. Hall, *Religious Education in the Public Schools of the State and City of New York* (Chicago, 1914), pp. 1-15.   C. Johnson, *Old-Time Schools and School Books* (New York, 1904), pp. 14-60.   J. A. Burns, *Catholic School System in the United States* (New York, 1908), p. 161.   C. H. Brewer, *History of Religious Education in the Protestant Episcopal Church to 1835* (Yale Studies in Religious Education, II, New Haven, 1924), pp. 27-28, 54 *et seq.*

[5] The first child's book written and printed in America was John Cotton's *Spiritual Milk for Babes in Either England.   Drawn out of the Brests of both Testaments for their souls nourishment.   But may be of like use to*

to the congregations of the ministers who compiled them; gradually, however, the *Shorter Catechism* adopted by the Westminster Assembly superseded nearly all others in New England. The Anglican, Baptist, Quaker, Dutch Reformed and Moravian congregations had their own catechisms. These might be printed separately, or incorporated in one of the numerous editions of the primer. The latter was a universal handbook, combining the features of an abecedarium, a speller, a reader and a catechism. With this single book parents could teach their children the minimum requirements of church and state. It was cheap enough for even the poorest families; for not a few it was the only book associated with their childhood. Its influence, therefore, in this formative period would be paramount.[6]

The average colonial child probably learned the alphabet not from a primer but from a hornbook. In its most characteristic form the hornbook consisted of a flat piece of wood to which was fastened a piece of paper or vellum containing the alphabet, a list of syllables, an invocation to the Holy Trinity, and the Lord's Prayer. The first row of letters was preceded by a cross and was called the criss-cross (Christ's cross) row. To protect the lesson, the paper was covered with a piece of thin horn and bound with a strip of brass. These hornbooks, popular in England in the sixteenth, seventeenth and eighteenth centuries, came to America with the colonists. Significantly enough, the New

---

any Children (Cambridge, 1656), N. Y. P. L. Increase Mather, a generation later, counted five hundred catechisms in use. L. A. Weigle, *Amer. Idealism*, p. 258 *et seq.*

[6] W. Eames, "Early New England Catechisms," American Antiquarian Society *Proceedings*, n. s. xii (Oct., 1897), p. 76 *et seq.* *Plymouth Church Records* (2 vols., Pub. Colonial Soc. Mass., xxii-xxiii), vol. i, pp. xix-xxi. R. V. Halsey, *Forgotten Books of the American Nursery* (Boston, 1911), pp. 6-7. P. L. Ford, *The New England Primer: a History of its Origin and Development* (New York, 1897), pp. 42-44.

England hornbooks effaced the cross from the first row, as tending to " popish idolatry." [7]

Although the *Shorter Catechism* of the Westminster Assembly omits the invidious reference to the " Man of Sin " contained in the larger edition, there were not wanting " explicatory catechisms " to supply the omission of the briefer texts.   One of these, *The Protestant Tutor for Children . . . To which is Added Verses made by Mr. John Rogers, a Martyr in Queen Maries Reign,* was printed by Samuel Green in 1685 for John Griffin, a Boston bookseller.   Its subtitle is " A Catechism." ´ Actually it is a reprint of a section of the first London edition of Benjamin Harris' *Protestant Tutor,*[8] and the John Rogers verses, which, although wanting in the first edition, were soon to become a characteristic feature of the *New England Primer.   The Protestant Tutor* has been discussed already.[9]

Another work of the same type was compiled by Thomas Vincent, who in his " Epistle to the Reader ", justifies its publication on the ground that the " popish axiom is long since exploded, that ignorance is the mother of devotion." With this premise the writer proceeds to enlighten his readers on the character of the Church of Rome and the nature of

---

[7] Morton's *New English Canaan* speaks of a minister who brought to New England "a great Bundell of Horne Books . . . and carefull hee was (good man) to blott out all the crosses of them for feare lest the people of the land should become Idolaters." Thomas Morton, *New English Canaan* (Amsterdam, 1637), p. 153. *Cf.* A. W. Tuer, *History of the Horn-Book* (2 vols., London, New York, 1896), vol. ii, p. 247. G. Littlefield, *Early Schools,* pp. 110-117. Ford, *New Eng. Primer,* pp. 23-48.

[8] There is a copy of this catechism (first leaf imperfect) in the library of the American Antiquarian Society.   It is referred to by George E. Littlefield in his *Early Boston Booksellers, 1642-1711* (Boston, 1900), pp. 147-161.   Mr. Littlefield seems to imply (pp. 109-110) that the Boston edition is a reprint of the London edition of 1679.

[9] See pp. 31-35.

her worship. The church herself he describes as " an apostate and corrupt church, and the seat of Antichrist." Of
Catholic worship he has more to say, enumerating thirteen
distinct practises, among " many more " which might have
been selected, as " superstitious and idolatrous." [10]

Of the primers strictly so-called, by far the most important is the *New England Primer*. For six generations it
formed the principal text of dissenters not only in New
England but in the colonies to the west and to a limited
extent in the south, and for another century it continued to
be reprinted in large editions. So great was the demand for
it in the heyday of its popularity that the New England
presses could not supply the trade, even though the editions
reached the tens of thousands. In Pennsylvania Benjamin
Franklin's press helped the good cause along, as did also the
presses of New York and New Jersey. Publishers in London and in Glasgow reaped their share of the profits, thus
swelling the magnitude of the sales which are said to have
totaled three million copies in one hundred and fifty years.
Small wonder that the *Primer* has been called " the little
Bible of New England," and that its influence in the formation of the New England character has been estimated to
have been but little less than that of the inspired text itself.[11]

[10] Thomas Vincent, *An Explicatory Catechism: or, an Explanation
of the Assembly's Shorter Catechism* (Northampton, 1805), pp. 16, 126,
230-31, 253; N. Y. P. L. Cotton Mather also contributed to these " explicatory " catechisms, adding to the Assembly's Catechism seven essays,
one of which was intended to fortify its readers against "the wiles of
popery." This new edition, called *The Man of God Furnished*, was
designed especially for New Englanders who were exposed to contamination from Canada. A like service was to be rendered to the frontier
settlements in the *Fall of Babylon*. See *Diary*, vol. i, pp. 572, 594-95.
Cf. W. Eames, " Early New Eng. Cat.," pp. 158-59.

[11] C. F. Adams, *Three Episodes of Massachusetts History* (2 vols.,
Boston, 1892), vol. ii, p. 778 *et seq.* A. J. Hall, *op. cit.*, pp. 26-36.
Clement Ferguson, " The New England Primer, 1690," in *Magazine*

Of the origin and authorship of the *Primer* much has been written.   It is now generally conceded that the early editions were compiled and published by Benjamin Harris.[12]   There is no known extant copy of the first edition, printed some time between 1687 and 1690.   It seems to have contained no anti-Catholic features.   In the second enlarged and subsequent editions, however, the account of the first Marian martyr, John Rogers, and the verses attributed to him are almost identical with those of the first London edition of the *Protestant Tutor*.   The prayer attributed to the young King Edward to " defend this Realm from Papistry " probably proved unpopular, or at least unsuited, to American texts, for it does not appear after the second edition.[13]   On the other hand, the John Rogers feature, appearing for the first time in the second edition, became one of the tests of a genuine *New England Primer*.   In its most characteristic form, the account of the martyrdom included a woodcut of the victim at the stake, his wife and children attending close by.   On the opposite page was this account:

of *American History*, vol. xx (1888), pp. 148-149.   P. L. Ford, *op. cit.*, p. 19.   Littlefield, *op. cit.*, pp. 147-161.   George Livermore, *The Origin, History and Character of the New England Primer*.   Being a Series of articles contributed to the *Cambridge Chronicle* (New York, 1915), reprint of edition of 1849, p. 26.   R. Rantoul, " Rantoul Genealogy," in Essex Inst. Hist. *Coll.*, vol. v, p. 149.   J. F. Watson, *Annals of Philadelphia and Pennsylvania* (2 vols., Philadelphia, 1868), vol. i, pp. 296-97.   S. M. Smith, *Relation of the State to Religious Education in Massachusetts* (Syracuse, N. Y., 1926), p. 46.

[12] P. L. Ford, *op. cit.*, p. 49 *et seq.*   W. C. Ford, " The New England Primer," in *Bibliographical Essays: A Tribute to Wilberforce Eames*, pp. 61-65.   C. Johnson, *Old-Time Schools*, p. 77.   Littlefield, *op. cit.*, pp. 147-161.

[13] It is interesting to note that it was included in *The New England Tutor, Enlarged* (c. 1702), published by Harris on his return to England. There is a photostatic reproduction of this text in P. L. Ford's *Hist. New Eng. Primer*.

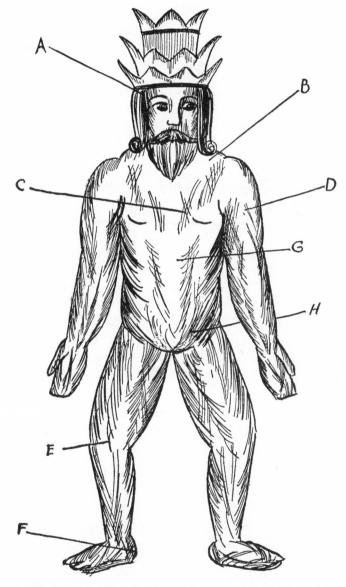

Paul L. Ford, *The New England Primer: a History of its Origin and Development* (New York, 1897), plate xix, p. 248. Dodd, Mead and Company.

Mr. John Rogers, Minister of the Gospel [14] in London, was the First Martyr in Queen Mary's Reign, and was burnt in Smithfield, February the 15th, 1554. His Wife, with Nine small Children at her Breast, follow'd him to the Stake, with which sorrowful Sight, he was not in the least daunted, but with wonderful Patience, Dyed coragiously for the Gospel of Jesus Christ. Some few days before his Death, he Writ the following Exhortation to his Children.

Then follow the famous John Rogers verses which include the lines:

> Abhor that arrant Whore of Rome,
>   And all her Blasphemies;
> And drink not of her cursed cup
>   Obey not her decrees.[15]

Another ear-mark of the genuine *New England Primer,* though absent from some editions, was the illustration of the Pope as the " Man of Sin." Borrowing the anatomy of the common almanac, so familiar in those days to every child, the compiler crowned the figure with a tiara, and placed over it the caption, " The Pope, or the Man of Sin." Lines designated by capital letters radiated from various parts of the body. The key on the opposite page explained the diagram:

Advise to Children

Child, behold that Man of Sin, the *Pope,* worthy of thy utmost hatred.

Thou shalt find in his Head, (A) Heresy.
In his Shoulders, (B) *The Supporters of Disorder.*
In his Heart, (C) *Malice, Murder, and Treachery.*
In his Arms, (D) Cruelty.

---

[14] *The Protestant Tutor* reads: "Minister of St. Sepulchers Church in London."

[15] *Cf. Protestant Tutor,* p. 45.

In his Knees, (E) False Worship and Idolatry.
In his Feet, (F) Swiftness to shed Blood.
In his Stomach, (G) Insatiable Covetousness.
In his Lyons, (H) The worst of Lusts.[16]

For over one hundred and fifty years this obviously one-sided version of the religious persecutions in England went unchallenged, until George Livermore in a series of articles in the *Cambridge Chronicle,* 1849, pointed out its inaccuracy and its unfairness. But Livermore is less concerned with the inaccuracies of the *Primer* than with the spirit which prompted their author. Without doubt, the latter intended to convey " the impression that the martyrs in Queen Mary's reign were all peaceable and passive subjects, directly the opposite in temper and spirit to their Catholic persecutors." Livermore agrees with Foxe that it was John Rogers who was responsible for the burning of Joan Bocher. Though Foxe's narrative has been questioned by Sidney Lee,[17] Livermore's contention that the *Primer* was intended to illustrate " the persecuting spirit of the Church of Rome " remains true. That John Rogers was done to death for refusing to recant the principles of Protestantism, was to the compiler the all-important fact; it was this that " gave to picture and poem their permanent place in the *Primer*." [18]

The sponsoring by Harvard of the third Dudleian lecture for over a century and a half, the colonial penal laws, the furor over the religious clauses of the Quebec Act, the retention of religious tests in the early state constitutions, the social discrimination against Catholics, the denunciation of Rome and her works by the Protestant pulpit, the fear of

---

[16] P. L. Ford, *op. cit.,* plate xix, p. 248.

[17] D. N. B., vol. xvii, p. 127. Lee refers to the 1563 edition of Foxe's *Actes and Monuments.*

[18] P. L. Ford, *op. cit.,* pp. 32-37. W. C. Ford, *loc. cit.* Livermore, *op. cit.,* p. 30 *et seq.* Weigle, *op. cit.,* p. 266.

the Jesuit, the hatred of France as a Catholic nation—all this is explicable in generations who were nurtured on the " spiritual milk " of the *New England Primer*.

What has been said of the dominance of the religious objective in elementary education during the colonial and Revolutionary periods, holds equally true of higher education. All but one of the colleges founded before the outbreak of the Revolution were under religious control from their inception; the exception, the College of Philadelphia, was for some time largely under Episcopalian influences. Most of these institutions were frankly intended to serve as seminaries for the ministry of a specific creed. One is not surprised, therefore, to find the presidency of such colleges restricted to the clergy of the controlling sect. The fellows, tutors, visitors and trustees were in some instances subjected to the same restrictions as the president, as in King's College and the College of Rhode Island. In others, the tests were broad enough to include all Protestants. Catholics, of course, were not even considered. Not until 1779 was a Catholic admitted to an office of trust in the pre-Revolutionary group of colleges.[19] In none of these institutions was a religious test required of students for admission. Some of the charters expressly forbade such tests, others were silent. But college regulations might be equivalent to a test. In the early days of Yale, all students were required to follow the divinity courses; at Harvard, 1734, the same obligation was imposed upon seniors and juniors.[20] Such regulations might or might not prove a hardship for Protestant students; for the practical Catholic they meant exclusion. On the other hand, no sectarian instruction was permitted in the class-

[19] F. N. Thorpe, *Benjamin Franklin and the University of Pennsylvania* (Washington, 1893), p. 83. *Cf. infra*, p. 154.

[20] *Harvard College Records* (2 vols., Pub. Col. Soc. Mass., xv-xvi), vol. i, p. 139. S. M. Smith, *op. cit.*, pp. 56, 58.

room at King's College or the colleges of New Jersey or Pennsylvania.[21]

Among the colonial colleges Harvard ranks first both in point of time and of influence. During the first half-century of its existence—a period when the Congregational clergy was still the dominant power in New England—fifty-two per cent of its graduates and forty per cent of its entire enrollment entered the ministry.[22] Many of them became important figures in church and state. The congregations of most of the smaller New England towns were supplied with ministers from the ranks of Harvard graduates. With the sons of Yale their influence spread in the eighteenth century through the middle and southern colonies, through the Ohio Valley and into the Northwest Territory.[23] All but the first two presidents of the college were Harvard alumni. In public, professional and private life, Harvard men were among the most distinguished members of the commonwealth. Of the nine colleges chartered before the Revolu-

[21] That does not mean however that religious instruction was neglected at King's College or at the College of New Jersey. See H. and C. Schneider, *Samuel Johnson*, vol. iv. pp. 115, 275 *et seq.*; John McLean, *History of the College of New Jersey* (2 vols., Phila., 1877), vol. i, pp. 140, 176, 213; vol. ii, pp. 50, 51, 57-59, 64, 106, 206. *Cf.* W. A. Bronson, *History of Brown University* (Providence, 1914), pp. 4, 29 *et seq.* Thomas Clapp, *The Answer to a Friend in the West, to a Letter from a Gentleman in the East, entitled: The present State of the Colony of Connecticut considered* (New Haven, 1755). Confrey, *op. cit.*, p. 19, n. *Sesquicentennial of Brown University, 1764-1914* (pub. by the Univ., 1915), p. 36. J. Quincy, *History of Harvard College* (2 vols., Boston, 1860), vol. i, p. 54.

[22] S. Morison, *Founding of Harvard College*, p. 247 n. *Cf.* Ezra Stiles, *Literary Diary*, vol. ii, p. 415.

[23] Thorpe, *op. cit.*, p. 140 *et seq.* J. L. Sibley, *Biographical Sketches of Those Who Attended Harvard College* (4 vols., Cambridge, 1873-1933, vol. iv by C. K. Shipton; introd. by S. Morison), pp. 3-6. H. C. White, *Abraham Baldwin* (Athens, Ga., 1926), pp. 19-27. E. Stiles, *Literary Diary*, vol. ii, p. 415-16.

tion, " five . . . were inaugurated under the direct or indirect influence of Harvard." Drawing its student body from the west and south as well as from New England, Harvard sent them forth again as witnesses of her " liberal and catholic spirit." [24]

However " liberal and catholic " its ideals were in theory, in practice the college absorbed and reflected the Puritan outlook of its environment. Controlled by the Congregational clergy whose Calvinistic convictions found expression in the Westminster and Saybrook Confessions, " they did not fail," says President Quincy, " to associate the college with the all-absorbing passions and prejudices of the times." [25] A bequest left to Harvard in 1750 by Paul Dudley gave the " standing order " a rare opportunity of indulging one of these pet " prejudices," and of inaugurating among the students a campaign of education against the Church of Rome which was to continue more or less uninterruptedly for a century and a half.

That the founder of the Dudleian lectureship should have had strong antipathies to the ancient faith is not surprising. In Elizabethan days his great-grandfather had fallen in the Protestant cause. Governor Thomas Dudley, his grandfather, left in his will a testimony of his hatred of " the old idolatry and superstition of popery." [26] Paul Dudley's New England environment was not likely to soften the inherited antagonism. Nor was it weakened by contact with non-English emigrants who fled from religious persecution in continental Europe. The year before he went

[24] S. K. Wilson, " The Genesis of American College Government," *Thought*, vol. i (Dec., 1925), pp. 415-433. G. G. Bush, *History of Higher Education in Massachusetts* (Washington, 1891), pp. 36-37. T. C. Wright, *Literary Culture in Early New England* (New Haven, 1920), pp. 16-22. Josiah Quincy, *op. cit.*, vol. i, pp. 44-50.

[25] Josiah Quincy, *op. cit.*, vol. i, pp. 44-45.

[26] Dean Dudley, *History of the Dudley Family* (2 vols., Wakefield, Mass., 1886-1892), vol. i, p. 88; vol. ii, p. 27.

to Harvard a band of Huguenots arrived in Boston and set up a church in School Street where young Dudley was at school. The story of their sufferings, remarked a nineteenth century Dudleian enthusiast, "lost nothing in the telling." [27]

Paul Dudley's career at Harvard, where he took his bachelor's and master's degrees in 1690 and 1693 respectively, was followed by a period of study in England at the Inner Temple. Law, however, was only one of his many interests, which included natural philosophy,[28] history, "sacred and profane", and theology. His advancement after his return to New England was rapid. He became successively attorney general of the province, member of the Massachusetts general court, judge of the superior court, and finally, chief justice. In all these capacities he served with ability and even with distinction.[29] It is significant that this representative of the highest culture of his day should deem it at once a privilege and a duty to found the lectureship named after him. "The public lectureship founded by him, is an evidence of his love of good learning, and of his reverence of pure religion," is the verdict of Alden Bradford.[30] Judge Dudley's contemporaries undoubtedly agreed with the biographer.

The purpose of the lectureship, as clearly set forth in the donor's will,[31] is to provide an annual discourse on various

[27] Prof. John Moore, in his edition of *Liberalism's Answer to the Claims of the Romish Church*, by the Rev. Brooke Herford, D.D. (American Citizen Co., Boston, n. d.), introd. Another ed., Boston, 1895.

[28] Paul Dudley was a member of the Royal Society of London.

[29] H. W. H. Knott, in D. A. B., vol. v, p. 483.

[30] Alden Bradford, *Life and Writings of Jonathan Mayhew* (Boston, 1868), p. 473. *Boston News Letter* (Feb. 7, 1751). Reprint of article in Dudleian Lecture by Ebenezar Gay, 1759, in *Dud. Lec. 1755-1770*, H. U. L.

[31] The passages of the will relating to the foundation were transcribed by President Quincy of Harvard and prefixed to the first manuscript

aspects of natural and revealed religion, of the doctrines and practices of the Church of Rome, and of the validity of Congregational ordinations. The cycle was to be completed every four years. Concerning the third of the series, the will reads:

> The Third Lecture to be for the detecting & convicting & exposing the Idolatry of the Romish Church, Their Tyranny, Usurpations, damnable Heresies, fatal Errors, abominable Superstitions, and other crying Wickednesses in their high Places; and Finally that the Church of Rome is that mystical Babylon, That Man of Sin, That apostate Church spoken of, in the New-Testament.

Some twenty years before he made his will the judge had himself written a pamphlet which might well have served as a model for the Dudleian lecturers. That it did in fact serve as such, a perusal of the sermons makes only too clear. In this *Essay on the Merchandise of Slaves and Souls of Men*,[32] he accuses the Church of deliberately prostituting the ceremonies connected with its liturgy and its sacramental system, that " sharpers " may make money for their own personal use. This " trafficking " or " Merchandizing " with the bodies and souls of men, he continues, proves beyond all doubt that the Church of Rome is the Man of Sin. We should never think or speak of her " without a holy Indignation and Abhorrence." As for the proposed union between Protestants and Catholics, " a communion of light with darkness, and concord between Christ and Belial, may as soon be expected."

volume of the lectures. *Dud. Lec., 1755-1770*, H. U. L. *Cf. Harvard Coll. Rec.* (Col. Soc. Mass., *Pub.*, xv-xvi), vols. i-ii, pp. 854-57.

[32] [Paul Dudley], *An Essay on the Merchandise of Slaves and Souls of Men. Rev. xviii, 13. With an Application thereof to the Church of Rome. By a Gentleman* (Boston, 1731).

The roll call of the Dudleian speakers is a distinguished one in Harvard and indeed in New England annals. The trustees of the foundation were the president of Harvard, the professor of Divinity, the senior tutor, the pastors of the First Churches of Cambridge and of Roxbury. Three of these, it will be noted, held offices of great honor and responsibility in the college. The president, Rev. Edward Holyoke, inaugurated the lectures in 1755. Two of his successors were among the speakers. Following the example of Rev. Edward Wigglesworth, the first of the " Popery " lecturers (though the third of the series), subsequent incumbents of the chair of divinity accepted invitations to deliver one or other of the lectures. The Harvard Corporation was frequently represented. In fact one is struck with the close association of the Dudleian lecturers with Harvard. Those who could not claim the college as their *Alma Mater,* or who in later life were not identified with her interests, constitute the exception. Of these Rev. William Gordon is an example. He illustrates, also, a class of interests, other than the purely academic and religious, with which the Congregational clergy of New England were so intimately connected; namely, the civic and the patriotic. Merely to mention the names of Charles Chauncy, Jonathan Mayhew and Samuel Cooper is to conjure up a host of associations connected with colonial and Revolutionary history.

Without doubt the Dudleian lecturers were a group whose opinions would carry weight. Whatever their interpretation of Roman Catholicism might be, it would be received by most Harvard undergraduates with a faith as completely credulous as any apostle of infallibility could wish. The average individual is a firm believer in the transfer of aptitudes and skills from one field of endeavor to another. Pious and godly in private life, " masters " in the Congregational " Israel ", eminent in secular and profane learning, skillful in controversy, eloquent in defense of civil and religious liberty—with all these claims to respect, to devotion, why should these speakers be doubted when they assayed an exposition of the " errors of popery "?

From 1757 to 1773 there were five Dudleian lectures on the " Errors of the Church of Rome." A detailed analysis of them would be but the repetition of an oft-told tale. All were delivered according to the letter and the spirit of Paul Dudley's will. The clause in the will already quoted seems to have guided the speakers in their choice of subject: " Infallibility," [33] " The Supremacy of the Bishop of Rome," [34] " Popish Idolatry," [35] " Popery a Complex of Falsehoods," [36] " The Church of Rome, the Man of Sin." [37] The list, it will be noted, offered an almost unrivaled opportunity to " hew Agag in pieces "—to borrow the apt phrasing of another. Indeed, as one peruses the finely written pages of the manuscripts, one cannot escape the deadly earnestness with which the writers approached their task. That it was a congenial one for the most part only added zest to what was obviously a religious duty. One is struck, also, by the lack of originality in treatment and in content. True, the speakers studiously avoided a repetition of subject, yet they managed to include with the exposition of their own chosen " error " a veritable litany of charges, religious and political, against the Church of Rome. These accusations were, of course, not new. They might be found in the works of

[33] Delivered by Rev. Edward Wigglesworth, May 11, 1737 (Printed Boston, 1757), H. U. L., N. Y. P. L., Boston Public Library.

[34] Rev. Thomas Foxcroft, May 13, 1761. H. U. L., N. Y. P. L.

[35] Rev. Jonathan Mayhew, May 8, 1765 (Boston, 1765), H. U. L., N. Y. P. L., Newberry Library, Chicago, L. C. Many copies extant.

[36] Rev. Samuel Mather, May 10, 1769. H. U. L. The four sermons just listed may be found in the Mss. volume in the Harvard Library, *Dudleian Lectures, 1755-1770.*

[37] Rev. Samuel Cooper, 1773 (Boston, 1773, 2nd ed., 1774).

many of the Anglican divines,[38] in Puritan manifestoes,[39] in
historical works such as Edward Johnson's *Wonder-Working Providence*[40] or in the more pretentious *Magnalia*[41] of
Cotton Mather, as well as in the private pages of the latter's
Diary.[42] To the lack of originality in method and content,
there is the added monotony of the vocabulary of invective
which has its limitations, especially when applied to a single
individual or institution.

But to the Harvard undergraduate who heard the third
Dudleian lecture but once, or at most twice, during his
college career, these limitations were not so obvious. On
the contrary, the summary of preceding lectures with which
the sermons usually began, and the peroration with its catalog of Rome's iniquities, would tend to round out a discussion otherwise restricted to a special phase. Occasionally
one meets with a lecture characterized with great—for the
subject and the times—moderation. Typical of this class
was the first of the series, delivered according to the terms
of the will, by the president of Harvard. Having demonstrated to his own satisfaction, and presumably to that of
his audience, that Rome's claim to infallibility is false, Dr.
Wigglesworth concludes with a clear statement of the opinion
which he would convey to the young divinity students before
him. He exhorts them to lay a deep foundation for their
theological studies in natural and revealed religion. That
done, they should turn their attention to the controversies

---

[38] *Cf. supra*, pp. 12-20, 47, 63 *et seq.*

[39] W. H. Frere, *Puritan Manifestoes, passim.*

[40] Edward Johnson, *Wonder-Working Providence, 1628-1651 (Original
Narratives of Early American History*, ed. by J. Franklin Jameson,
New York, 1910), pp. 23, 31, 50, 59, 122, 159.

[41] Cotton Mather, *Magnalia Christi Americana*, vol. i, pp. 65, 79, 162,
195, 229, 454; vol. ii, p. 229.

[42] Cotton Mather, *Diary*, vol. i, pp. 572, 594-95; vol. ii, pp. 207, 441-
42, 445-46. *Cf.* Mass. H. S. *Coll.*, vol. ii, pp. 133-35.

between Protestants and Catholics, because the Church of Rome is

a restless, incroaching, & implacable Enemy to Protestants of every Denomination. It is indefatigable in its Endeavours, compassing Land and Sea to make Proselytes. It utterly denies Salvation to any out of it's Communion. And its Heresies, Superstitions, Cruelties, Idolatries and other crying Wickednesses are such, that you will find it no easy Matter to persuade yourselves, that there can be any Salvation in it (pp. 30-31).[43]

Dr. Foxcroft's lecture in 1761 on " Papal Supremacy " need detain us only long enough to note its exemplification of that type of sermon which added to the exposition of its own special " error " a summary of European history from the Reformation to the " glorious revolution " of 1688. The recent fall of Quebec with its consequent transfer of territory to the British flag offered a current topic which might serve to quicken the zeal of the divinity students for the conversion of their " Popish and Pagan Adversaries." The concluding prayer, " May the Spirit of *Popery* be eternally banisht from every Breast! " runs through several pages. In fact the sermon was so lengthy that little more than half was delivered at the desk.[44]

Dr. Mayhew's Dudleian lecture was delivered when his international reputation was at its height, when everything he wrote, to quote John Adams, " was read by everybody, celebrated by friends, abused by enemies . . . To draw the character of Mayhew would be to transcribe a dozen volumes. This transcendent genius threw all the weight of his great

---

[43] *Cf.* C. E. L. Wingate, *Life and Letters of Paine Wingate* (2 vols., Medford, Mass., 1930), vol. i, p. 62. Paine Wingate, in a letter to the librarian of Harvard, May 5, 1831, quotes this passage as indicative of the " light in which Popery was regarded at that day."

[44] Note to Ms. copy in H. U. L. *Cf.* Sermon preached in Old Church in Boston, Oct. 9, 1760 (Boston, 1760).

fame into the scale of his country in 1761, and maintained it there with zeal and ardor till his death in 1766." [45]

There is nothing new in Dr. Mayhew's treatment of his subject, nor in his conclusion that every Roman Catholic is an idolater. He has, however, another quarrel with Rome besides the religious one, a quarrel which involves a

defense of our laws, liberties, and civil rights as men, in opposition to the proud claims and encroachments of ecclesiastical persons, who, under pretext of religion and saving men's souls, would engross all power and property to themselves and reduce us to the most abject slavery.

Transubstantiation, he continues, linking up religion and politics, denies the evidence of the senses. After the priest has " played a few tricks over a morsel of bread," we must believe it is God, " under pain of being burnt in this world and damned in the next." Such high-handed dogmatism is further evidence that " popery and liberty are incompatible . . . May gracious heaven ever preserve us from the one," he prays, " and deliver us from the other."

The son of Cotton Mather undoubtedly had a congenial task when he attempted to demonstrate in his Dudleian lecture of 1769 that the " Romish religion . . . is a complex Lie and a Compendium of Falsehood." To the prestige of family connections, he brought a reputation for zeal in the cause of liberty [46] which would give added weight to his exposition. His arguments were but restatements in syllogistic form of charges that might be found in his father's writings or in the anti-Catholic tracts with which Cotton

[45] John Adams, *Works*, ed. by C. F. Adams (10 vols., Boston, 1856), vol. x, p. 288. *Cf.* M. C. Tyler, *Literary History of the Revolution* (2 vols., New York, 1897), vol. i, pp. 121-24, 133.

[46] His brother-in-law, Governor Hutchinson, wrote to Sir Francis Barnard from Boston, Jan. 30, 1771, . . . " you know that he (Mather) has been as violent as any except Chauncy." *Hutchinson Correspondence*, vol. ii, p. 211, Bancroft Trans., N. Y. P. L.

Mather's library was so well supplied.[47] The sermon represents that type of lecture, already referred to,[48] which supplemented its specific topic with a historical disquisition after the manner of Foxe or Burnet. Mather's sermon proper is followed by an appendix in which he traces the development of the temporal power of the Papacy through stages which he terms " ten horrors."

Alumnus of Harvard and member of the Harvard corporation, doctor of divinity from Edinburgh and for forty years pastor of the Brattle Square Church, Rev. Samuel Cooper, Dudleian lecturer for the year 1773, was one of the most distinguished of that group of dissenting clergymen who were as ardent defenders of the " standing order " as they were stout opponents of every effort to subvert what they conceived to be the rights of his Majesty's " free Protestant subjects." Like Jonathan Mayhew and Charles Chauncy, he was as well known in political as in religious circles. His zeal for the patriot cause made Boston an unsafe place for him when the British army of occupation entered that city in 1775. So pronounced was his sympathy for France and his enthusiasm for the French alliance that his religious friends disapproved of his intimacy with a government so avowedly papistical.[49] If later he " viewed with alarm the hostility of the Bostonians and all the Congregational clergy toward France," and if, further, he " set himself to battle courageously against this current," succeeding so well that his Puritan congregation prayed for His Very Christian Majesty,[50] those who listened to his

[47] For a list of these tracts, see J. H. Tuttle, " The Libraries of the Mathers," Amer. Antiq. Soc. *Proc.*, n. s., vol. xx (1909-10), pp. 269-356.

[48] *Supra*, p. 132, Dr. Foxcroft.

[49] T. F. Persons in D. A. B., vol. iv, pp. 410-411. Sprague, *Annals*, vol. i, p. 440 *et seq.*

[50] B. Faÿ, *L'Ésprit Révolutionaire en France et aux États-Unis à la Fin du xviii Siècle* (Paris, 1925), pp. 87-88.

Dudleian lecture in 1773, or who read it in printed form (a second edition was called for in 1774), had little reason to be alarmed at his kindly feeling toward the religion of the vast majority of the Frenchmen of that day.[51]

Dr. Cooper's purpose is to prove that the Church of Rome is " That Man of Sin, That apostate Church spoken of in the New Testament." A consummate politician himself, it is not strange, perhaps, that the speaker should emphasize the human elements which in his opinion gave the Church such a firm hold on the minds and hearts of her children. After stating that " the Romish superstition " is " a surprising monument of human sagacity and weakness " (p. 5), Dr. Cooper proceeds to show that the Church advancing

by slow degrees to that fatal maturity it acquired before the Reformation, it was nurtured by the observation and experience of ages, and the abilities of a long succession of as deep politicians as perhaps the world ever produced. It discovers a thorough acquaintance with the frailty of the human mind: Its pomp and pageantry strike the senses; It manages with uncommon art and address, every object that can touch the passions; and while it flatters the corrupt inclinations of the heart, it is at the same time covered with a glare of devotion and austerity, and supported with a sophistry extremely adapted to dazzle and mislead the understanding (p. 6).

With the spread of Christianity and the increase of its power, the Church grew oppressive, but failed to veil her thirst for domination.

[51] A. H. Smyth, *Writings of Benjamin Franklin* (10 vols., New York, 1907), vol. vii, pp. 38-39; vol. ix, p. 91 n; vol. x, p. 248. E. E. Hale, *Franklin in France* (2 vols., Boston, 1887-88), vol. ii, p. 218 *et seq.* S. Cooper, *Sermon* . . . *Oct. 25, 1780*, pp. 42-45. [S. Cooper], "Address to the People of America on the treaty with France," *Affaires de l'Angleterre et de l'Amérique* (14 vols., Paris, 1776-1779), vol. xi, p. xciv *et seq.*, cxlix, ccx. *Cf.* Cooper's correspondence with Franklin in Smyth edition.

. . . Contrary to the spirit of dissimulation and subtilty by which it had been generally guided, it neglected to varnish its avarice, and venal dispensations for licentiousness, with the color of prudence and sobriety (p. 8).

It were unprofitable to follow the doctor through the course of his argument. By a process of selection and misinterpretation, he succeeds in "proving" that "popery is in the true and proper sense anti-Christian." To the Reformation which freed Europe from this anti-Christian bondage he pays a passing tribute. Then the scene changes to the new world, where in Canada "popery" has again reared her head in the guise of a "Romish bishop and a popish colony." Canada's proximity to New England prompts a word of warning. For

if Popery, deceitfully assuming a milder form, seems to be less dreaded and abhorred than it once was; let us be upon our guard, and remembering it is Popery still, be prepared to oppose it in every form. At best it is the extremest despotism . . .

Like Dr. Mayhew, Cooper argues that the Church which "tramples upon the rights of conscience" and presumes to absolve its subjects from "every sacred obligation" can offer no pledge "for the security of civil freedom."

Dr. Cooper's lecture was delivered almost on the eve of the Revolution. Before the cycle was again completed, that struggle was well on its way. Postponing to a later chapter the consideration of the Revolutionary and post-Revolutionary influences, let us pause here to sum up the probable influence of the lectureship sponsored by Harvard.

A comparison of the Dudleian Lectures with the early pages of this study will make it clear that the conception of Roman Catholicism conveyed by the series is in direct line with the English historical tradition. The Church of Rome is both unchristian and anti-Christian; unchristian, inasmuch as she has departed from the primitive teachings of Christianity; anti-Christian, because she is the implacable foe of those sects whose sole reliance is the Scriptures.[52] She has reverted to the grossest idolatry and the darkest superstitions of paganism.[53] She is, moreover, the most active enemy of Protestantism, seeking by means of her powerful organization to undo the liberalizing work of the Reformation.[54] Furthermore, individual Protestants are in grave danger of being enticed by the wiles of this Circe who has naught to feed them but the husks of swine. Protestantism as a spiritual force will never be safe while this inveterate enemy can compass land and sea.[55] It is war to the death between the two. Politically, Roman Catholicism is no less dangerous, for her teachings are directly subversive of all civil government.[56] As for intellectual development or social improvement, it is a matter of common knowledge that Catholic countries are the most benighted, the most ignorant, the poorest, the most superstitious, the lowest in the social scale. It is part of Rome's policy to keep her disciples thus enslaved, lest thinking for themselves, they might wish to throw off her yoke. True, there are some learned Catholics, but their enlightenment is directly owing to the Reformation and its liberalizing principles which by some miracle managed to penetrate the thick wall of " popish ignorance." [57] " Associated with civil and religious bondage, with perfidy and cruelty, as well as all that is absurd in doctrine and gross in

---

[52] S. Cooper, *Man of Sin*, 1773. E. Wigglesworth, *Tradition*, 1777.

[53] Paul Dudley's will, *Harv. Rec.*, vols. i-ii, pp. 854-59. *Essay*, p. 20. J. Mayhew, *Popish Idolatry*, 1765. S. Mather, *Popery, A Complex of Falsehoods*, 1769.

[54] E. Wigglesworth, *Infallibility*, 1759. S. Cooper, *Man of Sin*, 1773.

[55] E. Wigglesworth, *Infallibility*, 1759. T. Foxcroft, *Papal Supremacy*, 1761.

[56] S. Mather, *Popery, a Complex of Falsehoods*. S. Cooper, *Man of Sin*.

[57] S. Cooper, *Man of Sin*.

superstition," the Church of Rome, says a nineteenth-century lecturer, was "not only unfavorable to public liberty and social improvement, but utterly incompatible with either." [58]

William and Mary College, the second in time in the colonies, was as completely under Episcopalian as Harvard was under Congregational control. Founded in 1693 by Commissary Blair who was its first president, its three-fold purpose, as set forth in the charter, was to instruct the "Youth of Virginia" in "Learning and good Morals," to supply the churches of America, and especially of Virginia with "good Ministers after the Doctrine and Government of the Church of England," and to develop eventually a native Indian ministry. To attain these ends, the president, masters and visitors were to be members of the Church of England, and before beginning their duties were to declare publicly their adherence to the Thirty-nine Articles. In addition "they should be required to take the usual oaths of office, and subscribe the Test against Popery." [59] Down to the Revolution the bishops of London were chancellors of the college; its president was the head of the church in Virginia; its professors were ecclesiastics of the same church.

[58] Hosea Hildreth, *The Kingdom of Christ not of this World, May 13, 1829* (Cambridge, 1829).

[59] *Charter and Statutes of the College of William and Mary in Virginia. In Latin and English* (Williamsburg, 1736), L. C. Reprinted in *Bulletin of the College of William and Mary*, vol. vii, no. 3 (Jan., 1914). *Charter, Transfer and Statutes of the College of William and Mary in Virginia* (Williamsburg, 1758), L. C. The statutes are reprinted in *William and Mary College Quarterly*, vol. xvi (1907-08), pp. 239-256. Statutes of 1792, *ibid.*, vol. xx, p. 59 *et seq.* For administration of the test oaths, see "Journal of the Minutes of the President and Masters of William and Mary College, 1729-1784," *W. and M. Coll. Quar.*, vols. i, ii, iii, iv, xiii, xiv, xv. P. A. Bruce, *Institutional History of Virginia in the Seventeenth Century* (New York, 1910, 2 vols.), vol. i, pp. 385-86. See also chapters x, xi, xii for the history of the inception and founding of the college.

All students were to be taught the catechism of the Church of England.[60] These data afford no positive testimony of the attitude of the college toward Roman Catholics, yet they are not without significance.

In 1785,[61] according to a report of Bishop Carroll, there were but two hundred Catholics in Virginia. With the exception of the Brents and perhaps a few other families, they were mostly poor and obscure, without that social standing which would ensure an *entrée* into collegiate circles. The naturalization laws, together with the social and political ostracism resulting from the penal code, had effectively excluded Catholics from the province, or had rendered them objects of contempt, if no longer of fear.[62] It is unlikely that they would be welcome at William and Mary. Besides, the catechetical requirement, if strictly enforced, would exclude them. Moreover, the connection of the masters with the S. P. G.[63] would imply an unfriendly attitude towards Catholics who were not prepared to apostatize.

If colonial Harvard were a stronghold of what might be termed liberal Congregationalism, it was the boast of Yale that within her walls Calvinism, pure and undefiled, had found a refuge. True, economic and social factors were not without their influence in determining the foundation of the Connecticut college. The founders, however, made no

---

[60] *Chart. and Stat. of W. and M.* (1736). *Chart. Trans. and Stat. of W. and M.* (1758). N. Trott, *Laws of Brit. Plant.*, pp. 149-161.

[61] J. G. Shea, *Hist. Cath. Church in U. S.*, vol. ii, p. 257. Letter dated Feb. 27, 1785, to Cardinal Antonelli.

[62] That the term " Papist " connoted contempt as well as fear is attested by the many excerpts of this study. Another sidelight is furnished by a game with which the Virginia aristocracy were wont to amuse themselves, " Break the Pope's Neck." See P. V. Fithian, *Journal and Letters, 1767-1774*, ed. by J. R. Williams (Princeton, 1900), p. 74.

[63] See address of loyalty to the king transmitted by the clergy convened by the president of the college, Rev. Dr. Dawson, 1745. F. L. Hawks, *Eccles. Contrib.*, vol. i, p. 110.

secret of their lack of sympathy with what they chose to call the "apostasy" of certain members of the Harvard faculty, and they took care that officers and students of the new institution should be guarded against liberalizing tendencies.[64]   Classes were open to all Protestants. Religious instruction, which all students were obliged to attend, was to be based upon the *Shorter Catechism* and certain definitely prescribed Calvinistic texts.[65]   A synod of the Congregational Churches was to choose the first president and the twelve inspectors.   The same synod was to agree to "certain Articles relating to the purity of Religion", which the president, the inspectors, and the tutors were to sign.[66]   Notwithstanding these precautions, President Cutler, and his assistant, Tutor Brown, in 1722 departed from the straight and narrow path of Calvinism.   Whereupon, the trustees voted to "excuse" them from "all further service." [67]

By 1745 the expansion of the college warranted the conferring of a new charter for enlarging its "powers and privileges."   At that time addresses of sympathy and congratulation were being sent to the King by royal governors and colonial assemblies because of the abortive uprising in favor of the Pretender.

In 1752, when New England was torn with strife over the respective merits of the "New Lights" and the "Old Lights", the corporation of Yale reenacted the religious

[64] J. Quincy, *Hist. of Harvard*, vol. i, pp. 197-99.

[65] F. B. Dexter, *Documentary History of Yale University, 1701-1745* (New Haven, 1916), pp. 8, 16, 18, 27, 32, 47. E. Baldwin, *Annals of Yale College* (New Haven, 1831), pp. 20-22.

[66] F. B. Dexter, *Doc. Hist. Yale*, pp. 1-6, 231-34. "Founding of Yale College," New Haven H. S. *Papers*, vol. iii, p. 1 *et seq.* E. E. Beardsley, "Yale College and the Church," in W. S. Perry, *Hist. Am. Epis. Ch.*, vol. i, p. 561 *et seq.*

[67] H. E. Starr, in *D. A. B.*, vol. v, pp. 14-15. F. B. Dexter, *op. cit.*, pp. 229, 232. *Cf.* Conn, H. S. *Coll.*, vol. iv, p. 58, for Gov. John Talcott's letter to Jeremiah Dummer, Hartford, June 20, 1725.

tests, and stated emphatically that any officer who departed
from the Confession of Faith and the Assembly's Catechism
as " received and established in the churches of this colony "
should resign his office.[68] When Ezra Stiles was invited to
the presidency in 1778, he objected to this imposition of
creeds, and refused to accept the honor until the corporation
repealed the tests of 1753, " except an assent to the Saybrook
platform." Even as late as 1792, when a revision of the
charter introduced civilians into the corporation, and gave
them a part in the management of the college, the religious
tests for officers and students remained unchanged. It was
not until 1823 that all religious tests were eliminated.[69]

Yale's influence in New England, and indeed throughout
British America, was second only to that of Harvard. Nor
was she without champions who claimed for her the first
place. As Harvard supplied Massachusetts, so Yale's classes
in divinity trained most of the Congregational clergy of
Connecticut.[70] The president was divinity instructor of the
senior class. It is important to note that men of such diverse
outlooks as President Clapp who was largely responsible for
the tests of 1745 and 1753, and Ezra Stiles who refused
the presidency while such tests were required, were in substantial agreement as regards the Church of Rome. Stiles,
especially, was noted for his broad catholic sympathies, yet
he mistrusted men who had a " popish education " and deplored the Quebec Act as establishing " idolatry " over three-
fourths of British America.[71] And it is consistent with the

[68] E. Baldwin, *Annals*, pp. 68-72.

[69] S. E. Baldwin, " Ecclesiastical Constitution of Yale College," New
Haven H. S. *Papers*, vol. iii, pp. 405-442. E. E. Beardsley, " Yale College and the Church," p. 561 *et seq.*

[70] Ezra Stiles, *Literary Diary*, vol. ii, p. 415. Stiles notes that of
158 Congregational ministers in Connecticut in 1774, 131 were Yale men.

[71] E. Stiles, *op. cit.*, vol. i, p. 455. B. C. Steiner, *History of Education in Connecticut* (Washington, 1893), pp. 103-104, 122-23. H. C.
White, *Abraham Baldwin*, pp. 19-27.

liberalism of one who considered the Saybrook Platform a
sufficiently broad *modus vivendi,* that, reporting on the state
of religious liberty in New York in 1773, he should write
" that there are no laws in this colony disqualifying persons
for any civil office on account of their religious persuasion:
unless Quakers be considered an exception." [72] He was
surely aware of the anti-Catholic laws on the New York
statute books.   Were Catholics beyond his purview, or did
Stiles rest his argument on the Lockian theory that they
should be excluded from office because their principles were
dangerous to the state?

What Harvard and Yale were to New England, Princeton
was to the middle group of colonies.   Its fame however was
not confined to that section.   Like its northern contemporaries, the College of New Jersey extended its influence far
beyond the territorial limits of the region in which it was
located.   Founded by the " New Side " Presbyterians, who
in their zeal for a learned ministry had sponsored the Log
College movement, Princeton became the " mother of colleges " for that denomination, and " exerted a powerful
influence over the whole field of Presbyterian activity in
higher education." [73]   Its first four presidents came from
Yale, and the precedent thus established of having a Calvinist
clergyman as the head of the institution remained unbroken
until the twentieth century.[74]   Its connection with Scottish

[72] " Brief View of the State of Religious Liberty in the colony of
New York, read before the Reverend General Convention of the Delegates
from the consociated Churches of Connecticut, and the Synod of New
York and Philadelphia, met at Stanford, Sept. the 1st 1773," Mass.
H. S. *Coll.,* 2 ser., vol. i, pp. 140-155.

[73] D. C. Tewkesbury, *The Founding of American Colleges and Universities before the Civil War, with special reference to the religious
influences bearing upon the College movement* (New York, 1932), pp.
91-92.   *Cf.* J. McLean, *History of the College of New Jersey, 1746-1854,*
vol. i, pp. 61-69.   George Whitefield, *Works,* " Letters," vol. ii, pp. 348-49.

[74] V. L. Collins, *President Witherspoon* (2 vols., Princeton, 1925), vol.
i, p. 70.

Presbyterianism was equally close.[75] From Princeton's theological students the ranks of the Presbyterian ministry were recruited. In civil life, many of her sons became eminent lawyers, judges, physicians, educators, administrators. In the Continental Congresses and in the Constitutional Convention, Princeton alumni were both numerous and influential. In state politics, likewise, many of them followed distinguished careers.[76] Princeton's influence, therefore, was felt in every walk of public and private life.

The first charter of the institution, that of 1746, is not extant. The second, signed by Governor Belcher, September 14, 1748, provides for a board of twenty-three trustees, twelve of whom are ministers. The trustees are to take the oaths of I George I " for the further Security of his Majesty's Person and Government . . ." and of the act of 25 Charles II for " Preventing Dangers, which may happen from Popish Recusants . . ." The laws of the college must not be " repugnant to the laws of Great Britain " or of New Jersey, nor may they exclude " any Person of any religious Denomination whatsoever from free and equal liberty and Advantage of Education, nor from any of the Liberties, Privileges, or Immunities of the said College, on account of his, or their being of a religious Profession different from the said Trustees." [77]

[75] *New Jersey Archives*, ed. by A. W. Whitehead and others (Newark, 1880-1906), I ser., vol. xix, pp. 443-45, 433, 490; vol. viii, pt. I, p. II. *Cf.* Minutes of meeting of the Church of Scotland, May 31, 1754 in C. A. Briggs, *Amer. Presby.*, app. xxix. W. Gewehr, " Rise of Popular Churches in Virginia," *South Atlantic Quarterly*, vol. xxvii (1928), pp. 187-88.

[76] Rev. J. De Witt, in D. Murray, *History of Education in New Jersey* (Washington, 1899), pp. 245-246. For the influence of Princeton on the frontier, see *W. and M. Quar.*, vol. vi (1897-98), pp. 186-87.

[77] Charter of the College of New Jersey. Manuscript copy, Mss. Div. L. C., Force Coll., 1867.

According to the terms of this charter, Catholics, like students of all other denominations, would be admitted. The religious tests would, however, exclude them from the trusteeship, for in taking the oaths of allegiance, supremacy and abjuration, officers were obliged to declare their abhorrence of Transubstantiation and of " Popery." Furthermore, they were bound to receive the sacrament in the Church of England within three months of taking office.[78]   Here we have the anomalous situation of a royal governor, a New Englander suspected of Episcopalian sympathies,[79] granting a charter to a board of twenty-three trustees, the majority of whom were Presbyterians.   It is quite improbable that the non-Anglicans complied with the sacramental requirement just mentioned.[80]

The student body of the pre-Revolutionary college was small enough for the president and tutors to have a more or less intimate acquaintance with their young charges.   The

[78] Ruffhead, vol. v, p. 31, 1 Geo, I, ch. 13; *ibid.*, vol. iii, p. 377, 25 Chas. II, ch. 2. For administration of the oaths, see J. McLean, *op. cit.*, vol. i, pp. 134, 139.

[79] J. G. Palfrey, *History of New England* (5 vols., Boston, 1890), vol. iv, pp. 559-562.

[80] The same oaths were required at King's College on whose Board of Governors every Protestant sect then in New York was represented. While there is evidence that the official oaths were administered (*cf. supra*, note 78, and *infra*, notes 94, 95) in the colleges of New York and New Jersey, precise and detailed information is lacking.   The British statutes are lengthy and subdivided into many chapters and sections. Whether in America they were enforced wholly or only in part, we do not know.   Some sections would have less significance in the colonies than in England.   Certainly those who were responsible for the charters of the institutions under review, could not have been wholly unaware of their inconsistencies, nor of the embarrassing situations likely to arise in imposing their provisions on groups composed of both Anglicans and non-Anglicans. Perhaps the only practical ends sought were the allegiance of the college officers to the Crown and the exclusion of Roman Catholics from the governing boards and the faculties.   Other difficulties may have been tacitly ignored.

president usually taught one or more of the senior classes. His ideals—social, political, religious—would, consciously or unconsciously, be impressed upon his students. Of the pre-Revolutionary presidents, the first, Jonathan Dickinson, was in office about six months only. The second, Aaron Burr, held the presidency from 1748 to 1757. His sermons delivered during that period are of the politico-religious type which begins with the Roman Empire and the barbarian invasions, traces the triumphant career of Antichrist to the Reformation, which dispelled the " dark and dismal Night " brought on by " Popery and Mohamet ", reviews the " slaying of the Witnesses " (i. e., the Protestants) in the religious wars which followed, and concludes with a summary of the political situation in Europe and America. In the French and Indian War he sees what may be

the last Effort of the *Man of Sin,* and his Adherents, . . . one of the most *desperate Attacks* he has ever made on the *Reformed Churches. Satan* will seem to be loosed from the *bottomless Pit,* and will come in great Wrath, because his Time is short. But, blessed be God, tho' this will be a Time of great *Darkness* and *Distress,* yet it will soon be over.

The doom of the " Whore of Babylon ", the " Destruction of Antichrist " will be at hand.[81]

The power of Princeton's fourth president, Samuel Davies, as a recruiting agent has been discussed already. His anti-French animus, his enthusiasm for the House of Hanover as the embodiment of Protestantism, found expression in literary efforts which would reach circles untouched by his military sermons. One of these, an ode on

[81] Aaron Burr, *A Sermon Preached before the Synod of New York at Newark, Sept. 30, 1756* (New York, 1756). L. C. *Cf. A Discourse delivered at Newark, January 1, 1755, by Aaron Burr, President of the College of New Jersey.* Advertised and synopsized in the *New York Mercury,* March 3, 1755.

the " Military Glory of Great Britain," was given in the
form of a pageant at the commencement in 1762, the year
after his death.   Of no intrinsic literary merit, its allusions
to British heroes, to " Gallic rage " and " Iberian pride " as
contrasted with Hanoverian valor, would be sure to capture
the fancy of actors and audience as they experienced vicar-
iously the honors of war.[82]   The sectarian implications of
the ode would be the more effective because of their being
garbed in the mantle of patriotism.[83]

The Revolutionary president of Princeton, Rev. John
Witherspoon, was a man of wide scholarly attainments.
Few college presidents appear to have exercised so profound
an influence upon the young men who came under their care.
Like many of his confrères, he took a keen interest in the
politics of his adopted country.   He was an active member
of the Continental Congress.   It is interesting to note in
President Witherspoon's " first known writing on the American controversy " with Great Britain that he classes Roman
Catholics with the traditional enemies of the British colonies.   In his " Thoughts on American Liberty ", written
in 1774 prior to the meeting of the First Continental Congress, he suggests that " the great object of the approaching
Congress should be to unite the colonies, and make them as
one body in any measure of self-defense . . ."   To attain

---

[82] " The Military Glory of Great-Britain (1762). Rev. Samuel Davies.
An Entertainment given by the late Candidates for Bachelor's degree at
the close of the anniversary commencement held in Nassau-Hall, New
Jersey, September 29, 1762. Philadelphia, 1762," *Magazine of History
with notes and queries*. Extra number 114, vol. xxix, no. 2, p. 97 *et seq.*
At the same commencement was sung a chorus entitled " Britain's Glory,"
also by Davies, *loc. cit.*, pp. 105-06. *Cf. New York Mercury*, Oct. 1,
1759. See Commencement of that year, *N. J. Arch.*, 1 ser., vol. xx, pp.
383-84.

[83] Davies was succeeded by Rev. Samuel Finley, concerning whom, see
supra, p. 95.

this purpose, he submits a series of resolutions or recommendations, the sixth of which reads

That it be recommended to the legislature of every colony, to put their militia on the best footing; and to all Americans to provide themselves with arms, in case of a war with the Indian, French, or Roman Catholics or in case they should be reduced to the hard necessity of defending themselves from murder and assassination.

In view, then, of Princeton's inception and purpose, in view of the manifest antipathy of its presidents and of practically all who were prominently connected with the institutions in its early years,[84] it would seem that a Catholic student at Princeton would find himself in a thoroughly unsympathetic, if not actively hostile, atmosphere.

New York, like her sister colonies, was eager to have her own institution of higher education. Anglican interest in King's College was apparent in the offer, by the vestry of Trinity Church, of a portion of the Queen's Farm for the erection of the building, on condition that the president be an Anglican, and that morning and evening services be conducted according to the liturgy of the same church.[85] To the dissenters of the province this looked dangerously like Anglican control. Their protest, immediate and vigorous, was led by William Livingston, whose " Remarks on our intended College," published in *The Independent Reflector*,[86] inaugurated a lively newspaper controversy over the

---

[84] Gov. Belcher, the Tennents, the Caldwells, the Livingstons, to mention but a few.

[85] W. S. Perry, *Hist. Am. Epis. Ch.*, vol. i, pp. 429-446. F. Hathaway, "Columbia University," in *History of Higher Education in the State of New York*, ed. by S. Sherman (Washington, 1900), pt. ii, p. 133 *et seq.* *A History of Columbia University, 1754-1904* (New York, 1904), pp. 3-4, 11.

[86] *The Independent Reflector. Weekly Essays on Sundry and Important Subjects, more particularly adapted to the Province of New York. Printed (until tyrannically suppressed) in 1753.* See " Remarks on our

respective merits of sectarian and non-sectarian institutions. The debate attracted much attention throughout the country. Besides appearing in his own organ, *The Independent Reflector* (November, 1752-October, 1753), Livingston's contributions were published also in the " Watch Tower " column of the *New York Mercury*. He demanded (1) that the college should be " non-sectarian and catholic ", (2) that the charter should not come from the king but from the assembly, (3) that the officers and professors of the college should be subject to no religious test.[87]   For us the contest is significant, inasmuch as it reveals how completely Catholics were beyond the educational purview of liberal and conservative alike.

In his " Remarks on our intended college in New York," Livingston stressed the significance of a college in or near the city, and the still greater importance of its constitution to the bench, the bar, the pulpit, and the senate.   For, he argued, the students will imbibe the principles of the religious system of the college, and making them part of their philosophy of life, will carry them beyond the walls of their *Alma Mater* to their various careers and avocations.   Harvard and Yale are familiar examples of the extension of Presbyterian influence.   Undesirable religious principles may be propagated in the same way.   For

. . . In the Reign of King James II of arbitrary and papistical Memory, a Project jesuitically artful, was concerted to poison the Nation, by filling the Universities with popish-affected

intended College.   Shall it be sectarian or non-sectarian?   By Wm. Livingston, March 22, 1753," pp. 57-70.   Also in *Eccles. Rec.*, N. Y., vol. v, pp. 3338-39.

87 N. F. Moore, *An Historical Sketch of Columbia College in the City of New York* (New York, 1846), pp. 10-14.   W. S. Perry, *op. cit.*, vol. i, pp. 429-446.   F. Hathaway, *op. cit.*, p. 133.   T. Sedgwick, *Life of William Livingston* (New York, 1883), p. 74 *et seq.*

Tutors; and but for our glorious Deliverance, by the immortal William, the Scheme had been sufficient, in Process of Time, to have introduced and established, the sanguinary and anti-christian Church of Rome.[88]

In another contribution [89] he urged that the college be thrown open to "all Protestant denominations." Such a policy would not fail to attract students from other colleges. Moreover, he would leave officers and students free "to attend any Protestant church at their pleasure." [90] Morning and evening prayers should be such "as all Protestants can freely join in." [91] In conclusion, he earnestly exhorted all Protestants

By the numberless blessings of Liberty, heavenly-born;—by the uncontrollable dictates of Conscience, the Vicegerent of God; —by the horrors of Persecution, conceived in Hell and nursed in Rome;—by the awful name of Reason, the glory of the human race,

to defeat the scheme to rule them by a dominant party.[92]

In spite of the opposition of the dissenters, the royal charter was conferred October 31, 1754. Anglican control was insured by giving members of that communion a majority on the board of governors. The lands and funds offered by Trinity Church were accepted on the conditions mentioned above.[93] With the exception of the archbishop

[88] *Independent Reflector*, pp. 57-70.

[89] *Ibid.*, March 20, 1753, pp. 71-74. *Cf.* "The Watch Tower," *N. Y. Mercury*, Nov. 25, 1754, no. 120; Dec. 2, 1754, no. 121, and successive numbers to Dec., 1755. H. and C. Schneider, *Samuel Johnson, President of King's College*, vol. iv, p. 129.

[90] *Ind. Ref.*, April 19, 1753, no. 21.

[91] *Ibid.*

[92] *Ibid.*, Apr. 26, 1753, no. 22. *Cf.* H. and C. Schneider, *op. cit.*, vol. iv, p. 129. *Eccles. Rec. N. Y.*, vol v, p. 3364. For protests other than those of Livingston, see Schneider, vol. iv, pp. 208-212.

[93] *Cf. supra*, p. 147.

of Canterbury, the governors as well as the fellows, professors and tutors were to take the oaths mentioned in the Princeton charter. While no student was to be excluded because of his religious beliefs, the charter enjoined morning and evening services according to the Church of England.[94] The statutes of 1755 as well as the revision of 1763, made attendance at these services compulsory.[95] Besides the exclusion of religious tests for entrance, the liberals scored one other point in securing representation on the board of governors for every Protestant sect in New York City.[96]

The Minutes of the Governors furnish evidence of the faithful fulfillment of the terms of the charter. It must have been with distinct pleasure that Judge Horsmanden,[97] of Negro Plot fame, administered the oaths so freighted with hatred of Catholics. The zeal for Protestantism frequently emphasized in the speeches made at the inaugural meeting of the governors, recurs again and again in the correspondence of the authorities of King's College with prominent Anglican churchmen in England. Ten years after the formal opening of the college it was decided to make a "drive" for funds. In its choice of Sir James Jay as manager of the campaign in England the college selected an agent of Huguenot ancestry—one whose personal and hereditary hatred of "popish enemies" would be used to good

[94] *The Charter of the College of New York, in America. Published by Order of His Honour the Lieutenant Governor, in Council* (New York, Parker and Weyman, 1754), L. C.

[95] *Minutes of the Governors of the College of the Province of New York in the City of New York in America, 1755-1768, and of the Corporation of King's College in the City of New York, 1768-1770* (New York, 1932).

[96] *Charter.*

[97] The Judge qualified for governor by taking the same oaths, March 8, 1758. *Minutes of the Gov.* For his connection with the Negro Plot, see p. 57.

advantage. The petition which he presented to the King in behalf of the governors stressed the necessity of preserving America from the " slavish and destructive Tenets " of the " Emissaries of a false Religion." [98]

The first president of the college, Rev. Samuel Johnson of Stratford, Connecticut, was considered by at least one panegyrist to have been in his day the foremost Anglican clergyman in the colonies.[99] A graduate of Yale and later a tutor there, Johnson severed his connection with his *Alma Mater* in 1722, when he entered the Church of England. While pastor of the Anglican parish of Stratford, he wrote and published two letters in defense of that communion. To the charge that the church of his adoption " is little better than popery and symbolizes with the Church of Rome," he makes an emphatic denial, assuring his dissenting parishioners that " we have as much zeal against and hatred to popery as you can have." [100] The letter called forth a reply from " one J. G." who " wickedly " insinuated " that the archbishop of Canterbury is as bad as the pope of Rome ! " To refute this " intolerably abusive " accusation, Johnson goes into some detail to prove the difference between the two churches and their heads. When he has finished, the reader is under no illusion as to what he thinks of Rome.[101]

---

[98] *Gr. Brit. Trans.*, Lambeth Palace Mss., vol. 1123, pt. iii, no. 262. L. C. Mss. Div. *Documents Relating to the Colonial History of New York*, vol. vii, p. 643. These two sources supplement each other and contain many documents illustrative of the close connection between King's College and Canterbury.

[99] W. G. Andrews, *Samuel Johnson, D.D. An address delivered in Christ Church, New Haven, Conn., Nov. 4, 1892, Johnson Collection,* Columbia University.

[100] "A Letter from a Minister of the Church of England to his dissenting Parishioners, . . . New York. Printed by J. P. Zenger, 1753," in Schneider, *Samuel Johnson, Pres. of King's College,* vol. iii, pp. 20-21.

[101] "A Second Letter From a Minister of the Church of England To his Dissenting Parishioners, In Answer to Some Remarks made on the

Narrow as it was from a Catholic point of view, the liberal policy which included in the governing body of the college Protestants of every denomination in the state was destined to develop during the colonial and Revolutionary periods. Merged with the University of New York for a short time, Columbia College resumed its separate existence again in 1787, when the legislature ratified the original charter with the exception of certain provisions. Among these were the clauses which enjoined the taking of specified oaths, which required the president to be a member of the Church of England, and which prescribed Anglican forms of public prayer.[102] However the presidency of Columbia is still restricted by the Trinity Church deed of gift.[103]

Benjamin Franklin's " Proposals relative to the Education of Youth in Pennsylvania," 1749, bore fruit in the foundation of an academy of which he became the head. In 1750 he submitted, in the name of the trustees, to the Common Council of Philadelphia, a paper setting forth the purpose and benefits of the institution. The children of the wealthy and the fairly well-to-do would no longer have to send their children abroad, since the education offered at the academy would prepare the youth of Pennsylvania for distinguished service in public and private life. The charity school in connection with the academy would instruct poor children in the

former by one J. G. . . . (Boston, 1734), Schneider, *op. cit.*, vol. iii, p. 45 *et seq.* For further evidence of the same point of view, see Schneider, vol. i, p. 411; vol. iii, pp. 211, 222. "A Sermon on The Great Duty of Thankfulness to God & Especially for Public Blessings. . . . For the Fifth of November, being also appointed by the Government for a General Thanksgiving, 1740," Ms. *John. Coll.*, Col. Univ.

[102] Thomas Greenleaf, *Laws of the State of New York, comprising the Constitution and the Acts of the Legislature, since the Revolution, from the First to the Twentieth Session inclusive* (3 vols., 2d ed., New York, 1798), vol. i, p. 437.

[103] *History of Columbia University*, p. 13.

three " R's " and in " the first principles of virtue and piety." No " sect or party " was to be excluded. Not the least of the advantages of the charity school would be the training of teachers for the rural districts which were often " obliged . . .

to employ in their schools vicious imported servants or concealed Papists, who by their bad examples and instructions often deprave the morals or corrupt the principles of the children under their care." [104]

By 1754 the academy had expanded into a group of schools called collectively the College and Academy of Philadelphia. Under the provostship of Rev. William Smith (1754-1779), Episcopalian influence predominated in the institution.[105] This ascendency called forth no little criticism from the Quakers and other non-conformist groups. As the Revolution approached, the provost's unpopularity, the Tory sympathies of many of the trustees, and the English support [106] of the college increased the opposition to those in power. On November 27, 1779, the assembly passed an act dispossessing the trustees of the College of Philadelphia of their privileges and estates, on the ground that they had departed

---

[104] William Smith, *Life and Correspondence of*, ed. by H. W. Smith (Philadelphia, 1879), vol. i, p. 51. F. N. Thorpe, *Benjamin Franklin and the University of Pennsylvania*, pp. 215-232. W. S. Perry, *Hist. Am. Epis. Ch.*, vol. i, pp. 426-445. J. F. Watson, *Annals of Philadelphia and Pennsylvania*, vol. i, p. 286 *et seq.*

[105] F. N. Thorpe, *op. cit.*, pp. 215-232. However the vice-provost, Rev. Francis Alison, was a Presbyterian. *Cf. infra*, pp. 267.

[106] Smith was collecting for his institution at the same time that Jay was convassing for King's College. See broadside published Sept., 1762, "An Humble Representation by William Smith, D.D. and James Jay, M.D. In behalf of the lately erected colleges of Philadelphia and New York." L. C. *Coll. of Broadsides*, Gr. Brit., vol. 269. *Cf.* documents v and vi in F. N. Thorpe, *op. cit.*, pp. 77-79; also *Newport Mercury*, Oct. 17, 1763, and *New York Gazette*, May 16, 1763, no. 231, for excerpts from the sermon of John Brown, D.D., bishop of Newcastle. *Lambeth Palace Mss.*, vol. 1123, pt. iii, nos. 257, 260.

from the original " catholicism " of the charter.   Under the designation of the "University of the State of Pennsylvania," all the powers of the college, academy and charitable school were vested in a new board of control consisting among others of the senior members of the various churches, the Roman Catholic included.[107]   The Jesuit missionary, Father Farmer (Steinmeyer) was the first Catholic priest to serve on the governing board of a college within the present limits of the United States.

The three remaining colleges need not detain us long. When it became evident to the Baptists that it was impossible to train their own candidates for the ministry in colleges controlled by other denominations, Rhode Island, because of her tradition of religious liberty, was chosen as the seat of their venture.   The Baptists had themselves been through the fires of persecution; into the charter of their first college they would incorporate the broadest principles of toleration. It was enacted, therefore,

that into this Liberal and Catholic Institution shall never be admitted any Religious Tests, but on the Contrary all the Members hereof shall forever enjoy full free Absolute and un-interrupted Liberty of Conscience and that the Places of Professors, Tutors and all other Officers the President alone

[107] *Laws Enacted at the First Sitting of the Fourth General Assembly of the Commonwealth of Pennsylvania* (Philadelphia, October 25, 1779), ch. 136, pp. 271-272.   This act also abrogated the test oaths, 1 Geo. I, ch. 13, and 25 Chas. II, of the charter of 1755.   By an Act of Assembly, March 6, 1789, the dispossessed trustees were reinstated because they had not been given a trial by jury.   This repeal renewed the college, so that there were two institutions with the same purpose and claiming the same support.   They were united under the name of the University of Penn-sylvania by an Act of Assembly, Sept. 20, 1791.   See F. N. Thorpe, *op. cit.*, pp. 88, 92.   *Cf.* S. W. Pennypacker, " The University of Penn-sylvania in its Relations to the State of Pennsylvania," *Pennsylvania Mag. Hist. & Biog.*, vol. xv (1891), p. 88 *et seq.*

excepted shall be free and open to all Denominations of Protestants . . . [108]

That Jews were included in " all Denominations of Protestants," seems apparent from a letter drafted by Rev. James Manning, " at the direction of the corporation, in 1770," in reply to an inquiry of a Jewish merchant. " The committee," writes the historian of the university, " express their willingness to appoint a Jew as professor of Hebrew." [109] Catholics, according to the charter, might be admitted as students, but they were excluded from the faculty and from all other places of honor and trust. President Manning was sufficiently broad-minded to appreciate the bigotry of the apparently liberal clauses, for he asked a correspondent in France to assure the French King that the exclusion of Catholics from the faculty was a relic " from the Times of our Ignorance," and that if the disabilities were removed from the state constitution, he had no doubt but that the college charter would be amended also. Yet Brown was the institution which " recognized more broadly than any other the principle of denominational cooperation." [110]

Dartmouth, whose charter dates from 1769, was the outgrowth of an Indian school established in 1754 at Lebanon by Rev. Eleazar Wheelock, whose antagonism to Catholic missionary efforts among the Indians on the New Hampshire frontier is only too evident from his correspondence and " Narratives." [111] The incorporation of the Indian

---

[108] W. A. Bronson, *The History of Brown University*, p. 506. R. A. Guild, *Early History of Brown University, including the Life, Times, and Correspondence of President Manning* (Providence, 1897), p. 535 *et seq.*

[109] *Ibid.*, p. 100.   [110] *Ibid.*, pp. 30, 100.

[111] Letter of Wheelock to Sir William Johnson, June, 1761, in D. McClure, *Memoir of Rev. Eleazar Wheelock* (Newburyport, 1811), p. 227. E. Wheelock, *A Continuation of the Narrative of the Indian Charity School, begun in Lebanon, Connecticut, now incorporated with Dartmouth College, in Hanover, in the Province of New Hampshire* (Hartford, 1772), (From Sept. 26, 1772, to Sept. 26, 1773), pp. 5-8, 10, 14.

school with Dartmouth was not likely to lessen that antipathy. Theoretically non-sectarian, the control of the college by the " standing order " was as complete as if it had rested on legal sanctions. The Westminster Confession and Catechism constituted the spiritual norm for all who would serve Dartmouth in any capacity. Assuming that orthodoxy was at least as carefully guarded in the eighteenth as in the nineteenth century, we can form some notion of Dartmouth's thoroughly Calvinistic atmosphere by the care with which the religious sympathies of the faculty were watched. In 1835 a professor of chemistry, and in 1849 a professor of Greek were removed from office because of leanings towards Episcopalianism in the one case and Universalism in the other. As late as 1891 an instructor in public speaking was rejected because he was an Episcopalian.[112] What consideration would have been accorded a Catholic applicant?

The charter of Queen's College issued by George III in 1770 reflects the beginnings of relief legislation for the Catholics of England. The oaths required by the charter are those imposed by 6 George III, ch. 53, a simple oath of allegiance to the king and of abjuration of the Pretender.[113] In view of the purpose of the college, the education of candidates for the ministry of the Dutch Reformed Church, it is not surprising that the president should be a member of that denomination.[114] No religious tests were required of students.[115]

[112] L. B. Richardson, *History of Dartmouth College* (2 vols., Hanover, 1932), vol. i, pp. 445-52, 637-38. *Cf.* David McClure, *Diary, 1748-1820* (New York, 1899), p. 8.

[113] Ruffhead, vol. x, pp. 276-77.

[114] *Charter of a College To be erected in New-Jersey, By the Name of Queen's College, For the Education of the Youth of the said Province and the Neighboring Colonies in true Religion and useful Learning, and particularly for providing an able and learned Protestant Ministry, according to the Constitution of the Reformed Churches in the United*

Plainly, then, there was no place for the Roman Catholic in the colonial educational systems. The frankly denominational character of educational legislation effectively prevented Catholics from qualifying as teachers in schools established by the government. Their children presumably might have entered the schools as pupils, for drastic as were the immigration and naturalization laws, school legislation seems to have been free from such discrimination. That some Catholic children did, in fact, attend these schools seems beyond question. But it could only be at the cost of hearing their religion vilified. The very texts, as we have seen, were intended to inculcate an abiding hatred of " Popery." Matriculation at the higher institutions would not only plunge the student into a bitterly hostile atmosphere, but in most cases would involve apostasy.

There were, of course, the private schools. While these institutions were not confined to any particular colony or section, they were probably more numerous in the central and southern groups where up to the Revolution the governments did little or nothing for elementary or secondary education. It was in these schools that Catholics for the most part obtained their education. The Irish schoolmaster was ubiquitous.[116] Most of them were Presbyterians from

Provinces, using the Discipline approved and instituted by the National Synod of Dort, in the year 1618 and 1619, New York, printed by John Holt, 1770. Facsimile, L. C.

[115] W. H. S. Demarest, *History of Rutgers College* (New Brunswick, 1924), pp. 1, 6, 75, 274, 402, 546. In 1920 the legislature of New Jersey amended the charter annulling the requirement that the president be a member of the Dutch Reformed Church, *Acts of the One Hundred and Forty-fourth Legislature of the State of New Jersey* (Trenton, 1920), ch. cxxxv, p. 273.

[116] *Cf.* R. J. Purcell, "Education and Irish Teachers in Colonial Maryland," *Catholic Educational Review*, vol. xxxii (March, 1934), pp. 143-52; "Some Early Teachers in Connecticut," *Cath. Ed. Rev.*, vol. xxxii (June, 1934), p. 332 *et seq.*

the north of Ireland, but some also were Catholics. Catholic missionary priests, like their Protestant brethren, united in themselves the functions of pastor and teacher. The S. P. G. correspondence bears eloquent testimony to the untiring zeal of the " papist " schoolmaster, be he layman or Jesuit.[117] Wealthy Catholics like the Carrolls of Maryland could hire tutors or send their children to be educated abroad. Such opportunities, however, were closed to the poor, perhaps, also, to the Catholic in fairly easy circumstances. The vast majority of them were dependent upon home instruction, or upon the efforts, always uncertain and frequently interrupted, of the private schoolmaster.

Here and there, as circumstances of time and place permitted, foundations were made. Most of them were short-lived, however, and their story but emphasizes anew the prevailing antagonism of American public opinion. A Latin school in New York, founded during the liberal administration of Governor Dongan, flourished for a time. Jesuit supervision and Catholic patronage proved its undoing when the government was seized by Leisler at the downfall of James II.[118] Thereafter New York penal legislation with its liberal rewards to informers [119] obliged Catholics to carry on their educational activities with the utmost secrecy. In Virginia the story is much the same. Notwithstanding periods of relatively light enforcement of the penal laws,[120]

[117] W. S. Perry, *Historical Collections*, vol. ii, pp. 216, 219, 311, 316, 468-9, vol. iv, pp. 233-34, 241, 251.

[118] *Eccles. Rec., N. Y.*, vol. ii, p. 877 *et seq.* H. Foley, *Rec. Eng. Prov.*, vol. vii, pt. 1, pp. 282, 343, 335. *Doc. Hist. N. Y.*, vol. ii, pp. 14, 147. T. P. Phelan, " Thomas Dongan, Colonial Governor of New York," *Journal*, American Irish Historical Society, vol. xvi (1917), pp. 22 *et seq.* J. H. Kennedy, *Thomas Dongan, Governor of New York, 1682-1688*, p. 82.

[119] *Supra*, pp. 56-57, 60.

[120] D. R. Randall, *The Puritan Colony in Virginia* (Johns Hopkins Univ. Studies in History and Political Science, 4 ser., vol. vi, 1886), pp. 242-3. But *cf. supra*, pp. 56-60. Sadie Bell, *The Church, the State, and Education in Virginia*, pp. 105, 133-4.

organized educational effort by the comparatively few Catholics in Virginia was out of the question.

The difficulties under which Catholics labored in the education of their children can best be studied in Maryland, where they were most numerous. There, in 1671, a bill for the erection of a school or college was lost because of failure to agree upon the site and the religious affiliations of the teachers. The Puritan party objected to the location of the institution at St. Mary's, a thriving center of Catholicity, and wished the teachers to be of " the Reformed Church of England," or to be equally divided between Catholics and Protestants.[121] The Act of 1694 for the erection of a free school in every county, " that a perpetual succession of Protestant divines of the Church of England may be provided for the propagation of the true Christian religion," was slow of realization.[122] Even after the passage of the Act of 1723 " for the Encouragement of Learning ",[123] county schools were opened only gradually. These institutions were supposedly supervised by visitors, but " the only supervision of schoolmasters," remarks Steiner, " was undertaken with a view to prevent Catholics from teaching." [124]

The activity of Catholic schoolmasters was one of the grievances which the general meeting of the Anglican clergy at Annapolis, October, 1753, proposed to lay before the Lower House.[125] The same year a schoolmaster named Elston was reported by the Committee of Grievances and Courts of Justice for attending Mass, keeping school and

[121] *Md. Arch.*, Proceedings and Acts of the Assembly, April, 1666-June, 1676, vol. ii, p. 262.

[122] W. S. Perry, *Hist. Coll.*, vol. iv, pp. 1-2, 33.

[123] *Laws of Maryland at Large,* compiled by Thomas Bacon (Annapolis, 1765), 1723, ch. xix.

[124] B. C. Steiner, *History of Education in Maryland* (Washington, 1894), p. 34.

[125] *Calvert Papers, 1753,* no. 510. *Cf. supra,* p. 73.

teaching fifteen or sixteen pupils. In 1754 returns were made from various counties of schoolmasters who had taken the prescribed oaths and of those who had not. In Dorchester County, Edward McShehy, master of a free school, and eleven masters of private schools, had taken the oaths. One teacher had fled the country rather than take the test; another had refused, and two others, suspected of Catholicity, had been summoned to the next court. The administration of the tests in Frederick County caused several Catholic schoolmasters to flee to Pennsylvania where toleration was a fact.[126]

In the face of such efforts to eliminate the Catholic schoolmaster from the free schools, it would seem like temerity to attempt to establish distinctly Catholic schools. Yet this was done by both the laity and the clergy. The former are represented by a school called " My Lady's Manor ", established in 1752 by Daniel Connelly and Patrick Cavanaugh, and by another opened five years later in Baltimore by Mary Anne Marsh. The latter was brought to the attention of the assembly by Rev. Thomas Chase, who complained that the Protestant schoolmaster had lost many of his pupils " to the popish seminary." The assembly, as was expected, ordered the magistrates to call all keepers of public and private schools and to prosecute according to the law those who refused to take the oaths.[127]

The laity also gave whole-hearted cooperation to the clergy. The chaplains who served as tutors to the children of the manor, also counted among their pupils the children

---

[126] W. S. Perry, *op. cit.*, vol. iv, pp. 171-77. J. A. Burns, *The Catholic School System in the United States*, p. 106 *et seq.*; " Early Jesuit Schools in Maryland," *Catholic University Bulletin*, vol. xiii (July, 1907), pp. 361-381. R. J. Purcell, " Education and Irish Teachers in Colonial Maryland," *Catholic Educational Review*, vol. xxxii (March, 1934), pp. 143-52. J. T. Scharf, *History of Maryland* (3 vols., Baltimore, 1879), vol. i, p. 351 *et seq.*

[127] *Md. Arch.*, vol. xxxi, p. 208 *et seq.*

of the neighboring gentry as well. Wealthy planters left bequests for the endowment of schools. The preparatory school conducted by the Jesuit lay brother, Ralph Crouch, at Newton, probably owes its existence to the generosity of Edward Cotton,[128] who in 1653 left the bulk of his estate for the advancement of Catholic education. How long the school was in operation, or what became of it, is not known. Equally obscure is the history of another school at Newton established in 1677 through the gift of Luke Gardner, whose will was dated 1673. Father Burns thinks it was of collegiate grade and that to it belongs the honor of being the second college within the limits of the United States. Best known of the Jesuit institutions was the preparatory school at Bohemia Manor, near the Pennsylvania boundary. Here " Jacky " Carroll, the future archbishop, and probably his cousin, Charles Carroll, the Brents, the Neales, the Heaths, and the sons of other noted Maryland families, were prepared for St. Omer's. The list of students who went to Europe in 1745 is still extant. Isolated though it was, the school did not escape the vigilance of Rev. Mr. Reading of Apoquiniminck, who wished the law enforced against " this very considerable popish seminary." The school was in operation eleven years, being closed in 1765.[129]

A few bequests in a book of wills, evidence of two schools conducted by laymen, a few documents relating to two Jesuit secondary schools—this, in brief, constitutes the documentary history of the Catholic schools in the colony in which

[128] See J. A. Burns, " Early Jesuit Schools," for will of Edward Cotton, pp. 366-67.

[129] T. A. Hughes, *Jesuits in N. A.*, doc. i, pt. 1, pp. 25, 39, 48, 57-59. R. J. Purcell, " The Education of the Carrolls of Maryland," *Cath. Ed. Rev.*, vol. xxx (1932), p. 587 *et seq.* W. J. McGucken, *Jesuits and Education* (Milwaukee, 1932), pp. 46-59. W. S. Perry, *Hist. Coll.*, vol. ii, pp. 311-16, 468-69. S. P. G. *Journals, 1773-1776*, vol. xx, pt. 6, p. 410.

they were most numerous and which they had founded as a "land of sanctuary." The very paucity of the evidence testifies to the success of the penal laws. That they should so largely have attained their ends, notwithstanding frequent periods of lax or non-enforcement, points to a vigorous public opinion ever ready to take advantage of passing events either to revive the old or enact new legislation destined to keep the Catholic population in a despised and disfranchised minority.

It is with pleasure we turn to Pennsylvania, which had the second largest body of Catholics. Religious bigotry is by no means absent; persecution is not unknown. Catholics there, as in the other colonies, were through the test oaths excluded from all offices of trust and honor. Nor is there any recorded protest on the part of the Quakers.[130] Yet, although the Friends did not see fit to make equal political opportunity a practical corollary of their doctrine of religious liberty, Catholics were free to build their churches and chapels for the public worship of God and unmolested to educate their children in the tenets of their own faith. The Quakers near Chester, Pennsylvania, had even the bad taste to prefer as school master " a native Irish bigoted Papist ", much to the disgust of the S. P. G. appointee and his Anglican pastor.[131]

One of the objects of the Jesuits in locating Bohemia Manor near the Pennsylvania boundary was to have a center from which they might serve the German Catholics of that colony. Although the German emigration from the Rhine

[130] Charles Stillé, "Religious Tests in Provincial Pennsylvania," *Pa. Mag. Hist. and Biog.*, vol. ix (1885), p. 365 *et seq.* W. T. Root, *The Relations of Pennsylvania with the British Government, 1696-1765*, pp. 222-255. W. R. Shepherd, *History of the Proprietary Government in Pennsylvania*, pp. 368-369. Cf. *supra*, p. 105, n. 123.

[131] W. S. Perry, *op. cit.*, vol. ii, pp. 216, 219, 232. J. A. Burns, *op. cit.*, p. 119.

in 1717 and 1727 was largely Protestant, it included also many Catholics. A succession of learned and zealous Jesuits organized them into parishes, and although there seems to be no documentary proof of the foundation of Catholic schools among them, there are strong traditions that they were begun with the parishes. One of the most noted of these schools was that of Goshenhoppen, of which Father Schneider was in charge as early as 1741. After a brilliant career as student and professor, Father Schneider resigned the rectorship of the University of Heidelberg to minister to the spiritual needs of his fellow countrymen in the backwoods of Pennsylvania. His parish at Goshenhoppen was the center of a number of missions and schools. Begun in the rectory for the children of his own flock, the school was so well patronized that funds for a separate building were collected in 1745. And since Protestants as well as Catholics attended, the former contributed their share of the necessary funds. The school seems to have been kept open during the French and Indian War, and to have prospered so well that in 1763 a paid teacher was engaged. The high standard of instruction set by Father Schneider became a tradition in the school, for among the schoolmasters who served from 1763 to 1796 was the distinguished John L. Gubernator.[132]

[132] J. A. Burns, *op. cit.*, p. 125 *et seq.* L. G. and M. J. Walsh, *History and Organization of Education in Pennsylvania* (State Teachers College, Indiana, Pa., 1928), pp. 66-67. The authors of this work quote Wickersham, p. 115, as commenting on this school as "a curious combination of a church and public school." They further assert that the schoolhouse was owned by the church and furnished rent free to the town, that the salary of the principal teacher was paid by the board of directors of the district, while that of the assistant teacher was paid by the congregation, and that the school was attended only by Catholics. Father Burns states that the school was attended by both Protestants and Catholics, and adds (p. 127): "It is pleasant to record that the educational zeal of the first schoolmaster at Goshenhoppen was not forgotten by the

Pennsylvania, then, was the only colony at the outbreak of the Revolution where, despite the laws, despite the test oaths, despite the opposition of those who legally controlled education, Catholics seem to have worked out their own educational salvation publicly, and at times even with the cooperation of their Protestant neighbors. Father Schneider's twenty-three years of distinguished service at Goshenhoppen was not an isolated example. His work was ably seconded by Father Farmer (Steinmeyer 1752-58), and Father J. B. Causse (1785——) at Lancaster, by Father Wapeler at Conewego, and by other Jesuits who had charge of the Pennsylvania missions. Burns suggests that the indefinable change which took place during the Revolution in the attitude of America was due in no small measure to the broadmindedness, the learning, the culture, the charity which embraced Catholic and non-Catholic alike, and the truly civic virtues of such men as Father Schneider and Father Farmer.

early settlers. More than a century after, the public school authorities showed their appreciation of what he had done, by an arrangement which provided for the education of the children of the Goshenhoppen parish school at the public expense."

John L. Gubernator, born in or near Oppenheim, Germany, served in the Seven Years War under Frederick the Great. He came to America during the Revolution. He taught at Goshenhoppen and also at the " Little Seminary ", Hanover, in the Pigeon Hills. He was likewise organist at Conewago. During his twenty-five years of service in the classroom, he acquired a reputation which gave him first place among a group of teachers noted for their learning. See Reilly, J. T., *Life of Cardinal Gibbons* (2 vols., Martinsburg, W. Va., 1822-23), vol. ii, pp. 530-37.

CHAPTER V

The Tradition in Colonial Literature

Although sermons and other religious works bulk so large in early colonial bibliographies,[1] there were other types of literature which, while exercising a profound influence upon provincial society, were at the same time a reflection of it. The almanac was one of these. There were few households too poor to welcome this humble visitor. The absence of free public libraries and the expense of importing books made the almanac in many colonial homes almost the sole type of reading besides the Bible. The variety of its information, its excerpts from well-known English authors, its utility as a calendar and often as a diary, gave it an honored place in the household. In many families it was the custom to save the almanacs from year to year. When five or six had accumulated, they were stitched together and the resulting volume was set aside for the rising generation to pore over during the long winter evenings.[2] Enterprising pub-

---

[1] Charles Evans, *American Bibliography, 1637-1820* (Chicago, 1903), introd. to vols. i, ii, v.

[2] M. C. Tyler, *History of American Literature during the Colonial Period, 1607-1765* (2 vols., New York, 1879), vol. ii, p. 120 *et seq.* Joseph T. Buckingham, *Personal Memoirs and Recollections of an Editorial Life* (2 vols., Boston, 1852), vol. i, p. 20. Diary of Jacob Cushing in the Library of Congress, Mss. Div. The diaries cover the years 1749-1818, the entries being made in ten different almanacs. *Cf.* H. W. Cunningham, ed., *Diary of the Reverend Samuel Checkley, 1735,* reprinted from Col. Soc. Mass. *Pub.,* vol. xii, pp. 270-71 (Cambridge, 1909). J. C. Lyford, *History of Concord* (2 vols., Concord, N. H., 1896), vol. ii, p. 1213. M. A. Stickney, "Almanacs of Nathaniel Low," Essex Inst. H. *Coll.,* vol. viii, pp. 28-32.

lishers would be eager to increase their sales by including in their almanacs features which had already proved popular or innovations which would give them an advantage over their rivals. On the other hand, almanacs of tested reputation, such as those of Nathaniel Ames, father and son, which ran from 1726 to 1775, or those of Nathaniel Low, from 1762 to 1827, or again, *Poor Richard,* which for twenty-five years enjoyed a circulation of ten thousand,[3] would be able to exercise an appreciable influence upon readers who subscribed year after year.

Reflecting as they did " the various phases of thought . . . the scientific, literary and political growth of the years of their production," almanacs mirrored also the religious opinions and prejudices of the times.[4] Thus the title-page of Bickerstaff's *Boston Almanac* for 1777 reads:

Bickerstaff's Boston Almanac, For the Year of our Redemption, 1777, Being the First after Leap-Year, And from the Creation of the World, according to the best History, 5725. But the eighty-first from the horrid Popish, High-Church Jacobite Plot.

The last page of a Richardson Almanac advertises " A Perpetuall Calendar fitted for the Meridian of Babylon, where the Pope is elevated 42 Degr." [5] Indicative of a similar viewpoint, and found in almost all the almanacs of the colonial period, is the designation of November fifth as " Gun-

---

[3] James Parton, *Life and Times of Benjamin Franklin* (2 vols., New York, 1864), vol. i, p. 227. M. A. Stickney, *op. cit.,* vol. viii, pp. 28-32; vol. xiv, pp. 81-93, 212-233, 242-248.

[4] C. L. Nichols, " Massachusetts Almanacs, 1630-1850," *Amer. Antiq. Soc. Proc.,* n. s., vol. xxii (April–Oct., 1912), pp. 15-134. S. Briggs, *Essays, Humor and Poems of Nathaniel Ames, Father and Son, of Dedham, Massachusetts, from their Almanacks, 1726-1775, with notes and comments* (Cleveland, 1891), p. 20. G. L. Kittredge, *The Old Farmer and His Almanack* (Boston, 1904), pref. v.

[5] J. Richardson, *An Almanack . . . 1670* (Cambridge, 1670).

powder Plot Day," or " Pope Day," or " Papist Conspiracy."
Sometimes these brief identifications are expanded into
couplets, as in the Ames *Astronomical Diary* for 1735 :

> Gun Powder Plot
> We ha'n't forgot.

The *Diary* for 1737 is more explicit :

> Ere you pretend to burn the Pope
> Secure the Papists with a Rope.[6]

Another familiar feature of the early almanacs was a
stanza at the head of each page. Often the verses were
appropriate to the month or the season. To secure variety
was no slight tax upon the ingenuity of a compiler whose
almanacs were published for a considerable number of years.
Political events like the colonial wars or the Revolution
would prove a boon for the almanac-maker of little or no
creative ability. Patriotism combined with national and
religious bias would form a popular theme. Roger Sherman, whose almanacs ran from 1750 to 1761, found such a
theme in the French and Indian War. His annual for 1760
summarizes the conflict in thirteen head-page stanzas. The
emphasis on the British-Prussian alliance, the glorification
of Frederick II as the great Protestant hero, the insistence
on the Catholic faith of France, are all typical of the official
policy to keep before the public the religious elements of
the struggle. The stanza for April reads :

[6] For similar references, see *Astronomical Diary or Almanack* by
Nathaniel Ames (Boston, 1739, 1743, 1746, 1750). Nathaniel Ames, Jr.,
succeeded his father in 1766. The almanac for 1767 marks the beginning
of a change : " Powder Plot most forgot." In 1772 the younger Ames
wrote, " To burn the Pope is now a joke." *Cf. infra*, pp. 256-61.

> May Britain's Sons, with Prussian Pow'rs alli'd
> Conquer the French, humble the Sons of Pride
> Who are against the Prot'stant Cause combin'd;
> A Scourge of Nations, Murd'rers of Mankind ... [7]

Other almanac publishers made use of similar head-page attractions.[8]   The Ames almanacs helped to revive the old animosities against Spain, who in " an evil Planetary Hour " cast her lot with France

> And Briton's Friendship spurned with base Design.... [9]

Not content with the usual head-page references, the Ames publications devoted considerable space to the last of the colonial wars, summing up its progress year by year and celebrating British victories with a fervor that was equaled only by the bitterness with which they execrated the French and the Canadians.[10]   When it is recalled that the annual sales of the *Diary* in New England ran up to sixty thousand copies, one can readily agree with James Truslow Adams that the name of Ames " must have been a household word throughout " that section of the country.   There is evidence, also, that the almanac was distributed through the middle and southern colonies where it rivaled *Poor Richard* in popularity.   Such, indeed, was its reputation that an edition was scarcely off the press before it was pirated.   It would be difficult to overestimate the influence of such a publication

---

[7] *Cf.* Roger Sherman, *An Almanack* ... *1761* (Boston, 1761).

[8] Thomas More, *Poor Thomas Improved* (New York, 1760). Also *Poor Roger*, 1760, 1761. *Cf.* P. L. Ford, *Journals of Hugh Gaine* (2 vols., New York, 1902), vol. i, p. 30, for an account of Theophilus Greed (Thomas More) and his work.

[9] Nathaniel Ames, *The Astronomical Diary or Almanack* (Boston, 1763), Feb. page.

[10] See especially editions of 1747, 1751, 1756. The most significant portions of the Ames series have been collected by Samuel Briggs in his *Essays, Humor and Poems.*

in the average colonial household.   The experience of Joseph
T. Buckingham as recorded in his *Memoirs* is probably
typical of many another New England lad.[11]   The very
excellencies of the *Diary* would tend to blind its readers to
its limitations.

The elder Ames was not the only almanac-maker whose
pen was " dipped in gall."   There was Nathaniel Low, whose
almanacs are important because of the long duration of their
publication, 1762 to 1827, and also because they cover the
Revolutionary period.   His annuals often contained political
articles written and signed by himself.[12]   His " Address to
the Inhabitants of Boston " in 1775 takes the stand that the
home government's tolerant treatment of the religious question in Canada is but the prelude to the establishment of
" Popery " in British America.[13]   In subsequent issues Low

[11] Buckingham's home possessed a shelf of the Ames almanacs covering a period of fifty years. He found these a welcome change from the
New England Primer and the Bible. He was especially interested in the
accounts of the French and Indian War, and the Revolution. " The
Articles of Confederation between the colonies," he wrote, " Petitions to
the King, the Declaration of Independence, and many other papers connected with the history and politics of the country, were preserved in
these useful annuals, and afforded me ample food for study." J. T.
Buckingham, *Personal Memoirs*, vol. i, p. 20. *Cf.* J. T. Adams, in
D. A. B., vol. i, pp. 250-251. M. C. Tyler, *Amer. Lit. during Col. Period*,
vol. ii, pp. 122-130. M. A. Stickney in Essex Inst. H. *Coll.*, viii, p. 27;
vol. xiv, p. 82. S. Briggs, *op. cit.*, pp. 201, 262 and *passim*.

[12] M. A. Stickney (*loc. cit.*, vol. viii, p. 27), writes: " While Otis,
Adams and others, dared not to publish and sign their names, Low came
out boldly in his *Almanacs*, and signed his name to what might, if the
colonies had not succeeded, cost him his life." Another writer credits
Low's articles with exerting " great influence at the New England fireside,
inspiring young and old with a love of freedom." A. A. Spofford, "A
Brief History of Almanacs," in *An American Almanac ... for the year
1878* (New York, Washington, 1878), p. 25.

[13] N. Low, *An Astronomical Diary, or Almanack ... 1775*.   *Cf.* Benjamin West, *New England Almanack* (Providence, 1775), for an elaborate
" geographical account " of Canada.   West shares his rival's fears of
" Popery."

pays his respects to the Inquisition [14] and to Galileo.[15]   William Penn's alleged defection from Quakerism to join the Jesuits finds a place in John Tobler's *Almanack*.[16]   Isaac Bickerstaff reprints in 1778 an article on the persecution of Protestants in Ireland which had been featured by Hutchins in 1765.[17]

The sixteen numbers of John Tully's almanac, important because it was the first humorous publication of its kind in the colonies, are for the most part not concerned with religious topics.   To this general statement there are three exceptions, the issues for 1693, 1694, 1695.   These three numbers were printed by Benjamin Harris,[18] who probably could not resist the opportunity of indulging his anti-Catholic animus. The interpolations, moreover, both in subject-matter and style, are suggestive of Harris.   The page following the December calendar of 1693 [19] has " Some few lines by another Hand," which exhort " Albion " to " defie the Arts of Hell and Rome."   The following year a passage from the book of Daniel is interpreted as a prophecy of the " late Popish Reign " of James II and the landing of William of Orange at Torbay.[20]   The same issue has a twenty-line stanza on

---

[14] N. Low, *op. cit.*, 1776. *Cf. Poor Roger*, 1762.

[15] N. Low, *op. cit.*, 1785.

[16] John Tobler, *Pennsylvania Town and Countryman's Almanack* (Wilmington, 1777).

[17] J. N. Hutchins, *Improved…Almanack* (New York, 1765).

[18] *Cf. supra*, pp. 29, 118. That printers sometimes took the liberty of inserting matter in almanacs given them to print is evident from the corrections and apologies made by the compilers in the succeeding issues. See Roger Sherman's apology in the almanac for 1755. *Cf.* V. H. Paltsits, *The Almanacs of Roger Sherman* (Worcester, 1907), pp. 7-14. For an account of Tully and his work, see *History of Middlesex County, Conn.* (New York, 1860), p. 459.

[19] John Tully, *An Almanac for 1693. Boston, printed by Benjamin Harris.*

[20] John Tully, *Almanac for 1694* (Boston, 1694).

" The French King's Nativity ", to show how

> The *Tyrant* with the *Churches Rod*
> Murder'd the Protestants to please his God.

Harping on the same theme, Tully's almanac for 1695 prints " An Account of the Cruelty of the Papists; acted upon the Bodies of the Godly Martyrs." A comparison of this account with Harris' *Protestant Tutor* and Foxe's *Book of Martyrs* leaves little doubt as to its source.[21]

Owing to the popularity of the Tully annuals, these three issues were probably widely distributed. Belonging as they do to the closing decade of the seventeenth century, their chief influence would perhaps be exerted on the sires and grandsires of the Revolutionary generation. But in those days when opinions changed but slowly and the printed expression of those opinions was preserved with other household treasures, it is not unlikely that the Tully almanacs with others of their time played their part in molding the mental outlook of the actors of 1776. The dependence of eighteenth-century almanacs upon sixteenth- and seventeenth-century material has been noted in the foregoing pages. Witness, among others that might be cited, *Poor Roger* for 1762, the Low almanacs for 1776, 1785, and Tobler's for 1767 and 1777. An examination of some hundreds of pre-Revolutionary almanacs from New England to Georgia has failed to reveal a single sympathetic reference to Roman Catholics or their beliefs. The greater number do not touch upon religious or politico-religious matters. When they do, any reference to the Church of Rome or her activities is invariably unfriendly.

[21] Benj. Harris, *Protestant Tutor*, pp. 136, 163 *et seq.* John Foxe, *Acts and Monuments*, book Eleven. Cf. J. Tobler, *Pa. Almanack for 1767*, for the martyrdom of John Gardiner, " Taken from Foxe's *Acts and Monuments of Martyrs.*"

Unlike the almanac in almost every respect, the broadside was usually printed for a special occasion.   It was sure to appear in times of public excitement, and lent itself readily to political and religious propaganda.   If the pamphlet, that favorite medium of expression in the seventeenth and eighteenth centuries, was often a reasoned, well-balanced discussion of a current issue, the broadside was more likely to reflect the emotional reaction of the community to the same subject.   However varied its form and content, its appeal was but transitory.   Colonial authorities were quick to see the advantage of such a cheap, practical means of reaching the public.   The very first issue of Stephen Day's press at Cambridge was the " Freeman's Oath ", in broadside form. Confined largely, in the early days, to official or semi-official communications, such as colony laws, civil or religious proclamations, and the like, it was not long before the broadside began to cater to the taste for the lurid and the startling.   A disaster, an epidemic, the threat of war, a fifth of November celebration, the execution of a criminal, or the death of a village celebrity would call forth a warning, a tribute, or perhaps a ballad whose droll allusions and coarse innuendo constituted its chief claim to popularity.   Lacking in originality as it was, and crude in workmanship, the American broadside soon began to develop a " distinctly American flavor."   This was especially true of early American broadside verse, which " possesses significance, in that it recorded beliefs and loyalties which were living gospel when they were uttered." [22]

A thoroughly characteristic broadside of this type was issued shortly after the Revolution of 1688 by Benjamin

[22] M. A. Shaaber, *Forerunners of Newspapers in England* (Oxford Univ. Press, 1929), p. 184. Ola A. Winslow, *American Broadside Verse. From Imprints of the Seventeenth and Eighteenth Centuries* (New Haven, 1930), pp. xvii-xxvi. M. C. Tyler, *Literary History of the American Revolution, 1763-1783*, vol. i, pp. 26-27.

Harris and sold at his shop, the " London Coffee House ", in Boston. An analysis of it would add nothing to our knowledge of Harris' anti-Papal complex, and would, perhaps, over-emphasize his importance. It deserves notice, however, as one of the earliest political broadsides extant, and also because it illustrates that characteristic of American broadside verse which caught the humor of the hour, reflecting, rather than guiding the opinions of the multitude. The title of the broadside is, " The Plain Case Stated of Old— but especially of New England, in an Address to His Highness the Prince of Orange." [23]   Published in a New England seething with resentment at the " voiding " of its charter, and at what was deemed the high-handed procedure of Governor Andros, it undoubtedly reflected the point of view of that faction which had interpreted measures purely political or administrative as snares of the Catholic James to lure unsuspecting provincials into those twin evils, " Popery and slavery."   For the " Plain Case Stated " was simply this: William of Orange had delivered Old England from

> . . . a crew of mercenary Knaves,
> Jesuits & Priests, tools us'd to make us Slaves . . .

New England, in arresting Andros and instituting a provisional government, had only followed the great Protestant hero's example, and God had blessed their efforts.   Thus, Harris.   The Puritan theocracy was to find to its sorrow that the case was not so simple.   Meanwhile it would welcome this popular justification of its action.   Harris had a personal grievance against the Stuarts.   Into the " Plain Case Stated " he put all the venom of his vindictive pen.

Almost a century later we find in a popular ballad this same device of justifying by an appeal to religious prejudice,

[23] *English and American Political Ballads* (5 vols.), vol. v, no. 30, Newberry Library, Chicago, Collection of Broadsides.

state policies which were clearly motivated by political or economic considerations.   No military expedition of the pre-Revolutionary period took on the appearance of a religious crusade as did that of Louisbourg.   That it offered, likewise, a possibility of paying off an old score against France was an additional incentive.   The two motives find a place in a ballad entitled" An Endeavor to Animate and Incourage our Soldiers for the Present Expedition (1758). By M. B." [24]   First there is an exhortation to win " immortal honor " by joining the colonial forces.   Then

> Once France was our's, but did Rebel,
> And now we must their force Repel,
> And send old *Lewis* to his Cell,
>   Or else to Purgatory;
> There let him lie, and loud Complain,
> To Popes and Fryars, all in Vain,
> The Virgin *Mary* will not dain
>   To hear his Mournful Story ...

The ballad concludes:

> And may some kind propitious Stars,
> Assist you on the Field of Mars,
> And Heaven Crown our righteous Wars
>   To Papists utter Ruin.

Besides the political ballad or broadside which deliberately plays upon the religious antipathies of its readers, there is another group, varied in form and content, whose testimony is all the more valuable because of its indirect reflection of popular sentiment.   To this type belongs an " Elegie " called forth by the death of Governor John Winthrop.   It conjures up an image of the Jesuit quite in keeping with the conception conveyed by current political tracts.   Witness the couplet:

[24] O. A. Winslow, *Amer. Broad. Verse*, no. 59.

> Death like a murthering Jesuite
> Hath rob'd us of our hearts delight.[25]

So it is with other visitations, local or national. Comets, plagues, fires, wars and other disasters may be messengers of God's wrath; nevertheless the " Papists " are His willing instruments. The return of Halley's comet in April, 1759, brought a warning from the press of Richard Draper in Boston. Draper's press, closely affiliated with the royal authorities, could be counted on for the official viewpoint of the government. The ballad recounts the calamities which visited England after the appearance of the comet in 1664. The war with Holland was followed by a plague,

> Soon after which, even the next Year,
> The Papists do conspire
> And by their Craft and Subtilty,
> London they set on fire.[26]

An interesting example of how private economic interests combined with political and religious bias might be exploited for purely commercial purposes is found in a broadside issued by Benjamin Mecom, probably in 1765. Mecom, it will be recalled, was a nephew of Benjamin Franklin, under whom he served his apprenticeship in Philadelphia. A skillful printer, but a poor business manager, Mecom's enterprises were usually short-lived. One of these was the revival of the *Connecticut Gazette,* which had been suspended for a time pending a transfer of ownership.[27] The purpose of the broadside was to secure an adequate subscription list. The writer acknowledges that, owing to what we should today

---

[25] O. A. Winslow, *op. cit.*, no. 2.

[26] *Ibid.*, no. 33. Also in L. C. *Coll.*, Mass., vol. xxxv, ac. 1717. xxxv, ac. 1717.

[27] Isaiah Thomas, *History of Printing in America* (2 vols., Worcester, 1810), vol. i, pp. 215, 349, 411-12; vol. ii, p. 67.

call a post-war depression, the time is unpropitious. But there never was a time, he continues, when such a paper was more necessary. For never were Americans in such danger of slavery. He draws a vivid picture of the economic and moral changes which would be wrought by " the infernal Monster, called SLAVERY," who " will first persuade you to sin and then send you to the POPE of degenerate *Rome,* for Absolution . . . Behold SLAVERY afar off! he bends his Course this Way from Louisiana!" There follow details of the effects to be expected from the threatened evil, which the people of Connecticut are called upon to ward off. Presumably they can do this most effectively by subscribing for a newspaper which exposes the arts of the monster.[28]

We shall have occasion to notice as this study proceeds many other examples of this type of literature which included such diverse subjects as fast-day proclamations, western land schemes, ballads for " Pope Night ", the Anglican episcopate, Whig and Tory ballads, addresses of the Continental Congress, town and county resolves, and so on. No subject was too trivial or too important to be published in this popular form. Transitory as it was, both in its origin and its appeal, the broadside had also a permanent value. This is especially true of the ballad which soon passed into the "traditional balladry " of the country, as Mr. Shaaber points out, and was " preserved and handed down " from generation to generation.[29]

Partisan and ephemeral like the broadside, the pamphlet has been characterized by Paul Leicester Ford as a " photograph of public opinion." [30] Of the political pamphlets of

[28] *Broadsides, Conn.*, vol. iii, L. C. Mss. Div.

[29] M. A. Shaaber, *Forerunners of Newspapers*, p. 203. *Cf.* M. C. Tyler, *Lit. Hist. Rev.*, vol. i, pp. 26-27.

[30] P. L. Ford, *Pamphlets on the Constitution of the United States, published during its discussion by the People, 1787-1788* (Brooklyn, 1888), pref., p. v.

the Revolutionary period and their relation to this study, we shall have something to say later. Here we are concerned with the religious pamphlet, other than the sermon, the purpose of which, like Paul Dudley's " Essay ", was to expose the snares of "Popery." The S. P. C. K. and the S. P. G., as we have seen, made the publication and dissemination of these tracts one of their special cares. Most of the colonial libraries whose catalogues have come down to us possessed one or more of these expositions;[31] others, like those of Elder Brewster and the Mathers, were well stocked with them.[32] Booksellers[33] found a steady sale for Foxe's *Book of Martyrs,* and for many of the pamphlets of which Foxe was the fountainhead. Some of these tracts went through edition after edition until well into the nineteenth century.[34] They may be divided into two general classes; the first, on

[31] *William and Mary College Quarterly,* 1 ser., vol. ii (1893-94), pp. 169-175; vol. viii (1899-1900), pp. 77, 144 *et seq.* E. E. Atwater, *History of the Colony of New Haven* (Meriden, 1902), p. 105. Julius Gay, *An Address Delivered at the Annual Meeting of the Village Library Company of Farmington, Conn., Sept. 12, 1900* (Hartford, 1900). F. B. Dexter, "Early Private Libraries in New England," Amer. Antiq. Soc. *Proc.,* n. s., vol. xviii (1906-07), pp. 135-147. Thomas Hutchinson, *Diary and Letters,* ed. by P. O. Hutchinson (Boston, 1884), p. 47.

[32] F. B. Dexter, "Elder Brewster's Library," Mass. H. S. *Proc.,* 2 ser., vol. v (1889-90), pp. 37-85. There are at least fifteen titles. *Cf.* W. C. Ford, *The Boston Book Market, 1679-1700* (Boston, 1917), p. 3. J. H. Tuttle, "The Libraries of the Mathers," Amer. Antiq. Soc. *Proc.,* vol. xx (1909-1910), pp. 269-356. About twenty-five titles.

[33] W. C. Ford, *op. cit., passim. W. and M. Quar.,* vol. xv (1906-07), pp. 100-113. Books for sale by Dixon and Hunter, Williamsburg, Va., advertised in *Virginia Gazette,* Nov. 2, 1775. H. M. Jones, *America and French Culture* (Chapel Hill, 1927), pp. 37, 356. W. V. Wells, *Life and Public Services of Samuel Adams* (3 vols., Boston, 1865), vol. iii, pp. 197-98.

[34] Charles Evans, *American Bibliography, 1637-1820.* See first three volumes, especially numbers 438, 464, 504, 775, 1611, 1933, 2176, 3216, 5266, 5615, 5716, 5858, 6277, 6775, 7100, 7795, 9095, 8604, 6488. I. Thomas, *Hist. of Printing,* vol. ii, pp. 324-643.

a more or less high intellectual plane, represented a sincere attempt to state dispassionately the case against Rome; the second, on the other hand, was just as obviously an appeal to prejudice, sometimes by the distortion of half truths, more often by utterly false and vicious charges. The two groups would reach what Tyler characterizes as " the uppermost and undermost thought " [35] and emotion of a period.

The Church of Rome Evidently Proved Heretick by Peter Berault [36] may be cited as an example of the first class. The author, if one may credit the information given on the title page, had "abjured all the Errors of the Said Church in London, at the Savoy upon the 2d day of April, 1671." He states his argument against the church of his abjuration thus: "That Church which is obstinate in her errours, is Heretick; the Roman Church is obstinate in her errours, *Ergo*." [37] For readers who may be unconvinced by logic, the writer devotes the remainder of the sixty pages to other proofs of Rome's heterodoxy. Not a single link in the Reformation " chain of errors " is omitted, but the argument is free from the scurrility which so often defaces controversial pamphlets.

The *Newport Mercury* for May 9, 1774 (no. 818), and succeeding numbers, carried the following advertisement:

A Master-Key to Popery; In five parts; containing 300 large octavo pages, price 4s. being as cheap a book of the kind, as was ever printed in Europe or America: (And highly necessary to be kept in every protestant family in this country; that they may see to what a miserable state the people are reduced in all arbitrary and tyrannical governments, and be hereby excited to stand on their guard against the infernal machinations of the

[35] M. C. Tyler, *Lit. Hist. Rev.*, vol. i, pp. 5-6.

[36] Peter Berault, *The Church of Rome Evidently Proved Heretick* (London, 1680; Boston editions, 1685, 1745). C. Evans, *op. cit.*, no. 384.

[37] London ed., p. 2.

British ministry, and their vast *host* of tools, emissaries, etc., etc., sent hither to propagate the principles of popery and slavery, which go hand in hand as inseparable companions.)

The same advertisement was appended to the text of a broadside issue of the Boston Port Bill.[38] The militant note sounded in the lengthy parenthesis would find a ready response in a Boston aflame with resentment at the closing of her harbor. The publisher and seller of the tract was Solomon Southwick, editor of the *Newport Mercury,* the columns of which were always open to anti-Catholic propaganda. According to his own account, the forger of the *Master-Key,* Don Antonio Gavin, had belonged to the secular clergy of Spain, had abjured Catholicism, and had been a minister of the Church of England since 1715.[39] The edition published by Southwick in 1773 is represented on the title page as the " Third edition, completely corrected." In what the " correction " consisted does not appear; perhaps, as in the Boston edition of 1835, in the incorporation of other pamphlets which had previously been published separately.[40] It would

[38] A. C. H. *Researches*, o. s., vol. xxi (1904), pp. 15-18.

[39] Is this the Rev. Anthony Gavin mentioned by Bishop Meade as officiating in several Virginia parishes between 1738 and 1749, the year of his death? See William Meade, *Old Churches, Ministers, and Families in Virginia* (2 vols., Philadelphia, 1861), vol. i, p. 467. *Cf.* G. M. Brydon, " The Virginia Clergy," *Va. Mag. Hist. and Biog.*, vol. xxxii (1924), pp. 212, 333, n. L. W. Burton, *Annals of Henrico County, Va.* (Richmond, 1904), pp. 14, 17-20, 40. There is no mention in any of these accounts of *The Master-Key to Popery*, or of Gavin's career before his coming to Virginia.

[40] This 1835 edition is characteristic of the use made of tracts, sometimes centuries old, whenever a wave of religious bigotry sweeps the country, as happened in the 1830's. To the original title-page is added: "An Account of the Inquisition at Goa, by Dr. Buchanan; the Inquisition at Macerata, by M. Bowen; a Preservative against Popery, by Rev. Joseph Blanco-White, formerly chaplain to the King of Spain; a Summary of the Catholic Faith; Damnation and Excommunication of Elizabeth, Queen of England, and her adherents; and Francis Freeman

be hard to find a more vicious libel of Catholicism. Every doctrine and practice of the Catholic Church is made to appear false, sordid, or ridiculous—sometimes all three. The modern gangster is a paragon of virtue compared with the hypocrites who make up the hierarchy and the rank and file of the Catholic clergy. The women of the underworld are pure beside the nuns and Catholic matrons who figure in the pages of this tract. The greater part of the work is too irreverent, too obscene for quotation. On the other hand, excerpts from quotable passages would fail to give an adequate notion of the venom of the book.

Another type of anti-Catholic pamphlet, equally objectionable from a moral point of view, is that which borrows its technique from the novel, and relates the experiences of an individual or group of characters. *The French Convert* seems to have been one of the most widely circulated of this class. There were New York editions as early as 1724 [41] and as late as 1830.[42] The second quarter of the eighteenth century saw four editions in Boston [43] and at least one in Philadelphia.[44] The presses of Hartford [45] and New Haven, of Burlington, New Jersey, of Wilmington, Delaware, and

for embracing the Protestant Religion; also the Pope's Alum-Maker; and other interesting details carefully collected from Romish writers. By the Publisher to the Third American Edition, Boston. Published by Wm. C. Webster, 1835." Newberry. Copies of 1773 ed. in L. C., N. Y. P. L. For an account of the "No-Popery" campaign of the 1830's and subsequent movements of the same kind, see M. Williams, *Shadow of the Pope*, ch. 4, *et seq.*

[41] From W. Bradford's press. See "Issues of the Press in New York, 1736-1752," *Pa. Mag. Hist. and Biog.*, vol. xiii (1889), p. 90 *et seq.*

[42] Issued by G. G. Sickels under the title, *Maria, or the ever-Blooming flower* (A tale for young ladies).

[43] C. Evans, *op. cit.*, nos. 5399, 5599, 6322.

[44] *Ibid.*, no. 6143. *Cf.* I. Thomas, *Hist. of Printing*, vol. ii, pp. 402, 482, 497, 602.

[45] Copies of this edition and of those which follow in L. C.

Brookfield, Massachusetts, all profited by the sales. The main outlines of the story may be gathered from the complete title given below.[46] The arguments for and against Catholicism are discussed by the lady and her gardener. The priest, of course, is the villain, who, to the crime of attempted seduction, would add that of murder.

The S. P. G. ministers, as already noted,[47] sometimes sent for anti-Catholic tracts such as were " suited to the meanest capacities." Of these there was no dearth. Their specialty was garbled versions of history, illustrated by the most brutal and heart-rending tales imaginable. As with the types already discussed, pamphlets of this class went through numerous editions. The thirtieth edition of *Popish Cruelty Displayed* was on sale in Boston bookshops in 1753.[48] It opens with an address in doggerel " To all Haters of Popery," who are bidden

[46] *The French Convert; Being the true relation of the happy Conversion of A Noble French Lady, From the errors and superstitions of Popery, to the Reformed Religion, by means of a Protestant Gardner, her servant, wherein is shown, Her great and unparalleled Sufferings, on the account of her said Conversion: as also her Wonderful Deliverance from Two Assassins, Hired by a Popish Priest to murder her: and of her miraculous preservation In a wood for two years, And how she was at last providentially found by her Husband; who, together with her parents, were bro't over to the embracing of the true Religion, as were divers others also* (Hartford, printed by John Babcock, 1798).

[47] *Supra*, p. 75.

[48] *POPISH CRUELTY DISPLAYED: being A full and true Account of the Bloody and Hellish Massacre in Ireland. Perpetrated by the Instigation of the Jesuits, Priests and Fryars, who were the chief Promoters of those Morthers, unheard of Cruelties, barbarous Villanies and Inhuman practices, executed by the Irish Papists upon the ENGLISH PROTESTANTS. In the Year 1641. And intended to have been acted over again, on the 9th of December, 1688, being Sabbath Day; but by a wonderful Providence of God was prevented. Very proper to be in the hands of every honest PROTESTANT, of what country soever he may be. The Thirtieth edition. Boston: Printed and sold at the Bible & Heart in Cornhill (1753).* Cf. I. Thomas, *op. cit.*, vol. i, p. 518. C. Evans, *op. cit.*, no. 7100.

> Come, you that loathe this Brood, this murdering Crew,
> Your Predecessors well their Mercies knew.
> Take Courage now, and be both bold and wise;
> Stand for your Laws, Religion, Liberties.[49]

This exhortation is followed by the assertion that

The Priests gave the Sacrament unto divers of the Irish upon condition that they would neither spare Man, Woman, nor Child of the Protestants.[50]

Then begins the recital of tale after tale of the most revolting cruelty. Two brief examples will suffice to illustrate their character.

At Casel they put all the Protestants into a loathsom Dungeon, kept them twelve weeks in great misery. Some they barbarously mangled and left them languishing; some they hanged up twice or thrice, others they burnt alive . . . [51]

They broke the back of a Youth, and left him in the Fields; some days after he was found, having eaten the grass round about him; neither would they kill him outright, but removed him to better Pastures; therein was fulfilled that saying, *The tender mercies of the Wicked are cruelty.*[52]

To cite the colonial newspapers which printed anti-Catholic items would be to call the roll of the colonial press. In this as in so many other aspects of provincial society, British precedent served as a model. In England the press was largely, if not entirely, under government or party control. There was a conscious attempt to mold public opinion. The selection and presentation of foreign news was colored, in Whig and Tory organ alike, by the political and dynastic wars of continental Europe. References to France, to

---

[49] *Popish Cruelty Displayed*, p. 2.

[50] *Ibid.*

[51] *Ibid.*, p. 6.

[52] *Ibid.*, p. 13.

Spain, to the Jesuits, to the Papacy, reflected the traditional opposition to everything Catholic.[53] Until the Revolution colonial printers relied almost entirely upon the British press for the items reprinted in their foreign columns. The Whig papers were quoted more often than the Tory. Domestic news other than local happenings might be gleaned from other provincial newspapers. This practice of making up an issue from the clippings of contemporaries made it reasonably certain that an item or event of more than local interest would eventually find a place in nearly every important paper in the country. Official announcements, such as acts of assemblies, governors' proclamations, and the like, advertisements, a poem or two, perhaps, or a literary selection, and letters addressed to the editor or to the public made up the remainder of a given edition. There were no editorials as we understand the term, but the letters or essays just referred to, with the replies which they often called forth, constituted an open forum for the discussion of any topic of general interest. The writers of these articles frequently represented the best talent and the weightiest influence of the community, although presumably any one who had a grievance to air or an opinion to express might do so through this medium.[54]

Each of the characteristics mentioned above, in practically every newspaper from New England to the Carolinas, illustrated at one time or other, and some of them in many successive issues, the prevailing colonial attitude towards Roman Catholicism. The *Boston News Letter,* important because

[53] M. A. Shaaber, *Forerunners of Newspapers,* pp. 58, 65-74. W. T. Laprade, " The Power of the English Press in the Eighteenth Century," *South Atlantic Quarterly,* vol. xxvii (Oct., 1928), pp. 426-34. W. H. Lecky, *Eng.,* vol. iii (1883), pp. 262-65.

[54] Bernard Faÿ, *L'Ésprit Révolutionaire,* pp. 39-40. M. C. Tyler, *Lit. Hist. Rev.,* vol. i, pp. 18-19. W. G. Bleyer, *Main Currents in the History of American Journalism* (New York, 1927), p. 1. L. M. Salmon, *The Newspaper and the Historian* (New York, 1923), p. 181.

of its place in the history of American journalism,[55] set the fashion which was only too faithfully followed by its rivals and other contemporaries.[56]   The *New England Courant,* founded by the elder brother of Benjamin Franklin, even bettered the instruction of its competitor.   Its attacks upon Anglicans as well as Catholics were no small factor in its popularity.[57]   The *Courant's* issue for June 10-17, 1723, reprints a Roman dispatch, in which ridicule and sarcasm are combined to win popular favor.   The Pope, although partially recovered from a recent illness, runs the item,

still complains of a Pain in his Foot, which undoubtedly affects his Toes; and we all know that the honour and Happiness of a great Number of Catholicks depends upon the Health of his Holiness's Great Toe, which by this Account, I am afraid, is not in a kissing Condition.[58]

[55] Although the *Boston News Letter* is usually listed as our first American newspaper, its title to that honor is sometimes questioned, since Benjamin Harris had issued a news-sheet called *Public Occurrences both Foreign and Domestick,* in Boston, Sept. 25, 1690. Its life was limited to a single issue, for it was suppressed because of offensive references to the French King and the Mohawks. See facsimile copy in S. A. Green, *Ten Fac-simile Reproductions Relating to Old Boston and Neighborhood* (Boston, 1901), pp. 1-2. *Cf.* F. Monaghan, article on Harris in *D. A. B.,* vol. viii, pp. 303-05. For the evolution of the *Boston News Letter,* see Green, *op. cit.,* pp. 3-4.

[56] With the exception of the foreign news items, much of the material of the first three years of the *News-Letter's* existence may be found in L. H. Weeks and E. M. Bacon, *An Historical Digest of the Provincial Press* (Boston, 1911). For a succession of foreign news items see *News-Letter* for 1723.

[57] C. A. Dunaway, *Development of Freedom of the Press in Massachusetts* (Harvard Historical Studies, vol. xii, 1906), p. 97. B. Faÿ, *Franklin, the Apostle of Modern Times* (Boston, 1929), pp. 19, 60.

[58] *New-England Courant,* June 17, 1723. *Cf.* issue for March, 18-25, 1723. For other foreign news items, see *New Hampshire Gazette,* July 30, Aug. 6, 1762; Nov. 30, 1770; *New York Gazette,* April 24, 1763; *Maryland Gazette,* excerpts in E. Riley, " *The Antient City,*" *A History of Annapolis in Maryland* (Annapolis, 1887), pp. 101-02.

The New York Mercury for March 23, 1761, carried an advertisement for *The French Convert*,[59] while the issue of May 4 for the same year advertised *A seasonable Antidote against Popery* by William Romaine. The *Newport Mercury's* advertisement for Gavin's *Master-Key to Popery*[60] could be paralleled by many others of the same type. Hugh Jones' *Protest against Popery*, besides receiving frequent notice in the *Maryland Gazette* during 1745-46, was also advertised by the *Pennsylvania Gazette*, November 13, 1746, but no copy of the pamphlet has been located.[61]

After 1763 the *Boston Gazette*, published by Edes and Gill, was probably the most important newspaper of New England. Its office was the meeting place of the most influential political writers of the day—Samuel and John Adams, James Otis, John Hancock, Joseph Warren, Thomas Cushing, Josiah Quincy, Jr. There they discussed the latest encroachments of the British authorities upon the chartered privileges of the colony, there they reprobated among other policies the tolerance of the home government towards its new subjects in Canada. The fruit of these discussions was often given to the public in the form of letters to the editor, the identity of the authors being concealed under assumed names. Samuel Adams was one of the most frequent contributors. His practice of writing under various signatures he defended on the plea that his communications would have more weight if his readers thought they came from different persons.[62]

[59] *Supra*, pp. 180-181.

[60] *Supra*, pp. 178-180.

[61] See L. C. Wroth, *Hist. Printing in Col. Md.*, p. 191. A. C. H. *Researches*, o. s., vol. xv (1898), p. 184.

[62] Wells, *Life and Services of S. Adams*, vol. i, pp. 240, 244. Hosmer, *S. Adams*, pp. 116, 119-20. C. A. Dunaway, *op. cit.*, pp. 123-24. J. T. Buckingham, *Specimens of Newspaper Literature* (2 vols., Boston, 1852), pp. 165-67. M. C. Tyler, *Lit. Hist. Rev.*, vol. i, pp. 8-11.

In 1768, under the signature of " A Puritan ", Adams contributed to the *Gazette* a series of articles intended to arm his countrymen against the wiles of " Popery." As a disciple of Locke, Adams believed the political principles of Roman Catholics to be subversive of free government; as a staunch Congregationalist, " Popery and slavery " were to him synonymous, and the rites of the Catholic Church " the pitiable and worn-out superstitions of the ignorant." [63] Precisely what prompted this particular outburst on the part of Adams is not difficult to surmise. In all probability it was the vexed question of an Anglican episcopate. Colonial excitement over the repeal of the Stamp Act had abated, and although the Townshend Duty Act had been passed, it was being honored more in the breach than in the observance. Boston's " tea party " was still in the future. But there were other forms of tyranny against which the public should be warned. Episcopacy was in the air. That it savored of " Popery " was not the least of its titles to condemnation. And of course there was always " Popery " itself. A lull in the political storm could always be profitably filled in by a diatribe against Rome. No subject could be more congenial to Adams, none likely to receive a more sympathetic hearing from the readers of the *Boston Gazette*.[64]

The first of the series appeared in the *Gazette* for April 4, 1768. Its purpose, purely introductory, was to convince its readers in general, and the clergy in particular, that there was real danger that

[63] Wells, *op. cit.*, vol. i, pp 200, 447, 502-07. H. A. Cushing, ed., *Writings of Samuel Adams* (4 vols., New York, 1904-08), vol. ii, pp. 352-53, 355.

[64] For Adams' anti-Catholic complex and his power as a propagandist, see C. H. Van Tyne, " The Clergy and the American Revolution," *Amer. Hist. Rev.*, vol. xix (1913-14), pp. 44-46. Hosmer, *op. cit.*, pp. 321-26. J. H. Denison, *Emotional Currents in American History* (New York, 1932), p. 25. Wells, *op. cit.*, vol. ii, p. 283. Brooks Adams, *Emancipation of Massachusetts* (Boston and New York, 1887), p. 516.

this *enlightened* continent should become the *worshippers of the Beast* . . . There is a variety of ways in which POPERY, the idolatry of Christians, may be introduced into America, which at present I shall not so much as hint at . . . Yet, my dear countrymen,—suffer me at this time . . . to warn you all, as you value your precious *civil* liberty, and everything you call dear to you, to be upon your guard against POPERY.

The writer's travels through the continent have convinced him of the imminence of the peril. Then, with a thrust at the Anglicans, he exclaims,

Bless me! could our ancestors look out of their graves, and see how many of *their own* sons, deck'd with the worst of *foreign Superfluities*, the ornaments of the *whore of Babylon*, how it would break their sacred Repose! . . .

The " Puritan's " second contribution [65] listed a number of towns that were likely to be affected by the threatened evil. Personal investigation had proved that " the Image " had been set up in York and Haverhill, and that some of the deluded townsmen had " appeared in public with *crucifixes* at their breasts." Marblehead had been visited by a priest who had used his " arts and tricks " so successfully that some had begun " to wander after the beast." The letter began with a warning that " Popery " was worse than the Stamp Act or " any other Acts destructive of man's civil rights; " it closed with a recommendation that these rights be preserved by the choice of Protestant representatives.

The third letter [66] seems to have been written merely to sustain interest in the subject. A tale of Papal bulls was begun and abruptly broken off with a promise of continuance in the future. It does not appear that the promise was kept, however, for an examination of the files of the *Gazette*

[65] *Boston Gazette*, April 11, 1768.
[66] *Ibid.*, April 18, 1768.

for the remainder of the year 1768 and for 1769 failed to disclose further letters from the " Puritan." The essays already published had elicited some response.[67] It is probable, however, that local issues [68] so clamored for attention that Adams had little time to devote to so remote a danger as the introduction of Papal bulls into New England.

Among the newspapers of the South, the *Virginia Gazette* and the *South Carolina Gazette* developed towards the end of our period an interest in cultural subjects rather greater than that of their New England contemporaries. The literary quality of the essays of the *Virginia Gazette* attracted the attention of editors throughout the colonies.[69] Yet one of these essays, though redolent of the ivy-clad chapels and churchyards of the Old Dominion, reveals essentially the same viewpoint as the letters of the " Puritan." The writer, wandering among the ruins of an old abbey, soliloquizes—

Ye are fallen . . . ye dark and gloomy Mansions of mistaken Zeal, where the proud Priest and lazy Monk fattened upon the Riches of the Land, and crept like Vermin from their Cells to spread their poisonous Doctrines through the Nation, and disturb the Peace of Kings . . . [70]

With this brief sampling of three characteristic features of the colonial newspaper,[71] we turn to the question of dis-

[67] See communication of "Anti-Pope" in the issue of April 25, and of Andrew Marvell, May 2, 1768. There is a complete file of the *Gazette* in the Boston Public Library. The letters of Adams may be found with some changes and omissions in his *Writings*, vol. i, p. 201 *et seq.*

[68] The Non-importation agreement and the Circular Letter to all the colonies were drafted about this time.

[69] J. T. Adams, *Provincial Society, 1690-1763* (A History of American Life, 12 vols., New York, 1927), vol. iii, p. 266.

[70] *Virginia Gazette*, April 14, 1774, no. 1175.

[71] For further references, see " Catholic and Anti-Catholic Items in American Colonial Newspapers," in *U. S. Cath. Hist. Mag.*, vol. i (1887),

tribution. In pre-Revolutionary days, the newspaper was by no means so universally read as it is today. Relatively speaking, it was too expensive for the rank and file. True, every important town had its gazette, but an edition usually consisted of a few hundred, rarely of more than a thousand, copies. But the neighborly habit of borrowing and lending, and the practice of gathering at the tavern, where the host's copy was read and discussed, increased the number of readers far beyond that indicated by the subscription list. With the turn of the half century and Franklin's appointment as postmaster general, the newspapers throughout the country took on new life. From that time, their influence in molding public opinion grew steadily, if not always consciously, until at the opening of the Revolution both parties in the struggle recognized their value as instruments of propaganda. Towards Roman Catholicism, as will be seen later, there was a decided change of tone.[72]

The popularity of the purely literary features of some of the colonial newspapers, led more than one editor to think that the time had come for more ambitious efforts in that direction. The conclusion would appear to have been premature, for with one exception all of the pre-Revolutionary periodicals perished through lack of financial support. But a beginning had been made. Short-lived as they were, and depending even more than the newspaper upon English contemporaries, they nevertheless constitute an important source of colonial history. If the subscription lists were not ade-

pp. 81-91, 203-214; vol. ii (1888), pp. 93-99. There are also many items in A. C. H. *Researches.* See also *infra*, pp. 228, n. 52; 231, 295-301, 311, n. 2; 333-38.

[72] B. Faÿ, *L'Ésprit Rév.*, pp. 39-40; *Notes on Amer. Press*, pp. 2-7, 22-25. B. F. Stevens, *Facsimiles in European Archives relating to America, 1773-1783* (25 vols., London, 1889-1905), no. 2046, Ambrose Serle to Earl of Dartmouth, Nov. 26, 1776. J. T. Adams, *Prov. Soc.*, p. 265.

quate to their support, it was not because their editors failed
to provide attractions for readers of every social class, of
every profession and avocation.   The very titles of the magazines—*The American Museum, or Repository of Ancient
and Modern Fugitive Pieces; The Universal Asylum; The
Christian's, Scholar's and Farmer's Magazine*—suggest their
all-inclusive program.   Unlike the newspaper or the broadside, the magazine was concerned with contributions of a
more or less permanent nature; they were to be " museums "
or " repositories " of that which was most worthy of preservation in the past or the present.   Now and then an enterprising publisher would issue a prospectus for a periodical
devoted to a special group of readers, such as *Christian History*, a " chronicle of the Great Awakening," the *Arminian
Magazine*, the *American Musical Magazine*, or the *Children's
Magazine*.   Their clientele was apparently not a wide one,
for their lives were very short, some of them being limited to
a single issue.[73]

As might be expected from their comprehensive programs,
the early American magazines reflected the various religious
movements which swept the country from time to time.
They are summarized in his careful analysis of the content
of our early periodicals by Mr. L. N. Richardson, who has
this passage pertinent to our subject—

In religion, the magazine tells a story of . . . anti-Catholic
sentiment merged with political hatred for France and Spain
during the middle years—an aversion which was somewhat
mitigated during the Revolution, and which was absent from
the two important magazines edited by Mathew Carey.[74]

[73] F. L. Mott, *A History of American Magazines, 1741-1850* (New
York, 1930), pp. 2-3, 24-31. L. N. Richardson, *A History of Early
American Magazines, 1741-1789* (New York, 1931), pp. 1-5. J. T.
Adams, *Prov. Soc.*, pp. 268-69.

[74] L. N. Richardson, *op. cit.*, pp. 4-5.

Mathew Carey's affiliation with the Roman Catholic Church is the explanation of the last statement and of the editor's defense of his co-religionists.

Of the mid-eighteenth century periodicals, one of the most ambitious was the *American Magazine and Historical Chronicle: for All the British Plantations* (Boston, Printed by Rogers and Fowle). Its editor was Jeremiah Gridley, a lawyer of ability and so popular that even his defense of the British government in a celebrated speech on the "Writs of Assistance" seems to have increased rather than to have lessened the esteem in which he was held. He was, withal, a highly cultivated gentleman with decidedly literary tastes. Some twelve years before the appearance of the *American Magazine,* Gridley had edited the *Weekly Rehearsal,* a newspaper whose literary features were gradually superseded by news items, so that when it was finally taken over by Thomas Fleet in 1733, it had ceased to be a literary journal.[75]

Gridley's second venture drew so heavily upon British journals that it "did not adequately represent America in a period of ferment"; nevertheless, its comparatively long life of three years and four months (September, 1743 to December, 1746) would seem to indicate that the editor was fairly successful in catering to public taste.[76]

As regards the religious outlook of the *American Magazine,* the anti-Catholic note struck in the first number [77] is

[75] J. T. Adams, in *D. A. B.*, vol. vii, p. 611. I. Thomas, *Hist. of Printing*, vol. i, p. 125; vol. ii, pp. 42-46.

[76] I. Thomas, *op. cit.*, vol. i, pp. 122-23; vol. ii, pp. 67-68. L. N. Richardson, *op. cit.*, pp. 37-57, 364.

[77] *American Magazine and Historical Chronicle; for All the British Plantations* (Boston, Sept., 1743-Dec., 1746), vol. i (1743), pp. 19-45. An account of the capture of a Spanish prize gives occasion for a disquisition on the *Bula de la Crusada* found among its cargo, and on the Catholic doctrine of indulgences. The incident seems to have been rather widely noted by the press. See *New York Mercury,* Dec. 15, 1743;

heard with increasing frequency as the repercussions in America of the War of the Austrian Succession inflamed anew national and religious hatreds. Although the Jacobite uprising under the " Young Pretender " in 1745 and the capture of Louisbourg were but minor incidents in the European conflict, to the subjects of King George on either side of the Atlantic they were of prime significance. The rebellion which terminated in the battle of Culloden was one more proof—if proof were needed—that the downfall of the Protestant succession was still one of the major objects of Papal and French intrigue; the capture of Cape Breton, on the other hand, meant control of one of the chief strongholds of the same enemies in the new world. To the British press the rebellion and the consequent revival of the penal laws furnished a welcome opportunity for the renewal of the ever popular anti-Popery propaganda. Colonial publishers, too, were quick to take advantage of such a windfall. Among the periodicals, the *American Magazine* devoted a disproportionate amount of space during 1746 to articles on the Pretender, the Protestant succession, the " dangers of Popery," and kindred subjects. Nor did it neglect the Louisbourg expedition in which New Englanders were so keenly interested.

The January number for 1746 offers an essay on " The Difference between Popery and Protestantism." The gist of the article is found in the conclusion—

. . . Popery is, by the invention of Commutations & Dispensations for the Breach of the Moral Law, the *strongest Enforce-*

Pennsylvania Gazette, May 10, 1743; *Boston Evening Post*, quoted in J. Buckingham, *Specimens of Newspaper Literature*, vol. i, p. 142. The inaccuracies of these accounts have been pointed out in A. C. H. *Researches*, o. s., vol. vi (April, 1889), p. 76; vol. xviii (Jan., 1901), pp. 26-28. *Cf.* John England, *Works* (Messmer edition, Cleveland, 1908, 7 vols.), vol. iv, p. 195 *et seq.* S. F. Smyth, " Bula de la Crusada," *The Month*, vol. ciii (1904), pp. 119-130, 225-42.

ment of Vice, under the Sanction of Religion; Protestantism, by placing Religion in the Practice of universal Virtue, as that Virtue is the Will of God, is the *Strongest Enforcement* of the moral Law . . . [78]

In the same issue " Angelenus " contributes " The Nation Awakn'd at the Danger of Popery." [79] He regrets that his fellow citizens have ceased to persecute Catholics. " A Short Display of Popery " [80] is intended to arouse " the most stupid and lukewarm Protestants and undecisive Papists," by a rehearsal of scandals connected with the Papacy.

The Pretender, as the arch-enemy—after the Pope—of Protestantism, was given much space in letters either to or from Noble Lords,[81] in sermons of the Anglican clergy,[82] in speeches of the lord high chancellor,[83] in " poetical essays." They were not always easy reading. The ballad, set to a familiar tune, might catch the fancy which more formal contributions would leave cold. One of these, " A Song upon the Times," sung to the tune of " Derry down Derry," illustrates the facility with which the rhymsters bridged the apparent gap between European and American politics. The first stanza reads—

> Ye true *British subjects*, whose loyalty dares
> To face the Pretender, and all the Pope's snares,

---

[78] *Amer. Mag.*, vol. iii (1746), pp. 10-12.

[79] *Ibid.*, vol. iii, p. 19.

[80] *Ibid.*, vol. iii, pp. 22-24. For similar articles, see Feb., pp. 32-65, 74-77, 82-83; March, 117-120; April, pp. 172-76; July, pp. 323-24, 330-32; Oct., pp. 465-69; Nov., pp. 503-06, 506-09.

[81] *Ibid.*, vol. ii (Aug., 1745), pp. 509-10.

[82] *Ibid.*, vol. ii (Nov., 1745), pp. 499-500; vol. iii (1746), pp. 78-80, 117-120. *Cf.* Address of Synod of Glasgow, vol. ii, pp. 46-47.

[83] *Amer. Mag.*, vol. iii (Oct., 1746), pp. 465-69. *Cf.* "Address of Dissenting Ministers of London and Westminster," vol. iii, p. 429; "Address of Pastors of Massachusetts Bay," vol. iii, pp. 576-77.

> Exert all your might in found [sic] *liberties* cause,
> And stand by your nation, and stand by the laws.
> > Derry down, etc.

The next four stanzas recite the calamities that would come to England under the rule of " Jacobite knaves." Then with a quick transition, the ballad concludes,

> *Cape Breton* we've conquer'd, *Cape Breton* we'll *keep*,
> Nor suffer our *foes* to cajole us asleep;
> And *Jemmy's* adherents we'll bring to the block,
> The *Nation's united* as firm as a rock.[84]

Adult readers of Jeremiah Gridley's periodical were not the only object of his solicitude. He was not unmindful of the rising generation, and like pedagogues the world over, knew the value of rhymes as a means of imparting information and of fixing it in the memory. As a painless method of learning history, the magazine published certain model stanzas on " bloody Mary," Elizabeth's " great heroick Soul," James II, "a furious Popish King," and—

> *William* the third, with good Maria join'd,
> Approv'd himself a Lover of Mankind;
> But chief of Britains, whom he did set free
> From arbitrary Power and Popery.[85]

It was not Gridley's fault if the Revolutionary generation was not imbued with the principles of the Whig tradition.

---

[84] *Ibid.*, vol. ii (1745), p. 86. See in the same issue another ballad, "A Loyal Song, with a Chorus, to the Tune of Lillibullero," pp. 85-86. For other references to the Pretender and to Canada, see vol. iii (1746), pp. 12-17, 25-27, 27-30, 240-50, 490-92, 576-77.

[85] *Amer. Mag.*, vol. iii, pp. 514-515. For further examples of the anti-Catholic Policy of this periodical, see vol. ii (1745), pp. 111-114, 122-23; vol. iii (1746), pp. 20-22, 67-68, 126-27, 134-35, 164-65, 182-83, 205-06, 340-46, 503-06.

Some ten years after the discontinuance of the New England periodical just discussed, another *American Magazine* made its appearance in Philadelphia. It was published by the "patriot printer of 1776," William Bradford (III), and edited by "a Society of Gentlemen" of whom William Smith, provost of the College and Academy of Philadelphia, was the chief. The editorial policy included loyalty to the crown, to the proprietary, and to the interests of the Anglican clergy; it was likewise "an able exponent of renewed military activities against France." The magazine was well conducted and reflected the varied cultural interests of the best Philadelphia society of the mid-eighteenth century. Dr. Smith's influence secured for it contributions of writers of distinction in the South. It was the only pre-Revolutionary periodical whose subscription list was adequate to its support. Its circulation, while concentrated chiefly in Pennsylvania and New Jersey, extended from New England to North Carolina on the mainland, and abroad to the West Indies, England, Ireland and Scotland. But its extensive subscription list does not tell the entire story of "the influence of the magazine, for a great many of the subscribers were educators, physicians, ministers, and merchants of high standing, whose contacts were numerous and whose opinions were highly respected." [86] Notwithstanding these advantages, notwithstanding, also, its reputation of being the most original literary magazine of the period, the *American Magazine* lasted but a year. Exigencies of colonial politics rather than lack of interest or support, seem to have been the cause.

Although it is nowhere stated in the magazine, Smith was probably the editor-in-chief. How far the other members of the "Society of Gentlemen" shared his views on the Church

[86] J. M. Wallace, *An Old Philadelphian*, pp. 65-73. Richardson, *Early Amer. Mag.*, pp. 98-123, 365. Mott, *Hist. Amer. Mag.*, pp. 23-31. V. H. Paltsits, in *D. A. B.*, vol. ii, pp. 564-66.

of Rome and on the French and Indian problem can not be determined. Certain it is that Smith's views as expressed elsewhere in his writings color the pages of the publication. " The Antigallican ", thought by J. W. Wallace [87] to have been Smith himself, openly flaunted his antagonism to the French. From November, 1757, to July, 1758, he wrote seven essays, the purpose of which is thus expressed in the first—

As an Antigallican, and an irreconcilable foe to *French* power, *French* customs, *French* policy and every species of *Slavery*, it is my purpose, as far as I am able, to expose and check the enormous growth and influence of those evils, especially in these remoter parts of the globe.[88]

The ever-present Indian problem, Smith thought, could be handled effectively if French influence were eliminated. To further this end he carried on a well-planned campaign through the pages of the magazine, every department of which contributed its share. " Canada must be demolished," ran the slogan, the " Brood of French savages " must be destroyed, or the British colonies are undone.[89] " The Watchman ", in a letter addressed to the " Colonies of the Southern District," describes his French neighbors in Canada as " hoodwincked ", their " Consciences ridden by a set of priests and jesuits and monks and inquisitors, swarming in every corner." The account of their " mock adoration " is followed by a call to rally to the support of the Protestant religion.[90]

Running through the entire volume is a " History of the War in North America," including the " old war " which

[87] Wallace, *Old Philadelphian*, p. 66.

[88] *American Magazine, or Monthly Chronicle for the British Colonies* (1757-1758, Philadelphia), pub. by William Bradford, p. 78.

[89] (Bradford) *Amer. Mag.*, pp. 9-23.

[90] *Ibid.*, pp. 352-54.

terminated with the capture of Louisbourg, and the French and Indian War. The cuts at the head of each installment are intended to convey to the reader how much more humane and intelligent are England's methods of dealing with the natives than those of the French.[91] French expansion into the Mississippi Valley is motivated by a desire

to surround all the English colonies, . . . to murder the inhabitants, or drive them into the sea; or what is a thousand times worse, to enslave them to *French* Tyranny and Popish Superstition.[92]

In his treatment of the war in the " two Tobacco Colonies," the writer stresses the number and wealth of the Jesuits in Maryland, and the danger of having such a stronghold of " Popery " in the very heart of the colonies. What if they should unite with the French on the Ohio or with the Irish and German immigrants?[93]

From January to September, 1769, the Bradford brothers published another *American Magazine* under the editorship of Lewis Nicola. Religious topics were given comparatively little space; the importance of the periodical lay rather in its scientific interests.[94] The notion prevalent among Protestants that Catholics for the merest whim may secure Papal dispensation from the most solemn vows, was illustrated in

[91] Wallace, *Old Philadelphian*, pp. 65-73.

[92] (Bradford) *Amer. Mag.*, p. 345.

[93] *Ibid.*, p. 510. For further references, see pp. 315-19, 480-83, 537-41, 617-21; on previous wars between French and English, pp. 515-27, 361, 408, 460, 558, 562; the Indians, pp. 9-23, 195-98, 246-50, 447-53, 468-70; the " Watchman ", pp. 307-15, 349-54, 492-97, 546-50.

[94] The *Transactions of the American Philosophical Society* were published as supplements to every issue except the first. See art. on " Lewis Nicola" by Louise B. Dunbar, in *D. A. B.*, vol. xiii, pp. 509-10. I. Thomas, *Hist. of Printing*, vol. ii, p. 150.

the March issue by a letter to the editor.[95]   Those portions of a history of the Camisards which stress their sufferings under religious persecution ran through several numbers.[96] " A Caution against Jesuitical Conversions " was the caption of another letter to the editor.[97]   These few instances are sufficient to indicate that on the Catholic question the outlook of the *American Magazine* edited by Nicola was in essential agreement with that of its predecessor.

Among the New England magazines that enjoyed considerable popularity on the eve of the Revolution was the *Royal American Magazine, or Universal Repository of Instruction and Amusement.*   Begun in January, 1774, it was edited for the first six months by Isaiah Thomas, and thereafter by Joseph Greenleaf, until March, 1775, after which it was discontinued.   Lexington and the events which followed seem to have made its continuance impracticable.   It was the last magazine founded in Boston before the Revolution. Besides the New England territory, its subscription list included readers in New York, Maryland, Pennsylvania and South Carolina.   A special feature of the periodical was its full-page engravings, some of them by Paul Revere.[98]

A contribution in the first number of the *Royal American Magazine,* though not directly concerned with Catholic belief and practice, nevertheless cites it as an example of senseless idolatry.[99]   For the next five months the periodical has noth-

---

[95] *American Magazine, or General Repository* (Philadelphia, pub. by William and Thomas Bradford), edited by Lewis Nicola, Jan.-Sept., 1769, pp. 51-52.

[96] *Loc. cit.,* pp. 219-223, 248-253, 281-85.

[97] *Loc. cit.,* pp. 83-87.

[98] I. Thomas, *op. cit.,* vol. i, p. 175; vol. ii, pp. 72-73, 119.   Richardson, *Early Amer. Mag.,* pp. 163-74, 36-68.   Mott, *op. cit.,* pp. 24-31.   Art. on " Thomas Greenleaf," by V. H. Paltsits, in *D. A. B.,* vol. vii, p. 584.

[99] *Royal American Magazine, or Universal Repository of Instruction and Amusement* (Boston, Jan. 1774-March, 1775), vol. i, p. 11.

ing for our purpose, but beginning with August, 1774, and continuing through December of the same year, the *Royal American* contributed its share to the flood of protest and invective let loose by the passage of the Quebec Act. Whoever had a grievance, economic, political or religious, might find an outlet in the press. If he were not a writer he was sure to find that a kindred spirit, skillful with the pen, had given clear and vigorous expression to his own half-formulated opinions.[100]

Subscribers who held Churchmen and Tories in abhorrence might read for their delectation the " High Church Creed " as formulated in the " High-Church Catechism. . . . By Charles Tory." The " Creed ", after proclaiming James II the " true father of his people," runs thus:

. . . that the Pope is a good sort of Christian, that the holy mother the church of which he is the head, is not so great a whore as she is represented to be. That with very little alteration, Jacobites and Tories might hold in her the communion of saints, and for a proper sum of money receive the forgiveness of sins with a safe and speedy deliverance from the pains of purgatory.

James gave his followers Ten Commandments, the sixth of which reads:

Thou shalt count it no murder under my commission or by my order to kill any man, how great soever, for the sake of my cause.[101]

The section of the *Royal American* devoted to Mathematical Questions was for the most part what it was intended to be—a medium of exchange for readers interested in mathematics. But even mathematicians are children of

[100] For American reaction to the Quebec Act, see *infra*, p. 273 *et seq.*

[101] *Royal American Mag.*, vol. i, pp. 307-310.

their age and share the prepossessions of their environment. Was it a sense of humor or an inclination to ridicule that prompted the formulation of the following problem:

If a Cardinal can pray a soul out of purgatory by himself in an hour, a bishop in three hours, a priest in five, and a friar in seven.—In what time can they pray out three souls, all praying together?

The problem is solved without comment in the following issue.[102]   This number (October, 1774) also offers an account of the Gunpowder Plot [103] and reprints from the *London Magazine,* " The Mitered Minuet. A Vision."   The " elegant engraving " with which the article is " embellished " is a reproduction by Paul Revere of the caricature in the London periodical.   It represents four Anglican bishops dancing around the Quebec Bill, the manuscript of which is on the floor.   A group of churchmen form a semicircle to the right and back of the dancers.   To the left a Scotchman, an Englishman and a Canadian (?) delightedly look on while the Devil flies over their heads.[104]

The November number of the *Royal American* reprinted from the *South Carolina Gazette* another " Vision " describing with much detail a miscarriage of justice and drawing the inevitable application to " Popery." [105]   The periodical closed its first year [106] with an impassioned appeal by " Tertius Cato " for a strict adherence to the Non-importation and Non-exportation agreements.   Like others of his fellow-

---

[102] *Royal Amer. Mag.,* vol. i, pp. 327, 368.

[103] *Ibid.,* vol. i, p. 387.

[104] *Ibid.,* vol. i, pp. 365-66. For the content of the " Vision ", see *infra,* pp. 303-04.   *Cf.* W. L. Andrews, *Paul Revere and His Engravings* (New York, 1901), p. 73.

[105] *Royal Amer. Mag.,* vol. i, pp. 414-416.

[106] *Ibid.,* vol. i, pp. 454-56.

countrymen, the writer professed to see behind the punitive measures of Parliament the shadows of France and Rome. The Revolution was to prove how unsubstantial those shadows were. They find no place in the three issues of the *Royal American* for 1775.

A considerable portion of early American verse appeared in broadsides or found its way into the verse sections of the newspapers or among the " poetical essays " of the magazines. Little of the verse that was published independently and as a part of the *belles-lettres* of the period found its inspiration directly in the Church of Rome. There is one poem, however, which deserves mention, not for its intrinsic merit or originality, but because of its place in the first volume of verse published by a Connecticut author.[107] *The Daniel Catcher* by Richard Steere contains a lengthy poem entitled " Antichrist Display'd ", the subtitle of which furnishes a brief analysis of its content and makes unnecessary any comment upon its point of view:

Antichrist Display'd. In a brief Character of the Sordid Ignorance, and Implacable Cruelty of the Church of Rome Called in Scripture Mistery Babylon the Great. With the Certainty of her Total Fall, Final Destruction and Desolation, which produceth matter for Sion's *Ejaculation and Consolation.*

Other references to our subject—and they are few enough —are connected with other topics, especially with France

[107] Richard Steere, "Antichrist Display'd," in *The Daniel Catcher. The Life of the Prophet Daniel: in a Poem. To which is Added, Earth's Felicities, Heaven's Allowances, A Blank Poem. With several other Poems. By R. S. Printed in the Year 1713.* Reprinted in G. E. Littlefield, *The Early Massachusetts Press, 1638-1711* (2 vols., Boston, 1907), vol. ii, pp. 73-81. Mr. Littlefield notes (vol. ii, p. 93) that Steere was a resident of Connecticut for nearly a quarter of a century, and that although his volume of verse was printed outside of the colony, it antedated by forty-one years Roger Wolcott's volume of *Poetical Meditations,* the first book of verse printed in Connecticut.

and the colonial wars. They differ neither in quality nor pattern from the broadside or periodical verse. There is, moreover, a striking similarity in their viewpoint. Witness the little volume entitled *Poems on Divers Subjects* by Margaret Brewster of Lebanon. " Braddock's Defeat, July 9, 1755," glorifies the ambushed general. Eventually the god of war will see that he gets his deserts.

> New-England Boys shall pledge their Cup,
> And drink the Dregs of Fury up,
> 'Till both the Pagan and the Pope
> Shall stagger at the Blow.[108]

Two early American plays, both published in London, illustrate situations and characters which most Protestant Americans of the eighteenth century would have accepted as true to life. Charlotte Ramsay Lennox's comedy, *The Sister,* is built around the story of a young girl whose aunt, " a bigoted Roman Catholic," employed every argument to convert her niece. When the girl resisted, the aunt abandoned moral suasion and tried to force her into a convent. Whereupon her niece fled to Paris.[109] The notion of fair damsels being forced into convents is even yet not entirely exploded.

The scene of the second drama,[110] published three years earlier, is laid in the wilds of America at the time of Pontiac's war. The Indian chief, determined to make a last stand

---

[108] Margaret Brewster, of Lebanon, *Poems on Divers Subjects* (Boston, 1757), pp. 25-26. *Cf.* " On General Braddock's Defeat," in the *Patriot Muse,* by Benjamin Prime (London, 1764), pp. 9-17. Samuel Davies, *Military Glory of Great Britain* (Philadelphia, 1762). See *supra,* pp. 145-46; *infra,* p. 385.

[109] Mrs. Charlotte Lennox, *The Sister; a Comedy* (London, 1769), p. 4.

[110] Robert Rogers, *Ponteach; or, the Savages of America. A Tragedy* (London, 1766).

against the English, is assured by a priest, whom he has consulted regarding the outcome of the war, that he will be successful. God will bless a war against the English who killed His Son. Christ was an Indian, the priest further insists. Whoever, therefore, kills a Briton merits heaven and will be conveyed there by the angels. In proof of the truth of what he says, the cleric draws from his pocket a burning-glass bequeathed by the Lord to Saint Peter. By means of it the priest can bring down fire from heaven. He kneels, pretends to pray, then focuses the sun as a sign that the Indians should destroy the English. Pontiac, convinced by this charlatanry, takes up the bloody hatchet and vows vengeance. This bare outline of the narrative gives but a faint notion of the intrigue, the hypocrisy, the ambition of this clerical profligate, for he is that, also.[111] There is concentrated in the portrayal of his character, the accumulated distrust and hatred of generations of Indian warfare, almost invariably instigated, in the mind of the Anglo-American, by the missionary.

Colonial historians, far from softening the harsh lines of the conventional portrait of the typical Roman Catholic, rather accentuated them. The New England output in this field far exceeded that of other sections of British America. The writers were for the most part important figures in church and state, men who had helped to make much of the history of which they wrote. They were men, too, of high integrity, impressed with the seriousness of the historian's calling, and undoubtedly sincere in their claims to impartiality. Save for an occasional clerical visitor on a diplomatic mission, they had no contact with Roman Catholics, no prac-

---

[111] See Act iii, scenes 2, 3; Act iv, scene 1. For Rogers' career and a critical estimate of his work see introduction and biography by Allan Nevins in the edition of *Ponteach* sponsored by the Caxton Club, Chicago, 1914. *Cf.* F. Parkman, *Conspiracy of Pontiac* (2 vols., Boston, 1851), vol. ii, pp. 321, 332; M. C. Tyler, *Lit. Hist. Rev.*, vol. ii, pp. 188-192.

tical experience of Catholic life and practice under normal conditions. New England legislation saw to it that inherited traditions should not be disturbed. Nor did it occur to a Bradford,[112] a Winthrop [113] or a Prince [114] that in adopting the current phraseology and figures of speech when referring to the Church of Rome they were giving evidence of a bias which as historians they would be the first to disclaim.

The temporary loss of the Bradford and Winthrop manuscripts, gave the narrative of a town clerk the distinction of being the first printed history of New England. Decidedly inferior as a historical narrative to both the Bradford and the Winthrop histories,[115] Johnson's *Wonder-Working Providence* has a value peculiarly its own. An emigrant from Kent to the Bay Colony in 1630, the writer brought with him the preconceptions and the standards of the small English country gentlemen. In 1640 he moved from Cambridge to the new settlement of Woburn, of which he was the first citizen. For thirty years he was identified with the public life of the town, serving it as selectman, leader of the train-band, town clerk, and representative at the general court. In these capacities he had unrivaled opportunities of observing the intimate details of the daily life of the small New

[112] W. Bradford, *History of Plymouth Plantation.* Mass. H. S. *Coll.,* 4 ser., vol. iii, pp. 3, 5, 7, 8. The mss. have been reproduced in facsimile, London, 1896.

[113] J. Winthrop, *A Short Story of the Rise, reign and ruin of the Antinomians, Familists & Libertines that infected the Churches of New England* (London, 1644), *passim.* For the story of his *Journal* or *History of New England* and that of the Bradford manuscripts, see J. F. Jameson, *The History of Historical Writing in America* (Boston, 1891), pp. 13-29.

[114] Thomas Prince, *A Chronological History of New-England, in the form of Annals* (3rd ed. by Samuel G. Drake, Boston, 1736, 1826, 1852), pp. 416-417. *Cf.* J. F. Jameson, *op. cit.,* pp. 68-71.

[115] For the loss and misplacement of these manuscripts, see J. F. Jameson, *op. cit.,* pp. 13-15, 28.

England town—opportunities of which he fully availed himself. His narrative, therefore, is important because it reflects the viewpoint of " the rank and file "; their narrownesses and their prejudices, no less than their public spirit and their religious ideals.[116]

Like all good Puritans, Edward Johnson looked upon the Anglican tendency towards ritualism and its lax—to his mind —observance of the sabbath as a harking back to paganism and " Popery ", with the result that a " multitude of irreligious lascivious and popish affected persons spread the whole land like Grasshoppers." To deliver the country from this plague, " Christ creates a New England to muster up the first of his Forces. . . ." [117] As His chosen army they will meet with temptation and must consequently be warned " never to make a League with any of there seven Sectaries." In listing these sources of infection, Johnson gives local visitations precedence over the more remote. So the Gortonists [118] head the list, with the " Papists " a close second. The latter, he says,

with (almost) equall blasphemy and pride prefer their own Merits and Workes of Supererogation as equall with Christs unvaluable Death, and Sufferings.[119]

The rebuilding of the kingdom of God in New England was the beginning of a " thorough Reformation of the Churches of Christ." In vision he sees the downfall of Babylon. " Listen a while," he cries, " hear what the herauld proclaimes. Babylon is fallen, is fallen, both her Doctrine and

[116] Jameson, *Hist. Writing in Amer.*, pp. 29-40. See also introd. to Edward Johnson, *Wonder-Working Providence*, ed. by J. F. Jameson (Original Narratives of Early American History, New York, 1910), pp. 5-8, 14-16. Mass. H. S. *Coll.*, 2 ser., vol. ii, pp. 95-96.

[117] Johnson, *Wonder-Working Prov.*, p. 23.

[118] *Ibid.*, p. 31.

[119] *Ibid.*

Lordly rabble of Popes, Cardinals, Lordly-Bishops. . . ."
Before he finishes the enumeration, every grade of the hierarchy, every functionary of the Church to the " Bel-ringers ",
is included.[120] In chapter fifteen Johnson calls all nations
to join in advancing the kingdom of Christ. To Italy, " the
Seat and Center of the Beast," he holds out the hope that
Christ will make of her a chosen nation even as He has of
New England. " See here," he exclaims, " what wonders
hee works in little time." To Spain and Portugal he makes
a like appeal, but with a choice of metaphors even more
suggestive of Rome's vileness.[121] A haunting fear of episcopacy seems to have pursued the zealous town clerk. Even
among the Presbyterians, orthodox enough from the point
of doctrine, he finds, in their efforts to lord it over one
another, traces of the cloven foot.[192] So he cautions them
against the " Malignant Adversary ", lest it invade civil as
well as religious life. And he drives his lesson home by an
analogy which all Woburn would understand. The Indians,
he points out, never succeed in permanently taming the
wolves of the forest; let the elect of royalist leanings take
heed, for " your Lord Bishops, Deans, Prebends, etc. be
right whelps of the Roman litter." [123]

With this warning we turn from the small frontier settlement to the Boston of half a century later, where another
historian had just received a copy of what he fondly refers
to as " my Church History." Cotton Mather was in many
respects a contrast to Edward Johnson. His distinguished
family connections, his learning, his social prestige, his prominence in the religious and civil life of Boston for a period
of over fifty years, his contacts with persons of learning

---

120 Johnson, *op. cit.*, p. 50.
121 *Ibid.*, pp. 59-60.
122 *Ibid.*, p. 122.
123 *Ibid.*, p. 159.

and distinction at home and abroad—all these advantages would suggest a broader outlook on life than that revealed in *Wonder-Working Providence*. Yet the *Magnalia*, for all its pretensions, for all its ponderous learning, for all its store of information not easily accessible elsewhere,[124] has many points in common with its less ambitious predecessor. As a reflection of the Puritan mind—of what it thought, of what it esteemed, of what it hated—it does not point to the existence of any great chasm between the unlearned chronicler of Woburn's simple annals and the erudite Mather.

On the question of " Popery " and its evils, they were certainly one. They agreed on New England's exalted destiny to form a " bulwark against the kingdom of antichrist," [125] " to express and pursue the Protestant Reformation," [126] to eschew all mixtures of " paganry and popery ",[127] to reject an " imposed liturgy " from which sprang the "abomination of the Mass." [128] That book of the *Magnalia* called *Decennium Luctuosum* abounds in references to the evil effects of Catholic teaching upon the Indian.

[124] For brief estimates of Mather as a churchman and historian, see P. L. Ford, preface to *Diary*, p. xvii. W. S. Perry, *Hist. Am. Epis. Ch.*, vol. i, p. 182. C. H. Lincoln, *Narratives of the Indian Wars* (Orig. Nar. of Amer. History, New York, 1913). Introd. to "Decennium Luctuosum," by Cotton Mather (1699), pp. 175-78. J. F. Jameson, *op. cit.*, pp. 46-62. For more extended treatments, see Barrett Wendall, *Cotton Mather* (1891-1926). R. and L. Boas, *Cotton Mather* (1928). *Commonwealth History of Massachusetts*, ed. by A. B. Hart, vol. ii (1928), ch. xi, on Mather. I. W. Riley, *American Philosophy, The Early Schools* (1907), pp. 195-199.

[125] C. Mather, *Magnalia*, vol. i, p. 65.

[126] *Ibid.*, vol. i, p. 79.

[127] *Ibid.*, vol. i, p. 195.

[128] *Ibid.*, vol. i, p. 454. *Cf. supra*, pp. 205-06, notes 117, 118, 119, 120, 121, 122, 123. Also Mass. H. S. *Coll.*, vol. iii, pp. 133-36. *Diary*, vol. i, pp. 572, 594-95; vol. ii, pp. 207, 435, 445-46, 441-42.

Embalmed in the first published history of New England as well as in the most pretentious historical effort of the eighteenth century, it is not surprising that the Puritan estimate of Rome and her followers should find a place in other contemporary histories. About the middle of the century, there was published at first in pamphlet installments, and later in two volumes, an historical *Summary* by a Boston physician who included history among his many non-professional interests. Although marred by many inaccuracies, and based often upon hearsay or tradition, the work, like the *Magnalia,* has preserved information not readily obtained elsewhere and is still considered an important source for early colonial history.[129] As a busy practising physician in the days when a doctor went wherever he was called and attended to cases now relegated to the specialist, he had unusual opportunities of observing the point of view not only of his clients among the common folk, but also of the religious and professional groups in and around Boston. However unreliable his *Summary* may be in detail,[130] the doctor's Scottish birth and training and his Calvinistic prepossessions would make him a sympathetic medium for the transmission of Puritan prejudices.

Like most of his New England contemporaries, William Douglass thought Roman Catholics should be debarred from " all well-regulated governments." The " most evident political reasons for their exclusion " follow:

. . . the Constitution of their Religion, renders them a Nusance in Society; they have an Indulgence for Lying, Cheating, Robbing, Murdering, and not only may, but are in Christian

---

[129] J. F. Fulton in *D. A. B.*, vol. v, pp. 407-08.

[130] Thomas Hutchinson, who was a contemporary of Douglass, notes some of the erroneous statements of the *Summary.* See his *History of the Province of Massachusetts-Bay* (3rd ed., Boston, 1795), vol. i, pp. 191, 283, 317, 320; vol. ii, pp. 29, 52, 78.

Duty bound, to extirpate all mankind who are not of their Way
of thinking; they call them Hereticks . . . [131]

The Lockian principles thus enunciated are carried to their
logical conclusion in that section of the *Summary* devoted to
Maryland and Pennsylvania. Papists, he thinks, are too
much indulged in these two provinces, where the public exercise of their religion is actually tolerated. Since

that religion is pernicious to human society in general, and tends
to subvert our happy Constitution; why may it not be suppressed
as to publick worship by an act of Parliament? [132]

Reference has been made to Hutchinson's criticism of the
inaccuracies of the *Summary* just discussed.[133] The Revolutionary governor of Massachusetts had already published
two volumes of his history of the Bay colony before the
opening of the war. With access to sources which were not
then available to others, Hutchinson, like Douglass, was
obliged to utilize, as best he could, the odd moments of a
busy life. Unlike the Scottish doctor, however, he was free
from violent prejudices and partisanship. His *History of
the Province of Massachusetts Bay* is, on the whole, fair-
minded and will always remain among the first authorities
on the early history of New England.[134] True, he sees eye
to eye with other New England historians on the question
of the French and Indians,[135] but even when he lays at the

[131] William Douglass, *Summary, Historical and Political of the First
Planting, Progressive Settlements and Present State of the British
Settlements in North America* (Boston, vol. i, 1749, vol. ii 1751. Also
2 vols., Boston, 1754). L. C. has some numbers of the pamphlet edition.
See vol. i, p. 225 n.

[132] *Ibid.*, vol. i, p. 157.

[133] *Supra*, p. 208, note 130.

[134] J. K. Hosmer, *Life of Thomas Hutchinson* (Boston, 1896), pp.
85, 88. J. F. Jameson, *Hist. Writing in Amer.*, pp. 76-79.

door of the French missionary the responsibility of the
Indian raid, he does not, like his contemporaries—and not a
few of his successors—take occasion therefrom to launch
into a disquisition on the iniquities of the Papacy or the
" dangers of Popery."

The Virginia historians of the eighteenth century have
little for our purpose. One may gather from the vocabulary, the phraseology and passing references in Beverly,[136]
Jones,[137] and Stith [138] that they had little sympathy and less
esteem for the " Papists " or their beliefs. Beverly, for
example, discussing the detection of an Indian conspiracy and
subsequent reprisals by the whites, remarks

This gave the English a fair Pretense of endeavouring the total
Extirpation of the Indians . . . making use of the Roman
Maxim, (Faith is not to be kept with Hereticks) to obtain their
Ends.[139]

William Smith, the colonial historian of New York, thought
that the law [140] excluding priests from the province should be
made perpetual. His other references to Roman Catholics
are consistent with this opinion and in accord with the policy
of New York officialdom.[141] The historical collections of
the Carolinas and Georgia reprint the important pamphlet

[135] Thomas Hutchinson, *History of the Province of Massachusetts Bay,*
vol. ii, pp. 69, 124, 157, 198, 236, 279-84.

[136] Robert Beverly, *History of Virginia in Four Parts* (London, 1705).

[137] Rev. Hugh Jones, *The Present State of Virginia* (London, 1724).

[138] Rev. William Stith, *History of the First Discovery and Settlement
of Virginia* (Williamsburg, 1747).

[139] R. Beverley, *op. cit.,* p. 43.

[140] *Supra,* pp. 56-57.

[141] William Smith, *History of the Province of New York, from the
Discovery to the Year 1732 . . . with a continuation, From the Year
1732 to the Commencement of the Year 1814* (continuation by J. V. N.
Yates, Albany, 1814), pp. 80, 82, 99, 102, 111. Also in N. Y. Hist. Soc.
Colls., vol. iv (1826).

materials of the period. Much of it was intended for European consumption. There is, consequently, frequent reference to the religious liberty which these colonies offered to Protestant sects, a liberty which would appear all the more attractive against the background of the religious and dynastic wars of Europe. The English historical tradition would and did naturally find a place in the sketching of that background.

To this examination of certain outstanding types of colonial literature might be added a mass of official and semi-official documents—memorials, petitions, proclamations, statutes, correspondence of governors and of lesser dignitaries. Some of these will be referred to later. Here they would add only cumulative evidence to the data already presented. Whether we regard colonial literature from the viewpoint of writer or reader, as a reflection, that is, of the thought and emotion of the highest and lowest classes, or as an important influence in the molding of that thought and emotion, the inferences are clear enough. The Roman Catholic whose portrait has been preserved in that literature is the lineal descendant of the " Papist dogge " of the England of the Reformation; he is the counterpart of that " worshipper of the Beast " so often decried in the colonial pulpit; he is the incarnation of that monster of ignorance and cruelty denounced by the sponsors of the educational system which fed its babes on the " milk " of the *New England Primer* and its youths on the Dudleian lectures.

CHAPTER VI

The Tradition in Action

The foregoing chapters have been concerned, more or less theoretically, with the origin of British public opinion of Roman Catholicism in the seventeenth and eighteenth centuries, with its transit to British America, and with its manifestation in three important aspects of colonial life—religion, education and literature. It is the purpose of the present chapter to consider American opinion in some of its practical bearings on the civil and political life of Roman Catholics and their fellow colonists—the Spanish-French-Indian problem, immigration, naturalization, land-holding, the franchise, and the like.

America had her own Spanish and French problems which were bound up with the fisheries, the fur trade, boundary disputes, the conversion of the natives and the horrors of Indian warfare. To the south, in the Caribbean region, along the Georgia-Florida frontier and the backwoods of the Carolinas, the Spanish danger loomed large. To the north, along the Canadian border and the outposts of New York, Pennsylvania and Virginia, French activities, especially after the turn of the mid-century, assumed ever increasing importance.

The reaction caused by the Revolution of 1688 was still at its height in England and America when the first of the four inter-colonial wars broke out (1689-1697). Most of the colonial legislatures were at that time framing addresses of congratulation and loyalty to William and Mary, and thanking the Almighty for the advent of a Prince who had deliv-

ered them from the wiles of " Popery and arbitrary power." [1]
In New York, the Catholic Governor, Thomas Dongan, and
the few other Catholics in office, were overthrown by the
Leislerian revolution. The reactionaries justified their high-
handed methods by proclamations which hinted darkly at
" Popish plots " not unlike those which were then terroriz-
ing England.[2] In America, to the trio held responsible, over
seas, for these plots—the " Papists ", the French and the
Pretender—there was added the Indian. Only the frontier
settlements which had experienced the horrors of Indian
raids, could plumb the terrors suggested by an attack of
French and Indians. Connecticut's distrust of the Catholic,
armed or unarmed, is reflected in her response to Leisler's
proclamation,

. . . we doe advise you that you keep the Forte tenable and well
manned for the defense of the protestant religion and those ends
above mentioned and that you suffer no catholick to enter the
same armed or without arms within your government or citty . . . [3]

In New Hampshire, as in the other British provinces, officers
at their induction were obliged to take among other tests, the
Declaration Oath so impregnated with hatred of the Papacy.[4]
When, in 1696, news of the attempted assassination of
William III reached the colony, the danger from " Popery "
seemed so imminent that it was deemed advisable to administer these oaths to youths of sixteen and over.[5] As in

---

[1] Conn. *Rec.* (1687-79), vol. iii, pp. 463 *et seq.* *Doc. Hist. N. Y.*,
vol. iii, pp. 577-83.

[2] *Doc. Hist. N. Y.*, vol. iii, pp. 599, 608.

[3] Conn. *Rec.*, vol. iii, p. 467.

[4] A. S. Batchellor and H. H. Metcalf, eds., *Laws of the State of New
Hampshire, 1679-1792* (5 vols., Manchester–Concord, 1904-6), vol. i, p. 579.

[5] N. H. *State Papers*, vol. ii, pp. 188, 191 ; vol. iii, pp. 201-02.

the South, New Hampshire formed an " Association " to uphold the Protestant succession.[6]

In Maryland the " glorious Revolution " followed much the same course as in New York. A few malcontents, headed by John Coode, spread a report that the Senecas and the " Papists " were planning to massacre the Protestants of the isolated frontier districts. The Maryland *Archives* of the period abound in rumors of plots which investigation proved fictitious.[7] Catholics meanwhile were deprived of arms, removed from office, and subject to another period of penal legislation.[8] Eventually the arbitrary methods of Coode and his " Associators " brought about a reaction of the better class of Protestants, who petitioned the King to summon the leaders to England to answer charges against them.[9]

From Maryland the panic spread to Virginia where the activities of Rev. John Waugh matched those of Coode. Reports of plots to " cut the throats of Protestants " were received apparently with the same credulity as in Maryland.[10] So intense was the excitement, so over-wrought the imaginations of some witnesses, that when George Hack of Accomac County, was reported to have received a bull from the Pope, pardoning all his sins, there were not wanting those who would testify to having seen it.[11] The experience of

[6] *Ibid.*, vol. ii, p. 258.

[7] Md. *Arch.*, vol. viii, pref. v-vi; pp. 90-91, 341-509.

[8] Md. *Arch.*, vol. xix, pp. 36-37, 389-90; vol. xx, p. 224.

[9] Md. *Arch.*, vol. viii, pp. 115-212, 225-28.

[10] " Virginia Records, 1688-90," in *Va. Mag.*, vol. xx (1912), pp. 4, 11. *Cf.* Fairfax Harrison, " Parson Waugh's Tumult," *Va. Mag.*, vol. xxx (1922), pp. 31 *et seq.*

[11] For deposition of the witness see P. A. Bruce, *Institutional History of Virginia in the Seventeenth Century* (2 vols., New York, 1910), vol. i, p. 270 n.

George Brent, discussed later in this chapter,[12] would suggest that the life of a prominent Catholic, at that period, was not safe. The Pennsylvania *Archives* tell a similar tale of alleged connivance of the " Papists " with the northern Indians to " cutt off the Protestants, or at least to reduce them to the See of Rome." But the Pennsylvania Council, then as later, refused to become alarmed.[13]

That the outbreak of the first colonial war should confirm and even increase the suspicions and rumors noted above, was to be expected. Though hostilities were confined to the northern frontier, the progress of the war was closely watched by the governments to the west and south.[14] Synchronizing as they did with the so-called " Popish plots," the events of the struggle would give a tragic significance to every alarm that reached the isolated settlers in the backwoods.

A brief summary of the conflict is all that is necessary here. An Iroquois attack on the French village at LaChine, in August, 1688, convinced Frontenac, the French governor, of the necessity of drastic measures. Since the Iroquois were allies of the English, the latter were included in the French program of reprisals. Proceeding in three divisions from Montreal, Three Rivers and Quebec, the French and Indians attacked Schenectady, N. Y., Salmon Falls, N. H., and Fort Loyal at Falmouth, Me. For sheer cruelty and destruction the massacre of Schenectady stands out amid a series of raids and counter-raids noted for their barbarity. The inhabitants of Salmon Falls were either slain or taken prisoner. At Falmouth, Captain Sylvanus Davis bravely defended the fort; then convinced of the futility of resist-

---

[12] *Infra*, pp. 249-51.

[13] Pa. *Arch.*, 4 ser., vol. i, pp. 138, 141. Pa. *Col. Rec.*, vol. i, pp. 277, 279.

[14] *Cf.* Md. *Arch.*, vol. viii, pp. 456-69, 478-80, 513-16.

ance, surrendered on condition that all lives be spared. Once disarmed, they were treacherously massacred by the Indians.

The elation of the French was equalled only by the terror of the English, who in turn organized a punitive expedition against Port Royal, Acadia. Convinced of the complicity of the French clergy in the recent atrocities, and a firm believer in the *lex talionis*, the leader, Sir William Phipps, wrought such havoc at Port Royal that some New Englanders deprecated his excesses. If French accounts be credited, he also violated the terms of the surrender, desecrated the churches, and brought home two priests among the prisoners.

Success in Acadia was offset by failure before Quebec. The war dragged on until 1697, neither side being able to claim the victory. Since nothing was really settled, the Peace of Ryswick was merely a truce.[15]

In the interval between the Peace of Ryswick and the outbreak of Queen Anne's War, Anglo-French rivalry for control of the Mississippi was an important factor in keeping alive old animosities. The second inter-colonial war told the same sickening tale of Indian attacks on the settlements of Maine, New Hampshire and Western Massachusetts, with counter expeditions from New England against Acadia and Quebec. Wells, Saco and Ft. Casco in Maine, Berwick and York in New Hampshire, Haverhill in Massachusetts, and Deerfield in Connecticut, were some of the places which suffered. If the activities of the Abnakis at St. Francis and

---

[15] N. H. *State Papers*, vol. ii, pp. 49, 55-56, 125-26, 145, 147, 189. N. H. H. S., *Coll.*, vol. viii, p. 403 *et seq.* Mass. Hist. Soc., *Coll.*, 3 ser., vol. i, p. 85, 101-112; *Doc. Hist. N. Y.*, vol. ii, pp. 68, 75, 179. Mass. Hist. Soc. *Proc.*, 2 ser., vol. xv, p. 281. H. L. Osgood, *Amer. Colonies in the Eighteenth Century*, vol. ii, pp. 53-114. G. M. Wrong, *Rise and Fall of New France* (2 vols., New York, 1928), vol. ii, pp. 53-114. C. H. Lincoln, ed., *Narratives of the Indian Wars*. C. Mather, *Magnalia*, bk. ii. S. Penhallow, *History of the Wars of New England with the Eastern Indians* ... (Boston, 1726).

Norridgewock convinced the British of the evil influence of the Catholic priests, who, it was alleged, " blessed the Indian's tomahawk and scalping knife, and bade him God-speed in the work of destroying heretics," [16] the murder of Gourdault and his companions by Benjamin Church was not calculated to impress the French with the restraint of Puritan reprisals.

In the South, the English expedition against the Floridas (1702) inflicting considerable damage on St. Augustine, and the Spanish-Indian invasion of the Carolinas (1703-04) were indecisive. Territorial gains could be held by neither party.[17] But here, as in the North, religion was often the scapegoat of conflicting policies of Indian warfare, trade rivalry and territorial expansion. In the Treaty of Utrecht, the cession of Acadia to England was destined to inject a politico-religious issue which is still a vexed question in American history.

Between 1713 and the resumption of hostilities in the Anglo-Spanish War, 1739, the last of the British colonies on the mainland was founded. The philanthropic and religious motives which actuated the Trustees of Georgia did not blind the British government to the strategic value of a colony south of the Carolinas. Neither did Spain miss the significance of the last British settlement in what she regarded as Florida territory. It was a challenge which the governments of both countries recognized would have to be met sooner or later.[18] Nor were the subjects of the two nations

---

[16] B. Laboree, *Historical Address at the Dedication of a Monument in Charlestown, N. H.* (Aug. 30, 1870), p. 8. *Cf.* N. H. *State Papers,* vol. ii, p. 436. W. Allen, *History of Norridgewock* (Norridgewock, 1849), ch. 2. See appendix for letters of Father Râle. Osgood, *op. cit.,* vol. i, pp. 399-453. Wrong, *op. cit.,* vol. ii, p. 562 *et seq.*

[17] E. McCrady, *South Carolina, 1670-1719,* chs. xvi-xvii. Osgood, *op. cit.,* vol. i, pp. 455, 482 *et seq.*

[18] *Diary of Viscount Percival.* Historical Manuscripts Commission (2 vols., London, 1920-23), vol. i, pp. 44-46. (Feb. 13, 1729-30). V. W.

slow to provoke a quarrel. Commercial rivary in the Caribbean and Indian intrigues on land, to say nothing of other differences, were fertile sources of irritation. The incident of Jenkin's ear was the occasion rather than the cause of the war which was declared in 1739.

Osgood [19] points out that in this war a decided effort was made to break down the policy of isolation which had hitherto characterized colonial participation in European conflicts. With Spain as the declared enemy, and France as a possible second, it was inevitable that the religious issue should be exploited in the publicity which was intended to enlist the cooperation of colonies none too keenly interested in the welfare of Georgia. Indeed the religious element had been given special prominence from the very inception of the colony, for besides being a refuge for English debtors, the project was widely advertised as an asylum for persecuted Protestants the world over. The promoters [20] of the enterprise were personally hostile to the Church of Rome; the so-called " Georgia sermons," [21] delivered annually before the

Crane, *Promotion Literature of Georgia*, reprinted from *Bibliographical Essays: a Tribute to Wilberforce Eames*, pp. 6-7. *Cf.* Osgood, *Amer. Col. in Eighteenth Century*, vol. iii, pp. 62, 502-510.

[19] Osgood, *op. cit.*, vol. iii, pp. 402, 510.

[20] Five of the original Trustees were clergymen of the Church of England. Four other clergymen were added later. The president of the Trustees, Viscount Percival, was the author of " Some thoughts concerning religion and the reformation from popery, a discourse," and " The Idolatry of the Papists." *Diary*, vol. i, pp. 122, 385. *Colonial Records of the State of Georgia, 1732-1774*, ed. by A. D. Chandler (26 vols., Atlanta, 1904-1911), vol. ii, pp. 3-4.

[21] These sermons were delivered annually from 1731 to 1750. A bequest in the will of Dr. Bray of Virginia fame was used for the printing and distribution of the sermons. See *Diary of Viscount Percival*, vol. i, pp. 223-25. There is evidence that the choice of speakers was controlled by the Trustees. Only four of the eighteen sermons examined were free from anti-Catholic propaganda. See especially those of Rev. Philip Bearcroft, March 16, 1737/8 (London, 1738), and Rev. Wm.

Trustees, were an important part of the promotion literature widely distributed in Europe and America. Like their S. P. G. prototypes, these discourses frequently indict the Catholic Church for " altering " and even " reversing " the " whole tenor " [22] of Christianity. Running through them like a refrain is the glorification of England as the " bulwark and refuge of the Protestant interest." [23] Equally insistent is the note of enmity to Frenchman and Spaniard, neither of whom is ever dissociated from the cruelty and treachery of the Indian.

Georgia's position as a buffer state between South Carolina and the Spanish settlements to the south and the French to the west and southwest suggested the expediency of reviving old national antagonisms. Though France was determined to keep out of the struggle if possible,[24] both England and the colonies expected that she would enter the contest on the side of Spain. Her declaration of war was looked for daily. Meanwhile the call for aid went forth to the colonies to the north and with it tales of negro insurrections incited by Spain,[25] of Indian tribes alienated by France,[26] of the determination of both enemies to divide British America

Berriman, March 15, 1738/9 (London, 1739). For an account of the sermons and their place in the promotion literature of Georgia, see V. W. Crane, " Prom. Lit. of Georgia." For evidence that Trustees controlled choice of speaker, see *Diary of Viscount Percival*, vol. ii, pp. 463, 471, 147.

[22] Samuel Smith, *Sermon at . . . First Yearly Meeting, Feb. 23, 1730/31 . . .* (London, 1733).

[23] George Watts, *Sermon Preached before the Trustees For Establishing the Colony of Georgia in America . . . March 18, 1735* (London, 1736).

[24] *Archives Nationales*, Colonies, Ser. B., vols. 68, 70, 72, 74, L. C. Trans. France.

[25] E. McCrady, *South Carolina under Royal Government* (New York, 1899), p. 185.

[26] *Ga. Col. Rec.*, vol. xxii, pt. 2, pp. 68, 166, 178, 266.

between them.[27]   The state archives afford evidence of Anglo-American reaction to the appeal.[28]   In Maryland, to cite but one example, the loyalty of the Catholic population was made the subject of a recriminating debate between the Upper and Lower Houses.   The former, communicating to the Lower House a bill for encouraging enlistment in the army, hinted that while the Catholics would doubtless rejoice if France should enter the war against England, the Protestants would look upon it with horror.   To the Assembly's protest against such insinuations, the Upper House disclaimed any malicious intention; it had merely stated an obvious fact—that Catholics would be glad if their religion were established, even at the price of a conquest by France.   The mother country, the reply continued, had no such confidence in the loyalty of its Roman Catholic subjects; witness the proclamation of the preceding November by the Lord-Lieutenant of Ireland forbidding Catholics to keep or bear arms.   The Upper House could not answer for Roman Catholics where their religion was concerned.   The debate continued throughout the month of May, 1740, neither house agreeing on the details of the bill in question.   In a final effort to get it passed, the Upper House, on the twenty-ninth, begged its colleagues to consider that

We have an Actual War with Spain and expect One every day with France if it is not already declared. Our Province lies in a defenseless condition easily to be invaded by the French and Indians in Friendship with them, and the Papists among Ourselves and other Jacobites have arrived at a degree of

[27] *Colonial Records of North Carolina*, vol. v, p. 221.

[28] Among others see *Archives of Pennsylvania*, 4 ser., vol. i, pp. 686, 712, 717, 727, 729, 731, 734, 750, 753, 755, 760; vol. ii, p. 10. *Archives of the State of New Jersey*, 1 ser., vol. xv, pp. 85-89, 113-117, 126, 183, 237-38. *Ga. Col. Rec.*, vol. v, pp. 39, 48, 631, 659. *N. H. State Papers*, vol. v, pp. 47-53. *Conn. Rec.*, vol. viii, p. 324. *R. I. Rec.*, vol. iv, pp. 573, 576. *Doc. Hist. N. Y.*, vol. vi, pp. 147, 162-170.

Insolence beyond all imagination some of them not sparing his most Sacred Majesty himself others threatening the Destruction of Our Religion and Laws and the mildest of them haranguing daily upon the terrible and Irresistible Power of France and Spain . . . [29]

With the defeat of the Spaniards and the capture of St. Augustine, the scene of the war in America was transferred to the north. There the most important event was the capture of Louisbourg. Its place in the literary remains of the period has been pointed out in the preceding chapter. The capture of this stronghold which the French had built to compensate for the loss of Nova Scotia had become the darling project of the New Englanders. So convinced were they of its strategic and economic value to New England that they were willing to undertake its conquest without the aid of the home government. In an effort to enkindle enthusiasm Governor Shirley made the most of the " No-Popery " complex of the New Englanders. It was fanned to a white heat by the clergy who accompanied the forces singing hymns and praying with a fervor that would have done credit to Cromwell and his Model Army. George Whitefield furnished Pepperell with his motto, and although he refused to accompany the soldiers he

made a recruiting house of the sanctuary; and he not only preached *delenda est Carthago*, but one of his followers actually joined the troops as chaplain, and carried an axe at the shoulder, with which to hew down the Catholic images in the churches of that fated city.

Nor was Parson Moody, the chaplain in question, alone in his enthusiasm; rather was he the envy of those who remained at home. Writing to William Pepperell, old Parson Gray wistfully exclaims—

[29] *Md. Arch.*, Assemb. Proc., Apr. 23–June 5, 1740, vol. xl, pp. 444, 448, 455, 460, 465-66, 469-70, 475, 485-86, 495.

. . . And how sweet and pleasant it will be to you to be the person under God that shall reduce and pull down that stronghold of Satan, and sett up the kingdome of our exalted Saviour. O, that I could be with you and dear Mr. Moody in that single church to destroy the images their sett up . . . [30]

The prospect of hewing down the " idols " was not the only thought which comforted the elect. There were the fisheries. Once in their possession

. . . All the Papists in Christiandom will depend upon us for their Fast Day provisions, and must pay us greater Tax for their superstitions, than they pay even to the Pope himself . . .[31]

The ten years that intervened between the siege of Louisbourg and the outbreak of the French and Indian War were spent by England and France in preparation for what was hoped would be the final struggle. In the British settlements an heroic effort was made to secure contributions of men and money from the central and southern groups. These provinces had hitherto been content for the most part with offering their sympathy and moral support. Contributions were not unknown, but they were the exception rather than the rule. In the campaign of education which was undertaken more or less systematically, the religious question entered into every phase of the controversy and into practically every detail of the preparation. Neither the methods nor the charges were new. The experience of three colonial wars, the slow but steady expansion of the French

---

[30] *Pepperell Papers*, Mass. Hist. Soc. *Coll.*, ser. 6, vol. x, pp. 105-106. *Louisbourg Journals, 1745*, ed. by L. E. DeForest (New York, 1932), pp. 33, 84 n. Samuel Curwen, *Journal and Letters* (New York, 1842), Introductory memoir, p. 16. G. Whitefield, *Works*, vol. ii, pp. 81 *et seq.* Roger Wolcott, *Journal*, 1745, p. 13, in Stevens Trans. L. C. Mss. Div.

[31] *American Magazine* (Gridley), Nov., 1746, " The Importance of Cape Breton," pp. 490-492. See issues for 1744, 1745 and 1746 for speeches of Shirley and Pepperell. *Cf. supra*, pp. 190 *et seq.*

behind the seaboard colonies, the growing importance of the fur trade and of French influence over the Indian—these gave to the old methods a new vigor, to the old accusations a new significance.

There was first of all the Indian. If to the Catholic missionary the most important aspect of the French and Spanish occupation of America was the conversion of the native to the Church of Rome, to his Protestant brother, that spiritual change was nothing short of a calamity. There is no need here to repeat what the Protestant clergy thought of the ancient Church. Thinking as they did they could not but deplore a conversion which to their minds rendered the last state of the neophyte worse than the first. And deplore it they did in no uncertain terms. But when to the usual denunciations of " Popery ", there was added the special application of its tenets to the Indian—how he was taught by the missionaries that the Blessed Virgin Mary was a Frenchwoman, that the British crucified our Saviour, and that therefore was it not only an act of virtue but a duty to kill every Englishman, nay even women and children [32]— then indeed did that religion seem an evil thing.

[32] This accusation already noted in connection with the S. P. G. annual sermons (*supra*, pp. 66-67) seems to have made a deep impression on the Puritan mind, for it is found again and again in private correspondence, official reports, histories, newspapers, diaries — in fact in almost every form of composition. See for example such disparate productions as Mather's *Magnalia*, vol. i, p. 195; Rogers' *Ponteach*, p. 63; the *Memorial* of Jeremiah Dummer, agent for Massachusetts Bay, Mass. Hist. Soc. *Coll.*, 3 ser., vol. i, pp. 231-34; and a pamphlet advertising a trans-Alleghany colony at Charlotina (*infra*, p. 254). As late as 1837 the Massachusetts Sabbath School Society, Boston, printed an edition of *Hannah Swanton. The Casco Captive; or the Catholic Religion in Canada and its Influence on the Indians in Maine.* The advertisement reads: "What is here presented to the reader is taken chiefly from the Rev. Cotton Mather's *Magnalia, or Ecclesiastical History of New England.* The object has been to keep to the truth." See p. 11 *et seq.*, for passage from Mather.

Upon the question of Indian warfare it was difficult for our colonial forbears to think calmly. Scarcely a border settlement of Massachusetts and New Hampshire had escaped unscathed. At the door of the French missionary was laid the responsibility for these attacks. The ubiquitous Jesuit was to the mind of the Anglo-American at once the tool and the abettor of his countrymen. Even those who could appreciate the fine culture and zeal of a Brébeuf or a Jogues, of a Druilletes or a Râle, had an uneasy feeling that these heroes were being used in spite of themselves to further the dark designs of his Christian Majesty. Nay, the very zeal which inspired their dauntless courage was the most telling argument against them, for one of the hall-marks of " Popery " was its ability so to enslave its victims as to deaden in them all sense of fair dealing, even of humanity. How could one be sure that the very qualities which compelled admiration were not being employed for some fell purpose? [33]

With such a background of fact and theory, one can readily imagine the effect of the following passage from an election sermon.[34] Dr. Mayhew's inherited interest in the

[33] F. Parkman, *Half Century of Conflict* (2 vols., Boston, 1892), vol. i, pp. 212-213. L. W. Bacon, *History of American Christianity* (New York, 1900), pp. 28-29. C. W. Baird, *History of Huguenot Emigration to America* (2 vols., New York, 1885), vol. ii, pp. 274-76. For an account of Father Jean Le Loutre and the legends which grew up about him, see J. B. Brebner, *New England's Outpost* (New York, 1927), p. 119 *et seq.* For Father Râle see Thomas Hutchinson, *History of the Province of Massachusetts Bay from 1691 to 1774*, vol. ii, pp. 98, 236, 238, 279-84; vol. iii (London, 1828), pp. 69, 124, 128-29, 157. Mass. Hist. Soc. *Coll.*, 2 ser., vol. viii, pp. 245-267. W. D. Williamson, *History of the State of Maine, 1602-1820* (2 vols., Hallowell, 1832), vol. ii, pp. 101-102, 109, 129-132. Most of the available data is summarized in two articles in A. C. H. S. *Records*, vol. xviii and *Cath. Hist. Rev.*, 1 ser., vol. i, pp. 164-174. See also Louise P. Kellogg in *D. A. B.*, vol. xv, p. 330.

[34] *Cf. supra*, pp. 87-88.

Indian [35] would give to his eloquence the sanction of one speaking with authority. He has been pleading for the rescue of the red man from the " various artifices of the Romish missionaries, to convert them to their wicked religion." He has emphasized as one of the teachings of that " wicked religion " the duty " of butchering, and scalping Protestants." He now visualizes for his audience, the effects, as he sees them, of French domination in America:

. . . And what horrid scene is this, which restless, roving fancy, or something of an higher nature, presents to me and so chills my blood! Do I behold these territories of freedom, become the prey of arbitrary power? . . . Do I see the slaves of Lewis with their Indian allies, dispossessing the free-born subjects of King George, of the inheritance received from their forefathers, and purchased at the expense of their ease, their treasure, their blood! . . . Do I see a protestant, there, taking a look at his Bible, and being taking [sic] in the fact and punished like a felon! . . . Do I see all liberty, property, religion, happiness, changed, or rather transubstantiated, into slavery, poverty, superstition, wretchedness! . . . [36]

Such passages might be multiplied from the sermons of other New England orators, such as the " silver tongued " Cooper,[37] as Stiles calls him, and Rev. Thomas Frink,[38] to mention only one of the lesser lights. The recruiting sermons of Davies, Finley, Whitefield, Burr and the Tennents have

[35] He was the son of Rev. Experience Mayhew, an S. P. G. missionary, who with four brothers preached to the Indians. See F. Mood, in *D. A. B.*, vol. vii, pp. 454-455; W. Sprague, *Annals*, vol. viii, pp. 22 *et seq.*

[36] J. Mayhew, *Sermon preached before Gov. Shirley, May 29, 1754* (Boston, 1754), pp. 31-32, 37-38.

[37] Samuel Cooper, *Sermon on the Reduction of Quebec. Preached Oct. 16, 1759* (Boston, n. d.), p. 41.

[38] Thomas Frink, *Election Sermon, May 31, 1758* (Boston, 1758), *passim.*

been noted already.[39]   Parson Moody was not the only clergyman who beat recruits through the village streets.   If volunteers jostled each other in their eagerness to enlist, if the troops marched off with enthusiasm at white heat, if those who remained at home gave " until it hurt," the credit is due in no small measure to the efforts of the clergy.[40]

If to the missionary, Protestant or Catholic, the Indian was a soul to be rescued from the darkness of heathenism, to the government, French or British, he was in addition a potential friend or enemy.   Missionary and government official did not always see eye to eye in matters of Indian policy.[41]   Both recognized their spiritual obligations towards the native, both appreciated his friendship in peace and in war.   That the rival governments expected their missionaries to be patriots as well as clergymen has been pointed out more than once in the preceding pages.[42]   The missionaries may not have been blind to the economic advantages of the fur trade, but they were quick to utilize them to further the conversion of the red man.   On the other hand, trader and civil officer were equally alert to reap economic or political profit from the attachment of the neophyte to their religion.[43]

[39] *Supra*, pp. 82, 93-95 *et seq.*

[40] A. M. Baldwin, *New England Clergy and the American Revolution* pp. 87-88.   W. deL. Love, *Fast and Thanksgiving Days of New England* Boston, 1895), p. 312.   There is a list of sermons on the Louisbourg expedition in American Antiquarian Society *Proceedings*, vol. xx (1909-10), p. 179 *et seq.*

[41] Sister M. Celeste Leger, *Catholic Indian Missions in Maine, 1611-1820* (Washington, 1929), p. 65.

[42] *Supra*, pp. 67-68.   See also *Conn. Rec.*, vol. ii, pp. 387, 463, 336, 346, 371, 381, 418, 432, 459, 485.   *Pa. Gaz.* July 26, 1759, in *N. J. Arch.*, 1 ser., vol. xx, p. 369.   *Wolcott Papers*, in Conn. Hist. Soc. *Coll.*, vol. xvi, p. 194.

[43] For contemporary accounts see William Clarke, "Observations On the Late and present Conduct of the French with Regard to their Encroachments upon the British Colonies in North America...(Boston, 1755)," in *Magazine of History with Notes and Queries*, vol. xvi, (1917-

French and English exploited the Indian in the fur trade; French and English formed alliances with him and profited by his services in time of war. Each laid at the door of the other the failure of the red man to observe treaty obligations.[44] French and English offered bounties for the scalps of enemy tribes and organized punitive expeditions against them.[45] And, inconsistently enough, French and English justified in their own policies methods which they condemned unequivocally in their rivals.[46]

18), pp. 110-143. This was quoted by Franklin in his *Interest of Great Britain considered*... (London and Boston, 1760, Evans, 8601, Sabin, 35,450). See also Franklin's *Plain Truth, or a Serious Consideration of the Present State of the City of Philadelphia and the Province of Pennsylvania, by a Tradesman of Philadelphia, Boston Evening Post*, Sept. 8, 1755. No. 1045. Also issued in broadside at the Heart and Crown in Cornhill, Boston. *New Jersey Archives*, 1 ser., vol. viii, pp. 140-141. A. T. Volwiler, "George Croghan and the Western Movement, 1741-1782," in *Pa. Mag. Hist. Biog.*, vol. xlvi (1922), p. 273; vol. xlvii (1923), pp. 28, 115. C. H. McIlwaine, ed., *Abridgement of Indian Affairs* ... (Harvard Univ. Press, 1915), pp. xx-xxi, n. 1.

[44] *A Scheme to Drive the French Out of All the Continent of America* (n. p. 1754). Archibald Kennedy, *Serious Considerations on the Present State of the Affairs of the Northern Colonies* (New York, 1754), pp. 16, 18. W. Allen, *Hist. of Norridgewock*, pp. 12, 132 *et seq.* For Treaty with Catawbas and Cherokees, 1755, see *Va. Mag. Hist.*, vol. xiii (1905-06), pp. 225-64. *American Magazine, or Monthly Chronicle* (Philadelphia, by Wm. Bradford), 1757-58, p. 484.

[45] *Ga. Col. Rec.*, vol. vii, p. 546. *Ga. Council Journals*, 1755-61, Aug. 20, 1756, p. 22. Jan. 25, 1757. *Pa. Arch.*, 4 ser., vol. ii, p. 547. Robert Dinwiddie, *Official Records*...ed. by R. A. Brock, *Va. Hist. Soc. Coll.* (2 vols., Richmond, 1883-84, n. s., iii-iv), vol. ii, pp. 135, 176, 254, 507, 582, 645, 406. *Colonial Laws of New York* (Albany, 1894), vol. iii, p. 540. *N. H. State Papers*, vol. iv, p. 183; vol. v, pp. 410, 491, 587, 820, 912. Force Trans. *N. H. Miscel. 1736-1751*, Sept. 27, 1745. May 14, 1747, Act of N. H. Legislature, L. C. Mss. Div. J. Huske, *Present State of North America* (London, 1755), pp. 40, 41, 48. *Mass. Hist. Soc. Coll.*, 3 ser., vol. v, pp. 235, 239, 274; 4 ser., vol. vi, p. 313.

[46] Elizabeth White, *American Opinion of France from Lafayette to Poincaré* (New York, 1927), Introd., xii-xiii.

There is a mass of evidence to testify to British efforts to develop in the colonists what is termed today a war psychology. From the Mosquito Shore and the Caribbean,[47] from the frontiers of Georgia, Virginia, Maryland and Pennsylvania,[48] from Nova Scotia and the St. Lawrence,[49] came tales of Indian massacres and " Popish plots " in which the red man, the lay Catholic and the Jesuit were the chief protagonists. Every means then at the disposal of the provinces was utilized to play upon the fears of the populace. Pamphlets [50] poured from the press; the magazine,[51] the newspaper,[52] the almanac,[53] and the broadside [54] made their con-

[47] *New York Mercury*, Oct. 2, 1752, No. 8.

[48] J. Huske, *Present State of North America* (London, 1755).

[49] *Ibid., cf. Boston Evening Post*, Sept. 8, 1755. Aaron Hobart, *Historical Sketch of Abingdom* (Boston, 1839), pp. 103-04.

[50] *A Review of the Military Operations in North America, from the Commencement of the French Hostilities on the Frontier of Virginia in 1753, to the Surrender of Oswego, on the 14th of August, 1756; in a Letter to a Nobleman.* Reprinted in Mass. Hist. Soc. *Coll.*, 1 ser., vol. vii (1800), pp. 67-163. A foot-note (p. 6) states that the letter was written by "the late Governor Livingston, and his friends, Messrs. W. Smith and Scott, lawyers, New York."

[51] *American Magazine, or Monthly Chronicle* (Phila., by Wm. Bradford), 1757-58.

[52] *Supra*, p. 182 *et seq. Cf. New York Mercury*, Nov. 20, 1752; Sept. 16, 23, 1754; Jan. 13, Aug. 18, Nov. 10, Dec. 1, Dec. 22, 1755; Jan. 12, Feb. 16, 23, Mar. 8, 15, 22, May 3, Aug. 30, 1756; June 6, 1757. *Pennsylvania Gazette*, June 13, 1754; *Maryland Gazette*, Nov. 28, 1754. Similar citations might be given for every important organ of the provincial press.

[53] *Supra*, p. 167 *et seq.*

[54] Many of the governors' proclamations, militia acts, recruiting orders were issued in broadside. *Cf.* Broadside issued by Gov. Shirley, Boston, April 7, 1755. Among the "Beating Orders" we read: 3. "You are to inlist no Roman Catholick." Newberry Library *Coll.* Broadsides, vol. iii. "Dying Speech of Old Tenor, on the 31st of March, 1750;—being the Day appointed for his Execution. By Joseph Green," *Mag. of Hist.*, vol. xxiv, extra no. 94, p. 41. See also *Mag. Hist.*, extra numbers 84, 90; vol. xxiv, ex. no. 96.

tributions; college presidents [55] and tutors [56] mingled with the theses of commencement programs, classic odes and choruses commemorating British victories over " gallic slaves "; " governors addressed houses, houses addressed governors, and both addressed the crown " [57]—the immediate object of all this agitation finding its expression in the slogan, " Canada delenda est." [58]

[55] *Supra*, pp. 145-46; 202, n. 108.

[56] Benjamin Y. Prime, *The Patriot Muse, or Poems on Some of the Principle Events of the Late War; Together with a Poem on the Peace. . . . By an America Gentleman (London . . . 1764, Wegelin, 314)*. Benjamin Prime was tutor at Princeton in 1756-57. His " Britain's Glory or Gallic Pride Humbled " formed part of the commencement program. His little volume of verse, *The Patriot Muse*, is largely concerned with the events of the French and Indian war. Even when the subject of the poem is not immediately connected with the war, as in " Loyal Tears shed over Royal Dust, or An Elegy on the Death of his late Majesty King George II," he voices the contemporary Whig attitude toward the war as a struggle between Protestantism and Catholicism. For a time " Prussia trembles for her Frederick's throne." But George hurls " destruction on his foes . . .

> Then gay in rifled spoils of Gallic pride,
> Triumphant, in a blaze of glory, dy'd." See pp. 76, 77.

cf. pp. 12-17, 17-25, 32-39, 41-50, 51-52, 84-85, 86. His poems were widely circulated during the war. See Appleton's *Dic. Amer. Biog.* and *D. A. B.*

[57] A survey of this type of official document as preserved in the archival collections of the various states reveals a bitterness on the part of American officialdom that might be matched but scarcely surpassed by the most ardent demagogue unacquainted with the real state of affairs. Governor Sharpe of Maryland forms a notable exception, though even he saw no injustice in the double tax on Catholics. See among a multiplicity of references which might be cited, *N. C. Col. Rec.*, vol. v, pp. 214-15, 220, 235, 238, 635-38, 998-99; vol. vi, pp. 62-65, 266-67. *Legislative Journals of the Council of Colonial Virginia*, ed. by H. R. McIlwaine (Richmond, 1919), vol. iii, pp. 1125, 1126, 1144, 1145, 1156. *Md. Arch.*, Sharpe Corr., (1), vol. vi, pp. 13, 152-53, 240, 411, 419, 426, 496, 497, 501, 512, 518, 521, 540. *N. J. Arch.*, 1 ser., vol. xvii, pp. 6-8, 41-45, 62-66, 86, 103-04; vol. ix, p. 183; vol. viii, pt. 2, pp. 133, 158, 163, 218. *Pa. Col. Rec.*, vol. vii, p. 344. *Pa. Arch.*, vol. ii, pp. 174-76; 4 ser., vol. ii, pp. 336, 345, 697. Ga. Hist. Soc. *Coll.*, vol. ii, p. 316.

[58] *Supra*, pp. 196 *et seq.*, 221.

The eminent success of this anti-Catholic publicity is seen in the public reaction to it especially in the two provinces with the largest number of Catholics (Maryland and Pennsylvania), and in Virginia, whose proximity to Maryland exposed her, as she thought, to their evil designs. The *Maryland Gazette,* Nov. 28, 1754, published the instructions of the citizens of Prince George County to their delegates in the Assembly. They were to urge the passage of a law to dispossess the Jesuits of their lands, because as wealthy land owners they had become " formidable to his Majesty's good Protestant subjects "; to " exclude Papists from places of trust and profit; and to prevent them from sending their children to foreign popish seminaries for education. . . ."

The Justices of Berks County, Pennsylvania, registered their alarm in an address to the governor, July 23, 1755. Some Catholics had recently shown great joy at the news of Braddock's defeat; the Justices beg that they be disarmed or otherwise prevented from injuring others " who are not of their vile principles." It is reported that in the neighborhood of Goshenhoppen, where the Catholics have a " magnificent chapel," thirty Indians are now lurking, " well armed with Guns and Swords or Cutlasses." The priests who attend Reading and Goshenhoppen every four weeks have told their congregations that they will not return for nine weeks. This long absence is interpreted as a visit to Fort Duquesne to consult the French. The address concludes,

It is a great Unhappiness at this Time to the other People of this Province that the Papists should keep Arms in their Houses, against which the Protestants are not prepared, who therefore are subject to a Massacre whenever the Papists are ready. . . .[59]

---

[59] *Pa. Col. Rec.*, vol. vi, pp. 503, 533. *Cf. Md. Arch.*, vol. xxxi, pp. 47-49, 80-84, 121-25.

Another rumor reported that there were many Indians at the house of Father Schneider. The Assembly to whom this address was referred refused to be alarmed. The committee of investigation reported that the Indians at Father Schneider's rectory were beggars, six warriors with their wives and children, the recipients of his charity. In October still another alarm was raised. Thirteen hundred French and Indians were said to be approaching. Again investigation proved that the rumor was unfounded.[60]

Braddock's defeat seems to have made a profound impression on his colonial contemporaries. History has reversed the popular verdict which was inclined to regard him as a victim of French intrigue. The *Maryland Gazette* supplemented its account of the disaster with a lengthy parenthesis addressed to the " Protestant Reader ". He is reminded of the fate that awaits him should he become a vassal of France and a dupe of " the Romish Clergy, whose most tender Mercies are but hellish cruelties." [61]   Seth Pomeroy, writing to his wife from New York, likewise attributes Braddock's misfortune to the " hellish designs " of the French.[62]   Margaret Brewster, as we have seen,[63] dedicated a poem to this opening incident of the war, and Benjamin Prime [64] bemoaned the fate of Braddock

> to die by cruel savages,
> A sacrifice to Gallic perfidy !

[60] H. W. Kriebal, *The Schwenkfelders in Pennsylvania* (Lancaster, 1904). In Pa. German Society *Proceedings*, vol. xiii (1902), pp. 141-2.

[61] *Md. Gaz.*, July 31, 1755.

[62] Pomeroy was among the New England forces destined for the attack upon Crown Point. The letter is dated, " Camp at the Great Carrying Place, 23d August, 1755,'" Bancroft Trans., *American Papers*, vol. i, p. 263 *et seq.*

[63] *Supra*, p. 202.

[64] Benj. Prime, *Patriot Muse*, pp. 9-17. *Cf.* James Allen, *The Poem which the Committee of the Town of Boston had voted unanimously to be published with the late oration ... Boston, 1772.*

Charles Carroll of Doughoreghan Manor, writing to his son in 1756, speaks of the " most shocking barbarities " inflicted by the Indians after Braddock's defeat, on the back settlements of Maryland, Pennsylvania and Virginia; but he adds that the accounts "are vastly magnified in the English papers." [65]

These exaggerations were not without their effect upon the mob. In Philadelphia they were so incensed that they determined to attack the Roman Catholic Chapel. They were with difficulty dissuaded by the friendly Quakers.[66] Daniel Dulany is witness to a like fanaticism in Virginia where a priest at Alexandria was obliged to flee for his life. Dulany was of the opinion that had the priest fallen into the hands of the troops he would have been hanged as a spy. This prominent Maryland lawyer may be taken as representative of that group of so-called liberals who disclaimed all sympathy with religious persecution, who would therefore have conceded to Catholics liberty of worship, but with certain restraints upon both clergy and laity. Yet he was convinced that any attempt to secure moderate restrictions would be useless, for such was " the heat and ferment of the times," he wrote, " that nothing short of the total extermination " of the Catholic clergy would have satisfied the radicals.[67]

[65] K. M. Rowland, *Life of Charles Carroll of Carrollton, 1737-1832, with his Correspondence and Public Papers*, vol. i, p. 30. *Extracts from Chief Justice Allen's Letter Book* . . . (Pottsville, Pa., 1897), p. 22.

[66] " Extracts from the Diary of Daniel Fisher," *Pa. Mag. Hist. Biog.*, vol. xvii (1893), p. 274. Fisher came to America in 1750, settling at Williamsburg, Va. He was later a prominent citizen of Richmond. He made a trip from Williamsburg to Philadelphia where he stayed eleven weeks. The incident noted above is recorded July 18, 1755. *Cf. Journal of James Kenny, 1761-1763, Pa. Mag. Hist. Biog.*, vol. xxxvii (1913), pp. 1, 22, 142, and *passim*. Also Kenny's *Journal to the Westward*, 1758-59. *Ibid.*, p. 395 and *passim*.

[67] Daniel Dulany, "Military and Political Affairs of the Middle Colonies in 1755," *Pa. Mag. Hist. Biog.*, vol. iii, pp. 27-28.

That all this agitation should find expression in penal legislation similar to that enacted after the Revolution of 1688 is not surprising. Virginia, Maryland and Pennsylvania passed the Militia Acts or " Acts for Disarming Papists," to which passing reference has been made in the preceding pages.[68] Recruiting instructions forbade the enlistment of non-English recruits " unless you are sure that they are Protestants." [69] Spies were everywhere busily earning the reward of the informer and haling unoffending citizens before the courts.[70] The Irish extraction of George Croghan, the noted Indian trader, brought him under suspicion. He and Francis Campbell, another Indian trader suspected of being a Catholic, seem to have given the governors of four states some anxious moments.[71] The Archives of Maryland tell a tale of espionage, of recrimination, of legal oppression [72] which finally became so burdensome that Charles Carroll and a number of prominent Catholics planned to move across the Mississippi into what is now Arkansas. In 1757, Carroll while in Europe personally made application to the French King for a grant of land. The extent of the grant was greater than the King cared to make at the time, but he assured Carroll of sufficient land for his purpose.

[68] *Supra*, p. 58. For the Pennsylvania Act see *Pa. Arch.*, vol. iii, pp. 131-32. This act was disallowed by George III, not because of its discrimination against Catholics but because it gave the regiments the right to elect their own officers. It is but fair to note that the year in which the militia act was passed, Father Harding enlarged and improved St. Joseph's. J. L. J. Kirlin, *Catholicity in Philadelphia*, pp. 83-84.

[69] *Pa. Arch.*, 2 ser., vol. ii, pp. 594-95.

[70] *Pa. Arch.*, vol. iii, pp. 16-17. *Pa. Col. Rec.*, vol. vii, p. 344. J. T. Scharf and T. Westcott, *History of Philadelphia* (3 vols., Philadelphia, 1884), vol. i, pp. 652-53.

[71] *Pa. Arch.*, vol. ii, pp. 114, 228-29, 694. C. H. Browning, " Francis Campbell," *Pa. Mag. Hist. Biog.*, vol. xxvii (1904), pp. 63 *et seq.*

[72] *Md. Arch.*, vol. xxxi, pp. 47-49, 80-89, 121-125. For Governor Sharpe's summary of the situation see *ibid.*, vol. ix, pp. 313-315.

The migration was never effected, but public knowledge of the project seems to have caused some mitigation of the penal laws. The relief apparently was but temporary, for in 1760-61, Carroll is still thinking of Louisiana. In a lengthy letter to his son, July 14, 1760, he sums up the grievances of the Roman Catholics from the foundation of the colony. In conclusion he writes:

From what I have just said I leave you to judge whether Maryland be a tolerable residence for a Roman Catholic. Were I younger I would certainly quit it; at my age (as I wrote you) a change of climate would certainly shorten my days, but I am embracing every opportunity of getting rid of my real property, that if you please you may the sooner and with more ease and less loss, leave it.[73]

Given the attitude of British-America towards Catholic France, it requires little effort to conceive the reception accorded the seven or eight thousand Acadians or " French Neutrals " as they were called. Nowhere were they welcome. Doubly suspect because of their nationality and their religion, their destitution made them in addition an economic

---

[73] K. Rowland, *C. Carroll of Car.*, vol. i, pp. 42-43. L. A. Leonard, *Life of Charles Carroll of Carrollton* (New York, 1918), pp. 54, 80. T. M. Field, *Unpublished Letters of Charles Carroll of Carrollton and of his Father* (U. S. Cath. Hist. Soc. Monograph I, New York, 1902), pp. 41-47, 57-58, 68, 70. *Cf. Carroll Papers, Md. Hist. Soc.*, box, 1731-1761, letters dated June 22, 1759, Apr. 10, 1760; box, 1760-63, letters dated, Sept. 16, 1760, Jan. 1, Feb. 13, July 20, Oct. 13, 1761. These are all replies of the younger Carroll to his father. In 1767-68 another attempt was made by the Catholics of Maryland under the direction of Dr. Henry Jerningham, an English physician who had settled in the province. Like previous efforts the project seemed too extensive to receive royal sanction, and as before the position of Catholics began to improve. See Thomas F. O'Connor, " Maryland and the West," *Historical Bulletin*, vol. xii (Jan., 1934), pp. 27-28. T. A. Hughes, *Jesuits in N. A.* Text, vol. ii, pp. 491, 546-49. *Amer. Hist. Rev.*, vol. xvi, pp. 320 *et seq.*

burden. Georgia [74] and Virginia,[75] fearing their influence on the Indians and negroes, kept their quotas through the winter only. Governor Hutchinson of Massachusetts was sympathetic, but he knew too well the temper of the Bay Colony to allow the exiles public worship. Besides, the law against the entry of priests into the province was still on the statute books. It was owing to Hutchinson's tolerance that they were not molested in their private family devotions. Public sentiment, however, insisted that the exiles be scattered. The children were placed in Protestant families. Grateful as they were for the Governor's charity and sympathy, the Acadians felt themselves aliens in the Puritan community. Eventually most of them left the province.[76] South Carolina too was sympathetic, though not to the extent of wishing to keep her visitors. But she helped many of the Acadians to reach France or Louisiana.[77] New York indented her adult quota, and placed the children in Protestant homes.[78] In Connecticut, although the Neutral French were suspected of putting arsenic in the food of the

[74] *Georgia Council Journal*, 1755-61, p. 24, Force Trans. L. C. Mss. Div. *Ga. Col. Rec.*, vol. vii, pp. 302, 304, 506-07, 625; vol. xiii, p. 89. *N. J. Arch.*, I ser., vol. xx, pp. 42-43.

[75] *Dinwiddie Papers*, vol. ii, pp. 268, 306, 347, 401, 444, 396. W. Hening, *Statutes at Large*, vol. vii, p. 39. *Va. Mag. Hist. Biog.*, vol. vi (1898-99), pp. 386-89 (Reprint of Council Proceedings, *Va. Arch.*). C. Millard, "The Acadians in Virginia," *Va. Mag. Hist. Biog.*, vol. xl (1932), p. 241. A good summary with extracts from *Journals of House of Burgesses*, Hening, and *Dinwiddie Papers*.

[76] T. Hutchinson, *Hist. Mass. Bay*, vol. ii (1795), p. 93; vol. iii (1828), pp. 39-42. J. K. Hosmer, *Life of Thomas Hutchinson*, p. 41. G. F. Dow, "French Acadians in Essex County," Essex Inst. Hist. *Coll.*, vol. xlv, p. 299. W. A. Leahy, *History of the Archdiocese of Boston*, p. 3.

[77] D. D. Wallace, *History of South Carolina* (4 vols., New York, 1934), vol. ii, pp. 16-18.

[78] *Doc. Hist. N. Y.*, vol. vi, p. 954; vol. vii, p. 125; vol. x, pp. 11, 282, 380, 427, 518, 528, 540, 547, 973. *Laws of New York from 1691 to 1751* ... (New York, 1752), vol. ii, p. 103.

students at Yale, they were, for the most part kindly treated. Families were not separated as in so many of the other provinces.[79] In Pennsylvania, with its large foreign population, there was great fear that the Acadians would unite with the French and Indians in the back country. They were at first quartered in "neutral huts" in Philadelphia, where Anthony Benezet, the Quaker, and Father Harding did much for them. Later they were distributed throughout the province, one family to each township.[80] The feeling in Maryland was intense. It was the one colony where the co-religionists of the exiles were of sufficient competence to afford them substantial relief, but the government would not allow them to live with Catholics. Charles Carroll offered to support two families but was not permitted to do so.[81] The number of Acadians who eventually migrated to Canada, Louisiana or Santo Domingo from Maryland and other provinces attests the strength of anti-Catholic bias throughout the province.

[79] F. B. Dexter, *Biographical Sketches of the Graduates of Yale College with Annals of the College History* (New York, 1885-1907), vol. iii, pp. 57-58. T. S. Duggan, *Catholic Church in Connecticut* (New York, 1930), pp. 9-13. J. B. Felt, *History of Ipswich, Essex and Hamilton* (Cambridge, 1834), p. 66.

[80] *Votes and Proceedings of the House of Representatives of the Province of Pennsylvania, Met at Philadelphia, Oct. 14, 1758* (Phila., 1759). See entries for Nov. 24, Dec. 1, Dec. 2, Dec. 5, 1758. *Pa. Col. Rec.*, vol. vii, pp. 45, 55, 239, 408, 410, 241, 393, 446, 7, 5-20. *Pa. Arch.*, vol. ii, pp. 513; vol. iii, pp. 565-68; 4 ser., vol. i, pp. 549, 554, 579. W. B. Reed, "The Acadian Exiles, or French Neutrals, in Pennsylvania." To which is appended "A Relation of their Misfortunes," by John Baptiste Galeron, in *Memoirs of Historical Society of Pennsylvania*, vol. vi (1858), pp. 285, 289. S. M. Sener, "The Acadians of Lancaster County." Read before Lancaster County Historical Society, Sept. 4, 1896.

[81] L. A. Leonard, *Life of C. Carroll of Car.*, p. 63. K. M. Rowland, *C. Carroll of Car.*, vol. i, p. 27. *Md. Gaz.*, Sept. 4, 11, Dec. 4, 1755; Feb. 10, 1757. Basil Sollers, "The Acadians (French Neutrals) Transported to Maryland," *Md. Hist. Mag.*, vol. iii (1908), pp. 1-21. *Archivo General de Indias*, Legajo 2585, No. 18.

Colonial naturalization and immigration laws in their relation to Roman Catholics were of a piece with the policy of the mother country. Both were intimately bound up with the question of land holding. According to English law aliens could not own land, bequeath or inherit property, or exercise trading privileges. These disabilities might be partially removed by letters of denization conferred by the monarch or by a parliamentary act of naturalization, public or private. Neither denization nor naturalization conferred political rights, such as the exercise of the franchise or the holding of office.[82]   The precedent set by the naturalization act of 7 Jas. i, ch. 2, which reduced Catholics to the status of aliens, was followed by subsequent British legislation of the same kind.[83]   Similarly the welcome extended to the Huguenot, the Palatine, the Salzburger and other Protestant groups from continental Europe did not include the followers of Rome. Those who accompanied their Protestant countrymen were soon sifted by the test oaths and promptly sent home. England would risk contamination neither for herself nor her colonies.[84]

British immigrants it was understood brought with them the civil rights they had enjoyed under English common law.

[82] H. L. Osgood, *Amer. Col. in Eighteenth Century*, vol. ii, pp. 523-25. E. Channing, *History of the United States* (6 vols., New York, 1905-27), vol. ii, pp. 413-16. E. E. Proper, *Colonial Immigration Laws* . . . (Col. Univ. Studies in History, Economics and Public Law, vol. xii, no. 2, New York, 1900), pp. 14-15.

[83] 7 Jas. I, ch. 2, Ruffhead, vol. iii, pp. 73-74. For other laws affecting the naturalization of Catholics see 7 Anne, ch. 5, ss. 2, 3; 4 Geo. II, ch. 21, 13 Geo. II, ch. 7, 20 Geo. II, ch. 44, ss. 1, 2, 4, 6; 22 Geo. II, ch. 45, ss. 8, 9, 11; 2 Geo. III, ch. 25.

[84] Osgood, *op. cit.*, vol. ii, p. 494. S. G. Fisher, *The Making of Pennsylvania* (Phila., 1896), p. 97. F. R. Diffenderffer, "The German Exodus to England in 1709" (Lancaster, 1897), in Pa. German Soc. *Proc.*, vol. vii (1896), p. 277 *et seq. Cf.* Channing, *op. cit.*, vol. ii, p. 404 n. L. Schrott, *German Catholic Immigrants in the Colonies*, pp. 14-15.

It was not until 1740 that Parliament enacted a naturalization act for aliens in the plantations. The oaths required
by this act,[85] as well as the sacramental test imposed upon
all who took them, debarred Catholics from naturalization
and from offices of trust and honor in the provinces. With
a few minor changes it remained the general law for naturalization in the colonies until the Revolution.[86] The colonies
however, long before the passage of this act, had legislated
for their own aliens, and even after 1740 foreigners took
little advantage of the British law because the seven-year
period of residence was, in their opinion, too long. Even
though citizenship in one colony did not confer similar privileges in another,[87] aliens, induced by the shorter term of
residence and other advantages, preferred to qualify under
colonial regulations. Land at that time was the key to economic independence, to social distinction, to political preferment. To be sure colonial laws were sometimes disallowed,
but it is doubtful whether substantial acres acquired under
them would be forfeited.[88]

Unlike the middle and southern colonies, New England
did not welcome the immigration of non-English stocks;
nor even of British groups whose religious views differed
from their own. Not for nothing had God sifted the
peoples of the earth to transplant the wheat of His elect

---

[85] 13 Geo. 2, ch. 7, Ruffhead, vol. vi, p. 384.

[86] H. L. Osgood, *op. cit.*, vol. ii, pp. 528-29. E. Channing, *op. cit.*,
vol. ii, pp. 413-16. M. S. Guiseppi, ed., *Naturalization of Foreign Protestants in the American and West India Colonies Pursuant to Statute 13
George II, c. 7* (vols. xiii-xiv of *Pubs. Huguenot Society of London*,
Manchester, 1921). *Cf.* A. C. H. *Researches*, o. s. xi (1894), pp. 11-13.

[87] George Chalmers, *Opinions of Eminent Lawyers, on Various Points
of English Jurisprudence, Chiefly Concerning the Colonies, Fisheries and
Commerce of Great Britain*, vol. i, pp. 343-344.

[88] S. G. Fisher, "The Twenty-eight Charges against the King in the
Declaration of Independence," *Pa. Mag. Hist. Biog.*, vol. xxxi (1907),
p. 257 *et seq.*

to the new world; theirs it was to respect His winnowing and to preserve the good grain from the tares and the cockle. Strangers therefore were viewed with suspicion, were admitted grudgingly, and were to be " entertained " only with permission of the authorities and for a limited time. Those who could not give a satisfactory account of themselves were asked to leave. Permission to remain in the town or colony was secured only after a satisfactory probation; nor did permanent residence always include the right to hold land.[89]

Although the earliest regulations of this sort contained no reference to Catholics, discriminatory legislation was not slow in making its appearance as soon as their advent became a reality or even a probability. The measures adopted varied according to time and circumstance. Sometimes it was a law that voiced at once the Puritan hatred of " Popery " and the fear of physical violence, as in the Massachusetts Law against Catholic priests, already referred to,[90] or the proclamation at the outbreak of Queen Anne's War requiring the registration of all Frenchmen residing in the province and declaring all French Roman Catholics to be prisoners of war.[91] Again it took the form of naturalization laws,[92] of land regulations,[93] or of a tax on Irish servants.[94] In spite

[89] *Records of Massachusetts Bay Colony,* vol. i, p. 196. *New Haven Colony Records,* vol. i, p. 130; vol. ii, pp. 217, 610. *Conn. Records,* vol. i, pp. 283, 303, 308, 324, 351; vol. ii, p. 66; vol. iii, p. 111; vol. v, pp. 21-50. *N. H. State Papers,* vol. i, p. 407. *Early Records of Providence,* vol. ii, pp. 90, 112; vol. iii, pp. 13, 122; vol. iv, pp. 18, 36, 43; vol. viii, p. 104; vol. xii, p. 27; vol. xv, p. 112. *R. I. Rec.,* vol. i, p. 243.

[90] *Supra,* p. 56.

[91] Mass. *Acts and Resolves,* vol. viii, app. 3, pp. 54, 344. *Cf. N. H. State Papers,* vol. ii, p. 429.

[92] *Conn. Rec.,* vol. xiv (1772-75), p. 94. J. H. O'Donnell, *Diocese of Hartford* (Boston, 1899), pp. 21-23.

[93] See opinion of Solicitor General Northey on the right of Massachusetts to refuse lands to Roman Catholics. *Shelburne Papers,* vol. lxi, p. 115; vol. lviii, pp. 349-350. Cited, G. F. Donovan, *The Pre-*

of efforts to exclude them, some Catholics did get into New England and Gridley's *Weekly Rehearsal* for March 30, 1732, reported that Mass had been " performed " by an Irish priest for some of his compatriots " of whom it is not doubted," the *Rehearsal* remarks, " we have a considerable number among us." [95] As with the Acadians, the policy of Massachusetts with regard to Irish immigrants was to scatter them and deprive them of the ministrations of their clergy so that they might lose their faith. There are no exact contemporary statistics, but we have the testimony of William Douglass whose professional practice afforded unusual opportunities to observe the effect of such a policy. He writes approvingly of its success,

We have an Instance of this in New England, where many Irish in Language and Religion (I mean Roman Catholicks) have been imported some Years since; their children have lost their Language and Religion, and are good subjects.[96]

Revolutionary Irish in Massachusetts, 1620-1775 (Menasha, Wis., 1932), pp. 20-21. N. H. Hist. Soc. Coll., vol. i, pp. 155-156. N. Bouton, *History of Concord . . . 1725-1853* (Concord, 1856), pp. 62-71. W. R. Cochrane and G. K. Wood, *History of Francestown, N. H.* (Nashua, N. H., 1895), pp. 384-85.

[94] Conn. Hist. Soc. *Coll.*, vol. xxii, p. 173; *Conn. Rec.*, vol. i, 253; 303, 308, 324. *New Haven Col. Rec.*, vol. ii, p. 217. *R. I. Col. Rec.*, vol. i, p. 243. *Cf.* regulations of other colonies in this respect: *Md. Arch.*, vol. xxxix, pp. 218, 235; vol. xlii, p. 602; vol. xliv, p. 646; vol. xlvi, p. 615. S. C., *Statutes at Large*, vol. ii, p. 646. Va., Hening, vol. iii, p. 298; vol. v, p. 480; vol. vi, p. 338. *New York Col. Laws*, vol. ii, pp. 513-515. *Acts of the Province of Pennsylvania, 1729, 1730, 1734. Pa. Arch.*, vol. i, p. 455. *Pa. Col. Rec.*, vol. iii, p. 359.

[95] W. A. Leahy, *Archdiocese of Boston*, p. 6.

[96] W. Douglass, *Summary*, vol. i, p. 209. *Cf.* W. H. J. Kennedy, " Catholics in Massachusetts before 1750," *Cath. Hist. Rev.*, vol. xvii (1931), pp. 10-28. R. H. Lord, in *Commonwealth History of Massachusetts*, vol. v, pp. 508-09. For exclusion of Irish from office in the Charitable Irish Society of Boston see J. B. Cullen, *The Irish in Boston* (Boston, 1893), p. 19.

Recent investigations of the number of Irish in Massachusetts in the eighteenth century vary in their estimates from .018 (1770) [97] to 1% (1790).[98] Immigration from 1770 to 1790 was not sufficiently heavy to account for the discrepancy in these figures. Accepting them, however, as a maximum and minimum, with the real percentage lying somewhere between, it would seem that the Massachusetts policy of exclusion was highly successful. In striking contrast is the Bay State's welcome of the Huguenots whose Calvinism was regarded by the Congregational clergy as not far removed from orthodoxy. Their Protestantism, however, was not always proof against their French nationality, and in times of excitement even they fell under suspicion.[99]

To the middle and southern colonies, European immigrants were attracted by the mild climate, by the fertility of the soil, by the hope of religious liberty, above all by the promotion literature which was scattered throughout Europe and the salesmanship of public or private colonizing agencies. Generally speaking the colonists welcomed these accessions which promised so much for the undeveloped resources of their adopted country. Land grants were offered upon generous, even tempting, terms, such as exemption from taxes for a time, and security of tenure. The various religious groups did not always find the toleration, to say nothing of the complete religious liberty, they were led to expect. Anglican and dissenter, Methodist and Baptist,

---

[97] G. F. Donovan, *Pre-Rev. Irish in Mass.*, p. 209.

[98] American Council of Learned Societies. "Report of Committee on Linguistic and National Stocks in the Population of the United States." A. H. A. *Annual Report*, 1931 (Wash., 1932), vol. i, p. 117.

[99] Ezechiel Carré, *The Charitable Samaritan, A Sermon . . . Pronounced in the French Church at Boston* (Boston, 1689). G. Chinard, *Les Réfugiés Huguenots en Amérique avec un Introduction sur le Mirage Américain* (Paris, 1925), pp. 80, 102, 114, 118. H. M. Jones, *America and French Culture, 1750-1848*, pp. 80-81, 90.

Quaker and Jew—all experienced religious discrimination, not always or everywhere within the territory now under review, but to an extent which made clear the difference between the reality and the ideal. The Roman Catholic, abhorred by all these sects, could not and did not escape.

From the beginning, New York was a melting pot. Although the Dutch Reformed Church was the state religion under the Dutch regime, and although Stuyvesant's governorship witnessed the persecution of Quakers, Lutherans, and other non-Calvinistic groups,[100] generally speaking, there was practical toleration for everybody, even for the Catholic. For a short period under the English rule, " Papists began to settle under the smiles of the governor," but with the Revolution of 1688, there began a period of persecution of which the penal legislation already noted was the fruition.[101] Under the governorship of the Catholic Dongan, a liberal naturalization act had been passed for the purpose of encouraging immigration. All foreign Christians might avail themselves of it by taking a simple oath of allegiance.[102] During the confusion which followed the inauguration of the Revolution government, land purchases and transfers seem to have continued. In 1715 a new act was passed confirming the naturalization of all who had come into the colony in 1683 and who since that date had purchased lands. The act required, besides the oath of allegiance, oaths denying the spiritual supremacy of the Pope, Transubstantiation and the claims of the Pretender.[103] Not until 1821 were New York's naturalization laws sufficiently liberalized to include Catholics.

[100] E. B. O'Callaghan, *History of New Netherland under the Dutch* (2nd ed., 2 vols., New York, 1855), vol. ii, pp. 316, 345-55, 450, 451, 453.

[101] *Supra*, p. 37.

[102] *Col. Laws of New York* (Albany, 1894), vol. i, pp. 123-24.

[103] *Supra*, p. 38. *Cf.* James Kent, *Commentaries on American Law*, ed. by W. M. Tracy (4 vols., Phila., 1889), vol. ii, p. 73.

The difficulties which New York Catholics encountered in their efforts to secure the advantages usually open to land holders, may be illustrated by the career of Hector St. John de Crèvecoeur,[104] naturalized by a special act of the legislature and owner of large estates. His French biographer, while acknowledging that religion sat lightly enough on his great-grandfather, states expressly that the latter never abjured his religion.[105] But if Crèvecoeur took the oaths prescribed by the act of Dec. 23, 1765 [106]—and there is no reason to think that the tests were dispensed with—he solemnly renounced Roman Catholicism.[107] In 1769, he was married to a Protestant by the Huguenot minister, Jean Pierre Tétard, who also baptized Crévecoeur's three children in 1776.[108] According to Robert de Crèvecoeur, the two sons were reared Catholics, and the daughter a Protestant like her mother.[109] In those days such an arrangement was common in the case of mixed marriages. But the daughter in turn was married in St. Peter's (Roman Catholic) church in Barclay Street, of which her father was one of the trustees.[110] It would seem then that although Crèvecoeur did not allow his religion to stand in the way of his economic and social advancement,

---

[104] *Supra*, p. III, n. 146.

[105] Robert de Crèvecoeur, *Saint John de Crèvecoeur, sa vie et ses ouvrages, 1735-1813* (Paris, 1883), "Crèvecoeur était catholique, plus que tiède, il est vrai, mais il n'a jamais abjuré sa religion," p. 23, n.

[106] I W. and M., st. I, ch. 8; 13 Wm. III, ch. 6.

[107] *Colonial Laws of New York*, vol. iv, pp. 899-900. Text of oaths, vol. iii, p. 425. The act is reprinted in Julia P. Mitchell, *St. Jean de Crèvecoeur* (Columbia Studies in English and Comparative Literature, New York, 1916), pp. 307-09.

[108] R. de Crèvecoeur, *op. cit.*, pp. 22-23. Marriage and baptismal records, pp. 285-86. Also in Mitchell, p. 314.

[109] R. de Crèvecoeur, *op. cit.*, p. 23 n.

[110] J. P. Mitchell, *op. cit.*, pref. xiv. Robert de Crèvecoeur says, p. 23 n, that she married a Protestant. If the bride and groom were both Protestants they would hardly have been married in a Catholic Church.

he remained at heart a Catholic, and was ready enough to identify himself openly with the Church when the penal laws were abrogated. While funds were being collected for the erection of St. Peter's, Crèvecoeur presented a request to the city authorities to hold Catholic services in the Exchange, but the petition was not granted.[111]

About 1772 a group of Catholic Highlanders with their chaplain, Father McKenna, settled in the Mohawk Valley. So inhospitable did they find New York that their stay was of short duration. The story of their withdrawal to Canada, where they helped to swell the ranks of the royal forces, belongs to another chapter.[112]

Thus far the history of immigration, naturalization and land-holding has revealed tolerable consistency between theory and practice. The Catholic frankly was not wanted. Legislators and neighbors alike saw to it that he should be made as uncomfortable as possible, as degraded as legal discrimination could make him. Pennsylvania on the other hand presents strange contrasts between theory and practice. William Penn for all his lack of sympathy with the Church of Rome and her teachings,[113] made no distinction between Catholic and other alien freeholders. By the act of 1682 all might be naturalized by making a promise of fidelity to the proprietor.[114] With the accession of Queen Anne the halcyon days were over. From 1708 to 1742 a series of naturalization acts was passed in conformity with British emigration policies. While these laws offered every inducement to foreign Protestants, they excluded Catholics from

[111] J. P. Mitchell, *op. cit.*, pp. 146-47. R. de Crèvecoeur, *op. cit.*, pp. 109-10.

[112] J. G. Shea, *Cath. Ch. in U. S.*, vol. ii, p. 74. A. C. H. *Researches*, n. s. vol. iv (1908), pp. 231-249. *Cf. infra*, p. 317.

[113] *Cf. supra*, p. 103 *et seq.*

[114] *Charter and Laws of Pennsylvania, 1682-1700*, ed. by George Staughton, *et al.* (Harrisburg, 1879), p. 105.

citizenship, and debarred them from purchasing land.[115] Catholic church property was left without legal protection.[116] All this was contrary to the ideas of Penn, though consonant with the policy of the home government and the instructions of Penn's successors.[117]   Never backward in protesting when their own principles were involved, there is no record of the Quakers having lodged any formal objection to the tests against Catholics.[118]   Yet in practice they fell short of the instructions which forbade them to allow Catholics to settle in the province, and, as we have more than once noted, they resolutely refused to interfere or to allow others to interfere with the practice of Catholicism, private or public.

It was easy to keep alive the flame of religious hatred in a province exposed as Pennsylvania was to the attacks of the French and Indians and with a large foreign population many of whom it was said were Catholics.   The number of the latter in the constantly increasing German population has been variously estimated.   William Smith, provost of the College and Academy of Philadelphia, in a communication to Archbishop Secker, Nov. 27, 1759, reported the number of English, Irish and German Catholics to be ten thousand.[119] But Smith could never think coolly of non-English immigrants, least of all if they were Catholics.   Father Harding who had noted the exaggerations of the provost's pamphlet,

---

[115] *Pennsylvania Acts*, 1708, 1729, 1730, 1734, 1737, 1742.   For a sample certificate of naturalization see *Pa. Arch.*, vol. iv, p. 243.   For text of the oaths required, *ibid.*, 2 ser., vol. xvii, pp. 3-4.

[116] *Pennsylvania Acts*, 1730, p. 72.   *Cf.* M. F. Noonan, *A Catholic Colony in Pennsylvania* (Loretto), (Wash., 1932), p. 14.

[117] W. R. Shephard, *Proprietary Govt. in Pa.*, p. 369.

[118] C. Stillé, "Religious Tests," *Pa. Mag. Hist. Biog.*, vol. ix, p. 395. W. T. Root, *Relations of Pennsylvania with the British Government, 1696-1765*, p. 233 *et seq.*

[119] W. Smith, *Life and Correspondence*, vol. i, p. 219.

A Brief State of the Province of Pennsylvania, (1755)[120] made a careful census of the Catholics whom he and Father Schneider attended. Irish and Germans together totaled only 1365; allowing for those of whom no report could be obtained, the priests were sure that the number did not exceed 2,000.[121] Smith, in season and out of season, harped on the danger of these foreigners uniting with the French and Indians to cut the throats of all good Protestant Pennsylvanians.[122] Nor were there wanting those who agreed with him,[123] even while they pointed out his exaggerations. The legislation discussed above, the militia act of 1757, the tax on Irish servants, perhaps, also, the failure of the Quakers to protest against this discrimination, all point to a public opinion ready to take alarm at the slightest suggestion of danger, however unfounded.

The religious liberty which in Maryland was a fact long before it was given formal expression in the famous act of 1649 did not fail to attract immigrants. A generous land policy was another powerful inducement. But like Pennsylvania Maryland fell away from her first ideal. The penal laws directed against Catholics were intended not only to disable those already settled in the province but to discourage further immigration. The story is too familiar to require repetition here.[124] Not so generally known perhaps are the

---

120 W. Smith, *A Brief State of the Province of Pennsylvania . . . In a Letter from a Gentleman who resided many Years in Pennsylvania to his Friend in London,* 2nd ed. (London . . . 1755), pp. 19, 26, 31, 37, 41.

121 *Pa. Col. Rec.,* vol. vii, p. 447; *Pa. Arch.,* vol. iii, p. 144.

122 W. Smith, *Works,* ed. by H. W. Smith (2 vols., Phila., 1803), vol. ii, pp. 20, 22, 91, 101-03, 107. *Discourses on Several Public Occasions. . . . During the War in America . . .* (London, 1759). Discourses, iii, iv. *Life and Correspondence,* vol. i, pp. 51, 197. W. S. Perry, *Hist. Coll.,* vol. ii, pp. 546, 555-56.

123 Letter from Dr. Thomas Graeme of Philadelphia to Thomas Penn, July 1, 1755. Quoted in J. L. J. Kirlin, *Catholicity in Philadelphia,* pp. 79-80.

124 *Supra,* pp. 57-60, 159 *et seq.*

statutes governing Catholic land-ownership. Begun under the second Lord Baltimore, and intended originally to limit the capacity of religious corporations to acquire and administer wealth, they were later extended to individual Catholics who were thus deprived of power to acquire and possess. But this was not enough. Catholics were also deprived of the enjoyment of the profits of their land even though those profits were the fruits of their own labor. Moreover, no Catholic could be the beneficiary of a trust either in his own name or in that of another. And while Catholics were thus incapacitated, every effort was being made to attract foreign Protestants.[125]

Virginia's second charter, 1609, forbade the entrance into the colony of any person affecting " the superstitions of the church of Rome." [126] The third charter, 1612, provided for the admission of aliens to the franchise, but excluded the native English Catholic by a double oath of supremacy and allegiance.[127] To this policy of excluding " the sons of Anak " colonial Virginia consistently adhered. Certainly no colony copied more faithfully the illiberal portions of English law, and especially the British penal statutes.[128] For the first half-century or more partisan legislation was aimed at

---

[125] Wm. Kilty, *Report of English Statutes*, pp. 147, 185, 191, 196, 200. *Cf. Lower House Journal, 1762-75*, p. 105, for a typical "Act for preventing the Importation of German and French Papists, and Popish Priests and Jesuits into the Province, and of Irish Papists by way of Pennsylvania or the Government of New Castle, Kent and Sussex on Delaware..." See also article by L. A. Lilly, "Mortmain in Maryland," in *Historical Bulletin*, vol. xii (Jan., 1934), pp. 34-35. *Md. Gaz.*, Nov. 28, 1754.

[126] W. W. Hening, *Statutes at Large*, vol. i, pp. 97-98. S. Lucas, *Charters of the Old English Colonies in America*, pp. 18-19.

[127] W. W. Hening, *op. cit.*, vol. i, pp. 105-06. S. Lucas, *op. cit.*, pp. 20-25.

[128] C. J. Stillé, "Religious Liberty in Virginia and Patrick Henry," *Amer. Hist. Ass'n. Papers*, vol. iii (1889), pp. 205-211. *Cf.* Hening, vol. i, p. 268.

dissenters as well as Catholics;[129] then the hard logic of economic necessity suggested some lowering of the barriers in order to attract settlers. A beginning was made in 1671 when applicants for naturalization having taken the usual oaths might petition the assembly for the passage of a private act.[130] Lord Culpepper in 1680 was empowered by England to declare individuals naturalized.[131] This method was re-affirmed in 1705 and again in 1738.[132] Governor Spotswood's interest in the development of the iron industry secured special privileges and exemptions for the settlement at Germanna.[133] Governor Dinwiddie in a letter to the Lords of Trade, Feb. 23, 1756, suggested the founding of a buffer colony to the west with special inducements to foreign and English Protestants. The legislature with his approval had already exempted Protestant settlers from taxes, at first for ten and then for fifteen years, and had set aside an appropriation of ten thousand pounds for their defense.[134] The Huguenot and the Presbyterian from the North of Ireland also received special consideration.[135] Contemporan-

---

[129] Hening, *Statutes*, vol. i, pp. 122, 155, 267, 269, 532; vol. ii, pp. 46, 47, 49.

[130] Hening, *Statutes*, vol. ii, pp. 289, 290. *Cf. Va. Mag.*, vol. ix, p. 280. *William and Mary College Quar.*, 1 ser., vol. viii, p. 249.

[131] Hening, *Statutes*, vol. ii, pp. 464, 465. *Cf. Va. Mag.*, vol. x, p. 148; vol. xi, p. 156; vol. xiv, pp. 363, 367; vol. xxv, pp. 265, 270. *W. & M. Quar.*, 1 ser., vol. iii, pp. 11-12.

[132] Hening, *Statutes*, vol. iii, pp. 228, 434, 435, 479. *Cf. Va. Mag.*, vol. xxxv, p. 265. *W. & M. Quar.*, 1 ser., vol. iii, p. 39.

[133] *Spotswood Letters, 1710-1722* (Va. Hist. Soc. *Coll.*, i-ii, Richmond, 1882), vol. i, p. 20; vol. ii, pp. 70, 78, 95, 196, 215. *Cf. Council Journals*, vol. i, pp. 583, 584, 585; vol. ii, pp. 765, 767, 768.

[134] *Dinwiddie Papers*, vol. i, p. 156n; vol. ii, p. 343. *Cf.* Hening, vol. vi, pp. 258, 355, 417-20. J. W. Wayland, *The German Element in the Shenandoah Valley of Virginia* (Charlottsville, Va., 1907), pp. 106-07.

[135] Robert Beverly, *History and Present State of Virginia*, pp. 44, 45, 47. J. L. Peyton, *History of Augusta County, Va.* (Staunton, Va., 1882), pp. 5-7, 78, 96, 177. *Journals of the House of Burgesses*, 1773-76, p. 189.

eous with this encouragement of foreign Protestant immigration to the Old Dominion was the effort to exclude Roman Catholics as well as to outlaw and degrade the few who had gained entrance. Officials at the port of entry might be ever so exact in tendering the prescribed oaths; their vigilance might easily be outwitted by entrance over the border lines of Pennsylvania and Maryland. The presence in these two neighboring provinces of considerable bodies of Catholics was a constant source of irritation to Virginia. Her governors watched with a jealous eye the practical toleration of Pennsylvania with its constant accretion of Germans. " Popish plots " and Indian alarms in the Quaker colony or in Maryland were sure to be given credence in Virginia.[136] So efficacious was her vigilance that Lord Culpepper in 1681 reported to the Lords of Trade that there was only one Catholic in the colony.[137] Certainly there were more than that, but they were too obscure, too indigent, too fearful of being known as Catholics to have come to the notice of his lordship. The only Catholics of any prominence in the Old Dominion were the Brents. Their story like that of the Carrolls in Maryland illustrates the life of the Virginia Catholic under the most favorable circumstances.

Giles Brent and his sister, prominent in early Maryland history, left Maryland for Virginia in 1650. They settled in Stafford County where Giles acquired a large estate. He and his sister were closely watched; but since they made no attempt to proselytize, they were unmolested in the private practice of their religion, and even harbored Jesuits with impunity. Giles Brent's will was probated in 1671. The

---

[136] *Dinwiddie Papers*, vol. ii, pp. 207, 306, 415. *Va. Historical Register,* vol. vi, p. 155. *Va. Calendar of State Papers,* vol. i, p. 79; vol. iv, p. 96. P. S. Flippen, " William Gooch," *W. & M. Quar.,* 2 ser., vol. v (1925), pp. 225-58; vol. vi (1926), pp. 1-38, p. 21.

[137] " Minutes of the Committee of Trade and Plantations, Nov. 26, 1681," *Va. Mag.,* vol. xxvi (1918).

bulk of his estate went to his nephew who was known as George Brent of Woodstock.[138] Such was the confidence with which the master of Woodstock inspired his Protestant neighbors that even though he was a Catholic he was appointed by the Governor and Council, May 2, 1683, Receiver-General north of the Rappahannock, and on July 10, 1691, Ranger-General of the Northern Neck. He was also a member of the House of Burgesses for Stafford County in 1688. As a law partner of William Fitzhugh he seems to have made a name for himself in legal circles.[139]

The short reign of James II witnessed what appears to have been the only attempt at large scale immigration of Catholics to Virginia. Brent and four or five other gentlemen purchased before 1687 a tract of land of about 30,000 acres called Brent Town or Brenton. James II issued a proclamation granting religious liberty to all who would settle in the new colony. William Fitzhugh regarded the project sympathetically and hoped that it would be a buffer state against the Indians. Others characterized the scheme as " diabolical." The Revolution of 1688 put an end not only to all hopes of a Catholic settlement in Virginia but also it seems to George Brent's security. In the reign of terror inaugurated by Parson Waugh of Virginia and Coode of Maryland, Brent, accused with other Catholics of inciting the Indians, was forced to take refuge in the home of his friend Fitzhugh, who protected him at the risk of his life. The refugee remained in hiding for five months.[140]   Some

[138] E. R. Richardson, "Giles Brent, Catholic Pioneer in Virginia," *Thought*, vol. vi (1932), pp. 650-664. *Va. Mag.*, vol. i (1893-94), p. 123 n; vol. xvii (1909), p. 311.

[139] *Va. Mag.*, vol. i, p. 123 n; vol. xvii, pp. 309 *et seq.* *Council Journals*, vol. i, p. 126.

[140] *Va. Mag.*, vol. xvii, pp. 309, 421; vol. ii, pp. 275, 372. B. C. Steiner, "The Protestant Revolution in Maryland," *Amer. Hist. Ass'n. Report*, 1897, p. 296. *W. & M. Quar.*, vol. xi (1902-03), p. 247. F. Harrison,

years later, Brent and his brother Robert, were cited before the Stafford County Court to take the test oaths required for practicing law. They were to be presented not only as " Popish Recusants " but also to answer for " several wicked crimes." The Brents contended that they were not legally summoned and appealed to the General Court.[141] Two generations later the vote of another George Brent, probably the grandson of Brent of Woodstock, was being contested in the House of Burgesses, on the ground that as a Roman Catholic he had no right to vote.[142] One may conjecture from the experiences of the Brents what would have been the lot of the projected colony at Brenton. Perhaps the best commentary on the success of Virginia's policy is the number of Catholics reported by Bishop Carroll about 1785—a paltry two hundred.[143]

The history of naturalization and immigration in the Carolinas and Georgia repeats the story which by this time has become familiar—the encouragement of French, Swiss, German, Scotch-Irish Protestants and the exclusion of Roman Catholics.[144] The first definite attempt at anti-Catholic legislation in the Carolinas is recorded in the Journal of the Assembly of South Carolina, Feb. 24, 1696/7. A bill for naturalization was to be prepared granting liberty of conscience " to all except Roman Catholicks and That The Clause be Incerted in the act To putt in force the Severall

" Brent Town, Ravensworth and the Huguenots in Stafford," in *Tyler's Quarterly Magazine*, vol. v, pp. 164-183.

[141] *Va. Cal. of State Papers*, vol. i, pp. 46-47 ; County Court of Stafford, May 18, 1693.

[142] *Journal of the House of Burgesses, 1761-1765*, Friday, Dec. 3, 1762, p. 127. *Va. Mag.*, vol. xii, p. 439 for Brent genealogy.

[143] *Supra*, p. 139.

[144] *Public Record Office, Col. Off.*, 5 ser., vol. 196, pp. 105, 125, 132. Gr. Brit. Trans. L. C.

acts in The Kingdome of England." [145]   Catholics apparently took the hint, for during the pre-Revolutionary period there is no evidence of activity on their part.   They were also excluded from the benefits of an act for the importation of white servants.   Importers were obliged to declare under oath that none of the servants were " what is commonly called native Irish or persons of known scandalous characters or Roman Catholicks." [146]   At the opening of the Revolution the Carolinas and Georgia had a relatively large foreign population.   The European experience of the immigrants rendered them " peculiarly fitted," as Bishop England [147] points out, to imbibe the notions and confirm the opinions of the British settlers concerning Roman Catholicism.   The few Catholics in the territory, without spiritual ministration and unknown even to each other, were in no position to offer a corrective.

Georgia's system of land tenure to 1750 furnishes one of several keys [148] to her position on Roman Catholic immigrants.   There were several reasons for not allowing the settlers to hold their lands in fee simple, but one of the most weighty was the fear that they would dispose of their holdings to the French or Spanish.   Catholics would in this way get a foothold in the colony and serve as spies for their respective governments. [149]   Even the Indians with whom Oglethorpe and his associates made treaties promised " with

[145] *Journal of the Common House of the Assembly, Feb. 23–March 10, 1697*, ed. by A. S. Salley (Columbia, 1913), pp. 7, 13, 14, 18.

[146] *Statutes at Large*, vol. ii, p. 646.

[147] John England, " Early History of the Diocese of Charleston" (Dublin, 1832), in *Works* (Messmer ed.), vol. iv, pp. 298 *et seq. Cf.* J. J. O'Connell, *Catholicity in the Carolinas and Georgia* (New York, 1879), p. 27.

[148] For the attitude of the Georgia Trustees see *Diary of Viscount Percival*, vol. i, pp. 299, 370, 374; vol. ii, p. 201.

[149] *Ga. Col. Rec.*, vol. iii, pp. 374-75.

stout hearts " to encourage no other white people to settle among them and to have no " correspondence with the Spanish or French." [150] The Georgia records on the other hand furnish ample evidence that in the encouragement of immigrants national lines were not drawn save to exclude Roman Catholics. In addition to generous offers, the legislature frequently made appropriations to defray the expenses of prospective Protestant colonists.[151]

There were other land schemes besides those sponsored by colonial authorities which throw not a little light upon the Catholic question. When it became evident that in the duel between England and France for the trans-Alleghanian territory actual settlement would be an important factor, numerous land companies were formed for the purpose of exploiting the idea. The promotion literature, intended to " sell " the scheme as well as the land, failed not to appeal to a variety of motives, among which the national and the religious found an important place. A pamphlet issued in the interests of the projected colony at Charlotina made the most of the trade rivalry between the French and the British. The writer also pointed out the effects of French missionary efforts in alienating the affections of the natives from the British. The stock charges anent heretics, British responsibility for the Crucifixion, the French nationality of our Lady and the like, were all repeated. Cotton Mather's *Decennium Luctuosum* might well have furnished the model

[150] S. G. McLendon, *History of the Public Domain of Georgia* (Atlanta, 1924), p. 10.

[151] *Ga. Col. Rec.*, vol. i, pp. 200, 492; vol. ii, pp. 35, 53, 82; vol. v, index under Ebenezer; vol. x, pp. 432, 435; vol. xii, pp. 212-213; vol. xiv, pp. 70, 108, 271, 417; vol. xix, p. 182. There is a striking similarity between the naturalization, immigration and land laws of the southern colonies and those of the British plantations in the Caribbean. See N. Trott, *Laws of the British Plantations in America*, p. 388 *et seq.*

for this portion of the pamphlet.   The accusations, even much of the phraseology, are identical.[152]

One of the most widely advertised colonization projects, scattered in broadside throughout the country, concerned the Connecticut claims west of Pennsylvania.   Prominent Connecticut citizens, among whom were Theophilus Parsons and Silas Deane,[153] were interested in the scheme, but the memorial setting forth its purposes, its advantages and the qualifications for settlers seems to have been drawn up by Samuel Hazard, a Philadelphia merchant.   Connecticut is asked in the petition to release her claims to the land in question.   The designs of the French, " scenes of Blood and Rapin " and all the " mazes of popish error and superstition " are hinted at darkly.   An Anglo-American colony, Protestant to the core, must save the West and its natives from these impending calamities.   By a process of elimination the memorialist proves that only Presbyterians can be counted on for this hazardous undertaking.   Twelve of their ministers are ready to accompany the three thousand five hundred eight volunteers who by accretions will shortly number ten thousand.   Every Protestant over fourteen will be given a grant of land.   Protestants only shall be eligible to office. No Roman Catholic shall hold property, keep arms or ammunition, nor shall any " Mass House or Popish Chapels be

---

[152] *The Expediency of Securing our American Colonies by Settling the Country Adjoining the River Mississippi, and the Country upon the Ohio, Considered* ... Edinburgh, 1763.   Reprinted in Illinois State Historical Library *Collections*, vol. x (British Series i).   *The Critical Period, 1763-65*, ed. by C. W. Alvord and C. E. Carter (Springfield, 1915), pp. 135-161.   *Cf. ibid.*, vol. xi (Brit. Ser. ii), p. 256 for Governor William Franklin's proposal for a grant of 100,000 acres to a company of gentlemen on condition that at their own cost they settle thereon " One white Protestant Person for every hundred Acres."

[153] Conn. H. S. *Collections*, vol. ii, p. 133 n.   *Cf.* Silas Deane's " Loose Thoughts on the Subject of Western Lands," *Samuel Adams Papers*, vol. iii, Banc. *Coll.* N. Y. P. L.

allowed in the Province." The memorial is dated July 24, 1755.[154] Connecticut signified her willingness to release her claims, but referred the petitioners to the King for a transfer of title. The project never materialized. Hazard died July 8, 1758. In 1774 his son Ebenezer begged the privilege of carrying out his father's plan. It is significant that the broadside mentioned above with its accompanying petition was submitted without change to the Connecticut legislature on the eve of the Revolution, but with "unsuccessful results." [155]

It has been pointed out that while the naturalization laws of Great Britain and her colonies conferred certain civil rights, political privileges such as voting and office-holding were not included. Even if proof were lacking it would seem a foregone conclusion that the sect which was the pariah of the civil, social and religious life of British America should retain that status in the political world. But the proof is not wanting. Here as elsewhere, British and colonial legislation, test oaths, and political practice tell their story of ostracism. It would serve no useful purpose to discuss in detail this mass of legislation or the special studies which have been made for some of the colonies. McKinley's monograph [156] cites all the important documents. His conclusions have not been superseded. Everywhere, he finds, in British America, the Roman Catholic was disfranchised

---

[154] Fulham Palace Mss. Conn. No. 28. Also in the Force Trans. *Conn. Rec. Misc. Papers, 1637-1783*, p. 2368 *et seq.* Printed in Force's *Amer. Arch.*, 4 ser., vol. i, pp. 861-867. It will be noted that the date of this memorial coincides with the period of the militia acts of Pa., Md. and Va.

[155] *Conn. Rec.*, vol. x, pp. 382-83. *Susquehannah Company Papers*, ed. by J. P. Boyd (4 vols., Wilkes-Barre, Pa., 1930-33), vol. i, pp. 246-59, 278-83.

[156] Albert E. McKinley, *The Suffrage Franchise in the Thirteen English Colonies in America. Cf.* C. F. Bishop, *Elections in the American Colonies*, p. 62. C. Stillé, "Relig. Tests," *Pa. Mag.*, vol. ix, pp. 375-76.

and ineligible for office. Here and there an occasional Catholic like George Brent and his grandson,[157] or William Douglass in New Jersey,[158] would evade the law or be elected in spite of his religious disqualifications. But the law was there ready to be invoked; seldom were there wanting those who were willing to assume that thankless duty. In Maryland, notwithstanding the affluence of the Carrolls, Charles Carroll of Carrollton could be publicly taunted for his political disabilities by his antagonist Daniel Dulany.[159]

To what extent did public policy as evidenced in immigration, naturalization and suffrage regulations reflect popular sentiment? Not always articulate nor given overmuch to analyzing his opinions, the " man in the street " nevertheless can and usually does react to popular demonstrations in a fashion which leaves no doubt as to what he thinks on the question at issue. Popular anniversary celebrations, crude though they may be, are likely to embody traditional beliefs; frequently they are modified to give concrete expression to popular opinion of some recent occurrence, local or national.

The annual colonial celebration of November fifth was of this nature. In normal times it followed British precedent more or less closely. A special feature of the thanksgiving service [160] was a sermon in which the religious and

---

[157] *Supra*, pp. 249-51.

[158] *New Jersey Arch.*, I ser., vol. i, pp. 64, 88, 304, 306. R. P. Whitcomb, *History of Bayonne, N. J.* (Bayonne, 1904), p. 28. J. M. Flynn, *Catholic Church in New Jersey* (Morristown, 1904), p. 8.

[159] Elihu Riley, *The Correspondence of the First Citizen and Antilon. With a History of Governor Eden's Administration in Maryland, 1769-1776* (Balt., 1902), pp. 30, 95.

[160] A writer in the *Virginia Magazine* (xxxii [1924], p. 14 n) says of the annual thanksgiving service, . . . " there never was a time in which colonial Virginians did not heartily offer the following prayer: 'Accept also most Gracious God, of our unfeigned thanks for filling our hearts again with joy and gladness after the time that Thou hadst afflicted us and putting a new song in our mouths, by bringing his

patriotic notes were skillfully blended. If a grateful recognition of England's providential deliverance was insisted on, no less was the responsibility of Rome for the Gunpowder Plot.[161] Political excitement at home or international complications abroad were likely to be reflected in the pageants by the increased elaborateness of the floats, a greater number of episodes, lengthier processions and more inflammatory speeches. Simple or elaborate, these annual celebrations constituted an effective means of perpetuating religious bigotry.

In New England, November fifth was a gala day for the small boy who amused himself and the neighbors with his little Pope dressed up in the "most grotesque and fantastic manner," mounted on boards or on some wheeled contrivance. The older boys meanwhile, and even the adults, were busy preparing floats for the evening spectacle. In front of a moving stage was a "lanthorne" six or eight feet high, illuminated, and covered with satirical verses or political slogans. Sometimes a dancing boy was placed within. Occupying the center of the platform was the Pope, made as repulsive as possible. Behind him was the Devil with the traditional tail, cloven hoof and pitchfork. From time to time his Satanic Majesty would whisper confidentially to His Holiness; again he would belabor him lustily. Sharing the honors of the stage were other unpopular characters such as the Pretender, or, as Ezra Stiles records in his *Diary* in 1774, Lord North, Governor Hutchinson and General Gage.[162] Fiddlers and dancers were sometimes added to en-

Majesty King William upon this day for the deliverance of our Church and Nation from Popish Tyranny and Arbitrary Power.'"

[161] *Cf. supra*, pp. 31-33. The catalogue of Harvard, 1830, lists some forty of these sermons which the library possessed at that date. *Catalogue of the Library in Harvard University in Cambridge* (Cambridge, 1830-31), vol. iii, p. 39.

[162] Ezra Stiles, *Diary*, vol. i, Nov. 5, 1774. Force Trans. L. C. Mss. Div. Peter Oliver, "Origin and Progress of Rebellion..." *Egerton Mss.* 2671, pp. 16-17, 171-172. L. C. See *Pennsylvania Journal, Nov. 23,*

liven the pageant.   The celebration was quiet enough during
the day, but with the approach of evening and the gathering
of the crowd, the participants vied with each other in the
contribution of boisterously abusive features.   In Boston it
was long the custom to have a mock combat between two
rival Popes, sponsored respectively by the North and South
Ends of the city.   So intense was the rivalry that at times
spectators were injured in the fray.   The death of a child
in 1764 [163] aroused a public reaction, but it was not until ten
years later that Governor Hancock succeeded in reconciling
the factions.   Adopting the slogan, "Unity and No Popery,"
they compromised on a union Pope.[164]

"Pope Night" celebrations were not confined to New England, although the accounts from that section are most numerous.   The *New York Post-Boy* for Nov. 10, 1755, reports
the New York pageant for that year.[165]   Ten years later
Captain John Montrésor records in his journal for Nov. 5:

advertisements and many papers placarded throughout the city
declaring the storming of the Fort this Night under cover of
burning the Pope and pretender unless the Stamps were
delivered. . . . [166]

1774, No. 1668, for account of Nov. 5 in Newport, R. I.   Also *Virginia
Gaz.*, Nov. 24, Dec. 15, 1774.

[163] John Rowe, *Letters and Diary, 1759-1762, 1764-1779*, ed. by A. R.
Cunningham (Boston, 1903), pp. 67-68, 114, 195, 254, 287.

[164] John Rowe, *op. cit.*, p. 287.   W. Tudor, *Life of James Otis* (Boston,
1823), pp. 25-29.   For a typical New England celebration outside of
Boston see J. Coffin, *History of Newbury, Newburyport and West Newbury* (Boston, 1895), pp. 249-51.   *Cf. A. C. H. Researches*, n. s. vol. iii,
(1907), pp. 132-36; vol. iv (1908), pp. 259-274.   *Recollections of Samuel
Breck*, ed. by H. E. Scudder (Phila., 1877), pp. 19 n, 116-117.   *U. S.
Cath. Hist. Magazine*, vol. i, p. 1; vol. ii, pp. 3-6.   *New England Quarterly*, vol. vi, pp. 98-130, " Guy Fawks Day in Massachusetts."

[165] G. C. D. Odell, *Annals of the New York Stage* (7 vols., New York,
1927), vol. i, p. 71.

[166] " Journals of Captain John Montrésor," New York Hist. Soc. *Coll.*,
vol. xiv (1881), pp. 338, 346, 349, 357, 362.

The practice here indicated of associating the head of the Roman Catholic Church with the coercive measures of the British government in the decade immediately preceding the Revolution suggests the thoroughness with which colonial America had learned the lessons inculcated by generations of Guy Fawks celebrations. For Protestant America the Pope had become a symbol for all that was despicable, tyrannical and treacherous; what more natural than to identify him with the hirelings whose object was to enslave the colonies?

The arrival in America of the British customs clerks and the commissioners sent to enforce the revenue acts gave occasion for demonstrations of this sort. Ann Hulton, whose brother was a customs officer in Boston, tells of his welcome in that city, Nov. 5, 1767. The mob, he wrote her, carried " twenty Devils, Popes, & Pretenders, thro the Streets, with Labels on their breasts, Liberty & Property & No Commissioners." [167] Another account describes the five commissioners being escorted through the town with the Pope, the Devil and the Pretender.[168] A subscriber to the *Boston Gazette* asked the editor to insert a leaf from an old almanac (1697), " which may not be altogether useless AT THIS TIME." The leaf in question contained a conventional blood and thunder denunciation of " The Hellish Jacobite Plot" so common in British broadsides. The Jacobite, so the argument ran, whether Churchman, Whig, Quaker or Baptist is a traitor of equal dye with the " Papist," and therefore to be guarded against. The next issue of the *Gazette* refers to the celebration, on September 8, of the birthday anniversary of the commissioners, " who have ordered the Custom Houses Shut and Commerce obstructed." The Pope, it is added, may give orders for the insertion of the day in the " Popish calendar." [169]

[167] Ann Hulton, *Letters of a Loyalist Lady* (Harv. Univ. Press. 1921), p. 8.

[168] A. B. Forbes, in *Commonwealth Hist. Mass.*, vol. ii, p. 501.

[169] *Boston Gazette*, Sept. 5, 18 (nos. 701, 702), 1768.

British officials were by no means the only victims of the colonial mob. Among men of influence in British America there was an honest difference of opinion with regard to many of the administration's measures. Consequently, colonial reaction to opposition policies was neither uniform nor united. Non-importation was one of the burning issues which as might be expected aligned many of the merchant class on the side of the government. Sharing their viewpoint was, in the opinion of Schlesinger, " the shrewdest and most pertinacious controversialist in British America, John Mein of the *Boston Chronicle*." [170] Mein's championship of the British government as well as his attacks on persons in high places in Massachusetts, caused him to be suspected of being subsidized by the Crown. To escape the Boston mob he was forced into hiding until he secured passage to England. His departure under these circumstances obtained for him the doubtful distinction of being one of the leading actors in the Pope Day celebration of 1769. The *Boston Chronicle* for November 9 included in its " Description of the Pope, 1769 " an acrostic to its former editor:

> Insulting Wretch, we'll him expose
> O'er the whole world his deeds disclose,
> Hell now gaups wide to take him in,
> Now he is ripe, Oh lump of Sin.
>
> Mean is the man, M—n is his Name,
> Enough he's spread his hellish Fame,
> Infernal Furies hurl his Soul
> Nine million Times from Pole to Pole. . . . [171]

[170] A. M. Schlesinger, *The Colonial Merchant and the American Revolution, 1763-1776* (New York, 1917), pp. 157-160. *Cf.* I. Thomas, *Hist. of Printing*, vol. i, pp. 150-55; vol. ii, p. 60.

[171] C. K. Bolton, " Circulating Libraries in Boston, 1765-1865," Col. Soc. Mass. *Pub.*, vol. xi, p. 198. J. K. Hosmer, *Life of T. Hutchinson*, pp. 153-54. N. M. Tiffany and S. I. Kelsey, eds., *Letters of James Murray, Loyalist* (Boston, 1901), p. 168. The " Description of the Pope, 1769 " was also printed in broadside, copies of which are in L. C. and N. Y. H. S.

The continual association of patriotism with national and religious bias was not lost on the rising generation. In Philadelphia a group of school boys determined to have a tea party of their own on Guy Fawks day. The *Pennsylvania Journal* cooperated by publishing " A Card " from " An Association of Protestant School Boys." They like their elders had resolved to use no more tea after November first. On that day they would canvass the town

to request the gift of all such TEAS as may then remain in their houses, toward making a BONFIRE on the memorable fifth day of the said month, commonly called GUNPOWDER PLOT DAY: when the old custom is intended to be revived of exhibiting a piece of pageantry, to show their abhorrence and detestation of the *Pope,* Pretender, etc., and such of their *Adherents* as would overthrow the GOOD OLD ENGLISH CONSTITUTION. . . . [172]

It is apparent then that on the Catholic question " the man in the street " was in complete accord with his more sophisticated neighbor. To the one no less than to the other the Catholic was a *persona non grata*—if that euphemism is not altogether wide of the mark. Exclusion from the colony, if possible, or failing that, ostracism from every desirable avocation in life was the welcome extended to him at a period when save in New England every effort was being made to attract Protestant settlers to the colonies. In times of public danger his religion was the subject of execration by the mob; on public holidays the head of his Church was the butt of the mob's ridicule. Sometimes his life was in danger.

[172] *Pennsylvania Journals,* Nov. 9, 1774, no. 1666. Also in *Virginia Gazette,* Nov. 24, 1774, no. 446. *Cf.* R. T. H. Halsey, *The Boston Port Bill as Pictured by a Contemporary London Cartoonist* (New York, 1904), p. 319 *et seq.*

CHAPTER VII

THE TRADITION IN THE PRE-REVOLUTIONARY DECADE

THE pre-Revolutionary decade was one of violent controversies, one of the bitterest, perhaps, being that over the introduction of an Anglican episcopate. Although the Catholic hierarchy was not directly involved, a study of the arguments for and against the project brings out in sharp relief the attitude of the opposing groups to Roman Catholicism. Dissenter argued with Churchman and Churchman with dissenter, nay, even with his fellow Anglican, each intent upon convincing the other of the error of his ways, each eager to sway public opinion to his own point of view. Sometimes the controversy was dignified, and conducted on the high plane befitting the subject; more often it descended to personalities, even to invective. Through it all, whether it be accusation or defense, the reader is left in no doubt as to what the controversialists think of the Church of Rome. The evidence, moreover, is all the more valuable because of its indirect nature. For the writer or speaker is concerned with Rome and her teachings only so far as they strengthen or weaken, prove or disprove his argument. A brief outline of the controversy will help to clarify the issues of the debate.

Unlike the dissenting sects, the Anglican clergy considered orthodox only those ministers who had received episcopal ordination—an assumption highly resented by the dissenters, implying as it did the invalidity of their own ordination. If carried to its logical conclusion, the theory would, moreover, subordinate them to the Church of England. Furthermore, where church and state were so closely united, as they were in New England, any reflection on the orthodoxy of the ministry would seriously impair its political prestige. This prestige, it was claimed by some, the Anglican clergy wished to transfer to themselves. That the movement was dangerous to religious liberty, that it tended to strengthen the home government, that it was a scheme on the part of the clergy to detach themselves from the rest of the community and be a law unto themselves, were other objections urged by its opponents.

From the standpoint of the zealous Churchman there were many reasons for urging the appointment of a bishop for the colonies. Even under the most favorable circumstances, pioneer conditions in the plantations made it impossible to reproduce save to a limited extent the outward life of the Anglican Church in England. Questions of administration, of discipline, of ritual were continually arising. The absence of a bishop, to whom normally these problems would have been referred, left their solution to the commissary, or the governor, who not infrequently left them unsolved. One of the gravest of these problems was the ordination of candidates of American birth. The voyage to England was expensive, time-consuming, attended with hardship, and even hazardous to life. Given these conditions, it is not surprising that the authorities of the Church of England should listen with sympathy to appeals for a bishop for the colonies. From time to time during the century preceding the Revolution the project was agitated, only to be deferred because of the opposition both in England and America.[1]

Although the Anglican clergy were not unanimous in their approval of the plan,[2] the opposition came largely from dis-

[1] The best account of the controversy is the monograph of A. L. Cross, *The Anglican Episcopate and the American Colonies* (New York, 1902). For shorter accounts, see W. S. Perry, *Amer. Epis. Ch.*, vol. i, pp. 374-427. T. Sedgwick, *Life of William Livingston*, p. 130. A. Bradford, *Life and Writings of Jonathan Mayhew*, p. 240.

[2] A. L. Cross, *op. cit.*, pp. 231-35, 261.

senting groups. Their traditions, their views of ecclesiastical and of civil government, their political influence, their economic interests—these were the chief sources of their determined opposition to the introduction of an American bishop.[3] Many of them were descendants of those Nonconformists who had fled from the persecution of Laud.[4] In their opinion the Church of England was an instrument of persecution second only to that mighty engine of tyranny, the Church of Rome. For was she not the "brat of Popery," [5] whose highest ambition was to lord it over the godly? What else but persecution could be expected from the " illegitimate daughter " of such a mother? [6] The experience of the dissenters with many of the colonial governors and other crown officers had not been altogether happy. The high-handed procedure of these officials in religious no less than in civil affairs, their tactless, often ostentatious, preference for Anglican forms of worship,[7] tended only to emphasize the arbitrary connotation of episcopacy. The New England clergy in particular, champions of the house of Hanover and the Whig philosophy of resistance, had no mind to yield their power to an Establishment,

[3] A. L. Cross, *op. cit.*, chs. 6, 7, 8. *Cf.* Boston Committee of Correspondence, *General Correspondence of Committee of Correspondence, 1772-1775*, Statement of Rights and Grievances at Town Meeting, Faneuil Hall, Nov. 20, 1772. *Bancroft Coll.*, N. Y. P. L. Ezra Stiles, *Letters to, and documents*, Banc. Trans. (Stiles Papers).

[4] A. L. Cross, *op. cit.*, pp. 20-22. C. H. Van Tyne, *England and America* (Cambridge Univ. Press, 1929), pp. 68-70. *Eccles. Rec., N. Y.*, vol. vi, pp. 4084-85. W. S. Perry, *op. cit.*, vol. i, pp. 175-196. W. Smith, *Life and Correspondence*, vol. i, p. 385 *et seq.*

[5] Hawley Papers, Bancroft Coll., N. Y. P. L., Letter of Joseph Stewart (Colrain, Nov. 18, 1761).

[6] J. Shirley, "Early New Hampshire Jurisprudence," N. H. H. S., *Proc.*, vol. i, p. 307.

[7] W. S. Perry, *op. cit.*, vol. i, pp. 175-196. *Eccles. Rec. N. Y.*, vol. vi, pp. 4084-85. W. Tudor, *Life of James Otis*, pp. 443-44.

or to have their republican ideals undermined by the introduction of titles, spiritual courts and canon law. There was, besides, the financial burden. A hierarchy would have to be maintained with becoming dignity. Who was to pay the bill? There were precedents for taxing members of other denominations for the support of the Church of England. Little reason was there to doubt, if the request for a bishop were granted, that such precedents would be followed.[8]

In the pamphlet and newspaper warfare which the controversy provoked, the Catholic Church was made the target for prosecution and defense alike. In the earlier stages of the debate, about the time of the defection of Cutler and his associates, Samuel Mather's " testimony from Scripture against Idolatry and Superstition," was reprinted as a timely defense of Presbyterian ordination. In the course of the argument, the writer cites " ten principal ceremonies and idols of the Church of England." The source and character of these " idols " may be gathered from a single citation :

6. Popish Holy Days. As if the Lord Jesus Christ himself were not wise enough to appoint Days and Times Sufficient to keep his own Nativity, etc. in everlasting Remembrance in the hearts of his Saints but the Devil and the Pope must keep it out.[9]

---

[8] A. L. Cross, *op. cit.*, pp. 172-175, 196-97, 213. *Stiles Papers*, Letter to Ezra Stiles from Francis Alison, dated Phila., April 15, 1764, p. 29. *Cf.* pp. 137, 139-141, 195, *et seq.* Charles Turner, *Election Sermon, May 26, 1773* (Boston, 1773), p. 39. C. H. Van Tyne, *Causes of the War of Independence* (Boston, 1922), p. 349 *et seq.* S. P. G., Gr. Brit. Trans., ser. B, vol. ii, pts. 1, 2. G. M. Hill, *History of the Church in Burlington, N. J.* Many documents, *passim.*

[9] W. S. Perry, *op. cit.*, vol. i, p. 259. *Cf.* "A Faithful Relation of a Late Occurrence in the Churches of New England," Mass. H. S. *Coll.*, vol. ii, pp. 137-140. Also Cotton Mather's " To the brethren in Connecticut," Mass. H. S. *Coll.*, vol. iii, pp. 135-36.

It was an attack such as this that called forth the two letters of Dr. Johnson already mentioned.[10] Since the purpose of these letters is to review and refute " sundry false and groundless stories " that his readers may see how " wickedly you are imposed on and we abused," Dr. Johnson covers practically the same ground as his opponents. His discussion is not abusive, but his repudiation of the charges of " Popery " offer conclusive evidence that he and his antagonists were at agreement on at least one important question of the day.

With the entrance of the controversy into what Cross aptly calls the ecclesiastico-political stage, the debate became more acrimonious. To the attacks of a Livingston, a Chauncy and a Mayhew, the Anglicans could oppose the arguments of a Chandler, a Seabury or an Apthorp. The contributions of Livingston to the *New York Gazette* under the signature of " The American Whig " and of Francis Alison to the *Pennsylvania Journal* under the pseudonym of " The Centinel " emphasized the political aspect of the question. Analogies from British history were not far to seek. The old slogan, " Popery, the Pretender and arbitrary power," was used to point a moral if not to adorn a tale. The presence of a Roman Catholic bishop in the recently acquired territory of Canada gave the moral a significance which was not lost upon the opponents of episcopacy. Rev. Andrew Eliot, pastor of the New North Congregational Church in Boston, in a series of letters to Thomas Hollis, professed to see in this appointment the beginning of Roman Catholic domination of the British colonies, with the restoration of "Popery" in Ireland, and eventually in England.[11] Why not

---

[10] *Supra*, p. 151.

[11] " Letters from Andrew Eliot to Thomas Hollis," Mass. H. S. *Coll.*, 4 ser., vol. iv, pp. 400-461. *Cf.* Supplement to Charles Chauncy's *Letter to a Friend* (Boston, 1767). Referring to the appointment of Bishop

send candidates for orders to Canada, he suggested sarcastically. If ordination " comes from the sacred hands of a bishop," he continues, " though he is the professed offspring of the whore of Babylon, the mother of harlots, it is well enough." [12]

Provost Smith of Philadelphia entered the lists, under the pen name of " The Anatomist," against the vice-provost, " The Centinel ". From across the water came to Dr. Mayhew's *Observations,* an anonymous *Answer* of which, it was learned later, Thomas Secker,[13] archbishop of Canterbury, was the author. So the controversy continued. Merely to mention the principal names in the debate is to list writers who on other occasions had decried Rome with all her works and pomps.[14]   To their discussions were added those of scores of other writers, many of them anonymous, who in newspaper, magazine and pamphlet, helped to swell the chorus of approval or denunciation. The poetasters popularized the issue. A stanza from a ballad entitled " The Proselyte " may serve to illustrate this type of contribution in its bearing on this study. The ballad recounts the efforts

Briand, the writer says: " ... there is great reason to believe that whole ship-loads of Popish Priests and Jesuits have gone to Canada accordingly; from whence they will be able most commodiously to scatter and promote their base subversive principles throughout all North-America. I pray God the event of that *allowance* may not prove deeply *tragical*."

[12] *Ibid.,* pp. 410-11, 435, 448-89. See also, " Correspondence of Andrew Eliot, Jonathan Mayhew and Thomas Hollis, 1761-1776," Bancroft Trans., N. Y. P. L. For Chauncy's suggestion regarding the Moravian and Roman Catholic bishops, see A. L. Cross, *op. cit.,* pp. 180, 183-84. For Dr. Johnson's pained reaction to the proposal, see H. and C. Schneider, *Samuel Johnson,* vol. i, p. 411; Hawks and Perry, *Doc. Hist.,* vol. ii, p. 110; A. C. H. *Researches,* o. s., vol. vi (1889), p. 93.

[13] For the archbishop's attitude towards the Church of Rome, see *Five Sermons against Popery* (Windsor, Vt., 1827). Also in vol. vi of *Sermons* (7 vols., London, 1790, vols. i-iv; 1771, vols. v-vii).

[14] The principal contributions of the major writers are listed in A. L. Cross, *op. cit.,* pp. 351-357.

of the vestry " To build up the Church and to pull down the meeting." The last stanza reads:

> But if he from Rome greater Profit had hop'd,
> He who now is be-bishop'd, would have been be-poped,
> And annually run, to avoid being Poor,
> To the arms of the Church, or Babylon's Whore.[15]

The question of an Anglican bishop was not without its effect upon the Catholic population of the colonies. They, like the Anglicans, were without a bishop. Like them, too, Catholics felt keenly the absence of an ordinary and the consequent deprivation of the sacrament of confirmation. Candidates for the priesthood, like those for Anglican orders, were obliged to go to Europe for ordination. More than one petition had been sent to Rome through the vicar-apostolic at London, begging, not for a bishop—for Catholics realized how inopportune such an appointment would be— but for a vicar-apostolic with the powers of a bishop, though without the title and insignia. The result was that Bishop Briand, whose residence at Quebec was such a thorn in the side of Protestant America, was directed by the Holy See to proceed southward and administer confirmation in the English colonies. Bishop Briand doubted the feasibility of the project, but managed through Father Well to get in touch with the Jesuits of Maryland and Pennsylvania to see if the work might be undertaken with some chance of success.

Father Farmer's reply, far from being reassuring, expressed the fear that the advent of the Canadian bishop in the South might result in depriving Catholics of the few privileges they were then enjoying. These privileges, he remarked, were founded upon no legal right, but rested merely on the sufferance of the government and might be

[15] *Boston Gazette*, May 9, 1768.

revoked at any time. As an instance of the bitter feeling towards Catholics even in tolerant Pennsylvania, Father Farmer related an incident which had recently occurred in that colony. Father Diderick, in a conversation with a non-Catholic layman, had used harsh and insulting language. As a result he nearly lost his life from a musket which was twice discharged during the night into his dwelling and chapel. He was obliged to return to Maryland. Father Farmer then called his confrère's attention to the expressions of hatred which had been evoked by the appointment of Bishop Briand to Quebec and to the strong opposition to an Anglican bishop. Needless to say, the Canadian bishop remained at home.[16]

His residence in Quebec, however, continued to be a cause of grievance to disaffected Massachusetts whose Committees of Correspondence were not likely to overlook the unifying force of a common hatred. Boston's Committee in particular had an arch-agitator—Samuel Adams—who knew well how to make the most of the ingrained prejudices of his countrymen. The Committee, directed by the town meeting to report on the " Rights of the Colonists and of this Prov-

---

[16] Auguste Gosselin, *L'Église du Canada après la Conquête* (Quebec, 1916-17, 2 vols.), vol. i, p. 324; vol. ii, p. 10. Referring to Father Farmer's reply, the author writes : " La reponse fut des moins rassurantes ; la religion catholique n'était que tolerée au Maryland et en Pennsylvania ; et encore avec quelles restrictions !

L'arrivée ici d'un évêque, disait le Père Farmer, occassionera de grands troubles, et mettre en danger les privileges, si petite qu'ils soient, dont nous jouissons, sourtout au Maryland, ou l'exercise, même privé, de la religion n'est fondé sur aucun droit." Et il adjoutait, pour mettre encore en relief l'esprit vraiment diabolique des sectaires :

On n'a pas d'idee de la haine que portent les Americains non-catholiques au nom seul d'évêque. Ils ont été indignés de ce que l'on en a accordé un aux Canadiens, et ils ont mis des obstacles invincibles a l'envoie en Amerique d'un évêque anglican." *Archives de l'Eveque de Quebec.* Reponse du P. Farmer (Philadelphie, 22 avril, 1773, à la lettre du P. Well, datée du 15 fev., et recue à Philadelphie le 17 avril.)

ince in particular," did so November 20, 1772.   Among the natural rights enumerated in the report was liberty " to worship according to the dictates of one's own conscience." In practice this liberty was to be restricted by the Lockian limitation and denied to all whose doctrines were subversive of society.   The report continues:

The Roman Catholicks are excluded by Reason of such Doctrines as these, " that Princes excommunicated may be deposed, and those they call Hereticks may be destroyed without Mercy "; besides their recognizing the Pope in so absolute a manner, in Subversion of Government by introducing as far as possible into the States, under whose Protection they enjoy Life, Liberty and Property, that Solecism in Politicks *Imperium in Imperio,* leading directly to the worst Anarchy & Confusion, with Discord War and Bloodshed.

The exclusion of Catholics was reiterated in the second part of the report which discussed the rights of the colonists as Christians.   The British Toleration Act was cited as a precedent.[17]

Copies of this report were sent to the various towns throughout the province with an invitation to communicate their sentiments to the Boston committee.   The response was immediate, sympathetic and flattering, for in imitation of Boston nearly every town and hamlet drew up its own declaration of rights.   The Marlborough resolutions declared that when a prince governs tyrannically and uses " arbitrary power to introduce Popery," his subjects have a right to rebel.   The seventh resolve enumerates among the objectionable acts of Parliament, duties, salaries for judges, quartering troops, and " the Tolerating of a Romish Priest & Appointing Papists to high places of Trust in the British

[17] *Boston Committee of Correspondence, General Corr.,* Nov. 16-20, 1772.

Dominions." [18]   Worcester made the same complaint, but added to her list of grievances, " courts of Inquisition appointed, as arbitrary, and terrable as those under the Popes Jurisdiction." [19]   Tewkesbury thought it would be " grat Folley and Stupidity " as well as " vile Ingratitude to God " to give up the rights bestowed by His bounty; " for which Ingratitude and Contempt " God might deliver them up to the " Chains of Popery and Slavery, there to Condole and bewail though too late " the results of their apathy.[20]   These communications are all dated 1773, the year in which the correspondence between Father Farmer and the ecclesiastical authorities in Canada took place.   Although the middle and southern provinces had no grievances against the mother country comparable to those of Massachusetts, there was a community of sentiment on the Catholic question which would go far to unite sections otherwise divergent.   When the Quebec Act was passed the following year, agitators were quick to see in its religious clauses a possible bond of unity.

The toleration by the British government of a Roman Catholic bishop in the province of Quebec was the logical result of the fulfillment of the Articles of Capitulation drawn up after the surrender, in 1759, of Quebec and Montreal and of the Treaty of Paris of 1763.[21]   Both the articles and the treaty guaranteed to the king's " new subjects " the free exercise of their religion, with this difference, however, that Article IV of the treaty contained a qualifying clause which implied that in the practice of their religion the French

[18] *Bos. Com. Corr., Massachusetts Towns*, Marlborough, 1773.

[19] *Ibid.*, Worcester, July 18, 1773.

[20] *Bos. Com. Corr., Mass. Towns*, Tewkesbury, Feb., 1773.

[21] A. Shortt and A. G. Doughty, *Canadian Archives.   Documents Relating to the Constitutional History of Canada* (2 vols., Ottawa, 1918), vol. i, pp. 3, 5-18, 30-32, 100, 115-116.   W. M. P. Kennedy, *Statutes, Treaties, and Documents of the Canadian Constitution* (2nd ed., New York, 1930), pp. 23-31, 31-35.

would by no means be so " free " as they had been led to expect. The French plenipotentiaries had demurred at the restrictive clause, " so far as the Laws of Great Britain permit; " they had yielded only when assured that it was not within the power of the British sovereign to tolerate the Roman Catholic religion save under such limitations as were imposed by law. A bare toleration, therefore, was the most that could be expected. The continuation of the " Popish Hierarchy " was not to be thought of, since that was absolutely prohibited in any of the British dominions.[22]

These points were emphasized in a letter of the Earl of Egremont to Governor Murray, August 13, 1763. It was the intention of the government to establish eventually the Church of England both in principle and in practice. Murray was instructed to keep a watchful eye on the French clergy, and to do his utmost to further the conversion of the French into his Majesty's " good Protestant subjects." In the Governor's commission various agencies conducive to this desirable change were suggested, such as the establishment of schools whose masters were to be licensed by the Bishop of London or by Murray himself, and the multiplication of chapels served by the ministers of the Church of England. Furthermore, the transformation was to be accelerated by the introduction of large numbers of English Protestants whose immigration was to be fostered by the abolition of the *Coutume de Paris* and by the substitution of British civil and criminal law.[23] There were, of course, economic and

[22] For a discussion of the application of the penal laws to the colonies, whether occupied or conquered, see *supra*, pp. 55-56. The opinion of the Attorney-General and the Solicitor-General that the penal laws did not apply to Roman Catholics in the colonies was not delivered until June 1, 1765. See Shortt-Doughty, vol. i, p. 236. *Cf.* W. R. Riddell, " Status of Roman Catholicism in Canada," *Cath. Hist. Rev.*, n. s., vol. viii (Oct., 1928), pp. 305-328.

[23] Shortt-Doughty, vol. i, pp. 163, 169, 191-93. W. M. P. Kennedy, *op. cit.*, pp. 35, 47-48. R. Coupland, *The Quebec Act* (Oxford, 1925), pp. 21-22.

political reasons for these changes. The ecclesiastical viewpoint is stressed in order to make clear that the British government in 1763 had not the slightest intention of establishing " Popery " in its recently acquired dominions.

The Proclamation of 1763, which promised to solve so many
problems, did not work out so well in practice.[24] Under its
rule difficulties seemed to multiply rather than to lessen, lines
of cleavage to widen and deepen rather than to merge and
disappear. The assumption that the British penal laws
applied to the king's " new subjects " resulted in their exclusion from all participation in the government. Toleration of their religion without provision for ordination to
the priesthood meant the virtual extinction of the Catholic
Church in Canada. Fortunately the French had a sympathetic governor who persistently represented their grievances
to the home government. The report of the attorney-general that the Canadians were not subject to the disabilities
of English Catholics marked the beginning of a new policy,
slow though it was in getting into operation.[25] To avoid
an outcry in England against the appointment of a " Popish
bishop," Rev. Oliver Briand was told he might proceed
quietly to France for consecration. His official title was
" superintendent of the clergy "; his episcopal duties were
to be performed without the insignia of his office, and with
as little pomp and circumstance as possible.[26]

The liberal policy noted above was an earnest of a sincere
desire of the British government to conciliate the French
Canadians. Once inaugurated, it was developed, slowly and

[24] For the genesis of the Proclamation of 1763, see C. W. Alvord,
The Mississippi Valley in British Politics (2 vols., Cleveland, 1917),
vol. i, pp. 106-09, 253-264.

[25] Shortt-Doughty, vol. i, p. 236. W. R. Riddell, "Status of Roman
Catholicism in Canada," pp. 305-328. W. M. P. Kennedy, *op. cit.*, p. 40
et seq.

[26] A. Gosselin, *L'Église du Canada*, vol. i, pp. 148-56.

haltingly enough, but consistently, nevertheless, until it reached its fruition in the Quebec Act. The main outlines of the bill had been worked out in 1773 Professor Alvord points out, that is, before the coercive measures against Boston were considered. Unfortunately, its final passage through Parliament coincided with the adoption of the so-called "Intolerable Acts"; hence it has shared with them the odium of those punitive measures and was so regarded by Massachusetts and her sympathizers.[27] The opposition it aroused was intense and widespread. Here and there a voice was heard in its favor, but it was well-nigh drowned in the chorus of denunciation expressed in newspaper and in pamphlet, in private correspondence and in public proclamation, in resolutions of town, provincial or quasi-national assemblies.[28]

[27] C. W. Alvord, *op. cit.*, vol. ii, pp. 243-45. Cf. R. Coupland, *The American Revolution and the British Empire* (London, 1928), pp. 240-41. C. H. Van Tyne, *Causes of the War of Independence*, pp. 401-405. G. M. Wrong, *Canada and the American Revolution* (New York, 1935), pp. 240-260.

[28] For contemporary denunciations of the Act, see, P. Force, *American Archives* (Washington, 1737), 4 ser., vol. i, pp. 180, 184, 194, 202-06, 212, 215, 216, 218, 498-99, 513, 708-09, 777, 801, 816, 853-54, 912, 920-21, 927, 930, 959, 1104, 1146-47, 1310, 1315, 1836; vol. iii, p. 637; vol. v, pp. 411-12, 545-46, 1275; 5 ser., vol. i, pp. 777, 902, 1315; vol. ii, pp. 98, 546, 1048.

For debates in the House of Commons, together with addresses and petitions, both British and American: J. Wright, ed., *Cavendish's Debates of the House of Commons in the year 1774 on the bill for making more effectual provision for the government of the Province of Quebec* (London, 1839). Debates in House of Lords, *Parliamentary History*, vol. xvii. P. Force, *op. cit.*, 4 ser., vol. i, pp. 196-216. W. M. P. Kennedy, *op. cit.*, pp. 94-136.

For Catholic viewpoint, Amer. Cath. Hist. *Researches*, vol. vi, p. 150; vol. viii, p. 129; vol. xiv, p. 65.

The best collection of pamphlets is in the William Clements Library, Ann Arbor, Mich. Newberry Library, Chicago, has a collection of 574 tracts on the American Revolution, many of which discuss the Quebec Act.

An analysis of colonial opposition to the Quebec Act as indicated by various public and private utterances, reveals a threefold objection—political, economic and religious. First of all, the Act introduced into Canada an arbitrary form of government. Lord Mansfield's famous decision that the laws of a conquered country continue in force until altered by the conqueror, that is to say, by an act of Parliament, if the territory in question be a British conquest, was but the assertion in other words that French law was still in force in Canada. The Quebec Act provided for the substitution of English criminal law for the harsher French code. The only other change was indicated by Edmund Burke when he remarked pithily of the Canadians, " They will have George the Third instead of Louis the Sixteenth."

Here to the colonial mind was the actual consummation of the plot to foist upon British Protestants that trinity of evils, " Popery, France and arbitrary power," to escape which their forebears had fought and died. For included in the restoration of the French feudal tenure were the former rights and privileges of the Church of Rome. Under the Proclamation government, that Church had been merely tolerated; the payment of tithes, during the old regime the main support of the clergy, had been purely optional, and, one may gather from the opposition to the new arrangement, often evaded. Under the Quebec Act, tithes were once more legalized; that is, it was lawful for the Church to enforce their collection, but only from her own adherents. Protestants were expressly exempt from payment of tithes and ample provision was made for the support of the Church of England. This the opponents of the Act chose to ignore. The legalization of tithes in their opinion gave to the Church of Rome the status of an Establishment.

But that was not all. Not only was French despotism established in British territory to the exclusion of English civil law, trial by jury, habeas corpus, and other rights; not only was the Church of Rome reinstated in all her old rights and privileges; the boundaries of Quebec were extended to the Mississippi and the Ohio. In that territory, the Indian traders had long been doing a lucrative business. The seaboard colonies had regarded it as the theater of their future expansion. Provinces with land claims in the west and northwest had plans of their own regarding the development or disposal of their domains. Land companies had been formed to exploit the region and at the same time to save it from France and Rome. And here was the British Parliament not only checking all these legitimate projects, but doing for France and Rome what they had long planned to do for themselves![29]   And what was to prevent George III and his tools from doing in the British provinces what they had done in Canada? Was it not all part of one grand scheme to force the colonies to their knees? Thus they reasoned—or at least thus they talked.[30] As in the religious phase of the question, the Americans chose to ignore the provision for excepting from the feudal land tenure those lands already held in free and common socage. Nor did they advert to the proviso that the boundaries of the annexed portions should not effect the boundaries of any other colony.

---

[29] For text of the Quebec Act, see Shortt-Doughty, vol. i, p. 570 *et seq.* W. M. P. Kennedy, *op. cit.*, pp. 137-140. *Cf.* C. H. Van Tyne, *op. cit.*, p. 404. J. Winsor, "Virginia and the Quebec Bill," *Amer. Hist. Rev.*, vol. i (1895-96), p. 436 *et seq.*

[30] A. L. Burt in *Cambridge History of the British Empire*, vol. vi, p. 167 *et seq.* J. H. Stark, *Loyalists of Massachusetts* (Boston, 1907), pp. 29-32. J. Codman, *Arnold's Expedition to Quebec* (New York, 1901), pp. 6-8. D. McArthur, in *Camb. Hist. Brit. Emp.*, vol. vi, pp. 175-199. D. Ramsay, *History of the American Revolution* (2 vols., Philadelphia, 1789), vol. i, pp. 110-111. C. W. Alvord, *op. cit.*, vol. ii, pp. 243-45. W. Lecky, *England*, vol. iii, pp. 399-401. R. Coupland, *Amer. Rev.*, pp. 240-41; *Quebec Act*, pp. 118-121.

The keynote of colonial denunciation was sounded in the famous Suffolk Resolves passed only a few days after the Quebec Act went into force. Every town in the county is said to have been represented at the first session of the convention held at Dedham, September 5, 1774. Before adjourning to meet again at Milton on the ninth, the convention appointed a committee to carry out its various resolutions. The chairman of this committee was Joseph Warren, to whom is credited the drafting of the document known as the Suffolk Resolves.[31] Reported at the Milton meeting on the ninth, the Resolves were debated paragraph by paragraph and " unanimously adopted." Article 10 of these resolutions reads:

10. That the late act of Parliament for establishing the Roman Catholic Religion and the French laws in that extensive country now called Canada, is dangerous in an extreme degree to the Protestant religion and to the civil rights and liberties of all Americans; and, therefore, as men and Protestant Christians, we are indispensably obliged to take all proper measures for our security.[32]

Copies of the Resolves were sent to the Massachusetts press. The response was even more sympathetic and flattering than in 1772. The Suffolk committee was deluged with votes of thanks and commendation to which were added resolutions often expressive of local fears aroused by the peculiar situation of the town in question. Thus the towns of Cumberland County in what is now Maine visualized the Quebec Act as a prelude to a possible Indian raid. Writes their committee:

[31] R. Frothingham, *Life and Times of Joseph Warren* (Boston, 1865), pp. 360-61.

[32] *Journals of the Continental Congress*, ed. by W. C. Ford and others (Washington, 1904), vol. i, pp. 33-36. Cited hereafter as *Journals*.

As the very extraordinary and alarming Act for establishing the Roman Catholick religion and French laws in Canada, may introduce French and Indians into our frontier towns . . .

they recommend towns and individuals to store up military supplies and see to the proper training of the militia. In like manner, Stamford, Greenwich and Mansfield in Connecticut denounced the Act as threatening them with a " total loss of liberty and the introduction of *popery, that grand fountain of arbitrary power.*" [33]

Determined that the Resolves should get the widest possible publicity beyond the confines of New England, the Suffolk convention sent Paul Revere with a copy to the Massachusetts delegates of the Continental Congress. The gentlemen from the north lost no time in laying the paper before Congress, which not only approved of it by special resolution, but sent it to the press with directions that it be copied by the papers of the other provinces.[34] The news sheets of the middle and southern colonies promptly obeyed the behest and published in addition their own town and county resolves which again faithfully reflected the form and content of their Suffolk model. New York's protest is typical. The address to Lieutenant-Governor Colden expresses sympathy with the resistance of Massachusetts and

[33] Resolutions of (1) Cumberland County and Stamford, P. Force, *Amer. Arch.*, 4 ser., vol. i, pp. 800, 827. Rivington's *Gazette*, Oct. 31, 1774, no. 78. A. C. H. *Researches*, n. s., vols. vii-viii (1911-12), p. 388. (2) Greenwich, *History of Fairfield County, Conn.*, D. H. Hurd, ed. (Philadelphia, 1888), p. 371; S. P. Mead, *Ye Historie of ye Town of Greenwich* (New York, 1911), pp. 115-116. (3) Mansfield, J. R. Cole, *History of Tolland County, Conn.* (New York, 1888). The papers of the *Bos. Com. Corr.* contain the resolves of Middleborough and other Massachusetts towns. See also *Boston Gazette* for Oct. 3, 10, Nov. 14, 28, 1774; *Newport Mercury*, Aug. 30, 1774.

[34] For an account of the reception of the Suffolk Resolves by the Continental Congress and the return of Paul Revere, see *Boston Gazette,* Sept. 26, 1774. *Cf.* R. Frothingham, *Life of Joseph Warren*, pp. 366-67.

cites among those acts which it regards as dangerous to the "whole empire" that which extends the "bounds of Quebec" and establishes therein "Popery" and "arbitrary government." Then referring to the western problem,

Nor can we forbear mentioning the jealousies which have been excited in the colonies by the extension of the limits of the province of Quebec, in which the Roman Catholic religion has received such ample supports.[35]

New York was not content with its addresses to Massachusetts [36] and to the Lieutenant-Governor. His Majesty the King, the Anglican bishops, and the mayor and magistrates of London were all memorialized.[37] There are some historians who see in the Quebec Act one of the chief causes of the Revolution, and in the Suffolk Resolves the origin of the anti-Catholic phrases which almost invariably appear in the proclamations of the associations, conventions and congresses which broke out like a rash over the land after the historic meetings at Dedham and Milton.[38]

[35] P. Force, *op. cit.*, 4 ser., vol. i, pp. 1310-11, 1313-20. *Doc. Hist. N. Y.*, vol. vii, p. 584. *Parliamentary Register* (March 25, 1775), pp. 473-78. J. Almon, *The Remembrancer or impartial repository of public events, 1775-84* (17 vols.), vol. i, p. 215.

[36] See *Bos. Com. Corr., Other Colonies*, Banc. Trans., N. Y. P. L., for letters from New York and other provinces.

[37] Rivington's *Gazette*, April 20, May 18, 1775, nos. 105, 109. The New York addresses were given considerable publicity in the colonial press. See *Pennsylvania Gazette*, May 3, 1775; *Pennsylvania Packet*, May 1, 27, 1775; *Pennsylvania Journal*, May 24, 1775; *Maryland Gazette*, May 9, 1775.

[38] P. Guilday, *Carroll*, vol. i, p. 76. C. Martin, *Empire and Commonwealth* (Oxford Univ. Press, 1929), p. 138. C. H. Van Tyne, *op. cit.*, pp. 401, 405. D. McArthur, "Brit. N. A. and the Amer. Rev.," *Camb. Hist. Brit. Emp.*, vol. vi, p. 74. J. H. Stark, *Loyalists of Massachusetts*, pp. 29-30. A. L. Burt, "Problem of Government," *Camb. Hist. Brit. Emp.*, vol. vi, p. 167, *et seq.* For lists of historians who regard the Act as wise or unwise, see R. Coupland, *Amer. Rev. and Brit. Emp.*, pp. 317-322.

But approval and imitation of the work of the Suffolk assembly was not confined to town and county meetings, however important locally some of these may have been. Endorsement by the Continental Congress gave the Massachusetts precedent an almost national significance; and while it is true that there was no specific reference to number ten of the Resolves, such was not the case with subsequent Congressional utterances. On the contrary, the Continental Congress pointedly denounced the Quebec Act in a series of state papers, the language of which grew less and less restrained, until it descended to positive invective in the *Address to the People of Great Britain*. The *Address to the Inhabitants of Quebec* terminated the series in a complete *volte face*.[39]

That the First Continental Congress was a body of unusually able statesmen is generally conceded by historians, whether they be Americans evaluating their own countrymen, or writers from other lands with a supposedly more objective viewpoint. When the call came to send representatives to a convention which would discuss their common grievances, the provincial assemblies sent their ablest representatives. Forty of the fifty-six delegates, writes Schlesinger,

had taken an active part in the popular house of the provincial legislature; six of them had served in the Stamp Act Congress; practically all of them were members of committees of correspondence; and they must have felt a responsibility almost personal for the critical situation in which America found herself.[40]

[39] *Journals*, vol. i, pp. 33-36, 72, 76, 77-78, 88, 90-101, 105-113, 117. P. Force, *Amer. Arch.*, 4 ser., vol. i, pp. 893-938. Includes proceedings of Congress.

[40] A. M. Schlesinger, *Col. Merchant and the Rev.*, pp. 407-08. *Cf.* Charles Carroll of Carrollton, letter to his father, Sept. 12, 1774, *Carroll Papers, October, 1773–December, 1774*, box 6, Md. H. S. Joseph Reed, *Correspondence, 1764-1774*. Letter to Lord Dartmouth, Sept. 25, 1774, Banc. Trans., N. Y. P. L.

The official utterances of such a body, the repeated expression of their views, whether direct or indirect, on any question of common concern, would constitute a valuable cross-section of American public opinion at that period.

As a political and extra-legal body called in an emergency to consider the critical condition of the country, it was no part of the business of the Continental Congress to pronounce directly upon the orthodoxy or the heterodoxy of any particular creed, save in so far as the tenets of such a creed might affect practically the political fortunes of the colonies. Hence it is that we find most of its references to Catholicism incorporated in documents relating to the Quebec Act. Coming as it did in the company of the " Intolerable Acts " —though actually not concerned with them in any way—it not only shared their unpopularity, but was regarded by not a few as their fitting climax.

Having made its bow on the Congressional stage on September 17, in company with the Suffolk Resolves, the obnoxious Act appears again on October 5 in the *Address to the King,* who is assured that commerce with the colonies will be resumed when the acts enumerated—the Quebec Act among them—have been repealed. The *Declaration of Rights and Grievances,* adopted October 14, also mentions the act as part of the " systems formed to enslave America." On October 20, Congress approved the Continental Association, in Schlesinger's opinion the " most remarkable document put forth " by that body.[41] Its demands for redress of grievances are summed up under three heads, in the third of which is included the Quebec Act. While these repeated allusions leave no doubt as to the attitude of Congress towards a piece of legislation which, as regards its religious clauses at least, has been acknowledged as wise and liberal, their aspersions are mild compared with those in the

[41] A. M. Schlesinger, *Col. Merchant,* p. 423.

Address to the People of Great Britain, October 21, 1774.
The extension of the dominion of Canada, this document
asserts, has been affected in order to develop a territory con-
tiguous to the colonies, but so alien in civil government and
religious beliefs as to make it peculiarly adaptable, " in the
hands of power, to reduce the ancient, free Protestant colonies to . . . slavery . . . Nor can we suppress our aston-
ishment," the *Address* continues,

> that a British parliament should ever consent to establish in
> that country a religion that has deluged your island with blood,
> and dispersed impiety, bigotry, persecution, murder and rebellion
> through every part of the world.[42]

This effort of the Continental Congress to enlist the sympathies of their co-religionists across the water was paralleled
on the same day by a similar appeal to the racial and religious
prejudices of their fellow-countrymen.   The *Address to the
Inhabitants of the Colonies* but repeats the arguments already
noted.

As the hope of accomodation with Great Britain grew
fainter, Congress resolved to make another appeal to the
King.   What the answer might be only the future would
disclose.   The outlook was none too bright.   Not to make
what preparations they could would be folly.   If their rights
as Englishmen could be restored only by armed resistance,
the aid of the other British plantations would mean much.
Why wait until the British government mobilized their
neighbors to the north?   Why not forestall the action of
Parliament and convert the Catholic menace into an aid for
Protestant America?   In all history we have no more iron-
ical contrast than that between the documents signed by the
Continental Congress on October 21, quoted above, and the
Address to the Inhabitants of Quebec, signed, together with

[42] *Supra*, note 39.

the *Petition to the King,* on October 26. The latter lacked, indeed, the emotional appeal of the address to the British public five days before, but the grounds for grievance are no less clearly if less sensationally set forth. While this petition was being engrossed the *Address to the Inhabitants of Quebec* was read in its final form.

The document recalls the joy of the British Americans at the results of the last war, their hope that their " brave enemies would become their hearty friends," and their prayer that God would bless them with the " inestimable advantages of a free English constitution." Unfortunately that privilege was theirs only for a time. Venal ministers have deprived the Canadians of their treaty rights. " And what," the *Address* continues,

is offered you by the late act of Parliament in their place? Liberty of conscience in your religion? No. God gave it to you. . . . If laws, divine and human, could secure it against the despotic caprice of wicked men, it was secured before. . . . We are all too well acquainted with the liberality of sentiment distinguishing your nation, to imagine, that difference of religion will prejudice you against a hearty amity with us. You know, that the transcendant nature of freedom elevates those, who unite in her cause, above all such low-minded infirmities. The Swiss cantons furnish a memorable proof of this truth. Their union is composed of Roman Catholic and Protestant States, living in the utmost concord and peace with one another, and thereby enabled, ever since they bravely vindicated their freedom, to defy and defeat every tyrant that has invaded them.

This fulsome passage is followed by an invitation to send delegates from Canada to the Continental Congress the following May. The *Address* closes with a prayer that God may inspire them to unite their fortunes with those of their " sincere and affectionate fellow-subjects." The reading completed, the *Address* was approved, ordered to be signed by the president, to be printed, translated and distributed. And almost in the same breath was signed the second *Petition to the King* with the old complaint about establishing " the Roman Catholic religion." [43]

Were the signers as completely oblivious of the anomaly as the silence of the *Journals* might imply? Were there no dissenting voices? Did the members of the Continental Congress really fear that the toleration clauses of the Quebec Act were a " menace to the Protestant religion " and to the " civil and religious liberties " of all America? Or did they accept paragraph ten of the Suffolk Resolves because it formed part of a document which gave expression to their political and economic grievances? Was the repeated reference to Roman Catholicism and French laws, with its sensational amplification in the *Address to the People of Great Britain,* merely a clever piece of propaganda? Did the milder tone of the *Memorial to the Inhabitants of Quebec* voice the real sentiments of Congress, or was it adopted through motives of political expediency? By way of answer to these questions the *Journals* have but little to offer; they must be supplemented by the private minutes, the correspondence, and other papers of those who took part in the proceedings.

In the study of these documents, one must guard against attaching too much significance to a so-called unanimous vote. Whatever its representation in the Continental Congress each colony had but one vote.[44] " Entered unanimously " might be interpreted therefore as a majority vote. There is evidence that votes entered as " unanimous " were protested and that the request to have the protest recorded

[43] *Supra*, note 39. See also P. Guilday, *Carroll*, vol. i, p. 80, where the *Petition to the King*, the *Address to the People of Great Britain*, and *To the Inhabitants of Quebec* are printed in parallel columns and discussed.

[44] *Journals*, vol. i, p. 25.

was not granted.[45]   On the other hand, the committees which
drafted the manifestoes of Congress did not have things all
their own way.   Each document was subjected to a searching analysis and debated paragraph by paragraph.   Its final
form therefore represented the matured judgment of the
majority if not of all of the members present.

In the preliminary discussions of the fundamental principles upon which Congress proposed to base the series of state
papers which it was about to issue, the question as to whether
the Quebec Act should be one of the grievances was long
and earnestly debated.   James Duane of New York thought
the Act " dangerous from the religion and arbitrary constitution " which it established.   He consequently considered
it " good policy to complain of it as meeting the popular
clamour in England."   But while he " readily agreed to
mention it in the petition to the king," he was unwilling to
jeopardize New York's commerce by including the Act in
all of the Congressional proclamations.[46]   Richard Henry
Lee of Virginia thought the Act their " worst grievance,"
and would therefore have it included.   There was no safety
for Protestants when Catholics were in power, he argued.
To what end then was their religion confirmed in the extended province of Quebec, unless it was to keep the old
colonies in awe? [47]   John Jay, author of the *Address to the
People of Great Britain,* was of course for inclusion, as was

[45] *Ibid.,* vol. i, pp. 39-40, 138-157. James Duane, " Minutes of the Pro-
ceedings of the Continental Congress, 1774." Originals in New York
Historical Society, *Duane Papers,* Box 3. Transcripts in Banc. Coll.,
N. Y. P. L., *American Papers,* vol. ii, p. 99 *et seq.* Also printed in E. C.
Burnett, *Letters of Members of the Continental Congress* (vols. i-vii,
Wash., 1921-34), vol. i, pp. 77-79, no. 105. C. Stillé, *Life and Times of
John Dickinson* (2 vols., Phila., 1891-95), vol. i, pp. 138-39.

[46] *Duane Papers,* Box 3.

[47] *Letters of Richard Henry Lee,* ed. by J. C. Ballagh (2 vols., New
York, 1911-14), vol. i, p. 160.

also Thomas McKean, who thought that the Protestants of Quebec would join the colonies in their opposition. So the debate continued until October 17 when the vote was taken with apparently only one dissenting voice.[48]

Duane's memoranda are confirmed by a letter of John Sullivan, New Hampshire delegate to the Congress and later one of the generals of the northern army. " We have selected those Acts which we are determined to have a Repeal of," he wrote from Philadelphia. The " Canada Bill ", in his opinion, was the " most dangerous to American Liberties among the whole train." His vivid imagination conjures up a picture of Philadelphia as a " Refuge for Roman Catholicks," who aided by the Canadians and the Indians on the frontier and a " ministerial Fleet & the Army " from the sea, would force reluctant Protestants to embrace their religion. Were the Papists to have such power, he was " certain that no God may as well exist in the universe." [49]

Turning now from Congressional pronouncements to individual opinion of the Quebec Act, our inquiry might well begin with Samuel Adams, for none knew better than he how to manipulate the half-formed opinions of the " man in the street." An extremist in his political and religious views, he exercised rare skill in the choice of instruments to propagate them. He utilized to the full the advantage of the press. Of his use of religious animosities for political purposes, Van Tyne says,

. . . Samuel Adams and others taking their cue from him, so aroused the latent Puritan bigotry that pre-revolutionary literature is filled with denunciation of the wise act of the British

[48] *Duane Papers*, Box 3.

[49] *Langdon-Elwyn Papers*, Letters, 1774-1790, Banc. Trans., N. Y. P. L., pp. 27-31. *Letters and Papers of Major General John Sullivan* (Concord, 1930), (vol. xiii, N. H. H. S. *Coll.*), vol. i, p. 48. *Letters of Josiah Bartlett, William Whipple and Others* (Philadelphia, 1889), p. 5.

government, recognizing the Roman Catholic religion in the province of Quebec.[50]

His series of letters in the *Boston Gazette* in 1768 have been noted in the foregoing pages.[51] It was on the motion of Adams that the resolutions of the town of Boston were adopted in 1772 and sent out by the Committee of Correspondence.[52] Not content with appeals to his own race, he sought to arouse the fears of the Indian. In an address to the Mohawks, he cried:

. . . Brothers—They have made a law to establish the religion of the Pope in Canada which lies so near you. We much fear some of your children may be induced, instead of worshipping the only true God, to pay *his* dues to images made in their own hands.[53]

To the committees representing the Anglo-American traders at Quebec and Montreal he wrote, February 21, 1775, that all the colonies " from Nova Scotia to Georgia " have regarded the recent Act " not only as an Intolerable Injury to the Subjects of that Province, but as a capital Grievance on all." [54]

Compared with his cousin, John Adams was a liberal among liberals, yet he characterized the Quebec Act together with the " intolerable acts " as " a frightful system, as would have terrified any people, who did not prefer liberty to

---

[50] C. H. Van Tyne, "The Clergy and the American Revolution," *Amer. Hist. Rev.*, vol. xix (1913-1914), pp. 44-64. *Cf. Causes of War of Ind.*, pp. 291-96.

[51] *Supra*, pp. 186-88.

[52] *Supra*, pp. 269-70. B. Adams, *Emancipation of Massachusetts*, p. 516.

[53] W. V. Wells, *Life . . . of Samuel Adams*, vol. ii, p. 283. *Writings of Samuel Adams*, vol. iii, p. 213.

[54] *Boston Com. of Corr., Gen. Corr., 1772-1775. Writings of S. Adams*, vol. iii, pp. 185-87.

life." [55]   To James Bowdoin it was primarily " an Act for encouraging and establishing Popery." [56]   Joseph Warren, who drafted the Suffolk Resolves, wrote to the Committee of Montreal that the recent change in Canada was but " too well calculated to banish every idea of freedom and to familiarize the mind to slavery." [57]   New England's ever haunting fear of the French and Indians found expression in a letter of James Lovell to Josiah Quincy, Jr.   Previous attacks, he wrote, had been attributed to the instigation of French Catholics; but the British ministry appeared to have adopted that rôle.   In proof thereof he exclaimed, " I appeal to the framers of the Quebec Bill." [58]   Joseph Reed, writing from Philadelphia to Lord Dartmouth, September 25, 1774, described the growing opposition:

> The spirit of the people gradually arose, when it might have been expected to decline till the Quebec Bill added fuel to the fire; then all these deliberate measures of petitioning previous to any opposition were laid aside as inadequate to the apprehending danger and mischief, and now the people are ripe for the execution of any plan Congress advises, should it be war itself.[59]

Philip Livingston visualized the Act as an instrument of tyranny especially dangerous in the hands of an unscrupulous king.   " All the bigotry, all the superstition of a

[55] " Novanglus " in *Works*, vol. iv, pp. 42-43, 92-93, 118. For other indications of Adams' attitude towards the Church of Rome, see *Works,* vol. ii, p. 96; vol. iii, pp. 449-50; vol. ix, p. 355; vol. x, pp. 100, 185-88, 219, 229, 408-09.

[56] J. H. Stark, *Loyalists of Massachusetts*, p. 29.

[57] *Bos. Com. of Corr., Gen. Corr., Banc. Trans. Mass. H. S. Coll.,* 4 ser., vol. iv, p. 237, cited in R. Frothingham, *Life of Joseph Warren,* pp. 442-43.

[58] " Letters to Josiah Quincy, Jr.," Mass. H. S. *Proc.*, vol. l, p. 479.

[59] *Correspondence*, Banc. Trans.   Also in A. C. H. *Researches*, n. s. (1911-1912), vols. vii-viii, p. 391.

religion abounding in both beyond any which the world has beheld," he exclaimed, are at the disposal of the royal will.[60]

Young Alexander Hamilton undertook *A Full Vindication of the Measures of Congress.* Written in answer to Samuel Seabury's *Free Thoughts on the Proceedings of Congress* and *The Congress Canvassed* by a Westchester Farmer, the youthful apologist inquires of those who favor the policy of the British government, " Will they venture to justify the unparalleled stride to power by which Popery and arbitrary dominion were established in Canada? " The writer dwells sympathetically on the grievances of Boston and then passes on to Canada where, he says, conditions are " still worse." " Does not your blood run cold," he cries, " to think that an English Parliament should pass an act for the establishment of arbitrary power and Popery in such a country? " In another pamphlet, *Remarks on the Quebec Bill,* he sees in addition to the dangers enumerated in the *Vindication,* the establishment of the Inquisition in Canada, and fears that " priestly tyranny " may " find as propitious a soil in Canada as it ever has in Spain and Portugal." Furthermore, the Quebec Act is likely to hinder Protestant immigration and to encourage that of Catholics who " will be ready at all times to secure the oppressive designs of the administration against the other parts of the empire." [61]

The opinions considered thus far have been those of statesmen actively engaged in the political arena. Public servants in other departments were equally interested in the new legislative experiment in Canada. Even the judicial calm of the Sessions of the Peace felt the reverberations of the

[60] *The Other Side of the Question . . . by a Citizen* (New York, 1774), pp. 23-24. A. C. H. *Researches*, o. s. (1888-89), vols. vi-viii, p. 162.

[61] H. C. Lodge, ed., *Works of Alexander Hamilton* (9 vols., New York, 1885-86), vol. i, pp. 9, 36-38, 173-88.

political storm. In Essex County, New Jersey, Chief Justice Frederick Smyth warned the grand jury not to expose themselves to tyranny at home while guarding against imaginary tyranny abroad. The jury replied that no tyranny was imaginary; that " the scheme to establish French laws and the Popish religion to further the schemes of the British ministry in Canada had something more than a mental existence." [62] In South Carolina Judge Drayton, addressing the grand juries of his circuit, drew a lurid picture of the " tortures " and " flames which are lighted, blown up and fed with blood by the Roman Catholic doctrines," from which, happily, their own " sacred Christian Religion " had been released.[63] Judge Iredell, another famous Carolinian judge, deplored the Quebec Act as likely to increase the authority of a religion " persecuting in its principles, and horrid in its influence on the morals of mankind." [64]

The dissenting clergy, in whose breasts still rankled the bitterness engendered by the proposed establishment of the Anglican episcopate, saw in the Quebec Act a precedent which might be applied to the sea-board colonies. Firm in the belief that the coming of the bishops would spell the ruin of their own prestige, they welcomed the doctrine that " civil and religious liberty are inextricably bound together." The wish was father to the thought, and they preached it in season and out of season.[65]

[62] F. B. Lee, *New Jersey as a Colony and as a State* (2 vols., New York, 1902), vol. ii, p. 51.

[63] P. Force, *Amer. Arch.*, 4 ser., vol. i, p. 959; vol. v, pp. 1025-32. *Parliamentary Register*, vol. i, p. 95. H. Niles, *Principles and Acts of the Revolution in America* (Baltimore, 1822), p. 73. *Pennsylvania Ledger*, Jan. 28, 1775, no. 1.

[64] G. J. McRee, ed., *Life and Correspondence of James Iredell* (2 vols., New York, 1857-58), vol. i, p. 309.

[65] E. Stiles, *Literary Diary*, vol. i, pp. 490-496, 531, 585-87. A. M. Baldwin, *The New England Clergy and the American Revolution*, p. 170. W. H. Lecky, *England*, vol. iii, pp. 399-401.

To Ezra Stiles it seemed almost incredible that " a whole Protestant Parliament should expressly establish Popery over three Quarters of their Empire." To him " Popery " meant " IDOLATRY "—all in capitals, be it noted. One can almost feel his grief as he notes the fact in his *Diary*, and there is an implication of apostasy in his reproachful comment, " in this Act all the Bishops concurred." The sinister influence of this vast Popish Empire may extend, he fears, even to the members of Congress, to such, especially, who may have been tainted with " Popery " in their youth. On August 28, 1774, he writes of " General Charles Leigh " [Lee] :

He is now gone to Congress, talks, writes & prints for American Liberty. His having had a Popish education is a disagreeable Circumstance, especially as the Parliament have now established Idolatry & Popery over two Thirds of Eng. America.

On December 3, he records a conversation with the Quaker, John Pemberton, of whom he inquired whether there was not now more danger that the Quakers would suffer far greater persecution from the Romanists than they had from Protestants.

But there was a still more insidious design hidden in the notorious Act—that of exalting the Church of England at the expense of the Congregational and Presbyterian sects. The *Diary,* July 17, 1775, has a lengthy discussion of a pamphlet entitled *The Englishman's Answer to the Address of the Congress to the People of Great Britain.* The writer argues that the Quebec Act is really a detriment to the Church of Rome and an incentive to apostasy, since converts from that creed to Protestantism are no longer bound to pay tithes. Stiles not only dissents from this theory, but states his own : The Bill was intended to employ the " Romanists to subdue N. Engld Congregationalists a religious pple [people] abhored by Parliament." Both Congregationalists and Presbyterians would thus be forced to go west into the territory recently annexed to Quebec, where they would be caught " in a Net ", would become careless in the practice of their own peculiar tenets, and since they " would not become Romanists ", they would eventually join the Church of England. The Establishment would thus reap a great harvest at the expense of the " standing order." " May God defeat these Insidious Machiavellian hellish Designs against his Chh. in N. Engld! " is the diarist's concluding prayer.[66]

In Philadelphia there was a concerted effort to unite the dissenting clergy of Pennsylvania and through them their brethren of North Carolina. " If we are wrong now," ran the *Address to the Ministers and Presbyterian Congregations in North Carolina,*

our forefathers that fought for liberty at Londonderry and Enniskillen in King James' time, were wrong; nay they were rebels, when they opposed, and set aside their bigotted Prince, and the Stuart family, and set the Brunswick family on the throne of England. . . .

[66] E. Stiles, *Diary,* vol. i, pp. 455, 502-03, 585-87. Stiles' conviction of the malicious intentions of the Anglicans was apparently shared by many whose indignation found outlets less desirable than a diary. Rev. Mr. Cossit, an Anglican clergyman of Haverhill, N. H., had an unpleasant experience which is recorded in the S. P. G. *Journals, 1773-76* (vol. xx, pt. 5, p. 349 *et seq.*) : " The puritan Teachers have raised a great Hubbub about the Quebec Bill, abusing the King and the Church, as Papistical. Three hundred of them came armed with Clubs, headed by the Select men of Haverhill, Newbury & Peirmont (Fairmont?), with a determination to kill Mr. Cossit." Mr. Cossit escaped after signing certain promises. Rev. Wm. Edmiston of Maryland was cited before the Baltimore Committee for having approved publicly of the Quebec Bill. He was obliged to retract the statement and to promise for the future to express no opinions contrary to the decisions of the Continental Congress or of the Provincial Convention. *Journal of the Baltimore Committee,* Jan. 17, 1775, p. 13. L. C., Ms. copy. Cf. *Newport Mercury,* Feb. 13, 1775; *Pa. Journal,* Jan. 25, 1775.

There follows a list of grievances, including the establishment of " Popery in Quebec and the arbitrary Laws of France." Then comes the pertinent question, " Why may they not do the same in Pennsylvania and North Carolina? " [67]

Even the deliberations of an organization so remote from practical politics as the American Philosophical Society seem to have been affected by affairs in Canada, for among the reasons assigned for discontinuing their meetings, was the " Bill for establishing popery and arbitrary power in Quebec." [68]

The private correspondence of the period also reveals widespread dissatisfaction with Parliamentary plans for Canada. Josiah Quincy, Sr., wrote to his son, October 26, 1774,

. . . What! have we Americans spent so much of our Blood and Treasure in aiding Britain to conquer Canada, that Britons and Canadians in Conjunction may now subjugate us? Forbid it, Heaven! [69]

[67] *N. C. Rec.*, vol. x (1775-1776), pp. 86, 222. This appeal was signed by Francis Alison, James Sprout, George Duffield and Robert Davidson. It was given publicity in the newspapers. See *Cape Fear Mercury*, Aug. 25, 1775. As might be expected, the Quebec Act was a popular subject for pulpit denunciation, and that long after it had ceased to be a political issue. See the Election Sermon of Rev. Samuel Langdon (president of Harvard, 1774-1780) at Watertown, May 31, 1774, in J. W. Thornton, *The Pulpit of the American Revolution* (Boston, 1860). William Smith, *An Oration in Memory of General Montgomery, Feb. 19, 1776* (Philadelphia, 1776). J. Lathrop, *A Discourse Preached on March fifth, 1778* (Boston, 1778). Wm. Gordon, *Sermon*, Dec. 15, 1774. David Jones, *Fast Day Sermon* at Tredyffryn, Chester Co., Pa., 1775. John Carmichael, *Sermon to the Company of Captain Ross*, Lancaster, Pa., June 4, 1775.

[68] *Early Proceedings of the American Philosophical Society for the Promotion of Useful Knowledge* (Philadelphia, 1884), p. 87. The meetings apparently were discontinued from March 4 to Dec. 17, 1774.

[69] "Letters to Josiah Quincy, Jr.," Mass. H. S. *Proc.*, vol. 1 (1916-17), p. 481.

He writes in a similar strain to Franklin the following March.[70]   Thomas Wharton, merchant of Philadelphia, considered the act as the " greatest departure from the English constitution " up to that time attempted.   He agreed with Quincy that the concessions granted to the French Canadians were intended to attach them to ministerial policies of coercion.[71]   The same idea is expressed by James Allen of Philadelphia in a letter to Ralph Izard of South Carolina. Allen emphasizes the galvanizing effect of the Canadian policy which " has alarmed the most inattentive, and given us but one mind." [72]

What did the private in the Continental army think about the matter?   Fortunately, we have the memoirs of Private Daniel Barber, a native of Connecticut, who enlisted under Captain Elihu Humphrey in 1775.   Some time after the war Mr. Barber entered the ministry and was in charge of a church in Claremont, New Hampshire.   In 1818 he became a Roman Catholic.   In his *History of My Own Times,* he records his early impressions of the Quebec Act.   " We were all ready to swear," he writes,

that King George by granting the Quebec Bill . . . had thereby become a traitor, had broken his coronation oath, was secretly a Papist, and whose design was to oblige this country to submit itself to the unconstitutional power of the English Monarch, and under him, and by his authority, be given up and destroyed, soul and body, by that frightful image of 7 heads and 10 horns.   The real fear of Popery in New England had its influence; it stimulated many timorous people to send their sons to join the military

[70] Mass. H. S. *Proc.,* vol. vii (1863-64), p. 119.

[71] " Selections from the Letter-Books of Thomas Wharton of Philadelphia, 1773-1783," *Pa. Mag. Hist. Biog.,* vol. xxxiii (1909), pp. 319, 342 *et seq.,* 441-42.   *Cf. ibid.,* vol. xxxiv, p. 41.

[72] *Correspondence of Mr. Ralph Izard of South Carolina, 1774-1804,* ed. by Anne Izard Deas (New York, 1844), vol. i, p. 28.

ranks . . . The Common word then was " No King, No
Popery." [73]

This testimony is confirmed by a multiplicity of contemporary diaries, journals and letters. To it may be added an
abundance of material from one of the most powerful organs
for the " manufacture " of public opinion—the press. In
the colonial newspapers may be traced the rising tide of resentment from the first colorless notices of the passage of the
Act to the publication of British comment—mostly hostile—
followed by American reaction which, in the hands of skillful
leaders, rapidly crystallized into a hardened opposition which
no reasoning could move. The *Newport Mercury* is an
example in point. Its issue of July 18, 1774, published an
extract of the Act without comment. This was followed,
August 27, by an account of the debates in the House of
Commons. Again no comment. The next issue, August
29, under notes from London, stated that the recent Act " is
the only statute which has been passed these two hundred
years to establish Popery and arbitrary power in the British
dominions." It is " a well-concerted scheme," according to
a London correspondent in another note,

to give a check to the rest of our colonies. . . . A difference in
religion, laws, and dependency will keep up a strong animosity;
and there is no doubt but every encouragement that can possibly
be afforded these licensed slaves, these children of Popery, supported by a Protestant Court, will be given in order to subdue
these headstrong colonists, who pretend to be governed by
English laws.

These excerpts were in the usual anti-Catholic vein of the
Newport Mercury, as were further notes from London in
succeeding issues. With an eye to business, the printer, Sep-

[73] Daniel Barber, *History of My Own Times* (Washington, 1823),
p. 17.

tember 29, informed the public that he had still a *few* copies
of *A Master-Key to Popery,* " very necessary to be read by
every American Protestant at this alarming crisis!!!" A
dialogue between General Wolfe, " returned from the other
world," and General Gage revealed the sad news that the
" late proceedings of the British Parliament" had " produced a suspension " of the happiness of the "heroes of
Elysium." [74]

American reaction was noted by the *Mercury* in its report
of the Suffolk convention and the publication of its Resolves,
in Little Compton's vote of lack of confidence in the British
Parliament " until it be filled with men that seek the public,
before their own private good," [75] and the following account
of the celebration of Guy Fawkes day in Charleston, South
Carolina:

On the 5th of November, being the POWDER-PLOT, in the
morning there appeared a stage, fixed on the axle-tree of a
coach, the effigies of Lord North and Governor Hutchinson,
with the Devil and the POPE. North had in his hand the
Quebec Bill, and the Devil a canister of Tea, spitting fire at
North; and after being exposed to the public view the whole
day, thro' the principal streets, they were burnt with 75 barrels
of Tar.[76]

The *Boston Gazette,* like its Newport contemporary,
had served a long apprenticeship in anti-Catholic propaganda.
In its issue of October 10, 1774, a writer under the appropriate signature, " J. Tillotson ", quotes the British penal

[74] *Newport Mercury,* Jan. 23, 1775, no. 855. *Cf. Pennsylvania Journal,*
Jan. 4, 1775, no. 1674.

[75] *Newport Mercury,* Sept. 12, 1774, no. 836.

[76] *Newport Mercury,* Jan. 23, 1775, no. 855. For other references to
the Quebec Act, see July 18, Aug., 22, 29, Sept. 5, 12, 26, Oct. 3, Nov.
7, 14, Dec. 12, 1774; Jan. 23, Feb. 13, Mar. 15 (Sup.), June 12, 19,
Sept. 11, 1775.

law 11, 12 William III, ch. 4, inflicting perpetual imprisonment upon any Roman Catholic who presumes to teach
school or board youths within the realm or its dominions.
If such be the penalty for teaching or boarding youth, the
writer continues, what shall we think of the bishops who
have established Roman Catholicism in Quebec? St. Paul
would not recognize them as his lineal descendants. Coming
nearer home, the *Gazette* for October 17, reports that already
Protestants in Quebec are obliged to practice their religion
in secret through fear of offending Catholics. At the end
of the month another item by way of London pictures
Protestants fleeing across the Canadian border " from persecution, perhaps from torture." [77] Calculated· to excite
derision rather than fear was the news that the Pope had
invited Lord North to Rome, hoping thereby to cause another
revolution and thus induce George III to kiss his toe.[78]

The New York papers were not behind their rivals in
their condemnation of the Canadian measure. Rivington's
New York Gazette had some reference, though not always
unsympathetic, to the Act in almost every issue from June
to December, 1774. Less frequent, though by no means rare,
were its pertinent allusions in 1775. Besides printing the
proceedings of the House of Commons, the speeches of the
members of Parliament on the Quebec Act, and the addresses
and petitions of the various corporations against it, the
Gazette published the series of state papers issued by the
Continental Congress.[79] The *New York Journal or General
Advertiser* for November 3, 1774, reported from London
that General Carleton had orders to " embody THIRTY

[77] *Boston Gazette,* October 31, 1774. See also Oct. 17, 1774. *Cf.*
Pennsylvania Packet, Aug. 15, 1774; *Newport Mercury,* Nov. 7, 1774,
for similar items.

[78] *Boston Gazette,* Nov. 21, 1774, no. 1023.

[79] See issues for Feb. 23, June 21, Aug. 11, 18, 25, Sept. 2, 22, Oct. 6,
13, Nov. 3, 1774; Jan. 26, April 30, 1775.

THOUSAND Roman Catholic Canadians as militia." In view of such a formidable " Popish army " under a general of Carleton's ability, well might the writer ask, " Is it not high time for Protestants of all denominations in these kingdoms to take effectual means for the security of their civil and religious liberties? " [80] One meets such items not only during the preliminaries but during the early years of the Revolution. Sometimes the militia are united with the Indians " to cut our throats ", as the *Boston Gazette* intimated,[81] again they are associated with Irish immigration.[82] A toast frequently heard at festive gatherings was, " No Popish Army in a Protestant country," *The Massachusetts Gazette and Boston Post Boy* informed its readers.[83] It must have been with peculiar interest that Bostonians read the following in the *Boston Evening Post,*

London, July 5. It is reported that the Pope has been solicited to publish a Crusade against the rebellious Bostonians, to excite the Canadians, with the assistance of the British soldiery, to extirpate these bitter enemies to the Romish religion and monarchial power.[84]

Persecution of the Protestants in Europe was a favorite topic of the *Pennsylvania Gazette.* The war in the Cevennes, the Huguenots and the revocation of the Edict of Nantes, Philip II and Alva were all made to illustrate what might be expected from the change in Canada. Thus,

[80] For the same report, see *Pa. Gazette,* Oct. 19, 1774; *Pa. Journal,* Nov. 2, 1774; *Md. Gazette,* Nov. 10, 1774.

[81] April 4, 1768.

[82] *New Hampshire Gazette,* Sept. 16, 1774.

[83] Oct. 31–Nov. 7, 1774. Another popular toast of the period was " Confusion to the authors of the Canada Bill." See *Carroll Papers,* Oct., 1773–Dec., 1774 (Sept. 19, 1774). See also *Pa. Packet,* Sept. 19, *Pa. Journal,* Sept. 21, 1774.

[84] *Boston Evening Post,* supplement, Sept. 19, 1774. *N. H. Gazette,* Sept. 16, 1774.

. . . it remains to make the resemblance more complete, to introduce the inquisition at Quebec, and to erect Lord North's statue at Boston, in the posture of the Duke of Alva's at Antwerp, trampling upon the expiring liberties of America.[85]

George III, Lord North, the bishops—all who approved of the Quebec Act wholly or in part—received more than their share of obloquy. Tribunus, Scipio, Britannicus, and other pseudo-Romans addressed the King in abusive language, accusing him of everything but what he actually did.[86] The King's encounter with the London mob as he rode to Parliament to sign the Act, their hisses, the suspicion that the case of the sword of state contained a crucifix instead of a sword, were recounted again and again in the colonial press.[87] The bishops were cited before the self-appointed inquisition of American opinion, which treated them none too kindly. The *New Hampshire Gazette* printed this epigram " On the unanimous Vote of the right Rev. the Bench of Bishops to the Quebec Bill . . ."

Old Nick hugely pleased at what Yesterday past,
With Rapture exclaimed, " We have got it at last,
What Mary nor Charles nor James could achieve
We have partly obtained by the Crosier and Sleeve;
But let us be grateful (then calling an Imp)
Do you hear, my young Tycho, when next I want Drink
Instead of that liquid of Brimstone you dish up,
Pray let me be served, every day, with a Bishop." [88]

The Pennsylvania Gazette published a list of promotions among the members of Parliament who had favored the Act.

[85] *Pa. Gazette*, Sept. 28, 1774. *Cf.* issues for Sept. 21, 1774, July 26, 1775.

[86] *N. H. Gazette*, Sept. 30, 1774; *Pa. Gazette*, Sept. 14, Oct. 12, 1774; *Pa. Packet*, Aug. 19, 1774; *Pa. Journal*, Sept. 14, Oct. 5, 1774.

[87] *N. H. Gazette*, Aug. 16, 1774; *Pa. Gazette*, Aug. 24, 1774; *Va. Gazette*, Sept. 29, 1774.

[88] *N. H. Gazette*, Sept. 16, 1774.

Amusing as it may have been to contemporary readers, its appeal to their ingrained prejudices is clear. A few of the most significant titles follow:

Lord North—Commission of supplies to the College of Jesuits.
Jeremiah Dyson, Esq.—Clerk of the Inquisition.
Edmund Burke—Professor of Oratory in the University of Padua.
Lord Chatham—Superior of the Holy House of Loretto.
Archbishop of Canterbury—Sovereign Pontiff.
Mr. Horne—Crucifix-Maker to his most Catholic Majesty.
Lord Mayor—Tea-Man to the Pope.[89]

Both in England and in America light verse played its part in the " No-Popery " campaign. Set to the tunes of popular ballads which had done good service in previous political upheavals, these efforts of the poetasters went the rounds of the British and American press. America had more than one " Bob Jingle " who, Tory though he was, nevertheless agreed with the Whigs that of all the objectionable acts the

> . . . last and worst of all the Pack
> Is that Vile Act about Quebec.

" Bob's " poem, " The Association," is a satirical version of that document with a number of stanzas devoted to the " Vile Act ". The territorial and religious grounds of opposition are treated thus:

> Shall George the third presume to give
> To Provinces their bounds?
> And to our very noses bring
> The Whore of Bab'lon, Z——ds!

[89] *Pa. Gazette*, Oct. 5, 1774; *Newport Mercury*, Sept. 26, 1774. The compiler of the list was apparently unaware that although Burke approved of the toleration clauses of the Act, he opposed it on other grounds, and that Chatham, though ill, went to the House of Lords expressly to speak against it. See Cavendish, *Debates*, preface, and pp. 89, 222-23, 288-90.

> If Gallic Papists have a Right
> To worship their own way,
> Then farewell to the Liberties
> Of poor America.[90]

Of the English ballads, one of the most widely circulated was " A New Song ", reprinted from *St. James's Chronicle*. It represents " Goody " North singing a lullaby " to the foundling brat, the Popish Quebec Bill." The last stanza reads:

> Then heigh for the penance and pardons,
> And heigh for the faggots and fires;
> And heigh for the Popish Church wardens,
> And heigh for the Priests and the Friars;
> And heigh for the rareshew relics,
> To follow my Canada Bill-e,
> With all the Pope's mountebank tricks:
> So prithee, my baby, lie still-e.
>> Then up with the Papists, up, up,
>> And down with the Protestants, down-e;
>> Here we go backwards and forwards,
>> All for the good of the crown-e.[91]

To the examples already given, many others might be added; these are sufficient, however, to indicate the general attitude of the colonial press. Naturally the fear of the undesirable consequences of the Act was most intense in the colonies whose northern and western boundaries touched those of the extended province of Quebec; opposition to the

---

[90] *The Association . . . By Bob Jingle, Esq., Poet Laureat to the Congress, 1774* (Wegelin, *Early Amer. Poetry*, no. 496). See also *A Poor Man's Advice to His Neighbor* (New York, 1774). "A Rough Sketch for the Royal Academy" in *The Crisis*, no. xxii (London, 1775). Moore's *Diary of the American Revolution* (Hartford, 1876), gives excerpts not easily accessible elsewhere.

[91] *Va. Gazette*, Sept. 15, 1774; *Pa. Packet*, Aug. 29, 1774; *Newport Mercury*, March 15, 1775; *Massachusetts Spy*, Feb. 16, 1775. See also "Prophecy of Ruin," in the *Mass. Spy*, Nov. 3, 1775, and *The Crisis* (London), no. 12.

new legislation was, therefore, most articulate in the New England and the middle provinces. But comment on the Canadian question was by no means confined to the papers of those sections. The *Virginia* and *Maryland Gazettes* devoted proportionately as much space to it as their northern contemporaries. The papers of the Carolinas and Georgia are not easily accessible, but such copies as are available would suggest no marked difference in viewpoint.[92] Colonial printers made a practice of reprinting the most interesting articles of rival sheets. For almost a year after its passage the Quebec Act made good copy, copy altogether too popular to be neglected. Up to the time that the progress of the Revolution forced printers to take sides definitely with patriot or loyalist, a list of references to the Act in one of the more important newspapers could be fairly duplicated by almost any of its competitors. The citations given have included in most instances more than one reference for an excerpt; they make no pretense to completeness. The following note from the *Massachusetts Gazette,* October 10, 1774, sums up the situation:

London, Aug. 9, 1774. For Want of other Subjects, the Quebec Bill is still handled by the News Papers, and like some of the Boston News Papers, they repeat the same Thing fifty Times.

The implications as regards a uniform public opinion are obvious.

In a previous chapter we have discussed the popularity of the almanac and its importance as a factor in the formation of public opinion. It was pointed out then, that the amount of space which such a publication could devote to current topics was admittedly very small; consequently the compiler

[92] See *South Carolina and American General Gazette,* Aug. 19, 26, 1774; *South Carolina Gazette and Country Journal,* March 28, 1775; *Cape Fear Mercury,* Aug. 7, 25, Sept. 1, 1775; *Georgia Gazette,* Nov. 23, 1774.

would be careful to select issues which would have a wide appeal. During the French and Indian wars, as we have seen, popular almanacs reflected the general fear and hatred of the "hereditary foe." The hopes and fears of the Revolutionary era were likewise recorded in the same publications. Benjamin West's *New England Almanack* for 1775 devotes three pages following the regular calendar to *A Brief View of the Present Controversy between Great Britain and America, with Some Observations Thereon.* His "observations" on the Quebec Act voice the terror of the New England frontier. There is the usual complaint about establishing the old faith in Canada, and that with malicious intent. Of England's attitude, the writer says:

All her dispositions towards America, lately, have seemed inimical. We know not what may be attempted; fire and sword may be unexpectedly sent into our country.

Nathaniel Low's *Astronomical Diary* for 1775 has a signed "Address to the Inhabitants of Boston" in the true Suffolk manner. After citing the "vacating" of the Massachusetts charter and discussing the abuses that may arise from such tyranny, he continues:

And is not the cause of God in these Colonies at stake, and the religion of the gospel in danger of being wrested from her hands? Popery, we see, is already established in one Colony, and slavery is its never-failing concomitant; should the latter be established in the other Colonies, which is now attempted, the introduction of the former will not be difficult.

Paul Revere's engraving, "The Mitered Minuet", has been noted in the discussion of *The Royal American Magazine.* The "Vision" which the engraving illustrated was occasioned by the writer's concern lest the passage of the Quebec Act should be the forerunner of an era of persecution similar to that of Mary's reign. "I felt all the pains of those martyrs, who had been grilled in Smithfield," he exclaims. Small wonder that he dreamed of the Act which so aroused his emotions. In his dream the writer was conducted through various apartments of the royal household until he came to a room where the council was debating the bill in question. Lord North was beating his forehead as he was wont to do when Burke had the floor.

> In the next room I saw all the bishops seated in their mitres and pontifical dignity, excepting four, who were dancing a minuet to the bagpipe played by the Thane; and, just as I entered, they were taking hands across, and going around the Quebec Bill, which lay upon the floor. This part of the ceremony, I found upon reflection, had more meaning in it than I imagined at first: it was to sanctify and confirm the same; and the crossing hands was to show their approbation and countenance of the Roman religion. . . . Struck to the soul at the apostasy of the church, I awaked.[93]

No discussion of the Quebec Act in its relation to American thought would be complete without a consideration of the effect of British public opinion upon the views of their fellow-countrymen on this side of the Atlantic. In England, as in America, the reaction was violent and for the most part denunciatory. The petition of the Lord Mayor and the Aldermen of London that the King refuse his assent to the bill, was the prelude to a long series of letters, addresses, and speeches which deluged both King and Parliament after the passage of the Act. Just as in America, the Suffolk Resolves offered a precedent which was followed by town and county assemblies throughout the length and breadth of the land, so in England, the protests of the Lord Mayor and Aldermen, of the various liveries and guilds of London, were imitated by similar corporations throughout the British

---

[93] *Royal Amer. Mag.*, Oct., 1774, pp. 365-66, 478.

Isles. Appearing wholly or in part in the British press, these denunciations were reprinted in the colonial newspapers, helping thus in no small degree to crystallize American public opinion. Many of the excerpts quoted above were taken from the British press. Rivington's *New York Gazette*, August 25, 1774 (No. 71), published the protest of the Lord Mayor, the Aldermen and the Commons of London. There is no mistaking the attitude of his Majesty's memorialists:

. . . the Roman Catholic religion which is known to be idolatrous and bloody, is established by this bill, and no legal provisions made for the free exercise of our reformed faith, nor the security of our Protestant subjects of the Church of England. . . .[94]

Expressions of appreciation and sympathy soon poured in upon the London memorialists, proving how well they had taken the public pulse. The letter of the Guild of Merchants of the City of Dublin is only one of many that might be selected. They offer " their grateful acknowledgements as Protestants, for your steady opposition to the establishment of popery and slavery." The same theme, though with variations, forms the subject of the instructions of the Freeholders of Middlesex County to their representatives. The establishment of " Popery " in Quebec has armed " many of our fellow-subjects with a *crucifix* in one hand and a *dagger* in the other, against our Protestant brethren." While a Catholic bishop and his clergy are provided for, " the pastors of our own pure and excellent faith " are dependent upon " what *Romish* priests and Romish councils shall deign to afford them." [95] There was, of course, much

[94] In many colonial papers. See *Pa. Packet*, Aug. 15, 1774; *Pa. Journal*, Aug. 10, 1774; *Pa. Evening Post*, June 3, 1775; *Md. Gazette*, Aug. 25, 1774.

comment of a melodramatic nature, with references to the fires of Smithfield, the Stuarts and the Pretender, and " Popish crews of Jesuitcal priests," some of which, at least, was intended for American as well as British consumption.

Canadian reaction also found expression in the colonies. Some of it came directly over the border, and not a little by way of London. It was the British and the American traders who were disatisfied with the Act. Their complaints were undoubtedly the inspiration of much of the propaganda which came from Canada. Adding nothing to the arguments already noted, the Canadian contribution only helped to swell the chorus of denunciation.[96]

[95] *Pa. Gazette*, Dec. 20, 1775; *Pa. Evening Post*, Jan. 9, 1776. In many other papers. For British reaction, see also: J. Almon, *Remembrancer*, 1775, pp. 246, 295, 297. *The Crisis*, Jan. 21, 1775–Oct. 12, 1776 (92 numbers, London), no. i, p. 5; no. v, pp. 28-30; no. xii, pp. 76-77; no. xiii, p. 100; no. xxxii, p. 213; no. xxxiii, pp. 218-19; no. xxxvi, p. 239; no. xxxvii, p. 240; no. xlvii, p. 305 *et seq.* [Arthur Lee], *An appeal to the justice and interests of Great Britain, in the present disputes with America, By an old member of Parliament* (London, 1774), p. 43. [Charles Lee], *A speech intended to be delivered in the House of Commons, in support of the petition from the general Congress at Philadelphia* (London, 1775), p. 32 *et seq. An Essay on the nature of the colonies, and the conduct of the mother-country towards them* (London, 1775), p. 53 *et seq. A Defense of the resolutions and address of the American Congress, in reply to Taxation no Tyranny. By the author of Regulus* (London, 1775), p. 25. *A Letter to Sir William Meredith, Bart., in answer to his late letter to the Earl of Chatham* (London, 1774). *Mass. Gazette and Boston Post Boy and Advertiser*, Oct. 10, 1774. A. C. H. *Researches*, n. s., vols. vii-viii (1911-12), pp. 384, 387-88. *Cavendish's Debates.*

[96] J. Almon, *Remembrancer*, vol. i, pp. 210-213; vol. ii, pp. 130-135. P. Force, *Amer. Arch.*, 4 ser., vol. i, pp. 853, 891, 1850. [C. Inglis], *The True Interest of America Impartially Stated . . . By an American* (2nd ed., Philadelphia, 1776). J. Smith, *Our Struggle for the Fourteenth Colony* (2 vols., New York, 1907), vol. i, pp. 59-69, 199-200, 206-10; vol. ii, pp. 214-15. W. R. Riddell, " Benjamin Franklin and Canada," *Pa. Mag. Hist. Biog.*, vol. xlviii (1924), pp. 91-110. " Duane Correspondence," *Southern Hist. Ass'n Pub.*, vol. x (Sept., 1906), pp. 305-06. Letter of S. Metcalf to Jas. Duane, Montreal, Sept. 22, 1774.

Both in England and America the Act was not without its apologists. Defense was based, however, not on any favorable opinion of Roman Catholicism, but rather on the broad principles of toleration which the measure embodied. That the Act only fulfilled promises made at the capitulation was another argument of its defenders. This was the ground taken by Daniel Leonard who, over the signature of " Massachusettensis ", discussed with John Adams, " Novanglus ", the " controversy between Great Britain and her colonies." Leonard pointed out the absurdity of the reasoning which concluded that Great Britain intended to take from her old subjects the privileges she was extending to the new. He likewise deplored the " fresh stimulous " which the tolerant course of the British ministry gave to the " disaffected of all orders," as well as the use made of it by the clergy " to give pathos to public oratory." [97]

Jonathan Sewall's *The American Roused in a Cure for the Spleen* was a dramatic effort in which Sharp, a country parson, supports the Act as a just measure which was not intended to affect the older colonies. [98] On similar grounds the Act was defended by Rev. Myles Cooper, president of King's College. His pamphlet, *A Friendly Address to All Reasonable Americans,* called attention to the use of the Act for purposes of propaganda, and declared that " more lies and misrepresentations concerning this act have been circulated, than one would think malice and falsehood could invent." [99] Sincere as they were in the defense of the measure, Leonard, Sewall and Cooper, Tories all, were actuated by party loyalty and a spirit of fair play, rather than

[97] *Novanglus and Massachusettensis* (Boston, 1819).

[98] Jonathan Sewall, *The American Roused in a Cure for the Spleen* (New England, printed; New York, reprinted, 1775), pp. 22-24.

[99] Myles Cooper, *A Friendly Address to all reasonable Americans* (New York, 1774). This and most of the Tory pamphlets attributed to Cooper are now thought to have been written by Dr. Chandler.

sympathy with the Church of Rome. The same may be said of Samuel Seabury, also a loyalist, who undertook to answer Hamilton's *Vindication*. Seabury contended that the Roman Catholic Church was not established in Canada, it was only tolerated. The restoration of French laws was but a temporary expedient until the Canadians should become reconciled to the laws of England.[100]

In the correspondence of Silas Deane there is a letter from his son-in-law, Colonel Saltonstall, who thought the Quebec Act a timely measure, since the uproar which it was causing would make the ministry realize what a dangerous thing it was to tamper with the liberties of free British colonists.[101]

Shea calls attention to the fact that in spite of all this furor over the Quebec Act, there was no physical violence against the Catholic population of Pennsylvania and Mary-

[100] [Samuel Seabury], *A View of the Controversy between Great Britain and her Colonies ... By A. W. Farmer* (New York, printed; London, reprinted, 1775. Often attributed to Seabury and Wilkins), pp. 83-84.

[101] "Correspondence of Silas Deane, 1774-1776," Conn. Hist. Soc. *Coll.*, vol. ii, pp. 142-43, 152. Also in *Deane Papers* (N. Y. Hist. Soc. Coll., vols. xix-xxiii), vol. xix, pp. 4-5. Deane himself advocated defeating the operation of the Quebec Act by founding New England communities and governments in the annexed territory. See his "Loose Thoughts on the Subject of Western Lands," in *Samuel Adams Papers*, Banc. Coll., vol. iii. For British defense of the Act see William Knox, *The Justice and Policy of the Late Act of Parliament* (London, 1774) ; *A Short Appeal to the People of Great Britain* (London, 1775) ; [John Lind], *An Englishman's Answer to the Address from the Delegates ... in the late Continental Congress* (New York, 1775) ; [John Shebbeare], *An Answer to the Queries ... printed in the Public Ledger*, Aug. 10 (1775) ; "Lord Lyttleton's Defense," Rivington's *New York Gazette*, Sept. 2, 1774; J. Cartwright, *American Independence, the Interest and Glory of Great Britain* (London, 1775) ; Samuel Johnson, *The Patriot* (London, printed; Dublin, reprinted, 1774) ; *A Letter to Lord Germain, By a Gentleman, for many years a resident of America* (London, 1778).

land.[102]   Here and there individuals may have been intimi-
dated, but certainly there was nothing in America like the
Gordon Riots in London a few years later.   Yet there is no
doubt that the Act, condemned though it was because of
its association with the " Intolerable Acts ", and because of
its political and economic implications, was also cordially
detested on religious grounds.   As one wades through the
mass of literature on the subject, one cannot escape the
conviction that to the average colonial, Roman Catholicism
was an evil fiercely to be hated, deeply to be feared, and
unremittingly to be fought.   Politicians like Samuel Adams
and John Jay might employ " Popery and Arbitrary Power "
as a rallying cry to unite the disaffected of all classes; but
what of the New England mother who bravely sent her son
to battle lest " the Man of Sin " obtain a foothold in this
fair land to pollute its pure religion and undermine its free
institutions?   There is no gainsaying the fact that on the
eve of the Revolution the fear was very real and well-nigh
universal.   Now and then one might find individuals who,
however unsympathetic they might be with the teachings of
the Roman Catholic Church, were willing to extend to its
members the blessings of civil and religious liberty.   But
the masses had far to go and much to learn before they
would concede that " Papists " were entitled to those rights
about which they declaimed so vociferously.   The Revolution was to inaugurate a campaign of education which
would at least start them on the road to toleration, if indeed
they had not already learned their first lesson when they
issued the *Memorial to the Inhabitants of Quebec.*

[102] J. G. Shea, *Cath. Church in U. S.*, vol. ii, p. 139.   S. H. Cobb, *Relig.
Liberty in America*, p. 490.   For the effect of the Quebec Act upon the
lot of English Catholics, see Henry Harrington, " Catholic Emancipation in England," *Thought*, vol. iv, pp. 480-499.

CHAPTER VIII

The Revolution

In the history of religious liberty in America Lexington is an important landmark. The militia who there made things so uncomfortable for the redcoats formed the nucleus of an army which could ill afford to make distinction between Protestant and Catholic, Jew and Gentile, believer and unbeliever. Religious minorities found their status changed almost over night. One looks in vain for recruiting orders forbidding the enrollment of Roman Catholics. There were no new acts for disarming " Papists ", though as we shall see, the state of mind which prompted such legislation was not altogether a thing of the past. The Catholic who could shoulder a gun was everywhere welcome. It is true that his religious susceptibilities were often wounded, but it is not without significance that the commander-in-chief should forbid the usual celebration of November fifth by the army at Cambridge, or that the General Orders should call attention to the ineptitude of burning the Pope in effigy when the Continental Congress was doing its utmost to win the allegiance of the Canadians.[1]

[1] *Writings of George Washington*, ed. by John C. Fitzpatrick, (Bi-Centennial edition, Washington, 1931-), vol. iv, p. 65. Another instance of the same disregard for the religious opinions of others is the effort of the patriot army to break down the morale of their opponents by passing through the lines copies of the broadside, " Address to the Soldiers about to embark for America." The memorial, it is said, had been distributed among the British army as it was leaving England. It was an impassioned appeal from " An Old Soldier " not to imbrue their hands in the blood of their fellow-countrymen who were revolting only because they were forced to resist " popery and slavery." The address was reprinted in practically every colonial newspaper.

To many a thoughtful Catholic it must have been difficult to decide on which side he would cast his lot. Although there were signs that a better day was dawning, there was plenty of evidence that the old mentality persisted. In New York City the Sons of Freedom met at the Liberty Pole prior to marching to the Exchange where they were to choose delegates to a Provincial Congress. From the Pole waved a flag, one side of which bore the inscription, " George III —Rex. and the Liberties of America.—No Popery." The reverse side read, " The Union of the Colonies, and the Measures of Congress." The temper of the Sons of Freedom may be gathered from their treatment of William Cunningham and John Hill, each of whom was forcibly brought under the Liberty Pole and commanded to " go down on his knees and damn his Popish King George." Refusal brought mistreatment which was continued until officers of the peace rescued the culprits. The mob then marched to the Exchange, " attended by musick," and bearing a flag similar to that on the Liberty Pole.[2] New Jersey's Liberty Pole bore the Inscription, " Liberty, Prosperity and No Popery." [3]

The humor of the South was characterized by the same intolerance. In South Carolina two Catholics of Tory sympathies were tarred and feathered, and for the first time in the history of the province, dragged through the streets, for having behaved in an "improper manner" towards a member

---

[2] Force, *Amer. Arch.*, 4 ser., vol. ii, p. 48. F. Moore, *Diary of Amer. Rev.*, pp. 35-36. For accounts of the incident by Cunningham and Hill, see Rivington's *Gazette*, March 9, 1775, and Holt's *New York Journal*, March 23, 1775. When the New York delegates left for the Continental Congress a salutation of cannon, " and three huzzas, bid them go and proclaim to all nations, that they, and the virtuous people they represent, dare defend their rights as PROTESTANT ENGLISHMEN." *Virginia Gazette*, Sept. 22, 1774.

[3] N. J. H. S. *Proc.*, 4 ser., vol. iv (1919), p. 44.

of the Association. Their " improper " conduct arose from a remark made by the informer, one Michael Hubart, that Catholics and negroes should not be allowed to have arms lest they attack " Christians." James Dealy, to whom the remark had been reported by his friend Martin, without waiting for his wrath to cool, went immediately to Hubart's house, " mistreated " him, and sealed his own fate by drinking the toast, " Damnation to the Association and their proceedings." After the chastisement recorded above, both were sentenced to deportation. Later, Martin's public apology having been accepted, he was allowed to remain, but Dealy was sent to London to make an example of him.[4] The incident derives its significance not so much from the violence of the mob as from the fact that their activities were directed by the Secret Committee of the Association, men presumably of superior calibre. The sentence was signed by Judge Drayton, whose charge to the grand jury has been noted in the discussion on the Quebec Act.[5] On the other hand, the South Carolina Regulators, largely Scotch-Irish and Tory, were as little likely as the patriots to

[4] John Drayton, ed., *Memoirs of the American Revolution* (2 vols., Charleston, 1821), vol. i, pp. 273, 300. See also *ibid.*, vol. i, p. 226 *et seq.*, for an attempt by Judge Drayton and other prominent South Carolinians to crystallize public opinion against the British ministry. Figures representing Lord Grenville, Lord North, the Pope and the Devil were placed on a platform at a much frequented corner of the town. Whenever a crown officer passed, the Pope would bow obsequiously to him, only to be belabored lustily by the Devil. In the evening there was a parade and a bonfire, as was customary in November fifth celebrations. After recording the incident, the writer of the *Memoirs* tells how the small boy abandoning his ordinary games took to making similar figures, " with which, having amused themselves, and roused their youthful spirits into a detestation of oppression; they also committed them to the flames." See also *North Carolina Records*, vol. x, pp. 126-27, for deposition of Jacob Williams.

[5] *Supra*, p. 290.

deal kindly with Catholics whose political views differed from their own.[6]

Undoubtedly, the Roman Catholic was in a difficult position. On the one hand his experience with the British government, whether in Europe or America, offered little hope for religious liberty or for that economic, political and social equality which is its corollary. The best that could be hoped for was connivance at the non-enforcement of the penal laws which, unrepealed, could always be invoked at times of public excitement. True, the Quebec Act had marked a departure from the policy of centuries, but the opposition it had aroused in England and America proved how futile was the hope of similar liberality in these " free Protestant colonies." On the other hand, the most vigorous opponents of the British policy of coercion had been the bitterest persecutors of the Catholics.[7] More than one writer of the period has characterized the Revolution as a " Presbyterian rebellion." [8] As in previous wars, Calvinist preachers on the eve of the Revolution were fulminating against the anti-Christian, anti-social principles of " The stupid, bigoted Roman Catholics." [9]

[6] *Fulham Palace*, Mss. S. C. no. 52. Letter of the Regulators to Henry Laurens. L. C.

[7] J. Boucher, *Causes and Consequences of the American War of Independence* (London, 1791), p. 241 *et seq.*

[8] J. Boucher, *op. cit.*, pref., pp. xxiv-xxviii. Ambrose Serle to the Earl of Dartmouth, in Stevens' *Facsimiles*, vol. xxiv, no. 2045. " Journal of Samuel Rowland Fisher of Philadelphia, 1779-1781," *Pa. Mag. Hist. Biog.*, vol. xli (1917), p. 145 *et seq.* " Letter-Book of Capt. Johann Heinrichs of the Hessian Jager Corps, 1778-1789," *Pa. Mag. Hist. Biog.*, vol. xxii, p. 137 *et seq.* Joseph Galloway, *Historical and Political Reflections on the Rise and Progress of the American Rebellion* (London, 1780), p. 36 *et seq.* *Cf.* C. Evans, *Amer. Bibliog.*, vol. iv, introd., p. 9, vol. v, introd., p. 9. T. C. Hall, *Religious Background of American Culture*, pp. 168-171. G. O. Trevelyan, *The American Revolution* (4 vols., New York, 1905), vol. iii, pp. 280, 310.

[9] Rev. Samuel Cooke, " Sermons delivered April 6, 1775, April 12, 1778," quoted in Benj. and W. R. Cutter, *History of the Town of*

Hatred of the Church of Rome was still too useful a weapon to be dispensed with. If Massachusetts promised to send the Catholic Indians of Maine a Catholic chaplain, when she could, her missionaries went to the Mohawks and other tribes armed with the speech of Samuel Adams noted in the foregoing chapter.[10] While Washington and the Continental Congress were endeavoring to win the Canadians with promises of complete religious liberty, the Boston Committee of Correspondence, urging its agents in Quebec and Montreal to renewed efforts, were still citing the Quebec Act as an unfailing irritant. All the colonies from Nova Scotia to Georgia, ran the letter, feared that the Act or similar legislation would be extended to them; so although Canada had not been represented in the late Continental Congress, " the Quebeck Bill was considered then as not only an intolerable Injury to the Subjects of that Province but as a capital Grievance on all." [11] Through most of British America provincial conventions were being held; scarcely one of them, as will be seen, failed to make some offensive reference to the Catholic question. The radicals' summary methods with the Tories were not, it was suspected, wholly

Arlington, 1635-1789 (Boston, 1880), pp. 50-85. Samuel Langdon, *A Rational Explication of St. John's Vision of the Two Beasts* (Portsmouth, 1774). Samuel West, *Election Sermon, May 29, 1776* (Boston, 1776). General Gage, like all the crown officers, was suspected of Catholic sympathies. A versification of his Proclamation, 1775, represents him speaking thus :

> Did not your clergy, all as one,
> Vile protestants each mother's son . . .
> Persuade you Heav'n would help you out,
> Till you despised our threats so stout—
> While ev'ry sermon spread alarms,
> And ev'ry pulpit beat to arms?

Magazine of History, vol. xiii (1868), p. 5 *et seq.*

[10] *Supra*, p. 287.

[11] *Boston Com. Corr. General Corr., Feb. 21, 1775.* Banc. Trans. N. Y. P. L.

due to outraged patriotism. If the Puritans won, was it not possible that the same methods might be employed to confirm the " standing order "? History could furnish more than one precedent.[12]

In such a dilemma it is not surprising that Catholics should have hesitated. But to waver in those days was to be suspected; to be suspected was to invite persecution. Of that, Catholics, especially those of Maryland, had had enough. To spare them further suffering, and to win them perhaps to the loyalist cause, Rev. Jonathan Boucher, the rector of Queen Anne's parish, Maryland, preached a sermon " On the Toleration of Papists." [13] The discourse is a sympathetic summary of the Catholic position and an eloquent plea that, in the crisis confronting them, Catholics be treated with consideration. Whatever the practical effects of the sermon in ameliorating their lot, the Catholics of Maryland with some exceptions became under the leadership of Charles Carroll, " good Whigs " rather than ardent Tories. Elsewhere in

---

[12] S. P. G. *Journals*, vol. xx, part 5 (1773-1776), p. 349 *et seq.* C. H. Van Tyne, *War of Independence*, pp. 70-74. P. Force, *Amer. Arch.*, 4 ser., vol. i, pp. 711-717, 802. J. G. Shea, *Cath. Ch. in U. S.*, vol. ii, p. 145. *Doc. Hist. N. Y.*, vol. iii, p. 1050. J. Bouchier, ed., *Reminiscences of an American Loyalist* (New York, 1925), pp. 133-34. The fear of reprisals by a victorious Presbyterian party was given dramatic expression in a scene in *The Battle of Brooklyn. A Farce in Two Acts, as it was performed on Long Island on Tuesday, the 27th day of August, 1776, by the Representatives of the Tyrants of America assembled at Philadelphia* (New York, Rivington, 1776. Reprinted, Brooklyn, 1873). Gen. Putnam remarks to Snuffle, a New England parson, ". . . what a ripping reformation you Gentlemen will make in church affairs. Down goes Episcopacy and Quakerism, at least . . ." Snuffle, ". . . we shall be very apt to make free with those Gentlemen. We have long beheld, with a jealous eye, the growing power of the Episcopal Clergy, and considered them as the only obstacles to our becoming the heads of the Church in America. . . . As for the Quakers, who in general have joined the Tories against us, we shall not fail to produce an 'ancient testimony' in their behalf; I mean the testimony of our forefathers . . .", p. 15.

[13] *Supra*, note 7.

the colonies, though there were individuals and at least two groups who were loyalists, Catholics for the most part followed the example of their Maryland co-religionists. Years after, Rev. Daniel Barber, reviewing the experience of his youth, explained their choice as follows:

Now what must appear very singular, is that two parties, naturally so opposed to each other, should become even at the outset, united in opposing the efforts of the Mother country. And now we find the New England people and the Catholics of the Southern states fighting side by side, though stimulated by extremely different motives; the one acting through fear, lest the King of England should succeed in establishing among us, the Catholic Religion; the other, equally fearful lest the bitterness against the Catholic faith should increase till they were destroyed or driven to the mountains or waste places of the wilderness.[14]

Of the two loyalist groups one was the so-called " Roman Catholic Regiment " formed during Howe's occupation of Philadelphia. Shea [15] says that it existed only on paper, but it appears to have been more substantial than that. Captain John Montrésor's *Journals* [16] record the movement of " Allen's and Clifton Regt. of Provincials (the latter Roman Catholic) . . . into the Jersies ", and the *Colonial Records of Pennsylvania* [17] tell of the examination before the City

---

[14] D. Barber, *History of My own Times*, vol. ii, p. 8 *et seq.* *Cf.* Report of Bishop Carroll in J. C. Brent, *Biographical Sketch of the Most Rev. John Carroll, First Archbishop of Baltimore, with select portions of his writings* (Baltimore, 1843), pp. 68-69. For the activities of Catholics during the Revolution see M. I. J. Griffin, *Catholics and the American Revolution* (3 vols., Ridley Park, Pa., 1907). A. C. H. *Researches.* P. Guilday, *Carroll*, early chapters.

[15] J. G. Shea, *Cath. Ch. in U. S.*, vol. ii, pp. 169-70 n. G. Bancroft, *Hist. of U. S.*, vol. v, p. 295.

[16] "Journals of Captain John Montrésor," New York Hist. Soc. *Coll.*, vol. xiv (1881), p. 489. Also in *Pa. Mag. Hist. Biog.*, vol. vi, p. 190.

[17] *Pa. Col. Rec.*, vol. xii, pp. 176-177.

Council of Lieutenant Patrick Keane, " of the Roman Catholic Regiment of Volunteers in the British Service." There are other contemporary references.[18] So while there is no doubt that there was a unit of Catholic volunteers among the Tories, it probably was no larger than a battalion.[19]

The second group of Catholic loyalists, the Highlanders of the Mohawk Valley, were trebly suspect because of their former adherence to the Stuart cause, the oath—exacted of all Jacobites—never again to take up arms against their King, and their faith. The exposure of New York's frontier to Indian raids, the danger of a Canadian offensive, and the revival of the old stories of Catholic connivance with redskin and Frenchman were all factors in the decision to disarm the Highlanders and to demand hostages for their future loyalty. When in addition to these precautions it was determined to remove them from their homes, the greater number, including their patron Sir John Johnson, escaped to Canada. There some of them joined the Royal Greens organized by Johnson.[20]

On the northeastern frontier the Catholic Indians of Maine were offering their services to Washington on condition that he send them a Catholic chaplain. The Massachusetts leg-

[18] " Extracts from the Letter-Book of Captain Johann Heinrichs of the Hessian Jager Corps, 1778-1789," in *Pa. Mag. Hist. Biog.*, vol. xxii, p. 137 *et seq.* " Order Books of Lieut.-Col. Stephen Kemble... 1775-1778," in N. Y. Hist. Soc. *Coll.*, vol. xvi (1883). J. Adams, *Twenty-six letters... respecting the revolution of America* (London, 1786), pp. 13-14.

[19] C. W. Sloane, " Provincial Corps of Catholic Volunteers," U. S. Cath. Hist. Soc. *Records and Studies*, vol. ii, pp. 203-205. A. C. H. *Researches*, n. s., vol. iv, (1908), pp. 289-310. C. H. Van Tyne, *Eng. and America*, p. 135.

[20] J. G. Shea, *Cath. Ch. in U. S.*, vol. ii, pp. 76, 142. A. C. H. *Researches*, n. s., vol. iv (1908), pp. 231-249. *Doc. Hist. N. Y.*, vol. vii, p. 630, vol. viii, pp. 589, 663, 683. P. Guilday, " Father John McKenna, A Loyalist Catholic Priest," *Cath. World*, vol. cxxxiii, pp. 21-27. E. J. Macdonald, " Father Roderick Macdonell Missionary at St. Regis and the Glengarry Catholics," *Cath. Hist. Review*, vol. xix (1933), pp. 265-74.

islature, through whom the negotiations were conducted, had none to give. Their laws had seen to that. Nor did they know where to find one. Their promise to do so when they could was destined to be fulfilled through the illiberal policy of another province. New York, like Massachusetts, had still on her statute books the law against Catholic priests. Unlike the Bay Colony, however, she saw no necessity for suspending it during hostilities. When, in 1779, a French prize was brought into the harbor with its chaplain on board, the Catholics of New York asked the priest to say Mass. A request for permission to do so was refused by the British authorities then in control. Misinterpreting the refusal for assent, Father de la Motte said Mass, but found himself shortly after a prisoner. His exchange as a prisoner of war enabled Massachusetts to send him to Maine and Nova Scotia.[21]

Meanwhile Congress was doing its best to secure both the allegiance and the control of Canada. The fair phrases of the first address to the Canadians (Oct. 26, 1774) had been counteracted by the bigotry of the appeals to the British public and to the King. Convinced that the latter rather than the former expressed the real sentiments of the " perfidious, double-faced Congress," the Canadian clergy and their people saw in the second *Address to the Oppressed Inhabitants of Canada* only another evidence of American insincerity.[22] When the army of the invasion violated both

---

[21] *Amer. Arch.*, 4 ser., vol. vii, pp. 838-848, 1223. G. Washington, *Writings*, vol. iii, pp. 398-99, 423, 525; vol. iv, pp. 253-274, 280, 301. *Papers of John Holker, 1771-1782* (44 vols., L. C. Mss. Div.), Letter of De Valnais to Holker (June 10, 1779), vol. iv, pp. 620-621. *Journal of Claude Blanchard*, trans. by Wm. Duane (Albany, 1876). Entry Aug. 29, 1780.

[22] James Jeffry, " Journal kept in Quebec in 1775." Annotated by Wm. Smith, in Essex Inst. Hist. *Coll.*, vol. 1 (1914), p. 124. P. Force, *Amer. Arch.*, 4 ser., vol. i, pp. 987-99. J. Smith, *Fourteenth Colony*, vol. ii, pp. 214-15. J. Codman, *Arnold's Expedition to Quebec*, p. 9.

the spirit and the letter of Washington's proclamation to the Canadians and his instructions to Arnold,[23] when their clergy were insulted and even mistreated,[24] when Hazen's forces welcomed the services of a priest who in defiance of Bishop Briand's instruction was administering the sacraments,[25] the attitude of the *habitant,* friendly at first, changed to one of hostility. Acts of vandalism on the part of the American forces strengthened Canadian opposition, while the free use of the worthless continental currency instead of hard money filled up the measure of American transgressions.[26]

Canadian lack of response to American overtures was explained at least in part by a report of the Committee of Secret Correspondence. Among other reasons the offense given to the religious susceptibilities of the French Canadians was emphasized. The Tory press of New York, it was stated, had convinced them that the fair words of the Americans were merely a ruse to deprive them of their religion and their possessions. The report further asserted that the addresses sent by Congress had been read to the Canadians by their priests who did not fail to point out the inconsistencies of these appeals with other Congressional documents. On

[23] For Washington's proclamation and instructions to Arnold see *Writings,* vol. iii, pp. 478-80, 491-96. *Cf.* Letter to Gen. Schuyler, vol. iv, pp. 495-96.

[24] G. Washington, *Writings,* vol. iv, pp. 65 n, 495 n. P. Force, *Amer. Arch.,* 4 ser., vol. v, pp. 751-54, 869-71. A. Gosselin, *L'Église du Canada,* vol. ii, pp. 35, 70. *Journal of the Most Remarkable Occurrences in Quebec, the 14th of November, 1775, to the 7th of May, 1776.* By an Officer of the Garrison, in New York Hist. Soc. *Coll.,* vol. xiii (1880), pp. 220-21. J. Smith, *Fourteenth Colony,* vol. ii, pp. 225-26.

[25] A. Gosselin, *L'Église du Canada,* vol. ii, p. 72. A. H. Germain, *Catholic Military and Naval Chaplains, 1776-1917* (Wash., 1929), p. 11. For Father Floquet's own account to Bishop Briand, see A. C. H. *Researches,* vol. v, pp. 65-67.

[26] P. Force, *Amer. Arch.,* 4 ser., vol. v, p. 1098; vol. vi, pp. 413, 812, 1028, 1194. C. H. Van Tyne, *War of Ind.,* pp. 70-74.

the other hand, the clergy had been careful to call attention to British liberality as evidenced in the Quebec Act. The result was that the invitation of the revolting colonies to join their cause had failed to elicit a sympathetic response. The *habitants,* on the whole, were unwilling to take up arms against Great Britain. To counteract this pro-British influence the Committee recommended that a delegation be sent to Canada to explain to clergy and laity our desire not to conquer them but to share with them the blessings of civil and religious liberty.[27]

In accordance with this recommendation, Congress appointed a committee consisting of Benjamin Franklin, Samuel Chase and Charles Carroll of Carrollton. Carroll's education in France, his knowledge of the French language and his religious affiliations would, it was hoped, make him acceptable to our northern neighbors. And as if to make assurance doubly sure, he was asked to " persuade " his cousin, Father John Carroll, to accompany the delegation, that he might use his influence with the Canadian clergy. Congress, apparently, could not risk antagonizing public opinion by the appointment of two Roman Catholics, one of them a priest and an ex-Jesuit. John Adams was duly impressed with the exceptional character of this procedure, which he justified in a letter to his wife:

. . . This Gentleman will administer Baptism to the Canadian Children and bestow Absolution upon Such as have been refused it by the toryfied Priests in Canada. The Anathemas of the Church so terrible to the Canadians having had a disagreeable effect upon them.

[27] *Journals,* vol. iv, p. 148. For Bishop Briand's policy and influence see A. Gosselin, *L'Église du Canada,* vol. i, p. 28; vol. ii, p. 78 *et seq.* Shortt and Doughty, *Canada. Arch.,* vol. i, p. 455. P. Guilday, *Carroll,* vol. i, p. 93. Almon, *Remembrancer,* vol. i, p. 244. S. K. Wilson, " Bishop Briand and the American Revolution," *Cath. Hist. Rev.,* vol. xix (Apr., 1933–Jan., 1934), pp. 133-137.

He relies upon her " prudence " to disclose

the circumstances of the priest, the Jesuit, and the Romish religion, only to such persons as can judge of the measure upon large and generous principles, and will not indiscretely divulge it.[28]

Charles Carroll also felt that it would be the part of wisdom to be cautious in discussing the large powers granted the commission, especially in regard to religious toleration. " Keep this paragraph relating to the nature and content of our Instructions to yourself," he wrote to his father, " it ought not to be mentioned." [29]

The fifth paragraph of those instructions, liberal even in the light of twentieth-century standards, shows, nevertheless, that the Quebec Act was still a cause of grievance to Congress. The delegates were to urge the Canadians to place themselves under the protection of the United States. " Explain to them," the Instructions continue,

the nature and principles of government among freemen; developing, in contrast to those, the base, cruel, and insidious designs involved in the late act of parliament, for making a more effectual provision for the government of the province of Quebec. . . .

For the rest, they were to assure the Canadians that they would be guaranteed complete liberty of conscience, that their clergy would be confirmed in the possession of their estates, and finally, that the regulation of religious affairs would remain entirely in the hands of the people and such legislature as they should choose. There was the added

[28] *Warren-Adams Letters,* Mass. Hist. Soc. *Coll.* (2 vols., 1917-1923), vol. i, p. 207. John and Abigail Adams, *Familiar Letters,* ed. by C. F. Adams (Boston, 1875), pp. 135-36.

[29] *Carroll Papers, Feb., 1775 to March, 1776.* Letter dated Philadelphia, March 21, 1776.

proviso that all other religions should be tolerated and granted civil rights as well, and that the payment of tithes should not be obligatory.[30] This was a more liberal program than the majority of the provinces were ready to adopt when, having become independent, they drafted their first constitutions. But liberal as it was it could not tempt the Canadians. They were in fact living under a government quite as generous as that promised by the Americans; they were not at all sure that the latter would keep their word. They could and did point to several documents which denounced the British King for attempting to enslave the colonies by tolerating Roman Catholicism in Canada.[31]

If the Commission failed to attain its main purpose, that of winning the allegiance and active cooperation of the Canadians, it was not without tangible results. Two regiments for the American cause were enrolled, and the neutrality of the most of the *habitants* was secured.[32] It is not unlikely that a larger number of the French would have wavered were it not for the efforts of Bishop Briand and his clergy. They were determined that their flocks should prove their loyalty. And lest Father Carroll should influence spirits less determined than his own, the Bishop forbade his priests to have any intercourse with the American prelate.[33] When Frank-

[30] *Journals*, vol. iv, pp. 151, 215 *et seq.*

[31] John England, *Works*, vol. ii, p. 280; vol. iv, p. 254. W. R. Riddell, "Benjamin Franklin's Mission in Canada," *Pa. Mag. Hist. Biog.*, vol. xlviii (1924), pp. 91-100. P. Guilday, *Carroll*, vol. i, p. 98 *et seq.* J. Smith, *Fourteenth Colony*, vol. ii, pp. 334-35.

[32] *Carroll Papers*, April, 1776–Feb., 1777. See letters of Charles Carroll, April 15, 21, May 6, 17, 1776. *Papers of the Continental Congress*, vol. 166 for Report of Committee on Ticonderoga; reports of Franklin, Chase and Carroll. *Journal of most remarkable occurrences* . . . N. Y. H. S. *Coll.*, vol. xiii, p. 236.

[33] *Supra*, note 27. See also *Les Affaires Étrangères, Cor. Pol. États-Unis*, vol. 21, fol. 100, Luzerne to Vergennes, 23 June, 1782.

lin, whose health was poor, determined to return to Philadelphia, Father Carroll, convinced of the futility of a longer stay in Canada, accompanied him.[34]

Meanwhile the problem of securing foreign aid was engaging the attention of Congress. Supplies of every sort were needed, as well as money, ships and men. But far more than the sinews of war did the nascent nation need that moral support inherent in the recognition of their cause by the nations of Europe. So the Committee of Secret Correspondence sent its couriers to the various European courts to secure treaties of amity and commerce. In these efforts they were none too successful, yet the net result was the formation of an alliance, far-reaching in its political effects, and unique in the intellectual and spiritual reactions of the two nations concerned.[35]

For dire as was the need of the revolting colonies, it was not without much fear and trepidation that they contemplated an alliance with "papistical France." Their entire past history was against it. On the other hand, they argued that if England had a long list of grievances against France, the latter was not without her catalog of injuries for which she might not be loathe to take revenge. Here was her opportunity. What more effective means of humiliating England than by aiding the insurgents? From this standpoint, it was not difficult for the colonists to regard their once "natural enemy" as their equally "natural ally." And should France

[34] *Carroll Papers.* John Carroll to Charles Carroll of Doughoregan Manor, Philadelphia, June 2, 1776. Portfolio 6, paper 10, Md. Hist. Soc.

[35] *Journals,* vol. iv, entries under March 8, July 8, Aug. 7, Sept. 17, 28 and *passim.* B. Faÿ, *L'Ésprit Rév.,* pp. 314-19. E. C. Kite, "Catholic Aid to American Independence," *America,* vol. xxxix, Sept. 21, 29, 1928. J. J. Jusserand, "Rochambeau and the French in America: Why They Came and What They Did," *North Carolina Historical Commission,* Bulletin No. 15 (Raleigh, 1913), pp. 83-117.

be joined by Catholic Spain, who also had old scores to pay, so much the better.[36]

With the negotiations which in 1778 terminated in the treaties of commerce and friendship this study is not concerned. As to the expediency of the alliance, there was of course a sharp difference of opinion not only between Whig and Tory but also among the patriots themselves. In Congress the anti-French faction headed by Samuel Adams and Richard Henry Lee impugned the motives of France [37] and discussed the possible effects of French " finesse and flattery " [38] upon the unsophisticated colonists. Others feared the cloven hoof hidden under alluring offers of aid. Among the latter were Roger Sherman and Robert Treat Paine who opposed the appointment of a French artillery officer because he was a " Papist." [39] Fortunately the misgivings of the opposition were forced into the background by the hard logic of facts. The danger from England was immediate; that from " Foreign Papists ", remote, perhaps groundless. It was no time to question the source from which assistance could be obtained. So the negotiations continued. Though not at first ready to exchange treaties of commerce

---

[36] E. S. Corwin, *French Policy and the American Alliance of 1778* (Princeton, 1916), pp. 49-50. Francis Wharton, *Revolutionary Diplomatic Correspondence of the United States* (6 vols., Washington, 1889), vol. i, pp. 313, 340, 349-50. C. Van Tyne, *Eng. and Amer.*, p. 160. H. M. Jones, *America and French Culture*, pp. 352, 358, 386, 418, 508-11, 567-70. B. Faÿ, "The Course of French-American Friendship," *Yale Review*, vol. xviii (Spring, 1929), pp. 436-55. J. J. Jusserand, *With Americans of Past and Present Days* (New York, 1916), p. 11.

[37] J. Adams, *Works*, vol. i, p. 200. *Journals*, vol. vi, pp. 1073, 1087. Stevens, *Facsimiles*, vol. xii, no. 1264. *Life and Correspondence of Rufus King*, ed. by C. R. King (3 vols., New York, 1894-96), vol. i, p. 15 n.

[38] E. C. Burnett, *Letters*, vol. ii, pp. 379, 394, 417, 442; vol. iii, p. 418; vol. v, pp. 28-29.

[39] *Journal of Richard Smith*, Banc. Coll., N. Y. P. L., p. 67. Also in Burnett, vol. v, p. 208.

and friendship, France signified her willingness to give secret aid. This she had already extended through Beaumarchais and his agents. With the arrival of the *Amphitrite* at Portsmouth, N. H., March 17, 1777, the fulfilment of her recent pledges began. After Saratoga came the recognition of American Independence with the conclusion of the formal alliance.[40]

With the ratification of the treaties, May 4, 1778, Congress, besides passing a resolution expressive of its own appreciation, issued an address to the nation. Henceforth the French were to be treated by them as the subjects of a " magnanimous and generous ally." [41] The keynote thus sounded was a norm consistently adhered to by Congress, throughout the war, though not always and everywhere achieved by American diplomats or by the populace. As became good friends, the joys and sorrows of the one became the joys and sorrows of the other. The birth of a prince or princess, the birthday of the King, the death of a member of the royal family, called forth appropriate expressions of congratulation or condolence.[42] Diplomatic functions, such as the arrival or departure of ambassadors, receptions given in their honor, or celebrations arranged by them, as, for example, the public *Te Deum* after the victory at Yorktown—these and similar occasions afforded Congress opportunities of renewing its esteem, of repeating its sentiments of gratitude.[43]

---

[40] *Journals*, vol. xi, pp. 419-464. For the diplomatic history of the negotiations, see S. F. Bemis, *The Diplomacy of the American Revolution* (New York, 1935), pp. 17-69. For the activities of Beaumarchais see E. S. Kite, *Beaumarchais: and The War of American Independence* (2 vols., Boston, 1918).

[41] *Journals*, vol. xi, pp. 457-58, 468; vol. xiii, pp. 649-57. *The Treaties of 1778 and Allied Documents*, ed. by G. Chinard (Balt., 1828), pp. xiii-xv.

[42] *Journals*, vols. xiv, pp. 736, 737, 988-90; xxii, pp. 261-63, 327; xxviii, pp. 457-58. *Secret Journals*, vol. iii, pp. 107-09, 140-41, 461-62, 556-57.

[43] *Journals*, vols. xi, pp. 638, 753-57; xv, pp. 1-72, 75, 1085, 1238, 1279, 1780-83; xxi, pp. 1145-46; xxiv, pp. 1-2; xxvii, pp. 673-684.

And if the correspondence published in the *Letters of the Members of the Continental Congress* be accepted as fairly representative of the private convictions of the writers, they were in substantial agreement with the official attitude of Congress. Confidence in their new ally, renewed courage, hope of ultimate victory are their dominant notes.[44]

Yet there was much searching of hearts amid the general enthusiasm with which the Franco-American alliance was greeted. Protestant America had negotiated a treaty with Catholic France. To Elbridge Gerry this championship of a Protestant cause by France was nothing short of a " miraculous change in the political world." [45] To Benjamin Rush it seemed that " human nature " had " turned inside outwards " when a Protestant rejoiced at the " birth of a prince whose religion he had always been taught to consider as unfriendly to humanity." [46] There were other members of the Continental Congress who, if they did not go so far as to view the Revolution as a Protestant rebellion, nevertheless were not likely to overlook the possible religious implications of the alliance.

Elsewhere in the colonies there were similar misgivings. Boston [47] and Newport,[48] though at first violently opposed to

[44] E. C. Burnett, *Letters*, vols. v, pp. 34, 267, 337, 398, 433-34, 479; vi, 102, 206, 207, 210, 216, 343. " Excerpts from the Papers of Benjamin Rush," *Pa. Mag. Hist. Biog.*, vol. xxix (1905), p. 23. " Revolutionary Correspondence of James McHenry," *ibid.*, p. 54.

[45] J. T. Austin, *Life of Elbridge Gerry*... (2 vols., Boston, 1928-29), vol. i, p. 276. *Cf.* J. Fitzpatrick, *George Washington Himself* (Indianapolis, 1933), pp. 376-77.

[46] *Pa. Mag. Hist. Biog.*, vol. xxi, p. 257. Also in *Magazine of American History*, vol. i (1877), pp. 506-510. For other letters of Rush on the French alliance, see *Pa. Mag. Hist. Biog.*, vol. xxix (1905), pp. 23, 54.

[47] F. H. Smith, " The French in Boston during the Revolution," *Bostonian Society Proc.*, vol. x, pp. 9-75. *Warren-Adams Letters*, vol. ii, p. 51. J. Merlant, *Soldiers and Sailors of France during the American*

their foreign guests, later vied with each other in doing them honor. But their enthusiasm failed to penetrate the strongholds of orthodoxy in New Hampshire and Connecticut. New Hampshire in 1779 was discussing the adoption of a new constitution in which for the first time a religious test was proposed. William Plumer, an ardent advocate of religious liberty, says in reference to this test that it

was nearly contemporaneous with the alliance with France, which, however beneficial in other respects, was thought by many to favor the introduction of popery among us.[49]

At New Haven Silas Deane's offer to collect funds for the foundation of a professorship of French at Yale, though favored by President Stiles, was finally rejected by the trustees because of the " danger of Popery." [50]

For a complete picture of the religious import of the alliance, the opinions of the Whigs must be supplemented by those of the Tories. Many of the latter regarded the Revolution as a civil war. Vehement in their protest against the arbitrary acts of the British government, they were yet unwilling to follow the radicals to the point of secession. As the breach between the two groups widened with the progress of the war, the respective policies of Whig and Tory became the target of mutual denunciation. If to some of the patriots the French alliance was not an unmixed blessing, to the

War for Independence, 1776-1783. Trans. by M. E. Colman (New York, 1920), p. 66.

[48] J. Merlant, *op. cit.*, p. 117 *et seq.* There are some interesting entries in the *Diary* of Ezra Stiles who seems to have met most of the French celebrities. See vol. ii, pp. 371, 473, 459.

[49] W. Plumer, *Life of William Plumer*, ed. by A. P. Peabody (Boston, 1856), pp. 49-50.

[50] Ezra Stiles, *Diary*, vol. ii, pp. 296-98. A. C. H. *Researches*, vols. xviii-xix (1901-02), pp. 150-151. *Deane Papers*, vol. ii (1777-78), pp. 475-477.

average loyalist it was the acme of folly. From such a pact there could be but one issue—the deliverance of the " free Protestant colonies " into the toils of Rome.[51] In other words, it meant the exchange of freedom for slavery, of purity of worship for idolatry.

This is the burden of the complaints recorded in the *Journal and Letters* of Samuel Curwen, Salem merchant, impost officer of Essex County and judge of admiralty. An exile from the outbreak of the war until 1784, his extensive correspondence in America and England kept him in touch with the various currents of Tory opinion in both countries. Curwen was convinced that the alliance would eventually terminate in the permanent imposition of " French government, laws, religion, manners, and policy "—all so " alien to Americans " that they " will sit uneasy till custom and long use have familiarized them." [52] He returns to the same thought in 1782, when he writes to Richard Ward of Salem that should France succeed in obtaining control of " the late English colonies," no man " in his wits " would forego a bare subsistence in England for " French dominion and wooden shoes " in America." [53]

Samuel Rowland Fisher, of a prominent Quaker family in Philadelphia, regarded the French alliance as a punishment permitted by Providence for America's defection from the ideals of the Reformation. The Presbyterians, he wrote in his *Journal,* have permitted an altar to be erected in one of their meeting houses where the " popish mass " is " performed." That more than anything else will destroy their influence with other Protestants. Fisher rejoiced at the

[51] *Aff. Étr. Mém. et Doc.*, vol. ii, no. 10, p. 75 *et seq.* Also in Stevens, *Facsimiles*, no. 1616.

[52] Samuel Curwen, *Journal and Letters, from 1775 to 1784*, p. 95. Also in Force Trans., L. C. *Misc. Letters, C-H.*

[53] S. Curwen, *op. cit.*, pp. 344-45. *Cf.* pp. 178, 206, 324, 402-04.

failure of the French-American attack upon Savannah. The disaster would, he hoped, disunite the allies and restore peace to the land.[54] The admirable behavior of the French troops in passing through Philadelphia in 1781 was, he wrote, merely

a piece of French policy to gain the good opinion of the people of America . . . for can any man that has the use of his faculties, or is not deluded believe that they have meddled as it were in a Quarrell between Members of the same family, Religion & Language, upon any other motive than to serve their own purposes, which they study to keep covered till a suitable time may arrive to discover the cloven foot.[55]

Although the Quaker's pen is more caustic than the New Englander's, the two merchants are in essential agreement as to the motives of our Gallic friends and the baleful influence to be expected from their stay in America. Their views were committed to the privacy of their journals or exchanged in conversation or correspondence with a limited circle of friends. Not so the *Letters of Papinian,* intended to carry on an active propaganda and first published in two New York journals, Rivingston's *Royal Gazette* and Hugh Gaine's *New York Gazette and Weekly Mercury.* In 1779 they appeared in pamphlet form. Their author, for some time doubtful, is now generally conceded to have been Rev. Charles Inglis, the Anglican pastor of Trinity Church, New York, and later first Anglican bishop of Nova Scotia. As the subtitle of the pamphlet indicates, the purpose of the letters is to inquire into "the conduct, present state, and prospects, of the American Congress." To the writer's supreme disgust, Congress has reversed its attitude

---

[54] "Journal of Samuel Rowland Fisher, of Philadelphia, 1779-1781," *Pa. Mag. Hist. Biog.,* vol. xli (1917), pp. 177-79.

[55] *Ibid.,* pp. 456-57.

towards France and the French Canadians. " Professing to be patrons of liberty, candor and republicanism," he writes in Letter VIII to John Jay, they [Congress] exhaust our language in fulsom adulation to the most ambitious, restless and faithless monarchy in christiandom." [56] John Jay's own conduct is not free from the same reproach. To Mr. Inglis it is utterly unworthy of one whose ancestors fled from France because of religious persecution. In another letter, also addressed to Jay, he calls attention to one of the alleged reasons for entering the rebellion, " the legal toleration of Popery in Canada . . . yet you afterwards offered compleat establishment of this religion to the Canadians, provided they would join the rebellion." [57]

But it is in Letter IX addressed " To the people of North America," that the writer gives full expression to his fears as to the pernicious effect of the recent treaties with their one-time enemy. With Congress already perverted it behooves Protestants to be on their guard against the further progress of " Popery." " The French Alliance," he writes, " looks with no less malignant an aspect on the Protestant religion, than on the liberties of America." Inglis justifies the passage of the British penal laws and their extension to the colonies. Congress has reversed this procedure, it has thrown open the door to Catholic priests who meet with " every encouragement," while Protestant clergymen, " who will not *perjure* themselves to support the Congress," are persecuted with impunity. The reference to persecution

---

[56] [Charles Inglis], *Letters of Papinian: in which the conduct of the present state, and prospects, of the American Congress are examined...* (New York, by Hugh Gaine, 1777), p. 97. Also attributed to Rev. Jacob Duché, one-time chaplain to the Continental Congress. See *Washington-Duché Letters*, ed. by W. C. Ford (Brooklyn, 1890). For an estimate of Inglis's place among the loyalist writers, see M. C. Tyler, *Lit. Hist. Rev.*, vol. ii, p. 73.

[57] *Letters of Papinian*, p. 42.

recalls the Inquisition with its attendant horrors. These are sketched and followed by a list of " indubitable facts " to prove that the work of perversion is already well afoot: the dissenting clergy no longer declaim against the Church of Rome; on the contrary, they seek to palliate her errors; " popish beads " and other " such trumphery " are being imported and dispersed, even in New England; Catholic chaplains accompany the French ships; Congress and " the Rebel Legislature of Pennsylvania " attend " Te Deum's " at a Catholic church in Philadelphia. How different, this, from loyal New York which imprisoned Father de la Motte for saying Mass.[58]

Preeminent among the Tory pamphleteers was Joseph Galloway, who fought in America for reconciliation as long as there was hope, and, failing that, continued to work in England in behalf of the British government. Following the rejection by Congress of his " Plan of a Proposed Union between Great Britain and her Colonies," he made an appeal to the forum of public opinion in a pamphlet entitled " A Candid Examination of the Mutual Claims of Great Britain and the Colonies: With a Plan of Accommodation on Constitutional Principles." It is a sincere and able inquiry into actual conditions in America, accompanied by much destructive criticism, it is true, but offering also a constructive " Plan of Accommodation." It was probably one of the most widely circulated pamphlets of its day.[59] Referring to the lack of colonial cooperation with Great Britain during the French and Indian wars, Galloway dwells on the generosity of the mother country in bearing the brunt of the burden and in saving the colonies from " all the horrors of French slavery and popish superstition." With that introduction, he passes easily to the present danger of French

[58] *Ibid.*, pp. 113-118.
[59] M. C. Tyler, *Lit. Hist. Rev.*, vol. i, p. 380.

ambition and the certainty of becoming its victim if the protection of England is forfeited by rebellion. On the other hand, if the colonies succeed in establishing their independence, they will be between the upper and nether millstones; that is, they will either fall a prey to those twin evils already referred to or if they escape France and the " bloody superstition of Rome " they will be destroyed by their own internal dissensions.[60] In his " Historical and political reflections . . ." published in London Galloway reverts to the same theme. He points out also how the dissenting clergy in New England had recourse to that very " inquisitorial cruelty " against which they so eloquently inveighed.[61]

Minor pamphleteers borrowed arguments and analogies from the greater lights. *Candidus* in Philadelphia inquired whether no danger would come from " an army of French and Spaniards in the bosom of America? Would ye not dread their junction with the Canadians and Savages and with the numerous Roman Catholics, dispersed throughout the colonies? " [62] A Charleston writer, examining Great Britain's obligations to the loyalists, in the event of an unfavorable peace, insisted that it would be England's duty to stipulate for the advantageous disposal of their property, with liberty to move to " such of the Colonies or Dominions as may not be unfortunately surrendered at the end of the war, to a popish or arbitrary power." [63] With French domi-

---

[60] Joseph Galloway, *A Candid Examination of the Mutual Claims of Great Britain and the Colonies: With a Plan of Accommodation, on Constitutional Principles* (New York, Rivington, 1775). *Cf.* C. F. Van Tyne, *War of Ind.*, p. 466.

[61] Joseph Galloway, *Historical and Political Reflections on the Rise and Progress of the American Rebellion . . .*, pp. 4-5, 35.

[62] " PLAIN TRUTH Addressed to the Inhabitants of America containing Remarks on a late pamphlet entitled Common Sense," etc. By Candidus (Phila., 1776), p. 30. Cited, A. C. H. *Researches*, o. s., vol. xii (1895), p. 94.

[63] *The Candid Retrospect: or The American War examined by Whig Principles* (Charleston, printed. New York, reprinted, 1780), p. 28.

nation, another writer asserts, " the candle of Science would soon be extinguished, and ignorance introduced, in order to keep up a blind devotion and implicit obedience." [64]

While the war of the pamphlets went merrily on, anti-French propaganda was being dispersed industriously by the Tory press. The most influential as well as the most popular of these sheets was the *Royal Gazette,* whose editor, James Rivington, made effective " use of calumnies concerning the stupidity of the King, the frivolity of the Queen, the bad condition of French finances, and the wrath of the people " in his campaign against France.[65] Americans who favored the alliance were warned of their fate by a fable of the frogs who wanted a king. The alliance of the frogs with King Stork, his promise to make them independent of all lawful rule, and their final consumption by the King who

> . . . grew so fond of well-fed frogs
> He made a larder of the bogs,[66]

pointed a moral which needed no elucidation.

Franklin of course came in for his share of abuse. He was accused of having delivered Americans to the French King on condition that they be independent of England, enjoy the privileges of French citizenship, and, thanks to the generosity of the Pope, be freed from purgatory after their death.[67] The *Royal Gazette* for Sept. 10, 1778, announced that the Pope, overjoyed at the alliance, was sending his " favorite cardinal " to congratulate Louis XVI. The same legate would bring a special blessing to the " electrical

[64] John Morgan and others. *Four Dissertations on the Reciprocal Advantages of a Perpetual Union between Great Britain and her American Colonies...* (Phila., printed; London, reprinted, 1766).

[65] B. Faÿ, *L'Ésprit Rév.,* p. 74.

[66] Rivington's *Royal Gazette,* Dec. 8, 1778, no. 228.

[67] B. Faÿ, *L'Ésprit Rév.,* p. 74.

Doctor." These were mere pleasantries, however. Rivington knew well how to appeal to the sympathies, the fears, the prejudices of his readers. Most patrons of the *Gazette* would be amused by a bit of doggerel [68] which turned to ridicule the enthusiastic reception tendered to Monsieur Gérard; few of them would be alarmed at the mock solemnity with which the French ambassador kissed the bit of American turf presented to him by Silas Deane; [69] fewer still would believe with the "American Vicar of Bray" [70] that Americans would invite his Holiness with their "good ally." But when, as Professor Faÿ points out, Rivington published from the letters seized by the British cruisers, "extracts from the correspondence of Beaumarchais, Barbé-Marbois, etc., tending to prove that France far from being disinterested, had territorial ambitions;" when he gave detailed accounts of the attendance of Congress at Catholic functions; when he cited instances of Presbyterian and Congregational assemblies praying for the French monarch, readers were inclined to find a kernel of truth in every fable and lampoon, and to take at face value every forged letter or dispatch. [71]

[68] *Royal Gaz.*, Oct. 3, 1778. No. 210. "Yankee Doodle's Expedition at Rhode Island."

[69] *Royal Gaz.*, July 29, 1778. No. 191. *Cf. Royal Gaz.*, Aug. 22, 1778, cited in F. Moore, *Diary of Amer. Rev.* (1860), pp. 604-606. For Gérard's account to Vergennes see E. S. Kite in A. C. H. *Records,* vol. xxxii (1921), pp. 274-94. The *Gazette* for Sept. 16, 1778, No. 205, describes the landing of D'Estaing on the island of Coninicut and his taking possession of it in the name of the King.

[70] *Royal Gaz.*, June 20, 1779. No. 287.

[71] F. Wharton, *Rev. Dip. Cor.*, vol. i, p. 326. The territorial designs of France seem to have impressed the British authorities no less than naive provincials. Guy Carleton wrote to Lord Shelburne, New York, 16 Dec., 1782, "I have been informed that the French Minister at Philadelphia demanded of Congress that Rhode Island be delivered up as a pawn for the Money lent them by France, and that it be declared

The *Gazette* of March 17, 1779, assaying the role of prophet, set before its readers the probable effects of the treaty in a single decade. A subscriber to an American newspaper in 1789 would read of the enforcement of French navigation acts, the establishment of the Inquisition in Boston, the drafting of Americans for service in the French West Indies, the sentencing of Americans to the galleys, the suppression by French troops of a tax riot in Virginia and the granting of large tracts of American land to the French nobility. For his further delectation he would be informed of the abolition of trial by jury, the private execution of criminals in the " New Bastille ", the prohibition to keep arms, and the imposition of the *gabelle,* or salt tax. To these evidences of arbitrary government would be added information on the progress of religion—the " cargoes " of rosaries and Mass books, the conversion of the Old South Meeting House into a cathedral, the burning of Obadiah Steadfast, Quaker, the prohibition of the use of the Bible in the vernacular, with this triumph of proselytizing zeal:

This day being Sunday, the famous Samuel Adams read his recantation of heresy, after which he was present at Mass, and we hear that he will soon receive priests orders to qualify for a member of the American Sorbonne.[72]

Throughout 1779 every movement of the French army and fleet furnished grist to the Tory mill. This was particularly true when the news of any miscarriage of the allied plans or any disaster penetrated the British lines. A series of ballads contributed to the *Royal Gazette* by Joseph Stans-

The King's port till the debt be paid, and then to be restored to its former state..." Shelburne Mss. ELS 68, fol. 277. L. C. Transcript of original in William Clements Library, Ann Arbor, Mich.

[72] Quoted in F. Moore, *Diary of Rev.*, vol. i, p. 326. For similar items in the *Gazette* see Oct. 7, 10, 14, 17, 21, 31, 1778.

bury and Jonathan Odell effectively carried on the emotional phase of the anti-French propaganda. The dispersal of D'Estaing's fleet and the failure of the allied attack upon Savannah are instances in point. " The Congratulation " by Odell was a lengthy—it occupied twenty-one columns—attempt to felicitate Congress on the disappearance of the fleet. The following couplets indicate its tone and temper:

> What pains were taken, to procure D'Estaing!
> His fleet's dispers'd, and Congress may go hang . . .
>
> Oh brother! things are at a dreadful pass:
> Brother, we sinned in going to the Mass. . . .
>
> How wretched is their lot, to France and Spain
> Who look for succour, but who look in vain . . . [73]

The Mass to which the ballad just quoted referred was a solemn requiem celebrated at St. Mary's, Philadelphia, shortly after the death of the Spanish observer, Don Miralles.

---

[73] *Royal Gazette*, Oct. 6, 1779. Also in *Loyal Verses of Joseph Stansbury and Jonathan Odell; relating to the American Revolution*, ed. by W. Sargent (Albany, 1860), pp. 45-50. The "Feu de Joie" aims to congratulate Congress on the finding of the fleet and its escape to the West Indies. *Royal Gaz.*, Nov. 24, 1779. Also in *Loyal Verses*, pp. 51-58. Other ballads by the same authors are to be found in the *Gazette* for Nov. 27, 1779: " The Siege of Savannah," "A New Ballad," " The Jolly Tars of Old England." " Lords of the Main," by Stansbury is in *Loyal Verses*, pp. 61-62. "An Appeal, 1780," stressed the religious import of the conquest of America by the French. See F. Moore, *Songs and Ballads of the Revolution* (New York, 1856), p. 289. W. L. Stone, *Ballads and Poems relating to the Burgoyne Campaign* (Albany, 1893), p. 98. For the contribution of the loyalist writers to the literature of the Revolution see M. C. Tyler, *Lit. Hist. Rev.*, vol. ii, pp. 51-129. During the British occupation of Philaelphia the *Pennsylvania Ledger*, edited by Joseph Humphreys and the *Pennsylvania Evening Post*, by Benjamine Towne, were organs of the royalist cause. Their news was often copied by Rivington. Like their New York contemporary they inveighed against the French alliance and the supposedly Romeward trend of Congress. See *Pennsylvania Ledger*, May 13, 1778, and the *Pennsylvania Evening Post*, May 20, 1778.

Though there are numerous references to this memorial service in the private correspondence and journals of the time, Rivington's *Gazette* seems to have been the only newspaper which commented upon the attendance of Congress.[74] Among those who were present was the traitor Arnold. After his defection from the patriot cause, Arnold published in broadside a vindication of his conduct, with an appeal to his readers to follow his example. The French alliance and the apparent apostasy of Congress are offered as justification for his treason:

> Do you know that the eye which guides this pen, lately saw your mean and profligate Congress at Mass, for the soul of a Roman Catholic in Purgatory and participating in the rights of a Church against whose anti-Christian corruption your pious ancestors would have witnessed their blood? [75]

If Congress winced at Arnold's scathing denunciation, a letter of Silas Deane's was scarcely more calculated to soothe their feelings. Writing to Jesse Root from Paris, May 20, 1781, Deane says that the death of Don Miralles

> produced a remarkable instance of condescension and inconsistency, not to say hypocricy, in Congress, who, to liberate the soul of the deceased from Purgatory very devoutly attended one of the most superstitious rights of a religion which that body but a little time before, in addressing the people of England, had

[74] Rivington's *Royal Gazette*, May 20, 1780. See also James Thacher, *Military Journal during the Revolutionary War, from 1775 to 1783* (Boston, 1823), pp. 193, 228-30. E. C. Burnett, *Letters*, vol. v, p. 131. *Diary of Colonel Caleb Gibbs*, interleaved almanac by Anthony Sharp (Phila., 1780), with manuscript entries. Entry under April 28. L. C. Mss. Div. Letter of Ebenezer Hazard to Jeremy Belknap, June 27, 1780, Mass. Hist. Soc. *Coll.*, 5 ser., vol. ii, p. 61 *et seq.* For an account of the mission of Miralles see S. F. Bemis, *Diplomacy of the Rev.*, p. 88.

[75] A. C. H. *Researches*, o. s., vol. vi (1889), pp. 68-69. R. Maury, *Wars of the Godly* (New York, 1928), pp. 35-36. *Complot d'Arnold et de Sir H. Clinton* (Paris, 1816), p. 133.

described as "having dispersed impiety, bigotry, persecution, murder, and rebellion through every part of the world."

The letter fell into the hands of the British and was published in the *Royal Gazette*.[76]

The patriot press contains little for our purpose. Papers which before the Revolution were loud in their denunciations of the old faith, either ignored the religious affiliations of France or noticed them only to affirm their harmlessness. On the other hand they consistently supported the alliance. Reporting for the most part the same events as did the Tory press, the accounts of the Whig papers differed from those of their rivals largely in their interpretation of the news. Not only was there almost complete abstention from innuendo; there was also positive enthusiasm. Reports of banquets were sure to include all the toasts in honor of their generous ally and his representatives.[77] Receptions with their exchange of complimentary speeches,[78] were reported with a fervor calculated to awaken a like enthusiasm in the reader.

---

[76] *Deane Papers*, vol. iv, pp. 347-48. Had the letter reached Root it would have met with a sympathetic reception. In 1775 he had written to Deane in Philadelphia praying that the "American empire" would be preserved through the wisdom of Congress from all "craft and power of Tyranny, the Pope and the Devil." Conn. Hist. Soc. *Coll.*, vol. ii, p. 237.

[77] The *Boston Gazette*, March 1, 1779, No. 1279, prints an account of an "elegant entertainment" given by Boston in honor of the French consul, Monsieur de Valnais. See among many others that might be cited, *New Hampshire Gazette*, July 5, 1783. *Massachusetts Spy*, April 30, 1778, July 16, 1778. *Pennsylvania Packet*, July 4, 14, Dec. 5, 1778; April 19, 1783. *Pennsylvania Journal*, July 23, Sept. 13, 1783. *Providence Gazette*, May 3, 1783.

[78] *Pennsylvania Packet*, Aug. 11, 1778, May 13, 1783. *Pennsylvania Journal*, Aug. 13, 18, 1779; Jan. 4, 1783. *North Carolina Gazette*, May 22, 1778. *Boston Gazette*, Jan. 18, 1778. *New Jersey Gazette*, June 19, 1782, July 12, 1780, May 29, 1782. E. C. Burnett, *Letters*, vol. iv, pp. 56, 299. J. B. Perkins, *France in the American Revolution* (Boston, 1911), p. 307 *et seq.*

Comment on terms of the treaties,[79] often printed with the text complete, emphasized the generosity of France and the undeniable advantages to America. Occasionally a writer would be at some pains to prove how immune America was to French influence and quite inadvertently would betray the religious bias he sought to conceal. Thus " Gallo-Americanus " in a letter to the editor of the *Pennsylvania Packet* contrasts our " equal alliance " with that " mean dependence upon a protestant power " which has recently established " the Popish religion throughout a province the largest in America! " Far from being influenced by France, the writer is not without hope that we may there introduce " liberty and the Protestant religion." [80]

So completely, apparently, had the viewpoint of the American Whigs changed that the *Pennsylvania Packet,* the organ of Congress after the British evacuation of Philadelphia, deemed it necessary to explain, almost apologetically, some of the ways and means adopted by their ally. For a time there was question of a combined French and American attack upon Canada. Before the project was abandoned, D'Estaing had prepared an address to the Canadians. Fearing that his readers might take umbrage at that portion of the speech which reminded the Canadian clergy of the influence which, as a corporate body, they might exert upon French Catholics, the editor prefaces the text of the address with the following note:

[79] *Pennsylvania Journal,* Jan. 29, April 23, Oct. 25, 1783. *Providence Gazette,* Nov. 2, 1782. *Massachusetts Spy,* Oct. 8, 1778. *South Carolina and American General Gazette,* June 4, 1778. *North Carolina Gazette,* May 29, 1778.

[80] *Pennsylvania Packet,* Aug. 1, 1778. Letter dated Philadelphia, July 10, 1778. The same letter, unsigned, is quoted from the *South Carolina Gazette* in Almon's *Remembrancer,* vol. vii (1778-79), pp. 330-31. *Cf. Remembrancer,* vol. ix, pp. 287-290.

. . . It is evidently the design of Count D'Estaing . . . to induce the Canadians to comply with the invitation which Congress formerly gave them. . . . Accordingly he employs such persuasives as in their presentation are most likely to prove effectual; holding up to view how pleasing such a step would be to their Prince, and the whole French nation, as well as the absolute freedom respecting religion which Congress had engaged they should enjoy.[81]

Of all the changes of opinion, real or apparent, witnessed by the Revolution, none is more striking than that of the Calvinist clergy. It was they more than any other clerical group that had sown the seed of opposition to the British government; it was they also who continually denounced kings and princes as the authors of war. The King of France particularly had become the stock example of tyranny from which his religion was never dissociated. Such was the zest with which the dissenting clergy denounced " French tyranny and popish superstition," that the loyal Anglican clergy, seeking for a concrete expression of civil and religious treason, selected their dissenting brethren as the extreme example of perversion. That they should have dissolved political connection with Great Britain was bad enough; but that they should have allied themselves with Catholic France was well nigh inconceivable.[82] Nevertheless the inconceivable had become an actuality. Chauncy and Cooper were not content with preaching rebellion as a religious duty. The treaties with the court of Versailles were proclaimed from their very pulpits; prayers were offered for their " great and good ally "; the benefits of the alliance found a place in elec-

[81] *Pennsylvania Packet*, Dec. 19, 1778.

[82] A. Baldwin, *New Eng. Clergy*, pp. 88-89, 164, 170-71. C. H. Van Tyne, *England and America*, p. 60 et seq. *Causes of War of Ind.*, p. 360. Hugh Percy, *Letters of Hugh, Earl Percy* (Boston, 1902), p. 29. *Hutchinson Correspondence*, vol. ii, pp. 427, 536-37. Banc. Coll. N.Y.P.L. J. and A. Adams, *Familiar Letters*, pp. 46-47.

tion, anniversary and thanksgiving sermons.[83]   Ezra Stiles whose *Diary* [84] testifies to the change of mind produced by contact with the French, looked upon their advent as a special intervention of Divine Providence.   America's gratitude would be sung by her " future Homers, Livys and Tassos." They would "celebrate the names of a Washington and a Rochambeau, a Greene and Lafayette, a Lincoln and a Chatelleux, a Gates and a Viomenil, a Putnam and a Duc de Lauzon, a Morgan, and other heroes who rushed to arms." [85]

Rev. George Duffield, preaching in the Third Presbyterian Church of Philadelphia, felt it his duty to rebuke those cavilers who insisted that the court of Versailles was actuated by motives of self-interest.

. . . Let detraction, therefore, be silent, nor object the influence of interest, to sully the generous deed.   God has connected duty with interest, by indissoluble bonds; nor may neither of right assume the name alone.

The speaker then faces frankly the change that has taken place, and attributes it generously to personal intercourse with the French.   That intercourse not only dispelled inherited prejudices, it ripened into " cordial affection."

The citizens and subjects of both nations embraced as brethren; and fought side by side with united hands, in the then made

---

[83] See among others, S. Cooper, *A sermon preached before His Excellency, John Hancock,* . . . *Oct. 25, 1780* . . . (Boston, 1780), p. 42.   Zabdiel Adams, *A sermon preached before His Excellency, John Hancock* . . . *May 29, 1782* . . . (Boston, 1782), pp. 42, 47.   Jonathan Trumbull, *God is to be praised for the glory of His majesty* . . . (New Haven, 1784), p. 24. H. M. Brackenridge, *Eulogium of the brave who have fallen in the contest with Great Britain,* . . . July 5, 1779.   Quoted in Almon's *Remembrancer*, vol. xi, pp. 334-42.   Jonas Clark, *Sermon preached before His Excellency, John Hancock* . . . (Boston, 1781), pp. 42, 49.   S. Woodward, *The help of the Lord, in signal deliverances* . . . (Boston, 1779), p. 22.

[84] Stiles, *Diary*, vol. ii, pp. 371, 459, 473.

[85] Ezra Stiles, *The United States Elevated to Glory and Honor* . . . (Worcester, 1785), pp. 68, 75.

common cause. Their only strife was, who should display the noblest deeds, and render themselves more worthy each other's esteem.[86]

An idealized picture which exhibits only one side of the canvas, this description of the course of Franco-American friendship takes no account of the suspicions, the antagonisms, the jealousies which were its inevitable accompaniment. Nevertheless, within its limitations, it seems to be a faithful account of the experience of many a Calvinist, both lay and clerical. Innumerable letters and diaries of the period, in French and in English, support the passages quoted above.[87]

Sharing in much of the comment which this chapter has reviewed, Spain's vacillating policy obscured the extent and value of her services to the American colonies. In 1776 she expressed her willingness to extend secret aid and to share with France its financial burden. When later it became evident that the war was being waged for independence rather than the redress of grievances, Spain for a time lost interest in the struggle. A successful war of independence so close to her own colonies would furnish a dangerous precedent. Still less would it become her to countenance openly such a rebellion. Her observers in America and her ministers to

---

[86] George Duffield, *A sermon preached in the Third Presbyterian Church ... Philadelphia ... Dec. 11, 1783 ...* (Phila. printed; Boston, reprinted, ... 1784), pp. 12-13, 20-21. *Cf.* John A. M. Murray, *Jerubbaal, or Tyranny's Grove Destroyed ... A Discourse delivered at the Presbyterian Church in Newbury-Port, Dec. 11, 1783* (Newbury-Port, 1784), pp. 34-35.

[87] E. Stiles, *Diary, supra,* note 84. J. and A. Adams, *Familiar Letters,* pp. 242-243. Baron DeKalb, Letter to Duc de Broglie, May 7, 1778. Stevens' *Fac.,* vol. viii, no. 821. Chevalier de Fleury, "Summary of the political and military condition of America," Nov. 16, 1779, in Stevens' *Fac.,* vol. xvii, no. 1616. B. Rush, "Letter to a Lady," reprinted from *Portfolio* IV (1817) in *Mag. of Amer. Hist.,* vol. i (1877), pp. 506-10. Francis Hopkinson, Letter to Benj. Franklin, in G. E. Hastings, *Life and Works of Francis Hopkinson* (Chicago, 1926), p. 279. E. C. Burnett, *Letters,* vol. v, pp. 164-173, 328, 480.

the courts of France and Spain were meanwhile keeping her informed; her aid continued. When in 1779 she entered the war on the side of France, she was justly considered one of our allies, though she had not entered into a formal alliance with us.[88] Spanish troops rendered valuable assistance in the southwest; Spanish ships diverted units of the British fleet from American waters; but neither the Spanish government nor the Spanish nation [89] shared the enthusiasm which swept over France and sent the flower of her nobility to serve the American cause. Hence we do not find Americans vying with one another in singing her praises; neither on the other hand was she the object of such scorn and ridicule as was heaped upon France.

One finds however her name constantly coupled with that of France, especially after 1779. In its relations with Spain or with Spanish agents Congress was as meticulous in the observance of diplomatic amenities as it was with France. Don Miralles as we have seen, though only an informal observer, was accorded, unofficially, the honors of a formally accredited minister. Jay was instructed to express his country's grateful appreciation of Spanish aid " on all suitable occasions." [90] The army celebrated the entrance of our " new ally, the King of Spain " into the war.[91] Governor

---

[88] S. F. Bemis, *Diplomacy of the Amer. Rev.*, pp. 25-26 n, 27-28, 52-53, 75-76, 85-87, 110-111. F. Wharton, *Rev. Dip. Cor.*, vol. iii, pp. 707-34; vol. iv, pp. 112-50, 738-65; vol. v, pp. 336-37. C. H. McCarthy, "Attitude of Spain during the American Revolution," *Cath. Hist. Rev.*, vol. ii (1916-17), pp. 47-65.

[89] *N. C. State Records*, vol. xv, p. 57, letter of Hon. W. Hill to Dr. Burke, Phil., Aug. 20, 1780. *Cf.* G. O. Trevelyan, *George the Third and Charles Fox* (2 vols., New York, 1912-14), vol. i, pp. 184-85.

[90] *Journals*, vol. xx, pp. 551-53.

[91] Adam Hubly, Jr., Lieut.-Col. Commandant 11th Penna. Regt., *His Journal, Commencing at Wyoming, July 30, 1779*, ed. by J. W. Jordan, *Pa. Mag. Hist. Biog.*, vol. xxxiii (1909), p. 416. *Cf.* Burnett, *Letters*, vol. v, p. 337.

Patrick Henry of Virginia instructed Colonel John Todd to

embrace every opportunity to manifest the high regard and friendly sentiments of this Commonwealth towards all the subjects of his Catholic Majesty, for whose safety, prosperity and advantage you will give every possible advantage.[92]

Private opinion of Spain seemed to fluctuate with changes in Spanish policy. In 1777 James Lovell wrote to William Whipple, " Spain is unbounded in manly friendship." [93] But in February, 1780, when Spanish negotiations regarding the Mississippi and Florida seemed to stand in the way of an early peace, Lovell wrote to Samuel Adams,

We must cut Throats for another year at least, and we ought to do it vigorously. F and S will persist in strenuous Cooperation for the purpose of *securing* our Independ'ce and *indemnifying themselves.*[94]

John Collins, Rhode Island delegate to Congress, also wrote in 1780 that there would be no peace that year because Spain was not ready for it. She would see to it that the United States would not get too near her " Strong Box," Mexico, and for that reason would leave whatever she obtained east of the Mississippi and the Floridas a wilderness.[95] James Duane thought we relied too much upon foreign aid. Neither Holland nor Spain, he wrote to Washington, were inclined to imitate the liberality of France, but were waiting until they could obtain solid advantages.[96] James Madison's trust in both France and Spain was unshaken. He admitted

---

[92] *Va. Cal. State Papers*, vol. i, p. 312.

[93] *Langdon-Elwyn Papers*, vol. i, p. 267. Banc Trans. N. Y. P. L.

[94] E. C. Burnett, *Letters*, vol. v, pp. 28-29. See also Lovell to H. Laurens, *ibid.*, p. 34; to S. Adams, *ibid.*, p. 53; to James Warren, *ibid.*, p. 476.

[95] E. C. Burnett, *Letters*, vol. v, p. 47.

[96] *Ibid.*, vol. v, p. 479.

that their policies were not always clear, but because of their " wisdom and goodness " in the past,

> we ought not on slight grounds to abate our faith in them. For my part I have as yet great confidence in them.[97]

Elbridge Gerry, Samuel Holten, John Sullivan, Jared Ingersoll agree substantially with the writers quoted above.[98] In these letters, if there is little enthusiasm, there is no abuse, no inclination to invoke the Inquisition or the sins of the conquistadores in explanation of Spanish policy, intent on making a good bargain.

From the Tory pamphleteers and the ballad writers Spain received her share of opprobrium, though it was almost negligible compared with that showered upon France. To this the patriot writers contributed. Philip Freneau, the ablest and the bitterest of the Whig satirists, in his *Voyage to Boston,* compares General Gage to Cortez.

> Cortez was sent by Spain's black brotherhood
> Whose faith is murder, whose religion blood,
> Sent unprovok'd with his Iberian train,
> To fat the soil with millions of the slain.

The poet then calls upon Mexico and Peru to reveal their " hosts of murder'd dead " to

> Force a dumb voice and echo to the sky,
> The blasting curse of papal tyranny;
> And let your rocks, and let your hills proclaim
> That Gage and Cortez' errand are the same.[99]

There follows a speech by an American soldier who regrets that he must fight fellow Britons. But Liberty calls; he obeys.

[97] *Ibid.*, vol. v, pp. 433-34.

[98] *Ibid.*, vol. v, pp. 135, 144, 398, 405.

[99] [Philip Freneau], *A Voyage to Boston*. A Poem (New York, 1775), p. 9.

> Let Carleton arm his antichristian might,
> And sprinkle holy water ere he fight;
> And let him have to shield his limbs from hurt
> St. Stephen's breeches and St. Stephen's shirt . . .[100]

Of all the religious groups in America one would naturally expect the Catholics to be the loudest in their approbation of the French alliance. Catholic nations, Catholic rulers, had for generations been held up as lovers and exponents of tyranny. Louis XVI was now hailed as "the protector of the rights of mankind." Partly through French influence, another Catholic country had entered the war and had made substantial contributions to the cause of American independence. The French nation was hardly less enthusiastic for American liberty than the patriots themselves. Moreover, contact with individual Frenchmen, officers and privates, proved them to be the very antithesis of the "ignorant, bigoted Papists" of the Protestant tradition. Furthermore, the French clergy as exemplified in the hundred or more chaplains of the French military and naval forces, proved to be charming, cultured gentlemen, zealous in the discharge of their religious duties, but apparently devoid of that proselytizing propensity so generally attributed to them.[101] The fears of the Tories that Protestant America should become the dupe of Rome were obviously unfounded. Yet the Catholics were strangely inarticulate. A Carroll, a Barry, a Moylan, a Gibault, might and did give unstintingly of their best. There seems to be no evidence however that they were in any way identified with the French alliance.

[100] See also "Rivington's Reflections" in *Poems of Philip Freneau...* (Phila., 1786), pp. 269-270; "America Independent," *ibid.*, p. 159. *American Liberty...* (New York, 1775), pp. 4, 7. For an account of Freneau and his work see Tyler, *Lit. Hist. Rev.*, vol. ii, p. 246 *et seq.*

[101] For an account of the French chaplains and their work see A. H. Germain, *Catholic Military and Naval Chaplains, 1776-1917.*

After independence was won, Catholics like other religious denominations, presented their felicitations to President Washington. During the war they had been content to do their part quietly, hoping for the dawn of religious liberty. Many of them no doubt rejoiced at the aid given by Catholic France and Spain; yet, while victory hung in the balance, they dared not give expression to their joy. Royalist propaganda made the most of the " Popish " bogy. The Whigs did not disdain to use it on occasion. Catholics had not forgotten the outcry against the toleration clauses of the Quebec Act. Should the outcome of the war go against the colonists and their Catholic allies, the old charges of French treachery and Spanish cruelty would revive. Monsieur D'Anemours, French consul at Baltimore, probably summed up the situation accurately when he wrote to his colleague at the French legation in Philadelphia that the Maryland Catholics " fear an alliance with France, lest they be persecuted, and lest their priests be expelled." [102] Gérard, writing to Vergennes of the *Te Deum* in Philadelphia in 1779, said that it was thought that the celebration would react favorably for the Catholics of " whom a rather large number are suspected of not being strongly attached to the patriot cause." [103] It was the impression of Barbé-Marbois, French Chargé d'Affaires, writing to Vergennes in September, 1784,

[102] *French Legation Papers.* " Extrait divers. 1er Cahier. Observations du 8ième mois de 1777. Par M. D'Annemours. Religion. En Maryland les Catholiques forment moitie de la population. ils sont guides par les jesuites par consequence ils dissimulent mais on soupconne qu'ils craignent une alliance avec la France qui ferait chasser les Saints peres. en general toutes les sects redoutent l'intolerance des Puritans." L. C. Photostat of originals in William Mason Library, Evanston, Illinois.

[103] *Aff. Étr. Cor. Pol. États-Unis*, vol. ix, no. 6. Gérard writes: " C'est le premier Te Deum qui ait jamais été chanté dans les treize États et on croit que cet acte d'éclat produira un bon effect sur les Catholiques dont un asséz grand nombre sont suspectés de n'être pas bien fortement attachés à la cause Américaine."

that the Catholics were neither kindly disposed towards the Revolution nor towards the French.[104] If the Catholics in Maryland, where their services to the state had placed their reputation beyond cavil, were thus fearful of the reaction of the alliance, their silence there and in the other provinces is readily explained.

What then was the final effect of the French alliance upon American opinion of Roman Catholicism? It would be too much to claim that it caused any appreciable change in the American attitude toward Roman Catholicism as a religion. Catholic doctrine and practice were—and still are—reprobated by Protestants of strong religious convictions. As a political system Catholicism was considered equally undesirable. The " shadow of the Pope " fell heavily, as we shall presently see, upon the constitutional conventions of the various states, only four of which gave Catholics political equality with Protestants. It cannot be denied however that in practice Americans had grown more tolerant of the " Papist." Criticism had not been silent, misunderstandings were not unknown, friction had not been lacking in the intercourse between the two nations. Yet the total impression made upon the colonists by their allies was favorable. Americans had had a practical lesson which they would not entirely forget. Catholics, they had learned, could be true to their religious obligations and still be lovers of liberty; they could and did give " until it hurt." As a nation and as individuals they had kept their word with heretics. In spite of their religion, they exemplified in their lives many

---

[104] *Aff Étr. Cor. Pol. États-Unis*, vol. 28, folios 140-143. Marbois to Vergennes. "Phil. le 15 aout, 1784. Les Catholiques toujours dirigès par les Jesuites dans ce pais-ci, Msgr. ont été en géneral mal disposes pour la révolution. Ils ne sont pas mieux pour nous, mais plusieurs particuliers considérables n'ont pas les mêmes préjugés." *Cf.* J. Gurn, *Charles Carroll of Carrollton* (New York, 1932), pp. 101-102. John Carroll, in J. C. Brent, *Biog. Sketch*, pp. 68-69.

Christian virtues. The word Catholic no longer connoted of necessity all that was vile and despicable. In other words, the French alliance had made a breach in the wall of prejudice which hitherto had prevented intercourse with the enemy. This was especially true of the more responsible statesmen, of the best representatives of the clergy, of the highest types in the professional and business world. The masses then as now were at the beck and call of every demagogue. Witness the " No-Popery " waves in American history since the Revolution. But Protestant Americans had learned, for the time being at any rate, not to decry the religion of their friends; they had moreover admitted that a Roman Catholic in spite of, not because of, his religion, might be a desirable neighbor, a devoted friend, a loyal citizen. That at least was a step forward.[105]

---

[105] John England, *Works*, vol. iv, p. 182. C. H. Van Tyne, " Clergy and Amer. Rev.," *Amer. Hist. Rev.*, vol. xix (1913-14), p. 62.

CHAPTER IX

MAKING THE CONSTITUTIONS

WHILE the Revolution was being fought and won the colonies which had declared their independence from Great Britain were confronted with the necessity of establishing legal machinery to take the place of the government they had repudiated. It was soon found that government by extra-legal bodies such as Committees of Safety or Provincial Congresses was not in most cases satisfactory. Applied to for advice, the Continental Congress recommended the formation of governments which would best " conduce to the happiness and safety of their constituents in particular, and America in general." The result was that series of written instruments known as our state constitutions.

The statesmen who drafted these constitutions were in many cases members of the Continental Congress. Like that body, the provincial congresses were drawing up memorials to the King, declarations of rights and instructions to their delegates which contained many high-sounding phrases about natural rights and civil and religious liberty on the one hand, and statements of grievances on the other. The inconsistency between these two portions of the documents was often glaring. It is not surprising, therefore, that the bills of rights which prefaced many of the new constitutions should display the same divergence between theory and practice. In some of these declarations the God-given rights of liberty of conscience and freedom of worship were somehow found to be compatible with a state church. Others, a shade more liberal, would concede these rights to all Protestants. The political philosophy of Locke, which would exclude Catholics from all share in the government, was evident in all but four of the new constitutions.[1]

With the provincial congresses listing the Quebec Act among their grievances in their petitions to the King or in their declarations of rights,[2] it follows, almost as a matter of course, that it should appear as such in the state constitutions. In some of these its economic aspect alone is stressed; in others, as in that of South Carolina, the religious clauses of the Act are emphasized.[3] Yet, in spite of this emphasis, South Carolina's first constitution, hastily framed, contained no provisions regarding religion. The constitution of 1778, however, declared Protestantism the state religion; none but Protestants were eligible to the assembly and the senate.[4]

[1] W. C. Webster, "A Comparative Study of the State Constitutions of the American Revolution," *Annals of the American Academy of Political and Social Science*, vol. lx, pp. 380-420. James G. Dealey, *Growth of American State Constitutions* (New York, 1915), p. 36. J. F. Jameson, *Introduction to the Study of the Constitutional and Political History of the United States* (Johns Hopkins Studies in History and Political Sciences, 4 ser., no. 5, vol. iv, 1886), p. 195.

[2] See among others the *New York Committee of Safety, Mar. 3, 1775*, Force Trans. L. C. *Votes and Proceedings of the General Assembly of New Jersey, Perth Amboy, June 11, 1775–Feb. 13, 1776*, Force Trans. L. C., Petition to King, Feb. 13, 1775, p. 3287. Declaration of the Delegates of Maryland, July 3, 1776, *Carroll Papers, Apr., 1776–Feb., 1777*, Md. Hist. Soc. Indorsed: "My sons Rough Draft of the Maryland Declaration." Provincial Congress of Georgia, Petition to King, July 14, 1775, text in W. Harden, *History of Savannah and South Georgia* (Chicago and New York, 1913), vol. i, pp. 182. Va., *Journal of the House of Burgesses, 1773-1776*, pp. 213-219.

[3] *Statutes at Large*, vol. i, pp. 128-134. B. P. Poore, *Federal and State Constitutions, Colonial Charters, and other Organic Laws of the United States* (Wash., 1877), vol. ii, p. 1615.

[4] *Statutes at Large*, vol. i, pp. 137-146. B. P. Poore, *Fed. and State Const.*, vol. ii, p. 1622.

South Carolina's sister colony met in convention at Hillsboro in August 1775. Its constitutional provisions with regard to religion were foreshadowed in the instructions issued by Mecklenburg and Orange counties. Both of these districts were Scotch-Presbyterian strongholds where, according to the Presbyterian historian, Foote, the early settlers " had brought with them no kind remembrance of the Popish clergy and their adherents. Every page of their history," he says, " was stained with blood," for which the Irish Catholics and their clergy were responsible. To tolerate that sect would be to cherish the very enemy from which they had fled.[5] The Mecklenburg delegates therefore were instructed to resist every form of ecclesiastical oppression. More specifically, they were to oppose " the toleration of popish idolatrous worship." [6] The Orange County delegates were instructed to insist upon freedom of religion for everyone, but to see to it that those entrusted with any office

. . . give assurance that they do not acknowledge any supremacy ecclesiastical or civil in any foreign power or spiritual infallibility or authority to grant Divine pardon to any person who may violate moral duties or commit crimes injurious to the community.[7]

Owing to the antagonism between the conservatives and radicals, the Hillsboro congress adjourned without having framed a constitution. The following year the same task was undertaken at Halifax. Like its predecessor the convention found that constitution making was not so simple a matter as they thought. Although the final outcome was

[5] W. H. Foote, *Sketches of North Carolina*, p. 75.

[6] *N. C. Col. Rec.*, vol. x, p. 870d. Also quoted in Foote, *Sketches of N. Carolina*, pp. 70-73. J. M. Hurley, " The Political Status of Roman Catholics in North Carolina," A. C. H. *Records*, vol. xxxviii (1927), pp. 237-293.

[7] *N. C. Col. Rec.*, vol. x, p. 870 f-h.

a victory for the radicals, the constitution which eventually emerged bore the marks of the struggle. Article xix of the Declaration of Rights declared that " All men have a natural and inalienable right to worship Almighty God according to the dictates of their own conscience." In contrast with this liberalism, Article xxxii excluded from office those

who shall deny the being of God or the truth of the Protestant religion, or the divine authority of either the Old or the New Testament, or who shall hold religious principles incompatible with the freedom and safety of the State.[8]

This test, it is said, was introduced by Rev. David Caldwell and represented the views of many of the delegates. Its path through the convention was not a smooth one, however, and it was only after " much warm debate " and for the sake of peace that it was carried. Those who opposed it are said to have been responsible for Article xxxi which excluded clergymen from office.[9]

Having conceded that much to the religious prejudices of certain members of the convention, in practice North Carolina appears to have ignored the existence of the thirty-first and thirty-second articles, for there is no record of their having been invoked during the eighteenth century against Catholic, Jew or clergyman. Although documentary evidence is lacking, there is a well established tradition that the first governor under the state constitution, Thomas Burke, was a Catholic. Burke had been a member of the constitutional convention of 1776 and had represented North Carolina in the Continental Congress from 1777 to 1780. It

[8] B. P. Poore, *Fed. and State Const.*, vol. ii, p. 1410.

[9] G. J. McRee, *Life and Correspondence of James Iredell* (2 vols., New York, 1857-58). See letter of Samuel Johnson to his sister Mrs. Iredell, dated Halifax, Dec. 13, 1776, vol. i, p. 339. E. W. Sikes, *Transition of North Carolina from Colony to Commonwealth* (J. H. U. Studies, 16 ser., nos. 10-11, 1898), pp. 554-555. Allan Nevins, *American States during and after the Revolution* (New York, 1927), p. 438.

would seem that if a political candidate had reached the economic and social status of the ruling class nothing much was said about his religion.[10]

Georgia retained her Establishment and required her representatives to be Protestants.[11] As in North Carolina, however, Georgia seems to have dispensed on occasion with property and religious qualifications, for complaints were made in 1777 that a Roman Catholic was representing Chatham county in the state legislature.[12]

The proceedings of the New Jersey convention at Burlington give no clue to the authorship of the constitution of 1776.[13] John Witherspoon is said to have been one of the guiding spirits of the convention, though his biographer can find no evidence of his influence, and notes that on the day of its adoption Witherspoon was in Philadelphia debating the Declaration of Independence.[14] Rev. Jacob Green is also cited as one of its authors, especially of the religious clause excluding Catholics from office.[15] But again evidence is

[10] See correspondence on this subject between Dr. Guilday and Prof. R. W. D. Connor, of the University of North Carolina in Guilday's *England*, vol. i, pp. 129-30. Prof. W. K. Boyd of Duke University, Durham, N. C., is in substantial accord with the conclusions of Professor Connor (Letter of Prof. W. K. Boyd to the writer, Nov. 20, 1935).

[11] B. P. Poore, *Fed. and State Const.*, vol. i, p. 377.

[12] See letter of John Wereat to George Walton, Savannah, Aug. 30, 1777, in *Georgia Records, Misc. 1732-1796*, Force Trans. L. C. Also from the same to Henry Laurens in *Correspondence of Henry Laurens* (New York, 1861), pp. 45-46.

[13] *Journal of Votes and Proceedings of the Convention of New Jersey* ... (Burlington, 1776. Reprinted, Trenton, 1831).

[14] "History of the Constitution of New Jersey, adopted in 1776, and of the Government under it," L. Q. Elmer, N. J. Hist. Soc. *Proc.*, 2 ser., vol. ii, p. 133 *et seq.* D. W. Woods, *John Witherspoon*, pp. 213-214.

[15] F. B. Lee, *New Jersey as a Colony and a State*, vol. ii, pp. 412-13. J. Whitehead, *Judicial and Civil History of New Jersey* (Boston, 1897), p. 300. L. T. Stevens, *History of Cape May County* ... (Cape May City, 1897), pp. 183-84.

lacking. What is more important is that the New Jersey constitution was the first of the state instruments to discriminate against Catholics and that despite this bias it was praised for its liberality by some of the most distinguished personages of the time. Ezra Stiles, commenting upon its religious provisions, records approvingly in his *Diary*, " Universal Protestant Religious Liberty established." [16]   Witherspoon, whose influence at Princeton and through the middle states was comparable to that of Stiles in New England, wrote in answer to Barbé-Marbois's inquiry,

V. There is no profession of religion which has an exclusive legal establishment. Some particular churches have charters of incorporation; and probably they would not be refused to a body of any denomination. All professions are tolerated, and all protestants capable of electing and being elected, and indeed have every privilege belonging to citizens.[17]

Governor Livingston's pamphlet, " Remarks on the Origin of Government and on Religious Liberty (1788)," praised the " Catholic Constitution " of New Jersey. Mathew Carey, the Irish editor of the *American Museum,* failed to see its catholicity, and said so plainly in the fourth volume of his magazine,[18] and in the *General Advertiser.*   To his protest was added that of Bishop Carroll,

At that time the American army swarmed with Catholic soldiers, and the world would have held them justified, had they withdrawn themselves from the defense of a state which treated them with so much cruelty and injustice, and which they actually covered from the depredations of the British army.[19]

---

[16] Ezra Stiles, *Diary*, vol. ii, Aug. 12, 1776. Force Trans. L. C.

[17] *Works of John Witherspoon* (9 vols., Edinburgh, 1815), vol. ix, pp. 202-03.

[18] *The American Museum*, vol. iv, pp. 493-95. *Cf. ibid.*, vol. ii, p. 245.

[19] J. C. Brent, *Biog. Sketch*, p. 143. *Cf.* A. C. H. *Researches*, o. s., vol. xv (1898), pp. 62-64.

In the constitutional convention which met at Kingston on the Hudson, March 6, 1777, the religious clauses of the proposed frame of government for New York were the subject of frequent and protracted debates. After the reading on March 20 of the thirty-second paragraph, granting liberty of worship to " all mankind ", John Jay, whose religious antipathies have been noted in connection with the Quebec Act, offered an amendment which would exclude Catholics from the benefit of the clause. That is, he would exclude " any sect or denomination of Christians " whose principles were " inconsistent with the safety of civil society." Of this inconsistency the state legislature was to be the judge.[20]

The adoption of that amendment would have left every sect at the mercy of the legislature. The opposition forced Jay to be more specific. He therefore withdrew the amendment, substituting the following in its stead:

Except the professors of the religion of the church of Rome, who ought not to hold lands in, or be admitted to a participation in the civil rights enjoyed by the members of this State, until such time as the said professors shall appear in the Supreme Court of this State, and there most solemnly swear, that they verily believe in their consciences, that no pope, priest, or foreign authority on earth hath power to absolve the subjects of this State from their allegiance to the same. And further that they renounce and believe to be false and wicked, the dangerous and damnable doctrine, that the pope or any other earthly authority, have power to absolve men from sins . . . and particularly, that no pope, priest, or foreign authority on earth, hath power to absolve them from the obligation of this oath.[21]

The wording of this substitute was unequivocal. After prolonged debate it was defeated by a vote of nineteen to

[20] *Journals of the Provincial Congress, Provincial Convention, Committee of Safety and Council of Safety of the State of New York, 1775, 1776, 1777* (2 vols., Albany, 1842), vol. i, p. 844.

[21] *Ibid.*

ten. Nothing daunted, Jay moved for a postponement of the question to the following day, when he again offered an amendment, less objectionable in form but capable, in the opinion of some members of the convention, of the same construction. In the discussions which followed, Gouverneur Morris and Robert Livingston led the opposition in favor of religious liberty. Unfortunately the Journal of the convention records none of the debates, but enough is given to make it clear that the religious question was of vital concern. Eventually Morris's efforts to save the thirty-second article were successful, his motion being carried nineteen to seven.[22]

Although defeated in his efforts to exclude Catholics from the religious liberty guaranteed by the constitution, Jay was by no means discouraged. When the thirty-sixth article on the naturalization of foreigners was read, he was again ready with an amendment which, by depriving immigrant Catholics of citizenship, would also debar them from all offices of trust and profit. Once more the liberals led by Morris and the Livingstons offered substitute amendments which would leave at least a loophole for the " Romanist." But the forces of bigotry carried the day. When on April 22 the entire constitution was read the forty-second article gave the legislature power to naturalize foreigners on condition that the latter

take an oath of allegiance to this State, and abjure and renounce all allegiance and subjection to every foreign king, prince, potentate and State, in all matters ecclesiastical as well as civil.[23]

Of the thirty-four members present at this final reading, every one voted for the constitution except Colonel Peter Livingston, who asked that his dissent be entered in the

[22] *Ibid.*, vol. i, p. 845.

[23] *Ibid.*, p. 897.

[24] *Ibid.*, p. 982.

Journal.[24] That is, the New York convention, while unwilling to have the article on religious liberty restricted by the partisan amendment proposed by John Jay, was not ready to follow the ideal in all its implications.

This inconsistency was doubtless shared by others throughout the state. The work of the convention at Kingston was followed with an interest verging on anxiety by many New Yorkers who were not privileged to be present. Members of the same family did not always view the matter in the same light nor did they hesitate to enlarge upon their own views in the hope of making converts. Of this number was Rev. John Henry Livingston, who wrote a series of letters to his cousin, Robert Livingston, on the subject of religious liberty and its limitations. The clergyman had been reading Locke whose *Essay on Toleration,* he wrote, had " enlarged " his views. Since liberty of conscience was a natural right it should receive the careful consideration of the convention. The proposed constitution was deficient on this point, for it included no such detailed provisions to insure liberty of conscience as it did to secure property and civil rights. The writer offers a plan which he outlines in the first letter. The second letter disposes of objections to the plan, while the third concludes the series with some remarks upon the " toleration of papists." Locke's " enlarging " influence is here manifest. After a strangely familiar passage on " blood thirsty zeal " which has " deluged Europe with the blood of millions," the writer's conclusion is that Catholics can not be trusted with civil or political rights. Efforts to secure the cooperation of Canada and other " popish powers " make discrimination against them a delicate question, Livingston admits, but the matter can be managed if not in one clause, then in another, if not openly, then covertly. Caution while highly desirable, should not be allowed to obscure the issue. So he writes:

This could doubtless be managed in such a manner as to hold up no cause of suspicion, should any be indulged, and yet sufficiently secure us from the fatal influence of unbridled popery. Let the name be concealed (if the necessity of the day forces us to such caution) and enact as the closing Article upon religious liberty " that this free toleration and encouragement of religion shall extend only to such sects as hold no foreign jurisdiction or subordination in things temporal or spiritual whatsoever " and in the qualification for all offices. Surely it can give no alarm to insert a general article of abjuration in the Oath, worded in Such a manner or effectually to exclude all passive obedience to the Bishop of Rome or any other political monster that does or ever shall exist.[25]

Though there is no evidence to show that this letter was circulated in the convention, the constitution which it produced embodied Livington's advice. It left intact the article on religious liberty, but in voting for Jay's naturalization clause it effectively deprived immigrant Catholics of every opportunity to rise in the social and political world of New York.

Virginia's broad declaration of religious freedom was not contradicted by other clauses in the Bill of Rights itself.[26] Nevertheless in Virginia as elsewhere the statesmen who voted for it so enthusiastically hesitated to translate their ideal into practical legislation.[27] On the contrary, the constitution drawn up by the same convention declares that " the

[25] *Livingston Papers*, Banc. Trans. N. Y. P. L., vol. i, pp. 311-357. For further evidence of J. H. Livingston's anti-Catholic bias see *Sermon Preached before the New York Missionary Society*, at their annual meeting, April 3, 1804 ... (3rd ed. Providence, 1832).

[26] *Cf.* the Bills of Rights of the constitutions of Massachusetts, New Hampshire and Connecticut. B. P. Poore, *Fed. and State Const.*, vol. i, pp. 957-58.

[27] H. St. G. Tucker, *Commentaries on the Laws of Virginia . . .* (2 vols., Winchester, 1836), p. 10. J. A. C. Chandler, *The History of Suffrage in Virginia* (Richmond, 1901), p. 22.

right of suffrage in the election of members to both Houses shall remain as exercised at present. . . ." [28]   That is to say, the qualifications for voters as determined by the Acts of 1769 were to remain in force. These acts class recusants with convicts, negroes, mulattoes, and Indians, and exclude them, even though they are freeholders, from the franchise.[29] Although these qualifications remained on the statute books substantially unchanged until 1830, they were by implication repealed by Section III of Jefferson's act for religious liberty, 1785-86. After that date they were practically a dead letter.[30]

The privileged position of the Anglican clergy in Virginia had been challenged by their dissenting brethren long before the Revolution. As early as 1769 bills for granting toleration to "his Majesty's Subjects, being Protestant Dissenters" were introduced into the House of Burgesses.[31] In this struggle the Presbyterians and Baptists took the lead. The Baptist historian, C. F. James, commenting on the petitions of these two sects, asserts that until the Revolution all they asked for in Virginia was that measure of toleration accorded dissenters in England by the Act of 1689. This is an understatement which the petitions themselves disprove. Baptist and Presbyterian repeatedly beg for exemption from those clauses of the Toleration Act which require registration of ministers and places of worship. There is no

[28] W. W. Hening, *Statutes at Large*, vol. i, pp. 50-56. B. P. Poore, *Fed. and State Const.*, vol. ii, p. 1908.

[29] W. W. Hening, *op. cit.*, vol. vii, p. 517; vol. viii, p. 305. *Journal of the House of Burgesses, 1761-65*, p. 164. *A Collection of All such Public Acts of the General Assembly and Ordinances of the Conventions of Virginia, Passed since the Year 1768, as are now in force* ... (Richmond, 1785), p. 3 and n.

[30] W. W. Hening, *op. cit.*, vol. xii, pp. 84-86. B. P. Poore, *op. cit.*, vol. ii, p. 1912.

[31] *Journals of the House of Burgesses, 1766-69*, pp. 205, 252.

doubt, however, that the revolt against Great Britain broadened their objective. Thenceforth they aimed not at toleration but at equality of all religious sects before the law. " Liberty " had become the watchword instead of " toleration." [32] Thanks to the constant agitation of the dissenters, to the liberalizing influences of the Revolution and above all to the efforts of George Mason, Patrick Henry, James Madison and Thomas Jefferson, the goal was attained in 1785.[33]

The numerous petitions which poured into both houses of the Virginia legislature are not without their value for this study. On June 5, 1775, the Presbytery of Hanover presented a petition in " behalf of themselves and all the Presbyterians of Virginia." They recount in this document the circumstances of their coming to the Virginia frontier. They beg that no law may be passed that will not secure for them " equal liberties and advantages with their fellow Subjects." They are petitioning for a church, they continue, " neither contemptable nor obscure," one which claims in its membership " the greatest Monarch in the north of Europe," Holland, and above all Geneva, " the foremost of those, who at the Reformation emancipated themselves from the Slavery of Rome." [34] The following year the same Presbytery re-

[32] C. F. James, *Documentary History of the Struggle for Religious Liberty in Virginia* (Lynchburg, 1900), pp. 179-184.

[33] H. J. Eckenrode, *The Separation of the Church and State in Virginia* (Richmond, 1910), gives the story of the struggle in detail. See also *Journals House of Burg., 1773-76*, etc., *Writings of James Madison*, ed. by G. Hunt (9 vols., New York, 1900-1910), vol. iii, pp. 116-117, 526, 542, 605-606. G. Hunt, " James Madison and Religious Liberty," Amer. Hist. Assn. *Proc.*, Dec. 1901, pp. 165-171. Thomas Jefferson, *Writings*, Memorial ed. (Washington, 1905), vol. vi, pp. 387-388, 425, 454; vol. vii, pp. 96, 223, 311; vol. viii, p. 213; vol. xix, p. 57. C. J. Stillé, " Religious Liberty in Virginia and Patrick Henry," Amer. Hist. Assn. *Papers*, vol. iii (1889), pp. 205-211.

[34] *Council Journal*, vol. iii, pp. 1592-93. *Journal of House of Burg., 1773-76*, p. 189.

minded the House of Delegates that to show any preference among the various sects would " be to set up a chair of infallibility which would lead us back to the Church of Rome." [35] In 1779 came a plea from Lunenburg County that

the Christian religion free from the errors of popery, and a general contribution to the support thereof, ought to be established from the principles of public utility . . .[36]

This petition had been anticipated by Essex County which begged that only Protestants be allowed to exercise " civil authority " within the state.[37] If Catholics profited, as they certainly did, by the struggle for religious liberty in Virginia, it was not because their disabilities were sympathetically regarded by those who pleaded for it most persistently.

In New England, Connecticut and Rhode Island, content with their charter governments, formed no constitutions. The erasure of a word or two with the substitution of others sufficed to indicate the change from their nominal dependence upon Great Britain to the status of independent commonwealths.[38] Connecticut retained her state church until the second decade of the nineteenth century.[39] Some concessions were made perforce to dissenters. In 1777 they were exempt from the payment of taxes to the Establishment, on condition that they file each year with the " Secretary of the Established Order a certificate, verifying their attend-

---

[35] *Journal of House of Del.*, Oct. 7–Dec. 21, 1776, pp. 32-33.

[36] *Journal of House of Del.*, 1779 (fall session), p. 37.

[37] *Ibid.*, p. 20.

[38] *Conn. State Records*, vol. i, pp. 3-4.

[39] B. P. Poore, *Fed. and State Const.*, vol. i, pp. 257-58. *New Haven Historical Papers*, vol. iii, p. 402. H. Bronson, " Chapters on the Early Government of Connecticut," New Hav. Hist. Soc. *Papers*, vol. iii, pp. 292-403. J. H. Trumbull, *Historical Notes on the Constitution of Connecticut, 1639-1818* ... (Hartford, 1901), pp. 13-14.

ance upon and support of their own religious worship." [40]
This certificate had to be countersigned by the spiritual authorities of the dissenter's church. However liberal this exemption may have seemed to the " standing order," to nonconformists the " Certificate Law " was a burden. An agitation was begun for its repeal, with the result that in 1784 when the laws were revised they included an " Act for securing the Rights of Conscience." No Christian, soberly dissenting and professing his own worship, should incur penalty for not attending the Established Church. Church taxes were to be distributed according to the wishes of the tax-payer; if he attended no church he could be taxed for the Establishment. Certificates of attendance were still required. All Protestant dissenters should have power to maintain their societies according to law. This act, as Cobb observes, left out the Catholic and the Jew.[41] The act of 1817 omitted the adjective Protestant.[42] This included Catholics, but excluded Jews and deists, as did the constitution of 1818.[43]

Whether the familiar " except Papists " was deliberately inserted in Rhode Island laws or crept in through the inadvertence of a careless copyist, it was five times formally reenacted. That argues no great sympathy for Roman Catholics. Perhaps it was not repealed because Catholics never protested against it. This much is certain, however. As soon as Catholics came to Rhode Island in considerable

[40] *Conn. State Rec.*, vol. i, pp. 232-33.

[41] *Statute Laws of Connecticut* (Hartford, 1808), vol, i, p. 575. S. H. Cobb, *Relig. Liberty in America*, p. 501.

[42] M. L. Greene, *Development of Religious Liberty in Connecticut* (New York, 1905), pp. 479-480. J. H. Trumbull, *Hist. Notes on Const. Conn.*, p. 38.

[43] B. P. Poore, *Fed. and State Const.*, vol. i, pp. 258-59. Bill of Rights, Art. 1, secs. 3, 4. *Cf.* Art. 7 of Const. *ibid.*, p. 265. 1902 revision, pp. 37-38, 47.

numbers, steps were taken to remove their disabilities. Rhode Islanders were not slow to see the inconsistency between their statutes and the welcome they accorded Rochambeau and his army. The wording of the repealing act leaves no doubt as to its main purpose. The legislature of February, 1783, decreed

That all the Rights and Privileges of the Protestant citizens of this State, be fully extended to Roman Catholic citizens, and that they being of competent estates and of civil conversation and acknowledging and paying obedience to the Civil Magistrate, shall be admitted Freemen, and shall have liberty to choose and be chosen Civil or Military Officers within this state. . . .[44]

Since Rhode Island like Connecticut saw no reason to abrogate her liberal charter, she continued to be governed by that instrument until 1842. When in that year the charter of 1663 was superseded by a constitution, the new frame of government continued the tradition of the commonwealth and guaranteed full religious liberty.

The constitution first proposed for Massachusetts was submitted to the people in March, 1778. Article xxxix granted freedom of worship to all Protestants; it restricted to Protestants the offices of governor, lieutenant-governor, membership in the Senate and House of Representatives, and appointments to the judiciary.[45] Notwithstanding these concessions to the " standing order " the constitution was rejected by a vote of 9,972 to 2,083.[46] With the returns from the various towns came the reasons for their rejection, accompanied in not a few instances by constructive suggestions. Among the

[44] *R. I. (State) Records*, Feb., 1783, p. 412.

[45] J. F. Thorning, *Religious Liberty in Transition* (Washington and New York, 1931), p. 16.

[46] J. H. Edmunds, in *Commonwealth History of Massachusetts*, vol. iii, pp. 115-16.

many shortcomings listed, the omission of a bill of rights was most frequent.[47]

It was in accordance with these recommendations, and especially of those of the pamphlet called the *Essex Result,* that the constitutional convention of 1779 framed a new document. With the exception of Article III of the Bill of Rights it was largely the work of John Adams. In Article II Adams had declared the obligation of public worship and the right of the individual to perform that duty according to the light of his own conscience, provided that in so doing he did not disturb others. But to reconcile the inalienable rights of conscience with the public support of a state church in a commonwealth which embraced among its religious sects every form of dissent as well as Anglicans, Roman Catholics and Jews, was a problem which the logical mind of John Adams did not attempt to solve. Possibly he realized that he could not embody his ideas in a form which would be acceptable to the " standing order " and at the same time satisfy other religious groups which were clamoring for civil and religious equality. So he asked that the writing of the third section be assigned to someone else, perhaps to some clergyman who might phrase the article more happily. The convention appointed a committee of seven which in turn selected Rev. Noah Alden, pastor of the Baptist Church in Bellingham, as their draftsman.

The argument of Article III as reported by Alden and the convention ran as follows: good morals are necessary for the preservation of civil society. Religion is the only true foundation of morality. Therefore the state, the guardian of civil society, has the right and the duty to support religion at the expense of the subject, and to insist if necessary that

[47] *Result of the Convention of Delegates holden at Ipswich in the County of Essex* ... (Newburyport, 1778). This was probably the most constructive as well as the most influential of the reports on the rejected constitution.

individuals perform their religious obligation, provided there
is a church which they can conscientiously and conveniently
attend.[48]   Commenting upon the difference between this and
the amended article, Charles Francis Adams notes that it is
broad enough to include " the Catholic on the one side, and
the Deist on the other; and, doubtless, this was one of the
most serious objections to it." [49]   The journal of the convention, meager as it is, gives some indication of how
" largely " and " warmly " the question was debated for three
successive days.   There were those in the assembly who were
opposed to both compulsory worship and compulsory taxation; there were those also who were determined that the
Congregationalists should emerge from the contest with
their privileged position intact, and that while all religions
should be tolerated, Catholics should be debarred from the
positions of trust and honor open to all Protestants.   Again
and again amendments were introduced qualifying the words
" Christian " and " teacher " with " Protestant," or specifically excepting Catholics whose principles were said to be
inconsistent with the constitution as well as with " the peace
and safety of the state." [50]   Notwithstanding the opposition
of the liberals, among whom were many of the clergy, the
conservatives won.   Article III, as adopted in its amended
form, made public worship compulsory and restricted the
application of funds collected for this purpose " to protestant
teachers of piety, religion and morality." [51]

[48] J. Adams, *Works*, vol. iv, p. 221.

[49] *Ibid.*, vol. iv, p. 222 n.

[50] *Journal of the Convention for Framing a Constitution of Government for the State of Massachusetts Bay, 1779-80* (Boston, 1832), pp.
35-46.   J. Adams, *Works*, vol. iv, p. 222.

[51] B. P. Poore, *Fed. and State Const.*, vol. i, p. 596.   Pamphlet edition
(Boston, 1780), pp. 7-8.   *Journal*, pp. 75-77.   Though the word " Congregational " did not appear in Article III, the " standing order " was
so intrenched in Massachusetts, that in most towns the practical effect

Efforts to exclude Catholics from the offices of governor and lieutenant-governor, and from membership in the legislature were defeated, but the advantage thus gained was lost by the adoption of the oaths recommended by the committee to whom this matter had been referred. Catholics would have no difficulty in taking the first oath—that they believed in Christianity and that they had the requisite amount of property. The second oath which denied the spiritual supremacy of the Pope no Catholic could take.[52] The purpose of the oaths was explained in the address of the convention to its constituents. It was drawn up by Samuel Adams,[53] who quite frankly sought to disarm criticism for the apparent inconsistency between the high-sounding language of the Bill of Rights and the test oath required of all officers of the commonwealth. " Your Delegates," the Address explains,

did not conceive themselves vested with Power to set up one Denomination of Christian above another; for Religion must at all Times be a matter between God and individuals; But we have nevertheless, found ourselves obliged by a Solemn Test, to provide for the exclusion of those from Offices who will not disclaim those Principles of Spiritual Jurisdiction which Roman Catholics *in some Countries* have held, and which are subversive of a free Government established by the People.[54]

The votes, as they came trickling in from the towns, indicated that while a small minority agreed with John Adams [55] and Joseph Hawley [56] in condemning the test, by far the

of the provision for " protestant teachers " was confined to the Congregational clergy.

[52] B. P. Poore, *Fed. and State Const.*, vol. i, pp. 964-73. *Cf.* New York naturalization oath.

[53] W. V. Wells, *Samuel Adams*, vol. iii, pp. 90-96.

[54] *Journal of the Convention*, p. 218. Pamphlet ed., p. 17.

[55] J. F. Thorning, *Relig. Lib. in Transition*, p. 27.

[56] *Hawley Papers*, vol. ii., Banc. Trans. N. Y. P. L.

greater number of the Bay State voters approved of the intolerant clauses of the proposed constitution.   Many thought
it erred on the side of leniency.   For the few towns which
like Shelburne [57] and Westford [58] objected to state regulation of religion or to any curtailment of the most liberal
clauses of the Bill of Rights, many agreed with Westborough
and its pastor [59] that "the Protestant religion is not duly
guarded."   They would remedy this defect by the insertion
of the word " Protestant " before or in the place of " Christian " wherever it occurred in the constitution.   At least
forty towns in Worcester and Hampshire counties voted for
some qualification of this sort, some even going so far as to
deny the " protection of the law " to all but Protestants.[60]
Lexington sent a long disquisition supported by citations
from Robertson's *Charles V* against the admission of Catholics to office.[61]   Dunstable considered Article III so broad
as to " give protection to idolatrous worshippers of the
Church of Rome." [62]   Gorham, not content with pointing

[57] *Massachusetts Town Resolves, 1773-1787*, vols. iii-iv.   Force
Trans. L. C.

[58] J. F. Jameson, *Const. and Polit. Hist. of the States*, pp. 108-09.
Cf. J. E. A. Smith, *History of Pittsfield* (Boston, 1869), vol. i, p. 450.
Alden Bradford, *History of Massachusetts, 1764-1820*, vol. ii, pp. 185-187.

[59] Westborough, *Mass. Town Resolves*, vol. v, Force Trans. L. C.
Rev. Ebenezer Parkman, *Diary*, ed. by H. Forbes (Westborough Historical Society, 1899), p. 237.   Parkman's illiberal influence is thus recorded in his *Diary*: " May 24, 1780 . . . N. B. Strenuously insist that
the Govr. shall not only declare himself of the Christian Religion, but
a Protestant.   It was obtained to have the word Protestant inserted;
the vote had two against it, Capt. Fisher and Mr. Hannaniah Parker."

[60] S. E. Morison, " Struggle over the Adoption of the Constitution
of 1780," Mass. Hist. Soc. *Proc.*, vol. l (1916-1919), p. 381 *et seq.*   Cf.
Mass. Town Resolves, 1773-1778, vol. i-ii, for Wilbraham; vol. v for
Dudley, Worcester Co.

[61] S. E. Morison, *loc. cit.*

[62] S. E. Morison, *loc. cit.*

out the inconsistency between the second and third articles
of the Bill of Rights suggested the possible consequences of
state-imposed taxes for religion. Under pretense of promoting the common good, the report explained, the early Christian church abused this power,

until at last the haughty popes and prelates usurped a tyrannical
power over the consciences of men, and drew money out of
their pockets for pardons and indulgences, and praying them
out of purgatory, which was to their destruction and not to
their salvation.[63]

When the votes were all in it was found that the constitution with its Bill of Rights was approved by a vote of 5654
to 2047.[64] Catholics were debarred by the test oath from
any office of trust and honor, and like other religious groups,
were obliged to pay taxes for the support of the Congregational churches.

Beginning its career as a state with an instrument of government which contained no provisions regarding religion,
New Hampshire is now the only member of the Union with
a constitution prefaced by a sectarian Bill of Rights. The
explanation of this apparent contradiction is not far to seek.
The constitution of 1776 was but a temporary instrument
framed in accordance with the recommendations of the Continental Congress. It was intended to assert New Hampshire's position in the struggle with the mother country rather
than serve as a guide to religion and morality. It was not
long however before the defects of this hurriedly prepared
frame of government became apparent. Not the least of its
deficiencies was the failure to guarantee the permanent con-

---

[63] *Boston Gazette,* June 12, 1780, no. 1346. *Cf.* nos. 1350, 1355, 1356,
1365, 1370, 1373, 1374 for the newspaper controversy over the constitution.

[64] J. F. Thorning, *Relig. Lib. in Transition,* p. 33. *Cf.* J. C. Meyer,
Church and State in Massachusetts from 1740 to 1833 (Cleveland, 1930),
pp. 108, 186, 192, 217, 234.

trol of the government by the " standing order." With the adoption of the first constitution existing legislation concerning religion had not been abrogated; undoubtedly it was taken for granted that the " interlocking directorate " of church and state established by the old order should continue. Nevertheless with the movement to remedy the inadequacy of the constitution there developed a strong sentiment to preserve through its successor the religious *status quo*. That would also insure the exclusion, if not of all non-Congregationalists, at least of Roman Catholics.

In New Hampshire there were present all the elements of that politico-religious antipathy to Rome so characteristic of colonial British-America. There was in addition, an intensification of racial antagonisms due on the one hand to New Hampshire's proximity to the Canadian-French and on the other to the Scotch-Irish immigration. The frontier settlements of the province—itself an an outpost of New England—thought of their Canadian neighbors almost solely in terms of the Indian raid. Such a medium was calculated to soften neither Protestant hatred of " French idolatry " nor republican contempt of " wooden shoes." The New Hampshire immigrants of the eighteenth century brought with them the heritage of economic, political and religious grievances common to all Scotch-Irish exiles of that period. In New England insult was added to injury when they were taken for native Irish, ostracised, and even forcibly ejected from their settlements.[65] Given the historical background thus briefly sketched, the religious clauses of New Hampshire's constitution follow almost as a matter of course.

The second constitutional convention was called at Concord, June 10, 1778. The constitution which on June 5,

---

[65] Rev. W. R. Cochrane and G. K. Wood, *History of Francestown, N. H., 1758-1891*, pp. 384-85. *Cf.* L. A. Morrison, *History of Windham, 1719-1883*, p. 291.

1779,[66] it submitted to the people for ratification was rejected. The fifth article of the Bill of Rights forbade future legislatures to make laws infringing

the rights of conscience, or any other of the natural, unalienable Rights of Men, or contrary to the laws of God, or against the Protestant religion.[67]

Catholics, apparently, had neither "natural" nor "unalienable" rights. Article viii of the Plan of Government excluded them from the legislature and from the franchise.[68] Historians have pointed out that although this constitution was rejected, it was not because of its intolerance. On the contrary its religious bias would have recommended it to the majority of voters, first, because of the Quebec Act and the complete religious freedom which it had conferred upon the Canadians; secondly, because of the recently concluded French alliance discussed in the last chapter. To the fear that American territory might ultimately be transferred to France, there was the added danger that the wiles of the Jesuit would be supplemented by the sophistry of the French deist and the infidel.[69]

The Bill of Rights which prefaced the constitution drawn up by the third convention, June 1781-Sept. 1782, was both more explicit in its pretentious phrases about the inalienable rights of man and more illiberal in translating those phrases

[66] B. P. Poore, *Fed. and State Const.*, vol. ii, pp. 1279-1280 n. *N. H. State Papers*, vol. ix, pp. 834 *et seq.*

[67] B. P. Poore, *op. cit.*, vol. ii, p. 1280. *N. H. State Papers*, vol. ix, p. 838.

[68] *N. H. State Papers*, vol. ix, p. 839.

[69] Hon. Wm. Plumer, "The Constitution of New Hampshire," *Historical Magazine*, vol. xiv (n. s. iv), p. 178 *et seq.* M. B. V. Knox, "Intolerance in New Hampshire," *Granite Monthly* (1887), vol. x, p. 326 *et seq.* John A. McClintock, *History of New Hampshire* (Boston, 1888), p. 402.

into practice. These rights are discussed in the address to the people,[70] and their principles again laid down and applied in the fourth and fifth articles of the Bill of Rights.[71] Yet in the face of this very definite guarantee of religious liberty the sixth article empowers the legislature to authorize the towns, parishes and the like, to make provision for " Protestant teachers of piety, religion and morality." [72] Protestants only are eligible to the offices of governor, councillor, senator, representative, and delegate to the Congress of the United States.[73] If by chance a Catholic or a Jew should be chosen to any of these offices, he was confronted with a test oath which, like that of Massachusetts, derived its inspiration from its English prototype of 1689.[74] This constitution was also rejected. The fourth convention, which met in August 1782, made only one change which concerns this study. The test oath just referred to was so changed that the passage pertaining to the Pope was omitted.[75] But although a Catholic could now take the oath, he was still debarred from the offices mentioned above by the religious qualifications required. The fourth draft which was submitted to the people in the summer of 1783, accepted by them and proclaimed October 31 of the same year, retained the provisions in favor of Protestantism.[76] It was not until 1851 that

---

[70] *N. H. State Papers*, vol. ix, p. 851.

[71] *Ibid.*, vol. ix, p. 898. *Perpetual Laws of the State of New Hampshire, 1776-1789* (Portsmouth, 1910), pp. 9-10.

[72] *N. H. State Papers*, vol. ix, p. 898. Note the similarity of phraseology with Article III of the Massachusetts Bill of Rights. In most New Hampshire towns also the provision applied to the Congregational clergy.

[73] *N. H. State Papers*, vol. ix, pp. 863, 864, 867, 871, 873. *Perpetual Laws*, pp. 17-19, 20, 21, 27.

[74] *N. H. State Papers*, vol. ix, pp. 873-74. *Cf.* 1 Wm. and M. st. 1, ch. 8; Ruffhead, vol. iii, p. 417.

[75] *N. H. State Papers*, vol. ix, p. 892.

[76] *Ibid.*, vol. ix, pp. 906, 908-09.

the religious qualifications for governor, senator and representative were dispensed with.[77] The Bill of Rights as
already noted still retains the word " Protestant," although
it probably has no practical effect.

The triumph of religious intolerance in New Hampshire
in 1783-84 was not won without protest. In state convention and in town meeting there were ardent champions of
religious freedom. So continuous were the efforts of
William Plumer in the cause that his name has become a
synonym for religious liberty. In the convention at Concord
in 1781 he proposed an article conferring absolute religious
freedom which he would secure by prohibiting compulsory
attendance at public worship or the payment of any but voluntary taxes for religion. The article was broad enough to
include all shades of religious belief. Accepted by the convention, it was rejected by the people, getting a majority,
but not a two-thirds vote.[78] Undoubtedly the editor of
the *New Hampshire Gazette* gaged only too accurately the
prejudices of his readers when he refused to publish an article
by Plumer on behalf of religious freedom. It was not
until the writer offered to pay for the publication, that the
editor reluctantly consented to print it.[79]

As the reports from the towns came in, it became apparent
that here and there other voices were crying in the wilderness.
General John Sullivan called the attention of Durham to the
inconsistencies between theory and practice in the Bill of
Rights. His motion to substitute " public teachers of the
Christian religion " for " Protestant religion " was carried

[77] J. F. Colby, *Manual of the Constitution of the State of New Hampshire* (Concord, 1912), pp. 186, 188, 191.

[78] William Plumer, *Autobiography, 1759-1844.* Mss. L. C., pp. 14-15.

[79] William Plumer, Jr., *Life of William Plumer* (Boston, 1857), p.
116 *et seq.*

in Durham but not throughout the state.[80]   In August, 1782, the town of Plymouth recommended that the words " Protestant religion " be expunged from the constitution wherever they were mentioned as a qualification for office, and that no one be excluded from office because of his religious beliefs.[81]   Like Durham's recommendation, it failed to carry the state.[82]

It has been asserted by more than one apologist for New Hampshire that religious qualifications for office although carried repeatedly in popular·elections have fallen into desuetude almost as soon as they were enacted; that men not qualifying under the constitution have been elected and have held office, and that no effort has ever been made to exclude them.[83]   William Plumer is cited as an example.   A deist when he became a candidate for representative in March, 1785, he was warned that if he were elected his seat would be contested.   He persisted, won the election and took his seat as representative for Epping.[84]   Had Plumer been a Catholic the tale undoubtedly would have been different.   He was a member of the constitutional convention of 1781. Commenting on the religious provisions of the constitution, he notes that while they were more liberal than those of Massachusetts, they included nevertheless a " partial *test act*," the real object of which was to exclude " Papists." [85] That mentality has persisted in New Hampshire.   The

[80] J. E. Finan, *History of the Catholic Church in New England* (Boston, 1899), " New Hampshire," p. 570 *et seq.*

[81] E. S. Stearns, *History of Plymouth, New Hampshire* (2 vols., Cambridge, 1906), vol. i, pp. 200-203.

[82] *Ibid.*

[83] J. T. Perry, "Annual Address, 1878," N. H. H. S. *Proc.*, vol. i, p. 285. W. Plumer, Jr., *Life of Wm. Plumer*, p. 48 *et seq.*   J. E. Finan, *op. cit.*, p. 580.

[84] W. Plumer, Jr., *Life of Wm. Plumer*, p. 59.

[85] W. Plumer, *Autobiography*, pp. 14-15.

people, protected by the secret ballot, have repeatedly defeated every effort to purge the constitution of its discriminatory feature. Under the present constitution Catholics are not denied political privileges or legal protection. They have repeatedly held the highest office in the State. New Hampshire liberals deplore the retention of the word " Protestant " in the Bill of Rights, and no one apparently defends it openly. The ballot, however, is incontestable proof of the vitality of anti-Catholic bias. The story has been told by Dr. Thorning in his *Religious Liberty in Transition*. He sees in New Hampshire a typical, not

a pathological case, a remote or unusual instance of the social processes at work in this country. It seemed rather to typify the struggle religious liberty has had in every section of the Union and to afford some explanation of the periodical waves of prejudice which swept over the land.[86]

The complete political equality accorded the Catholic as a corollary to the religious liberty guaranteed him by the constitutions of Maryland, Pennsylvania, and Delaware formed a happy contrast to the restrictions imposed upon him in other commonwealths. This divergence between state and state as well as between conservatives and liberals within the state was a fact of prime importance which the Federal Convention of 1787 could not ignore. Many of its members had belonged to the Continental Congress which scored religious discrimination as a " low-minded infirmity " and which by proclamation and special commission had offered to the Canadians guarantees of religious liberty which left nothing to be desired. The drafting of these documents and the debates which they called forth were not without their educative value. The Federal Convention had also at its service the experience of the several states. Some of these

[86] Pp. 228 *et seq.*

had had considerable practice in making and rejecting constitutions. The heat with which the religious question had been debated in the state conventions and the wide divergence exhibited by the various constitutions convinced the Federal Convention of the utter impossibility of formulating religious legislation which would be accepted by the country as a whole. Wisely then it did not attempt the impossible. The Federal Constitution as submitted to the several states for ratification had only one religious clause—that which prohibits religious tests for office (Article VI). To this was added two years later, the first amendment forbidding the establishment of a state religion or the restriction of religious liberty.[87] These limitations did not, of course, affect the state governments, some of which retained established churches and tests for office until well into the nineteenth century.

Individual opinion, as recorded in the journals and proceedings of the state ratifying conventions, ranges from that of the liberal pragmatist at one end of the scale to the religious partisan at the other. The proceedings of the Massachusetts convention are among the fullest we have. Mr. Holmes of Rochester thought that Congress had too much power; it might establish the Inquisition, with racks, gibbets, and other instruments of torture.[88] Major Lusk also feared the Inquisition and " shuddered at the idea, that Roman Catholics, Papists, and Pagans might be introduced into office." [89]

---

[87] C. F. G. Zollman, *American Church Law* (St. Paul, 1933), pp. 5-7. Charles Warren, *The Making of the Constitution* (Boston, 1929), pp. 424-26. J. Elliot, *The Debates in the Several State Conventions on the Adoption of the Federal Constitution* ... (5 vols., Phila., 1836-45), vol. v, pp. 128-132, 446, 498, 578.

[88] *Debates, Resolutions and other Proceedings, of the Convention of the Commonwealth of Massachusetts* ... (Boston, 1788. Evans, 21242), p. 142.

[89] *Ibid.*, p. 181.

Among the liberals, Rev. Mr. Shute of Hingham thought that a religious test would injure some and be of no advantage to the country as a whole. There were worthy persons in all sects—even Papists, he argued, so none should be excluded.[90]

In North Carolina the Baptist elder, Henry Abbott, voiced the fears of those who saw in the treaty-making power the opportunity of forming alliances with Catholic countries and perhaps of engaging to introduce the Roman Catholic religion. Another member of the convention feared that the Pope might become president. A third saw danger in foreign immigration. Judge Iredell, one of the leaders of the convention, tried to point out the absurdity of such fears. He did not wholly succeed in banishing them, however, for Mr. Lancaster, while acknowledging that the qualifications for president rendered it unlikely that a foreigner should become president in the immediate future, thought it might be possible within a hundred years![91] Religious liberty should be safeguarded by a bill of rights or its equivalent. The lack of such a safeguard was discussed in almost every state convention. When the first Congress met James Madison offered the first amendment to supply the defect.[92]

A few years after the inauguration of the government under the Federal Constitution, Rev. Jonathan Boucher, commenting in London on the position of Maryland Catholics who had cast their lot with the Revolution, expressed the opinion that they had reaped no very substantial advantage. They had not been driven into exile, nor had their property been confiscated; but with the exception of the Carrolls, they

---

[90] *Ibid.*, p. 149 *et seq.*

[91] *Proceedings and Debates of the Convention of North Carolina...* (Edenton, 1789. Evans, 22037), pp. 217-25, 235, 242. *Cf.* L. I. Trenholme, *Ratification of the Federal Constitution in North Carolina* (New York, 1932), pp. 178-180.

[92] C. Warren, *Making of the Const.*, p. 769.

had not been distinguished by special honors. Under the liberal constitution of Maryland, he wrote,

> they, like other religionists, are no longer molested on account of their religion; nor are they stigmatized with any legal disqualifications. Still I do not hear of their having any weight or influence, as a body, in the State; so that as to any great privileges of citizenship which they have yet enjoyed, their emancipation . . . has been nominal rather than real.[93]

As regards Maryland the writer's estimate was accurate enough. Applied to other states it would need qualification. In no state were Catholics molested for the public exercise of their religion; nowhere were they forbidden by law to teach, to build their own schools, to educate their children in their own faith. On the other hand, in all but four states they were " stigmatized " with " legal disqualifications " of one sort or another. Public opinion sometimes ran ahead of the law and rendered it in special cases inoperative;[94] more often it lagged behind the law, or what the most liberal portions of the community would have made the law were they not held back by reactionary forces. The day was far distant when the nominal emancipation of which the Anglican clergyman wrote would become a reality. It was conceded in theory by Federal and state governments alike; in practice at least a beginning had been made; for Catholics these were the substantial gains of the Revolution.

Meanwhile in daily life the Catholic was confronted with the grim reality that much of the old prejudice remained. In New England Pope Day celebrations were revived and were to continue for more than a century.[95] At " the seat

---

[93] J. Boucher, *Causes and Consequences of the Amer. Rev.*, p. 243.

[94] *Supra*, pp. 353-54.

[95] Col. Soc. Mass. *Pub.*, vol. xii, pp. 291-92. M. E. Perkins, *Old Houses of the Antient Town of Norwich*, pp. 19-20. Wm. Bentley, *Diary* (4 vols., Salem, Mass.), vol. ii, pp. 164, 402, 456; vol. iii, p. 473; vol. iv, pp. 213, 296, 627.

of the Muses in Cambridge," the Dudleian Lectures were being continued. From 1777 to 1789 there were delivered four discourses on " Popery." The first and second of these, " The Authority of Tradition " by Rev. Edward Wigglesworth, and " Transubstantiation " by Rev. William Gordon, the Revolutionary historian, were, compared with most of their predecessors, remarkably temperate in treatment. But since the object of the lectureship was to point out the " errors " of the Church of Rome, the findings of the speakers were predetermined. They had nothing but condemnation for the Church's teaching on the two points in question. One is inclined to think that politics had something to do with the moderate tone of the sermon on Transubstantiation. Gordon's opinion of the Church may be gathered from scattered references in his history, and especially from the opening pages. His Dudleian lecture closes with a reference to our " alliance with Popish powers " and a warning lest our political connections with such nations and our willingness to grant toleration to all, should blind us to the errors of " Popery " or make us indifferent to them.[96]

" Persecution opposite to the genius of the Gospel " is the title of the 1785 lecture delivered by Rev. Joseph Willard, then President of Harvard. In severity of denunciation he is the equal of his most scathing colonial predecessors. His thesis is that the spirit of the Church of Rome is " hatred, malice and persecution." Reviving the fashion of an earlier day, the preacher reviews the alleged crimes of the Church and her pontiffs. He draws the indictment from the

---

[96] Rev. Edward Wigglesworth, *The Authority of Tradition ... Nov. 5, 1777* (Boston, 1778). Rev. William Gordon, *The Doctrine of Transubstantiation considered and refuted . . . Sept. 5, 1781* (Ms. H. U. L.). W. Gordon, *History of the Rise, Progress, and Establishment of the Independence of the United States of America* (4 vols., London, 1787), vol. i, p. 1 *et seq.*

Foxe-Burnet school of historians, proving—provided one grants his premises—that no church had ever equalled her in persecution.[97] The period closes in 1789, with Rev. Jason Haven's " The Doctrine of Merit and Supererogation as Held and Applied in the Romish Church." [98] It is as free from invective as its predecessor is full of it. True, the speaker finds the doctrine dangerous, unreasonable and unchristian; therefore would he warn his audience against such pervisions of the " truth delivered to the saints."

Outside of New England there were contrasts similar to those just noted—survivals of old prejudices with unmistakable signs of a new era. New York's naturalization law and the refusal of the city authorities to allow the Exchange to be used for Catholic services [99] are evidences of the one; the emergence of Catholic life from its catacumbal obscurity

[97] J. Willard, *Persecution opposite to the genius of the gospel* (Ms. H. U. L.).

[98] (Ms. H. U. L.). The subsequent history of the Dudleian foundation may be of interest. The lectures were continued until 1833 when they were interrupted for about sixty years to allow the fund to accumulate. At their revival in 1890, Bishop Keane of the Catholic University of America was invited to deliver the lecture on Revealed Religion. The intention of the University was to recognize a Catholic churchman of scholarship and distinction. In May, 1891, fifty-eight members of the University Faculty of Arts and Sciences petitioned the Harvard Corporation to suppress the third Dudleian lecture, urging that its continuance was " both impolitic and unbecoming, and even more than unbecoming, it would be ' indecent and unjust.' " Better surrender the whole trust, they urged, if by discontinuing this third lecture against Roman Catholicism the terms of the will should be violated. The Corporation declined to take the course suggested. There seems to have been no further protest. The lectures were given to the academic year 1908-09. In 1910 the President and Fellows of Harvard with the concurrence of the Trustees decided that the third lecture should be omitted and the other three continued. (Letter from the secretary of President Lowell, dated May 24, 1933. For the Faculty protest in 1891 and the correspondence thereon see *Harvard Univ. Bulletin*, 1892, vol. vi, pp. 342-43.)

[99] *Supra*, pp. 244, 357-58.

suggests the other. Tradition has it that, thanks to the charity of its Protestant owner, Mass was celebrated in the attic of a carpenter shop near Barclay Street until a more suitable place could be rented. The collection of funds for St. Peter's was given a new impetus and the lowly congregation much desirable prestige when the government fixed its seat in New York and with it the foreign legations. The French and Spanish legations were then available for services. The King of Spain gave a substantial donation. In 1784 Father Whelan, formerly chaplain to the troops of Comte de Grasse, took permanent charge of the little congregation. Hector St. John de Crévecoeur was one of its active members.[100]

In the South also there was new activity in Catholic circles. In 1786, a vessel bound for South America put in at Charleston. Learning that there was an Italian priest on board, the little congregation—about twelve—asked him to say Mass for them. So far as is known, that was the first Mass said in South Carolina. The see of Charleston, which included in Bishop England's time the two Carolinas and Georgia, did not have a Catholic church until 1790, when the Gaston family erected one at Newbern.[101]

[100] *Eccles. Rec. N. Y.*, vol. iii, pp. 1449-52. N. H. Miller, "Pioneer Capuchin Missionaries in the United States," U. S. Cath. Hist. Soc. *Records and Studies*, vol. xxi (1932), pp. 170-234. J. R. Bayley, *A Brief Sketch of the Catholic Church in New York* (New York, 1853), p. 39. J. G. Shea, *op. cit.*, vol. ii, pp. 265-68. The documents relating to the aid given by the Spanish King are printed in *Amer. Hist. Rev.*, vol. i (1915-16), p. 68 *et seq.*

[101] *Charleston Year Book, 1883*, p. 389. The early history of the Church in Charleston affords many illustrations of the survival of religious prejudice. Its story is beyond the scope of this study. See J. England, *Works*, vol. iv, p. 298 *et seq.* P. Guilday, *Life and Times of John England*, vol. i, p. 133 *et seq.* J. J. O'Connell, *Catholicity in the Carolinas and Georgia*, p. 140 *et seq.*

The penal laws removed, the development of Catholic life in Pennsylvania and Maryland went on apace. One of the most noteworthy signs of progress was the founding of Georgetown College, the credit of which is largely due to " Jacky " Carroll of Bohemia Manor days.[102] The elevation of this distinguished prelate to the episcopate was an event of prime importance, not only for the internal development of the Church itself, but also because of the light it sheds upon the changed status of a question that had been such a fertile source of controversy in pre-Revolutionary days. Moreover, it elicited from Congress a statement of its position in matters of church and state.

It will be recalled that so great was the opposition in colonial days to a bishop of any religious denomination that neither Bishop Briand of Canada nor the clergy of Maryland thought it prudent for the former to visit the colonies for the purpose of administering the sacrament of confirmation. Less acceptable still would have been the appointment of a Catholic bishop for the British provinces, since at that time such appointments were in the hands of Henry, Cardinal Stuart of York, brother of the Young Pretender. A nomination by him would almost certainly have exposed the Catholic clergy and laity to suspicion of disaffection. Under the circumstances, Bishop Challoner of London, vicar-apostolic of the American colonies, appointed Rev. John Lewis of Maryland as his representative. No change was made during the war, but when in 1783 two priests applied to Rome for faculties, the attention of the Propaganda was directed to the destitute condition of Catholics in the United States. The papal nuncio at Versailles sent a note to Benjamin Frank-

---

[102] J. S. Easby-Smith, *Georgetown University, 1789-1907* (2 vols., New York, 1907), pp. 1-40. J. F. McLaughlin, *College Days at Georgetown and Other Papers* (Phila., 1899), pp. 34-38. M. F. Morris, *Address at the Centennial Celebration of Georgetown*, Feb. 21, 1889 (Wash., 1889).

lin suggesting that the French monarch be asked to nominate for vicar-apostolic or bishop a prelate who would at the same time be agreeable to the American Congress. Approached on the matter by Franklin, Vergennes, the French minister, said that the nominee should be a resident of the United States. Franklin then submitted the entire correspondence to Congress. The reply of that body, sent without the knowledge of American Catholics, was as follows:

Resolved: That Doctor Franklin be desired to notify the Apostolic Nuncio at Versailles, that Congress will always be pleased to testify their respect to his sovereign and state; but that the subject of his application to Doctor Franklin, being purely spiritual, is without the jurisdiction and powers of Congress, who have no authority to permit or refuse it, these powers being reserved to the several states individually.[103]

The position thus taken by the Federal government has been consistently maintained. Father Carroll's appointment caused none of the political ferment which the advent of Bishop Briand or the proposed erection of an Anglican episcopate had stirred up before the war. That was a dead issue in politics. So far as the Federal government was concerned the Roman Catholic Church in the United States was free to develop from within according to the laws of its own organism.

As before the Revolution and during it, the press continued to reflect and to some extent mold public opinion.

[103] *Secret Journals of the Acts and Proceedings of Congress,* vol. iii, p. 493. J. G. Shea, *op. cit.,* vol. ii, p. 204 *et seq. Aff. Étr. Cor. Pol. États-Unis,* vol. 27, fol. 31; vol. 28, fols. 140-143; vol. 29, fols. 123-125. P. Guilday, *Carroll,* vol. i, pp. 151, 178-230, 343-391. T. J. Campbell, "The Beginnings of the Hierarchy of the United States," U. S. C. H. Soc. *Records and Studies* (New York, 1900), vol. i, pp. 251-277. The most recent study which takes issue with Shea and Guilday on the part played by France is by J. S. Baisnée, *France and the Establishment of the American Hierarchy* (Baltimore, 1934).

Newspapers and magazines published the state and Federal constitutions as they appeared, and, when they could be obtained, the debates of the conventions. There was much discussion of religious liberty, much commendation of those groups in the constitutional conventions who talked eloquently about inalienable rights yet were unwilling to concede them to any but Protestants. A writer in the *Pennsylvania Gazette,* Nov. 14, 1787, relates a conversation with a number of persons who condemned

the new government as a vile system of tyranny. A fifth exclaimed against it because a Roman Catholic and a Jew stood as good a chance of being President of the United States as a Christian or a Protestant.[104]

The *Georgia Gazette,* on the other hand, reporting the debates on the state constitution, records the objection of one speaker to the clause requiring representatives to be Protestants. Such qualification, he argued, is inconsistent with that liberty of conscience which every citizen should enjoy.[105]

The events of the French Revolution were followed with much interest in the United States. In its religious aspect it was hailed at first as a revolt against the Church of Rome rather than against Christianity. The day of religious liberty, so it was thought, had at last dawned for France. American press comment reveals much latent opposition to the Church. Lafayette's motion, together with that of the Archbishop of Toulouse for religious liberty in the broadest sense of the term, was published throughout the country. Sometimes the tone of the report is that of hearty admiration for the nation which is sufficiently enlightened to have

[104] Quoted in A. C. H. *Researches,* o. s., vol. vii (1890), p. 142.

[105] *Gazette of the State of Georgia,* Feb. 19, 1784, No. 54. See also *Pennsylvania Packet,* Dec. 1, 1778; *New Jersey Gazette,* Sept. 30, 1778, in *New Jersey Arch.,* ser. 2, vol. ii, pp. 445.

followed our example; again there is a covert sneer that " Popery " is still in the ascendency.[106]

The magazines followed the newspapers. The *Boston Magazine*, which ran from 1783 to 1786, had a distinguished board of editors, including Harvard graduates, business and professional men of note, and clergymen. Half of them later became members of the Massachusetts Historical Society.[107] The section of the periodical devoted to the Monthly Chronicle gave much space to the French alliance— the services of Comte de Grasse, the text of the treaties, banquets in honor of our guests and similar items.[108] " An Essay on the Rights to a free Exercise of Conscience in Religious Matters," by Judge James Sullivan ran through four issues.[109] The writer sees no inconsistency in the public support of Protestant teachers, but he does apologize for the clause of the constitution which limits the protection of the law to Christians. This crept in, he says, because of the many " prejudices " operating in so large an assembly.[110]

The friendly attitude of the *United States Magazine* is worthy of note because its editor, Hugh Henry Brackenridge, was a divinity student of Princeton. During the French and Indian wars, it will be remembered, Princeton commencement programs were wont to include odes and heroic poems which vilified the French " as knaves, moral lepers of cunning intrigue, and envoys of dreaded Catholicism." [111] The contributions of President Davies and Benjamin Prime to these programs have been noted. Before the French alliance

---

[106] *Pennsylvania Journal*, Sept. 15, 1787, Dec. 13, 1788, Nov. 21, 1789; *Pennsylvania Packet*, March 5, August 9, 1788.

[107] L. N. Richardson, *Early American Magazines*, pp. 211-28, 369.

[108] *The Boston Magazine*, Nov., Dec., 1783; March, 1784.

[109] Dec., 1783; Feb., March, April, 1784.

[110] April, 1784, pp. 230-233.

[111] L. N. Richardson, *Early Amer. Magazines*, pp. 196-210, 368-9.

Brackenridge's own poetic efforts were not free from such references.[112] With France as our friend none—figuratively speaking—responded more readily than the *United States Magazine* to the toasts so frequently printed in its pages, " To His Most Christian Majesty," and " To the perpetual union of France and the United States." [113]

Indicative of the greater freedom of discussion and especially of the admission that Catholics are entitled to a hearing is the answer to an article which appeared in the *Columbian Magazine*. A writer who signed himself " A. Z." contributed an article entitled " Considerations on Religion in General." Among other things he refers to the invocation of the saints and of the Blessed Virgin Mary as a species of idolatry.[114] A letter signed " A Reader " replies to " A. Z." The passages cited in the *Columbian* are identical with the reply of Bishop Carroll quoted in Brent's *Sketch*.[115] Mathew Carey was one of the editors of the *Columbian Magazine* in 1786-87. That probably accounts for the publication of the reply to " A. Z." Carey shortly severed his connection with the *Columbian* for another venture.[116] As editor of the *American Museum* he welcomed contributions from writers of every shade of thought, though he did not

---

[112] See his *Battle of Bunker Hill* (Phila., 1776), p. 21; *The Death of General Montgomery* (Phila., 1777). His *Poem on Divine Revelation* (Phila., 1774), delivered at the Princeton commencement Sept., 1774, is a glorification of the Reformation in contrast with "hell-born popery," pp. 13-18.

[113] *United States Magazine, a Repository of History, Politics and Literature* (Phila., Jan.-Dec., 1779).

[114] *Columbia Magazine, or Monthly Miscellany*, Sept., 1786–Feb., 1790, vol. i, pp. 459-61, 519-21, 881-82.

[115] *Supra*, p. 355, n. 19.

[116] For an estimate of Carey's work as editor see L. N. Richardson, *op. cit.*, pp. 272, 276-93, 370-371, 314-34. See also B. Faÿ, *Notes on Amer. Press*, pp. 13-14. E. Bradsher, *Mathew Carey, Editor, Author and Publisher* (New York, 1912).

hesitate to voice his dissent when he thought justice demanded it. That an Irish Catholic editor could do so with impunity argues a degree of tolerance in American subscribers rare, if not unknown, up to that time.

The deism which had begun to show itself in America during the colonial wars received a fresh impetus during the American Revolution and was making greater inroads into the intellectual and religious life of the post-war generation. The war had been accompanied and followed by looseness of morals and relaxation in religion; the prestige of the clergy had noticeably declined. The debonair Frenchman with his charming manners and his indifference to religion had proved a successful proselytizer, but in a far different sense than those who feared the inroads of " Popery " had imagined. The French Revolution coming at a time when America was ripe for change had given a stimulus to deism and other disrupting forces. The clergy had tried in vain to stem the tide. Two writers, both from Yale,[117] exemplify the opposing currents and their attitude towards the Church of Rome.

Joel Barlow, " poet, scholar, diplomat, cosmopolitan, and deist," assayed many rôles, but is chiefly remembered now as one of the " Hartford wits " whose disruptive influence Timothy Dwight felt called upon to check. Barlow had paid a graceful tribute to France in a poem entitled *The Prospect of Peace,* delivered at the Yale Commencement in 1778.[118] In 1787 he published a more ambitious effort, *The Vision of Columbus,* later expanded into the *Columbiad.* It was widely read at the time and did much to enhance his

[117] For an account of this movement at Yale see R. J. Purcell, *Connecticut in Transition* (Wash., 1918), pp. 5-22. I. W. Riley, *American Philosophy: The Early Schools* (New York, 1907), pp. 209-218.

[118] Joel Barlow, *The Prospect of Peace. A Poetical Composition, Delivered in Yale College* . . . July 23, 1778 (New Haven, 1778).

reputation. Columbus is represented as seeing in vision the results of his discovery of America. The part played by the Jesuits gives occasion for a pen-picture of St. Ignatius as a political meddler—

> Thro' courts and camps, by secret skill to wind;
> To mine whole states and over-reach mankind.

The poet passes to the Reformation. The Inquisition and the Spanish wars in the Netherlands, the Armada, the Marian persecutions are reviewed in gruesome details of which the following lines are typical:

> What shrines and altars flow with christian gore!
> What dismal shrieks! what agonizing cries!
> What prayers are wafted to the listening skies!

But when the scene changes to the new world Barlow recognizes the tolerance of " Blest Baltimore " and his followers

> who catch the liberal flame,
> Partake of freedom and extend the same.

The Vision of Louis XVI, of French and Spanish aid are very laudatory. Most of the French heroes appear to receive their meed of praise.[119]

Barlow's disruptive tendencies are best seen in his *Political Writings*. The thesis of his " Advice to the Privileged Orders " is, " The existence of any kind of liberty is incompatible with the existence of any kind of church." This proposition he develops by a detailed examination of the characteristics of the various churches. He does not think the Catholic Church worse than others, he says; if he discusses her characteristics oftener it is because she is the dominant " church in those parts of Europe where revolutions are

[119] J. Barlow, *The Vision of Columbus; A Poem in Nine Books...* (Hartford, 1787), pp. 137-39, 155, 179.

soonest expected." One sentence will illustrate the facility with which the author connects the practice of private religion with the civic life of the individual. Of the Catholic custom of going to confession he says:

I cannot conceive of any person going seriously to a confessional and believing in the equality of rights, or possessing one moral sentiment, that is worthy of a rational being.[129]

To the orthodox New England clergyman whose idea of religious liberty was public worship established by law, that is, the Congregational system as set up in New Hampshire, Massachusetts and Connecticut, Joel Barlow's political ideas were heresy. Small wonder that Timothy Dwight felt called upon to stem the tide which threatened to subvert all religion. Yet if the heretical Barlow and " Pope Dwight " could have calmly compared their ideas, unquestionably they would have found that they agreed in their opinion of the Roman Catholic Church. They would part company, however, when Barlow attempted to show that his strictures applied equally to the " standing order."

In the American Revolution and in contemporary events in Europe, Timothy Dwight saw Divine Providence working for the destruction of Antichrist, that is, for the Church of Rome. On Nov. 28, 1781, he preached in Northampton a sermon in commemoration of the surrender of Cornwallis. Quoting the text [121] which Protestant divines have commonly interpreted as St. Paul's description of Antichrist, he attempts to prove that it has been " literally verified " for ages in " the clergy, especially the Popes, of the Romish church."

---

[120] J. Barlow, *The Political Writings of Joel Barlow* (New York, 1796), pp. 40-46. For an account of Barlow's political philosophy see V. L. Parrington, *The Colonial Mind, 1620-1800* (New York, 1927), pp. 382-389. *Cf.* C. B. Todd, *Life and Letters of Joel Barlow*, 1886.

[121] II Thes. 2: 4.

They have not only made themselves equal to God, but they have set themselves above Him, claiming " the power of indulging in sin." Providence, however, is preparing for the downfall of this usurper. The dissolution of the Jesuits was the beginning. Persecution for religion's sake is falling into disuse in Europe. The recent annulment of the revocation of the Edict of Nantes is another sign of the downfall of Antichrist.[122]

Dwight was a many-sided individual whose interests included the law, the ministry, education, *belles lettres,* and travel. During his life-time his reputation was extraordinary. His religious writings embraced sermons, hymns, and a complete system of theology. In the educational field he taught so well that he is said to have attracted students from other institutions. In *belles lettres* his range included verse. epic and pastoral, satire and the familiar travel essay. It is in this last type that he seems to have been most successful. His *Travels in New England and New York* is still valuable for the social history of the period. In fact it is about the only one of Dwight's works that is still read, for his claim to greatness has not stood the test of time.

Dwight's narrow theological outlook, writes a recent biographer, colored " his views of life, his political and social doctrines, all his judgments and all that he wrote. . . ."[123] He seems to have been untouched by the wave of liberalism which swept over America during the Revolution. His *Travels* furnish many instances of his conservatism as well as of his inaccurate judgments. In the course of his wanderings he came across a community of Shakers. He saw

[122] T. Dwight, *A sermon preached at Northampton on the twenty-eighth of November, 1781; occasioned by the capture of the British army under the command of Earl Cornwallis* (Hartford, 1781). See also Dwight's *Nature and Danger of Infidel Philosophy* (New Haven, 1798).

[123] H. E. Starr, in *D. A. B.,* vol. v, pp. 573-77. *Cf.* V. L. Parrington, *Colonial Mind,* pp. 360-62.

in their doctrine and discipline a striking resemblance to those of the Church of Rome. He gives a summary of their beliefs and practices, taken, he says, from Thomas Brown's "An Account of the people called Shakers." The fifth point of the summary reads,

The Shakers hold that the end justifies the means; therefore it is lawful to lie, defraud, quarrel, etc., for the good of the church. They also teach "that ignorance is the mother of devotion."

Dwight closes the summary with, "It is impossible not to remark the striking coincidence between these dogmas and those of popery."[124]

Among the historians of this period there are two whose histories were long authorities in their respective fields— Jeremy Belknap's *History of New Hampshire* and William Gordon's *History of the Rise, Progress and Establishment of the Independence of the United States of America*. In some respects, indeed, Belknap's work has not yet been superseded; but we cannot entirely indorse the verdict of his latest biographer, that the work is "remarkable for its research, impartiality, and literary merit."[125] Impartial in its treatment of Catholic topics, it certainly is not. Even when the historian's facts are accurate, his interpretation of them is often wholly unwarranted. His attention was called to these distortions of the truth by a Catholic clergyman of Boston in 1792 when a new edition of his history was published. Belknap made no defense, but neither did he make the changes suggested.[126]

[124] T. Dwight, *Travels in New England and New York* (4 vols., New Haven, 1821-22), vol. iii, p. 162. *Cf. ibid.*, pp. 446, 532. For Dwight's impressions of Canada see *ibid.*, vol. i, p. 294 n.

[125] L. S. Mayo in *D. A. B.*, vol. ii, p. 147.

[126] For the correspondence between Belknap and Rev. John Thayer see *Belknap Papers*, Mass. Hist. Soc. *Coll.*, 6 ser., vol. iv, p. 539 *et seq.* See also "Correspondence between Jeremy Belknap and Ebenezer Hazard,"

For over a hundred years Gordon's history was considered an authority on the Revolution, and although it has since been discredited [127] its value for this investigation remains unimpaired. The opening pages of the first volume are as clear an exposition of the writer's attitude towards Roman Catholicism as they are of Puritan opposition to the English Act of Uniformity.[128] In fact his references to "popish ceremonies" and other liturgical rites, which to his thinking had been "degraded to idolatry," are so suggestive of sixteenth- and seventeenth-century writers, that one might be inclined to think them mere borrowings, like other portions of the history. But if these subsequent passages are checked with his sermons, and especially with his Dudleian lecture, they will be found to be perfectly consistent.

The contributions of two southern writers form a contrast to those just considered. Jonathan Boucher's *Causes and Consequences of the American Revolution* was not published in London until 1797, but with the exception of the introduction the lectures of which it is composed were delivered in Maryland between 1763 and 1775. The introduction, however, was written after the war, presumably about 1791.[129] The Tory clergyman was no lover of Roman Catholicism nor was he in sympathy with the adherence of the majority of Maryland Catholics to the patriot cause, yet he represents a tolerance unknown to most of his confrères

Mass. Hist. Soc. *Coll.*, 5 ser., vol. ii, pp. 1-500; vol. iii, pp. 1-371. J. Belknap, *History of New Hampshire*, ed. by John Farmer (3 vols., Dover, 1831). See vol. i, chs. x, xii, xiv, xxii and *passim*. Cf. M. H. S. *Colls.*, 6 ser., vol. iv, p. 253 *et seq.*

[127] G. O. Libby, Amer. Hist. Ass'n. *Report*, vol. i (1899), pp. 367-388.

[128] William Gordon, *History of the Rise, Progress and Establishment of the Independence of the United States of America*, vol. i, p. 1 *et seq.* Cf. *supra*, p. 379.

[129] Jonathan Boucher, *A View of the Causes and Consequences of the American Revolution; in thirteen discourses, Preached in North America between the Years 1763 and 1775* (London, 1797).

until the close of the war. The same may be said of David Ramsay, a physician who worked in the field with the army. He also served South Carolina in the state legislature and in the Continental Congress. He was consequently a participant in many of the events which he recorded. His works are compilations rather than original narratives, expressing views which in many cases are in the direct line with the Protestant tradition; nevertheless the fairness and the broad tolerance of the historian are apparent.[130]

In summary, American public opinion of Roman Catholicism in the closing decades of the eighteenth century was " in transition." If much of the old prejudice remained, much also had disappeared. Both tendencies are reflected in the various phases of American life—in its legal aspects, its literary output, its human relationships. The most important single gain perhaps was the opportunity for the Catholic to live a normal social life, to slough off his own prejudices and to help his Protestant or deistic neighbor to do the same in the give and take of everyday life. In neighborly intercourse, in business contacts, in professional life, distrust would gradually disappear. Eventually, the American sense of fair play, as some one has well phrased it, would see to it that political disabilities also would cease to exist.

[130] David Ramsay, *History of the Revolution in South Carolina* (2 vols., Trenton, 1785), vol. i, p. 11. See also his *History of South Carolina from its settlement in 1670 to the year 1808* (2 vols., Charleston, 1809), vol. ii, p. 38.

CONCLUSION

THE sixteenth-century notion of controversy, whatever the subject, was summed up in the maxim, " Keep your enemy in the wrong." Convinced of their own rectitude, the Protestant Reformers adopted the slogan, and aided in no small measure by political events, domestic and foreign, built up a conception of " Popery " as a composite monster reaching out its tentacles to draw all good Protestants to destruction. This travesty of Roman Catholicism was brought to America by the early immigrants as part of their intellectual and religious equipment. Its vitality was insured by new-world conditions: by the dominant influence for several generations of a clergy almost uniformly hostile to the Church of Rome; by an educational system, equally antagonistic, from which Catholics were excluded except at the price of apostasy; by a press which catered to political, racial and religious antipathies; by colonial governments which, with few exceptions, would exclude the Catholic from the province or penalize him after he had entered; by non-English immigration with a European experience that had been for the most part an education in intolerance.

To these factors were added two that were peculiarly American. There were generations of colonists who had had no contact whatever with a Catholic in the flesh. Naturalization and immigration laws, land regulations, penal statutes had seen to that. There was no opportunity therefore for the amenities of social relationships to soften the harsh outlines of their mental picture. Where contact did exist, as in Maryland, Virginia, in early New York, or on the Indian frontier, relationships were so complicated by

394

political, economic or international rivalry that religious partisanship was strengthened rather than weakened. Religion was the scapegoat which bore the onus of many a selfish or sordid policy that could not bear the light. This applies especially to the Indian question whether on the northern, western or southern frontiers.

In the eighteenth century, the " Popish " frenzy reached its height during the French and Indian War. After the Treaty of 1763 there was a period of comparative peace when the British colonists were more concerned with what they deemed the repressive measures of the home government than with the real or imaginary intrigues of the " Papists." But the old hatreds were merely quiescent, not dead, or even dying, as the passage of the Quebec Act demonstrated. Colonial anger had not yet burned itself out before the preliminaries of the Revolution had begun their lessons in conciliation. The aid of Catholic Canada was lost, but that of Catholic France and Spain was won. Catholic blood flowed freely in the cause of the Revolution. The record of the Catholic private seems to have been as good as that of his comrade of other denominations, while the services of a Carroll, a Barry, a Lafayette are a matter of common knowledge. The Revolution silenced once and for all the old assumption that the Roman Catholic must of necessity be an actual or a potential traitor.

But ingrained prejudices die hard. The Lockian philosophy was still invoked. With the adoption of the state constitutions Catholics were still the objects of political discrimination, though there were substantial gains. In every state they were free to practice their religion publicly, to build their churches, and, when they could, their schools. Gradually their civil disabilities were lessened, until, by the middle of the nineteenth century, they were in most cases removed. In time, came political preferment in city and in state. Under the federal government the chief justiceship of the Supreme Court has twice been held by Catholics, Roger B. Taney and Edward D. White. A Catholic has even succeeded in winning the nomination for the presidency. If, in the political campaign which followed, the success of anti-Catholic propaganda revealed how strong and wide-spread, even in our own day, is the old distrust of the Roman Catholic Church, it demonstrated also how far American public opinion has travelled along the road of real toleration. One has only to compare the protest with which this outburst of bigotry was deplored by the best and wisest in the land, with the denunciations of governor, clergyman, or average colonial, in the early eighteenth century, to realize what progress has been made. Even at the close of that period, the candidacy of a Catholic for the presidency was unthinkable.

But the ideal of religious liberty embodied in constitutional bill of rights, together with the conception of social and political equality which was gradually accepted as the corollary of that vision, was destined for fuller, if not complete realization. In spite of its waves of anti-Catholic fanaticism, the nineteenth century made notable progress toward the desired goal. Today, however unsympathetic the average citizen may be towards the tenets of a particular creed, he is likely to condemn as un-American the exploitation of racial and religious antipathies. Unless his own interests are concerned, however, he is unlikely to give his active, not to say enthusiastic, cooperation for the solution of social, economic or political problems involving religious issues. Until he is willing to do so, progress must be slow and halting. Meanwhile it is encouraging to note the efforts of a small but influential group for the better understanding of those problems and for that inter-denominational action which should do much to foster cordial relationships. In such an atmosphere old prejudices should weaken, perhaps disappear.

BIBLIOGRAPHICAL NOTES

Generally speaking, only the titles which have proved most useful for this study are listed in the bibliography. Others are referred to in the footnotes.

THE EUROPEAN BACKGROUND

CHAPTERS I-II

A. BIBLIOGRAPHIES

Godfrey Davies, *Bibliography of British History, Stuart Period, 1603-1714* (Oxford, 1928).

[Edward Gee], *A Catalogue of all the Discourses Published against Popery, During the Reign of James II, by the members of the Church of England, and by the Non-conformists* ... (London, 1689). There are 228 titles by members of the Church of England, and 2 by Non-conformists.

Thomas Jones, ed., *A Catalogue of the Collection of Tracts for and against Popery (published in or about the reign of James II) in the Manchester Library founded by Humphrey Chetham, in which is incorporated, with large additions and bibliographical notes, the whole of Peck's list of tracts in the controversy, with his references* (2 vols., Manchester, 1859-65).

Thomas G. Law, *Catholic Tractates of the Sixteenth Century, 1573-1600* ... (London, 1901).

Conyers Read, *Bibliography of British History, Tudor Period, 1485-1603* (Oxford, 1933).

Joseph Smith, *Bibliotheca Anti-Quakeriana; or, a catalogue of books adverse to the Society of Friends* ... (London, 1873).

——, *A Descriptive Catalogue of Friends' Books, or books written by members of the Society of Friends, commonly called Quakers, from their first rise to the present time* ... (2 vols., London, 1867).

B. COLLECTIONS AND DIGESTS OF LAWS

There are many good editions of the British Statutes at Large. That most frequently cited in this study is Owen Ruffhead's compilation, *Statutes at Large from Magna Carta to the 20th Year of George III* (14 vols., London, 1763-1780). Ruffhead gives only the titles of statutes that have expired or were repealed, so that it is sometimes necessary to consult other editions for the text. There is a 24 volume edition by

Danby Pickering (Cambridge, 1769-1794), with a serviceable subject index. The compilation by John Raithby (29 vols., London, 1800-1869) has also been used.

Of the Irish statutes, a satisfactory edition is that of William Ball, *Statutes at Large, passed in the Parliaments held in Ireland: from the Third Year of Edward the Second, A. D. 1310 to the Thirty-eighth Year of George the Third, A. D. 1798, inclusive. With Marginal Notes and a complete index to the Whole* . . . (18 vols., Dublin, 1799). A useful digest is the *Abridgement of the Statutes of Ireland . . . and of all the English and British Statutes which extend to and bind Ireland* . . . (Dublin, 1754). Under the heading " Papist," the Irish penal laws are brought together in non-technical language.

A standard edition of the statutes of Scotland is that entitled *Acts of the Parliament of Scotland, A. D. 1124-1707. Printed by command of her Majesty Queen Victoria* (11 vols., 1844—). The Scottish dialect makes it difficult reading. Henry, Lord Kames, has edited a convenient compilation, *Statute Law of Scotland abridged. With historical notes* (2nd ed., Edinburgh, 1769). Pp. 237-242 give an abstract of the penal laws against Roman Catholics.

For the colonies, *Laws of the British Plantations . . . relating to the Church and the Clergy, Religion and Learning,* edited by Nicholas Trott (London, 1725), has the merit of including the laws of the island as well of as the mainland colonies. The date of publication is an obvious limitation.

C. OTHER SOURCE MATERIAL FALLS NATURALLY INTO TWO DIVISIONS: THAT EMANATING FROM PROTESTANT AUTHORITIES, SUCH AS ECCLESIASTICAL DOCUMENTS, SERMONS, PETITIONS, TRACTS, AND THE LIKE; AND RECORDS MEMORIALS, DIARIES AND SIMILAR MATERIAL OF CATHOLIC AUTHORSHIP

1. Protestant Sources

[John Bale], *The Pageant of the Popes, Contayninge the lyves of all the Bishops of Rome from the beginning to the year of Grace 1555* . . . (London, 1574).
——, *Select Works . . . containing the Examination of Lord Cobham, William Thorpe, and Anne Askewe, and the Image of Both Churches* (Parker Society, Cambridge, 1849).
——, *The Apology of John Bale agaynst a rank Papyst* . . . (1550).
Robert Barclay, *Anarchy of the Ranters* . . . (London, 1733).
Robert Barnes, " The Works of Doctour Barnes," in *The Whole Works of W. Tyndall, John Frith and Doct. Barnes* . . . (London . . . 1573).
Richard Baxter, *A Call to the Unconverted* (Reprint, Pittsburg, 1900).
——, *Jesuit Juggling. Forty Popish Frauds Detected and Disclosed* (First American Ed., New York, 1825).

Charles Blount, "An Appeal from the Country to the City for the preservation of his Majesties Person, Liberty and Property and the Protestant Religion" (1695), in *Miscellaneous Works of Charles Blount, Esq.*

Book of Common Prayer from the Original Manuscript attached to the Act of Uniformity of 1662 ... (London, 1892).

John Brown, *Quakerism the Path-Way to Paganism* . . . (Edinburgh, 1675).

Gilbert Burnet, *A Collection of Eighteen Papers, Relating to the Affairs of Church and State During the Reign of James the Second* . . . (London, 1689).

——, *A Discourse Wherein is held forth The Opposition of the Doctrine, Worship, and Practices of the Roman Church. To the Nature, Designs, and Characters of the Christian Faith* ... (London, 1688).

——, *A Sermon before the House of Peers ... 5th Nov., 1689* (London, 1689).

——, *A Sermon Concerning Popery* ... (Edinburgh, 1746).

——, *A Sermon preached ... Before His Highness the Prince of Orange, 23d Dec., 1688* (London, 1689).

——, *The Bishop of Salisbury, His Speech in the House of Lords on the First Article of the Impeachment of Dr. Henry Sacheverell* (London, 1710).

——, *The Royal Martyr Lamented, in a Sermon preached at the Savoy, on King Charles the Martyr's Day, 1674/5* ... (London, 1710).

Edward Cardwell, ed., *Documentary Annals of the Reformed Church of England ... with notes historical and explanatory* (2 vols., Oxford, 1844).

——, *Synodalia. A collection of articles of religion, canons and proceedings of Convocation in Canterbury* (2 vols., Oxford, 1842).

Certaine Sermons appoynted by the Queen's Majestie, to be declared and readde, by al Parsons, Vicars, and curates, every Sunday and Holydaye in their churches; and by her Graces advice perused and overseene, for the better understanding of the simple people. Newly imprinted in partes, according as is mentioned in the book of common prayers, 1574 (n. p., n. d. In black letter type. Another edition, London, 1850, edited by G. E. Corrie. It contains also the Thirty-nine Articles, the Constitutions and Ecclesiastical Canons).

John Dunton, *Life and Errors of John Dunton* (2 vols., London, 1818).

John Foxe, *Actes and Monuments* ... (2 vols., London, 1610). Many editions.

W. H. Frere and C. D. Douglas, eds., *Puritan Manifestoes* (Church Historical Society, vol. lxxxii, London, 1907).

Benjamin Harris, ed., *Protestant (Domestick) Intelligence, or News both from City and Country. Published to prevent false reports* (London, 1679-80). Photostat of original issues in British Museum.

——, *The Protestant Tutor* ... (London, 1679-80). Photo.

John Jewel, *A Defense of the Apologie of the Church of Englande* ... (London, 1571).

——, *Certaine Sermons preached before the Queene's Majestie* ... (London, 1571).

——, *A Exposition of the two Epistles of the Apostle Sainct Paule to the Thessalonians* ... (London, 1583).

Journals of the House of Commons ... *From November the 8th, 1547* ... [*to August the 14th, 1885*], [London] 1803-[85], 140 vols. in 142; 7 vols. of index.

Rev. Joseph Ketley, ed., *The Two Liturgies, A. D. 1549 and A. D. 1552: with other Documents set forth by authority in the Reign of King Edward VI* ... (Cambridge, 1844). Edited for the Parker Society.

John Knox, *The Historie of the Reformation of the Church of Scotland* ... (London, 1644).

William Laud, *A Relation of the Conference between William Laud* ... *and Mr. Fisher the Jesuite, by the Command of King James of ever Blessed Memory* ... (London, 1639).

——, *A Speech Delivered in the Starre-Chamber, on Wednesday the xivth of June, 1637* ... (London, 1637).

John Locke, *Letters Concerning Toleration* (London, 1765).

Michael Malard, *The French and Protestant Companion, Or a Journey into Europe, Asia and Africa;* ... *With the Defense of the Protestant Religion, and the Death of Popery. For the Use of Young Princesses* ... (London, 1719). [Intended to put the reader] into a condition of being never seduced by Popery. Pref., p. 6.

William Penn, *A Collection of the Works of William Penn* ... (2 vols., London, 1726).

John Percival, First Earl of Egmont, *Diary* (3 vols., Historical Manuscripts Commission, London, 1920-23).

[Nicholas Perrault], *The Jesuits Morals* ... *Englished by Ezrel Tonge, D.D.,* ... (London, 1679).

Henry Sacheverell, *The Perils of False Brethren* ... (London, 1709).

——, *The Perils of being Zealously Affected, but not Well* ... (London, 1709).

Thomas Secker, *Five Sermons against Popery* (Windsor, Vt., 1827).

——, *Sermons* (7 vols., London, 1771-1790).

Matthew Sylvester, ed., *Reliquiae Baxterianae: Or, Mr. Richard Baxter's Narrative of the most Memorable Passages of His Life and Times* ... (London, 1696).

John Tillotson, *A Seasonable New-Years gift against Popery* ... (London, n. d.).

——, *A Sermon Preached at Lincoln's-Inn-Chapel, On the 31st of January, 1688* ... (London, 1689).

——, *Works* (10 vols., London, 1820).

John Wycliffe, *Select English Works*, ed. by Thomas Arnold (3 vols., Oxford, 1869-71).

2. *Catholic Sources*

William, Cardinal Allen, *A Briefe Historie of Twelve Reverend Priests, Father Edmund Campion & His Companions* . . . ed. by Rev. J. H. Pollen, S.J. (London, St. Louis, n. d.). A contemporary record.

Catholic Record Society Publications (34 vols., London, 1904—).

Robert Chambers, *Domestic Annals of Scotland from the Reformation to the Revolution* (2 vols., 2nd ed., Edinburgh, 1859). A chronological compilation from many sources.

Henry Foley, *Records of the English Province of the Society of Jesus* (7 vols. in 8, London, 1877-83). Much valuable material.

William Forbes-Leith, *Memoirs of Scottish Catholics during the xviith and xviiith Centuries* (2 vols., London and New York, 1909).

——, *Narratives of Scottish Catholics under Mary Stuart and James VI* (London, 1889).

John Morris, *Troubles of Our Catholic Forefathers* (2 vols., London, 1872-75). A compilation of documents.

W. M. P. O'Reilly, *Memorials of those who suffered for the Catholic faith in Ireland in the sixteenth, seventeenth and eighteenth centuries* (London, 1868). Collected and edited from original sources.

D. SECONDARY AUTHORITIES

John E. (Lord) Acton, *The History of Freedom and other Essays* (London, 1909).

——, *Lectures on Modern History* (London, 1906).

W. J. Amherst, *History of Catholic Emancipation, 1771-1820* (2 vols., London, 1886).

T. C. Anstey, *A Guide to the Laws of England affecting Roman Catholics* (London and Dublin, 1842).

——, *The Queen's Supremacy* (Supplement to above. London, 1850).

A. H. Atteridge, *The Elizabethan Persecution* . . . (London, 1928).

A. Bellesheim, *Geschichte der Katholischen Kirche in Schottland* . . . (2 vols., Mainz, 1883).

Hilaire Belloc, *James the Second* (London, 1928).

H. N. Birt, *The Elizabethan Religious Settlement* (London, 1907).

William Blackstone, *Commentaries on the Laws of England* . . . (10th ed., London, 1787).

H. F. Bourne, *Life of John Locke* (2 vols., London, 1876).

Gilbert Burnet, *History of His Own Time* (6 vols., Oxford, 1823).

——, *History of the Reformation of the Church of England.* New and revised edition by Nicholas Pocock (7 vols., Oxford, 1865). From more than one point of view these two titles may also be regarded as sources.

Charles Butler, *Historical Memoirs of the English, Irish and Scottish Catholics* (3rd ed., 4 vols., London, 1822). Original documents in appendixes.

J. Paul de Castro, *The Gordon Riots* (London, 1926). Many contemporary records.

Richard Challoner, *Memoirs of Missionary Priests . . . and of other Catholics . . .* (London, 1844. Revised ed. by J. H. Pollen, London, 1924).

George N. Clark, *The Later Stuarts, 1660-1714* (Oxford, 1934).

Henry W. Clark, *History of English Non-conformity from Wiclif to Close of the Nineteenth Century* (2 vols., London, 1911-13).

William Cobbett, *Parliamentary History of England from 1066 to 1803.* Continued from 1803 as *Parliamentary Debates* (12 vols., London, 1806-12).

Charles Dodd, *Church History of England, 1500-1688. With Notes, Additions, and a Continuation by Rev. M. A. Tierney* (5 vols., London, 1839-1843). Valuable source material appended to each volume.

John N. Figgis, *The Divine Right of Kings* (2nd ed., Cambridge Univ. Press, 1914).

W. H. Frere, *The English Church in the Reigns of Elizabeth and James I, 1558-1625* (London, 1904).

Henry Gee, *The Elizabethan Prayer-Book and Ornaments . . .* (London, 1902), App. iii, *Distresses of the Commonwealth with the Means to Remedy Them . . .* (London, 1902).

John Gerard, *John Foxe and His "Book of Martyrs"* (London, n. d., Cath. Truth Society Pub.).

Peter Guilday, *English Catholic Refugees on the Continent, 1558-1795* (New York, 1914).

Dennis Gwynn, *The Struggle for Catholic Emancipation, 1750-1829* (New York, 1928). Gives special attention to the Irish phase.

T. C. Hall, *The Religious Background of American Culture* (Boston, 1930).

Henry Hallam, *Constitutional History of England from Henry VII to George II* (3 vols., New York, 1930).

Charles Hardwicke, *A History of the Articles of Religion*, ed. by F. Proctor (London, 1895).

M. V. Hay, *A Chain of Errors in Scottish History* (New York, 1927).

Philip Hughes, *The Catholic Question* (London, 1929).

William Hunt, *History of England . . . 1760-1801* (New York, 1905).

St. George K. Hyland, *A Century of Persecution under Tudor and Stuart Sovereigns from Contemporary Records* (London, 1920). Much source material.

W. K. Jordan, *Development of Religious Toleration...to the Death of Queen Elizabeth* (Harvard Univ. Press, 1932).

A. J. Klein, *Intolerance in the Reign of Elizabeth* (Boston, 1917).

Onno Klopp, *Der Fall des Hauses Stuart und die Succession des Hauses Hanover in Gross-Britannien und Ireland . . .* (14 vols. in 7, Wien, 1875-88).

I. S. Leadam, *History of England, 1702-1763* (New York, 1909).

William H. Lecky, *History of England in the Eighteenth Century* (8 vols., New York, 1891).

——, *History of Ireland in the Eighteenth Century* (5 vols., New York, 1895).

W. S. Lilly and J. E. P. Wallis, *Manual of Law Especially Affecting Roman Catholics* (London, 1893).

John Lingard, *History of England*. Revised edition edited by Hilaire Belloc (11 vols., New York, 1912).

R. Lodge, *History of England, 1660-1702* (New York, 1910).

F. C. Montague, *History of England, 1603-1660* (New York, 1907).

J. G. Muddiman, *The King's Journalist, 1659-1689* (London, 1923).

J. H. Overton and F. Relton, *The English Church, 1714-1800* (London, 1906).

Ludwig Pastor, *History of the Popes from the Close of the Middle Ages* (24 vols., London, 1898-1933).

J. O. Payne, *Records of the English Catholics of 1715* (London, 1889). Many source passages.

A. F. Pollard, *Factors in Modern History* (London, 1926).

Frederick Pollock, *Essays in Jurisprudence and Ethics* (London, 1882).

J. Pollock, *The Popish Plot* (London, 1903).

J. Powicke, *Life of the Reverend Richard Baxter, 1615-1691* (London, 1924).

Leopold von Ranke, *History of England principally in the Seventeenth Century* (Eng. trans., 6 vols., Oxford, 1875).

Alexander A. Seaton, *The Theory of Toleration under the Later Stuarts* (Cambridge Univ. Press, 1911).

H. J. Somers, *Life and Times of Hon. and Rt. Rev. Alexander Macdonell* (Washington, 1931).

Joseph Story, *Commentaries on the Conflict of Laws, Foreign and Domestic...* (Boston, 1834).

Charles J. Tarring, *Chapters on the Law relating to the Colonies...* (London, 1893).

James W. Thompson, *Wars of Religion in France, 1559-1576* (Chicago, 1909).

Herbert Thurston, *No-Popery* (London, 1930).

George M. Trevelyan, *England under Queen Anne* (3 vols., New York, 1930-34).

——, *England under the Stuarts* (12th ed., London, 1925).

Bernard Ward, *Dawn of the Catholic Revival in England, 1781-1803* (2 vols., New York, 1909).

Michael Williams, *The Shadow of the Pope* (New York, 1932).

J. R. Willington, *The Dark Pages of English History, Being a Short Account of the Penal Laws against Catholics from Henry the Eighth to George the Fourth* (London, 1902).

E. PERIODICAL AND ENCYCLOPEDIC ARTICLES

Edwin Burton, "English Recusants," *Catholic Encyclopedia*, vol. xii, p. 677.

——, "Penal Laws," *Cath. Ency.*, vol. xi, p. 614.

L. M. Friedman, "The Parental Right to Control the Religious Education of a Child," *Harvard Law Review*, vol. xxix (March, 1916), pp. 485-500.

John Gerard, "Titus Oates at School," *The Month*, vol. c (Aug., 1903), p. 121-132.

——, "History 'ex Hypothesi' and the Popish Plot," *ibid.*, vol. c (July, 1903), pp. 2-22.

Charles Gérin, "Le Pape Innocent XI et la Révocation de l'Édit de Nantes," *Révue des Quéstions Historiques*, vol. xxiv (1878), pp. 377-441.

——, "Le Pape Innocent XI et la Révolution anglaise de 1688," *ibid.*, vol. xx (1876).

Charles P. Keith, "Henry Compton, Bishop of London," Church Historical Society *Pub.*, No. iii (Phila., 1920).

F. W. Maitland, "Elizabethan Gleanings," *English Historical Review*, vol. xv (1900), p. 324 *et seq.* Reviews the relationships between Elizabeth and Paul IV.

Roger B. Merriman, "Some Notes on the Treatment of English Catholics in the Reign of Elizabeth," *American Historical Review*, vol. xiii (1908), pp. 480-500.

Louis O'Brien, "The Huguenot Policy of Louis XIV and Pope Innocent XI," *Catholic Historical Review*, vol. xvi (April, 1931), pp. 29-42.

J. H. O'Donnell, comp., "Gleanings from Early Catholic Journals," No. ii, "The Last of the Penal Laws," *Historical Records and Studies*, U. S. Catholic Historical Society, vol. ii (1901), pp. 338-344.

J. H. Pollen, "English Post-Reformation Oaths," *Cath. Ency.*, vol. xi, pp. 177-180.

——, "The Politics of English Catholics during the Reign of Elizabeth," *The Month*, vols. xcix-c (1902). A series of six articles from January to August.

——, "Religious Persecutions under Elizabeth," *ibid.*, vol. civ (1904), pp. 501-517.

Patrick Purcell, " The Jacobite Rising of 1715 and the English Catholics,"
English Historical Review, vol. xliv (1920), pp. 418-32.

THE AMERICAN CONTRIBUTION

A. BIBLIOGRAPHIES

William H. Allison, *Inventory of Unpublished Material for American
Religious History in Protestant Church Archives and Other Repositories* ... (Carnegie Inst. of Wash., 1910).

Charles M. Andrews, *Guide to the Materials for American History to
1783 in the Public Record Office of Great Britain* (Carnegie Inst.
of Wash., 1912-1914).

C. M. Andrews and F. G. Davenport, *Guide to the Manuscript Materials
for the History of the United States to 1783, in the British Museum*
... (Carnegie Inst. of Wash., Pub. No. 90, 1908).

S. J. Case, *A Bibliographical Guide to the History of Christianity* (Univ.
of Chicago Press, 1931).

*Checklist of Collections of Personal Papers in Historical Societies, Uni-
versities and Public Libraries, and other Learned Institutions in the
United States* (L. C., Wash., 1918).

Charles Evans, *American Bibliography* (vol. i—, 1903—).

P. L. Ford, *Bibliography and Reference List of the History and Literature Relating to the Adoption of the Constitution of the United
States, 1787-88* (Brooklyn, 1888).

Evarts B. Greene and R. B. Morris, comps., *Guide to the Principal
Sources for Early American History (1600-1800) in the City of
New York* (Col. Univ. Press, New York, 1929).

Grace G. Griffin, *Writings on American History* (1906—, various places
of publication; now Govt. Printing Office, Washington).

Roscoe R. Hill, *Descriptive Catalogue of the Documents relating to the
History of the United States in the Papeles Procedentes de Cuba
deposited in the Archivo General de Indias at Seville* (Wash., 1916).

*Inventaire Sommaire des Archives du Département des Affaires Étran-
gères, Mémoires et Documents—France* (3 vols., Paris, 1883-96).

Inventaire Sommaire ... Mémoires et Documents—Fonds Divers (Paris,
1892). See pp. 219-223 for *États-Unis*.

Frank Monaghan, *French Travellers in the United States, 1765-1932*
(New York Public Library, 1933).

William Nelson, *The American Episcopate Controversy, 1767-1774* ...
(Paterson, N. J., 1909).

*Newberry Library, A Checklist of American Revolutionary War Pamph-
lets*, compiled by Ruth Lapham (Chicago, 1922). 574 tracts about
equally proportioned between England and America.

E. G. Swem, ed., *Virginia Historical Index* (2 vols., vol. i, A-K, Roanoke,
1934-).

Oscar Wegelin, *Early American Plays, 1740-1830* (2nd ed., revised, New York, 1905).

——, *Early American Poetry* (2 vols. in 1, 2nd ed., New York, 1930).

B. CHARTERS, STATUTES, ACTS, COLONIAL AND STATE ARCHIVES

Samuel Lucas, comp., *Charters of the Old English Colonies in America* (London, 1850).

Connecticut. *Public Records of the Colony of Connecticut, 1636-1776.* Compiled by J. H. Trumbull and C. J. Hoadley (15 vols., Hartford, 1850-1890. 3 additional vols. of *State Records*, Hartford, 1894—).
Statute Laws of Connecticut (Hartford, 1808).

Georgia. *Colonial Records of the State of Georgia, 1732-1774*, ed. by A. D. Chandler (26 vols., Atlanta, 1905-11).
Digest of the Laws of Georgia (Savannah, 1802).

Maryland. *Archives of Maryland*, ed. by William H. Browne (Baltimore, vol. i—1883—).
Compleat Collection of the Laws of Maryland... (Annapolis, 1727). Contains penal laws against Catholics. Md. State Library and L. C.
Laws of Maryland...comp. by William Kilty (2 vols., Annapolis, 1779).
Laws of Maryland at Large, comp. by Thomas Bacon (Annapolis, 1765).
Lower House Journal, 1762-1775 (Mss. 5 vols., State House Library).
Upper House Journal, 1762-1775 (Mss. 5 vols., State House Library).

Massachusetts. *Acts and Resolves, Public and Private, of Massachusetts Bay* (21 vols., Boston, 1867-1912).

New Hampshire. *Perpetual Laws of the State of New Hampshire, 1776-1789* (Portsmouth, 1910).
Laws of New Hampshire, 1679-1745, comp. by A. S. Batchellor (2 vols., Manchester, 1904-1913).
New Hampshire State Papers (33 vols., Concord, 1867-1915).

New Jersey. *Archives of the State of New Jersey*, ed. by W. A. Whitehead and others (1 ser., 34 vols., relating to colonial history; 2 ser., 3 vols., relating to Revolutionary history, Newark, 1880-1906).
Acts of the One Hundred and Forty-fourth Legislature of the State of New Jersey (Trenton, 1920).
Laws of the State of New Jersey, comp. by Wm. Patterson (New Brunswick, 1800).

New York. *The Colonial Laws of New York, from the Year 1664 to the Revolution, Including the Acts of the Colonial Legislature from 1691 to 1775 Inclusive* (5 vols., Albany, 1894).
The Laws of the State of New York, comprising the Constitution and the Acts of the Legislature, since the Revolution, from the First

to the Twentieth Session inclusive (3 vols., 2nd ed., Thomas Greenleaf, editor, New York, 1798).

North Carolina. *Colonial Records of North Carolina, 1662-1790*, ed.
by W. L. Saunders and others (26 vols. with 4 vols. of index,
Raleigh, 1886-1914). Includes 3 vols. of laws, 1715-1790 (vols.
xxiii-xxv).

Laws of the State of North Carolina, ed. by James Iredell (Edenton,
1791).

Pennsylvania. *Archives of Pennsylvania*. 1 ser., vols. 1-12; 2 ser., vols.
1-19; 3 ser., vols. 1-30; 4 ser., vols. 1-12; 5 ser., vols. 1-8; 6 ser.,
vols. 1-15; 7 ser., vols. 1-5 (Phila., 1852-56; Harrisburg, 1874-1914).

*Charter to William Penn, and Laws of the Province of Pennsylvania,
passed between the years 1682 and 1700* ... compiled and edited by
George Staughton and others ... (Harrisburg, 1879).

Colonial Records, 1683-1790 (16 vols., Phila., 1852-53. General index,
Phila., 1860).

Statutes at Large of Pennsylvania from 1682 to 1801, comp. by
J. T. Mitchell and H. Flanders (15 vols., Harrisburg, 1896-1911),
vols. ii-xiii (1700-1790).

Rhode Island. *Records of the Colony of Rhode Island and Providence
Plantations in New England, 1636-1792*, comp. by J. R. Bartlett (10
vols., Providence, 1856-86).

South Carolina, *Journal of the Common House of the Assembly, Feb. 23–
March 10, 1697*, ed. by A. S. Salley (Columbia, 1913).

Statutes at Large, comp. by Thomas Cooper and David McCord
9 vols., Columbia, 1836-41).

Virginia. *Calendar of Virginia State Papers* (11 vols., Richmond, 1875-
1893).

Journals of the Council of Colonial Virginia, ed. by H. R. McIlwaine
(Richmond, 1919).

Journals of the House of Burgesses of Virginia (1727-1776), ed. by
H. R. McIlwaine and J. P. Kennedy (8 vols., Richmond, 1905-10).

Journals of the House of Delegates, 1775, 1777, 1778, 1779, 1786
(Richmond, 1827-28).

Statutes at Large, ed. by W. W. Hening (13 vols., Richmond, 1809-
23).

C. PUBLICATIONS OF HISTORICAL SOCIETIES

American Antiquarian Society Proceedings (new series, Worcester,
1880—).

American Catholic Historical Researches, ed. by M. I. J. Griffin (29 vols.,
Pittsburg-Philadelphia, 1884-1912. Index, 1916).

American Historical Association, Annual Reports (Washington, 1889—).

American Historical Association, Papers (5 vols., New York, 1885-91).

American Irish Historical Society, Journal (vol. i—, 1898—), vols. xii-xxx.

American Society of Church History, Papers, ed. by S. M. Jackson, (vols. i-viii, New York, 1889-97).

Connecticut Historical Society, Collections (vol. i—, Hartford, 1860).

Essex Institute Historical Society Collections (50 vols., Salem, 1859-1914).

Maryland Historical Society, Fund Publications (Nos. 1-37, Balt., 1867-1901).

Massachusetts Historical Society Collections (vol. i—, 1792—); *Proceedings* (vol. i—, 1791—).

Memoirs of the Historical Society of Pennsylvania (14 vols., Phila., 1826-95).

New Hampshire Historical Society, Collections (11 vols., Concord, 1824-1915); *Proceedings* (5 vols., Concord, 1874-1917).

New Jersey Historical Society, Collections (vol. i—, 1847—); *Proceedings* (vol. i—1845——).

New York Historical Society Collections (vols. i-v, 1809-30; 2 ser., vols. i-iv, 1831-59; 3 ser., vol. i—, 1868—).

Pennsylvania German Society Proceedings (17 vols., 1891-1906).

Records of the American Catholic Historical Society of Philadelphia (vol. i—, 1884—. Index, vols. i-xxxi).

Southern Historical Association Publications (11 vols., Washington, 1897-1907).

United States Catholic Historical Society, Historical Records and Studies (New York, 25 vols., vol. xxv, 1935).

D. PERIODICALS

American Historical Review (vol. i—, 1895—).

Catholic Educational Review (vol. i—, 1911—).

Catholic Historical Review (vol. i—, 1915—).

Catholic University Bulletin (33 vols., 1895-1927).

Catholic World (vol. i—, 1865—).

Georgia Historical Quarterly (vol. i—, 1917—).

Historical Bulletin (vol. i—, St. Louis, 1922—).

Historical Magazine with Notes and Queries . . . (23 vols., Boston, 1857-1875).

Lower Norfolk County Virginia Antiquary (5 vols., c. 1895-1906).

Magazine of American History (vols. i-xxx, New York, 1877-93; vols. xxx-xlvi, Mt. Vernon, N. Y., 1901-17).

Maryland Historical Magazine (vol. i—, Balt., 1906—).

The Month (vol. i—, London, 1864—), vols. xcix-civ.

New England Quarterly (vol. i—, 1928—).

Pennsylvania Magazine of History and Biography (vol. i—, 1877—).

Thought (vol. i—, 1926—).

United States Catholic Historical Magazine (4 vols., New York, 1887-1893).

Virginia Historical Register (6 vols., 1848-1853).

Virginia Magazine of History and Biography (vol. i—, 1893-94—).

William and Mary College Quarterly (1 ser., 27 vols., 1892-1919; 2 ser., 1921—).

E. THE FOLLOWING WORKS AND COMPILATIONS HAVE BEEN IN CONSTANT USE THROUGHOUT THIS INVESTIGATION

James R. Bayley, *A Brief Sketch of the Catholic Church ... of New York* (New York, 1853).

Edward Channing, *History of the United States* (6 vols., New York, 1905-27), vols. i-iii.

Sanford H. Cobb, *The Rise of Religious Liberty in America* (New York, 1902).

Documents Relating to the Colonial History of New York (15 vols., Albany, 1853-87).

Ecclesiastical Records of the State of New York (7 vols., Albany, 1901-1916).

Peter Guilday, *Life and Times of John Carroll* (2 vols., New York, 1922).

Albert B. Hart, ed., *Commonwealth History of Massachusetts* (5 vols., New York, 1927-32).

Thomas A. Hughes, *History of the Society of Jesus in North America* (5 vols., 2 of Text, 3 of Documents, New York, 1907-17).

Allan Nevins, *The American States during and after the Revolution* (New York, 1927).

Herbert L. Osgood, *The American Colonies in the Seventeenth Century* (3 vols., New York, 1904-07).

——, *The American Colonies in the Eighteenth Century* (4 vols., New York, 1924-25).

William T. Russell, *Maryland, Land of Sanctuary* (Baltimore, 1907). Valuable documents in the appendix.

Arthur M. Schlesinger and Dixon R. Fox, eds., *History of American Life* (New York, 1927—), vols. ii-iii.

John G. Shea, *History of the Catholic Church in the United States* (4 vols., New York, 1886-92).

Moses C. Tyler, *A History of American Literature during the Colonial Period, 1607-1765* (2 vols., New York, 1879).

——, *The Literary History of the American Revolution, 1763-1783* (2 vols., New York, 1897).

THE TRADITION AND THE COLONIAL CLERGY

CHAPTER III

A. MANUSCRIPT SOURCES

Archives of the Roman Catholic Archdiocese of Westminster, vol. xli,
no. 207; vol. xlii, nos. 45, 55. *Great Britain, Transcripts, L. C.*
Useful also for ch. nine.

"Comparative View of the Different Religious Persuasions," *Public
Record Office, Colonial Office,* 318, vol. ii, pt. i. *Gr. Brit. Trans.,
L. C.*

Dudleian Lectures, Widener Library, Harvard University. See section
on Education.

Society for Propagating the Gospel in Foreign Parts. The Library of
Congress has a hundred and fifty odd volumes of transcripts and
photostats of the S. P. G. Journals and Correspondence. The following have been useful for many aspects of this study:

Journals, 1755-1787, vols. xiii-xxiv. Photostats.

Correspondence, Series B, vols. i-vi; xxi-xxiv. Transcripts.

Fulham Palace Library, 15 vols., Trans.

Lambeth Palace Library, 3 vols., Trans.

Mss. of Dr. Bray's Associates, *Bibliothecae Provinciales Americanae,*
vols. i-iii (Andrews and Davenport, *Guide,* pp. 334-335).

Miscellaneous Unbound Documents, Package i, *Correspondence of
Commissary Blair.* Package vii, packets 2-4.

B. PRINTED SOURCES

Amos Adams, *Concise Historical View of the Perils, Hardships, Difficulties and Discouragements which have attended the Planting and
Progressive Improvement of New England* (Boston, 1769).

——, *Religious Liberty an Invaluable Blessing: Illustrated in Two Discourses Preached at Roxbury, Dec. 3, 1767* (Boston, 1768).

Isaac Backus, *The Infinite Importance of the Obedience of Faith, and of
a Separation from the World* (Boston, 1791).

——, *The Nature and Necessity of an Internal Call to Preach the Gospel*
(Boston, 1754).

——, *A Seasonable Plea for Liberty of Conscience . . .* (Boston, 1770).

Baptists. *An Address from the Baptist Church in Philadelphia, to their
Sister Churches of the same denomination, throughout the Confed-
erated States of North America . . .* (Phila., 1781).

Baptist Confession of Faith . . . (Phila., 1765).

Robert Barclay, *A Catechism and Confession of Faith* (Phila., 1773).

Belknap Papers. "Correspondence between Jeremy Belknap and Ebenezer Hazard," Mass. Hist. Soc. *Coll.,* ser. 5, vol. ii, pp. 1-500; vol. iii,
pp. 1-371. "Belknap Papers," *ibid.,* ser. 6, vol. iv.

The Book of Discipline, agreed on by the Yearly Meeting of Friends for New England ... (Providence, 1785).

Aaron Burr, *A Discourse delivered at Newark, Jan. 1, 1755.*

——, *Sermon preached before the Synod of New York, at Newark, Sept. 30, 1756* (New York, 1756).

Charles Chauncy, *A Letter to a Friend* ... (London, 1767; reprinted, 1768).

Richard Claridge, *Life and Posthumous Works* ... Collected by Joseph Besse (London, 1726).

Josiah Coale, *The Books and Divers Epistles of the Faithful Servant of the Lord, Josiah Coale* ... (1671).

Congregational Catechism, containing a General Survey of the Organization, Government and Discipline of Christian Churches, by E. R. Tyler (New Haven, 1844).

Congregational Church. *An Historical Narrative and Declaration. Shewing the Cause and Rise of the Strict Congregational Churches.* ... (Providence, 1781).

Samuel Cooper, *Sermon on the Reduction of Quebec, Preached Oct. 16, 1759* (Boston, n. d.).

William Crashaw, *A Newyeares Gift to Virginea* ... (London, 1610). L. C.

Samuel Davies, *The Curse of Cowardice* ... (London, 1758).

——, *The Good Soldier* ... (London, 1756).

——, *Religion and Patriotism* ... (Phila., 1756).

——, *Virginia's Danger and Remedy* ... (Williamsburg, 1756). Useful also for chapters four and six.

John England, *Works* (Messmer ed., 7 vols., Cleveland, 1908).

Samuel Finley, *The Curse of Meroz* ... (Phila., 1757). Useful for chapters four and six.

Peter Force, *Tracts and other Papers, relating principally to the Origin, Settlement, and Progress of the Colonies in North America, from the Discovery to the Year 1776* (Washington, 1836-46).

P. L. Ford, ed., *Diary of Cotton Mather.* Mass. Hist. Soc. *Coll.,* 7 ser., vols. vii, viii (1911-1912).

[George Fox], *The Arraignment of Popery* ... By G. F. and E. H. Printed in the year 1669.

——, *Gospel Truth Demonstrated* ... (London, 1706).

——, *Journal,* ed. from mss. by Norman Penny (2 vols., Cambridge Univ. Press, 1911).

Friends. *Discipline for the Yearly Meeting of Friends, Held in Baltimore* ... (Balt., 1821) Source material in appendix.

Georgia Sermons. Delivered annually from 1731 to 1750 before the Trustees and Associates of Dr. Bray at St. Mary-le-Bow, London. Useful for many aspects of this study.

John Griffith, *A Journal of the Life, Travels, and Labours in the Work of the Ministry of John Griffith* ... (London, 1780).

Francis L. Hawks, *Contributions to American Church History* (2 vols., New York, 1836-1839). Vol. i, Virginia; vol. ii, Maryland.

Francis L. Hawks and William S. Perry, *Documentary History of the Protestant Episcopal Church in the United States.* Connecticut (2 vols., New York, 1863-64).

Charles Hodge, *Constitutional History of the Presbyterian Church in the United States of America* (Phila., 1851).

H. E. Jacobs, *The Book of Concord: or the Symbolical Books of the Evangelical Lutheran Church* ... (2 vols., Phila., 1882-83), vol. i.

W. J. McGlothlin, ed., *Baptist Confessions of Faith* (Phila., 1911).

Jonathan Mayhew, *A Discourse Concerning Unlimited Submission* ... (Boston, 1750).

——, *A Sermon preached in the audience of his excellency William Shirley, esq.* ... (Boston, 1754).

——, *The Snare Broken* ... (Boston, 1766).

William Penn, "A Seasonable Caveat against Popery," in *Works* (London, 1726), vol. i, pp. 467-485.

William S. Perry, *Historical Collections Relating to the American Colonial Church* (5 vols., 1870-1878), vol. i, Va.; vol. ii, Pa.; vol. iii, Mass.; vol. iv, Md.; vol. v, Del.

Presbyterian Church. *Constitution of the Presbyterian Church in the United States of America* ... (Phila., 1815).

——, *Records of the Presbyterian Church in the United States of America* (Phila., 1841).

C. Robinson and R. A. Brock, eds., *Abstract of the Proceedings of the Virginia Company of London, 1619-1624* (2 vols., Richmond, 1888-89).

Philip Schaff, ed., *Creeds of Christendom* (3 vols., New York, 1877), vol. iii.

Society for Propagating the Gospel in Foreign Parts. Abstract of the Proceedings of the Society appended to the Sermon preached at the Annual Meetings held in the parish church of St. Mary-le-Bow, 1701-1783. Valuable for education, Indian relations, episcopacy and the loyalist clergy.

William Symonds, *Virginia* ... (London, 1609). With Crashaw's sermon noted above, gives attitude of Virginia Company towards Catholic immigration.

Gilbert Tennent, *The Blessedness of Peace-Makers represented; and the Danger of Persecution considered* ... (Phila., 1765).

——, *The Happiness of Rewarding the Enemies of our Religion and Liberty* ... (Phila., 1756).

——, *Sermons on Important Subjects* ... (Phila., 1758). French and Indian problem.

John Wesley, *Journals* (Standard ed., 8 vols., New York, 1909-16).
——, *Works...with a life of the author by the Rev. John Beecham, D.D.* (11th ed., 14 vols., London, 1856).
George Whitefield, *Works* (8 vols., London, 1771).
Samuel Willard, *A Compleat Body of Divinity in Two Hundred and Fifty Lectures on the Assembly's Shorter Catechism . . .* (Boston, 1726).
Roger Williams, *The Bloody Tenent of Persecution...* (Narrangansett Club Pub., 1 ser., vol. iii, Providence, 1867).
——, *George Fox Digg'd out of His Burrows*, ed. by J. L. Diman (Nar. Club. Pub., 1 ser., vol. v, Providence, 1875).
——, *Letters of Roger Williams, 1632-1682*, ed. by J. R. Bartlett (Providence, 1874).

C. SECONDARY AUTHORITIES

W. O. B. Allen and Edmund McClure, *Two Hundred Years: The History of the Society for the Promotion of Christian Knowledge, 1698-1898* (London, 1898). Much valuable source material.
C. W. Baird, *History of the Huguenot Emigration to America* (2 vols., New York, 1865).
Alice M. Baldwin, *The New England Clergy and the American Revolution* (Durham, N. C., 1928).
Bedford. *History of Bedford*, pub. by the Town (Concord, N. H., 1903).
David Benedict, *A General History of the Baptist Denomination in the United States of America* (2 vols., Boston, 1813).
G. D. Bernheim, *History of the German Settlements and of the Lutheran Church in North and South Carolina* (Phila., 1872). Also useful for Huguenot and Palatine immigration.
James Bowden, *History of the Society of Friends in America* (2 vols., London, 1850-54).
L. P. Bowen, *The Days of Makemie; or, the Vine Planted, 1680-1708* (Phila., 1885). Based on writings of Makemie.
W. C. Braithwaite, *Second Period of Quakerism* (London, 1819).
C. A. Briggs, *American Presbyterianism* (New York, 1885). Important documents in the appendixes.
Alexander Brown, *Genesis of the United States* (Boston, 1890). Valuable for old-world background; much source material).
F. K. Brown, *The Annapolitan Library at St. John's College* (privately printed, St. John's College, Annapolis, n. d.).
John Brown, *The Pilgrim Fathers of New England and their Puritan Successors* (London, 1895. Revised Amer. ed., 1896).
W. D. Brown, *History of the Reformed Church in America* (New York, 1928).

Charles H. Browning, *The Welsh Settlement of Pennsylvania* (Phila., 1912).

Ezra H. Byington, *The Puritan in England and in New England* (Boston, 1897).

W. Byrne, ed., *History of the Catholic Church in the New England States* (2 vols., Boston, 1899).

Gilbert Chinard, *Les Réfugiés Huguenots en Amérique avec une Introduction sur le Mirage Américain* (Paris, 1925).

W. R. Cochrane, *History of the Town of Antrim* (Manchester, N. H., 1880).

E. T. Corwin, *Manual of the Reformed Church in America, 1628-1902* (4th ed., New York, 1902).

J. G. Craighead, *Scotch and Irish Seeds in American Soil* . . . (Phila., 1878).

Samuel Davies, *Memoir of Rev. Samuel Davies, formerly President of the College of New Jersey* (Boston, 1832). (Depositary of the Mass. Sunday School Society, no. 24, Cornhill.)

J. H. Denison, *Emotional Currents in American History* (New York, 1932).

Henry M. Dexter, *The Congregationalism of the Last Three Hundred Years as Seen in Its Literature* (New York, 1880).

Jonathan Edwards, *Life and Character of the Late Reverend Mr. Jonathan Edwards, President of the College of New Jersey. Together with a Number of his Sermons on Various Important Subjects* (Boston, 1765).

Eliza C. K. Fludd, *Biographical Sketches of the Huguenot, Solomon Legaré, and of his Family* (Charleston, 1886).

William H. Foote, *The Huguenots, or the Reformed French Church* (Richmond, 1870).

——, *Sketches of North Carolina, historical and biographical* (New York, 1846).

——, *Sketches of Virginia, historical and biographical* (Phila., 1850; 2 series, 1855). Presbyterian viewpoint in all three.

Wesley M. Gewehr, *The Great Awakening in Virginia, 1740-1790* (Durham, 1930).

Louis de Goesbriand, *Catholic Memoirs and Biographies of Vermont and New Hampshire* (Burlington, Vt., 1886).

Peter Guilday, *Life and Times of John England* (2 vols., New York, 1927).

G. E. Hageman, *Sketches of the History of the Church* (St. Louis, n. d.).

Ernest Hawkins, *Historical Notices of the Missions of the Church of England in the North American Colonies, previous to the Independ-*

ence of the United States: chiefly from Ms. Documents of the S. P. G.
(London, 1845). Valuable also for the struggle for the Episcopate.

E. L. Hazelius, *History of the American Lutheran Church, 1685-1842*
(Zanesville, Ohio, 1846).

Henry U. Heilman, *The Old Hill Church and a Court Trial* (Lebanon
County Historical Society, vol. ix, no. 4).

G. M. Hill, *History of the Church in Burlington, N. J.* (Trenton, 1876).
Much source material.

Arthur H. Hirsch, *The Huguenots of Colonial South Carolina* (Durham,
1928).

History of the Town of Litchfield, Connecticut (Phila., 1881).

Robert B. Howell, *The Early Baptists of Virginia* (Phila., 1876).

Huguenot Society of America. *Commemoration of the Bi-Centenary of
the Revocation of the Edict of Nantes, Oct. 22, 1885 at New York*
(New York, 1886).

——, *Proceedings* (5 vols., New York, 1883-1906).

——, *Tercentenary Celebration of the Promulgation of the Edict of
Nantes, April 13, 1898* (New York, 1900).

Huguenot Society of South Carolina, *Transactions, 1889-1933* (Charleston, 1889-1933).

David Humphreys, *An Historical Account of the Incorporated Society
for the Propagation of the Gospel in Foreign Parts* (London, 1730).
A first hand account by the general secretary of the society.

John F. Hurst, *Parochical Libraries in the Colonial Period* (New York,
1890). Reprint of paper read before the American Society of
Church History, New York, Dec. 30-31, 1889.

H. E. Jacobs, *The Books of Concord; or the Symbolical Books of the
Evangelical Lutheran Church* ... (2 vols., Phila., 1882-83), vol. ii.

H. E. Jacobs and H. A. W. Haas, eds., *Lutheran Cyclopedia* (New York,
1899).

Charles F. James, *Documentary History of the Struggle for Religious
Liberty in Virginia* (Lynchburg, 1900). The story of Baptist participation in the struggle.

Samuel M. Janney, *The Life of William Penn; with selections from his
correspondence and auto-biography* (Phila., 1852).

H. M. Jones, *America and French Culture, 1750-1848* (Chapel Hill, N. C.,
1927). Useful for almost every phase of this study.

Joseph L. J. Kirlin, *Catholicity in Philadelphia from the earliest missionaries to the present time* (Philadelphia, 1909).

A. A. Lambing, ed., *The Baptismal Register of Fort Duquesne* (Pittsburg, 1885). Suggestive for many phases of our study, especially
for the use made by colonial governments of missionaries among the
Indians and traders.

Umphry Lee, *The Historical Backgrounds of Early Methodist Enthusiasm* (New York, 1931).

William de L. Love, Jr., *The Fast and Thanksgiving Days of New England* (Boston, 1895).

C. H. Maxson, *The Great Awakening in the Middle Colonies* (Chicago, 1920).

L. A. Morrison, *History of Windham* (Boston, 1883).

——, *Supplement to the History of Windham in New Hampshire* (Boston, 1892).

C. F. Pascoe, *Two Hundred Years of the S. P. G....* (London, 1901). An expansion and revision of the same author's *Classified Digest* of the Society's Records published in 1893.

William S. Perry, *History of the American Episcopal Church, 1587-1883* (2 vols., Boston, 1885). Valuable also for education, episcopacy.

F. B. Sanborn, *President Langdon: a Biographical Tribute* (Boston, 1904). Reprinted from Mass. Hist. Soc. *Proc.*, 2 ser., vol. xvii (1904), pp. 192-232.

Scotch-Irish Society of America. *Proceedings of the Scotch-Irish Congress at Columbia, Tenn.* (Cincinnati, 1889).

C. H. Smith, *The Mennonite Immigration to Pennsylvania in the Eighteenth Century* (Norristown, Pa., 1929).

George Smith, *History of Delaware County, Pennsylvania* (Phila., 1862).

H. S. Smith, *Colonial Days and Ways* (New York, 1900). Huguenots and the Edict of Nantes.

John T. Smith, *The Catholic Church in New York, 1808-1905* (2 vols., New York, 1905). The Prologue has a good summary of Catholic church history to the appointment of Bishop Carroll.

S. P. C. K., *A General Account of the Society for Promoting Christian Knowledge, to which are subjoined, the standing rules and orders, ...and other documents* (London, 1816).

William Sprague, *Annals of the American Pulpit* (8 vols., New York, 1857-1885).

Joseph Tracy, *The Great Awakening...* (Boston, 1842).

W. Walker, *Creeds and Platforms of Congregationalism* (New York, 1893). Source material.

Luther A. Weigle, *American Idealism* (New York, 1928, vol. x of *Pageant of America*).

Charles B. Williams, *A History of the Baptists in North Carolina* (Raleigh, 1901).

E. J. Wolf, *The Lutherans in America...* (New York, 1890).

W. D. Woods, *John Witherspoon* (New York, 1908).

D. ARTICLES, ADDRESSES, ETC., IN PERIODICALS AND OTHER SERIALS

John Q. Adams, "Address delivered before the Massachusetts Historical Society, May 20, 1843," in *Memoir of the Life of John Quincy Adams* by Josiah Quincy (Boston, 1858).

Edward Breck, "Letters on the Quakers, 1655," Col. Soc. Mass. *Pub.*, vol. xiv, pp. 49-58.

P. S. P. Connor, "Early Registers of the Catholic Church in Pennsylvania," Amer. Cath. Hist. Soc. *Records*, vol. ii (1886-88).

W. M. Gewehr, "The Rise of Popular Churches in Virginia, 1740-1790," *South Atlantic Quarterly*, April, 1928.

Stuart D. Goulding, "Honest Roger Williams," *Commonweal*, vol. xix (Jan. 19, 1934), pp. 317-319.

Stuart D. Goulding, "Rhode Island and Liberty," *Commonweal*, vol. xxiii (March 13, 1936), pp. 540-542.

J. Moss Ives, "Roger Williams, Apostle of Religious Bigotry," *Thought*, vol. vi (Dec., 1931), pp. 478-492.

John Nicum, "The Confessional History of the Evangelical Lutheran Church in the United States," *Papers of the American Society of Church History* (vol. iv, New York, 1892).

"Papers relating to the administration of Governor Nicholson and to the founding of William and Mary College," *Virginia Magazine*, vol. vii (1899-1900), p. 171.

John F. Quirk, "Rev. Ferdinand Farmer, S.J.," U. S. Cath. Hist. Soc., *Records and Studies*, vol. vi (1912), pp. 235-248.

Jeremiah Smith, "Centennial Address of the Honorable Jeremiah Smith delivered at the celebration of the Second Century from the time Exeter was settled by John Wheelright and others, July 4, 1838," N. H. H. Soc. *Coll.*, vol. vi, pp. 167-204.

G. A. Stead, "Roger Williams and the Massachusetts Bay," *New Eng. Quar.*, vol. vii (June, 1934), p. 252.

"A Vindication of William Penn by Philip Ford, and Other Papers relating to the Settlement of Pennsylvania," *Pa. Mag.*, vol. vi, p. 74 *et seq.*

J. E. Vose, "Centennial Address" (1874) in W. R. Cochrane, *History of the Town of Antrim* (Manchester, N. H.), pp. 121-130.

Charles G. Washburn, "Jasper Mauduit, Agent in London for the Province of the Massachusetts Bay, 1762-65," Mass. Hist. Soc. *Coll.*, vol. xxiii (1918), p. 74.

Henry Watts, "Goshenhoppen: An early Jesuit foundation in Philadelphia," *Records and Studies*, U. S. Cath. Hist. Soc., vol. xxi 1932), pp. 138-169.

W. Winslow, "Pilgrims in Holland and America," Col. Soc. Mass. *Pub.*, vol. xviii, pp. 132-152.

The Tradition and Colonial Education

Chapter IV

A. SOURCES

John Adams, *Works*, ed. by C. F. Adams (10 vols., Boston, 1856). Useful for almost every phase of this study, and especially for chapters seven, eight and nine.

Calvert Papers, 1576-1763. Nos. 509-510, 556, 558. Mss. Md. Hist. Soc. A portion of these papers has been published by the Society in the *Fund Publication*, Nos. 28, 34, 35-37 (Balt., 1889-1901). Useful also for chapter on clergy.

Charter and Statutes of the College of William and Mary in Virginia. In Latin and English (Williamsburg, 1736), L. C.

Charter, Transfer, and Statutes of the College of William and Mary in Virginia (Williamsburg, 1758). For the Statutes of 1792 see *William and Mary College Quarterly*, vol. xx, pp. 52-59.

Charter of a College to be erected in New Jersey . . . (New York, 1770). Facsimile, L. C. There is a contemporary manuscript copy in the Force Collection, Mss. Div., L. C.

The Charter of the College in New York, in America. Published by the Order of His Honour the Lieutenant Governor, in Council (New York, 1754), L. C.

Thomas Clapp, *The Answer to a Friend in the West, to a Letter from a Gentleman in the East, entitled: The present State of the Colony of Connecticut considered* (New Haven, 1755).

John Cotton, *Spiritual Milk for Babes in Either England . . .* (Cambridge, 1656). N. Y. P. L.

Samuel Davies, "The Military Glory of Great Britain" (1762), Rev. Samuel Davies. An Entertainment given by the late Candidates for Bachelor's degree at the close of the anniversary commencement held in Nassau-Hall, New Jersey, September 29, 1762. Philadelphia, 1762." *Magazine of History with Notes and Queries*, vol. xxix, No. 2, Extra No. 114, p. 97.

Franklin B. Dexter, *Documentary History of Yale University, 1701-1745* (New Haven, 1916).

[Paul Dudley], *An Essay on the Merchandise of Slaves and Souls of Men. Rev. xviii, 13. With an Application thereof to the Church of Rome.* By a Gentleman (Boston, 1731), N. Y. P. L.

Dudleian Lectures. The entire series may be found printed or in manuscript in the Widener Library, Harvard University. The lectures discussed or cited in this study are as follows:

Edward Wigglesworth, *The Spirit of Infallibility, May 11, 1757* (Boston, 1757).

Thomas Foxcroft, *The Supremacy of the Bishop of Rome, May 13, 1761.*

J. Mayhew, *Popish Idolatry, May 8, 1765* (Boston, 1765).

Samuel Mather, *Popery a Complex of Falsehoods, May 10, 1769.*

Samuel Cooper, *The Church of Rome, the Man of Sin, 1773.*

Edward Wigglesworth, *The Authority of Tradition, Nov. 5, 1777.*

William Gordon, *The Doctrine of Transubstantiation considered and refuted* ... Sept. 8, 1781.

Joseph Willard, *The Persecuting Spirit of the Church of Rome, Sept. 7, 1785.*

Jason Haven, *The Doctrine of Merit and Supererogation as Held and Applied in the Church of Rome, Sept. 2, 1789.*

Hosea Hildreth, *The Kingdom of Christ not of this World, May 13, 1829* (Cambridge, 1829).

Brooke Herford, *Liberalism's Answer to the Claims of the Romish Church* (Boston, 1895). Another edition edited by Prof. John Moore, American Citizen Company, Boston, n. d.).

Timothy Dwight, *Statistical Account of the City of New Haven* (New Haven, 1811).

Philip Vickers Fithian, *Journal and Letters, 1767-1774,* ed. by J. R. Williams (Princeton, 1900).

Harvard College Records (2 vols., Col. Soc. Mass. Pub., vols. xv-xvi), vol. i.

Hutchinson Correspondence, 3 vols., Banc. Trans., N. Y. P. L.

Journal of the Meetings of the President and Masters of William and Mary College, 1729-1784. Wm. and Mary College Quar., vols. i-v, xiii-xvi; 2 ser., vol. i. Administration of test oaths.

Lambeth Palace Mss., vol. 1123, pt. III (1760-1763). Trans. Much correspondence about the colleges of New York and Philadelphia.

William Livingston, *The Independent Reflector. Weekly Essays on Sundry and Important Subjects, more particularly adapted to the Province of New York. Printed (until tyranically suppressed) in 1753.*

Minutes of the Governors of the College of the Province of New York in America, 1755-1768, and of the Corporation of King's College in the City of New York, 1768-1770 (New York, 1932).

New York Mercury, Nov. 25, Dec. 2, Dec. 30, 1754; Jan. 13, 1755. "The Watch Tower," the question of sectarianism in King's College.

New England Primer Enlarged. For the more easy attaining the true Reading of English. To which is added, The Assembly of Divines Catechism (Boston, 1727). N. Y. P. L. Earliest extant edition.

New English Tutor Enlarged; For the more easy attaining the True Reading of English. To which is added Milk for Babes (1710?), Photo. N. Y. P. L.

Thomas Norton, *New English Canaan* (Amsterdam, 1637), L. C.

Plymouth Church Records (2 vols., Col. Soc. Mass. *Pub.*, xxii-xxiii), vol. i.

H. and C. Schneider, *Samuel Johnson, President of King's College* (4 vols., New York, 1929). Education, episcopal controversy, clergy.

A. R. Smyth, ed., *Writings of Benjamin Franklin* (10 vols., New York, 1907). Education, French and Indian problem, Canada, French alliance and other topics.

Thomas Vincent, *An Explicatory Catechism: or, an Explanation of the Assembly's Shorter Catechism* (Northampton, 1805), N. Y. P. L.

Eleazar Wheelock, *A Continuation of the Narrative of the Indian Charity School, begun in Lebanon, Connecticut, now incorporated with Dartmouth College, in Hanover, in the Province of New Hampshire* (Hartford, 1772).

B. SECONDARY AUTHORITIES

Charles F. Adams, *Three Episodes in Massachusetts History* (2 vols., Boston, 1892).

H. B. Adams, *The College of William and Mary* (Washington, 1887).

W. G. Andrews, *Samuel Johnson, D.D. An address delivered in Christ Church, New Haven, Conn., Nov. 4, 1892.* Johnson Collection, Columbia University.

E. E. Beardsley, *Life and Correspondence of Samuel Johnson, 1696-1772* (2nd ed., New York, 1874).

——, " Yale College and the Church," Monograph vii in W. S. Perry, *Hist. Amer. Epis. Church* (Boston, 1885), vol. i, p. 561 *et seq.*

Sadie Bell, *The Church, the State, and Education in Virginia* (Lancaster, Pa., 1930).

Bibliographical Essays: A Tribute to Wilberforce Eames (Cambridge, 1924). See W. C. Ford, " The New England Primer," pp. 60-65.

Alden Bradford, *Life and Writings of Jonathan Mayhew* (Boston, 1868).

C. H. Brewer, *History of Religious Education in the Episcopal Church to 1835* (New Haven, 1924). *Yale Studies in Religious Education, II.*

W. A. Bronson, *History of Brown University* (Providence, 1914).

Samuel W. Brown, *The Secularization of American Education…* (New York, 1912). *Contributions to Education, Teachers' College, Columbia Univ.*, no. 29.

James A. Burns, *The Catholic School System in the United States* (New York, 1908).

G. G. Bush, *History of Higher Education in Massachusetts* (Washington, 1891).

Joshua L. Chamberlain, ed., *Universities and their Sons* (2 vols., Boston, 1902).

Frederick Chase, *The History of Dartmouth College and the Town of Hanover, N. H.* (2 vols., Cambridge, 1891).

Elsie W. Clews, *Educational Legislation and Administration of the Colonial Governments* (New York, 1899). *Col. Univ. Contrib. to Philosophy, Psychology and Education,* vol. vi, nos. 1-4.

V. L. Collins, *President Witherspoon* (2 vols., Princeton, 1925).

Burton Comfrey, *Secularism in American Education: Its History* (Washington, 1931). *Catholic University of America, Educational Research Monographs,* vol. vi, no. 1.

W. H. S. Demarest, *History of Rutgers College* (New Brunswick, 1924).

Dean Dudley, *History of the Dudley Family* (2 vols., Wakefield, Mass., 1886-1892).

Paul L. Ford, *The New England Primer: a History of its Origin and Development* (New York, 1897). Facsimiles of the *Primer* and of the *New English Tutor.*

R. A. Guild, *Early History of Brown University including the Life, Times and Correspondence of President Manning* (Providence, 1897).

Arthur J. Hall, *Religious Education in the Public Schools of the State and City of New York*... (Univ. of Chicago Press, 1914).

Historical Sketch of the College of William and Mary, 1693-1870 (Baltimore, 1870).

A History of Columbia University, 1754-1904... (New York, 1904).

M. W. Jernegan, *Laboring and Dependent Classes in Colonial America, 1607-1783* (Chicago, 1931).

Clifton Johnson, *Old-Time Schools and School Books* (New York, 1904).

W. W. Kemp, *The Support of Schools in Colonial New York, by the Society for the Propagation of the Gospel in Foreign Parts* (New York, 1913). *Contrib. to Education, Teachers' College, Columbia Univ.,* no. 56.

George L. Littlefield, *Early Boston Booksellers, 1642-1711* (Boston, 1900).

——, *Early Schools and School-Books in New England* (Boston, 1904).

George Livermore, *The Origin, History and Character of the New England Primer. Being a Series of Articles Contributed to the Cambridge Chronicle* (New York, 1915; reprint of 1849 edition).

David McClure, *Memoir of Eleazar Wheelock* (Newburyport, 1811).

William J. McGucken, *The Jesuits and Education* (Milwaukee, 1932).

John McLean, *History of the College of New Jersey, 1746-1854* (2 vols., Phila., 1877).

Memorial Book of the Sesquicentennial Celebration of Princeton University (Princeton University Press, 1898).

N. F. Moore, *An Historical Sketch of Columbia College in the City of New York* (New York, 1846).

Samuel E. Morison, *Tercentennial History of Harvard College and University, 1636-1936.* Vol. i, *The Founding of Harvard College* (Cambridge, 1935).

Clara F. Purcell, *Pioneer Irish Teachers in America* (Wash., 1932). Master's Thesis, Mullen Library, Cath. Univ. of America).

Josiah Quincy, *History of Harvard College* (2 vols., Boston, 1860).

L. B. Richardson, *History of Dartmouth College* (2 vols., Hanover, 1932).

T. Sedgwick, *Life of William Livingston* (New York, 1883). Episcopacy, French and Indians, King's College.

Sesquicentennial of Brown University, 1764-1914 (pub. by the Univ., 1915).

R. F. Seybolt, *The Public Schools of Colonial Boston, 1635-1775* (Cambridge, 1935).

John G. Shea, *Memorial of the First Centenary of Georgetown College* (Wash., 1891).

J. L. Sibley, *Biographical Sketches of Those Who Attended Harvard College* (4 vols., Cambridge, 1873-1933. Vol. iv by G. K. Shipton).

S. M. Smith, *The Relation of the State to Religious Education in Massachusetts* (Syracuse, N. Y., 1926).

Henry S. Spalding, *Catholic Colonial Maryland* (Milwaukee, 1931).

Bernard C. Steiner, *History of Education in Connecticut* (Wash., 1893).

——, *History of Education in Maryland* (Wash., 1894).

D. C. Tewkesbury, *The Founding of American Colleges and Universities before the Civil War, with particular reference to the religious influences bearing upon the College movement* (New York, 1932).

Francis N. Thorpe, *Benjamin Franklin and The University of Pennsylvania* (Wash., 1893).

William Treacy, *Old Catholic Maryland and its Early Jesuit Missionaries* (Swedensboro, N. J., 1889).

Andrew W. Tuer, *History of the Horn-Book* (2 vols., London and New York, 1896).

L. G. and M. J. Walsh, *History and Organization of Education in Pennsylvania* (State Teachers' College, Indiana, Pa., 1928).

John F. Watson, *Annals of Philadelphia and Pennsylvania in the Olden Time* ... (2 vols., Phila., 1868).

H. C. White, *Abraham Baldwin* (Athens, Ga., 1926). Influence of Yale in the South.

C. E. L. Wingate, ed., *Life and Letters of Paine Wingate* (2 vols., Medford, Mass., 1931).

Thomas G. Wright, *Literary Culture in Early New England, 1620-1730.* Edited by his wife (New York, 1920).

THE TRADITION IN COLONIAL LITERATURE

CHAPTER V

A. ALMANACS. THE COLLECTIONS IN THE LIBRARY OF CONGRESS, THE NEW YORK PUBLIC LIBRARY AND THE NEWBERRY LIBRARY, CHICAGO, HAVE BEEN EXAMINED, BUT THEY HAVE YIELDED RELATIVELY LITTLE FOR OUR PURPOSE. THE FOLLOWING HAVE BEEN MOST USEFUL

Nathaniel Ames, *Astronomical Diary or Almanack* [Boston], 1747-51. 1756, 1763. The pertinent passages of the Ames' almanacs are conveniently brought together in Samuel Briggs' *Essays, Humor and Poems of Nathaniel Ames, Father and Son, of Dedham, Massachusetts, from their Almanacks, 1726-1775, with notes and comments* (Cleveland, 1891).

Bickerstaff's *Boston Almanack* ... 1777.

J. N. Hutchins, Improved ... Almanack (New York), 1762, 1765, 1766.

Nathaniel Low, *Astronomical Diary or Almanack*, 1775, 1776, 1785.

Thomas Moore, *Poor Thomas Improved* [New York], 1760, 1764.

——, *Poor Roger*, 1760, 1761, 1762.

J. Richardson, *An Almanack* ... (Cambridge), 1670.

Roger Sherman, *An Almanack* ... (Boston), 1760, 1761.

John Tobler, *Pennsylvania Town and Countryman's Almanack* (Wilmington), 1777.

——, *Pennsylvania Almanack for 1767*.

D. Travis, *An Almanack for 1716* (New London).

John Tully, *An Almanack* (Boston), 1693, 1694, 1695.

Benjamin West, *New England Almanack* (Providence), 1775, 1776.

B. BALLADS AND BROADSIDES. THE LIBRARY OF CONGRESS COLLECTION OF AMERICAN BROADSIDES COMPRISES 180 VOLUMES DISTRIBUTED OVER THE YEARS 1760-1789. THEY ARE ARRANGED ALPHABETICALLY BY STATES. THE FOLLOWING VOLUMES HAVE BEEN MOST USEFUL: 3, 28, 35, 36, 39, 107, 108, 111, 141, 142, 144, 146, 147, 172

The collection in the New York Historical Society, arranged in folders by years, yielded many items. See folders for 1774, 1775, 1778, 1779.

The Lenox Broadsides in the New York Public Library have many interesting items for the years 1755, 1756, 1758, 1759, 1771, 1774. This collection is described in the Library *Bulletin*, vol. iii, pp. 23-33, 43-44.

The following bound collections have also proved useful:

English and American Political Ballads (5 vols., Collection of Broadsides, Newberry Library, Chicago), vols. 3, 4, 5.

W. C. Ford, ed., *Broadsides, Ballads, etc., printed in Massachusetts, 1639-1800* (Mass. Hist. Soc., 1922).

Charles F. Heartman, *The Cradle of the United States, 1765-1789* (Metuchen, N. J., 1923).

Frank Moore, *Songs and Ballads of the American Revolution* (New York, 1856).

Winthrop Sargent, ed., *The Loyalist Verses of Joseph Stansbury and Doctor Jonathan Odell, relating to the American Revolution* (Albany, 1860).

W. L. Stone, *Ballads and Poems relating to the Burgoyne Campaign* (Albany, 1893).

Ola S. Winslow, *American Broadside Verse; From Imprints of the Seventeenth and Eighteenth Centuries* (New Haven, 1930).

C. MAGAZINES

American Magazine and Historical Chronicle; for all the British Plantations (Boston, Sept., 1743–Dec., 1746).

American Magazine, or General Repository, ed. by Lewis Nicola (Phila., Jan.–Sept., 1769).

American Magazine, or Monthly Chronicle for the British Colonies, ed. by "a Society of Gentlemen" (Phila., Oct., 1757–Oct., 1758).

The American Museum; or Repository of Ancient and Modern Fugitive Pieces...ed. by Mathew Carey (Phila., Jan., 1787–Dec., 1792).

The Boston Magazine (Boston, 1783–Dec., 1786).

Columbian Magazine; or a Monthly Miscellany (Sept., 1786–Feb., 1790).

Royal American Magazine, or Universal Repository of Instruction and Amusement (Boston, Jan., 1774–March, 1775).

United States Magazine; a Repository of History, Politics and Literature, ed. by Hugh Henry Brackenridge (Phila., Jan.–Dec., 1779).

D. NEWSPAPERS

I. Foreign

Affaires de l'Angleterre et de l'Amérique, ed. by Benjamin Franklin and others (14 vols., Paris, 1776-1779).

The Crisis, Jan. 21, 1775–Oct. 12, 1776 (92 numbers, London).

The Remembrancer, ed. by John Almon (17 vols., London, 1775-1784).

II. American

Boston Gazette, Boston Evening Post, Boston News Letter, Cape Fear Mercury (Wilmington), *Connecticut Courant, Exeter Journal, Georgia Gazette, Maryland Gazette* (Annapolis), *Massachusetts Spy, New England Courant, New Hampshire Gazette and General Advertiser* (Portsmouth), *New Hampshire Gazette and Morning Chronicle* (Exeter), *New Jersey Gazette* (Trenton), *New York Evening Post, New York Journal, New York Mercury, North Carolina Gazette* (New-Bern), *Pennsylvania Evening Post, Pennsylvania Gazette, Pennsylvania Journal or Weekly Advertiser, Pennsylvania Ledger,*

Pennsylvania Packet, Providence Gazette, Rivington's *Royal Gazette, Salem Mercury, South Carolina Gazette* (Charleston), *Virginia Gazette* (Williamsburg).

J. T. Buckingham, ed., *Specimens of Newspaper Literature* (2 vols., Boston, 1850).

Wm. Nelson, ed., *Extracts from American Newspapers, relating to New Jersey* (Paterson, N. J., 1894-1906), 1 ser., vols. i-viii; 2 ser., vols. i-iii of *New Jersey Archives.*

E. EARLY AMERICAN POETRY AND DRAMA (NOT INCLUDED UNDER B)

[James Allen], *The Poem which the Committee of the Town of Boston had voted unanimously to be published with the late oration . . .* (Boston, 1772). Louisbourg and the French.

The Association . . . by Bob Jingle, Esq., Poet Laureat to the Congress . . . (Rivington?, 1774).

Joel Barlow, *The Prospect of Peace . . .* (New Haven 1778).

——, *The Vision of Columbus . . .* (Hartford, 1787).

[Hugh Henry Brackenridge], *The Battle of Bunker Hill. A Dramatic Piece in Five Acts, in Heroic measure, by a Gentleman of Maryland . . .* (Phila., 1776).

——, *The Death of General Montgomery . . .* (Phila., 1776).

——, *A Poem on Divine Revelation . . .* (Phila., 1774).

Margaret Brewster, of Lebanon, *Poems, On Divers Subjects . . .* (Boston, 1757).

Nathaniel Evans, *Poems on Several Occasions . . .* (Phila., 1772).

[Philip Freneau], *American Liberty . . .* (New York, 1775).

——, *The Poems of Philip Freneau. Written chiefly during the Late War* (Phila., 1786).

——, *A Voyage to Boston . . .* (New York [1775]), 1st ed.

David Humphreys, *Poems* (2nd ed., Phila., 1789). See "Address to the Armies of the United States of America," p. 23.

——, *The Glory of America . . .* (Phila., 1783).

[John Leacock], *The Fall of British Tyranny, or American Liberty Triumphant . . .* (Phila., 1776).

Charlotte Ramsey Lennox, *The Sister: A Comedy* (London, 1769).

The Poor Man's Advice to His Poor Neighbors . . . (New York, 1774).

Benjamin Y. Prime, *Columbia's Glory, or British Pride Humbled . . .* (New York, 1791).

——, *The Patriot Muse . . .* (London . . . 1764).

Robert Rogers, *Ponteach: or, the Savages of America . . .* (London, 1766). See also edition sponsored by Caxton Club (Chicago, 1914) with introduction by Allan Nevins.

Richard Steere, "Antichrist Displayed," in the *Daniel Catcher . . .* Reprinted in G. E. Littlefield, *The Early Massachusetts Press, 1638-1711* (2 vols., Boston, 1907).

F. EARLY HISTORIANS

Jeremy Belknap, *History of New Hampshire* (3 vols., ed. by John Farmer, Dover, 1831).

Robert Beverly, *History of Virginia, in four parts* (London, 1705).

Jonathan Boucher, *A View of the Causes and Consequences of the American Revolution* ... (London, 1797).

William Bradford, *A History of Plymouth Plantation* (Boston, 1856). Mass. Hist. Soc. *Coll.*, 4 ser., vol. iii. Facsimile ed., London, 1896.

William Douglass, *A Summary, Historical and Political of the First Planting, Progressive Settlement and Present State of the British Settlements in North America* (2 vols., Boston, 1749-51).

William Gordon, *History of the Rise, Progress and Establishment of the Independence of the United States of North America* (4 vols., London, 1787).

Thomas Hutchinson, *The History of Massachusetts, from the first settlement thereof in 1628, until the year 1750* (3d ed., 2 vols., Boston, 1795). Volume iii under the title of *History of the Province of Massachusetts Bay from 1749 to 1774*, ed. by Rev. John Hutchinson (London, 1828).

Edward Johnson, *Wonder-Working Providence, 1628-1651* (*Original Narratives of Early American History*, ed. by J. F. Jameson, New York, 1910).

Hugh Jones, *The Present State of Virginia* ... (London, 1724. Reprinted in Sabin's Reprints, New York, 1865).

Charles H. Lincoln, ed., *Narratives of the Indian Wars* (*Orig. Nar. of Early Amer. Hist.*, New York, 1913).

Cotton Mather, *Magnalia Christi Americana* ... (Hartford, 1820).

Samuel Penhallow, *The History of the Wars of New England with the Eastern Indians* ... (Boston, 1726). New Hamp. Hist. Soc. *Coll.*, vol. i, 1824.

David Ramsay, *History of the American Revolution in South Carolina* (2 vols., Trenton, 1785).

——, *History of South Carolina from its Settlement in 1670 to the year 1808* (2 vols., Charleston, 1809).

William Smith, *The History of the Province of New York, from Its Discovery to the Appointment of Governor Colden in 1762* . . . New York Hist. Soc. *Coll.*, vol. iv (1826).

William Stith, *The History of the First Discovery and Settlement of Virginia* ... (Williamsburg, 1747. Sabin reprint, New York, 1865).

John Winthrop, *Journal, 1630-1649*, ed. by J. K. Hosmer (2 vols., New York, 1908).

G. OTHER CONTEMPORARY MATERIAL

Samuel Adams, *Writings*, ed. by H. A. Cushing (4 vols., Boston, 1904-08).

Peter Berault, *The Church of Rome Evidently Proved Heretick* (London, 1680; Boston, 1685, 1745).

H. W. Cunningham, ed., *Diary of Rev. Samuel Checkley, 1735*. Reprinted from Col. Soc. Mass. *Pub.*, vol. xii, pp. 270-271 (Cambridge, 1909).

The French Convert ... (New York, 1724). Many editions.

Hugh Gaine, *Journals*, ed. by P. L. Ford, (2 vols., New York, 1902).

Don Antonio Gavin, *Master-Key to Popery* . . . (Boston, 1773, 1835). Many editions.

Samuel A. Green, comp., *Ten Fac-Simile Reproductions Relating to Old Boston and Neighborhood* (Boston, 1901).

Popish Cruelty Displayed ... (Boston, 1753). Many editions.

Isaiah Thomas, *History of Printing in America* (2 vols., Worcester, 1810). Contemporaneous in part.

H. SECONDARY AUTHORITIES

Brooks Adams, *The Emancipation of Massachusetts* (Boston and New York, 1887).

James T. Adams, *Revolutionary New England, 1691-1776* (Boston, 1923).

W. L. Andrews, *Paul Revere and His Engravings* (New York, 1901).

E. E. Atwater, *History of the Colony of New Haven* (Meriden, 1902).

E. M. Bacon, *An Historical Digest of the Provincial Press* (Boston, 1911).

Joseph T. Buckingham, *Personal Memoirs of an Editorial Life* (2 vols., Boston, 1852).

Bernard Faÿ, *L'Ésprit Révolutionaire en France et aux États-Unis à la Fin du xviii Siècle* (Paris, 1925).

——, *Franklin the Apostle of Modern Times* (Boston, 1929).

——, *Notes on the American Press at the End of the Eighteenth Century* (New York, 1927).

W. C. Ford, *The Boston Book Market, 1679-1700* (Boston, 1917).

Julius Gay, *An Address Delivered at the Annual Meeting of the Village Library Company of Farmington, Conn., Sept. 12, 1900* (Hartford, 1900).

J. K. Hosmer, *Samuel Adams* (New York, 1899).

——, *Life of Thomas Hutchinson* ... (Boston, 1896).

J. Franklin Jameson, *History of Historical Writing in America* (New York, 1891).

George L. Kittredge, *The Old Farmer and His Almanack* (Boston, 1904).

George E. Littlefield, *The Early Massachusetts Press, 1638-1711* (2 vols., Boston, 1907).

J. C. Lyford, *History of Concord* (2 vols., Concord, N. H., 1896).

F. L. Mott, *A History of American Magazines, 1741-1850* (New York, 1930).

William Nelson, *American Newspapers in the Eighteenth Century as Sources of History* (Washington, 1910).

Victor H. Paltsits, *The Almanacs of Roger Sherman* (Worcester, 1907).

James Parton, *Life and Times of Benjamin Franklin* (2 vols., New York, 1864).

Lyon N. Richardson, *A History of Early American Magazines, 1741-1789* (New York, 1931).

Elihu Riley, "*The Antient City*," *A History of Annapolis in Maryland* (Annapolis, 1887).

M. A. Shaaber, *Some Forerunners of Newspapers in England, 1476-1662* (Oxford Univ. Press, 1929).

J. W. Wallace, *An Old Philadelphian, Colonel William Bradford, The Patriot Printer of 1776* (Philadelphia, 1884).

W. V. Wells, *Life and Public Services of Samuel Adams* (3 vols., Boston, 1865).

Lawrence C. Wroth, *History of Printing in Colonial Maryland, 1686-1776* (Baltimore, 1922).

I. ARTICLES IN PERIODICALS AND OTHER SERIALS

F. B. Dexter, "Early Private Libraries in New England," Amer. Antiq. Soc. *Proc.*, n. s., vol. xviii (1906-07), pp. 135-147.

——, "Elder Brewster's Library," Mass. Hist. Soc. *Proc.*, 2 ser., vol. v (1889-90), pp. 37-85.

W. T. Laprade, "The Power of the English Press in the Eighteenth Century," *South Atlantic Quarterly*, vol. xxvii (Oct., 1928), pp. 426-34.

G. L. Nichols, "Massachusetts Almanacs, 1630-1850," Amer. Antiq. Soc. *Proc.*, n. s., vol. xxii (Apr.-Oct., 1912), pp. 15-134.

A. A. Spofford, "A Brief History of Almanacs," in *An American Almanac...for the year 1878* (New York, Wash., 1878).

M. A. Stickney, "Almanacs of Nathaniel Low," Essex Inst. Hist. *Coll.*, vol. viii, pp. 28-32.

Julius H. Tuttle, "The Libraries of the Mathers," Amer. Antiq. Soc. *Proc.*, vol. xx (1909-10). pp. 269-356.

The Tradition in Action
Chapter VI

A. MANUSCRIPT SOURCES

Archives Nationales. Colonies. Series B, vols. lxviii, lxx, lxxii, lxxiv. L. C. Trans. France. French policy in Spanish War, 1739.

Archivo General de Indias, Legajo, 2585, No. 18, Photostat, L. C. Acadians from Maryland.

Belknap Papers, 3 vols., vol. i, Gov. Shirley's correspondence with Gov. Wentworth, 1742-1756. Force *Coll.,* L. C.

Egerton Mss., No. 2671. "Origin and Progress of the Rebellion," by Peter Oliver. Great Brit. Trans., L. C.

Public Record Office, Colonial Office, series 5, vols. 196-204. Great Brit., Trans. L. C. Instructions to governors; encouragement to Protestant immigration.

B. PRINTED SOURCES

J. P. Boyd, *Susquehannah Company Papers* (4 vols., Wilkes-Barre, Pa., 1930-33).

R. A. Brock, ed., *Official Records of Robert Dinwiddie* (2 vols., Richmond, 1883-84). Va. Hist. Soc. *Coll.* Cited as *Dinwiddie Papers.*

Canadian Archives, Annual Report, 1883 (Ottawa, 1884).

William Clarke, "Observations On the Late and present Conduct of the French with regard to their Encroachments upon the British Colonies in North America... (Boston, 1755)" in *Magazine of History with Notes and Queries,* vol. xvi (1917-18), pp. 110-143.

Hector St. John de Crèvecoeur, *Letters from an American Farmer* (New York, 1904).

——, *Sketches of Eighteenth Century America. More "Letters from an American Farmer"* (New York, 1925).

A. R. Cunningham, ed., *Diary and Letters of John Rowe, 1759-1762* (Boston, 1903).

Daniel Dulany, "Military and Political Affairs of the Middle Colonies in 1755," *Pa. Mag.,* vol. iii, pp. 27-28.

"The Expediency of Securing our American Colonies by Settling the Country Adjoining the Mississippi, and the Country upon the Ohio, Considered... Edinburgh, 1763." Reprinted in Illinois State Historical Library *Collections,* vol. x (British Series i), *The Critical Period, 1763-65,* ed. by C. W. Alvord and C. E. Carter (Springfield, 1915), pp. 135-161.

Extracts from Chief Justice Allen's Letter Book... (Pottsville, Pa., 1897).

Thomas M. Field, ed., *Unpublished Letters of Charles Carroll of Carrollton and of His Father* (New York, 1902). U. S. Cath. Hist. Soc., Monograph 1.

Benjamin Franklin, *The Interest of Great Britain Considered*... (London and Boston, 1760).

——, *Plain Truth: or Serious Considerations on the Present State of the City of Philadelphia, and the Province of Pennsylvania. By a Tradesman of Philadelphia* (1747).

Theodore Frelinghüysen, *A Sermon Delivered to the New England Forces proceeding against Crown Point in the French and Indian War* (Albany, 1754).

——, *A Sermon Preached on the Occasion of the Treaty Held in Albany* ... (New York, 1754).

Thomas Frink, *Election Sermon, May 31, 1758* (Boston, 1758).

M. S. Giuseppi, ed., *Naturalization of Foreign Protestants in the American and West Indian Colonies Pursuant to Statute 13 George II, c. 7* (Manchester, 1921, vols. xiii-xiv, *Pubs.* of the Huguenot Society of London).

Daniel Horsmanden, *The New York Conspiracy, or a History of the Negro Plot with the Journal of the Proceedings against the Conspirators at New York in the Years 1741-1742* ... (New York, 1810).

Gaillard Hunt, ed., " Journal of Major Henry Livingston, of the Third New York Continental Line, August to December, 1775." *Pa. Mag.*, vol. xxii (1899), p. 9 *et seq.*

Archibald Kennedy, *Serious Considerations on the Present State of the Affairs of the Northern Colonies* (New York, 1754).

James Kenny, "Journal of James Kenny, 1761-1763," *Pa. Mag.*, vol. xxxvii (1913), pp. 22, 142 *et seq.*

——, " Journey to the Westward, 1758-59," *ibid.*

Louisbourg Journals, 1745, ed. by L. E. De Forest (New York, 1932).

"Pepperell Papers," Mass. Hist. Soc. *Coll.*, 6 ser., vol. x, p. 105 *et seq.*

John Percival, First Earl of Egmont, *Journal of the Transactions of the Trustees for Establishing the Colony of Georgia in America* (Wormsloe, 1886).

"A Review of the Military Operations in North America, from the Commencement of the French Hostilities on the Frontier of Virginia in 1753, to the Surrender of Oswego, on the 14th of August, 1756; in a letter to a Nobleman." Reprinted in Mass. Hist. Soc. *Coll.*, vol. vii (1800), pp. 67-163.

Elihu Riley, ed., *The Correspondence of the First Citizen and Antilon. With a History of Governor Eden's Administration in Maryland, 1769-1776* (Baltimore, 1902).

A Scheme to Drive the French out of All the Continent of America (n. p., 1754).

H. W. Smith, ed., *Life and Correspondence of William Smith* (Phila., 1879).

William Smith, *A Brief State of the Province of Pennsylvania ... in a Letter from a Gentleman who resided many Years in Pennsylvania to his Friend in London* (2nd ed., London, 1755).
——, *Works* (2 vols., Phila., 1803).
Alexander Spotswood, *Official Letters* (2 vols. in 1, Richmond, 1882). Va. Hist. Soc. *Coll.*, n. s., vols. i-ii.
N. M. Tiffany and S. I. Kelsey, eds., *Letters of James Murray, Loyalist* (Boston, 1901).

C. SECONDARY AUTHORITIES

William Allen, *The History of Norridgewock* . . . (Norridgewock, Me., 1849).
American Council of Learned Societies, "Report of Committee on Linguistic and National Stocks in the Population of the United States," Amer. Hist. Assn. *Annual Report,* for 1931 (Wash., 1932), vol. i, pp. 103-441.
C. F. Bishop, *History of Elections in the American Colonies* (New York, 1893). *Columbia Studies in History, Economics and Public Law, iii.*
John B. Brebner, *New England's Outpost* (New York, 1927).
William H. Browne, *Maryland: the History of a Palatinate* (Baltimore, 1884).
George Chalmers, *Opinions of Eminent Lawyers, on Various Points of English Jurisprudence, Chiefly Concerning the Colonies, Fisheries and Commerce of Great Britain* (2 vols., London, 1814).
——, *Opinions on Interesting Subjects of Public Law and Commercial Policy, arising from American Independence* (London, 1784).
L. F. Church, *Oglethorpe: A Study in Philanthropy in England and Georgia* (London, 1932).
J. Coffin, *History of Newbury, Newburyport, and West Newbury* (Boston, 1895).
V. W. Crane, *Promotion Literature of Georgia.* Reprinted from *Bibliographical Essays: A Tribute to Wilberforce Eames* (Cambridge, 1924).
Robert de Crèvecoeur, *Saint John de Crèvecoeur, sa vie et ses ouvrages, 1735-1813* (Paris, 1883).
Frank R. Diffenderffer, *The German Immigration into Pennsylvania ... 1700-1775* (Lancaster, 1900).
George F. Donovan, *The Pre-Revolutionary Irish in Massachusetts, 1620-1775* (Menasha, Wis., 1932).
T. S. Duggan, *The Catholic Church in Connecticut* (New York, 1930).
J. B. Felt, *History of Ipswich, Essex and Hamilton* (Cambridge, 1834).
S. G. Fisher, *The Making of Pennsylvania* (Phila., 1896).
J. M. Flynn, *The Catholic Church in New Jersey* (Morristown, 1904).

R. T. H. Halsey, *The Boston Port Bill as Pictured by a Contemporary London Cartoonist* (New York, 1904).

George H. Haynes, *Representation and Suffrage in Massachusetts, 1620-1691* (Baltimore, 1894). *Johns Hopkins University Studies in History and Political Science*, 12 ser., vol. viii.

Aaron Hobart, *Historical Sketch of Abingdon* (Boston, 1839).

C. C. Jones, *History of Georgia* (2 vols., Boston, 1883).

J. W. Jordan, *History of Delaware County, Pa., and Its People* (3 vols., New York, 1914).

John E. Kennedy, *Thomas Dongan, Governor of New York, 1682-88* (Wash., 1930). *Cath. Univ. Studies in Amer. Church History, ix.*

James Kent, *Commentaries on American Law* (4 vols., Phila., 1889).

Sister M. Celeste Leger, *Catholic Indian Missions in Maine, 1611-1820* (Washington, 1929).

J. R. McCain, *Georgia as a Proprietary Province* (Boston, 1917).

Edward McCrady, *History of South Carolina under the Proprietary Government, 1690-1719* (New York, 1897).

——, *South Carolina under Royal Government* (New York, 1899).

C. H. McIlwaine, ed., *An abridgement of the Indian Affairs contained in folio volumes, transacted in the colony of New York from the year 1678 to the year 1751, by Peter Wraxall* ... (Cambridge, 1915).

Albert E. McKinley, *The Suffrage Franchise in the Thirteen English Colonies in America* (Phila., 1905). *Univ. of Pa. Series in History, no. 2.*

S. G. McLendon, *History of the Public Domain of Georgia* (Atlanta, 1924).

William Meade, *Old Churches, Ministers and Families in Virginia* (2 vols., Phila., 1857).

Julia P. Mitchell, *St. Jean de Crèvecoeur* (New York, 1916). *Columbia Studies in English and Comparative Literature.*

E. B. O'Callaghan, *History of New Netherland under the Dutch* (2nd ed., 2 vols., New York, 1855).

G. C. Odell, *Annals of the New York Stage* (7 vols., New York, 1927-1931), vol. i.

Francis Parkman, *Half Century of Conflict* (2 vols., Boston, 1892).

Mary E. Perkins, *Old Houses of the Antient Town of Norwich, 1660-1800* (Norwich, Conn., 1895).

J. L. Peyton, *History of Augusta County, Virginia* (Staunton, Va., 1882).

Thomas P. Phelan, *Thomas Dongan, Colonial Governor of New York,* (New York, 1935).

Edward E. Proper, *Colonial Immigration Laws* (New York, 1900). *Columbia Studies in History, Economics and Public Law, vol. xii, no. 8.*

M. J. Riordan, *Cathedral Records* (Balt., 1906).

W. T. Root, *The Relations of Pennsylvania with the British Government, 1696-1765* (New York, 1912).

Kate M. Rowland, *Life of Charles Carroll of Carrollton, 1737-1832, with his Correspondence and Public Papers* (2 vols., New York, 1898).

I. D. Rupp, *History and Topography of Dauphin, Cumberland, Franklin, Bedford, Adams, and Perry Counties* ... (Lancaster, 1846).

——, *History and Topography of Northumberland, Huntingdon, Mifflin* ... (Lancaster, 1847).

J. T. Scharf, *History of Maryland* (3 vols., Baltimore, 1879).

J. T. Scharf and T. Westcott, *History of Philadelphia* (3 vols., Phila., 1884).

Arthur M. Schlesinger, *The Colonial Merchant and the American Revolution, 1763-1776* (New York, 1917).

Lambert Schrott, *Pioneer German Catholics in the American Colonies, 1734-1784* (New York, 1933). *U. S. Cath. Hist. Soc. Monograph xiii.*

H. E. Scudder, ed., *Recollections of Samuel Breck* (Phila., 1877).

William R. Shepherd, *History of the Proprietary Government in Pennsylvania* (New York, 1896). *Columbia Studies in History, Economics and Public Law, vi.*

George Smith, *History of Delaware County, Pennsylvania* (Phila., 1862).

W. B. Stevens, *History of Georgia* (2 vols., New York, 1847, Phila., 1859).

Hannah Swanton, the Casco Captive: Or the Catholic Religion in Canada and Its Influence on the Indians in Maine ... (Boston, 1837).

William Tudor, *James Otis* (Boston, 1823).

D. D. Wallace, *History of South Carolina* (4 vols., New York, 1934).

J. W. Wayland, *The German Element in the Shenandoah Valley of Virginia* (Charlottesville, Va., 1907).

Elizabeth White, *American Opinion of France from Lafayette to Poincaré* (New York, 1927).

D. ARTICLES IN PERIODICALS AND OTHER SERIALS

C. H. Browning, "Francis Campbell," *Pa. Mag.,* vol. xxvii (1904), p. 63 *et seq.*

Luther Dame, "Life and Character of William Pepperell," Essex Inst. Hist. *Coll.,* vol. xxi, pp. 161-176.

F. R. Diffenderffer, "The German Exodus to England in 1709" (Lancaster, 1897). Pa. German Society *Proc.,* vol. vii (1896), p. 277 *et seq.*

G. F. Dow, "French Acadians in Essex County," Essex Inst. Hist. *Coll.,* vol. xiv, p. 299 *et seq.*

W. F. Dunaway, "The French Racial Strain in Colonial Pennsylvania," *Pa. Mag.,* vol. iv, p. 322 *et seq.*

F. Harrison, " Brent Town, Ravensworth and the Huguenots in Stafford," *Tyler's Quarterly Magazine*, vol. v, pp. 164-183.

W. H. J. Kennedy, " Catholics in Massachusetts before 1750," *Catholic Historical Review*, vol. xvii (1931), pp. 10-28.

Ethel King, " The New York Negro Plot of 1741," U. S. Cath. Hist. Soc., *Records and Studies*, vol. xx (1931), pp. 173-180.

H. W. Kriebal, " The Schwenkfelders in Pennsylvania " (Lancaster, 1904), Pa. Ger. Soc. *Proc.*, vol. xii (1902), pp. 141-42.

Linus A. Lilly, " Mortmain in Maryland," *Historical Bulletin*, vol. xii (Jan., 1934), pp. 34-35.

C. Millard, " The Acadians in Virginia," *Va. Mag.*, vol. xi (1932), p. 241.

Thomas F. O'Connor, " Maryland and the West," *Hist. Bulletin*, vol. xii (1934), pp. 27-28.

W. B. Reed, " The Acadian Exiles, or French Neutrals in Pennsylvania, to which is appended 'A Relation of their Misfortunes,' by John Baptiste Galeron," in *Memoirs of the Historical Society of Pennsylvania*, vol. vi (1858), pp. 285-289.

E. R. Richardson, " Giles Brent, Catholic Pioneer in Virginia," *Thought*, vol. vi (1932), pp. 650-654.

S. M. Sener, " The Acadians in Lancaster County," Paper read before the Lancaster County Historical Society, Sept. 4, 1796.

Basil Sollers, " The Acadians (French Neutrals) Transported to Maryland," *Md. Hist. Mag.*, vol. iii (1908), pp. 1-21.

Bernard C. Steiner, " The Protestant Revolution in Maryland," Amer. Hist. Assn. *Report*, 1897, p. 296 *et seq.*

Charles Stillé, " Religious Tests in Provincial Pennsylvania," *Pa. Mag.*, vol. ix (1885), p. 365 *et seq.*

A. T. Volwiler, " George Croghan and the Western Movement, 1741-1782," *Pa. Mag.*, vol. xlvi (1922), p. 273 *et seq.*, vol. xlvii (1923), pp. 28, 115 *et seq.* Reprinted, Cleveland, 1926.

THE REVOLUTION AND ITS PRELIMINARIES

CHAPTERS VII-VIII

A. MANUSCRIPT SOURCES

Archives Nationales, Paris, Series G. Photo, Binder Title: *France and Loan to U. S., 1780*, L. C. Mss. Div.

Samuel Adams Papers, 8 vols., Banc. Coll., N. Y. P. L.

American Papers, 3 vols., Banc. Coll., N. Y. P. L.

Archives des Affaires Étrangères, 1775-1789. Correspondence Politique, États-Unis., vols. i-xxxv. Trans. L. C. Duplicates much of the material in Stevens *Facsimiles*.

Boston Committee of Correspondence, General Correspondence, 1772-1775, 3 vols., Banc. Coll., N. Y. P. L.

——, *Minutes of the Boston Committee of Correspondence, 1772-1774,* 13 vols., Banc. Coll., N. Y. P. L.

Carroll Papers, 1731-1834. 16 boxes, arranged by dates. Md. Hist. Soc.

Correspondence of Andrew Eliot, Jonathan Mayhew and Thomas Hollis, 1761-1776. Banc. Trans., N. Y. P. L.

James Duane Papers, New York Historical Society.

French Legation Papers. L. C. Photostats of originals in William Mason Library, Evanston, Illinois.

Hawley Papers, 2 vols., Banc. Coll., N. Y. P. L.

John Holker Papers, 1771-1782. 44 vols., L. C. Photostats of originals in William Mason Library. Evanston, Ill., vol. iv.

Samuel Johnson Papers, Columbia University.

Journal of the Baltimore Committee, Jan. 17, 1775. L. C.

Langdon-Elwyn Papers, Banc. Coll., N. Y. P. L.

Joseph Reed, *Correspondence, 1764-1774,* Banc. Coll., N. Y. P. L.

Richard Smith, *Private Journal of the Continental Congress, 1775-1776,* Trans. Banc. Coll., N. Y. P. L. Also useful for ch. nine.

Benjamin F. Stevens, *Facsimiles of Manuscripts in European Archives relating to America, 1773-1783* . . . (25 vols., London, 1889-1905).

Ezra Stiles, *Diary, 1769-1795.* Transcript in Mss. Div., L. C. Also edited by F. B. Dexter (3 vols., New York, 1901).

——, *Papers.* Letters and documents. 1 vol., Banc. Coll., N. Y. P. L.

Tory Letters to Joseph Galloway. L. C. Force Trans., Miscellaneous Letters, C.-H.

B. PRINTED SOURCES

John and Abigail Adams, *Familiar Letters,* ed. by C. F. Adams (Boston, 1875).

J. C. Ballagh, ed., *Letters of Richard Henry Lee* (2 vols., New York, 1914).

Daniel Barber, *History of My Own Times* (Washington, 1823).

Charles Biddle, *Autobiography* (Phila., 1883).

J. Bouchier, ed., *Reminiscences of an American Loyalist* (New York, 1925).

H. H. Brackenridge, *Eulogium of the Brave who have fallen in the contest with Great Britain* . . . July 5, 1779.

Edmund C. Burnett, *Letters of Members of the Continental Congress* (vols. i-vii, Wash., 1921-34).

Sir Henry Cavendish, *Government of Canada. Debates in the House of Commons in the year 1774* . . . ed. by J. Wright (London, 1839).

Gilbert Chinard, ed., *The Treaties of 1778 and Allied Documents* (Baltimore, 1928).

Complot d'Arnold et de Sir Henry Clinton (Paris, 1816). Attributed by F. Monaghan (no. 1507) to Barbé-Marbois, Francois Marquis de.

[Myles Cooper], *A Friendly Address to all reasonable Americans* (New York, 1774).

Samuel Cooper, "Address to the People of America on the Treaty with France," *Affaires de l'Angleterre et de l'Amérique*, vol. xi, p. xciv *et seq.*

Correspondence of Washington and Comte de Grasse, Aug. 17–Nov. 4, 1781 (Senate Document 211, Wash., 1931).

Samuel Curwen, *Journal and Letters, from 1775 to 1784* (New York, 1842).

Sir John Dalrymple, *Address of the People of Great Britain to the Inhabitants of America* (London, 1775).

Deane Papers (5 vols., New York Hist. Soc. *Coll.*, vols. xix-xxiii. "Correspondence of Silas Deane," Conn. Hist. Soc. *Coll.*, vol. ii, pp. 126-368.

Anne Izard Deas, ed., *Correspondence of Ralph Izard, 1774-1804* (New York, 1844).

F. B. Dexter, ed., *Extracts from the Itineraries and other Miscellanies of Ezra Stiles, 1755-1794, with a selection from his correspondence* (New Haven, 1916).

John Drayton, ed., *Memoirs of the American Revolution* (2 vols., Charleston, 1820). Valuable documents in appendix.

"Duane Correspondence," Southern Historical Association *Publications,* vol. x (1906), pp. 305-06.

Early Proceedings of the American Philosophical Society for the Promotion of Useful Knowledge, 1744-1838 (Phila., 1884).

William Eddis, *Letters from America, 1769-1777* (London, 1792).

Exiles in Virginia: with observations on the conduct of the Society of Friends during the Revolutionary War . . . (Phila., 1848).

"Extracts from the Letter-Book of Captain Johann Heinrichs of the Hessian Jager Corps, 1778-1789," *Pa. Mag.*, vol. xxii, p. 137 *et seq.*

"Journal of Samuel Rowland Fisher of Philadelphia, 1779-1781," *Pa. Mag.*. vol. xli (1917), p. 145 *et seq.*

John C. Fitzpatrick, ed., *Writings of George Washington* (Washington, 1931—).

Peter Force, *American Archives: a collection of authentic state papers* . . . . (sers. 4-5, 9 vols., Wash., 1921-28).

W. C. Ford and others, eds., *Journals of the Continental Congress* (Washington, 1904—).

[Joseph Galloway], *A Candid Examination of the Mutual Claims of Great Britain and the Colonies: With a Plan of Accommodation on Constitutional Principles* (New York, 1775).

——, *Historical and Political Reflections on the Rise and Progress of the American Rebellion. . .* (London, 1780).

G. E. Hastings, ed., *Life and Works of Francis Hopkinson* (Chicago, 1926).

H——[istoricus] P——[opicola], pseud. *America poised in the balance of justice*... (London, 1776).

[Charles Inglis], *Letters of Papinian*... (New York, 1779).

——, *The True Interest of America Impartially Stated*... By an American (2nd ed., Phila., 1776).

James Jeffry, "Journal Kept in Quebec in 1775," annotated by William Smith, Essex Inst. Hist. *Coll.*, vol. 1 (1914), p. 124 *et seq.*

H. P. Johnson, ed., *Correspondence and Public Papers of John Jay, 1763-1781* (4 vols., New York, 1890-93).

J. W. Jordan, ed., "Adam Hubly, Jr., Col. Commandant 11th Penna. Regt. His Journal, Commencing at Wyoming, July 30, 1779," *Pa. Mag.*, vol. xxxiii (1909), p. 416 *et seq.*

"Journal of the Most Remarkable Occurrences in Quebec, from the 14th of November, 1775, to the 7th of May, 1776. By an Officer of the Garrison." New York Hist. Soc. *Coll.*, vol. xiii (1880), pp. 220-221.

Stephen Kemble, "Order Books of Lieutenant Colonel Stephen Kemble ...1775-1778," New York, Hist. Soc. *Coll.*, vol. xvi (1883).

W. M. P. Kennedy, ed., *Statutes, Treaties and Documents of the Canadian Constitution, 1713-1929* (2nd ed., New York, 1930).

[John Knox, Esq.], *An American Crisis, by a citizen of the World, inscribed to those members of the community, vulgarly named patriots* (London, 1777).

William Knox, *The Justice and Policy of the Late Act of Parliament* (London, 1774).

"Letters from Andrew Eliot to Thomas Hollis," Mass. Hist. Soc. *Coll.*, 4 ser., vol. iv, pp. 400-461.

Letters of Josiah Bartlett, William Whipple and Others (Phila., 1889).

H. C. Lodge, ed., *Works of Alexander Hamilton* (9 vols., New York, 1885-86).

N. D. Mereness, ed., *Travels in the American Colonies* (New York, 1916).

Frank Monaghan, *John Jay*... (New York and Indianapolis, 1935).

Frank Moore, *Diary of the Revolution*... (Hartford, 1876).

Hugh Percy, *Letters of Hugh, Earl Percy* (Boston, 1902).

Plain Truth Addressed to the Inhabitants of America containing Remarks on a late pamphlet entitled Common Sense, etc. By Candidus (Phila., 1776).

Benjamin Rush, "Letter to a Lady," reprinted from Portfolio, vol. iv (1817) in *Mag. of Amer. History*, vol. i (1877), pp. 506-510.

G. D. Scull, ed., *The Montrésor Journals*, New York Hist. Soc. *Coll.*, vol. xiv (1881). 5 Journals by Col. James Montrésor, 1757-59; 14 Journals by Capt. John Montrésor, 1757-1778.

Adam Shortt and A. G. Doughty, *Canadian Archives, Documents Relating to the Constitutional History of Canada* (2 vols., Ottawa, 1918).

Ezra Stiles, "Brief View of the State of religious liberty in the Colony of New York...", Mass. Hist. Soc. *Coll.*, 2 ser., vol. i, pp. 140-155.

James Thacher, *Military Journal during the Revolutionary War, from 1775-1783* (Boston, 1823).

Warren-Adams Letters... Mass. Hist. Soc. *Coll.*, lxxii, lxxiii.

Francis Wharton, *Revolutionary Diplomatic Correspondence of the United States* (6 vols., Washington, 1889).

Thomas Wharton, "Selections from the Letter-Book of Thomas Wharton of Philadelphia, 1773-1783," *Pa. Mag.*, vol. xxxiii (1909), pp. 319, 342 *et seq.*

C. THE PULPIT OF THE REVOLUTION

Zabdiel Adams, *A Sermon preached before His Excellency, John Hancock ... May 29, 1782* ... (Boston, 1782).

John Carmichael, *Sermon preached to the Company of Captain Ross, Lancaster, Pa., June 4, 1775.*

Jonas Clark, *Sermon preached before His Excellency, John Hancock* . . . (Boston, 1781).

Samuel Cooper, *A Sermon preached before His Excellency, John Hancock ... Oct. 25, 1780* ... (Boston, 1780).

George Duffield, *A Sermon Preached in the Third Presbyterian Church in the City of Philadelphia, Thursday, Dec. 11, 1783* ... (Phila., 1783).

William Gordon, *Sermon ... Dec. 15, 1774.*

David Jones, *Fast Day Sermon*, at Tredyffryn, Chester Co., Pa., 1775.

Samuel Langdon, *A Rational Explication of St. John's Vision of the Two Beasts* ... (Portsmouth, 1774).

J. Lathrop, *A Discourse Preached on March the fifth, 1778* (Boston, 1778).

Frank Moore, ed., *The Patriot Preachers of the American Revolution* (New York, 1862).

William Smith, *Oration in Memory of General Montgomery, Feb. 10, 1776* (Phila., 1776).

Ezra Stiles, *The United States Elevated to Glory and Honor* . . . (Worcester, 1785).

J. W. Thornton, *The Pulpit of the American Revolution* (Boston, 1860).

Jonathan Trumbull, *God is to be praised for the glory of His majesty* . . . (New Haven, 1784).

Charles Turner, *Election Sermon, May 26, 1773* (Boston, 1773).

Samuel West, *Election Sermon, May 29, 1776* (Boston, 1776).

S. Woodward, *The help of the Lord, in signal deliverances* ... (Boston, 1779).

D. SECONDARY AUTHORITIES

R. G. Adams, *Political Ideas of the American Revolution*... (Durham, 1922).

C. W. Alvord, *The Mississippi Valley in British Politics* (2 vols., Cleveland, 1917).

J. T. Austin, *Life of Elbridge Gerry, with contemporary letters to the close of the Revolution*... (2 vols., Boston, 1828-29).

Thomas Balch, trans., *The French in America during the War of Independence*... (2 vols., Phila., 1891).

Samuel F. Bemis, *The Diplomacy of the American Revolution* (New York, 1935).

John Carroll Brent, *Biographical Sketch of the Most Rev. John Carroll, First Archbishop of Baltimore, with select portions of his writings* (Baltimore, 1843).

E. Francis Brown, *Joseph Hawley, Colonial Radical* (New York, 1931).

Cambridge History of the British Empire, vol. vi, *Canada.*

J. Codman, *Arnold's Expedition to Quebec* (New York, 1901).

E. C. Corwin, *French Policy and the American Alliance of 1778* (Princeton, 1916).

Reginald Coupland, *The American Revolution and the British Empire* (London, 1928).

——, *The Quebec Act* (Oxford, 1925).

Arthur L. Cross, *The Anglican Episcopate and the American Revolution* (New York, 1902).

James B. Cullen, *The Story of the Irish in Boston* (Boston, 1893).

Benjamin and W. R. Cutter, *History of the Town of Arlington, 1635-1789* (Boston, 1880).

Richard Frothingham, *Life and Times of Joseph Warren* (Boston, 1865).

Alexander Garden, *Anecdotes of the American Revolution* (Brooklyn, 1865).

Dom Aiden Germain, *Catholic Military and Naval Chaplains, 1776-1917* (Wash., 1929).

Auguste Gosselin, *L'Église du Canada après la Conquete* (2 vols., Quebec, 1916-17).

Martin I. J. Griffin, *Catholics and the American Revolution* (3 vols., Ridley Park, Pa., 1907).

Edward E. Hale, *Franklin in France* (2 vols., Boston, 1887-88).

D. H. Hurd, ed., *History of Fairfield County, Conn.* (Phila., 1881).

William Jay, *Life of John Jay* (2 vols., 1833).

J. J. Jusserand, *With Americans of Past and Present Days* (New York, 1916).

C. R. King, *Life and Correspondence of Rufus King* (3 vols., New York, 1894-96).

E. S. Kite, *Beaumarchais and the War of American Independence* (2 vols., Boston, 1918).

F. B. Lee, *New Jersey as a Colony and as a State* (2 vols., New York, 1902).

L. A. Leonard, *Life of Charles Carroll of Carrollton* (New York, 1918).

G. J. McRee, *Life and Correspondence of James Iredell* (New York, 1857-58).

Chester Martin, *Empire and Commonwealth* (Oxford Univ. Press, 1929).

Joachim Merlant, *Soldiers and Sailors of France in the American War for Independence, 1776-1783.* Trans. by Mary E. Colman (New York, 1920).

M. J. O'Brien, *A Hidden Phase of American History: Ireland's Part in America's Struggle for Liberty* (New York, 1920).

James B. Perkins, *France in the American Revolution* (Boston and New York, 1911).

Josiah Quincy, *Memoir of the Life of John Quincy Adams* (Boston, 1858).

John Sanderson, *Biography of the Signers of the Declaration of Independence* (9 vols., Phila., 1827), vol. vii, Charles Carroll.

J. Smith, *Our Struggle for the Fourteenth Colony* (2 vols., New York, 1907).

J. H. Stark, *Loyalists in Massachusetts* (Boston, 1907).

C. J. Stillé, *Life and Times of John Dickinson, 1732-1808* (2 vols., Phila., 1891-95).

George Otto Trevelyan, *The American Revolution* (4 vols., New York, 1905-1912).

Claude H. Van Tyne, *Causes of the War of Independence* (New York, 1922).

——, *The War of Independence: The American Phase* (New York, 1929).

George M. Wrong, *Canada and the American Revolution* (New York, 1935).

E. ARTICLES IN PERIODICALS AND OTHER SERIALS

Bernard U. Campbell, "Memoirs of the Life and Times of the Most Rev. John Carroll," *United States Catholic Magazine*, vols. ii-vi (1844-1847).

Bernard Faÿ, "The Course of French-American Friendship," *Yale Review*, vol. xviii (Spring, 1929), pp. 436-55.

Sidney G. Fisher, "The Twenty-eight Charges against the King in the Declaration of Independence," *Pa. Mag.*, vol. xxxi (1907), pp. 257 *et seq.*

Peter Guilday, "Father John McKenna, a Loyalist Catholic Priest," *Catholic World*, vol. cxxxiii, pp. 21-27.

J. J. Jusserand, "Rochambeau and the French in America: Why They Came and What They Did." An Address by the French Ambassador, Raleigh, Nov. 21, 1913. North Carolina Historical Commission, *Bulletin*, No. 15 (Raleigh, 1913), pp. 83-117.

Elizabeth S. Kite, "Catholic Aid in American Independence," *America*, vol. xxxix (Sept. 21, 29, 1928).

Charles H. McCarthy, "The Attitude of Spain during the American Revolution," *Cath. Hist. Rev.*, vol. ii (1916-17), pp. 49-65.

W. R. Riddell, "Benjamin Franklin's Mission to Canada," *Pa. Mag.*, vol. xlviii (1924), pp. 91-110.

——, "Status of Roman Catholicism in Canada," *Cath. Hist. Rev.*, n. s., vol. viii (Oct., 1928), pp. 305-328.

C. W. Slone, "Provincial Corps of Catholic Volunteers," U. S. Cath. Hist. Soc. *Records and Studies*, vol. ii, pp. 203-205.

F. H. Smith, "The French in Boston during the Revolution," Bostonian Society, *Proc.*, vol. x, pp. 9-75.

F. J. Zwierlein, "The Catholic Contribution to Liberty in the United States," U. S. Cath. Hist. Soc. *Records and Studies*, vol. xv (1921), pp. 112-136.

MAKING THE CONSTITUTIONS

CHAPTER IX

A. MANUSCRIPT SOURCES

George Mason Papers, 1763-1791, L. C.

Livingston Papers (Robert R.) Banc. Coll., N. Y. P. L.

Massachusetts Town Resolves, 1783-1787. Force Trans., L. C., vols. i-v.

New Jersey. *Votes and Proceedings of the General Assembly of New Jersey, Perth-Amboy, June 11, 1775–Feb. 13, 1776. Force Trans.*, L. C.

New York Committee of Safety, March 3, 1775. Force Trans., L. C.

William Plumer, *Autobiography*, L. C.

B. PRINTED SOURCES

Joel Barlow, *Political Writings* (New York, 1796).

William Bentley, *Diary* (4 vols., Salem, 1905-14).

Debates, Resolutions and other Proceedings, of the Convention of the Commonwealth of Massachusetts, Convened at Boston, on the 9th of January, 1788, and continued until the 7th of February following, for the purpose of assenting to and ratifying the Constitution recommended by the Grand Federal Convention... (Boston, 1788).

Timothy Dwight, *The Nature and Danger of Infidel Philosophy*... (New Haven, 1792).

——, *Sermon Preached at Northampton on the twenty-eighth of November, 1781* (Hartford, 1781).

——, *Travels in New England and New York, 1796-1815* (4 vols., New Haven, 1821-22; London, 1823).

J. Elliot, *Debates in the Several State Conventions on the Adoption of the Federal Constitution* ... (5 vols., Phila., 1836-45).

The Federal and State Constitutions, Colonial Charters and other Organic Laws of the United States (Senate Misc. Docs., B. P. Poore, compiler. 44 Cong., 2 sess. Also separately in two parts, Wash., 1877. New ed., compiled by F. N. Thorpe, House Doc. 59 Cong., 2 sess., No. 357. 7 vols., Wash., 1909).

Harriette Forbes, ed., *Diary of Rev. Ebenezer Parkman* (Westborough Historical Society, 1899).

Journal of the Convention for Framing a Constitution of Government for the State of Massachusetts Bay, 1779-80 (Boston, 1832).

Journals of the Provincial Congress, Provincial Convention, Committee of Safety and Council of Safety of the State of New York, 1775, 1776, 1777 (2 vols., Albany, 1842).

Journal of the Votes and Proceedings of the Convention of New Jersey. Begun at Burlington the 10th of June, 1776, and thence continued by Adjournment at Trenton and New-Brunswick to the 21st of August following ... (Burlington, 1776).

Henry Laurens, *Correspondence* (New York, 1861).

Proceedings and Debates of the Convention of North-Carolina. Convened at Hillsborough, on Monday 21st Day of July, 1788, for the Purpose of deliberating and determining on the Constitution recommended by the General Convention at Philadelphia, the 17th Day of September, 1787 ... (Edenton ... 1789).

Result of the Convention of Delegates holden at Ipswich in the County of Essex ... (Newburyport, 1778).

John Witherspoon, *Works* (9 vols., Edinburgh, 1815).

C. SECONDARY AUTHORITIES

J. A. Baisnée, *France and the Establishment of the American Hierarchy* (Baltimore, 1934).

Alden Bradford, *History of Massachusetts, 1764-1820* (3 vols., Boston, 1822-29).

J. A. C. Chandler, *The History of Suffrage in Virginia* (Richmond, 1901).

Charleston Year Book, 1882, 1883, 1897.

W. R. Cochrane and G. K. Wood, *History of Francestown, N. H., 1758-1891* (Nashua, N. H., 1895).

J. F. Colby, *Manual of the Constitution of the State of New Hampshire* (Concord, 1912).

James G. Dealy, *Growth of American State Constitutions* (New York, 1915).

J. E. Easby-Smith, *Georgetown University, 1789-1907* (2 vols., New York, 1907).

H. J. Eckenrode, *The Separation of Church and State in Virginia* (Richmond, 1910).

John E. Finan, *Diocese of Manchester* (Boston, 1899).

M. Louise Greene, *Development of Religious Liberty in Connecticut* (New York, 1905).

E. Harden, *History of Savannah and South Georgia* (Chicago and New York, 1913).

Henry Hitchcock, *American State Constitutions: A Study of their Growth* (New York, 1887).

J. Franklin Jameson, *Introduction to the Study of the Constitutional and Political History of the States* (Balt., 1886). *Johns Hopkins Studies in History and Political Science*, 4 ser., vol. 4, no. 5.

John A. McClintock, *History of New Hampshire* (Boston, 1886).

J. F. McLaughlin, *College Days at Georgetown and Other Papers* (Phila., 1899).

Jacob C. Meyer, *Church and State in Massachusetts, 1740-1833* (Cleveland, Western Reserve Univ. Press, 1930).

M. F. Morris, *Address at the Centennial Celebration of Georgetown College, Feb. 21, 1889* (Wash., 1889).

Vernon L. Parrington, *The Colonial Mind, 1620-1800* (New York, 1927).

G. W. Paschal, *History of the North Carolina Baptists* (2 vols., Raleigh, 1930).

William Plumer, Jr., *Life of William Plumer* (Boston, 1857).

Richard Purcell, *Connecticut in Transition* (Wash., 1918).

I. Woodbridge Riley, *American Philosophy; The Early Schools* (New York, 1907).

E. W. Sikes, *Transition of North Carolina from Colony to Commonwealth* (Balt., 1898). *Johns Hopkins Studies*, 16 ser., nos. 10-11.

J. E. A. Smith, *History of the Town of Pittsfield* (2 vols., Boston, 1869).

E. S. Stearns, *History of Plymouth, New Hampshire* (2 vols., Cambridge, 1906).

L. T. Stevens, *History of Cape May County*... (Cape May City, 1897).

Louise I. Trenholme, *The Ratification of the Federal Constitution in North Carolina* (New York, 1932).

J. H. Trumbull, *Historical Notes on the Constitution of Connecticut, 1639-1818* (Hartford, 1901, reprint of 1873).

H. St. G. Tucker, *Commentaries on the Laws of Virginia*... (2 vols., Winchester, 1836).

Charles Warren, *The Making of the Constitution* (Boston, 1928).

J. Whitehead, *Judicial and Civil History of New Jersey* (Boston, 1897).

C. Zollman, *American Civil Church Law* (New York, 1917). *Columbia Studies in History, Economics and Public Law*, vol. lxxvii, no. 181. (Revised ed., St. Paul, 1933).

D. ARTICLES IN PERIODICAL AND OTHER SERIALS

T. J. Campbell, " The Beginnings of the Hierarchy of the United States,"
U. S. Catholic Hist. Soc. *Records and Studies*, New York, 1900,
pp. 251-277.

L. Q. Elmer, " History of the Constitution of New Jersey, adopted in
1776, and of the Government under it," New Jersey Hist. Soc. *Proc.*,
2 ser., vol. ii, p. 133 *et seq.*

J. M. Hurley, " The Political Status of Roman Catholics in North
Carolina," Amer. Cath. Hist. Soc., *Records*, vol. xxxviii (Sept., 1927),
no. 3.

K. B. V. Knox, " Intolerance in New Hampshire," *Granite Monthly*,
vol. x (1887), p. 326 *et seq.*

W. C. Morey, " The First State Constitutions," *Annals of American
Academy of Political Science*, vol. iv (Sept., 1893), pp. 201-232.

Samuel E. Morison, " The Struggle over the Adoption of the Constitution of 1780," Mass. Hist. Soc. *Proc.*, vol. l (1916-19), pp. 381 *et seq.*

Hon. William Plumer, " The Constitution of New Hampshire," *Historical Magazine*, vol. xiv (n. s. iv), p. 178 *et seq.*

W. C. Webster, "A Comparative Study of the State Constitutions of
the American Revolution," *Annals of the American Academy of
Political Science*, vol. ix, pp. 380-420.

F. J. Zwierlein, " How Religious Liberty Was Won," *Thought*, vol.
iii (March, 1929), pp. 639-661.

INDEX

Abbott, Henry, 377
Acadia, 216-17; Acadians, 234-36
Accounts of the Cruelties done to Protestants . . . See Tracts
Acts and Monuments. See Foxe, John
Adams, Amos, of Roxbury, 88
Adams, Charles Francis, quoted, 366
Adams, John, 132, 287-88, 307, 320-21, 365, 367
Adams, John Quincy, 100
Adams, Samuel, 186-88, 269-70, 286-87, 309, 314, 324, 335, 344, 367
Addison, Henry, 76
Address to the Inhabitants of the Colonies, Address to the Inhabitants of Quebec, Address to the King, Address to the Oppressed Inhabitants of Canada, Address to the People of Great Britain. See Continental Congress, Quebec Act
Address to the Soldiers about to Embark for America, 310, n.
Alden, Noah, 365
Alison, Francis, vice-provost of College of Phila., 153, n., 266, 267
Allegiance, 15, 16, 20, 22, 23, 48, 79. See also Oaths
Allen, James, of Phila., 294
Almanacs, 165-171
Alva, Duke of, 298-299
American Magazine . . . See Magazines, Bradford, William; Gridley, Jeremiah; Nicola, Lewis
American Museum . . . See Carey, Mathew
American Philosophical Society, 293
American Roused in a Cure for the Spleen. See Sewall, Jonathan
Ames, Nathaniel, 166, 168-70
Anabaptists, 21, 29. See also, Harris, Benjamin
Anarchy of the Ranters. See Barclay, George
"The Anatomist." See Smith, William

Anglican Episcopate. See Episcopate, Anglican
Anglicans. See Church of England
Anglo-Spanish War (1739-43), 217-22
Anne, Queen, 37, 39, 59, 216, 239, 244
"Antichrist," 15, 22, 34, 84, 100-101, 102, 109, 119, 136, 145, 201, 389-90. See also, Confessions of Faith, Dudleian Lectures, Pope, "Popery"
"Antichrist Display'd." See Steere, Richard
"Antigallican." See Smith, William
Apology. See Barclay, George
Apoquiniminck, Pa., 71, 161
Apthorp, East, 266
Armada, Spanish, 23, 33, 388
Arminianism, 85, 87
Arnold, Benedict, 319, 337
Arraignment of Popery. See Fox, George
Articles of Religion, Anglican, 84
The Association, by Bob Jingle. See Quebec Act
The Association, Protestant, 214
Augsburg Confession. See Confessions of Faith, Lutheran

Backhouse, R., S.P.G. missionary, 70
Backus, Isaac, 100, 102
Bacon, Thomas, of Md., 72-75
Bale, John, 12
Baptists, 21, 81, 99-100, 112, 154, 241, 259, 360-61, 377. See also Backus, Isaac; Williams, Roger; Confessions of Faith
Barbé-Marbois, François, marquis de, 334, 347-48, 355
Barber, Daniel, 294-95, 316
Barclay, George, 103-04
Barlow, Joel, 387-89
Barnes, Robert, 12
Barry, Commodore John, 346, 395
"Beast," the. See Roman Catholic Church
Beaumarchais, Pierre Augustin Caron de, 325, 334

445